Little Lord Fauntleroy

Frances Hodgson Burnett

Little Lord Fauntleroy

Copyright © 2020 Bibliotech Press
All rights reserved

ISBN: 978-1-64799-756-4

CONTENTS

CONTENTS

I

Cedric himself knew nothing whatever about it. It had never been even mentioned to him. He knew that his papa had been an Englishman, because his mamma had told him so; but then his papa had died when he was so little a boy that he could not remember very much about him, except that he was big, and had blue eyes and a long mustache, and that it was a splendid thing to be carried around the room on his shoulder. Since his papa's death, Cedric had found out that it was best not to talk to his mamma about him. When his father was ill, Cedric had been sent away, and when he had returned, everything was over; and his mother, who had been very ill, too, was only just beginning to sit in her chair by the window. She was pale and thin, and all the dimples had gone from her pretty face, and her eyes looked large and mournful, and she was dressed in black.

"Dearest," said Cedric (his papa had called her that always, and so the little boy had learned to say it),—"dearest, is my papa better?"

He felt her arms tremble, and so he turned his curly head and looked in her face. There was something in it that made him feel that he was going to cry.

"Dearest," he said, "is he well?"

Then suddenly his loving little heart told him that he'd better put both his arms around her neck and kiss her again and again, and keep his soft cheek close to hers; and he did so, and she laid her face on his shoulder and cried bitterly, holding him as if she could never let him go again.

"Yes, he is well," she sobbed; "he is quite, quite well, but we— we have no one left but each other. No one at all."

Then, little as he was, he understood that his big, handsome young papa would not come back any more; that he was dead, as he had heard of other people being, although he could not comprehend exactly what strange thing had brought all this sadness about. It was because his mamma always cried when he spoke of his papa that he secretly made up his mind it was better not to speak of him very often to her, and he found out, too, that it was better not to let her sit still and look into the fire or out of the window without moving or talking. He and his mamma knew very few people, and lived what might have been thought very lonely lives, although Cedric did not know it was lonely until he grew older and heard why it was they had no visitors. Then he was told that his mamma was an orphan, and quite alone in the world when his papa had married her. She was very pretty, and had been living as companion to a rich old lady who was not kind to her, and one day Captain Cedric Errol, who was calling at the house, saw her run up the stairs with tears on her eyelashes; and she looked so sweet and innocent and sorrowful that the Captain could not forget her. And after many strange things had happened, they knew each other well and loved each other dearly, and were married, although their marriage brought them the ill-will of several persons. The one who was most angry of all, however, was the Captain's father, who lived in England, and was a very rich and important old nobleman, with a very bad temper and a very violent dislike to America and Americans. He had two sons older than Captain Cedric; and it was the law that the elder of these sons should inherit the family title and estates, which were very rich and splendid; if the eldest son died, the next one would be heir; so, though he was a member of such a great family, there was little chance that Captain Cedric would be very rich himself.

But it so happened that Nature had given to the youngest son gifts which she had not bestowed upon his elder brothers. He had a beautiful face and a fine, strong, graceful figure; he had a bright smile and a sweet, gay voice; he was brave and generous, and had the kindest heart in the world, and seemed to have the power to make every one love him. And it was not so with his elder brothers; neither of them was handsome, or very kind, or clever. When they were boys at Eton, they were not popular; when they were at college, they cared nothing for study, and wasted both time and money, and made few real friends. The old Earl, their father, was constantly disappointed and humiliated by them; his heir was no honor to his noble name, and did not promise to end in being anything but a selfish, wasteful, insignificant man, with no manly or noble qualities. It was very bitter, the old Earl thought, that the son who was only third, and would have only a very small fortune, should be the one who had all the gifts, and all the charms, and all the strength and beauty. Sometimes he almost hated the handsome young man because he seemed to have the good things which should have gone with the stately title and the magnificent estates; and yet, in the depths of his proud, stubborn old heart, he could not help caring very much for his youngest son. It was in one of his fits of petulance that he sent him off to travel in America; he thought he would send him away for a while, so that he should not be made angry by constantly contrasting him with his brothers, who were at that time giving him a great deal of trouble by their wild ways.

But, after about six months, he began to feel lonely, and

longed in secret to see his son again, so he wrote to Captain Cedric and ordered him home. The letter he wrote crossed on its way a letter the Captain had just written to his father, telling of his love for the pretty American girl, and of his intended marriage; and when the Earl received that letter he was furiously angry. Bad as his temper was, he had never given way to it in his life as he gave way to it when he read the Captain's letter. His valet, who was in the room when it came, thought his lordship would have a fit of apoplexy, he was so wild with anger. For an hour he raged like a tiger, and then he sat down and wrote to his son, and ordered him never to come near his old home, nor to write to his father or brothers again. He told him he might live as he pleased, and die where he pleased, that he should be cut off from his family forever, and that he need never expect help from his father as long as he lived.

The Captain was very sad when he read the letter; he was very fond of England, and he dearly loved the beautiful home where he had been born; he had even loved his ill-tempered old father, and had sympathized with him in his disappointments; but he knew he need expect no kindness from him in the future. At first he scarcely knew what to do; he had not been brought up to work, and had no business experience, but he had courage and plenty of determination. So he sold his commission in the English army, and after some trouble found a situation in New York, and married. The change from his old life in England was very great, but he was young and happy, and he hoped that hard work would do great things for him in the future. He had a small house on a quiet street, and his little boy was born there, and everything was so gay and cheerful, in a simple way, that he was never sorry for a moment that he had married the rich old lady's pretty companion just because she was so sweet and he loved her and she loved him. She was very sweet, indeed, and her little boy was like both her and his father. Though he was born in so quiet and cheap a little home, it seemed as if there never had been a more fortunate baby. In the first place, he was always well, and so he never gave any one trouble; in the second place, he had so sweet a temper and ways so charming that he was a pleasure to every one; and in the third place, he was so beautiful to look at that he was quite a picture. Instead of being a bald-headed baby, he started in life with a quantity of soft, fine, gold-colored hair, which curled up at the ends, and went into loose rings by the time he was six months old; he had big brown eyes and long eyelashes and a darling little face; he had so strong a back and such splendid sturdy legs, that at nine months he learned suddenly to walk; his manners were so good, for a baby, that it was delightful to

3

make his acquaintance. He seemed to feel that every one was his friend, and when any one spoke to him, when he was in his carriage in the street, he would give the stranger one sweet, serious look with the brown eyes, and then follow it with a lovely, friendly smile; and the consequence was, that there was not a person in the neighborhood of the quiet street where he lived—even to the groceryman at the corner, who was considered the crossest creature alive—who was not pleased to see him and speak to him. And every month of his life he grew handsomer and more interesting.

When he was old enough to walk out with his nurse, dragging a small wagon and wearing a short white kilt skirt, and a big white hat set back on his curly yellow hair, he was so handsome and strong and rosy that he attracted every one's attention, and his nurse would come home and tell his mamma stories of the ladies who had stopped their carriages to look at and speak to him, and of how pleased they were when he talked to them in his cheerful little way, as if he had known them always. His greatest charm was this cheerful, fearless, quaint little way of making friends with people. I think it arose from his having a very confiding nature, and a kind little heart that sympathized with every one, and wished to make every one as comfortable as he liked to be himself. It made him very quick to understand the feelings of those about him. Perhaps this had grown on him, too, because he had lived so much with his father and mother, who were always loving and considerate and tender and well-bred. He had never heard an unkind or uncourteous word spoken at home; he had always been loved and caressed and treated tenderly, and so his childish soul was full of kindness and innocent warm feeling. He had always heard his mamma called by pretty, loving names, and so he used them himself when he spoke to her; he had always seen that his papa watched over her and took great care of her, and so he learned, too, to be careful of her.

So when he knew his papa would come back no more, and saw how very sad his mamma was, there gradually came into his kind little heart the thought that he must do what he could to make her happy. He was not much more than a baby, but that thought was in his mind whenever he climbed upon her knee and kissed her and put his curly head on her neck, and when he brought his toys and picture-books to show her, and when he curled up quietly by her side as she used to lie on the sofa. He was not old enough to know of anything else to do, so he did what he could, and was more of a comfort to her than he could have understood.

"Oh, Mary!" he heard her say once to her old servant; "I am sure he is trying to help me in his innocent way—I know he is. He looks at me sometimes with a loving, wondering little look, as if he were sorry for me, and then he will come and pet me or show me something. He is such a little man, I really think he knows."

As he grew older, he had a great many quaint little ways which amused and interested people greatly. He was so much of a companion for his mother that she scarcely cared for any other. They used to walk together and talk together and play together. When he was quite a little fellow, he learned to read; and after that he used to lie on the hearth-rug, in the evening, and read aloud— sometimes stories, and sometimes big books such as older people read, and sometimes even the newspaper; and often at such times Mary, in the kitchen, would hear Mrs. Errol laughing with delight at the quaint things he said.

"And, indade," said Mary to the groceryman, "nobody cud help laughin' at the quare little ways of him—and his ould-fashioned sayin's! Didn't he come into my kitchen the noight the new Prisident was nominated and shtand afore the fire, lookin' loike a pictur', wid his hands in his shmall pockets, an' his innocent bit of a face as sayrious as a jedge? An' sez he to me: 'Mary,' sez he, 'I'm very much int'rusted in the 'lection,' sez he. 'I'm a 'publican, an' so is Dearest. Are you a 'publican, Mary?' 'Sorra a bit,' sez I; 'I'm the bist o' dimmycrats!' An' he looks up at me wid a look that ud go to yer heart, an' sez he: 'Mary,' sez he, 'the country will go to ruin.' An' nivver a day since thin has he let go by widout argyin' wid me to change me polytics."

Mary was very fond of him, and very proud of him, too. She had been with his mother ever since he was born; and, after his father's death, had been cook and housemaid and nurse and everything else. She was proud of his graceful, strong little body and his pretty manners, and especially proud of the bright curly hair which waved over his forehead and fell in charming love-locks on his shoulders. She was willing to work early and late to help his mamma make his small suits and keep them in order.

"'Ristycratic, is it?" she would say. "Faith, an' I'd loike to see the choild on Fifth Avey-NOO as looks loike him an' shteps out as handsome as himself. An' ivvery man, woman, and choild lookin' afther him in his bit of a black velvet skirt made out of the misthress's ould gownd; an' his little head up, an' his curly hair flyin' an' shinin'. It's loike a young lord he looks."

Cedric did not know that he looked like a young lord; he did not know what a lord was. His greatest friend was the groceryman at the corner—the cross groceryman, who was never cross to him. His name was Mr. Hobbs, and Cedric admired and respected him very much. He thought him a very rich and powerful person, he had so many things in his store,—prunes and figs and oranges and biscuits,—and he had a horse and wagon. Cedric was fond of the milkman and the baker and the apple-woman, but he liked Mr. Hobbs best of all, and was on terms of such intimacy with him that he went to see him every day, and often sat with him quite a long time, discussing the topics of the hour. It was quite surprising how many things they found to talk about—the Fourth of July, for instance. When they began to talk about the Fourth of July there really seemed no end to it. Mr. Hobbs had a very bad opinion of "the British," and he told the whole story of the Revolution, relating very wonderful and patriotic stories about the villainy of the enemy and the bravery of the Revolutionary heroes, and he even generously repeated part of the Declaration of Independence.

Cedric was so excited that his eyes shone and his cheeks were red and his curls were all rubbed and tumbled into a yellow mop. He could hardly wait to eat his dinner after he went home, he was so anxious to tell his mamma. It was, perhaps, Mr. Hobbs who gave him his first interest in politics. Mr. Hobbs was fond of reading the newspapers, and so Cedric heard a great deal about what was going on in Washington; and Mr. Hobbs would tell him whether the President was doing his duty or not. And once, when there was an election, he found it all quite grand, and probably but for Mr. Hobbs and Cedric the country might have been wrecked.

Mr. Hobbs took him to see a great torchlight procession, and many of the men who carried torches remembered afterward a stout man who stood near a lamp-post and held on his shoulder a handsome little shouting boy, who waved his cap in the air.

It was not long after this election, when Cedric was between seven and eight years old, that the very strange thing happened which made so wonderful a change in his life. It was quite curious, too, that the day it happened he had been talking to Mr. Hobbs about England and the Queen, and Mr. Hobbs had said some very severe things about the aristocracy, being specially indignant against earls and marquises. It had been a hot morning; and after playing soldiers with some friends of his, Cedric had gone into the store to rest, and had found Mr. Hobbs looking very fierce over a piece of the Illustrated London News, which contained a picture of some court ceremony.

"Ah," he said, "that's the way they go on now; but they'll get enough of it some day, when those they've trod on rise and blow 'em up sky-high,—earls and marquises and all! It's coming, and they may look out for it!"

Cedric had perched himself as usual on the high stool and

pushed his hat back, and put his hands in his pockets in delicate compliment to Mr. Hobbs.

"Did you ever know many marquises, Mr. Hobbs?" Cedric inquired,—"or earls?"

"No," answered Mr. Hobbs, with indignation; "I guess not. I'd like to catch one of 'em inside here; that's all! I'll have no grasping tyrants sittin' 'round on my cracker-barrels!"

And he was so proud of the sentiment that he looked around proudly and mopped his forehead.

"Perhaps they wouldn't be earls if they knew any better," said Cedric, feeling some vague sympathy for their unhappy condition.

"Wouldn't they!" said Mr. Hobbs. "They just glory in it! It's in 'em. They're a bad lot."

They were in the midst of their conversation, when Mary appeared.

Cedric thought she had come to buy some sugar, perhaps, but she had not. She looked almost pale and as if she were excited about something.

"Come home, darlint," she said; "the misthress is wantin' yez."

Cedric slipped down from his stool.

"Does she want me to go out with her, Mary?" he asked. "Good-morning, Mr. Hobbs. I'll see you again."

He was surprised to see Mary staring at him in a dumfounded fashion, and he wondered why she kept shaking her head.

"What's the matter, Mary?" he said. "Is it the hot weather?"

"No," said Mary; "but there's strange things happenin' to us."

"Has the sun given Dearest a headache?" he inquired anxiously.

But it was not that. When he reached his own house there was a coupe standing before the door and some one was in the little parlor talking to his mamma. Mary hurried him upstairs and put on his best summer suit of cream-colored flannel, with the red scarf around his waist, and combed out his curly locks.

"Lords, is it?" he heard her say. "An' the nobility an' gintry. Och! bad cess to them! Lords, indade—worse luck."

It was really very puzzling, but he felt sure his mamma would tell him what all the excitement meant, so he allowed Mary to bemoan herself without asking many questions. When he was dressed, he ran downstairs and went into the parlor. A tall, thin old gentleman with a sharp face was sitting in an arm-chair. His mother was standing near by with a pale face, and he saw that there were tears in her eyes.

"Oh! Ceddie!" she cried out, and ran to her little boy and

caught him in her arms and kissed him in a frightened, troubled way. "Oh! Ceddie, darling!"

The tall old gentleman rose from his chair and looked at Cedric with his sharp eyes. He rubbed his thin chin with his bony hand as he looked.

He seemed not at all displeased.

"And so," he said at last, slowly,—"and so this is little Lord Fauntleroy."

II

There was never a more amazed little boy than Cedric during the week that followed; there was never so strange or so unreal a week. In the first place, the story his mamma told him was a very curious one. He was obliged to hear it two or three times before he could understand it. He could not imagine what Mr. Hobbs would think of it. It began with earls: his grandpapa, whom he had never seen, was an earl; and his eldest uncle, if he had not been killed by a fall from his horse, would have been an earl, too, in time; and after his death, his other uncle would have been an earl, if he had not died suddenly, in Rome, of a fever. After that, his own papa, if he had lived, would have been an earl, but, since they all had died and only Cedric was left, it appeared that HE was to be an earl after his grandpapa's death—and for the present he was Lord Fauntleroy.

He turned quite pale when he was first told of it.

"Oh! Dearest!" he said, "I should rather not be an earl. None of the boys are earls. Can't I NOT be one?"

But it seemed to be unavoidable. And when, that evening, they sat together by the open window looking out into the shabby street, he and his mother had a long talk about it. Cedric sat on his footstool, clasping one knee in his favorite attitude and wearing a bewildered little face rather red from the exertion of thinking. His grandfather had sent for him to come to England, and his mamma thought he must go.

"Because," she said, looking out of the window with sorrowful eyes, "I know your papa would wish it to be so, Ceddie. He loved his home very much; and there are many things to be thought of that a little boy can't quite understand. I should be a selfish little mother if I did not send you. When you are a man, you will see why."

Ceddie shook his head mournfully.

"I shall be very sorry to leave Mr. Hobbs," he said. "I'm afraid he'll miss me, and I shall miss him. And I shall miss them all."

When Mr. Havisham—who was the family lawyer of the Earl of Dorincourt, and who had been sent by him to bring Lord Fauntleroy to England—came the next day, Cedric heard many things. But, somehow, it did not console him to hear that he was to be a very rich man when he grew up, and that he would have castles here and castles there, and great parks and deep mines and grand estates and tenantry. He was troubled about his friend, Mr. Hobbs, and he went to see him at the store soon after breakfast, in great anxiety of mind.

9

He found him reading the morning paper, and he approached him with a grave demeanor. He really felt it would be a great shock to Mr. Hobbs to hear what had befallen him, and on his way to the store he had been thinking how it would be best to break the news.

"Hello!" said Mr. Hobbs. "Mornin'!"

"Good-morning," said Cedric.

He did not climb up on the high stool as usual, but sat down on a cracker-box and clasped his knee, and was so silent for a few moments that Mr. Hobbs finally looked up inquiringly over the top of his newspaper.

"Hello!" he said again.

Cedric gathered all his strength of mind together.

"Mr. Hobbs," he said, "do you remember what we were talking about yesterday morning?"

"Well," replied Mr. Hobbs,—"seems to me it was England."

"Yes," said Cedric; "but just when Mary came for me, you know?"

Mr. Hobbs rubbed the back of his head.

"We WAS mentioning Queen Victoria and the aristocracy."

"Yes," said Cedric, rather hesitatingly, "and—and earls; don't you know?"

"Why, yes," returned Mr. Hobbs; "we DID touch 'em up a little; that's so!"

Cedric flushed up to the curly bang on his forehead. Nothing so embarrassing as this had ever happened to him in his life. He was a little afraid that it might be a trifle embarrassing to Mr. Hobbs, too.

"You said," he proceeded, "that you wouldn't have them sitting 'round on your cracker-barrels."

"So I did!" returned Mr. Hobbs, stoutly. "And I meant it. Let 'em try it—that's all!"

"Mr. Hobbs," said Cedric, "one is sitting on this box now!"

Mr. Hobbs almost jumped out of his chair.

"What!" he exclaimed.

"Yes," Cedric announced, with due modesty; "I am one—or I am going to be. I won't deceive you."

Mr. Hobbs looked agitated. He rose up suddenly and went to look at the thermometer.

"The mercury's got into your head!" he exclaimed, turning back to examine his young friend's countenance. "It IS a hot day! How do you feel? Got any pain? When did you begin to feel that way?"

He put his big hand on the little boy's hair. This was more embarrassing than ever.

"Thank you," said Ceddie; "I'm all right. There is nothing the matter with my head. I'm sorry to say it's true, Mr. Hobbs. That was what Mary came to take me home for. Mr. Havisham was telling my mamma, and he is a lawyer."

Mr. Hobbs sank into his chair and mopped his forehead with his handkerchief.

"ONE of us has got a sunstroke!" he exclaimed.

"No," returned Cedric, "we haven't. We shall have to make the best of it, Mr. Hobbs. Mr. Havisham came all the way from England to tell us about it. My grandpapa sent him."

Mr. Hobbs stared wildly at the innocent, serious little face before him.

"Who is your grandfather?" he asked.

Cedric put his hand in his pocket and carefully drew out a piece of paper, on which something was written in his own round, irregular hand.

"I couldn't easily remember it, so I wrote it down on this," he said. And he read aloud slowly: "'John Arthur Molyneux Errol, Earl of Dorincourt.' That is his name, and he lives in a castle—in two or three castles, I think. And my papa, who died, was his youngest son; and I shouldn't have been a lord or an earl if my papa hadn't died; and my papa wouldn't have been an earl if his two brothers hadn't died. But they all died, and there is no one but me,—no boy,—and so I have to be one; and my grandpapa has sent for me to come to England."

Mr. Hobbs seemed to grow hotter and hotter. He mopped his forehead and his bald spot and breathed hard. He began to see that something very remarkable had happened; but when he looked at the little boy sitting on the cracker-box, with the innocent, anxious expression in his childish eyes, and saw that he was not changed at all, but was simply as he had been the day before, just a handsome, cheerful, brave little fellow in a blue suit and red neck-ribbon, all this information about the nobility bewildered him. He was all the more bewildered because Cedric gave it with such ingenuous simplicity, and plainly without realizing himself how stupendous it was.

"Wha—what did you say your name was?" Mr. Hobbs inquired.

"It's Cedric Errol, Lord Fauntleroy," answered Cedric. "That was what Mr. Havisham called me. He said when I went into the room: 'And so this is little Lord Fauntleroy!'"

"Well," said Mr. Hobbs, "I'll be—jiggered!"

This was an exclamation he always used when he was very

11

much astonished or excited. He could think of nothing else to say just at that puzzling moment.

Cedric felt it to be quite a proper and suitable ejaculation. His respect and affection for Mr. Hobbs were so great that he admired and approved of all his remarks. He had not seen enough of society as yet to make him realize that sometimes Mr. Hobbs was not quite conventional. He knew, of course, that he was different from his mamma, but, then, his mamma was a lady, and he had an idea that ladies were always different from gentlemen.

He looked at Mr. Hobbs wistfully.

"England is a long way off, isn't it?" he asked.

"It's across the Atlantic Ocean," Mr. Hobbs answered.

"That's the worst of it," said Cedric. "Perhaps I shall not see you again for a long time. I don't like to think of that, Mr. Hobbs."

"The best of friends must part," said Mr. Hobbs.

"Well," said Cedric, "we have been friends for a great many years, haven't we?"

"Ever since you was born," Mr. Hobbs answered. "You was about six weeks old when you was first walked out on this street."

"Ah," remarked Cedric, with a sigh, "I never thought I should have to be an earl then!"

"You think," said Mr. Hobbs, "there's no getting out of it?"

"I'm afraid not," answered Cedric. "My mamma says that my papa would wish me to do it. But if I have to be an earl, there's one thing I can do: I can try to be a good one. I'm not going to be a tyrant. And if there is ever to be another war with America, I shall try to stop it."

His conversation with Mr. Hobbs was a long and serious one. Once having got over the first shock, Mr. Hobbs was not so rancorous as might have been expected; he endeavored to resign himself to the situation, and before the interview was at an end he had asked a great many questions. As Cedric could answer but few of them, he endeavored to answer them himself, and, being fairly launched on the subject of earls and marquises and lordly estates, explained many things in a way which would probably have astonished Mr. Havisham, could that gentleman have heard it.

But then there were many things which astonished Mr. Havisham. He had spent all his life in England, and was not accustomed to American people and American habits. He had been connected professionally with the family of the Earl of Dorincourt for nearly forty years, and he knew all about its grand estates and its great wealth and importance; and, in a cold, business-like way, he felt an interest in this little boy, who, in the future, was to be the master and owner of them all,—the future Earl of Dorincourt. He had known all about the old Earl's disappointment in his elder sons and all about his fierce rage at Captain Cedric's American marriage, and he knew how he still hated the gentle little widow and would not speak of her except with bitter and cruel words. He insisted that she was only a common American girl, who had entrapped his son into marrying her because she knew he was an earl's son. The old lawyer himself had more than half believed this was all true. He had seen a great many selfish, mercenary people in his life, and he had not a good opinion of Americans. When he had been driven into the cheap street, and his coupe had stopped before the cheap, small house, he had felt actually shocked. It seemed really quite dreadful to think that the future owner of Dorincourt Castle and Wyndham Towers and Chorlworth, and all the other stately splendors, should have been born and brought up in an insignificant house in a street with a sort of green-grocery at the corner. He wondered what kind of a child he would be, and what kind of a mother he had. He rather shrank from seeing them both. He had a sort of pride in the noble family whose legal affairs he had conducted so long, and it would have annoyed him very much to have found himself obliged to manage a woman who would seem to him a vulgar, money-loving person, with no respect for her dead husband's country and the dignity of his name. It was a very old name and a very splendid one, and Mr. Havisham had a great respect for it himself, though he was only a cold, keen, business-like old lawyer.

When Mary handed him into the small parlor, he looked around it critically. It was plainly furnished, but it had a home-like look; there were no cheap, common ornaments, and no cheap, gaudy pictures; the few adornments on the walls were in good taste and about the room were many pretty things which a woman's hand might have made.

"Not at all bad so far," he had said to himself; "but perhaps the Captain's taste predominated." But when Mrs. Errol came into the room, he began to think she herself might have had something to do with it. If he had not been quite a self-contained and stiff old gentleman, he would probably have started when he saw her. She looked, in the simple black dress, fitting closely to her slender figure, more like a young girl than the mother of a boy of seven. She had a pretty, sorrowful, young face, and a very tender, innocent look in her large brown eyes,—the sorrowful look that had never quite left her face since her husband had died. Cedric was used to seeing it there; the only times he had ever seen it fade out had been when he was playing with her or talking to her, and had said some old-fashioned thing, or used some long word he had picked up out of the newspapers or in his conversations with Mr. Hobbs. He was fond of

13

using long words, and he was always pleased when they made her laugh, though he could not understand why they were laughable; they were quite serious matters with him. The lawyer's experience taught him to read people's characters very shrewdly, and as soon as he saw Cedric's mother he knew that the old Earl had made a great mistake in thinking her a vulgar, mercenary woman. Mr. Havisham had never been married, he had never even been in love, but he divined that this pretty young creature with the sweet voice and sad eyes had married Captain Errol only because she loved him with all her affectionate heart, and that she had never once thought it an advantage that he was an earl's son. And he saw he should have no trouble with her, and he began to feel that perhaps little Lord Fauntleroy might not be such a trial to his noble family, after all. The Captain had been a handsome fellow, and the young mother was very pretty, and perhaps the boy might be well enough to look at.

When he first told Mrs. Errol what he had come for, she turned very pale.

"Oh!" she said; "will he have to be taken away from me? We love each other so much! He is such a happiness to me! He is all I have. I have tried to be a good mother to him." And her sweet young voice trembled, and the tears rushed into her eyes. "You do not know what he has been to me!" she said.

The lawyer cleared his throat.

"I am obliged to tell you," he said, "that the Earl of Dorincourt is not—is not very friendly toward you. He is an old man, and his prejudices are very strong. He has always especially disliked America and Americans, and was very much enraged by his son's marriage. I am sorry to be the bearer of so unpleasant a communication, but he is very fixed in his determination not to see you. His plan is that Lord Fauntleroy shall be educated under his own supervision; that he shall live with him. The Earl is attached to Dorincourt Castle, and spends a great deal of time there. He is a victim to inflammatory gout, and is not fond of London. Lord Fauntleroy will, therefore, be likely to live chiefly at Dorincourt. The Earl offers you as a home Court Lodge, which is situated pleasantly, and is not very far from the castle. He also offers you a suitable income. Lord Fauntleroy will be permitted to visit you; the only stipulation is, that you shall not visit him or enter the park gates. You see you will not be really separated from your son, and I assure you, madam, the terms are not so harsh as—as they might have been. The advantage of such surroundings and education as Lord Fauntleroy will have, I am sure you must see, will be very great."

He felt a little uneasy lest she should begin to cry or make a

14

scene, as he knew some women would have done. It embarrassed and annoyed him to see women cry.

But she did not. She went to the window and stood with her face turned away for a few moments, and he saw she was trying to steady herself.

"Captain Errol was very fond of Dorincourt," she said at last. "He loved England, and everything English. It was always a grief to him that he was parted from his home. He was proud of his home, and of his name. He would wish—I know he would wish that his son should know the beautiful old places, and be brought up in such a way as would be suitable to his future position."

Then she came back to the table and stood looking up at Mr. Havisham very gently.

"My husband would wish it," she said. "It will be best for my little boy. I know—I am sure the Earl would not be so unkind as to try to teach him not to love me; and I know—even if he tried—that my little boy is too much like his father to be harmed. He has a warm, faithful nature, and a true heart. He would love me even if he did not see me; and so long as we may see each other, I ought not to suffer very much."

"She thinks very little of herself," the lawyer thought. "She does not make any terms for herself."

"Madam," he said aloud, "I respect your consideration for your son. He will thank you for it when he is a man. I assure you Lord Fauntleroy will be most carefully guarded, and every effort will be used to insure his happiness. The Earl of Dorincourt will be as anxious for his comfort and well-being as you yourself could be."

"I hope," said the tender little mother, in a rather broken voice, "that his grandfather will love Ceddie. The little boy has a very affectionate nature; and he has always been loved."

Mr. Havisham cleared his throat again. He could not quite imagine the gouty, fiery-tempered old Earl loving any one very much; but he knew it would be to his interest to be kind, in his irritable way, to the child who was to be his heir. He knew, too, that if Ceddie were at all a credit to his name, his grandfather would be proud of him.

"Lord Fauntleroy will be comfortable, I am sure," he replied. "It was with a view to his happiness that the Earl desired that you should be near enough to him to see him frequently."

He did not think it would be discreet to repeat the exact words the Earl had used, which were in fact neither polite nor amiable.

Mr. Havisham preferred to express his noble patron's offer in smoother and more courteous language.

He had another slight shock when Mrs. Errol asked Mary to

15

find her little boy and bring him to her, and Mary told her where he was.

"Sure I'll foind him aisy enough, ma'am," she said; "for it's wid Mr. Hobbs he is this minnit, settin' on his high shtool by the counther an' talkin' pollytics, most loikely, or enj'yin' hisself among the soap an' candles an' pertaties, as sinsible an' shwate as ye plase."

"Mr. Hobbs has known him all his life," Mrs. Errol said to the lawyer. "He is very kind to Ceddie, and there is a great friendship between them."

Remembering the glimpse he had caught of the store as he passed it, and having a recollection of the barrels of potatoes and apples and the various odds and ends, Mr. Havisham felt his doubts arise again. In England, gentlemen's sons did not make friends of grocerymen, and it seemed to him a rather singular proceeding. It would be very awkward if the child had bad manners and a disposition to like low company. One of the bitterest humiliations of the old Earl's life had been that his two elder sons had been fond of low company. Could it be, he thought, that this boy shared their bad qualities instead of his father's good qualities?

He was thinking uneasily about this as he talked to Mrs. Errol until the child came into the room. When the door opened, he actually hesitated a moment before looking at Cedric. It would, perhaps, have seemed very queer to a great many people who knew him, if they could have known the curious sensations that passed through Mr. Havisham when he looked down at the boy, who ran into his mother's arms. He experienced a revulsion of feeling which was quite exciting. He recognized in an instant that here was one of the finest and handsomest little fellows he had ever seen.

His beauty was something unusual. He had a strong, lithe, graceful little body and a manly little face; he held his childish head up, and carried himself with a brave air; he was so like his father that it was really startling; he had his father's golden hair and his mother's brown eyes, but there was nothing sorrowful or timid in them. They were innocently fearless eyes; he looked as if he had never feared or doubted anything in his life.

"He is the best-bred-looking and handsomest little fellow I ever saw," was what Mr. Havisham thought. What he said aloud was simply, "And so this is little Lord Fauntleroy."

And, after this, the more he saw of little Lord Fauntleroy, the more of a surprise he found him. He knew very little about children, though he had seen plenty of them in England—fine, handsome, rosy girls and boys, who were strictly taken care of by their tutors and governesses, and who were sometimes shy, and sometimes a trifle boisterous, but never very interesting to a ceremonious, rigid old lawyer. Perhaps his personal interest in little Lord Fauntleroy's fortunes made him notice Ceddie more than he had noticed other children; but, however that was, he certainly found himself noticing him a great deal.

Cedric did not know he was being observed, and he only behaved himself in his ordinary manner. He shook hands with Mr. Havisham in his friendly way when they were introduced to each other, and he answered all his questions with the unhesitating readiness with which he answered Mr. Hobbs. He was neither shy nor bold, and when Mr. Havisham was talking to his mother, the lawyer noticed that he listened to the conversation with as much interest as if he had been quite grown up.

"He seems to be a very mature little fellow," Mr. Havisham said to the mother.

"I think he is, in some things," she answered. "He has always been very quick to learn, and he has lived a great deal with grownup people. He has a funny little habit of using long words and expressions he has read in books, or has heard others use, but he is very fond of childish play. I think he is rather clever, but he is a very boyish little boy, sometimes."

The next time Mr. Havisham met him, he saw that this last was quite true. As his coupe turned the corner, he caught sight of a group of small boys, who were evidently much excited. Two of them were about to run a race, and one of them was his young lordship, and he was shouting and making as much noise as the noisiest of his companions. He stood side by side with another boy, one little red leg advanced a step.

"One, to make ready!" yelled the starter. "Two, to be steady. Three—and away!"

Mr. Havisham found himself leaning out of the window of his coupe with a curious feeling of interest. He really never remembered having seen anything quite like the way in which his lordship's lordly little red legs flew up behind his knickerbockers and tore over the ground as he shot out in the race at the signal word. He shut his small hands and set his face against the wind; his bright hair streamed out behind.

"Hooray, Ced Errol!" all the boys shouted, dancing and shrieking with excitement. "Hooray, Billy Williams! Hooray, Ceddie! Hooray, Billy! Hooray! 'Ray! 'Ray!"

"I really believe he is going to win," said Mr. Havisham. The way in which the red legs flew and flashed up and down, the shrieks of the boys, the wild efforts of Billy Williams, whose brown legs were not to be despised, as they followed closely in the rear of the red legs, made him feel some excitement. "I really—I really can't help hoping he will win!" he said, with an apologetic sort of cough. At that moment, the wildest yell of all went up from the dancing, hopping boys. With one last frantic leap the future Earl of Dorincourt had reached the lamp-post at the end of the block and touched it, just two seconds before Billy Williams flung himself at it, panting.

"Three cheers for Ceddie Errol!" yelled the little boys. "Hooray for Ceddie Errol!"

Mr. Havisham drew his head in at the window of his coupe and leaned back with a dry smile.

"Bravo, Lord Fauntleroy!" he said.

As his carriage stopped before the door of Mrs. Errol's house, the victor and the vanquished were coming toward it, attended by the clamoring crew. Cedric walked by Billy Williams and was speaking to him. His elated little face was very red, his curls clung to his hot, moist forehead, his hands were in his pockets.

"You see," he was saying, evidently with the intention of making defeat easy for his unsuccessful rival, "I guess I won because my legs are a little longer than yours. I guess that was it. You see, I'm three days older than you, and that gives me a 'vantage. I'm three days older."

And this view of the case seemed to cheer Billy Williams so much that he began to smile on the world again, and felt able to swagger a little, almost as if he had won the race instead of losing it. Somehow, Ceddie Errol had a way of making people feel comfortable. Even in the first flush of his triumphs, he remembered that the person who was beaten might not feel so gay as he did, and might like to think that he MIGHT have been the winner under different circumstances.

That morning Mr. Havisham had quite a long conversation with the winner of the race—a conversation which made him smile his dry smile, and rub his chin with his bony hand several times.

Mrs. Errol had been called out of the parlor, and the lawyer and Cedric were left together. At first Mr. Havisham wondered what he should say to his small companion. He had an idea that perhaps it would be best to say several things which might prepare Cedric for meeting his grandfather, and, perhaps, for the great change that was to come to him. He could see that Cedric had not the least idea of the sort of thing he was to see when he reached England, or of the sort of home that waited for him there. He did not even know yet that his mother was not to live in the same house with him. They had thought it best to let him get over the first shock before telling him.

Mr. Havisham sat in an arm-chair on one side of the open

window; on the other side was another still larger chair, and Cedric sat in that and looked at Mr. Havisham. He sat well back in the depths of his big seat, his curly head against the cushioned back, his legs crossed, and his hands thrust deep into his pockets, in a quite Mr. Hobbs-like way. He had been watching Mr. Havisham very steadily when his mamma had been in the room, and after she was gone he still looked at him in respectful thoughtfulness. There was a short silence after Mrs. Errol went out, and Cedric seemed to be studying Mr. Havisham, and Mr. Havisham was certainly studying Cedric. He could not make up his mind as to what an elderly gentleman should say to a little boy who won races, and wore short knickerbockers and red stockings on legs which were not long enough to hang over a big chair when he sat well back in it.

But Cedric relieved him by suddenly beginning the conversation himself.

"Do you know," he said, "I don't know what an earl is?"

"Don't you?" said Mr. Havisham.

"No," replied Ceddie. "And I think when a boy is going to be one, he ought to know. Don't you?"

"Well—yes," answered Mr. Havisham.

"Would you mind," said Ceddie respectfully—"would you mind 'splaining it to me?" (Sometimes when he used his long words he did not pronounce them quite correctly.) "What made him an earl?"

"A king or queen, in the first place," said Mr. Havisham. "Generally, he is made an earl because he has done some service to his sovereign, or some great deed."

"Oh!" said Cedric; "that's like the President."

"Is it?" said Mr. Havisham. "Is that why your presidents are elected?"

"Yes," answered Ceddie cheerfully. "When a man is very good and knows a great deal, he is elected president. They have torch-light processions and bands, and everybody makes speeches. I used to think I might perhaps be a president, but I never thought of being an earl. I didn't know about earls," he said, rather hastily, lest Mr. Havisham might feel it impolite in him not to have wished to be one,—"if I'd known about them, I dare say I should have thought I should like to be one."

"It is rather different from being a president," said Mr. Havisham.

"Is it?" asked Cedric. "How? Are there no torch-light processions?"

Mr. Havisham crossed his own legs and put the tips of his

19

fingers carefully together. He thought perhaps the time had come to explain matters rather more clearly.

"An earl is—is a very important person," he began.

"So is a president!" put in Ceddie. "The torch-light processions are five miles long, and they shoot up rockets, and the band plays! Mr. Hobbs took me to see them."

"An earl," Mr. Havisham went on, feeling rather uncertain of his ground, "is frequently of very ancient lineage——"

"What's that?" asked Ceddie.

"Of very old family—extremely old."

"Ah!" said Cedric, thrusting his hands deeper into his pockets. "I suppose that is the way with the apple-woman near the park. I dare say she is of ancient lin-lenage. She is so old it would surprise you how she can stand up. She's a hundred, I should think, and yet she is out there when it rains, even. I'm sorry for her, and so are the other boys. Billy Williams once had nearly a dollar, and I asked him to buy five cents' worth of apples from her every day until he had spent it all. That made twenty days, and he grew tired of apples after a week; but then—it was quite fortunate—a gentleman gave me fifty cents and I bought apples from her instead. You feel sorry for any one that's so poor and has such ancient lin-lenage. She says hers has gone into her bones and the rain makes it worse."

Mr. Havisham felt rather at a loss as he looked at his companion's innocent, serious little face.

"I am afraid you did not quite understand me," he explained. "When I said 'ancient lineage' I did not mean old age; I meant that the name of such a family has been known in the world a long time; perhaps for hundreds of years persons bearing that name have been known and spoken of in the history of their country."

"Like George Washington," said Ceddie. "I've heard of him ever since I was born, and he was known about, long before that. Mr. Hobbs says he will never be forgotten. That's because of the Declaration of Independence, you know, and the Fourth of July. You see, he was a very brave man."

"The first Earl of Dorincourt," said Mr. Havisham solemnly, "was created an earl four hundred years ago."

"Well, well!" said Ceddie. "That was a long time ago! Did you tell Dearest that? It would int'rust her very much. We'll tell her when she comes in. She always likes to hear cur'us things. What else does an earl do besides being created?"

"A great many of them have helped to govern England. Some of them have been brave men and have fought in great battles in the old days."

"I should like to do that myself," said Cedric. "My papa was a soldier, and he was a very brave man—as brave as George Washington. Perhaps that was because he would have been an earl if he hadn't died. I am glad earls are brave. That's a great 'vantage—to be a brave man. Once I used to be rather afraid of things—in the dark, you know; but when I thought about the soldiers in the Revolution and George Washington—it cured me."

"There is another advantage in being an earl, sometimes," said Mr. Havisham slowly, and he fixed his shrewd eyes on the little boy with a rather curious expression. "Some earls have a great deal of money."

He was curious because he wondered if his young friend knew what the power of money was.

"That's a good thing to have," said Ceddie innocently. "I wish I had a great deal of money."

"Do you?" said Mr. Havisham. "And why?"

"Well," explained Cedric, "there are so many things a person can do with money. You see, there's the apple-woman. If I were very rich I should buy her a little tent to put her stall in, and a little stove, and then I should give her a dollar every morning it rained, so that she could afford to stay at home. And then—oh! I'd give her a shawl. And, you see, her bones wouldn't feel so badly. Her bones are not like our bones; they hurt her when she moves. It's very painful when your bones hurt you. If I were rich enough to do all those things for her, I guess her bones would be all right."

"Ahem!" said Mr. Havisham. "And what else would you do if you were rich?"

"Oh! I'd do a great many things. Of course I should buy Dearest all sorts of beautiful things, needle-books and fans and gold thimbles and rings, and an encyclopedia, and a carriage, so that she needn't have to wait for the street-cars. If she liked pink silk dresses, I should buy her some, but she likes black best. But I'd, take her to the big stores, and tell her to look 'round and choose for herself. And then Dick——"

"Who is Dick?" asked Mr. Havisham.

"Dick is a boot-black," said his young lordship, quite warming up in his interest in plans so exciting. "He is one of the nicest boot-blacks you ever knew. He stands at the corner of a street downtown. I've known him for years. Once when I was very little, I was walking out with Dearest, and she bought me a beautiful ball that bounced, and I was carrying it and it bounced into the middle of the street where the carriages and horses were, and I was so disappointed, I began to cry—I was very little. I had kilts on. And Dick was blacking a man's shoes, and he said 'Hello!' and he ran in between the horses and caught the ball for me and wiped it off with

21

his coat and gave it to me and said, 'It's all right, young un.' So Dearest admired him very much, and so did I, and ever since then, when we go down-town, we talk to him. He says 'Hello!' and I say 'Hello!' and then we talk a little, and he tells me how trade is. It's been bad lately."

"And what would you like to do for him?" inquired the lawyer, rubbing his chin and smiling a queer smile.

"Well," said Lord Fauntleroy, settling himself in his chair with a business air, "I'd buy Jake out."

"And who is Jake?" Mr. Havisham asked.

"He's Dick's partner, and he is the worst partner a fellow could have! Dick says so. He isn't a credit to the business, and he isn't square. He cheats, and that makes Dick mad. It would make you mad, you know, if you were blacking boots as hard as you could, and being square all the time, and your partner wasn't square at all. People like Dick, but they don't like Jake, and so sometimes they don't come twice. So if I were rich, I'd buy Jake out and get Dick a 'boss' sign—he says a 'boss' sign goes a long way; and I'd get him some new clothes and new brushes, and start him out fair. He says all he wants is to start out fair."

There could have been nothing more confiding and innocent than the way in which his small lordship told his little story, quoting his friend Dick's bits of slang in the most candid good faith. He seemed to feel not a shade of a doubt that his elderly companion would be just as interested as he was himself. And in truth Mr. Havisham was beginning to be greatly interested; but perhaps not quite so much in Dick and the apple-woman as in this kind little lordling, whose curly head was so busy, under its yellow thatch, with good-natured plans for his friends, and who seemed somehow to have forgotten himself altogether.

"Is there anything——" he began. "What would you get for yourself, if you were rich?"

"Lots of things!" answered Lord Fauntleroy briskly; "but first I'd give Mary some money for Bridget—that's her sister, with twelve children, and a husband out of work. She comes here and cries, and Dearest gives her things in a basket, and then she cries again, and says: 'Blessin's be on yez, for a beautiful lady.' And I think Mr. Hobbs would like a gold watch and chain to remember me by, and a meerschaum pipe. And then I'd like to get up a company."

"A company!" exclaimed Mr. Havisham.

"Like a Republican rally," explained Cedric, becoming quite excited. "I'd have torches and uniforms and things for all the boys and myself, too. And we'd march, you know, and drill. That's what I should like for myself, if I were rich."

The door opened and Mrs. Errol came in.

"I am sorry to have been obliged to leave you so long," she said to Mr. Havisham; "but a poor woman, who is in great trouble, came to see me."

"This young gentleman," said Mr. Havisham, "has been telling me about some of his friends, and what he would do for them if he were rich."

"Bridget is one of his friends," said Mrs. Errol; "and it is Bridget to whom I have been talking in the kitchen. She is in great trouble now because her husband has rheumatic fever."

Cedric slipped down out of his big chair.

"I think I'll go and see her," he said, "and ask her how he is. He's a nice man when he is well. I'm obliged to him because he once made me a sword out of wood. He's a very talented man."

He ran out of the room, and Mr. Havisham rose from his chair. He seemed to have something in his mind which he wished to speak of.

He hesitated a moment, and then said, looking down at Mrs. Errol:

"Before I left Dorincourt Castle, I had an interview with the Earl, in which he gave me some instructions. He is desirous that his grandson should look forward with some pleasure to his future life in England, and also to his acquaintance with himself. He said that I must let his lordship know that the change in his life would bring him money and the pleasures children enjoy; if he expressed any wishes, I was to gratify them, and to tell him that his grand-father had given him what he wished. I am aware that the Earl did not expect anything quite like this; but if it would give Lord Fauntleroy pleasure to assist this poor woman, I should feel that the Earl would be displeased if he were not gratified."

For the second time, he did not repeat the Earl's exact words. His lordship had, indeed, said:

"Make the lad understand that I can give him anything he wants. Let him know what it is to be the grandson of the Earl of Dorincourt. Buy him everything he takes a fancy to; let him have money in his pockets, and tell him his grandfather put it there."

His motives were far from being good, and if he had been dealing with a nature less affectionate and warm-hearted than little Lord Fauntleroy's, great harm might have been done. And Cedric's mother was too gentle to suspect any harm. She thought that perhaps this meant that a lonely, unhappy old man, whose children were dead, wished to be kind to her little boy, and win his love and confidence. And it pleased her very much to think that Ceddie would be able to help Bridget. It made her happier to know that the very first result of the strange fortune which had befallen her little boy was that he could do kind things for those who needed kindness. Quite a warm color bloomed on her pretty young face.

"Oh!" she said, "that was very kind of the Earl; Cedric will be so glad! He has always been fond of Bridget and Michael. They are quite deserving. I have often wished I had been able to help them more. Michael is a hard-working man when he is well, but he has been ill a long time and needs expensive medicines and warm clothing and nourishing food. He and Bridget will not be wasteful of what is given them."

Mr. Havisham put his thin hand in his breast pocket and drew forth a large pocket-book. There was a queer look in his keen face. The truth was, he was wondering what the Earl of Dorincourt would say when he was told what was the first wish of his grandson that had been granted. He wondered what the cross, worldly, selfish old nobleman would think of it.

"I do not know that you have realized," he said, "that the Earl of Dorincourt is an exceedingly rich man. He can afford to gratify any caprice. I think it would please him to know that Lord Fauntleroy had been indulged in any fancy. If you will call him back and allow me, I shall give him five pounds for these people."

"That would be twenty-five dollars!" exclaimed Mrs. Errol. "It will seem like wealth to them. I can scarcely believe that it is true."

"It is quite true," said Mr. Havisham, with his dry smile. "A great change has taken place in your son's life, a great deal of power will lie in his hands."

"Oh!" cried his mother. "And he is such a little boy—a very little boy. How can I teach him to use it well? It makes me half afraid. My pretty little Ceddie!"

The lawyer slightly cleared his throat. It touched his worldly, hard old heart to see the tender, timid look in her brown eyes.

"I think, madam," he said, "that if I may judge from my interview with Lord Fauntleroy this morning, the next Earl of Dorincourt will think for others as well as for his noble self. He is only a child yet, but I think he may be trusted."

Then his mother went for Cedric and brought him back into the parlor. Mr. Havisham heard him talking before he entered the room.

"It's infam-natory rheumatism," he was saying, "and that's a kind of rheumatism that's dreadful. And he thinks about the rent not being paid, and Bridget says that makes the inf'ammation worse. And Pat could get a place in a store if he had some clothes."

His little face looked quite anxious when he came in. He was very sorry for Bridget.

"Dearest said you wanted me," he said to Mr. Havisham. "I've been talking to Bridget."

Mr. Havisham looked down at him a moment. He felt a little awkward and undecided. As Cedric's mother had said, he was a very little boy.

"The Earl of Dorincourt——" he began, and then he glanced involuntarily at Mrs. Errol.

Little Lord Fauntleroy's mother suddenly kneeled down by him and put both her tender arms around his childish body.

"Ceddie," she said, "the Earl is your grandpapa, your own papa's father. He is very, very kind, and he loves you and wishes you to love him, because the sons who were his little boys are dead. He wishes you to be happy and to make other people happy. He is very rich, and he wishes you to have everything you would like to have. He told Mr. Havisham so, and gave him a great deal of money for you. You can give some to Bridget now; enough to pay her rent and buy Michael everything. Isn't that fine, Ceddie? Isn't he good?" And she kissed the child on his round cheek, where the bright color suddenly flashed up in his excited amazement.

He looked from his mother to Mr. Havisham.

"Can I have it now?" he cried. "Can I give it to her this minute? She's just going."

Mr. Havisham handed him the money. It was in fresh, clean greenbacks and made a neat roll.

Ceddie flew out of the room with it.

"Bridget!" they heard him shout, as he tore into the kitchen. "Bridget, wait a minute! Here's some money. It's for you, and you can pay the rent. My grandpapa gave it to me. It's for you and Michael!"

"Oh, Master Ceddie!" cried Bridget, in an awe-stricken voice. "It's twenty-foive dollars is here. Where be's the misthress?"

"I think I shall have to go and explain it to her," Mrs. Errol said.

So she, too, went out of the room and Mr. Havisham was left alone for a while. He went to the window and stood looking out into the street reflectively. He was thinking of the old Earl of Dorincourt, sitting in his great, splendid, gloomy library at the castle, gouty and lonely, surrounded by grandeur and luxury, but not really loved by any one, because in all his long life he had never really loved any one but himself; he had been selfish and self-indulgent and arrogant and passionate; he had cared so much for the Earl of Dorincourt and his pleasures that there had been no time for him to think of other people; all his wealth and power, all the benefits from his noble name and high rank, had seemed to him to be things only to

25

be used to amuse and give pleasure to the Earl of Dorincourt; and now that he was an old man, all this excitement and self-indulgence had only brought him ill health and irritability and a dislike of the world, which certainly disliked him. In spite of all his splendor, there was never a more unpopular old nobleman than the Earl of Dorincourt, and there could scarcely have been a more lonely one. He could fill his castle with guests if he chose. He could give great dinners and splendid hunting parties; but he knew that in secret the people who would accept his invitations were afraid of his frowning old face and sarcastic, biting speeches. He had a cruel tongue and a bitter nature, and he took pleasure in sneering at people and making them feel uncomfortable, when he had the power to do so, because they were sensitive or proud or timid.

Mr. Havisham knew his hard, fierce ways by heart, and he was thinking of him as he looked out of the window into the narrow, quiet street. And there rose in his mind, in sharp contrast, the picture of the cheery, handsome little fellow sitting in the big chair and telling his story of his friends, Dick and the apple-woman, in his generous, innocent, honest way. And he thought of the immense income, the beautiful, majestic estates, the wealth, and power for good or evil, which in the course of time would lie in the small, chubby hands little Lord Fauntleroy thrust so deep into his pockets.

"It will make a great difference," he said to himself. "It will make a great difference."

Cedric and his mother came back soon after. Cedric was in high spirits. He sat down in his own chair, between his mother and the lawyer, and fell into one of his quaint attitudes, with his hands on his knees. He was glowing with enjoyment of Bridget's relief and rapture.

"She cried!" he said. "She said she was crying for joy! I never saw any one cry for joy before. My grandpapa must be a very good man. I didn't know he was so good a man. It's more—more agreeabler to be an earl than I thought it was. I'm almost glad—I'm almost QUITE glad I'm going to be one."

III

Cedric's good opinion of the advantages of being an earl increased greatly during the next week. It seemed almost impossible for him to realize that there was scarcely anything he might wish to do which he could not do easily; in fact, I think it may be said that he did not fully realize it at all. But at least he understood, after a few conversations with Mr. Havisham, that he could gratify all his nearest wishes, and he proceeded to gratify them with a simplicity and delight which caused Mr. Havisham much diversion. In the week before they sailed for England he did many curious things. The lawyer long after remembered the morning they went down-town together to pay a visit to Dick, and the afternoon they so amazed the apple-woman of ancient lineage by stopping before her stall and telling her she was to have a tent, and a stove, and a shawl, and a sum of money which seemed to her quite wonderful.

"For I have to go to England and be a lord," explained Cedric, sweet-temperedly. "And I shouldn't like to have your bones on my mind every time it rained. My own bones never hurt, so I think I don't know how painful a person's bones can be, but I've sympathized with you a great deal, and I hope you'll be better."

"She's a very good apple-woman," he said to Mr. Havisham, as they walked away, leaving the proprietress of the stall almost gasping for breath, and not at all believing in her great fortune. "Once, when I fell down and cut my knee, she gave me an apple for nothing. I've always remembered her for it. You know you always remember people who are kind to you."

It had never occurred to his honest, simple little mind that there were people who could forget kindnesses.

The interview with Dick was quite exciting. Dick had just been having a great deal of trouble with Jake, and was in low spirits when they saw him. His amazement when Cedric calmly announced that they had come to give him what seemed a very great thing to him, and would set all his troubles right, almost struck him dumb. Lord Fauntleroy's manner of announcing the object of his visit was very simple and unceremonious. Mr. Havisham was much impressed by its directness as he stood by and listened. The statement that his old friend had become a lord, and was in danger of being an earl if he lived long enough, caused Dick to so open his eyes and mouth, and start, that his cap fell off. When he picked it up, he uttered a rather singular exclamation. Mr. Havisham thought it singular, but Cedric had heard it before.

27

"I soy!" he said, "what're yer givin' us?" This plainly embarrassed his lordship a little, but he bore himself bravely.

"Everybody thinks it not true at first," he said. "Mr. Hobbs thought I'd had a sunstroke. I didn't think I was going to like it myself, but I like it better now I'm used to it. The one who is the Earl now, he's my grandpapa; and he wants me to do anything I like. He's very kind, if he IS an earl; and he sent me a lot of money by Mr. Havisham, and I've brought some to you to buy Jake out."

And the end of the matter was that Dick actually bought Jake out, and found himself the possessor of the business and some new brushes and a most astonishing sign and outfit. He could not believe in his good luck any more easily than the apple-woman of ancient lineage could believe in hers; he walked about like a boot-black in a dream; he stared at his young benefactor and felt as if he might wake up at any moment. He scarcely seemed to realize anything until Cedric put out his hand to shake hands with him before going away.

"Well, good-bye," he said; and though he tried to speak steadily, there was a little tremble in his voice and he winked his big brown eyes. "And I hope trade'll be good. I'm sorry I'm going away to leave you, but perhaps I shall come back again when I'm an earl. And I wish you'd write to me, because we were always good friends. And if you write to me, here's where you must send your letter." And he gave him a slip of paper. "And my name isn't Cedric Errol any more; it's Lord Fauntleroy and—and good-bye, Dick."

Dick winked his eyes also, and yet they looked rather moist about the lashes. He was not an educated boot-black, and he would have found it difficult to tell what he felt just then if he had tried; perhaps that was why he didn't try, and only winked his eyes and swallowed a lump in his throat.

"I wish ye wasn't goin' away," he said in a husky voice. Then he winked his eyes again. Then he looked at Mr. Havisham, and touched his cap. "Thanky, sir, fur bringin' him down here an' fur wot ye've done, He's—he's a queer little feller," he added. "I've allers thort a heap of him. He's such a game little feller, an'—an' such a queer little un."

And when they turned away he stood and looked after them in a dazed kind of way, and there was still a mist in his eyes, and a lump in his throat, as he watched the gallant little figure marching gayly along by the side of its tall, rigid escort.

Until the day of his departure, his lordship spent as much time as possible with Mr. Hobbs in the store. Gloom had settled upon Mr. Hobbs; he was much depressed in spirits. When his young friend brought to him in triumph the parting gift of a gold watch and chain, Mr. Hobbs found it difficult to acknowledge it properly. He laid the case on his stout knee, and blew his nose violently several times.

"There's something written on it," said Cedric,—"inside the case. I told the man myself what to say. 'From his oldest friend, Lord Fauntleroy, to Mr. Hobbs. When this you see, remember me.' I don't want you to forget me."

Mr. Hobbs blew his nose very loudly again.

"I sha'n't forget you," he said, speaking a trifle huskily, as Dick had spoken; "nor don't you go and forget me when you get among the British arrystocracy."

"I shouldn't forget you, whoever I was among," answered his lordship. "I've spent my happiest hours with you; at least, some of my happiest hours. I hope you'll come to see me sometime. I'm sure my grandpapa would be very much pleased. Perhaps he'll write and ask you, when I tell him about you. You—you wouldn't mind his being an earl, would you, I mean you wouldn't stay away just because he was one, if he invited you to come?"

"I'd come to see you," replied Mr. Hobbs, graciously.

So it seemed to be agreed that if he received a pressing invitation from the Earl to come and spend a few months at Dorincourt Castle, he was to lay aside his republican prejudices and pack his valise at once.

At last all the preparations were complete; the day came when the trunks were taken to the steamer, and the hour arrived when the carriage stood at the door. Then a curious feeling of loneliness came upon the little boy. His mamma had been shut up in her room for some time; when she came down the stairs, her eyes looked large and wet, and her sweet mouth was trembling. Cedric went to her, and she bent down to him, and he put his arms around her, and they kissed each other. He knew something made them both sorry, though he scarcely knew what it was; but one tender little thought rose to his lips.

"We liked this little house, Dearest, didn't we?" he said. "We always will like it, won't we?"

"Yes—yes," she answered, in a low, sweet voice. "Yes, darling."

And then they went into the carriage and Cedric sat very close to her, and as she looked back out of the window, he looked at her and stroked her hand and held it close.

And then, it seemed almost directly, they were on the steamer in the midst of the wildest bustle and confusion; carriages were driving down and leaving passengers; passengers were getting into a state of excitement about baggage which had not arrived and threatened to be too late; big trunks and cases were being bumped down and dragged about; sailors were uncoiling ropes and hurrying to and fro; officers were giving orders; ladies and gentlemen and children and nurses were coming on board,—some were laughing and looked gay, some were silent and sad, here and there two or three were crying and touching their eyes with their handkerchiefs. Cedric found something to interest him on every side; he looked at the piles of rope, at the furled sails, at the tall, tall masts which seemed almost to touch the hot blue sky; he began to make plans for conversing with the sailors and gaining some information on the subject of pirates.

It was just at the very last, when he was standing leaning on the railing of the upper deck and watching the final preparations, enjoying the excitement and the shouts of the sailors and wharfmen, that his attention was called to a slight bustle in one of the groups not far from him. Some one was hurriedly forcing his way through this group and coming toward him. It was a boy, with something red in his hand. It was Dick. He came up to Cedric quite breathless.

"I've run all the way," he said. "I've come down to see ye off. Trade's been prime! I bought this for ye out o' what I made yesterday. Ye kin wear it when ye get among the swells. I lost the paper when I was tryin' to get through them fellers downstairs. They didn't want to let me up. It's a hankercher."

He poured it all forth as if in one sentence. A bell rang, and he made a leap away before Cedric had time to speak.

"Good-bye!" he panted. "Wear it when ye get among the swells." And he darted off and was gone.

A few seconds later they saw him struggle through the crowd on the lower deck, and rush on shore just before the gang-plank was drawn in. He stood on the wharf and waved his cap.

Cedric held the handkerchief in his hand. It was of bright red silk ornamented with purple horseshoes and horses' heads.

There was a great straining and creaking and confusion. The people on the wharf began to shout to their friends, and the people on the steamer shouted back:

"Good-bye! Good-bye! Good-bye, old fellow!" Every one seemed to be saying, "Don't forget us. Write when you get to Liverpool. Good-bye! Good-bye!"

Little Lord Fauntleroy leaned forward and waved the red handkerchief.

"Good-bye, Dick!" he shouted, lustily. "Thank you! Good-bye, Dick!"

And the big steamer moved away, and the people cheered again, and Cedric's mother drew the veil over her eyes, and on the shore there was left great confusion; but Dick saw nothing save that bright, childish face and the bright hair that the sun shone on and the breeze lifted, and he heard nothing but the hearty childish voice calling "Good-bye, Dick!" as little Lord Fauntleroy steamed slowly away from the home of his birth to the unknown land of his ancestors.

IV

It was during the voyage that Cedric's mother told him that his home was not to be hers; and when he first understood it, his grief was so great that Mr. Havisham saw that the Earl had been wise in making the arrangements that his mother should be quite near him, and see him often; for it was very plain he could not have borne the separation otherwise. But his mother managed the little fellow so sweetly and lovingly, and made him feel that she would be so near him, that, after a while, he ceased to be oppressed by the fear of any real parting.

"My house is not far from the Castle, Ceddie," she repeated each time the subject was referred to—"a very little way from yours, and you can always run in and see me every day, and you will have so many things to tell me! and we shall be so happy together! It is a beautiful place. Your papa has often told me about it. He loved it very much; and you will love it too."

"I should love it better if you were there," his small lordship said, with a heavy little sigh.

He could not but feel puzzled by so strange a state of affairs, which could put his "Dearest" in one house and himself in another.

The fact was that Mrs. Errol had thought it better not to tell him why this plan had been made.

"I should prefer he should not be told," she said to Mr. Havisham. "He would not really understand; he would only be shocked and hurt; and I feel sure that his feeling for the Earl will be a more natural and affectionate one if he does not know that his grandfather dislikes me so bitterly. He has never seen hatred or hardness, and it would be a great blow to him to find out that any one could hate me. He is so loving himself, and I am so dear to him! It is better for him that he should not be told until he is much older, and it is far better for the Earl. It would make a barrier between them, even though Ceddie is such a child."

So Cedric only knew that there was some mysterious reason for the arrangement, some reason which he was not old enough to understand, but which would be explained when he was older. He was puzzled; but, after all, it was not the reason he cared about so much; and after many talks with his mother, in which she comforted him and placed before him the bright side of the picture, the dark side of it gradually began to fade out, though now and then Mr. Havisham saw him sitting in some queer little old-fashioned

32

attitude, watching the sea, with a very grave face, and more than once he heard an unchildish sigh rise to his lips.

"I don't like it," he said once as he was having one of his almost venerable talks with the lawyer. "You don't know how much I don't like it; but there are a great many troubles in this world, and you have to bear them. Mary says so, and I've heard Mr. Hobbs say it too. And Dearest wants me to like to live with my grandpapa, because, you see, all his children are dead, and that's very mournful. It makes you sorry for a man, when all his children have died—and one was killed suddenly."

One of the things which always delighted the people who made the acquaintance of his young lordship was the sage little air he wore at times when he gave himself up to conversation;— combined with his occasionally elderly remarks and the extreme innocence and seriousness of his round childish face, it was irresistible. He was such a handsome, blooming, curly-headed little fellow, that, when he sat down and nursed his knee with his chubby hands, and conversed with much gravity, he was a source of great entertainment to his hearers. Gradually Mr. Havisham had begun to derive a great deal of private pleasure and amusement from his society.

"And so you are going to try to like the Earl," he said.

"Yes," answered his lordship. "He's my relation, and of course you have to like your relations; and besides, he's been very kind to me. When a person does so many things for you, and wants you to have everything you wish for, of course you'd like him if he wasn't your relation; but when he's your relation and does that, why, you're very fond of him."

"Do you think," suggested Mr. Havisham, "that he will be fond of you?"

"Well," said Cedric, "I think he will, because, you see, I'm his relation, too, and I'm his boy's little boy besides, and, well, don't you see—of course he must be fond of me now, or he wouldn't want me to have everything that I like, and he wouldn't have sent you for me."

"Oh!" remarked the lawyer, "that's it, is it?"

"Yes," said Cedric, "that's it. Don't you think that's it, too? Of course a man would be fond of his grandson."

The people who had been seasick had no sooner recovered from their seasickness, and come on deck to recline in their steamer-chairs and enjoy themselves, than every one seemed to know the romantic story of little Lord Fauntleroy, and every one took an interest in the little fellow, who ran about the ship or walked with his mother or the tall, thin old lawyer, or talked to the sailors.

Every one liked him; he made friends everywhere. He was ever ready to make friends. When the gentlemen walked up and down the deck, and let him walk with them, he stepped out with a manly, sturdy little tramp, and answered all their jokes with much gay enjoyment; when the ladies talked to him, there was always laughter in the group of which he was the center; when he played with the children, there was always magnificent fun on hand. Among the sailors he had the heartiest friends; he heard miraculous stories about pirates and shipwrecks and desert islands; he learned to splice ropes and rig toy ships, and gained an amount of information concerning "tops'ls" and "mains'ls," quite surprising. His conversation had, indeed, quite a nautical flavor at times, and on one occasion he raised a shout of laughter in a group of ladies and gentlemen who were sitting on deck, wrapped in shawls and overcoats, by saying sweetly, and with a very engaging expression:

"Shiver my timbers, but it's a cold day!"

It surprised him when they laughed. He had picked up this sea-faring remark from an "elderly naval man" of the name of Jerry, who told him stories in which it occurred frequently. To judge from his stories of his own adventures, Jerry had made some two or three thousand voyages, and had been invariably shipwrecked on each occasion on an island densely populated with bloodthirsty cannibals. Judging, also, by these same exciting adventures, he had been partially roasted and eaten frequently and had been scalped some fifteen or twenty times.

"That is why he is so bald," explained Lord Fauntleroy to his mamma. "After you have been scalped several times the hair never grows again. Jerry's never grew again after that last time, when the King of the Parromachaweekins did it with the knife made out of the skull of the Chief of the Wopslemumpkies. He says it was one of the most serious times he ever had. He was so frightened that his hair stood right straight up when the king flourished his knife, and it never would lie down, and the king wears it that way now, and it looks something like a hair-brush. I never heard anything like the asperiences Jerry has had! I should so like to tell Mr. Hobbs about them!"

Sometimes, when the weather was very disagreeable and people were kept below decks in the saloon, a party of his grown-up friends would persuade him to tell them some of these "asperiences" of Jerry's, and as he sat relating them with great delight and fervor, there was certainly no more popular voyager on any ocean steamer crossing the Atlantic than little Lord Fauntleroy. He was always innocently and good-naturedly ready to do his small best to add to the general entertainment, and there was a charm in the very unconsciousness of his own childish importance.

"Jerry's stories int'rust them very much," he said to his mamma. "For my part—you must excuse me, Dearest—but sometimes I should have thought they couldn't be all quite true, if they hadn't happened to Jerry himself; but as they all happened to Jerry—well, it's very strange, you know, and perhaps sometimes he may forget and be a little mistaken, as he's been scalped so often. Being scalped a great many times might make a person forgetful."

It was eleven days after he had said good-bye to his friend Dick before he reached Liverpool; and it was on the night of the twelfth day that the carriage in which he and his mother and Mr. Havisham had driven from the station stopped before the gates of Court Lodge. They could not see much of the house in the darkness. Cedric only saw that there was a drive-way under great arching trees, and after the carriage had rolled down this drive-way a short distance, he saw an open door and a stream of bright light coming through it.

Mary had come with them to attend her mistress, and she had reached the house before them. When Cedric jumped out of the carriage he saw one or two servants standing in the wide, bright hall, and Mary stood in the door-way.

Lord Fauntleroy sprang at her with a gay little shout.

"Did you get here, Mary?" he said. "Here's Mary, Dearest," and he kissed the maid on her rough red cheek.

"I am glad you are here, Mary," Mrs. Errol said to her in a low voice. "It is such a comfort to me to see you. It takes the strangeness away." And she held out her little hand, which Mary squeezed encouragingly. She knew how this first "strangeness" must feel to this little mother who had left her own land and was about to give up her child.

The English servants looked with curiosity at both the boy and his mother. They had heard all sorts of rumors about them both; they knew how angry the old Earl had been, and why Mrs. Errol was to live at the lodge and her little boy at the castle; they knew all about the great fortune he was to inherit, and about the savage old grandfather and his gout and his tempers.

"He'll have no easy time of it, poor little chap," they had said among themselves.

But they did not know what sort of a little lord had come among them; they did not quite understand the character of the next Earl of Dorincourt.

He pulled off his overcoat quite as if he were used to doing things for himself, and began to look about him. He looked about the broad hall, at the pictures and stags' antlers and curious things that ornamented it. They seemed curious to him because he had never seen such things before in a private house.

"Dearest," he said, "this is a very pretty house, isn't it? I am glad you are going to live here. It's quite a large house."

It was quite a large house compared to the one in the shabby New York street, and it was very pretty and cheerful. Mary led them upstairs to a bright chintz-hung bedroom where a fire was burning, and a large snow-white Persian cat was sleeping luxuriously on the white fur hearth-rug.

"It was the house-kaper up at the Castle, ma'am, sint her to yez," explained Mary. "It's herself is a kind-hearted lady an' has had iverything done to prepar' fur yez. I seen her meself a few minnits, an' she was fond av the Capt'in, ma'am, an' graivs fur him; and she said to say the big cat slapin' on the rug moight make the room same homeloike to yez. She knowed Capt'in Errol whin he was a bye—an' a foine handsum' bye she ses he was, an' a foine young man wid a plisint word fur every one, great an' shmall. An' ses I to her, ses I: 'He's lift a bye that's loike him, ma'am, fur a foiner little felly niver sthipped in shoe-leather.'"

When they were ready, they went downstairs into another big bright room; its ceiling was low, and the furniture was heavy and beautifully carved, the chairs were deep and had high massive backs, and there were queer shelves and cabinets with strange, pretty ornaments on them. There was a great tiger-skin before the fire, and an arm-chair on each side of it. The stately white cat had responded to Lord Fauntleroy's stroking and followed him downstairs, and when he threw himself down upon the rug, she curled herself up grandly beside him as if she intended to make friends. Cedric was so pleased that he put his head down by hers, and lay stroking her, not noticing what his mother and Mr. Havisham were saying.

They were, indeed, speaking in a rather low tone. Mrs. Errol looked a little pale and agitated.

"He need not go to-night?" she said. "He will stay with me to-night?"

"Yes," answered Mr. Havisham in the same low tone; "it will not be necessary for him to go to-night. I myself will go to the Castle as soon as we have dined, and inform the Earl of our arrival."

Mrs. Errol glanced down at Cedric. He was lying in a graceful, careless attitude upon the black-and-yellow skin; the fire shone on his handsome, flushed little face, and on the tumbled, curly hair spread out on the rug; the big cat was purring in drowsy content,— she liked the caressing touch of the kind little hand on her fur.

Mrs. Errol smiled faintly.

"His lordship does not know all that he is taking from me," she said rather sadly. Then she looked at the lawyer. "Will you tell him, if you please," she said, "that I should rather not have the money?"

"The money!" Mr. Havisham exclaimed. "You can not mean the income he proposed to settle upon you!"

"Yes," she answered, quite simply; "I think I should rather not have it. I am obliged to accept the house, and I thank him for it, because it makes it possible for me to be near my child; but I have a little money of my own,—enough to live simply upon,—and I should rather not take the other. As he dislikes me so much, I should feel a little as if I were selling Cedric to him. I am giving him up only because I love him enough to forget myself for his good, and because his father would wish it to be so."

Mr. Havisham rubbed his chin.

"This is very strange," he said. "He will be very angry. He won't understand it."

"I think he will understand it after he thinks it over," she said. "I do not really need the money, and why should I accept luxuries from the man who hates me so much that he takes my little boy from me—his son's child?"

Mr. Havisham looked reflective for a few moments.

"I will deliver your message," he said afterward.

And then the dinner was brought in and they sat down together, the big cat taking a seat on a chair near Cedric's and purring majestically throughout the meal.

When, later in the evening, Mr. Havisham presented himself at the Castle, he was taken at once to the Earl. He found him sitting by the fire in a luxurious easy-chair, his foot on a gout-stool. He looked at the lawyer sharply from under his shaggy eyebrows, but Mr. Havisham could see that, in spite of his pretense at calmness, he was nervous and secretly excited.

"Well," he said; "well, Havisham, come back, have you? What's the news?"

"Lord Fauntleroy and his mother are at Court Lodge," replied Mr. Havisham. "They bore the voyage very well and are in excellent health."

The Earl made a half-impatient sound and moved his hand restlessly.

"Glad to hear it," he said brusquely. "So far, so good. Make yourself comfortable. Have a glass of wine and settle down. What else?"

"His lordship remains with his mother to-night. To-morrow I will bring him to the Castle."

The Earl's elbow was resting on the arm of his chair; he put his hand up and shielded his eyes with it.

"Well," he said; "go on. You know I told you not to write to me about the matter, and I know nothing whatever about it. What kind of a lad is he? I don't care about the mother; what sort of a lad is he?"

Mr. Havisham drank a little of the glass of port he had poured out for himself, and sat holding it in his hand.

"It is rather difficult to judge of the character of a child of seven," he said cautiously.

The Earl's prejudices were very intense. He looked up quickly and uttered a rough word.

"A fool, is he?" he exclaimed. "Or a clumsy cub? His American blood tells, does it?"

"I do not think it has injured him, my lord," replied the lawyer in his dry, deliberate fashion. "I don't know much about children, but I thought him rather a fine lad."

His manner of speech was always deliberate and unenthusiastic, but he made it a trifle more so than usual. He had a shrewd fancy that it would be better that the Earl should judge for himself, and be quite unprepared for his first interview with his grandson.

"Healthy and well-grown?" asked my lord.

"Apparently very healthy, and quite well-grown," replied the lawyer.

"Straight-limbed and well enough to look at?" demanded the Earl.

A very slight smile touched Mr. Havisham's thin lips. There rose up before his mind's eye the picture he had left at Court Lodge,—the beautiful, graceful child's body lying upon the tiger-skin in careless comfort—the bright, tumbled hair spread on the rug—the bright, rosy boy's face.

"Rather a handsome boy, I think, my lord, as boys go," he said, "though I am scarcely a judge, perhaps. But you will find him somewhat different from most English children, I dare say."

"I haven't a doubt of that," snarled the Earl, a twinge of gout seizing him. "A lot of impudent little beggars, those American children; I've heard that often enough."

"It is not exactly impudence in his case," said Mr. Havisham. "I can scarcely describe what the difference is. He has lived more with older people than with children, and the difference seems to be a mixture of maturity and childishness."

38

"American impudence!" protested the Earl. "I've heard of it before. They call it precocity and freedom. Beastly, impudent bad manners; that's what it is!"

Mr. Havisham drank some more port. He seldom argued with his lordly patron,—never when his lordly patron's noble leg was inflamed by gout. At such times it was always better to leave him alone. So there was a silence of a few moments. It was Mr. Havisham who broke it.

"I have a message to deliver from Mrs. Errol," he remarked.

"I don't want any of her messages!" growled his lordship; "the less I hear of her the better."

"This is a rather important one," explained the lawyer. "She prefers not to accept the income you proposed to settle on her."

The Earl started visibly.

"What's that?" he cried out. "What's that?"

Mr. Havisham repeated his words.

"She says it is not necessary, and that as the relations between you are not friendly——"

"Not friendly!" ejaculated my lord savagely; "I should say they were not friendly! I hate to think of her! A mercenary, sharp-voiced American! I don't wish to see her."

"My lord," said Mr. Havisham, "you can scarcely call her mercenary. She has asked for nothing. She does not accept the money you offer her."

"All done for effect!" snapped his noble lordship. "She wants to wheedle me into seeing her. She thinks I shall admire her spirit. I don't admire it! It's only American independence! I won't have her living like a beggar at my park gates. As she's the boy's mother, she has a position to keep up, and she shall keep it up. She shall have the money, whether she likes it or not!"

"She won't spend it," said Mr. Havisham.

"I don't care whether she spends it or not!" blustered my lord. "She shall have it sent to her. She sha'n't tell people that she has to live like a pauper because I have done nothing for her! She wants to give the boy a bad opinion of me! I suppose she has poisoned his mind against me already!"

"No," said Mr. Havisham. "I have another message, which will prove to you that she has not done that."

"I don't want to hear it!" panted the Earl, out of breath with anger and excitement and gout.

But Mr. Havisham delivered it.

"She asks you not to let Lord Fauntleroy hear anything which would lead him to understand that you separate him from her because of your prejudice against her. He is very fond of her, and

39

she is convinced that it would cause a barrier to exist between you. She says he would not comprehend it, and it might make him fear you in some measure, or at least cause him to feel less affection for you. She has told him that he is too young to understand the reason, but shall hear it when he is older. She wishes that there should be no shadow on your first meeting."

The Earl sank back into his chair. His deep-set fierce old eyes gleamed under his beetling brows.

"Come, now!" he said, still breathlessly. "Come, now! You don't mean the mother hasn't told him?"

"Not one word, my lord," replied the lawyer coolly. "That I can assure you. The child is prepared to believe you the most amiable and affectionate of grandparents. Nothing—absolutely nothing has been said to him to give him the slightest doubt of your perfection. And as I carried out your commands in every detail, while in New York, he certainly regards you as a wonder of generosity."

"He does, eh?" said the Earl.

"I give you my word of honor," said Mr. Havisham, "that Lord Fauntleroy's impressions of you will depend entirely upon yourself. And if you will pardon the liberty I take in making the suggestion, I think you will succeed better with him if you take the precaution not to speak slightingly of his mother."

"Pooh, pooh!" said the Earl. "The youngster is only seven years old!"

"He has spent those seven years at his mother's side," returned Mr. Havisham; "and she has all his affection."

V

It was late in the afternoon when the carriage containing little Lord Fauntleroy and Mr. Havisham drove up the long avenue which led to the castle. The Earl had given orders that his grandson should arrive in time to dine with him; and for some reason best known to himself, he had also ordered that the child should be sent alone into the room in which he intended to receive him. As the carriage rolled up the avenue, Lord Fauntleroy sat leaning comfortably against the luxurious cushions, and regarded the prospect with great interest. He was, in fact, interested in everything he saw. He had been interested in the carriage, with its large, splendid horses and their glittering harness; he had been interested in the tall coachman and footman, with their resplendent livery; and he had been especially interested in the coronet on the panels, and had struck up an acquaintance with the footman for the purpose of inquiring what it meant.

When the carriage reached the great gates of the park, he looked out of the window to get a good view of the huge stone lions ornamenting the entrance. The gates were opened by a motherly, rosy-looking woman, who came out of a pretty, ivy-covered lodge. Two children ran out of the door of the house and stood looking with round, wide-open eyes at the little boy in the carriage, who looked at them also. Their mother stood courtesying and smiling, and the children, on receiving a sign from her, made bobbing little courtesies too.

"Does she know me?" asked Lord Fauntleroy. "I think she must think she knows me." And he took off his black velvet cap to her and smiled.

"How do you do?" he said brightly. "Good-afternoon!"

The woman seemed pleased, he thought. The smile broadened on her rosy face and a kind look came into her blue eyes.

"God bless your lordship!" she said. "God bless your pretty face! Good luck and happiness to your lordship! Welcome to you!"

Lord Fauntleroy waved his cap and nodded to her again as the carriage rolled by her.

"I like that woman," he said. "She looks as if she liked boys. I should like to come here and play with her children. I wonder if she has enough to make up a company?"

Mr. Havisham did not tell him that he would scarcely be allowed to make playmates of the gate-keeper's children. The lawyer thought there was time enough for giving him that information.

The carriage rolled on and on between the great, beautiful trees which grew on each side of the avenue and stretched their broad, swaying branches in an arch across it. Cedric had never seen such trees,—they were so grand and stately, and their branches grew so low down on their huge trunks. He did not then know that Dorincourt Castle was one of the most beautiful in all England; that its park was one of the broadest and finest, and its trees and avenue almost without rivals. But he did know that it was all very beautiful. He liked the big, broad-branched trees, with the late afternoon sunlight striking golden lances through them. He liked the perfect stillness which rested on everything. He felt a great, strange pleasure in the beauty of which he caught glimpses under and between the sweeping boughs—the great, beautiful spaces of the park, with still other trees standing sometimes stately and alone, and sometimes in groups. Now and then they passed places where tall ferns grew in masses, and again and again the ground was azure with the bluebells swaying in the soft breeze. Several times he started up with a laugh of delight as a rabbit leaped up from under the greenery and scudded away with a twinkle of short white tail behind it. Once a covey of partridges rose with a sudden whir and flew away, and then he shouted and clapped his hands.

"It's a beautiful place, isn't it?" he said to Mr. Havisham. "I never saw such a beautiful place. It's prettier even than Central Park."

He was rather puzzled by the length of time they were on their way.

"How far is it," he said, at length, "from the gate to the front door?"

"It is between three and four miles," answered the lawyer.

"That's a long way for a person to live from his gate," remarked his lordship.

Every few minutes he saw something new to wonder at and admire. When he caught sight of the deer, some couched in the grass, some standing with their pretty antlered heads turned with a half-startled air toward the avenue as the carriage wheels disturbed them, he was enchanted.

"Has there been a circus?" he cried; "or do they live here always? Whose are they?"

"They live here," Mr. Havisham told him. "They belong to the Earl, your grandfather."

It was not long after this that they saw the castle. It rose up before them stately and beautiful and gray, the last rays of the sun casting dazzling lights on its many windows. It had turrets and battlements and towers; a great deal of ivy grew upon its walls; all the broad, open space about it was laid out in terraces and lawns and beds of brilliant flowers.

"It's the most beautiful place I ever saw!" said Cedric, his round face flushing with pleasure. "It reminds any one of a king's palace. I saw a picture of one once in a fairy-book."

He saw the great entrance-door thrown open and many servants standing in two lines looking at him. He wondered why they were standing there, and admired their liveries very much. He did not know that they were there to do honor to the little boy to whom all this splendor would one day belong,—the beautiful castle like the fairy king's palace, the magnificent park, the grand old trees, the dells full of ferns and bluebells where the hares and rabbits played, the dappled, large-eyed deer couching in the deep grass. It was only a couple of weeks since he had sat with Mr. Hobbs among the potatoes and canned peaches, with his legs dangling from the high stool; it would not have been possible for him to realize that he had very much to do with all this grandeur. At the head of the line of servants there stood an elderly woman in a rich, plain black silk gown; she had gray hair and wore a cap. As he entered the hall she stood nearer than the rest, and the child thought from the look in her eyes that she was going to speak to him. Mr. Havisham, who held his hand, paused a moment.

"This is Lord Fauntleroy, Mrs. Mellon," he said. "Lord Fauntleroy, this is Mrs. Mellon, who is the housekeeper."

Cedric gave her his hand, his eyes lighting up.

"Was it you who sent the cat?" he said. "I'm much obliged to you, ma'am."

Mrs. Mellon's handsome old face looked as pleased as the face of the lodge-keeper's wife had done.

"I should know his lordship anywhere," she said to Mr. Havisham. "He has the Captain's face and way. It's a great day, this, sir."

Cedric wondered why it was a great day. He looked at Mrs. Mellon curiously. It seemed to him for a moment as if there were tears in her eyes, and yet it was evident she was not unhappy. She smiled down on him.

"The cat left two beautiful kittens here," she said; "they shall be sent up to your lordship's nursery."

Mr. Havisham said a few words to her in a low voice.

"In the library, sir," Mrs. Mellon replied. "His lordship is to be taken there alone."

A few minutes later, the very tall footman in livery, who had escorted Cedric to the library door, opened it and announced: "Lord Fauntleroy, my lord," in quite a majestic tone. If he was only a footman, he felt it was rather a grand occasion when the heir came home to his own land and possessions, and was ushered into the presence of the old Earl, whose place and title he was to take.

Cedric crossed the threshold into the room. It was a very large and splendid room, with massive carven furniture in it, and shelves upon shelves of books; the furniture was so dark, and the draperies so heavy, the diamond-paned windows were so deep, and it seemed such a distance from one end of it to the other, that, since the sun had gone down, the effect of it all was rather gloomy. For a moment Cedric thought there was nobody in the room, but soon he saw that by the fire burning on the wide hearth there was a large easy-chair and that in that chair some one was sitting—some one who did not at first turn to look at him.

But he had attracted attention in one quarter at least. On the floor, by the arm-chair, lay a dog, a huge tawny mastiff, with body and limbs almost as big as a lion's; and this great creature rose majestically and slowly, and marched toward the little fellow with a heavy step.

Then the person in the chair spoke. "Dougal," he called, "come back, sir."

But there was no more fear in little Lord Fauntleroy's heart than there was unkindness—he had been a brave little fellow all his life. He put his hand on the big dog's collar in the most natural way in the world, and they strayed forward together, Dougal sniffing as he went.

And then the Earl looked up. What Cedric saw was a large old man with shaggy white hair and eyebrows, and a nose like an eagle's beak between his deep, fierce eyes. What the Earl saw was a graceful, childish figure in a black velvet suit, with a lace collar, and with love-locks waving about the handsome, manly little face, whose eyes met his with a look of innocent good-fellowship. If the Castle was like the palace in a fairy story, it must be owned that little Lord Fauntleroy was himself rather like a small copy of the fairy prince, though he was not at all aware of the fact, and perhaps was rather a sturdy young model of a fairy. But there was a sudden glow of triumph and exultation in the fiery old Earl's heart as he saw what a strong, beautiful boy this grandson was, and how unhesitatingly he looked up as he stood with his hand on the big dog's neck. It pleased the grim old nobleman that the child should show no shyness or fear, either of the dog or of himself.

Cedric looked at him just as he had looked at the woman at the lodge and at the housekeeper, and came quite close to him.

"Are you the Earl?" he said. "I'm your grandson, you know, that Mr. Havisham brought. I'm Lord Fauntleroy."

He held out his hand because he thought it must be the polite and proper thing to do even with earls. "I hope you are very well," he continued, with the utmost friendliness. "I'm very glad to see you."

The Earl shook hands with him, with a curious gleam in his eyes; just at first, he was so astonished that he scarcely knew what to say. He stared at the picturesque little apparition from under his shaggy brows, and took it all in from head to foot.

"Glad to see me, are you?" he said.

"Yes," answered Lord Fauntleroy, "very."

There was a chair near him, and he sat down on it; it was a high-backed, rather tall chair, and his feet did not touch the floor when he had settled himself in it, but he seemed to be quite comfortable as he sat there, and regarded his august relative intently but modestly.

"I've kept wondering what you would look like," he remarked. "I used to lie in my berth in the ship and wonder if you would be anything like my father."

"Am I?" asked the Earl.

"Well," Cedric replied, "I was very young when he died, and I may not remember exactly how he looked, but I don't think you are like him."

"You are disappointed, I suppose?" suggested his grandfather.

"Oh, no," responded Cedric politely. "Of course you would like any one to look like your father; but of course you would enjoy the way your grandfather looked, even if he wasn't like your father. You know how it is yourself about admiring your relations."

The Earl leaned back in his chair and stared. He could not be said to know how it was about admiring his relations. He had employed most of his noble leisure in quarreling violently with them, in turning them out of his house, and applying abusive epithets to them; and they all hated him cordially.

"Any boy would love his grandfather," continued Lord Fauntleroy, "especially one that had been as kind to him as you have been."

Another queer gleam came into the old nobleman's eyes.

"Oh!" he said, "I have been kind to you, have I?"

"Yes," answered Lord Fauntleroy brightly; "I'm ever so much obliged to you about Bridget, and the apple-woman, and Dick."

"Bridget!" exclaimed the Earl. "Dick! The apple-woman!"

"Yes!" explained Cedric; "the ones you gave me all that money for—the money you told Mr. Havisham to give me if I wanted it."

"Ha!" ejaculated his lordship. "That's it, is it? The money you were to spend as you liked. What did you buy with it? I should like to hear something about that."

He drew his shaggy eyebrows together and looked at the child sharply. He was secretly curious to know in what way the lad had indulged himself.

"Oh!" said Lord Fauntleroy, "perhaps you didn't know about Dick and the apple-woman and Bridget. I forgot you lived such a long way off from them. They were particular friends of mine. And you see Michael had the fever——"

"Who's Michael?" asked the Earl.

"Michael is Bridget's husband, and they were in great trouble. When a man is sick and can't work and has twelve children, you know how it is. And Michael has always been a sober man. And Bridget used to come to our house and cry. And the evening Mr. Havisham was there, she was in the kitchen crying, because they had almost nothing to eat and couldn't pay the rent; and I went in to see her, and Mr. Havisham sent for me and he said you had given him some money for me. And I ran as fast as I could into the kitchen and gave it to Bridget; and that made it all right; and Bridget could scarcely believe her eyes. That's why I'm so obliged to you."

"Oh!" said the Earl in his deep voice, "that was one of the things you did for yourself, was it? What else?"

Dougal had been sitting by the tall chair; the great dog had taken its place there when Cedric sat down. Several times it had turned and looked up at the boy as if interested in the conversation. Dougal was a solemn dog, who seemed to feel altogether too big to take life's responsibilities lightly. The old Earl, who knew the dog well, had watched it with secret interest. Dougal was not a dog whose habit it was to make acquaintances rashly, and the Earl wondered somewhat to see how quietly the brute sat under the touch of the childish hand. And, just at this moment, the big dog gave little Lord Fauntleroy one more look of dignified scrutiny, and deliberately laid its huge, lion-like head on the boy's black-velvet knee.

The small hand went on stroking this new friend as Cedric answered:

"Well, there was Dick," he said. "You'd like Dick, he's so square."

This was an Americanism the Earl was not prepared for.

"What does that mean?" he inquired.

Lord Fauntleroy paused a moment to reflect. He was not very sure himself what it meant. He had taken it for granted as meaning something very creditable because Dick had been fond of using it.

"I think it means that he wouldn't cheat any one," he

exclaimed; "or hit a boy who was under his size, and that he blacks people's boots very well and makes them shine as much as he can. He's a perfessional bootblack."

"And he's one of your acquaintances, is he?" said the Earl.

"He is an old friend of mine," replied his grandson. "Not quite as old as Mr. Hobbs, but quite old. He gave me a present just before the ship sailed."

He put his hand into his pocket and drew forth a neatly folded red object and opened it with an air of affectionate pride. It was the red silk handkerchief with the large purple horse-shoes and heads on it.

"He gave me this," said his young lordship. "I shall keep it always. You can wear it round your neck or keep it in your pocket. He bought it with the first money he earned after I bought Jake out and gave him the new brushes. It's a keepsake. I put some poetry in Mr. Hobbs's watch. It was, 'When this you see, remember me.' When this I see, I shall always remember Dick."

The sensations of the Right Honorable the Earl of Dorincourt could scarcely be described. He was not an old nobleman who was very easily bewildered, because he had seen a great deal of the world; but here was something he found so novel that it almost took his lordly breath away, and caused him some singular emotions. He had never cared for children; he had been so occupied with his own pleasures that he had never had time to care for them. His own sons had not interested him when they were very young—though sometimes he remembered having thought Cedric's father a handsome and strong little fellow. He had been so selfish himself that he had missed the pleasure of seeing unselfishness in others, and he had not known how tender and faithful and affectionate a kind-hearted little child can be, and how innocent and unconscious are its simple, generous impulses. A boy had always seemed to him a most objectionable little animal, selfish and greedy and boisterous when not under strict restraint; his own two eldest sons had given their tutors constant trouble and annoyance, and of the younger one he fancied he had heard few complaints because the boy was of no particular importance. It had never once occurred to him that he should like his grandson; he had sent for the little Cedric because his pride impelled him to do so. If the boy was to take his place in the future, he did not wish his name to be made ridiculous by descending to an uneducated boor. He had been convinced the boy would be a clownish fellow if he were brought up in America. He had no feeling of affection for the lad; his only hope was that he should find him decently well-featured, and with a respectable share of sense; he had been so disappointed in his other sons, and had

47

been made so furious by Captain Errol's American marriage, that he had never once thought that anything creditable could come of it. When the footman had announced Lord Fauntleroy, he had almost dreaded to look at the boy lest he should find him all that he had feared. It was because of this feeling that he had ordered that the child should be sent to him alone. His pride could not endure that others should see his disappointment if he was to be disappointed. His proud, stubborn old heart therefore had leaped within him when the boy came forward with his graceful, easy carriage, his fearless hand on the big dog's neck. Even in the moments when he had hoped the most, the Earl had never hoped that his grandson would look like that. It seemed almost too good to be true that this should be the boy he had dreaded to see—the child of the woman he so disliked—this little fellow with so much beauty and such a brave, childish grace! The Earl's stern composure was quite shaken by this startling surprise.

And then their talk began; and he was still more curiously moved, and more and more puzzled. In the first place, he was so used to seeing people rather afraid and embarrassed before him, that he had expected nothing else but that his grandson would be timid or shy. But Cedric was no more afraid of the Earl than he had been of Dougal. He was not bold; he was only innocently friendly, and he was not conscious that there could be any reason why he should be awkward or afraid. The Earl could not help seeing that the little boy took him for a friend and treated him as one, without having any doubt of him at all. It was quite plain as the little fellow sat there in his tall chair and talked in his friendly way that it had never occurred to him that this large, fierce-looking old man could be anything but kind to him, and rather pleased to see him there. And it was plain, too, that, in his childish way, he wished to please and interest his grandfather. Cross, and hard-hearted, and worldly as the old Earl was, he could not help feeling a secret and novel pleasure in this very confidence. After all, it was not disagreeable to meet some one who did not distrust him or shrink from him, or seem to detect the ugly part of his nature; some one who looked at him with clear, unsuspecting eyes,—if it was only a little boy in a black velvet suit.

So the old man leaned back in his chair, and led his young companion on to telling him still more of himself, and with that odd gleam in his eyes watched the little fellow as he talked. Lord Fauntleroy was quite willing to answer all his questions and chatted on in his genial little way quite composedly. He told him all about Dick and Jake, and the apple-woman, and Mr. Hobbs; he described the Republican Rally in all the glory of its banners and

48

transparencies, torches and rockets. In the course of the conversation, he reached the Fourth of July and the Revolution, and was just becoming enthusiastic, when he suddenly recollected something and stopped very abruptly.

"What is the matter?" demanded his grandfather. "Why don't you go on?"

Lord Fauntleroy moved rather uneasily in his chair. It was evident to the Earl that he was embarrassed by the thought which had just occurred to him.

"I was just thinking that perhaps you mightn't like it," he replied. "Perhaps some one belonging to you might have been there. I forgot you were an Englishman."

"You can go on," said my lord. "No one belonging to me was there. You forgot you were an Englishman, too."

"Oh! no," said Cedric quickly. "I'm an American!"

"You are an Englishman," said the Earl grimly. "Your father was an Englishman."

It amused him a little to say this, but it did not amuse Cedric. The lad had never thought of such a development as this. He felt himself grow quite hot up to the roots of his hair.

"I was born in America," he protested. "You have to be an American if you are born in America. I beg your pardon," with serious politeness and delicacy, "for contradicting you. Mr. Hobbs told me, if there were another war, you know, I should have to—to be an American."

The Earl gave a grim half laugh—it was short and grim, but it was a laugh.

"You would, would you?" he said.

He hated America and Americans, but it amused him to see how serious and interested this small patriot was. He thought that so good an American might make a rather good Englishman when he was a man.

They had not time to go very deep into the Revolution again— and indeed Lord Fauntleroy felt some delicacy about returning to the subject—before dinner was announced.

Cedric left his chair and went to his noble kinsman. He looked down at his gouty foot.

"Would you like me to help you?" he said politely. "You could lean on me, you know. Once when Mr. Hobbs hurt his foot with a potato-barrel rolling on it, he used to lean on me."

The big footman almost periled his reputation and his situation by smiling. He was an aristocratic footman who had always lived in the best of noble families, and he had never smiled; indeed, he would have felt himself a disgraced and vulgar footman if he had allowed himself to be led by any circumstance whatever into such an indiscretion as a smile. But he had a very narrow escape. He only just saved himself by staring straight over the Earl's head at a very ugly picture.

The Earl looked his valiant young relative over from head to foot.

"Do you think you could do it?" he asked gruffly.

"I THINK I could," said Cedric. "I'm strong. I'm seven, you know. You could lean on your stick on one side, and on me on the other. Dick says I've a good deal of muscle for a boy that's only seven."

He shut his hand and moved it upward to his shoulder, so that the Earl might see the muscle Dick had kindly approved of, and his face was so grave and earnest that the footman found it necessary to look very hard indeed at the ugly picture.

"Well," said the Earl, "you may try."

Cedric gave him his stick and began to assist him to rise. Usually, the footman did this, and was violently sworn at when his lordship had an extra twinge of gout. The Earl was not a very polite person as a rule, and many a time the huge footmen about him quaked inside their imposing liveries.

But this evening he did not swear, though his gouty foot gave him more twinges than one. He chose to try an experiment. He got up slowly and put his hand on the small shoulder presented to him with so much courage. Little Lord Fauntleroy made a careful step forward, looking down at the gouty foot.

"Just lean on me," he said, with encouraging good cheer. "I'll walk very slowly."

If the Earl had been supported by the footman he would have rested less on his stick and more on his assistant's arm. And yet it was part of his experiment to let his grandson feel his burden as no light weight. It was quite a heavy weight indeed, and after a few steps his young lordship's face grew quite hot, and his heart beat rather fast, but he braced himself sturdily, remembering his muscle and Dick's approval of it.

"Don't be afraid of leaning on me," he panted. "I'm all right— if—if it isn't a very long way."

It was not really very far to the dining-room, but it seemed rather a long way to Cedric, before they reached the chair at the head of the table. The hand on his shoulder seemed to grow heavier at every step, and his face grew redder and hotter, and his breath shorter, but he never thought of giving up; he stiffened his childish muscles, held his head erect, and encouraged the Earl as he limped along.

"Does your foot hurt you very much when you stand on it?" he asked. "Did you ever put it in hot water and mustard? Mr. Hobbs used to put his in hot water. Arnica is a very nice thing, they tell me."

The big dog stalked slowly beside them, and the big footman followed; several times he looked very queer as he watched the little figure making the very most of all its strength, and bearing its burden with such good-will. The Earl, too, looked rather queer, once, as he glanced sidewise down at the flushed little face. When they entered the room where they were to dine, Cedric saw it was a very large and imposing one, and that the footman who stood behind the chair at the head of the table stared very hard as they came in.

But they reached the chair at last. The hand was removed from his shoulder, and the Earl was fairly seated.

Cedric took out Dick's handkerchief and wiped his forehead.

"It's a warm night, isn't it?" he said. "Perhaps you need a fire because—because of your foot, but it seems just a little warm to me."

His delicate consideration for his noble relative's feelings was such that he did not wish to seem to intimate that any of his surroundings were unnecessary.

"You have been doing some rather hard work," said the Earl.

"Oh, no!" said Lord Fauntleroy, "it wasn't exactly hard, but I got a little warm. A person will get warm in summer time."

And he rubbed his damp curls rather vigorously with the gorgeous handkerchief. His own chair was placed at the other end of the table, opposite his grandfather's. It was a chair with arms, and intended for a much larger individual than himself; indeed, everything he had seen so far,—the great rooms, with their high ceilings, the massive furniture, the big footman, the big dog, the Earl himself,—were all of proportions calculated to make this little lad feel that he was very small, indeed. But that did not trouble him; he had never thought himself very large or important, and he was quite willing to accommodate himself even to circumstances which rather overpowered him.

Perhaps he had never looked so little a fellow as when seated now in his great chair, at the end of the table. Notwithstanding his solitary existence, the Earl chose to live in some state. He was fond of his dinner, and he dined in a formal style. Cedric looked at him across a glitter of splendid glass and plate, which to his unaccustomed eyes seemed quite dazzling. A stranger looking on might well have smiled at the picture,—the great stately room, the big liveried servants, the bright lights, the glittering silver and glass, the fierce-looking old nobleman at the head of the table and the very small boy at the foot. Dinner was usually a very serious matter with the Earl—and it was a very serious matter with the cook, if his lordship was not pleased or had an indifferent appetite. To-day, however, his appetite seemed a trifle better than usual, perhaps because he had something to think of beside the flavor of the entrees and the management of the gravies. His grandson gave him something to think of. He kept looking at him across the table. He did not say very much himself, but he managed to make the boy talk. He had never imagined that he could be entertained by hearing a child talk, but Lord Fauntleroy at once puzzled and amused him, and he kept remembering how he had let the childish shoulder feel his weight just for the sake of trying how far the boy's courage and endurance would go, and it pleased him to know that his grandson had not quailed and had not seemed to think even for a moment of giving up what he had undertaken to do.

"You don't wear your coronet all the time?" remarked Lord Fauntleroy respectfully.

"No," replied the Earl, with his grim smile; "it is not becoming to me."

"Mr. Hobbs said you always wore it," said Cedric; "but after he thought it over, he said he supposed you must sometimes take it off to put your hat on."

"Yes," said the Earl, "I take it off occasionally."

And one of the footmen suddenly turned aside and gave a singular little cough behind his hand.

Cedric finished his dinner first, and then he leaned back in his chair and took a survey of the room.

"You must be very proud of your house," he said, "it's such a beautiful house. I never saw anything so beautiful; but, of course, as I'm only seven, I haven't seen much."

"And you think I must be proud of it, do you?" said the Earl.

"I should think any one would be proud of it," replied Lord Fauntleroy. "I should be proud of it if it were my house. Everything about it is beautiful. And the park, and those trees,—how beautiful they are, and how the leaves rustle!"

Then he paused an instant and looked across the table rather wistfully.

"It's a very big house for just two people to live in, isn't it?" he said.

"It is quite large enough for two," answered the Earl. "Do you find it too large?"

His little lordship hesitated a moment.

"I was only thinking," he said, "that if two people lived in it who were not very good companions, they might feel lonely sometimes."

"Do you think I shall make a good companion?" inquired the Earl.

"Yes," replied Cedric, "I think you will. Mr. Hobbs and I were great friends. He was the best friend I had except Dearest."

The Earl made a quick movement of his bushy eyebrows.

"Who is Dearest?"

"She is my mother," said Lord Fauntleroy, in a rather low, quiet little voice.

Perhaps he was a trifle tired, as his bed-time was nearing, and perhaps after the excitement of the last few days it was natural he should be tired, so perhaps, too, the feeling of weariness brought to him a vague sense of loneliness in the remembrance that to-night he was not to sleep at home, watched over by the loving eyes of that "best friend" of his. They had always been "best friends," this boy and his young mother. He could not help thinking of her, and the more he thought of her the less was he inclined to talk, and by the time the dinner was at an end the Earl saw that there was a faint shadow on his face. But Cedric bore himself with excellent courage, and when they went back to the library, though the tall footman walked on one side of his master, the Earl's hand rested on his grandson's shoulder, though not so heavily as before.

When the footman left them alone, Cedric sat down upon the hearth-rug near Dougal. For a few minutes he stroked the dog's ears in silence and looked at the fire.

The Earl watched him. The boy's eyes looked wistful and thoughtful, and once or twice he gave a little sigh. The Earl sat still, and kept his eyes fixed on his grandson.

"Fauntleroy," he said at last, "what are you thinking of?"

Fauntleroy looked up with a manful effort at a smile.

"I was thinking about Dearest," he said; "and—and I think I'd better get up and walk up and down the room."

He rose up, and put his hands in his small pockets, and began to walk to and fro. His eyes were very bright, and his lips were pressed together, but he kept his head up and walked firmly. Dougal moved lazily and looked at him, and then stood up. He walked over to the child, and began to follow him uneasily. Fauntleroy drew one hand from his pocket and laid it on the dog's head.

"He's a very nice dog," he said. "He's my friend. He knows how I feel."

"How do you feel?" asked the Earl.

It disturbed him to see the struggle the little fellow was having with his first feeling of homesickness, but it pleased him to see that he was making so brave an effort to bear it well. He liked this childish courage.

"Come here," he said.

Fauntleroy went to him.

"I never was away from my own house before," said the boy, with a troubled look in his brown eyes. "It makes a person feel a strange feeling when he has to stay all night in another person's castle instead of in his own house. But Dearest is not very far away from me. She told me to remember that—and—and I'm seven—and I can look at the picture she gave me."

He put his hand in his pocket, and brought out a small violet velvet-covered case.

"This is it," he said. "You see, you press this spring and it opens, and she is in there!"

He had come close to the Earl's chair, and, as he drew forth the little case, he leaned against the arm of it, and against the old man's arm, too, as confidingly as if children had always leaned there.

"There she is," he said, as the case opened; and he looked up with a smile.

The Earl knitted his brows; he did not wish to see the picture, but he looked at it in spite of himself; and there looked up at him from it such a pretty young face—a face so like the child's at his side—that it quite startled him.

"I suppose you think you are very fond of her," he said.

"Yes," answered Lord Fauntleroy, in a gentle tone, and with simple directness; "I do think so, and I think it's true. You see, Mr. Hobbs was my friend, and Dick and Bridget and Mary and Michael, they were my friends, too; but Dearest—well, she is my CLOSE friend, and we always tell each other everything. My father left her to me to take care of, and when I am a man I am going to work and earn money for her."

"What do you think of doing?" inquired his grandfather.

His young lordship slipped down upon the hearth-rug, and sat there with the picture still in his hand. He seemed to be reflecting seriously, before he answered.

"I did think perhaps I might go into business with Mr. Hobbs," he said; "but I should LIKE to be a President."

"We'll send you to the House of Lords instead," said his grandfather.

"Well," remarked Lord Fauntleroy, "if I COULDN'T be a President, and if that is a good business, I shouldn't mind. The grocery business is dull sometimes."

Perhaps he was weighing the matter in his mind, for he sat very quiet after this, and looked at the fire for some time.

The Earl did not speak again. He leaned back in his chair and watched him. A great many strange new thoughts passed through the old nobleman's mind. Dougal had stretched himself out and gone to sleep with his head on his huge paws. There was a long silence.

In about half an hour's time Mr. Havisham was ushered in. The great room was very still when he entered. The Earl was still leaning back in his chair. He moved as Mr. Havisham approached, and held up his hand in a gesture of warning—it seemed as if he had scarcely intended to make the gesture—as if it were almost involuntary. Dougal was still asleep, and close beside the great dog, sleeping also, with his curly head upon his arm, lay little Lord Fauntleroy.

VI

When Lord Fauntleroy wakened in the morning,—he had not wakened at all when he had been carried to bed the night before,—the first sounds he was conscious of were the crackling of a wood fire and the murmur of voices.

"You will be careful, Dawson, not to say anything about it," he heard some one say. "He does not know why she is not to be with him, and the reason is to be kept from him."

"If them's his lordship's orders, mem," another voice answered, "they'll have to be kep', I suppose. But, if you'll excuse the liberty, mem, as it's between ourselves, servant or no servant, all I have to say is, it's a cruel thing,—parting that poor, pretty, young widdered cre'tur' from her own flesh and blood, and him such a little beauty and a nobleman born. James and Thomas, mem, last night in the servants' hall, they both of 'em say as they never see anythink in their two lives—nor yet no other gentleman in livery—like that little fellow's ways, as innercent an' polite an' interested as if he'd been sitting there dining with his best friend,—and the temper of a' angel, instead of one (if you'll excuse me, mem), as it's well known, is enough to curdle your blood in your veins at times. And as to looks, mem, when we was rung for, James and me, to go into the library and bring him upstairs, and James lifted him up in his arms, what with his little innercent face all red and rosy, and his little head on James's shoulder and his hair hanging down, all curly an' shinin', a prettier, takiner sight you'd never wish to see. An' it's my opinion, my lord wasn't blind to it neither, for he looked at him, and he says to James, 'See you don't wake him!' he says."

Cedric moved on his pillow, and turned over, opening his eyes.

There were two women in the room. Everything was bright and cheerful with gay-flowered chintz. There was a fire on the hearth, and the sunshine was streaming in through the ivy-entwined windows. Both women came toward him, and he saw that one of them was Mrs. Mellon, the housekeeper, and the other a comfortable, middle-aged woman, with a face as kind and good-humored as a face could be.

"Good-morning, my lord," said Mrs. Mellon. "Did you sleep well?"

His lordship rubbed his eyes and smiled.

"Good-morning," he said. "I didn't know I was here."

"You were carried upstairs when you were asleep," said the

housekeeper. "This is your bedroom, and this is Dawson, who is to take care of you."

Fauntleroy sat up in bed and held out his hand to Dawson, as he had held it out to the Earl.

"How do you do, ma'am?" he said. "I'm much obliged to you for coming to take care of me."

"You can call her Dawson, my lord," said the housekeeper with a smile. "She is used to being called Dawson."

"MISS Dawson, or MRS. Dawson?" inquired his lordship.

"Just Dawson, my lord," said Dawson herself, beaming all over. "Neither Miss nor Missis, bless your little heart! Will you get up now, and let Dawson dress you, and then have your breakfast in the nursery?"

"I learned to dress myself many years ago, thank you," answered Fauntleroy. "Dearest taught me. 'Dearest' is my mamma. We had only Mary to do all the work,—washing and all,—and so of course it wouldn't do to give her so much trouble. I can take my bath, too, pretty well if you'll just be kind enough to 'zamine the corners after I'm done."

Dawson and the housekeeper exchanged glances.

"Dawson will do anything you ask her to," said Mrs. Mellon.

"That I will, bless him," said Dawson, in her comforting, good-humored voice. "He shall dress himself if he likes, and I'll stand by, ready to help him if he wants me."

"Thank you," responded Lord Fauntleroy; "it's a little hard sometimes about the buttons, you know, and then I have to ask somebody."

He thought Dawson a very kind woman, and before the bath and the dressing were finished they were excellent friends, and he had found out a great deal about her. He had discovered that her husband had been a soldier and had been killed in a real battle, and that her son was a sailor, and was away on a long cruise, and that he had seen pirates and cannibals and Chinese people and Turks, and that he brought home strange shells and pieces of coral which Dawson was ready to show at any moment, some of them being in her trunk. All this was very interesting. He also found out that she had taken care of little children all her life, and that she had just come from a great house in another part of England, where she had been taking care of a beautiful little girl whose name was Lady Gwyneth Vaughn.

"And she is a sort of relation of your lordship's," said Dawson. "And perhaps sometime you may see her."

"Do you think I shall?" said Fauntleroy. "I should like that. I never knew any little girls, but I always like to look at them."

57

When he went into the adjoining room to take his breakfast, and saw what a great room it was, and found there was another adjoining it which Dawson told him was his also, the feeling that he was very small indeed came over him again so strongly that he confided it to Dawson, as he sat down to the table on which the pretty breakfast service was arranged.

"I am a very little boy," he said rather wistfully, "to live in such a large castle, and have so many big rooms,—don't you think so?"

"Oh! come!" said Dawson, "you feel just a little strange at first, that's all; but you'll get over that very soon, and then you'll like it here. It's such a beautiful place, you know."

"It's a very beautiful place, of course," said Fauntleroy, with a little sigh; "but I should like it better if I didn't miss Dearest so. I always had my breakfast with her in the morning, and put the sugar and cream in her tea for her, and handed her the toast. That made it very sociable, of course."

"Oh, well!" answered Dawson, comfortingly, "you know you can see her every day, and there's no knowing how much you'll have to tell her. Bless you! wait till you've walked about a bit and seen things,—the dogs, and the stables with all the horses in them. There's one of them I know you'll like to see——"

"Is there?" exclaimed Fauntleroy; "I'm very fond of horses. I was very fond of Jim. He was the horse that belonged to Mr. Hobbs' grocery wagon. He was a beautiful horse when he wasn't balky."

"Well," said Dawson, "you just wait till you've seen what's in the stables. And, deary me, you haven't looked even into the very next room yet!"

"What is there?" asked Fauntleroy.

"Wait until you've had your breakfast, and then you shall see," said Dawson.

At this he naturally began to grow curious, and he applied himself assiduously to his breakfast. It seemed to him that there must be something worth looking at, in the next room; Dawson had such a consequential, mysterious air.

"Now, then," he said, slipping off his seat a few minutes later; "I've had enough. Can I go and look at it?"

Dawson nodded and led the way, looking more mysterious and important than ever. He began to be very much interested indeed.

When she opened the door of the room, he stood upon the threshold and looked about him in amazement. He did not speak; he only put his hands in his pockets and stood there flushing up to his forehead and looking in.

He flushed up because he was so surprised and, for the

moment, excited. To see such a place was enough to surprise any ordinary boy.

The room was a large one, too, as all the rooms seemed to be, and it appeared to him more beautiful than the rest, only in a different way. The furniture was not so massive and antique as was that in the rooms he had seen downstairs; the draperies and rugs and walls were brighter; there were shelves full of books, and on the tables were numbers of toys,—beautiful, ingenious things,—such as he had looked at with wonder and delight through the shop windows in New York.

"It looks like a boy's room," he said at last, catching his breath a little. "Whom do they belong to?"

"Go and look at them," said Dawson. "They belong to you!"

"To me!" he cried; "to me? Why do they belong to me? Who gave them to me?" And he sprang forward with a gay little shout. It seemed almost too much to be believed. "It was Grandpapa!" he said, with his eyes as bright as stars. "I know it was Grandpapa!"

"Yes, it was his lordship," said Dawson; "and if you will be a nice little gentleman, and not fret about things, and will enjoy yourself, and be happy all the day, he will give you anything you ask for."

It was a tremendously exciting morning. There were so many things to be examined, so many experiments to be tried; each novelty was so absorbing that he could scarcely turn from it to look at the next. And it was so curious to know that all this had been prepared for himself alone; that, even before he had left New York, people had come down from London to arrange the rooms he was to occupy, and had provided the books and playthings most likely to interest him.

"Did you ever know any one," he said to Dawson, "who had such a kind grandfather!"

Dawson's face wore an uncertain expression for a moment. She had not a very high opinion of his lordship the Earl. She had not been in the house many days, but she had been there long enough to hear the old nobleman's peculiarities discussed very freely in the servants' hall.

"An' of all the wicious, savage, hill-tempered hold fellows it was ever my hill-luck to wear livery hunder," the tallest footman had said, "he's the wiolentest and wust by a long shot."

And this particular footman, whose name was Thomas, had also repeated to his companions below stairs some of the Earl's remarks to Mr. Havisham, when they had been discussing these very preparations.

"Give him his own way, and fill his rooms with toys," my lord

59

had said. "Give him what will amuse him, and he'll forget about his mother quickly enough. Amuse him, and fill his mind with other things, and we shall have no trouble. That's boy nature."

So, perhaps, having had this truly amiable object in view, it did not please him so very much to find it did not seem to be exactly this particular boy's nature. The Earl had passed a bad night and had spent the morning in his room; but at noon, after he had lunched, he sent for his grandson.

Fauntleroy answered the summons at once. He came down the broad staircase with a bounding step; the Earl heard him run across the hall, and then the door opened and he came in with red cheeks and sparkling eyes.

"I was waiting for you to send for me," he said. "I was ready a long time ago. I'm EVER so much obliged to you for all those things! I'm EVER so much obliged to you! I have been playing with them all the morning."

"Oh!" said the Earl, "you like them, do you?"

"I like them so much—well, I couldn't tell you how much!" said Fauntleroy, his face glowing with delight. "There's one that's like baseball, only you play it on a board with black and white pegs, and you keep your score with some counters on a wire. I tried to teach Dawson, but she couldn't quite understand it just at first—you see, she never played baseball, being a lady; and I'm afraid I wasn't very good at explaining it to her. But you know all about it, don't you?"

"I'm afraid I don't," replied the Earl. "It's an American game, isn't it? Is it something like cricket?"

"I never saw cricket," said Fauntleroy; "but Mr. Hobbs took me several times to see baseball. It's a splendid game. You get so excited! Would you like me to go and get my game and show it to you? Perhaps it would amuse you and make you forget about your foot. Does your foot hurt you very much this morning?"

"More than I enjoy," was the answer.

"Then perhaps you couldn't forget it," said the little fellow anxiously. "Perhaps it would bother you to be told about the game. Do you think it would amuse you, or do you think it would bother you?"

"Go and get it," said the Earl.

It certainly was a novel entertainment this,—making a companion of a child who offered to teach him to play games,—but the very novelty of it amused him. There was a smile lurking about the Earl's mouth when Cedric came back with the box containing the game, in his arms, and an expression of the most eager interest on his face.

"May I pull that little table over here to your chair?" he asked.

"Ring for Thomas," said the Earl. "He will place it for you."

"Oh, I can do it myself," answered Fauntleroy. "It's not very heavy."

"Very well," replied his grandfather. The lurking smile deepened on the old man's face as he watched the little fellow's preparations; there was such an absorbed interest in them. The small table was dragged forward and placed by his chair, and the game taken from its box and arranged upon it.

"It's very interesting when you once begin," said Fauntleroy. "You see, the black pegs can be your side and the white ones mine. They're men, you know, and once round the field is a home run and counts one—and these are the outs—and here is the first base and that's the second and that's the third and that's the home base."

He entered into the details of explanation with the greatest animation. He showed all the attitudes of pitcher and catcher and batter in the real game, and gave a dramatic description of a wonderful "hot ball" he had seen caught on the glorious occasion on which he had witnessed a match in company with Mr. Hobbs. His vigorous, graceful little body, his eager gestures, his simple enjoyment of it all, were pleasant to behold.

When at last the explanations and illustrations were at an end and the game began in good earnest, the Earl still found himself entertained. His young companion was wholly absorbed; he played with all his childish heart; his gay little laughs when he made a good throw, his enthusiasm over a "home run," his impartial delight over his own good luck and his opponent's, would have given a flavor to any game.

If, a week before, any one had told the Earl of Dorincourt that on that particular morning he would be forgetting his gout and his bad temper in a child's game, played with black and white wooden pegs, on a gayly painted board, with a curly-headed small boy for a companion, he would without doubt have made himself very unpleasant; and yet he certainly had forgotten himself when the door opened and Thomas announced a visitor.

The visitor in question, who was an elderly gentleman in black, and no less a person than the clergyman of the parish, was so startled by the amazing scene which met his eye, that he almost fell back a pace, and ran some risk of colliding with Thomas.

There was, in fact, no part of his duty that the Reverend Mr. Mordaunt found so decidedly unpleasant as that part which compelled him to call upon his noble patron at the Castle. His noble patron, indeed, usually made these visits as disagreeable as it lay in his lordly power to make them. He abhorred churches and charities, and flew into violent rages when any of his tenantry took the liberty of being poor and ill and needing assistance. When his gout was at its worst, he did not hesitate to announce that he would not be bored and irritated by being told stories of their miserable misfortunes; when his gout troubled him less and he was in a somewhat more humane frame of mind, he would perhaps give the rector some money, after having bullied him in the most painful manner, and berated the whole parish for its shiftlessness and imbecility. But, whatsoever his mood, he never failed to make as many sarcastic and embarrassing speeches as possible, and to cause the Reverend Mr. Mordaunt to wish it were proper and Christian-like to throw something heavy at him. During all the years in which Mr. Mordaunt had been in charge of Dorincourt parish, the rector certainly did not remember having seen his lordship, of his own free will, do any one a kindness, or, under any circumstances whatever, show that he thought of any one but himself.

He had called to-day to speak to him of a specially pressing case, and as he had walked up the avenue, he had, for two reasons, dreaded his visit more than usual. In the first place, he knew that his lordship had for several days been suffering with the gout, and had been in so villainous a humor that rumors of it had even reached the village—carried there by one of the young women servants, to her sister, who kept a little shop and retailed darning-needles and cotton and peppermints and gossip, as a means of earning an honest living. What Mrs. Dibble did not know about the Castle and its inmates, and the farm-houses and their inmates, and the village and its population, was really not worth being talked about. And of course she knew everything about the Castle, because her sister, Jane Shorts, was one of the upper housemaids, and was very friendly and intimate with Thomas.

"And the way his lordship do go on!" said Mrs. Dibble, over the counter, "and the way he do use language, Mr. Thomas told Jane herself, no flesh and blood as is in livery could stand—for throw a plate of toast at Mr. Thomas, hisself, he did, not more than two days since, and if it weren't for other things being agreeable and the society below stairs most genteel, warning would have been gave within a' hour!"

And the rector had heard all this, for somehow the Earl was a favorite black sheep in the cottages and farm-houses, and his bad behavior gave many a good woman something to talk about when she had company to tea.

And the second reason was even worse, because it was a new one and had been talked about with the most excited interest.

Who did not know of the old nobleman's fury when his

handsome son the Captain had married the American lady? Who did not know how cruelly he had treated the Captain, and how the big, gay, sweet-smiling young man, who was the only member of the grand family any one liked, had died in a foreign land, poor and unforgiven? Who did not know how fiercely his lordship had hated the poor young creature who had been this son's wife, and how he had hated the thought of her child and never meant to see the boy—until his two sons died and left him without an heir? And then, who did not know that he had looked forward without any affection or pleasure to his grandson's coming, and that he had made up his mind that he should find the boy a vulgar, awkward, pert American lad, more likely to disgrace his noble name than to honor it?

The proud, angry old man thought he had kept all his thoughts secret. He did not suppose any one had dared to guess at, much less talk over what he felt, and dreaded; but his servants watched him, and read his face and his ill-humors and fits of gloom, and discussed them in the servants' hall. And while he thought himself quite secure from the common herd, Thomas was telling Jane and the cook, and the butler, and the housemaids and the other footmen that it was his opinion that "the hold man was wuss than usual a-thinkin' hover the Capting's boy, an' hanticipatin' as he won't be no credit to the fambly. An' serve him right," added Thomas; "hit's 'is hown fault. Wot can he iggspect from a child brought up in pore circumstances in that there low Hamerica?"

And as the Reverend Mr. Mordaunt walked under the great trees, he remembered that this questionable little boy had arrived at the Castle only the evening before, and that there were nine chances to one that his lordship's worst fears were realized, and twenty-two chances to one that if the poor little fellow had disappointed him, the Earl was even now in a tearing rage, and ready to vent all his rancor on the first person who called—which it appeared probable would be his reverend self.

Judge then of his amazement when, as Thomas opened the library door, his ears were greeted by a delighted ring of childish laughter.

"That's two out!" shouted an excited, clear little voice. "You see it's two out!"

And there was the Earl's chair, and the gout-stool, and his foot on it; and by him a small table and a game on it; and quite close to him, actually leaning against his arm and his ungouty knee, was a little boy with face glowing, and eyes dancing with excitement. "It's two out!" the little stranger cried. "You hadn't any luck that time, had you?"—And then they both recognized at once that some one had come in.

63

The Earl glanced around, knitting his shaggy eyebrows as he had a trick of doing, and when he saw who it was, Mr. Mordaunt was still more surprised to see that he looked even less disagreeable than usual instead of more so. In fact, he looked almost as if he had forgotten for the moment how disagreeable he was, and how unpleasant he really could make himself when he tried.

"Ah!" he said, in his harsh voice, but giving his hand rather graciously. "Good-morning, Mordaunt. I've found a new employment, you see."

He put his other hand on Cedric's shoulder,—perhaps deep down in his heart there was a stir of gratified pride that it was such an heir he had to present; there was a spark of something like pleasure in his eyes as he moved the boy slightly forward.

"This is the new Lord Fauntleroy," he said. "Fauntleroy, this is Mr. Mordaunt, the rector of the parish."

Fauntleroy looked up at the gentleman in the clerical garments, and gave him his hand.

"I am very glad to make your acquaintance, sir," he said, remembering the words he had heard Mr. Hobbs use on one or two occasions when he had been greeting a new customer with ceremony.

Cedric felt quite sure that one ought to be more than usually polite to a minister.

Mr. Mordaunt held the small hand in his a moment as he looked down at the child's face, smiling involuntarily. He liked the little fellow from that instant—as in fact people always did like him. And it was not the boy's beauty and grace which most appealed to him; it was the simple, natural kindliness in the little lad which made any words he uttered, however quaint and unexpected, sound pleasant and sincere. As the rector looked at Cedric, he forgot to think of the Earl at all. Nothing in the world is so strong as a kind heart, and somehow this kind little heart, though it was only the heart of a child, seemed to clear all the atmosphere of the big gloomy room and make it brighter.

"I am delighted to make your acquaintance, Lord Fauntleroy," said the rector. "You made a long journey to come to us. A great many people will be glad to know you made it safely."

"It WAS a long way," answered Fauntleroy, "but Dearest, my mother, was with me and I wasn't lonely. Of course you are never lonely if your mother is with you; and the ship was beautiful."

"Take a chair, Mordaunt," said the Earl. Mr. Mordaunt sat down. He glanced from Fauntleroy to the Earl.

"Your lordship is greatly to be congratulated," he said warmly.

But the Earl plainly had no intention of showing his feelings on the subject.

"He is like his father," he said rather gruffly. "Let us hope he'll conduct himself more creditably." And then he added: "Well, what is it this morning, Mordaunt? Who is in trouble now?"

This was not as bad as Mr. Mordaunt had expected, but he hesitated a second before he began.

"It is Higgins," he said; "Higgins of Edge Farm. He has been very unfortunate. He was ill himself last autumn, and his children had scarlet fever. I can't say that he is a very good manager, but he has had ill-luck, and of course he is behindhand in many ways. He is in trouble about his rent now. Newick tells him if he doesn't pay it, he must leave the place; and of course that would be a very serious matter. His wife is ill, and he came to me yesterday to beg me to see about it, and ask you for time. He thinks if you would give him time he could catch up again."

"They all think that," said the Earl, looking rather black.

Fauntleroy made a movement forward. He had been standing between his grandfather and the visitor, listening with all his might. He had begun to be interested in Higgins at once. He wondered how many children there were, and if the scarlet fever had hurt them very much. His eyes were wide open and were fixed upon Mr. Mordaunt with intent interest as that gentleman went on with the conversation.

"Higgins is a well-meaning man," said the rector, making an effort to strengthen his plea.

"He is a bad enough tenant," replied his lordship. "And he is always behindhand, Newick tells me."

"He is in great trouble now," said the rector.

"He is very fond of his wife and children, and if the farm is taken from him they may literally starve. He can not give them the nourishing things they need. Two of the children were left very low after the fever, and the doctor orders for them wine and luxuries that Higgins can not afford."

At this Fauntleroy moved a step nearer.

"That was the way with Michael," he said.

The Earl slightly started.

"I forgot YOU!" he said. "I forgot we had a philanthropist in the room. Who was Michael?" And the gleam of queer amusement came back into the old man's deep-set eyes.

"He was Bridget's husband, who had the fever," answered Fauntleroy; "and he couldn't pay the rent or buy wine and things. And you gave me that money to help him."

The Earl drew his brows together into a curious frown, which somehow was scarcely grim at all. He glanced across at Mr. Mordaunt.

"I don't know what sort of landed proprietor he will make," he said. "I told Havisham the boy was to have what he wanted—anything he wanted—and what he wanted, it seems, was money to give to beggars."

"Oh! but they weren't beggars," said Fauntleroy eagerly. "Michael was a splendid bricklayer! They all worked."

"Oh!" said the Earl, "they were not beggars. They were splendid bricklayers, and bootblacks, and apple-women."

He bent his gaze on the boy for a few seconds in silence. The fact was that a new thought was coming to him, and though, perhaps, it was not prompted by the noblest emotions, it was not a bad thought. "Come here," he said, at last.

Fauntleroy went and stood as near to him as possible without encroaching on the gouty foot.

"What would YOU do in this case?" his lordship asked.

It must be confessed that Mr. Mordaunt experienced for the moment a curious sensation. Being a man of great thoughtfulness, and having spent so many years on the estate of Dorincourt, knowing the tenantry, rich and poor, the people of the village, honest and industrious, dishonest and lazy, he realized very strongly what power for good or evil would be given in the future to this one small boy standing there, his brown eyes wide open, his hands deep in his pockets; and the thought came to him also that a great deal of power might, perhaps, through the caprice of a proud, self-indulgent old man, be given to him now, and that if his young nature were not a simple and generous one, it might be the worst thing that could happen, not only for others, but for himself.

"And what would YOU do in such a case?" demanded the Earl.

Fauntleroy drew a little nearer, and laid one hand on his knee, with the most confiding air of good comradeship.

"If I were very rich," he said, "and not only just a little boy, I should let him stay, and give him the things for his children; but then, I am only a boy." Then, after a second's pause, in which his face brightened visibly, "YOU can do anything, can't you?" he said.

"Humph!" said my lord, staring at him. "That's your opinion, is it?" And he was not displeased either.

"I mean you can give any one anything," said Fauntleroy. "Who's Newick?"

"He is my agent," answered the Earl, "and some of my tenants are not over-fond of him."

"Are you going to write him a letter now?" inquired

66

Fauntleroy. "Shall I bring you the pen and ink? I can take the game off this table."

It plainly had not for an instant occurred to him that Newick would be allowed to do his worst.

The Earl paused a moment, still looking at him. "Can you write?" he asked.

"Yes," answered Cedric, "but not very well."

"Move the things from the table," commanded my lord, "and bring the pen and ink, and a sheet of paper from my desk."

Mr. Mordaunt's interest began to increase. Fauntleroy did as he was told very deftly. In a few moments, the sheet of paper, the big inkstand, and the pen were ready.

"There!" he said gayly, "now you can write it."

"You are to write it," said the Earl.

"I!" exclaimed Fauntleroy, and a flush overspread his forehead. "Will it do if I write it? I don't always spell quite right when I haven't a dictionary, and nobody tells me."

"It will do," answered the Earl. "Higgins will not complain of the spelling. I'm not the philanthropist; you are. Dip your pen in the ink."

Fauntleroy took up the pen and dipped it in the ink-bottle, then he arranged himself in position, leaning on the table.

"Now," he inquired, "what must I say?"

"You may say, 'Higgins is not to be interfered with, for the present,' and sign it, 'Fauntleroy,'" said the Earl.

Fauntleroy dipped his pen in the ink again, and resting his arm, began to write. It was rather a slow and serious process, but he gave his whole soul to it. After a while, however, the manuscript was complete, and he handed it to his grandfather with a smile slightly tinged with anxiety.

"Do you think it will do?" he asked.

The Earl looked at it, and the corners of his mouth twitched a little.

"Yes," he answered; "Higgins will find it entirely satisfactory." And he handed it to Mr. Mordaunt.

What Mr. Mordaunt found written was this:

"Dear mr. Newik if you pleas mr. higins is not to be intur feared with for the present and oblige. Yours rispecferly,

"FAUNTLEROY."

"Mr. Hobbs always signed his letters that way," said Fauntleroy; "and I thought I'd better say 'please.' Is that exactly the right way to spell 'interfered'?"

"It's not exactly the way it is spelled in the dictionary," answered the Earl.

67

"I was afraid of that," said Fauntleroy. "I ought to have asked. You see, that's the way with words of more than one syllable; you have to look in the dictionary. It's always safest. I'll write it over again."

And write it over again he did, making quite an imposing copy, and taking precautions in the matter of spelling by consulting the Earl himself.

"Spelling is a curious thing," he said. "It's so often different from what you expect it to be. I used to think 'please' was spelled p-l-e-e-s, but it isn't, you know; and you'd think 'dear' was spelled d-e-r-e, if you didn't inquire. Sometimes it almost discourages you."

When Mr. Mordaunt went away, he took the letter with him, and he took something else with him also—namely, a pleasanter feeling and a more hopeful one than he had ever carried home with him down that avenue on any previous visit he had made at Dorincourt Castle.

When he was gone, Fauntleroy, who had accompanied him to the door, went back to his grandfather.

"May I go to Dearest now?" he asked. "I think she will be waiting for me."

The Earl was silent a moment.

"There is something in the stable for you to see first," he said. "Ring the bell."

"If you please," said Fauntleroy, with his quick little flush. "I'm very much obliged; but I think I'd better see it to-morrow. She will be expecting me all the time."

"Very well," answered the Earl. "We will order the carriage." Then he added dryly, "It's a pony."

Fauntleroy drew a long breath.

"A pony!" he exclaimed. "Whose pony is it?"

"Yours," replied the Earl.

"Mine?" cried the little fellow. "Mine—like the things upstairs?"

"Yes," said his grandfather. "Would you like to see it? Shall I order it to be brought around?"

Fauntleroy's cheeks grew redder and redder.

"I never thought I should have a pony!" he said. "I never thought that! How glad Dearest will be. You give me EVERYthing, don't you?"

"Do you wish to see it?" inquired the Earl.

Fauntleroy drew a long breath. "I WANT to see it," he said. "I want to see it so much I can hardly wait. But I'm afraid there isn't time."

68

"You MUST go and see your mother this afternoon?" asked the Earl. "You think you can't put it off?"

"Why," said Fauntleroy, "she has been thinking about me all the morning, and I have been thinking about her!"

"Oh!" said the Earl. "You have, have you? Ring the bell."

As they drove down the avenue, under the arching trees, he was rather silent. But Fauntleroy was not. He talked about the pony. What color was it? How big was it? What was its name? What did it like to eat best? How old was it? How early in the morning might he get up and see it?

"Dearest will be so glad!" he kept saying. "She will be so much obliged to you for being so kind to me! She knows I always liked ponies so much, but we never thought I should have one. There was a little boy on Fifth Avenue who had one, and he used to ride out every morning and we used to take a walk past his house to see him."

He leaned back against the cushions and regarded the Earl with rapt interest for a few minutes and in entire silence.

"I think you must be the best person in the world," he burst forth at last. "You are always doing good, aren't you?—and thinking about other people. Dearest says that is the best kind of goodness; not to think about yourself, but to think about other people. That is just the way you are, isn't it?"

His lordship was so dumfounded to find himself presented in such agreeable colors, that he did not know exactly what to say. He felt that he needed time for reflection. To see each of his ugly, selfish motives changed into a good and generous one by the simplicity of a child was a singular experience.

Fauntleroy went on, still regarding him with admiring eyes— those great, clear, innocent eyes!

"You make so many people happy," he said. "There's Michael and Bridget and their ten children, and the apple-woman, and Dick, and Mr. Hobbs, and Mr. Higgins and Mrs. Higgins and their children, and Mr. Mordaunt,—because of course he was glad,—and Dearest and me, about the pony and all the other things. Do you know, I've counted it up on my fingers and in my mind, and it's twenty-seven people you've been kind to. That's a good many— twenty-seven!"

"And I was the person who was kind to them—was I?" said the Earl.

"Why, yes, you know," answered Fauntleroy. "You made them all happy. Do you know," with some delicate hesitation, "that people are sometimes mistaken about earls when they don't know them. Mr. Hobbs was. I am going to write him, and tell him about it."

"What was Mr. Hobbs's opinion of earls?" asked his lordship.

"Well, you see, the difficulty was," replied his young companion, "that he didn't know any, and he'd only read about them in books. He thought—you mustn't mind it—that they were gory tyrants; and he said he wouldn't have them hanging around his store. But if he'd known YOU, I'm sure he would have felt quite different. I shall tell him about you."

"What shall you tell him?"

"I shall tell him," said Fauntleroy, glowing with enthusiasm, "that you are the kindest man I ever heard of. And you are always thinking of other people, and making them happy and—and I hope when I grow up, I shall be just like you."

"Just like me!" repeated his lordship, looking at the little kindling face. And a dull red crept up under his withered skin, and he suddenly turned his eyes away and looked out of the carriage window at the great beech-trees, with the sun shining on their glossy, red-brown leaves.

"JUST like you," said Fauntleroy, adding modestly, "if I can. Perhaps I'm not good enough, but I'm going to try."

The carriage rolled on down the stately avenue under the beautiful, broad-branched trees, through the spaces of green shade and lanes of golden sunlight. Fauntleroy saw again the lovely places where the ferns grew high and the bluebells swayed in the breeze; he saw the deer, standing or lying in the deep grass, turn their large, startled eyes as the carriage passed, and caught glimpses of the brown rabbits as they scurried away. He heard the whir of the partridges and the calls and songs of the birds, and it all seemed even more beautiful to him than before. All his heart was filled with pleasure and happiness in the beauty that was on every side. But the old Earl saw and heard very different things, though he was apparently looking out too. He saw a long life, in which there had been neither generous deeds nor kind thoughts; he saw years in which a man who had been young and strong and rich and powerful had used his youth and strength and wealth and power only to please himself and kill time as the days and years succeeded each other; he saw this man, when the time had been killed and old age had come, solitary and without real friends in the midst of all his splendid wealth; he saw people who disliked or feared him, and people who would flatter and cringe to him, but no one who really cared whether he lived or died, unless they had something to gain or lose by it. He looked out on the broad acres which belonged to him, and he knew what Fauntleroy did not—how far they extended, what wealth they represented, and how many people had homes on their soil. And he knew, too,—another thing Fauntleroy did not,—that in all those homes, humble or well-to-do, there was probably not one person, however much he envied the wealth and stately name and power, and however willing he would have been to possess them, who would for an instant have thought of calling the noble owner "good," or wishing, as this simple-souled little boy had, to be like him.

And it was not exactly pleasant to reflect upon, even for a cynical, worldly old man, who had been sufficient unto himself for seventy years and who had never deigned to care what opinion the world held of him so long as it did not interfere with his comfort or entertainment. And the fact was, indeed, that he had never before condescended to reflect upon it at all; and he only did so now because a child had believed him better than he was, and by wishing to follow in his illustrious footsteps and imitate his example, had suggested to him the curious question whether he was exactly the person to take as a model.

Fauntleroy thought the Earl's foot must be hurting him, his brows knitted themselves together so, as he looked out at the park; and thinking this, the considerate little fellow tried not to disturb him, and enjoyed the trees and the ferns and the deer in silence.

But at last the carriage, having passed the gates and bowled through the green lanes for a short distance, stopped. They had reached Court Lodge; and Fauntleroy was out upon the ground almost before the big footman had time to open the carriage door.

The Earl wakened from his reverie with a start.

"What!" he said. "Are we here?"

"Yes," said Fauntleroy. "Let me give you your stick. Just lean on me when you get out."

"I am not going to get out," replied his lordship brusquely.

"Not—not to see Dearest?" exclaimed Fauntleroy with astonished face.

"'Dearest' will excuse me," said the Earl dryly. "Go to her and tell her that not even a new pony would keep you away."

"She will be disappointed," said Fauntleroy. "She will want to see you very much."

"I am afraid not," was the answer. "The carriage will call for you as we come back.—Tell Jeffries to drive on, Thomas."

Thomas closed the carriage door; and, after a puzzled look, Fauntleroy ran up the drive. The Earl had the opportunity—as Mr. Havisham once had—of seeing a pair of handsome, strong little legs flash over the ground with astonishing rapidity. Evidently their owner had no intention of losing any time. The carriage rolled slowly away, but his lordship did not at once lean back; he still looked out. Through a space in the trees he could see the house

71

door; it was wide open. The little figure dashed up the steps; another figure—a little figure, too, slender and young, in its black gown—ran to meet it. It seemed as if they flew together, as Fauntleroy leaped into his mother's arms, hanging about her neck and covering her sweet young face with kisses.

VII

On the following Sunday morning, Mr. Mordaunt had a large congregation. Indeed, he could scarcely remember any Sunday on which the church had been so crowded. People appeared upon the scene who seldom did him the honor of coming to hear his sermons.

There were even people from Hazelton, which was the next parish. There were hearty, sunburned farmers, stout, comfortable, apple-cheeked wives in their best bonnets and most gorgeous shawls, and half a dozen children or so to each family. The doctor's wife was there, with her four daughters. Mrs. Kimsey and Mr. Kimsey, who kept the druggist's shop, and made pills, and did up powders for everybody within ten miles, sat in their pew; Mrs. Dibble in hers; Miss Smiff, the village dressmaker, and her friend Miss Perkins, the milliner, sat in theirs; the doctor's young man was present, and the druggist's apprentice; in fact, almost every family on the county side was represented, in one way or another.

In the course of the preceding week, many wonderful stories had been told of little Lord Fauntleroy. Mrs. Dibble had been kept so busy attending to customers who came in to buy a pennyworth of needles or a ha'porth of tape and to hear what she had to relate, that the little shop bell over the door had nearly tinkled itself to death over the coming and going. Mrs. Dibble knew exactly how his small lordship's rooms had been furnished for him, what expensive toys had been bought, how there was a beautiful brown pony awaiting him, and a small groom to attend it, and a little dog-cart, with silver-mounted harness. And she could tell, too, what all the servants had said when they had caught glimpses of the child on the night of his arrival; and how every female below stairs had said it was a shame, so it was, to part the poor pretty dear from his mother; and had all declared their hearts came into their mouths when he went alone into the library to see his grandfather, for "there was no knowing how he'd be treated, and his lordship's temper was enough to fluster them with old heads on their shoulders, let alone a child."

"But if you'll believe me, Mrs. Jennifer, mum," Mrs. Dibble had said, "fear that child does not know—so Mr. Thomas hisself says; an' set an' smile he did, an' talked to his lordship as if they'd been friends ever since his first hour. An' the Earl so took aback, Mr. Thomas says, that he couldn't do nothing but listen and stare from under his eyebrows. An' it's Mr. Thomas's opinion, Mrs. Bates, mum, that bad as he is, he was pleased in his secret soul, an' proud, too; for a handsomer little fellow, or with better manners, though so old-fashioned, Mr. Thomas says he'd never wish to see."

And then there had come the story of Higgins. The Reverend Mr. Mordaunt had told it at his own dinner table, and the servants who had heard it had told it in the kitchen, and from there it had spread like wildfire.

And on market-day, when Higgins had appeared in town, he had been questioned on every side, and Newick had been questioned too, and in response had shown to two or three people the note signed "Fauntleroy."

And so the farmers' wives had found plenty to talk of over their tea and their shopping, and they had done the subject full justice and made the most of it. And on Sunday they had either walked to church or had been driven in their gigs by their husbands, who were perhaps a trifle curious themselves about the new little lord who was to be in time the owner of the soil.

It was by no means the Earl's habit to attend church, but he chose to appear on this first Sunday—it was his whim to present himself in the huge family pew, with Fauntleroy at his side.

There were many loiterers in the churchyard, and many lingerers in the lane that morning. There were groups at the gates and in the porch, and there had been much discussion as to whether my lord would really appear or not. When this discussion was at its height, one good woman suddenly uttered an exclamation.

"Eh," she said, "that must be the mother, pretty young thing." All who heard turned and looked at the slender figure in black coming up the path. The veil was thrown back from her face and they could see how fair and sweet it was, and how the bright hair curled as softly as a child's under the little widow's cap.

She was not thinking of the people about; she was thinking of Cedric, and of his visits to her, and his joy over his new pony, on which he had actually ridden to her door the day before, sitting very straight and looking very proud and happy. But soon she could not help being attracted by the fact that she was being looked at and that her arrival had created some sort of sensation. She first noticed it because an old woman in a red cloak made a bobbing courtesy to her, and then another did the same thing and said, "God bless you, my lady!" and one man after another took off his hat as she passed. For a moment she did not understand, and then she realized that it was because she was little Lord Fauntleroy's mother that they did so, and she flushed rather shyly and smiled and bowed too, and said, "Thank you," in a gentle voice to the old woman who had blessed her. To a person who had always lived in a bustling, crowded American city this simple deference was very novel, and at first just a little embarrassing; but after all, she could not help liking and being touched by the friendly warm-heartedness of which it seemed to speak. She had scarcely passed through the stone porch into the church before the great event of the day happened. The carriage from the Castle, with its handsome horses and tall liveried servants, bowled around the corner and down the green lane.

"Here they come!" went from one looker-on to another.

And then the carriage drew up, and Thomas stepped down and opened the door, and a little boy, dressed in black velvet, and with a splendid mop of bright waving hair, jumped out.

Every man, woman, and child looked curiously upon him.

"He's the Captain over again!" said those of the on-lookers who remembered his father. "He's the Captain's self, to the life!"

He stood there in the sunlight looking up at the Earl, as Thomas helped that nobleman out, with the most affectionate interest that could be imagined. The instant he could help, he put out his hand and offered his shoulder as if he had been seven feet high. It was plain enough to every one that however it might be with other people, the Earl of Dorincourt struck no terror into the breast of his grandson.

"Just lean on me," they heard him say. "How glad the people are to see you, and how well they all seem to know you!"

"Take off your cap, Fauntleroy," said the Earl. "They are bowing to you."

"To me!" cried Fauntleroy, whipping off his cap in a moment, baring his bright head to the crowd and turning shining, puzzled eyes on them as he tried to bow to every one at once.

"God bless your lordship!" said the courtesying, red-cloaked old woman who had spoken to his mother; "long life to you!"

"Thank you, ma'am," said Fauntleroy. And then they went into the church, and were looked at there, on their way up the aisle to the square, red-cushioned and curtained pew. When Fauntleroy was fairly seated, he made two discoveries which pleased him: the first that, across the church where he could look at her, his mother sat and smiled at him; the second, that at one end of the pew, against the wall, knelt two quaint figures carven in stone, facing each other as they kneeled on either side of a pillar supporting two stone missals, their pointed hands folded as if in prayer, their dress very antique and strange. On the tablet by them was written something of which he could only read the curious words:

"Here lyeth ye bodye of Gregorye Arthure Fyrst Earle of Dorincourt Allsoe of Alisone Hildegarde hys wyfe."

"May I whisper?" inquired his lordship, devoured by curiosity.

"What is it?" said his grandfather.

"Who are they?"

"Some of your ancestors," answered the Earl, "who lived a few hundred years ago."

"Perhaps," said Lord Fauntleroy, regarding them with respect, "perhaps I got my spelling from them." And then he proceeded to find his place in the church service. When the music began, he stood up and looked across at his mother, smiling. He was very fond of music, and his mother and he often sang together, so he joined in with the rest, his pure, sweet, high voice rising as clear as the song of a bird. He quite forgot himself in his pleasure in it. The Earl forgot himself a little too, as he sat in his curtain-shielded corner of the pew and watched the boy. Cedric stood with the big psalter open in his hands, singing with all his childish might, his face a little uplifted, happily; and as he sang, a long ray of sunshine crept in and, slanting through a golden pane of a stained glass window, brightened the falling hair about his young head. His mother, as she looked at him across the church, felt a thrill pass through her heart, and a prayer rose in it too,—a prayer that the pure, simple happiness of his childish soul might last, and that the strange, great fortune which had fallen to him might bring no wrong or evil with it. There were many soft, anxious thoughts in her tender heart in those new days.

"Oh, Ceddie!" she had said to him the evening before, as she hung over him in saying good-night, before he went away; "oh, Ceddie, dear, I wish for your sake I was very clever and could say a great many wise things! But only be good, dear, only be brave, only be kind and true always, and then you will never hurt any one, so long as you live, and you may help many, and the big world may be better because my little child was born. And that is best of all, Ceddie,—it is better than everything else, that the world should be a little better because a man has lived—even ever so little better, dearest."

And on his return to the Castle, Fauntleroy had repeated her words to his grandfather.

"And I thought about you when she said that," he ended; "and I told her that was the way the world was because you had lived, and I was going to try if I could be like you."

"And what did she say to that?" asked his lordship, a trifle uneasily.

"She said that was right, and we must always look for good in people and try to be like it."

Perhaps it was this the old man remembered as he glanced through the divided folds of the red curtain of his pew. Many times he looked over the people's heads to where his son's wife sat alone, and he saw the fair face the unforgiven dead had loved, and the eyes

76

which were so like those of the child at his side; but what his thoughts were, and whether they were hard and bitter, or softened a little, it would have been hard to discover.

As they came out of church, many of those who had attended the service stood waiting to see them pass. As they neared the gate, a man who stood with his hat in his hand made a step forward and then hesitated. He was a middle-aged farmer, with a careworn face.

"Well, Higgins," said the Earl.

Fauntleroy turned quickly to look at him.

"Oh!" he exclaimed, "is it Mr. Higgins?"

"Yes," answered the Earl dryly; "and I suppose he came to take a look at his new landlord."

"Yes, my lord," said the man, his sunburned face reddening. "Mr. Newick told me his young lordship was kind enough to speak for me, and I thought I'd like to say a word of thanks, if I might be allowed."

Perhaps he felt some wonder when he saw what a little fellow it was who had innocently done so much for him, and who stood there looking up just as one of his own less fortunate children might have done—apparently not realizing his own importance in the least.

"I've a great deal to thank your lordship for," he said; "a great deal. I——"

"Oh," said Fauntleroy; "I only wrote the letter. It was my grandfather who did it. But you know how he is about always being good to everybody. Is Mrs. Higgins well now?"

Higgins looked a trifle taken aback. He also was somewhat startled at hearing his noble landlord presented in the character of a benevolent being, full of engaging qualities.

"I—well, yes, your lordship," he stammered, "the missus is better since the trouble was took off her mind. It was worrying broke her down."

"I'm glad of that," said Fauntleroy. "My grandfather was very sorry about your children having the scarlet fever, and so was I. He has had children himself. I'm his son's little boy, you know."

Higgins was on the verge of being panic-stricken. He felt it would be the safer and more discreet plan not to look at the Earl, as it had been well known that his fatherly affection for his sons had been such that he had seen them about twice a year, and that when they had been ill, he had promptly departed for London, because he would not be bored with doctors and nurses. It was a little trying, therefore, to his lordship's nerves to be told, while he looked on, his eyes gleaming from under his shaggy eyebrows, that he felt an interest in scarlet fever.

"You see, Higgins," broke in the Earl with a fine grim smile, "you people have been mistaken in me. Lord Fauntleroy understands me. When you want reliable information on the subject of my character, apply to him. Get into the carriage, Fauntleroy."

And Fauntleroy jumped in, and the carriage rolled away down the green lane, and even when it turned the corner into the high road, the Earl was still grimly smiling.

VIII

Lord Dorincourt had occasion to wear his grim smile many a time as the days passed by. Indeed, as his acquaintance with his grandson progressed, he wore the smile so often that there were moments when it almost lost its grimness. There is no denying that before Lord Fauntleroy had appeared on the scene, the old man had been growing very tired of his loneliness and his gout and his seventy years. After so long a life of excitement and amusement, it was not agreeable to sit alone even in the most splendid room, with one foot on a gout-stool, and with no other diversion than flying into a rage, and shouting at a frightened footman who hated the sight of him. The old Earl was too clever a man not to know perfectly well that his servants detested him, and that even if he had visitors, they did not come for love of him—though some found a sort of amusement in his sharp, sarcastic talk, which spared no one. So long as he had been strong and well, he had gone from one place to another, pretending to amuse himself, though he had not really enjoyed it; and when his health began to fail, he felt tired of everything and shut himself up at Dorincourt, with his gout and his newspapers and his books. But he could not read all the time, and he became more and more "bored," as he called it. He hated the long nights and days, and he grew more and more savage and irritable. And then Fauntleroy came; and when the Earl saw him, fortunately for the little fellow, the secret pride of the grandfather was gratified at the outset. If Cedric had been a less handsome little fellow, the old man might have taken so strong a dislike to him that he would not have given himself the chance to see his grandson's finer qualities. But he chose to think that Cedric's beauty and fearless spirit were the results of the Dorincourt blood and a credit to the Dorincourt rank. And then when he heard the lad talk, and saw what a well-bred little fellow he was, notwithstanding his boyish ignorance of all that his new position meant, the old Earl liked his grandson more, and actually began to find himself rather entertained. It had amused him to give into those childish hands the power to bestow a benefit on poor Higgins. My lord cared nothing for poor Higgins, but it pleased him a little to think that his grandson would be talked about by the country people and would begin to be popular with the tenantry, even in his childhood. Then it had gratified him to drive to church with Cedric and to see the excitement and interest caused by the arrival. He knew how the people would speak of the beauty of the little lad; of his fine, strong, straight body; of his erect bearing, his handsome face, and his bright hair, and how they would say (as the Earl had heard one woman exclaim to another) that the boy was "every inch a lord." My lord of Dorincourt was an arrogant old man, proud of his name, proud of his rank, and therefore proud to show the world that at last the House of Dorincourt had an heir who was worthy of the position he was to fill.

The morning the new pony had been tried, the Earl had been so pleased that he had almost forgotten his gout. When the groom had brought out the pretty creature, which arched its brown, glossy neck and tossed its fine head in the sun, the Earl had sat at the open window of the library and had looked on while Fauntleroy took his first riding lesson. He wondered if the boy would show signs of timidity. It was not a very small pony, and he had often seen children lose courage in making their first essay at riding.

Fauntleroy mounted in great delight. He had never been on a pony before, and he was in the highest spirits. Wilkins, the groom, led the animal by the bridle up and down before the library window.

"He's a well plucked un, he is," Wilkins remarked in the stable afterward with many grins. "It weren't no trouble to put HIM up. An' a old un wouldn't ha' sat any straighter when he WERE up. He ses—ses he to me, 'Wilkins,' he ses, 'am I sitting up straight? They sit up straight at the circus,' ses he. An' I ses, 'As straight as a arrer, your lordship!'—an' he laughs, as pleased as could be, an' he ses, 'That's right,' he ses, 'you tell me if I don't sit up straight, Wilkins!'"

But sitting up straight and being led at a walk were not altogether and completely satisfactory. After a few minutes, Fauntleroy spoke to his grandfather—watching him from the window:

"Can't I go by myself?" he asked; "and can't I go faster? The boy on Fifth Avenue used to trot and canter!"

"Do you think you could trot and canter?" said the Earl.

"I should like to try," answered Fauntleroy.

His lordship made a sign to Wilkins, who at the signal brought up his own horse and mounted it and took Fauntleroy's pony by the leading-rein.

"Now," said the Earl, "let him trot."

The next few minutes were rather exciting to the small equestrian. He found that trotting was not so easy as walking, and the faster the pony trotted, the less easy it was.

"It j-jolts a g-goo-good deal—do-doesn't it?" he said to Wilkins. "D-does it j-jolt y-you?"

"No, my lord," answered Wilkins. "You'll get used to it in time. Rise in your stirrups."

"I'm ri-rising all the t-time," said Fauntleroy.

He was both rising and falling rather uncomfortably and with many shakes and bounces. He was out of breath and his face grew red, but he held on with all his might, and sat as straight as he could. The Earl could see that from his window. When the riders came back within speaking distance, after they had been hidden by the trees a few minutes, Fauntleroy's hat was off, his cheeks were like poppies, and his lips were set, but he was still trotting manfully.

"Stop a minute!" said his grandfather. "Where's your hat?"

Wilkins touched his. "It fell off, your lordship," he said, with evident enjoyment. "Wouldn't let me stop to pick it up, my lord."

"Not much afraid, is he?" asked the Earl dryly.

"Him, your lordship!" exclaimed Wilkins. "I shouldn't say as he knowed what it meant. I've taught young gen'lemen to ride afore, an' I never see one stick on more determiner."

"Tired?" said the Earl to Fauntleroy. "Want to get off?"

"It jolts you more than you think it will," admitted his young lordship frankly. "And it tires you a little, too; but I don't want to get off. I want to learn how. As soon as I've got my breath I want to go back for the hat."

The cleverest person in the world, if he had undertaken to teach Fauntleroy how to please the old man who watched him, could not have taught him anything which would have succeeded better. As the pony trotted off again toward the avenue, a faint color crept up in the fierce old face, and the eyes, under the shaggy brows, gleamed with a pleasure such as his lordship had scarcely expected to know again. And he sat and watched quite eagerly until the sound of the horses' hoofs returned. When they did come, which was after some time, they came at a faster pace. Fauntleroy's hat was still off; Wilkins was carrying it for him; his cheeks were redder than before, and his hair was flying about his ears, but he came at quite a brisk canter.

"There!" he panted, as they drew up, "I c-cantered. I didn't do it as well as the boy on Fifth Avenue, but I did it, and I staid on!"

He and Wilkins and the pony were close friends after that. Scarcely a day passed in which the country people did not see them out together, cantering gayly on the highroad or through the green lanes. The children in the cottages would run to the door to look at the proud little brown pony with the gallant little figure sitting so straight in the saddle, and the young lord would snatch off his cap and swing it at them, and shout, "Hullo! Good-morning!" in a very unlordly manner, though with great heartiness. Sometimes he would stop and talk with the children, and once Wilkins came back to the castle with a story of how Fauntleroy had insisted on dismounting near the village school, so that a boy who was lame and tired might ride home on his pony.

"An' I'm blessed," said Wilkins, in telling the story at the stables,—"I'm blessed if he'd hear of anything else! He wouldn't let me get down, because he said the boy mightn't feel comfortable on a big horse. An' ses he, 'Wilkins,' ses he, 'that boy's lame and I'm not, and I want to talk to him, too.' And up the lad has to get, and my lord trudges alongside of him with his hands in his pockets, and his cap on the back of his head, a-whistling and talking as easy as you please! And when we come to the cottage, an' the boy's mother come out all in a taking to see what's up, he whips off his cap an' ses he, 'I've brought your son home, ma'am,' ses he, 'because his leg hurt him, and I don't think that stick is enough for him to lean on; and I'm going to ask my grandfather to have a pair of crutches made for him.' An' I'm blessed if the woman wasn't struck all of a heap, as well she might be! I thought I should 'a' hex-plodid, myself!"

When the Earl heard the story he was not angry, as Wilkins had been half afraid that he would be; on the contrary, he laughed outright, and called Fauntleroy up to him, and made him tell all about the matter from beginning to end, and then he laughed again. And actually, a few days later, the Dorincourt carriage stopped in the green lane before the cottage where the lame boy lived, and Fauntleroy jumped out and walked up to the door, carrying a pair of strong, light, new crutches shouldered like a gun, and presented them to Mrs. Hartle (the lame boy's name was Hartle) with these words: "My grandfather's compliments, and if you please, these are for your boy, and we hope he will get better."

"I said your compliments," he explained to the Earl when he returned to the carriage. "You didn't tell me to, but I thought perhaps you forgot. That was right, wasn't it?"

And the Earl laughed again, and did not say it was not. In fact, the two were becoming more intimate every day, and every day Fauntleroy's faith in his lordship's benevolence and virtue increased. He had no doubt whatever that his grandfather was the most amiable and generous of elderly gentlemen. Certainly, he himself found his wishes gratified almost before they were uttered; and such gifts and pleasures were lavished upon him, that he was sometimes almost bewildered by his own possessions. Apparently, he was to have everything he wanted, and to do everything he wished to do. And though this would certainly not have been a very wise plan to pursue with all small boys, his young lordship bore it amazingly well. Perhaps, notwithstanding his sweet nature, he might have been somewhat spoiled by it, if it had not been for the hours he spent with his mother at Court Lodge. That "best friend" of his watched over him ever closely and tenderly. The two had many long talks together, and he never went back to the Castle with her kisses on his cheeks without carrying in his heart some simple, pure words worth remembering.

There was one thing, it is true, which puzzled the little fellow very much. He thought over the mystery of it much oftener than any one supposed; even his mother did not know how often he pondered on it; the Earl for a long time never suspected that he did so at all. But, being quick to observe, the little boy could not help wondering why it was that his mother and grandfather never seemed to meet. He had noticed that they never did meet. When the Dorincourt carriage stopped at Court Lodge, the Earl never alighted, and on the rare occasions of his lordship's going to church, Fauntleroy was always left to speak to his mother in the porch alone, or perhaps to go home with her. And yet, every day, fruit and flowers were sent to Court Lodge from the hot-houses at the Castle. But the one virtuous action of the Earl's which had set him upon the pinnacle of perfection in Cedric's eyes, was what he had done soon after that first Sunday when Mrs. Errol had walked home from church unattended. About a week later, when Cedric was going one day to visit his mother, he found at the door, instead of the large carriage and prancing pair, a pretty little brougham and a handsome bay horse.

"That is a present from you to your mother," the Earl said abruptly. "She can not go walking about the country. She needs a carriage. The man who drives will take charge of it. It is a present from YOU."

Fauntleroy's delight could but feebly express itself. He could scarcely contain himself until he reached the lodge. His mother was gathering roses in the garden. He flung himself out of the little brougham and flew to her.

"Dearest!" he cried, "could you believe it? This is yours! He says it is a present from me. It is your own carriage to drive everywhere in!"

He was so happy that she did not know what to say. She could not have borne to spoil his pleasure by refusing to accept the gift even though it came from the man who chose to consider himself her enemy. She was obliged to step into the carriage, roses and all, and let herself be taken to drive, while Fauntleroy told her stories of his grandfather's goodness and amiability. They were such innocent stories that sometimes she could not help laughing a little, and then she would draw her little boy closer to her side and kiss him, feeling glad that he could see only good in the old man, who had so few friends.

The very next day after that, Fauntleroy wrote to Mr. Hobbs. He wrote quite a long letter, and after the first copy was written, he brought it to his grandfather to be inspected.

"Because," he said, "it's so uncertain about the spelling. And if you'll tell me the mistakes, I'll write it out again."

This was what he had written:

"My dear mr hobbs i want to tell you about my granfarther he is the best earl you ever new it is a mistake about earls being tirents he is not a tirent at all i wish you new him you would be good friends i am sure you would he has the gout in his foot and is a grate sufrer but he is so pashent i love him more every day becaus no one could help loving an earl like that who is kind to every one in this world i wish you could talk to him he knows everything in the world you can ask him any question but he has never plaid base ball he has given me a pony and a cart and my mamma a bewtifle cariage and I have three rooms and toys of all kinds it would serprise you you would like the castle and the park it is such a large castle you could lose yourself wilkins tells me wilkins is my groom he says there is a dungon under the castle it is so pretty everything in the park would serprise you there are such big trees and there are deers and rabbits and games flying about in the cover my granfarther is very rich but he is not proud and orty as you thought earls always were i like to be with him the people are so polite and kind they take of their hats to you and the women make curtsies and sometimes say god bless you i can ride now but at first it shook me when i troted my granfarther let a poor man stay on his farm when he could not pay his rent and mrs mellon went to take wine and things to his sick children i should like to see you and i wish dearest could live at the castle but i am very happy when i dont miss her too much and i love my granfarther every one does plees write soon

"your afechshnet old frend

"Cedric Errol

"p s no one is in the dungon my granfarfher never had any one langwishin in there.

"p s he is such a good earl he reminds me of you he is a unerversle favrit"

"Do you miss your mother very much?" asked the Earl when he had finished reading this.

"Yes," said Fauntleroy, "I miss her all the time."

He went and stood before the Earl and put his hand on his knee, looking up at him.

"YOU don't miss her, do you?" he said.

"I don't know her," answered his lordship rather crustily.

"I know that," said Fauntleroy, "and that's what makes me

84

wonder. She told me not to ask you any questions, and—and I won't, but sometimes I can't help thinking, you know, and it makes me all puzzled. But I'm not going to ask any questions. And when I miss her very much, I go and look out of my window to where I see her light shine for me every night through an open place in the trees. It is a long way off, but she puts it in her window as soon as it is dark, and I can see it twinkle far away, and I know what it says."

"What does it say?" asked my lord.

"It says, 'Good-night, God keep you all the night!'—just what she used to say when we were together. Every night she used to say that to me, and every morning she said, 'God bless you all the day!' So you see I am quite safe all the time——"

"Quite, I have no doubt," said his lordship dryly. And he drew down his beetling eyebrows and looked at the little boy so fixedly and so long that Fauntleroy wondered what he could be thinking of.

IX

The fact was, his lordship the Earl of Dorincourt thought in those days, of many things of which he had never thought before, and all his thoughts were in one way or another connected with his grandson. His pride was the strongest part of his nature, and the boy gratified it at every point. Through this pride he began to find a new interest in life. He began to take pleasure in showing his heir to the world. The world had known of his disappointment in his sons; so there was an agreeable touch of triumph in exhibiting this new Lord Fauntleroy, who could disappoint no one. He wished the child to appreciate his own power and to understand the splendor of his position; he wished that others should realize it too. He made plans for his future.

Sometimes in secret he actually found himself wishing that his own past life had been a better one, and that there had been less in it that this pure, childish heart would shrink from if it knew the truth. It was not agreeable to think how the beautiful, innocent face would look if its owner should be made by any chance to understand that his grandfather had been called for many a year "the wicked Earl of Dorincourt." The thought even made him feel a trifle nervous. He did not wish the boy to find it out. Sometimes in this new interest he forgot his gout, and after a while his doctor was surprised to find his noble patient's health growing better than he had expected it ever would be again. Perhaps the Earl grew better because the time did not pass so slowly for him, and he had something to think of beside his pains and infirmities.

One fine morning, people were amazed to see little Lord Fauntleroy riding his pony with another companion than Wilkins. This new companion rode a tall, powerful gray horse, and was no other than the Earl himself. It was, in fact, Fauntleroy who had suggested this plan. As he had been on the point of mounting his pony, he had said rather wistfully to his grandfather:

"I wish you were going with me. When I go away I feel lonely because you are left all by yourself in such a big castle. I wish you could ride too."

And the greatest excitement had been aroused in the stables a few minutes later by the arrival of an order that Selim was to be saddled for the Earl. After that, Selim was saddled almost every day; and the people became accustomed to the sight of the tall gray horse carrying the tall gray old man, with his handsome, fierce, eagle face, by the side of the brown pony which bore little Lord Fauntleroy.

And in their rides together through the green lanes and pretty country roads, the two riders became more intimate than ever. And gradually the old man heard a great deal about "Dearest" and her life. As Fauntleroy trotted by the big horse he chatted gayly. There could not well have been a brighter little comrade, his nature was so happy. It was he who talked the most. The Earl often was silent, listening and watching the joyous, glowing face. Sometimes he would tell his young companion to set the pony off at a gallop, and when the little fellow dashed off, sitting so straight and fearless, he would watch him with a gleam of pride and pleasure in his eyes; and when, after such a dash, Fauntleroy came back waving his cap with a laughing shout, he always felt that he and his grandfather were very good friends indeed.

One thing that the Earl discovered was that his son's wife did not lead an idle life. It was not long before he learned that the poor people knew her very well indeed. When there was sickness or sorrow or poverty in any house, the little brougham often stood before the door.

"Do you know," said Fauntleroy once, "they all say, 'God bless you!' when they see her, and the children are glad. There are some who go to her house to be taught to sew. She says she feels so rich now that she wants to help the poor ones."

It had not displeased the Earl to find that the mother of his heir had a beautiful young face and looked as much like a lady as if she had been a duchess; and in one way it did not displease him to know that she was popular and beloved by the poor. And yet he was often conscious of a hard, jealous pang when he saw how she filled her child's heart and how the boy clung to her as his best beloved. The old man would have desired to stand first himself and have no rival.

That same morning he drew up his horse on an elevated point of the moor over which they rode, and made a gesture with his whip, over the broad, beautiful landscape spread before them.

"Do you know that all that land belongs to me?" he said to Fauntleroy.

"Does it?" answered Fauntleroy. "How much it is to belong to one person, and how beautiful!"

"Do you know that some day it will all belong to you—that and a great deal more?"

"To me!" exclaimed Fauntleroy in rather an awe-stricken voice. "When?"

"When I am dead," his grandfather answered.

"Then I don't want it," said Fauntleroy; "I want you to live always."

"That's kind," answered the Earl in his dry way; "nevertheless, some day it will all be yours—some day you will be the Earl of Dorincourt."

Little Lord Fauntleroy sat very still in his saddle for a few moments. He looked over the broad moors, the green farms, the beautiful copses, the cottages in the lanes, the pretty village, and over the trees to where the turrets of the great castle rose, gray and stately. Then he gave a queer little sigh.

"What are you thinking of?" asked the Earl.

"I am thinking," replied Fauntleroy, "what a little boy I am! and of what Dearest said to me."

"What was it?" inquired the Earl.

"She said that perhaps it was not so easy to be very rich; that if any one had so many things always, one might sometimes forget that every one else was not so fortunate, and that one who is rich should always be careful and try to remember. I was talking to her about how good you were, and she said that was such a good thing, because an earl had so much power, and if he cared only about his own pleasure and never thought about the people who lived on his lands, they might have trouble that he could help—and there were so many people, and it would be such a hard thing. And I was just looking at all those houses, and thinking how I should have to find out about the people, when I was an earl. How did you find out about them?"

As his lordship's knowledge of his tenantry consisted in finding out which of them paid their rent promptly, and in turning out those who did not, this was rather a hard question. "Newick finds out for me," he said, and he pulled his great gray mustache, and looked at his small questioner rather uneasily. "We will go home now," he added; "and when you are an earl, see to it that you are a better earl than I have been!"

He was very silent as they rode home. He felt it to be almost incredible that he who had never really loved any one in his life, should find himself growing so fond of this little fellow,—as without doubt he was. At first he had only been pleased and proud of Cedric's beauty and bravery, but there was something more than pride in his feeling now. He laughed a grim, dry laugh all to himself sometimes, when he thought how he liked to have the boy near him, how he liked to hear his voice, and how in secret he really wished to be liked and thought well of by his small grandson.

"I'm an old fellow in my dotage, and I have nothing else to think of," he would say to himself; and yet he knew it was not that altogether. And if he had allowed himself to admit the truth, he would perhaps have found himself obliged to own that the very things which attracted him, in spite of himself, were the qualities he had never possessed—the frank, true, kindly nature, the affectionate trustfulness which could never think evil.

It was only about a week after that ride when, after a visit to his mother, Fauntleroy came into the library with a troubled, thoughtful face. He sat down in that high-backed chair in which he had sat on the evening of his arrival, and for a while he looked at the embers on the hearth. The Earl watched him in silence, wondering what was coming. It was evident that Cedric had something on his mind. At last he looked up. "Does Newick know all about the people?" he asked.

"It is his business to know about them," said his lordship. "Been neglecting it—has he?"

Contradictory as it may seem, there was nothing which entertained and edified him more than the little fellow's interest in his tenantry. He had never taken any interest in them himself, but it pleased him well enough that, with all his childish habits of thought and in the midst of all his childish amusements and high spirits, there should be such a quaint seriousness working in the curly head.

"There is a place," said Fauntleroy, looking up at him with wide-open, horror-stricken eye—"Dearest has seen it; it is at the other end of the village. The houses are close together, and almost falling down; you can scarcely breathe; and the people are so poor, and everything is dreadful! Often they have fever, and the children die; and it makes them wicked to live like that, and be so poor and miserable! It is worse than Michael and Bridget! The rain comes in at the roof! Dearest went to see a poor woman who lived there. She would not let me come near her until she had changed all her things. The tears ran down her cheeks when she told me about it!"

The tears had come into his own eyes, but he smiled through them.

"I told her you didn't know, and I would tell you," he said. He jumped down and came and leaned against the Earl's chair. "You can make it all right," he said, "just as you made it all right for Higgins. You always make it all right for everybody. I told her you would, and that Newick must have forgotten to tell you."

The Earl looked down at the hand on his knee. Newick had not forgotten to tell him; in fact, Newick had spoken to him more than once of the desperate condition of the end of the village known as Earl's Court. He knew all about the tumble-down, miserable cottages, and the bad drainage, and the damp walls and broken windows and leaking roofs, and all about the poverty, the fever, and the misery. Mr. Mordaunt had painted it all to him in the strongest words he could use, and his lordship had used violent language in response; and, when his gout had been at the worst, he said that the sooner the people of Earl's Court died and were buried by the parish the better it would be,—and there was an end of the matter. And yet, as he looked at the small hand on his knee, and from the small hand to the honest, earnest, frank-eyed face, he was actually a little ashamed both of Earl's Court and himself.

"What!" he said; "you want to make a builder of model cottages of me, do you?" And he positively put his own hand upon the childish one and stroked it.

"Those must be pulled down," said Fauntleroy, with great eagerness. "Dearest says so. Let us—let us go and have them pulled down to-morrow. The people will be so glad when they see you! They'll know you have come to help them!" And his eyes shone like stars in his glowing face.

The Earl rose from his chair and put his hand on the child's shoulder. "Let us go out and take our walk on the terrace," he said, with a short laugh; "and we can talk it over."

And though he laughed two or three times again, as they walked to and fro on the broad stone terrace, where they walked together almost every fine evening, he seemed to be thinking of something which did not displease him, and still he kept his hand on his small companion's shoulder.

X

The truth was that Mrs. Errol had found a great many sad things in the course of her work among the poor of the little village that appeared so picturesque when it was seen from the moor-sides. Everything was not as picturesque, when seen near by, as it looked from a distance. She had found idleness and poverty and ignorance where there should have been comfort and industry. And she had discovered, after a while, that Erleboro was considered to be the worst village in that part of the country. Mr. Mordaunt had told her a great many of his difficulties and discouragements, and she had found out a great deal by herself. The agents who had managed the property had always been chosen to please the Earl, and had cared nothing for the degradation and wretchedness of the poor tenants. Many things, therefore, had been neglected which should have been attended to, and matters had gone from bad to worse.

As to Earl's Court, it was a disgrace, with its dilapidated houses and miserable, careless, sickly people. When first Mrs. Errol went to the place, it made her shudder. Such ugliness and slovenliness and want seemed worse in a country place than in a city. It seemed as if there it might be helped. And as she looked at the squalid, uncared-for children growing up in the midst of vice and brutal indifference, she thought of her own little boy spending his days in the great, splendid castle, guarded and served like a young prince, having no wish ungratified, and knowing nothing but luxury and ease and beauty. And a bold thought came in her wise little mother-heart. Gradually she had begun to see, as had others, that it had been her boy's good fortune to please the Earl very much, and that he would scarcely be likely to be denied anything for which he expressed a desire.

"The Earl would give him anything," she said to Mr. Mordaunt. "He would indulge his every whim. Why should not that indulgence be used for the good of others? It is for me to see that this shall come to pass."

She knew she could trust the kind, childish heart; so she told the little fellow the story of Earl's Court, feeling sure that he would speak of it to his grandfather, and hoping that some good results would follow.

And strange as it appeared to every one, good results did follow.

The fact was that the strongest power to influence the Earl was his grandson's perfect confidence in him—the fact that Cedric always believed that his grandfather was going to do what was right and generous. He could not quite make up his mind to let him discover that he had no inclination to be generous at all, and that he wanted his own way on all occasions, whether it was right or wrong. It was such a novelty to be regarded with admiration as a benefactor of the entire human race, and the soul of nobility, that he did not enjoy the idea of looking into the affectionate brown eyes, and saying: "I am a violent, selfish old rascal; I never did a generous thing in my life, and I don't care about Earl's Court or the poor people"—or something which would amount to the same thing. He actually had learned to be fond enough of that small boy with the mop of yellow love-locks, to feel that he himself would prefer to be guilty of an amiable action now and then. And so—though he laughed at himself—after some reflection, he sent for Newick, and had quite a long interview with him on the subject of the Court, and it was decided that the wretched hovels should be pulled down and new houses should be built.

"It is Lord Fauntleroy who insists on it," he said dryly; "he thinks it will improve the property. You can tell the tenants that it's his idea." And he looked down at his small lordship, who was lying on the hearth-rug playing with Dougal. The great dog was the lad's constant companion, and followed him about everywhere, stalking solemnly after him when he walked, and trotting majestically behind when he rode or drove.

Of course, both the country people and the town people heard of the proposed improvement. At first, many of them would not believe it; but when a small army of workmen arrived and commenced pulling down the crazy, squalid cottages, people began to understand that little Lord Fauntleroy had done them a good turn again, and that through his innocent interference the scandal of Earl's Court had at last been removed. If he had only known how they talked about him and praised him everywhere, and prophesied great things for him when he grew up, how astonished he would have been! But he never suspected it. He lived his simple, happy, child life,—frolicking about in the park; chasing the rabbits to their burrows; lying under the trees on the grass, or on the rug in the library, reading wonderful books and talking to the Earl about them, and then telling the stories again to his mother; writing long letters to Dick and Mr. Hobbs, who responded in characteristic fashion; riding out at his grandfather's side, or with Wilkins as escort. As they rode through the market town, he used to see the people turn and look, and he noticed that as they lifted their hats their faces often brightened very much; but he thought it was all because his grandfather was with him.

"They are so fond of you," he once said, looking up at his lordship with a bright smile. "Do you see how glad they are when they see you? I hope they will some day be as fond of me. It must be nice to have EVERYbody like you." And he felt quite proud to be the grandson of so greatly admired and beloved an individual.

When the cottages were being built, the lad and his grandfather used to ride over to Earl's Court together to look at them, and Fauntleroy was full of interest. He would dismount from his pony and go and make acquaintance with the workmen, asking them questions about building and bricklaying, and telling them things about America. After two or three such conversations, he was able to enlighten the Earl on the subject of brick-making, as they rode home.

"I always like to know about things like those," he said, "because you never know what you are coming to."

When he left them, the workmen used to talk him over among themselves, and laugh at his odd, innocent speeches; but they liked him, and liked to see him stand among them, talking away, with his hands in his pockets, his hat pushed back on his curls, and his small face full of eagerness. "He's a rare un," they used to say. "An' a noice little outspoken chap, too. Not much o' th' bad stock in him." And they would go home and tell their wives about him, and the women would tell each other, and so it came about that almost every one talked of, or knew some story of, little Lord Fauntleroy; and gradually almost every one knew that the "wicked Earl" had found something he cared for at last—something which had touched and even warmed his hard, bitter old heart.

But no one knew quite how much it had been warmed, and how day by day the old man found himself caring more and more for the child, who was the only creature that had ever trusted him. He found himself looking forward to the time when Cedric would be a young man, strong and beautiful, with life all before him, but having still that kind heart and the power to make friends everywhere, and the Earl wondered what the lad would do, and how he would use his gifts. Often as he watched the little fellow lying upon the hearth, conning some big book, the light shining on the bright young head, his old eyes would gleam and his cheek would flush.

"The boy can do anything," he would say to himself, "anything!"

He never spoke to any one else of his feeling for Cedric; when he spoke of him to others it was always with the same grim smile. But Fauntleroy soon knew that his grandfather loved him and always liked him to be near—near to his chair if they were in the library, opposite to him at table, or by his side when he rode or drove or took his evening walk on the broad terrace.

"Do you remember," Cedric said once, looking up from his book as he lay on the rug, "do you remember what I said to you that first night about our being good companions? I don't think any people could be better companions than we are, do you?"

"We are pretty good companions, I should say," replied his lordship. "Come here."

Fauntleroy scrambled up and went to him.

"Is there anything you want," the Earl asked; "anything you have not?"

The little fellow's brown eyes fixed themselves on his grandfather with a rather wistful look.

"Only one thing," he answered.

"What is that?" inquired the Earl.

Fauntleroy was silent a second. He had not thought matters over to himself so long for nothing.

"What is it?" my lord repeated.

Fauntleroy answered.

"It is Dearest," he said.

The old Earl winced a little.

"But you see her almost every day," he said. "Is not that enough?"

"I used to see her all the time," said Fauntleroy. "She used to kiss me when I went to sleep at night, and in the morning she was always there, and we could tell each other things without waiting."

The old eyes and the young ones looked into each other through a moment of silence. Then the Earl knitted his brows.

"Do you NEVER forget about your mother?" he said.

"No," answered Fauntleroy, "never; and she never forgets about me. I shouldn't forget about YOU, you know, if I didn't live with you. I should think about you all the more."

"Upon my word," said the Earl, after looking at him a moment longer, "I believe you would!"

The jealous pang that came when the boy spoke so of his mother seemed even stronger than it had been before; it was stronger because of this old man's increasing affection for the boy.

But it was not long before he had other pangs, so much harder to face that he almost forgot, for the time, he had ever hated his son's wife at all. And in a strange and startling way it happened. One evening, just before the Earl's Court cottages were completed, there was a grand dinner party at Dorincourt. There had not been such a party at the Castle for a long time. A few days before it took place, Sir Harry Lorridaile and Lady Lorridaile, who was the Earl's only sister, actually came for a visit—a thing which caused the greatest excitement in the village and set Mrs. Dibble's shop-bell tinkling madly again, because it was well known that Lady Lorridaile had only been to Dorincourt once since her marriage, thirty-five years before. She was a handsome old lady with white curls and dimpled, peachy cheeks, and she was as good as gold, but she had never approved of her brother any more than did the rest of the world, and having a strong will of her own and not being at all afraid to speak her mind frankly, she had, after several lively quarrels with his lordship, seen very little of him since her young days.

She had heard a great deal of him that was not pleasant through the years in which they had been separated. She had heard about his neglect of his wife, and of the poor lady's death; and of his indifference to his children; and of the two weak, vicious, unprepossessing elder boys who had been no credit to him or to any one else. Those two elder sons, Bevis and Maurice, she had never seen; but once there had come to Lorridaile Park a tall, stalwart, beautiful young fellow about eighteen years old, who had told her that he was her nephew Cedric Errol, and that he had come to see her because he was passing near the place and wished to look at his Aunt Constantia of whom he had heard his mother speak. Lady Lorridaile's kind heart had warmed through and through at the sight of the young man, and she had made him stay with her a week, and petted him, and made much of him and admired him immensely. He was so sweet-tempered, light-hearted, spirited a lad, that when he went away, she had hoped to see him often again; but she never did, because the Earl had been in a bad humor when he went back to Dorincourt, and had forbidden him ever to go to Lorridaile Park again. But Lady Lorridaile had always remembered him tenderly, and though she feared he had made a rash marriage in America, she had been very angry when she heard how he had been cast off by his father and that no one really knew where or how he lived. At last there came a rumor of his death, and then Bevis had been thrown from his horse and killed, and Maurice had died in Rome of the fever; and soon after came the story of the American child who was to be found and brought home as Lord Fauntleroy.

"Probably to be ruined as the others were," she said to her husband, "unless his mother is good enough and has a will of her own to help her to take care of him."

But when she heard that Cedric's mother had been parted from him she was almost too indignant for words.

"It is disgraceful, Harry!" she said. "Fancy a child of that age being taken from his mother, and made the companion of a man like my brother! He will either be brutal to the boy or indulge him until he is a little monster. If I thought it would do any good to write——"

"It wouldn't, Constantia," said Sir Harry.

"I know it wouldn't," she answered. "I know his lordship the Earl of Dorincourt too well;—but it is outrageous."

Not only the poor people and farmers heard about little Lord Fauntleroy; others knew him. He was talked about so much and there were so many stories of him—of his beauty, his sweet temper, his popularity, and his growing influence over the Earl, his grandfather—that rumors of him reached the gentry at their country places and he was heard of in more than one county of England. People talked about him at the dinner tables, ladies pitied his young mother, and wondered if the boy were as handsome as he was said to be, and men who knew the Earl and his habits laughed heartily at the stories of the little fellow's belief in his lordship's amiability. Sir Thomas Asshe of Asshawe Hall, being in Erleboro one day, met the Earl and his grandson riding together, and stopped to shake hands with my lord and congratulate him on his change of looks and on his recovery from the gout. "And, d' ye know," he said, when he spoke of the incident afterward, "the old man looked as proud as a turkey-cock; and upon my word I don't wonder, for a handsomer, finer lad than his grandson I never saw! As straight as a dart, and sat his pony like a young trooper!"

And so by degrees Lady Lorridaile, too, heard of the child; she heard about Higgins and the lame boy, and the cottages at Earl's Court, and a score of other things,—and she began to wish to see the little fellow. And just as she was wondering how it might be brought about, to her utter astonishment, she received a letter from her brother inviting her to come with her husband to Dorincourt.

"It seems incredible!" she exclaimed. "I have heard it said that the child has worked miracles, and I begin to believe it. They say my brother adores the boy and can scarcely endure to have him out of sight. And he is so proud of him! Actually, I believe he wants to show him to us." And she accepted the invitation at once.

When she reached Dorincourt Castle with Sir Harry, it was late in the afternoon, and she went to her room at once before seeing her brother. Having dressed for dinner, she entered the drawing-room. The Earl was there standing near the fire and looking very tall and imposing; and at his side stood a little boy in black velvet, and a large Vandyke collar of rich lace—a little fellow whose round bright face was so handsome, and who turned upon her such beautiful, candid brown eyes, that she almost uttered an exclamation of pleasure and surprise at the sight.

As she shook hands with the Earl, she called him by the name she had not used since her girlhood.

"What, Molyneux!" she said, "is this the child?"

"Yes, Constantia," answered the Earl, "this is the boy. Fauntleroy, this is your grand-aunt, Lady Lorridaile."

"How do you do, Grand-Aunt?" said Fauntleroy.

Lady Lorridaile put her hand on his shoulders, and after looking down into his upraised face a few seconds, kissed him warmly.

"I am your Aunt Constantia," she said, "and I loved your poor papa, and you are very like him."

"It makes me glad when I am told I am like him," answered Fauntleroy, "because it seems as if every one liked him,—just like Dearest, eszackly,—Aunt Constantia" (adding the two words after a second's pause).

Lady Lorridaile was delighted. She bent and kissed him again, and from that moment they were warm friends.

"Well, Molyneux," she said aside to the Earl afterward, "it could not possibly be better than this!"

"I think not," answered his lordship dryly. "He is a fine little fellow. We are great friends. He believes me to be the most charming and sweet-tempered of philanthropists. I will confess to you, Constantia,—as you would find it out if I did not,—that I am in some slight danger of becoming rather an old fool about him."

"What does his mother think of you?" asked Lady Lorridaile, with her usual straightforwardness.

"I have not asked her," answered the Earl, slightly scowling.

"Well," said Lady Lorridaile, "I will be frank with you at the outset, Molyneux, and tell you I don't approve of your course, and that it is my intention to call on Mrs. Errol as soon as possible; so if you wish to quarrel with me, you had better mention it at once. What I hear of the young creature makes me quite sure that her child owes her everything. We were told even at Lorridaile Park that your poorer tenants adore her already."

"They adore HIM," said the Earl, nodding toward Fauntleroy. "As to Mrs. Errol, you'll find her a pretty little woman. I'm rather in debt to her for giving some of her beauty to the boy, and you can go to see her if you like. All I ask is that she will remain at Court Lodge and that you will not ask me to go and see her," and he scowled a little again.

"But he doesn't hate her as much as he used to, that is plain enough to me," her ladyship said to Sir Harry afterward. "And he is a changed man in a measure, and, incredible as it may seem, Harry, it is my opinion that he is being made into a human being, through nothing more nor less than his affection for that innocent, affectionate little fellow. Why, the child actually loves him—leans on his chair and against his knee. His own children would as soon have thought of nestling up to a tiger."

The very next day she went to call upon Mrs. Errol. When she returned, she said to her brother:

"Molyneux, she is the loveliest little woman I ever saw! She has a voice like a silver bell, and you may thank her for making the boy what he is. She has given him more than her beauty, and you make a great mistake in not persuading her to come and take charge of you. I shall invite her to Lorridaile."

"She'll not leave the boy," replied the Earl.

"I must have the boy too," said Lady Lorridaile, laughing.

But she knew Fauntleroy would not be given up to her, and each day she saw more clearly how closely those two had grown to each other, and how all the proud, grim old man's ambition and hope and love centered themselves in the child, and how the warm, innocent nature returned his affection with most perfect trust and good faith.

She knew, too, that the prime reason for the great dinner party was the Earl's secret desire to show the world his grandson and heir, and to let people see that the boy who had been so much spoken of and described was even a finer little specimen of boyhood than rumor had made him.

"Bevis and Maurice were such a bitter humiliation to him," she said to her husband. "Every one knew it. He actually hated them. His pride has full sway here." Perhaps there was not one person who accepted the invitation without feeling some curiosity about little Lord Fauntleroy, and wondering if he would be on view.

And when the time came he was on view.

"The lad has good manners," said the Earl. "He will be in no one's way. Children are usually idiots or bores,—mine were both,—but he can actually answer when he's spoken to, and be silent when he is not. He is never offensive."

But he was not allowed to be silent very long. Every one had something to say to him. The fact was they wished to make him talk. The ladies petted him and asked him questions, and the men asked him questions too, and joked with him, as the men on the steamer had done when he crossed the Atlantic. Fauntleroy did not quite understand why they laughed so sometimes when he answered them, but he was so used to seeing people amused when he was quite serious, that he did not mind. He thought the whole evening delightful. The magnificent rooms were so brilliant with lights, there were so many flowers, the gentlemen seemed so gay, and the ladies wore such beautiful, wonderful dresses, and such sparkling ornaments in their hair and on their necks. There was one young lady who, he heard them say, had just come down from London, where she had spent the "season"; and she was so charming that he could not keep his eyes from her. She was a rather tall young lady with a proud little head, and very soft dark hair, and large eyes the color of purple pansies, and the color on her cheeks and lips was like that of a rose. She was dressed in a beautiful white dress, and had pearls around her throat. There was one strange thing about this young lady. So many gentlemen stood near her, and seemed anxious to please her, that Fauntleroy thought she must be something like a princess. He was so much interested in her that without knowing it he drew nearer and nearer to her, and at last she turned and spoke to him.

"Come here, Lord Fauntleroy," she said, smiling; "and tell me why you look at me so."

"I was thinking how beautiful you are," his young lordship replied.

Then all the gentlemen laughed outright, and the young lady laughed a little too, and the rose color in her cheeks brightened.

"Ah, Fauntleroy," said one of the gentlemen who had laughed most heartily, "make the most of your time! When you are older you will not have the courage to say that."

"But nobody could help saying it," said Fauntleroy sweetly. "Could you help it? Don't YOU think she is pretty, too?"

"We are not allowed to say what we think," said the gentleman, while the rest laughed more than ever.

But the beautiful young lady—her name was Miss Vivian Herbert—put out her hand and drew Cedric to her side, looking prettier than before, if possible.

"Lord Fauntleroy shall say what he thinks," she said; "and I am much obliged to him. I am sure he thinks what he says." And she kissed him on his cheek.

"I think you are prettier than any one I ever saw," said Fauntleroy, looking at her with innocent, admiring eyes, "except Dearest. Of course, I couldn't think any one QUITE as pretty as Dearest. I think she is the prettiest person in the world."

"I am sure she is," said Miss Vivian Herbert. And she laughed and kissed his cheek again.

She kept him by her side a great part of the evening, and the group of which they were the center was very gay. He did not know how it happened, but before long he was telling them all about America, and the Republican Rally, and Mr. Hobbs and Dick, and in

the end he proudly produced from his pocket Dick's parting gift,—
the red silk handkerchief.

"I put it in my pocket to-night because it was a party," he said.
"I thought Dick would like me to wear it at a party."

And queer as the big, flaming, spotted thing was, there was a
serious, affectionate look in his eyes, which prevented his audience
from laughing very much.

"You see, I like it," he said, "because Dick is my friend."

But though he was talked to so much, as the Earl had said, he
was in no one's way. He could be quiet and listen when others
talked, and so no one found him tiresome. A slight smile crossed
more than one face when several times he went and stood near his
grandfather's chair, or sat on a stool close to him, watching him and
absorbing every word he uttered with the most charmed interest.
Once he stood so near the chair's arm that his cheek touched the
Earl's shoulder, and his lordship, detecting the general smile, smiled
a little himself. He knew what the lookers-on were thinking, and he
felt some secret amusement in their seeing what good friends he
was with this youngster, who might have been expected to share the
popular opinion of him.

Mr. Havisham had been expected to arrive in the afternoon,
but, strange to say, he was late. Such a thing had really never been
known to happen before during all the years in which he had been a
visitor at Dorincourt Castle. He was so late that the guests were on
the point of rising to go in to dinner when he arrived. When he
approached his host, the Earl regarded him with amazement. He
looked as if he had been hurried or agitated; his dry, keen old face
was actually pale.

"I was detained," he said, in a low voice to the Earl, "by—an
extraordinary event."

It was as unlike the methodic old lawyer to be agitated by
anything as it was to be late, but it was evident that he had been
disturbed. At dinner he ate scarcely anything, and two or three
times, when he was spoken to, he started as if his thoughts were far
away. At dessert, when Fauntleroy came in, he looked at him more
than once, nervously and uneasily. Fauntleroy noted the look and
wondered at it. He and Mr. Havisham were on friendly terms, and
they usually exchanged smiles. The lawyer seemed to have forgotten
to smile that evening.

The fact was, he forgot everything but the strange and painful
news he knew he must tell the Earl before the night was over—the
strange news which he knew would be so terrible a shock, and which
would change the face of everything. As he looked about at the
splendid rooms and the brilliant company,—at the people gathered

together, he knew, more that they might see the bright-haired little fellow near the Earl's chair than for any other reason,—as he looked at the proud old man and at little Lord Fauntleroy smiling at his side, he really felt quite shaken, notwithstanding that he was a hardened old lawyer. What a blow it was that he must deal them!

He did not exactly know how the long, superb dinner ended. He sat through it as if he were in a dream, and several times he saw the Earl glance at him in surprise.

But it was over at last, and the gentlemen joined the ladies in the drawing-room. They found Fauntleroy sitting on the sofa with Miss Vivian Herbert,—the great beauty of the last London season; they had been looking at some pictures, and he was thanking his companion as the door opened.

"I'm ever so much obliged to you for being so kind to me!" he was saying; "I never was at a party before, and I've enjoyed myself so much!"

He had enjoyed himself so much that when the gentlemen gathered about Miss Herbert again and began to talk to her, as he listened and tried to understand their laughing speeches, his eyelids began to droop. They drooped until they covered his eyes two or three times, and then the sound of Miss Herbert's low, pretty laugh would bring him back, and he would open them again for about two seconds. He was quite sure he was not going to sleep, but there was a large, yellow satin cushion behind him and his head sank against it, and after a while his eyelids drooped for the last time. They did not even quite open when, as it seemed a long time after, some one kissed him lightly on the cheek. It was Miss Vivian Herbert, who was going away, and she spoke to him softly.

"Good-night, little Lord Fauntleroy," she said. "Sleep well."

And in the morning he did not know that he had tried to open his eyes and had murmured sleepily, "Good-night—I'm so—glad—I saw you—you are so—pretty——"

He only had a very faint recollection of hearing the gentlemen laugh again and of wondering why they did it.

No sooner had the last guest left the room, than Mr. Havisham turned from his place by the fire, and stepped nearer the sofa, where he stood looking down at the sleeping occupant. Little Lord Fauntleroy was taking his ease luxuriously. One leg crossed the other and swung over the edge of the sofa; one arm was flung easily above his head; the warm flush of healthful, happy, childish sleep was on his quiet face; his waving tangle of bright hair strayed over the yellow satin cushion. He made a picture well worth looking at.

As Mr. Havisham looked at it, he put his hand up and rubbed his shaven chin, with a harassed countenance.

"Well, Havisham," said the Earl's harsh voice behind him. "What is it? It is evident something has happened. What was the extraordinary event, if I may ask?"

Mr. Havisham turned from the sofa, still rubbing his chin.

"It was bad news," he answered, "distressing news, my lord—the worst of news. I am sorry to be the bearer of it."

The Earl had been uneasy for some time during the evening, as he glanced at Mr. Havisham, and when he was uneasy he was always ill-tempered.

"Why do you look so at the boy!" he exclaimed irritably. "You have been looking at him all the evening as if—See here now, why should you look at the boy, Havisham, and hang over him like some bird of ill-omen! What has your news to do with Lord Fauntleroy?"

"My lord," said Mr. Havisham, "I will waste no words. My news has everything to do with Lord Fauntleroy. And if we are to believe it—it is not Lord Fauntleroy who lies sleeping before us, but only the son of Captain Errol. And the present Lord Fauntleroy is the son of your son Bevis, and is at this moment in a lodging-house in London."

The Earl clutched the arms of his chair with both his hands until the veins stood out upon them; the veins stood out on his forehead too; his fierce old face was almost livid.

"What do you mean!" he cried out. "You are mad! Whose lie is this?"

"If it is a lie," answered Mr. Havisham, "it is painfully like the truth. A woman came to my chambers this morning. She said your son Bevis married her six years ago in London. She showed me her marriage certificate. They quarrelled a year after the marriage, and he paid her to keep away from him. She has a son five years old. She is an American of the lower classes,—an ignorant person,—and until lately she did not fully understand what her son could claim. She consulted a lawyer and found out that the boy was really Lord Fauntleroy and the heir to the earldom of Dorincourt; and she, of course, insists on his claims being acknowledged."

There was a movement of the curly head on the yellow satin cushion. A soft, long, sleepy sigh came from the parted lips, and the little boy stirred in his sleep, but not at all restlessly or uneasily. Not at all as if his slumber were disturbed by the fact that he was being proved a small impostor and that he was not Lord Fauntleroy at all and never would be the Earl of Dorincourt. He only turned his rosy face more on its side, as if to enable the old man who stared at it so solemnly to see it better.

The handsome, grim old face was ghastly. A bitter smile fixed itself upon it.

"I should refuse to believe a word of it," he said, "if it were not such a low, scoundrelly piece of business that it becomes quite possible in connection with the name of my son Bevis. It is quite like Bevis. He was always a disgrace to us. Always a weak, untruthful, vicious young brute with low tastes—my son and heir, Bevis, Lord Fauntleroy. The woman is an ignorant, vulgar person, you say?"

"I am obliged to admit that she can scarcely spell her own name," answered the lawyer. "She is absolutely uneducated and openly mercenary. She cares for nothing but the money. She is very handsome in a coarse way, but——"

The fastidious old lawyer ceased speaking and gave a sort of shudder.

The veins on the old Earl's forehead stood out like purple cords.

Something else stood out upon it too—cold drops of moisture. He took out his handkerchief and swept them away. His smile grew even more bitter.

"And I," he said, "I objected to—to the other woman, the mother of this child" (pointing to the sleeping form on the sofa); "I refused to recognize her. And yet she could spell her own name. I suppose this is retribution."

Suddenly he sprang up from his chair and began to walk up and down the room. Fierce and terrible words poured forth from his lips. His rage and hatred and cruel disappointment shook him as a storm shakes a tree. His violence was something dreadful to see, and yet Mr. Havisham noticed that at the very worst of his wrath he never seemed to forget the little sleeping figure on the yellow satin cushion, and that he never once spoke loud enough to awaken it.

"I might have known it," he said. "They were a disgrace to me from their first hour! I hated them both; and they hated me! Bevis was the worse of the two. I will not believe this yet, though! I will contend against it to the last. But it is like Bevis—it is like him!"

And then he raged again and asked questions about the woman, about her proofs, and pacing the room, turned first white and then purple in his repressed fury.

When at last he had learned all there was to be told, and knew the worst, Mr. Havisham looked at him with a feeling of anxiety. He looked broken and haggard and changed. His rages had always been bad for him, but this one had been worse than the rest because there had been something more than rage in it.

He came slowly back to the sofa, at last, and stood near it.

"If any one had told me I could be fond of a child," he said, his harsh voice low and unsteady, "I should not have believed them. I always detested children—my own more than the rest. I am fond of

103

this one; he is fond of me" (with a bitter smile). "I am not popular; I never was. But he is fond of me. He never was afraid of me—he always trusted me. He would have filled my place better than I have filled it. I know that. He would have been an honor to the name."

He bent down and stood a minute or so looking at the happy, sleeping face. His shaggy eyebrows were knitted fiercely, and yet somehow he did not seem fierce at all. He put up his hand, pushed the bright hair back from the forehead, and then turned away and rang the bell.

When the largest footman appeared, he pointed to the sofa.

"Take"—he said, and then his voice changed a little—"take Lord Fauntleroy to his room."

XI

When Mr. Hobbs's young friend left him to go to Dorincourt Castle and become Lord Fauntleroy, and the grocery-man had time to realize that the Atlantic Ocean lay between himself and the small companion who had spent so many agreeable hours in his society, he really began to feel very lonely indeed. The fact was, Mr. Hobbs was not a clever man nor even a bright one; he was, indeed, rather a slow and heavy person, and he had never made many acquaintances. He was not mentally energetic enough to know how to amuse himself, and in truth he never did anything of an entertaining nature but read the newspapers and add up his accounts. It was not very easy for him to add up his accounts, and sometimes it took him a long time to bring them out right; and in the old days, little Lord Fauntleroy, who had learned how to add up quite nicely with his fingers and a slate and pencil, had sometimes even gone to the length of trying to help him; and, then too, he had been so good a listener and had taken such an interest in what the newspaper said, and he and Mr. Hobbs had held such long conversations about the Revolution and the British and the elections and the Republican party, that it was no wonder his going left a blank in the grocery store. At first it seemed to Mr. Hobbs that Cedric was not really far away, and would come back again; that some day he would look up from his paper and see the little lad standing in the door-way, in his white suit and red stockings, and with his straw hat on the back of his head, and would hear him say in his cheerful little voice: "Hello, Mr. Hobbs! This is a hot day—isn't it?" But as the days passed on and this did not happen, Mr. Hobbs felt very dull and uneasy. He did not even enjoy his newspaper as much as he used to. He would put the paper down on his knee after reading it, and sit and stare at the high stool for a long time. There were some marks on the long legs which made him feel quite dejected and melancholy. They were marks made by the heels of the next Earl of Dorincourt, when he kicked and talked at the same time. It seems that even youthful earls kick the legs of things they sit on;—noble blood and lofty lineage do not prevent it. After looking at those marks, Mr. Hobbs would take out his gold watch and open it and stare at the inscription: "From his oldest friend, Lord Fauntleroy, to Mr. Hobbs. When this you see, remember me." And after staring at it awhile, he would shut it up with a loud snap, and sigh and get up and go and stand in the door-way—between the box of potatoes and the barrel of apples—and look up the street. At night, when the store was closed, he would light his pipe and walk slowly along the pavement until he reached the house where Cedric had lived, on which there was a sign that read, "This House to Let"; and he would stop near it and look up and shake his head, and puff at his pipe very hard, and after a while walk mournfully back again.

This went on for two or three weeks before any new idea came to him. Being slow and ponderous, it always took him a long time to reach a new idea. As a rule, he did not like new ideas, but preferred old ones. After two or three weeks, however, during which, instead of getting better, matters really grew worse, a novel plan slowly and deliberately dawned upon him. He would go to see Dick. He smoked a great many pipes before he arrived at the conclusion, but finally he did arrive at it. He would go to see Dick. He knew all about Dick. Cedric had told him, and his idea was that perhaps Dick might be some comfort to him in the way of talking things over.

So one day when Dick was very hard at work blacking a customer's boots, a short, stout man with a heavy face and a bald head stopped on the pavement and stared for two or three minutes at the bootblack's sign, which read:

"PROFESSOR DICK TIPTON CAN'T BE BEAT."

He stared at it so long that Dick began to take a lively interest in him, and when he had put the finishing touch to his customer's boots, he said:

"Want a shine, sir?"

The stout man came forward deliberately and put his foot on the rest.

"Yes," he said.

Then when Dick fell to work, the stout man looked from Dick to the sign and from the sign to Dick.

"Where did you get that?" he asked.

"From a friend o' mine," said Dick,—"a little feller. He guv' me the whole outfit. He was the best little feller ye ever saw. He's in England now. Gone to be one o' them lords."

"Lord—Lord—" asked Mr. Hobbs, with ponderous slowness, "Lord Fauntleroy—Goin' to be Earl of Dorincourt?"

Dick almost dropped his brush.

"Why, boss!" he exclaimed, "d' ye know him yerself?"

"I've known him," answered Mr. Hobbs, wiping his warm forehead, "ever since he was born. We was lifetime acquaintances— that's what WE was."

It really made him feel quite agitated to speak of it. He pulled the splendid gold watch out of his pocket and opened it, and showed the inside of the case to Dick.

"'When this you see, remember me,'" he read. "That was his parting keepsake to me. 'I don't want you to forget me'—those was his words—I'd ha' remembered him," he went on, shaking his head, "if he hadn't given me a thing an' I hadn't seen hide nor hair on him again. He was a companion as ANY man would remember."

"He was the nicest little feller I ever see," said Dick. "An' as to sand—I never seen so much sand to a little feller. I thought a heap o' him, I did,—an' we was friends, too—we was sort o' chums from the fust, that little young un an' me. I grabbed his ball from under a stage fur him, an' he never forgot it; an' he'd come down here, he would, with his mother or his nuss and he'd holler: 'Hello, Dick!' at me, as friendly as if he was six feet high, when he warn't knee high to a grasshopper, and was dressed in gal's clo'es. He was a gay little chap, and when you was down on your luck, it did you good to talk to him."

"That's so," said Mr. Hobbs. "It was a pity to make a earl out of HIM. He would have SHONE in the grocery business—or dry goods either; he would have SHONE!" And he shook his head with deeper regret than ever.

It proved that they had so much to say to each other that it was not possible to say it all at one time, and so it was agreed that the next night Dick should make a visit to the store and keep Mr. Hobbs company. The plan pleased Dick well enough. He had been a street waif nearly all his life, but he had never been a bad boy, and he had always had a private yearning for a more respectable kind of existence. Since he had been in business for himself, he had made enough money to enable him to sleep under a roof instead of out in the streets, and he had begun to hope he might reach even a higher plane, in time. So, to be invited to call on a stout, respectable man who owned a corner store, and even had a horse and wagon, seemed to him quite an event.

"Do you know anything about earls and castles?" Mr. Hobbs inquired. "I'd like to know more of the particklars."

"There's a story about some on 'em in the Penny Story Gazette," said Dick. "It's called the 'Crime of a Coronet; or, The Revenge of the Countess May.' It's a boss thing, too. Some of us boys 're takin' it to read."

"Bring it up when you come," said Mr. Hobbs, "an' I'll pay for it. Bring all you can find that have any earls in 'em. If there aren't earls, markises'll do, or dooks—though HE never made mention of any dooks or markises. We did go over coronets a little, but I never happened to see any. I guess they don't keep 'em 'round here."

"Tiffany 'd have 'em if anybody did," said Dick, "but I don't know as I'd know one if I saw it."

Mr. Hobbs did not explain that he would not have known one if he saw it. He merely shook his head ponderously.

"I s'pose there is very little call for 'em," he said, and that ended the matter.

This was the beginning of quite a substantial friendship. When Dick went up to the store, Mr. Hobbs received him with great hospitality. He gave him a chair tilted against the door, near a barrel of apples, and after his young visitor was seated, he made a jerk at them with the hand in which he held his pipe, saying:

"Help yerself."

Then he looked at the story papers, and after that they read and discussed the British aristocracy; and Mr. Hobbs smoked his pipe very hard and shook his head a great deal. He shook it most when he pointed out the high stool with the marks on its legs.

"There's his very kicks," he said impressively; "his very kicks. I sit and look at 'em by the hour. This is a world of ups an' it's a world of downs. Why, he'd set there, an' eat crackers out of a box, an' apples out of a barrel, an' pitch his cores into the street; an' now he's a lord a-livin' in a castle. Them's a lord's kicks; they'll be a earl's kicks some day. Sometimes I says to myself, says I, 'Well, I'll be jiggered!'"

He seemed to derive a great deal of comfort from his reflections and Dick's visit. Before Dick went home, they had a supper in the small back-room; they had crackers and cheese and sardines, and other canned things out of the store, and Mr. Hobbs solemnly opened two bottles of ginger ale, and pouring out two glasses, proposed a toast.

"Here's to HIM!" he said, lifting his glass, "an' may he teach 'em a lesson—earls an' markises an' dooks an' all!"

After that night, the two saw each other often, and Mr. Hobbs was much more comfortable and less desolate. They read the Penny Story Gazette, and many other interesting things, and gained a knowledge of the habits of the nobility and gentry which would have surprised those despised classes if they had realized it. One day Mr. Hobbs made a pilgrimage to a book store down town, for the express purpose of adding to their library. He went to the clerk and leaned over the counter to speak to him.

"I want," he said, "a book about earls."

"What!" exclaimed the clerk.

"A book," repeated the grocery-man, "about earls."

"I'm afraid," said the clerk, looking rather queer, "that we haven't what you want."

"Haven't?" said Mr. Hobbs, anxiously. "Well, say markises then—or dooks."

108

"I know of no such book," answered the clerk.

Mr. Hobbs was much disturbed. He looked down on the floor,—then he looked up.

"None about female earls?" he inquired.

"I'm afraid not," said the clerk with a smile.

"Well," exclaimed Mr. Hobbs, "I'll be jiggered!"

He was just going out of the store, when the clerk called him back and asked him if a story in which the nobility were chief characters would do. Mr. Hobbs said it would—if he could not get an entire volume devoted to earls. So the clerk sold him a book called "The Tower of London," written by Mr. Harrison Ainsworth, and he carried it home.

When Dick came they began to read it. It was a very wonderful and exciting book, and the scene was laid in the reign of the famous English queen who is called by some people Bloody Mary. And as Mr. Hobbs heard of Queen Mary's deeds and the habit she had of chopping people's heads off, putting them to the torture, and burning them alive, he became very much excited. He took his pipe out of his mouth and stared at Dick, and at last he was obliged to mop the perspiration from his brow with his red pocket handkerchief.

"Why, he ain't safe!" he said. "He ain't safe! If the women folks can sit up on their thrones an' give the word for things like that to be done, who's to know what's happening to him this very minute? He's no more safe than nothing! Just let a woman like that get mad, an' no one's safe!"

"Well," said Dick, though he looked rather anxious himself; "ye see this 'ere un isn't the one that's bossin' things now. I know her name's Victory, an' this un here in the book, her name's Mary."

"So it is," said Mr. Hobbs, still mopping his forehead; "so it is. An' the newspapers are not sayin' anything about any racks, thumb-screws, or stake-burnin's,—but still it doesn't seem as if 't was safe for him over there with those queer folks. Why, they tell me they don't keep the Fourth o' July!"

He was privately uneasy for several days; and it was not until he received Fauntleroy's letter and had read it several times, both to himself and to Dick, and had also read the letter Dick got about the same time, that he became composed again.

But they both found great pleasure in their letters. They read and re-read them, and talked them over and enjoyed every word of them. And they spent days over the answers they sent and read them over almost as often as the letters they had received.

It was rather a labor for Dick to write his. All his knowledge of reading and writing he had gained during a few months, when he had lived with his elder brother, and had gone to a night-school; but, being a sharp boy, he had made the most of that brief education, and had spelled out things in newspapers since then, and practiced writing with bits of chalk on pavements or walls or fences. He told Mr. Hobbs all about his life and about his elder brother, who had been rather good to him after their mother died, when Dick was quite a little fellow. Their father had died some time before. The brother's name was Ben, and he had taken care of Dick as well as he could, until the boy was old enough to sell newspapers and run errands. They had lived together, and as he grew older Ben had managed to get along until he had quite a decent place in a store.

"And then," exclaimed Dick with disgust, "blest if he didn't go an' marry a gal! Just went and got spoony an' hadn't any more sense left! Married her, an' set up housekeepin' in two back rooms. An' a hefty un she was,—a regular tiger-cat. She'd tear things to pieces when she got mad,—and she was mad ALL the time. Had a baby just like her,—yell day 'n' night! An' if I didn't have to 'tend it! an' when it screamed, she'd fire things at me. She fired a plate at me one day, an' hit the baby— cut its chin. Doctor said he'd carry the mark till he died. A nice mother she was! Crackey! but didn't we have a time— Ben 'n' mehself 'n' the young un. She was mad at Ben because he didn't make money faster; 'n' at last he went out West with a man to set up a cattle ranch. An' hadn't been gone a week 'fore one night, I got home from sellin' my papers, 'n' the rooms wus locked up 'n' empty, 'n' the woman o' the house, she told me Minna 'd gone— shown a clean pair o' heels. Some un else said she'd gone across the water to be nuss to a lady as had a little baby, too. Never heard a word of her since—nuther has Ben. If I'd ha' bin him, I wouldn't ha' fretted a bit—'n' I guess he didn't. But he thought a heap o' her at the start. Tell you, he was spoons on her. She was a daisy-lookin' gal, too, when she was dressed up 'n' not mad. She'd big black eyes 'n' black hair down to her knees; she'd make it into a rope as big as your arm, and twist it 'round 'n' 'round her head; 'n' I tell you her eyes 'd snap! Folks used to say she was part Itali-un—said her mother or father 'd come from there, 'n' it made her queer. I tell ye, she was one of 'em—she was!"

He often told Mr. Hobbs stories of her and of his brother Ben, who, since his going out West, had written once or twice to Dick.

Ben's luck had not been good, and he had wandered from place to place; but at last he had settled on a ranch in California, where he was at work at the time when Dick became acquainted with Mr. Hobbs.

"That gal," said Dick one day, "she took all the grit out o' him. I couldn't help feelin' sorry for him sometimes."

They were sitting in the store door-way together, and Mr. Hobbs was filling his pipe.

"He oughtn't to 've married," he said solemnly, as he rose to get a match. "Women—I never could see any use in 'em myself."

As he took the match from its box, he stopped and looked down on the counter.

"Why!" he said, "if here isn't a letter! I didn't see it before. The postman must have laid it down when I wasn't noticin', or the newspaper slipped over it."

He picked it up and looked at it carefully.

"It's from HIM!" he exclaimed. "That's the very one it's from!"

He forgot his pipe altogether. He went back to his chair quite excited and took his pocket-knife and opened the envelope.

"I wonder what news there is this time," he said.

And then he unfolded the letter and read as follows:

"DORINCOURT CASTLE" My dear Mr. Hobbs

"I write this in a great hury becaus i have something curous to tell you i know you will be very mutch suprised my dear frend when i tel you. It is all a mistake and i am not a lord and i shall not have to be an earl there is a lady whitch was marid to my uncle bevis who is dead and she has a little boy and he is lord fauntleroy becaus that is the way it is in England the earls eldest sons little boy is the earl if every body else is dead i mean if his farther and grandfarther are dead my grandfarther is not dead but my uncle bevis is and so his boy is lord Fauntleroy and i am not becaus my papa was the youngest son and my name is Cedric Errol like it was when i was in New York and all the things will belong to the other boy i thought at first i should have to give him my pony and cart but my grandfarther says i need not my grandfarther is very sorry and i think he does not like the lady but preaps he thinks dearest and i are sorry because i shall not be an earl i would like to be an earl now better than i thout i would at first becaus this is a beautifle castle and i like every body so and when you are rich you can do so many things i am not rich now becaus when your papa is only the youngest son he is not very rich i am going to learn to work so that i can take care of dearest i have been asking Wilkins about grooming horses preaps i might be a groom or a coachman. The lady brought her little boy to the castle and my grandfarther and Mr. Havisham talked to her i think she was angry she talked

111

loud and my grandfarther was angry too i never saw him angry before i wish it did not make them all mad i thort i would tell you and Dick right away becaus you would be intrusted so no more at present with love from

"your old frend

"CEDRIC ERROL (Not lord Fauntleroy)."

Mr. Hobbs fell back in his chair, the letter dropped on his knee, his pen-knife slipped to the floor, and so did the envelope.

"Well!" he ejaculated, "I am jiggered!"

He was so dumfounded that he actually changed his exclamation. It had always been his habit to say, "I WILL be jiggered," but this time he said, "I AM jiggered." Perhaps he really WAS jiggered. There is no knowing.

"Well," said Dick, "the whole thing's bust up, hasn't it?"

"Bust!" said Mr. Hobbs. "It's my opinion it's a put-up job o' the British ristycrats to rob him of his rights because he's an American. They've had a spite agin us ever since the Revolution, an' they're takin' it out on him. I told you he wasn't safe, an' see what's happened! Like as not, the whole gover'ment's got together to rob him of his lawful ownin's."

He was very much agitated. He had not approved of the change in his young friend's circumstances at first, but lately he had become more reconciled to it, and after the receipt of Cedric's letter he had perhaps even felt some secret pride in his young friend's magnificence. He might not have a good opinion of earls, but he knew that even in America money was considered rather an agreeable thing, and if all the wealth and grandeur were to go with the title, it must be rather hard to lose it.

"They're trying to rob him!" he said, "that's what they're doing, and folks that have money ought to look after him."

And he kept Dick with him until quite a late hour to talk it over, and when that young man left, he went with him to the corner of the street; and on his way back he stopped opposite the empty house for some time, staring at the "To Let," and smoking his pipe, in much disturbance of mind.

XII

A very few days after the dinner party at the Castle, almost everybody in England who read the newspapers at all knew the romantic story of what had happened at Dorincourt. It made a very interesting story when it was told with all the details. There was the little American boy who had been brought to England to be Lord Fauntleroy, and who was said to be so fine and handsome a little fellow, and to have already made people fond of him; there was the old Earl, his grandfather, who was so proud of his heir; there was the pretty young mother who had never been forgiven for marrying Captain Errol; and there was the strange marriage of Bevis, the dead Lord Fauntleroy, and the strange wife, of whom no one knew anything, suddenly appearing with her son, and saying that he was the real Lord Fauntleroy and must have his rights. All these things were talked about and written about, and caused a tremendous sensation. And then there came the rumor that the Earl of Dorincourt was not satisfied with the turn affairs had taken, and would perhaps contest the claim by law, and the matter might end with a wonderful trial.

There never had been such excitement before in the county in which Erleboro was situated. On market-days, people stood in groups and talked and wondered what would be done; the farmers' wives invited one another to tea that they might tell one another all they had heard and all they thought and all they thought other people thought. They related wonderful anecdotes about the Earl's rage and his determination not to acknowledge the new Lord Fauntleroy, and his hatred of the woman who was the claimant's mother. But, of course, it was Mrs. Dibble who could tell the most, and who was more in demand than ever.

"An' a bad lookout it is," she said. "An' if you were to ask me, ma'am, I should say as it was a judgment on him for the way he's treated that sweet young cre'tur' as he parted from her child,—for he's got that fond of him an' that set on him an' that proud of him as he's a'most drove mad by what's happened. An' what's more, this new one's no lady, as his little lordship's ma is. She's a bold-faced, black-eyed thing, as Mr. Thomas says no gentleman in livery 'u'd bemean hisself to be gave orders by; and let her come into the house, he says, an' he goes out of it. An' the boy don't no more compare with the other one than nothin' you could mention. An' mercy knows what's goin' to come of it all, an' where it's to end, an' you might have knocked me down with a feather when Jane brought the news."

In fact there was excitement everywhere at the Castle: in the library, where the Earl and Mr. Havisham sat and talked; in the servants' hall, where Mr. Thomas and the butler and the other men and women servants gossiped and exclaimed at all times of the day; and in the stables, where Wilkins went about his work in a quite depressed state of mind, and groomed the brown pony more beautifully than ever, and said mournfully to the coachman that he "never taught a young gen'leman to ride as took to it more nat'ral, or was a better-plucked one than he was. He was a one as it were some pleasure to ride behind."

But in the midst of all the disturbance there was one person who was quite calm and untroubled. That person was the little Lord Fauntleroy who was said not to be Lord Fauntleroy at all. When first the state of affairs had been explained to him, he had felt some little anxiousness and perplexity, it is true, but its foundation was not in baffled ambition.

While the Earl told him what had happened, he had sat on a stool holding on to his knee, as he so often did when he was listening to anything interesting; and by the time the story was finished he looked quite sober.

"It makes me feel very queer," he said; "it makes me feel— queer!"

The Earl looked at the boy in silence. It made him feel queer, too—queerer than he had ever felt in his whole life. And he felt more queer still when he saw that there was a troubled expression on the small face which was usually so happy.

"Will they take Dearest's house from her—and her carriage?" Cedric asked in a rather unsteady, anxious little voice.

"NO!" said the Earl decidedly—in quite a loud voice, in fact. "They can take nothing from her."

"Ah!" said Cedric, with evident relief. "Can't they?"

Then he looked up at his grandfather, and there was a wistful shade in his eyes, and they looked very big and soft.

"That other boy," he said rather tremulously—"he will have to—to be your boy now—as I was—won't he?"

"NO!" answered the Earl—and he said it so fiercely and loudly that Cedric quite jumped.

"No?" he exclaimed, in wonderment. "Won't he? I thought—"

He stood up from his stool quite suddenly.

"Shall I be your boy, even if I'm not going to be an earl?" he said. "Shall I be your boy, just as I was before?" And his flushed little face was all alight with eagerness.

How the old Earl did look at him from head to foot, to be sure!

114

How his great shaggy brows did draw themselves together, and how queerly his deep eyes shone under them—how very queerly!

"My boy!" he said—and, if you'll believe it, his very voice was queer, almost shaky and a little broken and hoarse, not at all what you would expect an Earl's voice to be, though he spoke more decidedly and peremptorily even than before,—"Yes, you'll be my boy as long as I live; and, by George, sometimes I feel as if you were the only boy I had ever had."

Cedric's face turned red to the roots of his hair; it turned red with relief and pleasure. He put both his hands deep into his pockets and looked squarely into his noble relative's eyes.

"Do you?" he said. "Well, then, I don't care about the earl part at all. I don't care whether I'm an earl or not. I thought—you see, I thought the one that was going to be the Earl would have to be your boy, too, and—and I couldn't be. That was what made me feel so queer."

The Earl put his hand on his shoulder and drew him nearer.

"They shall take nothing from you that I can hold for you," he said, drawing his breath hard. "I won't believe yet that they can take anything from you. You were made for the place, and—well, you may fill it still. But whatever comes, you shall have all that I can give you—all!"

It scarcely seemed as if he were speaking to a child, there was such determination in his face and voice; it was more as if he were making a promise to himself—and perhaps he was.

He had never before known how deep a hold upon him his fondness for the boy and his pride in him had taken. He had never seen his strength and good qualities and beauty as he seemed to see them now. To his obstinate nature it seemed impossible—more than impossible—to give up what he had so set his heart upon. And he had determined that he would not give it up without a fierce struggle.

Within a few days after she had seen Mr. Havisham, the woman who claimed to be Lady Fauntleroy presented herself at the Castle, and brought her child with her. She was sent away. The Earl would not see her, she was told by the footman at the door; his lawyer would attend to her case. It was Thomas who gave the message, and who expressed his opinion of her freely afterward, in the servants' hall. He "hoped," he said, "as he had wore livery in 'igh famblies long enough to know a lady when he see one, an' if that was a lady he was no judge o' females."

"The one at the Lodge," added Thomas loftily, "'Merican or no 'Merican, she's one o' the right sort, as any gentleman 'u'd reckinize with all a heye. I remarked it myself to Henery when fust we called there."

The woman drove away; the look on her handsome, common face half frightened, half fierce. Mr. Havisham had noticed, during his interviews with her, that though she had a passionate temper, and a coarse, insolent manner, she was neither so clever nor so bold as she meant to be; she seemed sometimes to be almost overwhelmed by the position in which she had placed herself. It was as if she had not expected to meet with such opposition.

"She is evidently," the lawyer said to Mrs. Errol, "a person from the lower walks of life. She is uneducated and untrained in everything, and quite unused to meeting people like ourselves on any terms of equality. She does not know what to do. Her visit to the Castle quite cowed her. She was infuriated, but she was cowed. The Earl would not receive her, but I advised him to go with me to the Dorincourt Arms, where she is staying. When she saw him enter the room, she turned white, though she flew into a rage at once, and threatened and demanded in one breath."

The fact was that the Earl had stalked into the room and stood, looking like a venerable aristocratic giant, staring at the woman from under his beetling brows, and not condescending a word. He simply stared at her, taking her in from head to foot as if she were some repulsive curiosity. He let her talk and demand until she was tired, without himself uttering a word, and then he said:

"You say you are my eldest son's wife. If that is true, and if the proof you offer is too much for us, the law is on your side. In that case, your boy is Lord Fauntleroy. The matter will be sifted to the bottom, you may rest assured. If your claims are proved, you will be provided for. I want to see nothing of either you or the child so long as I live. The place will unfortunately have enough of you after my death. You are exactly the kind of person I should have expected my son Bevis to choose."

And then he turned his back upon her and stalked out of the room as he had stalked into it.

Not many days after that, a visitor was announced to Mrs. Errol, who was writing in her little morning room. The maid, who brought the message, looked rather excited; her eyes were quite round with amazement, in fact, and being young and inexperienced, she regarded her mistress with nervous sympathy.

"It's the Earl hisself, ma'am!" she said in tremulous awe.

When Mrs. Errol entered the drawing-room, a very tall, majestic-looking old man was standing on the tiger-skin rug. He had a handsome, grim old face, with an aquiline profile, a long white mustache, and an obstinate look.

"Mrs. Errol, I believe?" he said.

"Mrs. Errol," she answered.

"I am the Earl of Dorincourt," he said.

He paused a moment, almost unconsciously, to look into her uplifted eyes. They were so like the big, affectionate, childish eyes he had seen uplifted to his own so often every day during the last few months, that they gave him a quite curious sensation.

"The boy is very like you," he said abruptly.

"It has been often said so, my lord," she replied, "but I have been glad to think him like his father also."

As Lady Lorridaile had told him, her voice was very sweet, and her manner was very simple and dignified. She did not seem in the least troubled by his sudden coming.

"Yes," said the Earl, "he is like—my son—too." He put his hand up to his big white mustache and pulled it fiercely. "Do you know," he said, "why I have come here?"

"I have seen Mr. Havisham," Mrs. Errol began, "and he has told me of the claims which have been made——"

"I have come to tell you," said the Earl, "that they will be investigated and contested, if a contest can be made. I have come to tell you that the boy shall be defended with all the power of the law. His rights——"

The soft voice interrupted him.

"He must have nothing that is NOT his by right, even if the law can give it to him," she said.

"Unfortunately the law can not," said the Earl. "If it could, it should. This outrageous woman and her child——"

"Perhaps she cares for him as much as I care for Cedric, my lord," said little Mrs. Errol. "And if she was your eldest son's wife, her son is Lord Fauntleroy, and mine is not."

She was no more afraid of him than Cedric had been, and she looked at him just as Cedric would have looked, and he, having been an old tyrant all his life, was privately pleased by it. People so seldom dared to differ from him that there was an entertaining novelty in it.

"I suppose," he said, scowling slightly, "that you would much prefer that he should not be the Earl of Dorincourt."

Her fair young face flushed.

"It is a very magnificent thing to be the Earl of Dorincourt, my lord," she said. "I know that, but I care most that he should be what his father was—brave and just and true always."

"In striking contrast to what his grandfather was, eh?" said his lordship sardonically.

"I have not had the pleasure of knowing his grandfather,"

replied Mrs. Errol, "but I know my little boy believes——" She stopped short a moment, looking quietly into his face, and then she added, "I know that Cedric loves you."

"Would he have loved me," said the Earl dryly, "if you had told him why I did not receive you at the Castle?"

"No," answered Mrs. Errol, "I think not. That was why I did not wish him to know."

"Well," said my lord brusquely, "there are few women who would not have told him."

He suddenly began to walk up and down the room, pulling his great mustache more violently than ever.

"Yes, he is fond of me," he said, "and I am fond of him. I can't say I ever was fond of anything before. I am fond of him. He pleased me from the first. I am an old man, and was tired of my life. He has given me something to live for. I am proud of him. I was satisfied to think of his taking his place some day as the head of the family."

He came back and stood before Mrs. Errol.

"I am miserable," he said. "Miserable!"

He looked as if he was. Even his pride could not keep his voice steady or his hands from shaking. For a moment it almost seemed as if his deep, fierce eyes had tears in them. "Perhaps it is because I am miserable that I have come to you," he said, quite glaring down at her. "I used to hate you; I have been jealous of you. This wretched, disgraceful business has changed that. After seeing that repulsive woman who calls herself the wife of my son Bevis, I actually felt it would be a relief to look at you. I have been an obstinate old fool, and I suppose I have treated you badly. You are like the boy, and the boy is the first object in my life. I am miserable, and I came to you merely because you are like the boy, and he cares for you, and I care for him. Treat me as well as you can, for the boy's sake."

He said it all in his harsh voice, and almost roughly, but somehow he seemed so broken down for the time that Mrs. Errol was touched to the heart. She got up and moved an arm-chair a little forward.

"I wish you would sit down," she said in a soft, pretty, sympathetic way. "You have been so much troubled that you are very tired, and you need all your strength."

It was just as new to him to be spoken to and cared for in that gentle, simple way as it was to be contradicted. He was reminded of "the boy" again, and he actually did as she asked him. Perhaps his disappointment and wretchedness were good discipline for him; if he had not been wretched he might have continued to hate her, but just at present he found her a little soothing. Almost anything would have seemed pleasant by contrast with Lady Fauntleroy; and this one had so sweet a face and voice, and a pretty dignity when she spoke or moved. Very soon, through the quiet magic of these influences, he began to feel less gloomy, and then he talked still more.

"Whatever happens," he said, "the boy shall be provided for. He shall be taken care of, now and in the future."

Before he went away, he glanced around the room.

"Do you like the house?" he demanded.

"Very much," she answered.

"This is a cheerful room," he said. "May I come here again and talk this matter over?"

"As often as you wish, my lord," she replied.

And then he went out to his carriage and drove away, Thomas and Henry almost stricken dumb upon the box at the turn affairs had taken.

XIII

OF course, as soon as the story of Lord Fauntleroy and the difficulties of the Earl of Dorincourt were discussed in the English newspapers, they were discussed in the American newspapers. The story was too interesting to be passed over lightly, and it was talked of a great deal. There were so many versions of it that it would have been an edifying thing to buy all the papers and compare them. Mr. Hobbs read so much about it that he became quite bewildered. One paper described his young friend Cedric as an infant in arms,— another as a young man at Oxford, winning all the honors, and distinguishing himself by writing Greek poems; one said he was engaged to a young lady of great beauty, who was the daughter of a duke; another said he had just been married; the only thing, in fact, which was NOT said was that he was a little boy between seven and eight, with handsome legs and curly hair. One said he was no relation to the Earl of Dorincourt at all, but was a small impostor who had sold newspapers and slept in the streets of New York before his mother imposed upon the family lawyer, who came to America to look for the Earl's heir. Then came the descriptions of the new Lord Fauntleroy and his mother. Sometimes she was a gypsy, sometimes an actress, sometimes a beautiful Spaniard; but it was always agreed that the Earl of Dorincourt was her deadly enemy, and would not acknowledge her son as his heir if he could help it, and as there seemed to be some slight flaw in the papers she had produced, it was expected that there would be a long trial, which would be far more interesting than anything ever carried into court before. Mr. Hobbs used to read the papers until his head was in a whirl, and in the evening he and Dick would talk it all over. They found out what an important personage an Earl of Dorincourt was, and what a magnificent income he possessed, and how many estates he owned, and how stately and beautiful was the Castle in which he lived; and the more they learned, the more excited they became.

"Seems like somethin' orter be done," said Mr. Hobbs. "Things like them orter be held on to—earls or no earls."

But there really was nothing they could do but each write a letter to Cedric, containing assurances of their friendship and sympathy. They wrote those letters as soon as they could after receiving the news; and after having written them, they handed them over to each other to be read.

This is what Mr. Hobbs read in Dick's letter:

"DERE FREND: i got ure letter an Mr. Hobbs got his an we are sory u are down on ure luck an we say hold on as longs u kin an dont let no one git ahed of u. There is a lot of ole theves wil make al they kin of u ef u dont kepe ure i skined. But this is mosly to say that ive not forgot wot u did fur me an if there aint no better way cum over here an go in pardners with me. Biznes is fine an ile see no harm cums to u Enny big feler that trise to cum it over u wil hafter setle it fust with Perfessor Dick Tipton. So no more at present

"DICK."

And this was what Dick read in Mr. Hobbs's letter:

"DEAR SIR: Yrs received and wd say things looks bad. I believe its a put up job and them thats done it ought to be looked after sharp. And what I write to say is two things. Im going to look this thing up. Keep quiet and Ill see a lawyer and do all I can And if the worst happens and them earls is too many for us theres a partnership in the grocery business ready for you when yure old enough and a home and a friend in
"Yrs truly,

"SILAS HOBBS."

"Well," said Mr. Hobbs, "he's pervided for between us, if he aint a earl."

"So he is," said Dick. "I'd ha' stood by him. Blest if I didn't like that little feller fust-rate."

The very next morning, one of Dick's customers was rather surprised. He was a young lawyer just beginning practice—as poor as a very young lawyer can possibly be, but a bright, energetic young fellow, with sharp wit and a good temper. He had a shabby office near Dick's stand, and every morning Dick blacked his boots for him, and quite often they were not exactly water-tight, but he always had a friendly word or a joke for Dick.

That particular morning, when he put his foot on the rest, he had an illustrated paper in his hand—an enterprising paper, with pictures in it of conspicuous people and things. He had just finished looking it over, and when the last boot was polished, he handed it over to the boy.

"Here's a paper for you, Dick," he said; "you can look it over when you drop in at Delmonico's for your breakfast. Picture of an English castle in it, and an English earl's daughter-in-law. Fine young woman, too,—lots of hair,—though she seems to be raising

121

rather a row. You ought to become familiar with the nobility and gentry, Dick. Begin on the Right Honorable the Earl of Dorincourt and Lady Fauntleroy. Hello! I say, what's the matter?"

The pictures he spoke of were on the front page, and Dick was staring at one of them with his eyes and mouth open, and his sharp face almost pale with excitement.

"What's to pay, Dick?" said the young man. "What has paralyzed you?"

Dick really did look as if something tremendous had happened. He pointed to the picture, under which was written:

"Mother of Claimant (Lady Fauntleroy)."

It was the picture of a handsome woman, with large eyes and heavy braids of black hair wound around her head.

"Her!" said Dick. "My, I know her better 'n I know you!"

The young man began to laugh.

"Where did you meet her, Dick?" he said. "At Newport? Or when you ran over to Paris the last time?"

Dick actually forgot to grin. He began to gather his brushes and things together, as if he had something to do which would put an end to his business for the present.

"Never mind," he said. "I know her! An I've struck work for this mornin'."

And in less than five minutes from that time he was tearing through the streets on his way to Mr. Hobbs and the corner store.

Mr. Hobbs could scarcely believe the evidence of his senses when he looked across the counter and saw Dick rush in with the paper in his hand. The boy was out of breath with running; so much out of breath, in fact, that he could scarcely speak as he threw the paper down on the counter.

"Hello!" exclaimed Mr. Hobbs. "Hello! What you got there?"

"Look at it!" panted Dick. "Look at that woman in the picture! That's what you look at! SHE aint no 'ristocrat, SHE aint!" with withering scorn. "She's no lord's wife. You may eat me, if it aint Minna—MINNA! I'd know her anywheres, an' so 'd Ben. Jest ax him."

Mr. Hobbs dropped into his seat.

"I knowed it was a put-up job," he said. "I knowed it; and they done it on account o' him bein' a 'Merican!"

"Done it!" cried Dick, with disgust. "SHE done it, that's who done it. She was allers up to her tricks; an' I'll tell yer wot come to me, the minnit I saw her pictur. There was one o' them papers we saw had a letter in it that said somethin' 'bout her boy, an' it said he had a scar on his chin. Put them two together—her 'n' that there scar! Why, that there boy o' hers aint no more a lord than I am! It's BEN'S boy,—the little chap she hit when she let fly that plate at me."

Professor Dick Tipton had always been a sharp boy, and earning his living in the streets of a big city had made him still sharper. He had learned to keep his eyes open and his wits about him, and it must be confessed he enjoyed immensely the excitement and impatience of that moment. If little Lord Fauntleroy could only have looked into the store that morning, he would certainly have been interested, even if all the discussion and plans had been intended to decide the fate of some other boy than himself.

Mr. Hobbs was almost overwhelmed by his sense of responsibility, and Dick was all alive and full of energy. He began to write a letter to Ben, and he cut out the picture and inclosed it to him, and Mr. Hobbs wrote a letter to Cedric and one to the Earl. They were in the midst of this letter-writing when a new idea came to Dick.

"Say," he said, "the feller that give me the paper, he's a lawyer. Let's ax him what we'd better do. Lawyers knows it all."

Mr. Hobbs was immensely impressed by this suggestion and Dick's business capacity.

"That's so!" he replied. "This here calls for lawyers."

And leaving the store in the care of a substitute, he struggled into his coat and marched down-town with Dick, and the two presented themselves with their romantic story in Mr. Harrison's office, much to that young man's astonishment.

If he had not been a very young lawyer, with a very enterprising mind and a great deal of spare time on his hands, he might not have been so readily interested in what they had to say, for it all certainly sounded very wild and queer; but he chanced to want something to do very much, and he chanced to know Dick, and Dick chanced to say his say in a very sharp, telling sort of way.

"And," said Mr. Hobbs, "say what your time's worth a' hour and look into this thing thorough, and I'LL pay the damage,—Silas Hobbs, corner of Blank street, Vegetables and Fancy Groceries."

"Well," said Mr. Harrison, "it will be a big thing if it turns out all right, and it will be almost as big a thing for me as for Lord Fauntleroy; and, at any rate, no harm can be done by investigating. It appears there has been some dubiousness about the child. The woman contradicted herself in some of her statements about his age, and aroused suspicion. The first persons to be written to are Dick's brother and the Earl of Dorincourt's family lawyer."

And actually, before the sun went down, two letters had been written and sent in two different directions—one speeding out of New York harbor on a mail steamer on its way to England, and the

123

other on a train carrying letters and passengers bound for California. And the first was addressed to T. Havisham, Esq., and the second to Benjamin Tipton.

And after the store was closed that evening, Mr. Hobbs and Dick sat in the back-room and talked together until midnight.

XIV

It is astonishing how short a time it takes for very wonderful things to happen. It had taken only a few minutes, apparently, to change all the fortunes of the little boy dangling his red legs from the high stool in Mr. Hobbs's store, and to transform him from a small boy, living the simplest life in a quiet street, into an English nobleman, the heir to an earldom and magnificent wealth. It had taken only a few minutes, apparently, to change him from an English nobleman into a penniless little impostor, with no right to any of the splendors he had been enjoying. And, surprising as it may appear, it did not take nearly so long a time as one might have expected, to alter the face of everything again and to give back to him all that he had been in danger of losing.

It took the less time because, after all, the woman who had called herself Lady Fauntleroy was not nearly so clever as she was wicked; and when she had been closely pressed by Mr. Havisham's questions about her marriage and her boy, she had made one or two blunders which had caused suspicion to be awakened; and then she had lost her presence of mind and her temper, and in her excitement and anger had betrayed herself still further. All the mistakes she made were about her child. There seemed no doubt that she had been married to Bevis, Lord Fauntleroy, and had quarreled with him and had been paid to keep away from him; but Mr. Havisham found out that her story of the boy's being born in a certain part of London was false; and just when they all were in the midst of the commotion caused by this discovery, there came the letter from the young lawyer in New York, and Mr. Hobbs's letters also.

What an evening it was when those letters arrived, and when Mr. Havisham and the Earl sat and talked their plans over in the library!

"After my first three meetings with her," said Mr. Havisham, "I began to suspect her strongly. It appeared to me that the child was older than she said he was, and she made a slip in speaking of the date of his birth and then tried to patch the matter up. The story these letters bring fits in with several of my suspicions. Our best plan will be to cable at once for these two Tiptons,—say nothing about them to her,—and suddenly confront her with them when she is not expecting it. She is only a very clumsy plotter, after all. My opinion is that she will be frightened out of her wits, and will betray herself on the spot."

125

And that was what actually happened. She was told nothing, and Mr. Havisham kept her from suspecting anything by continuing to have interviews with her, in which he assured her he was investigating her statements; and she really began to feel so secure that her spirits rose immensely and she began to be as insolent as might have been expected.

But one fine morning, as she sat in her sitting-room at the inn called "The Dorincourt Arms," making some very fine plans for herself, Mr. Havisham was announced; and when he entered, he was followed by no less than three persons—one was a sharp-faced boy and one was a big young man and the third was the Earl of Dorincourt.

She sprang to her feet and actually uttered a cry of terror. It broke from her before she had time to check it. She had thought of these new-comers as being thousands of miles away, when she had ever thought of them at all, which she had scarcely done for years. She had never expected to see them again. It must be confessed that Dick grinned a little when he saw her.

"Hello, Minna!" he said.

The big young man—who was Ben—stood still a minute and looked at her.

"Do you know her?" Mr. Havisham asked, glancing from one to the other.

"Yes," said Ben. "I know her and she knows me." And he turned his back on her and went and stood looking out of the window, as if the sight of her was hateful to him, as indeed it was. Then the woman, seeing herself so baffled and exposed, lost all control over herself and flew into such a rage as Ben and Dick had often seen her in before. Dick grinned a trifle more as he watched her and heard the names she called them all and the violent threats she made, but Ben did not turn to look at her.

"I can swear to her in any court," he said to Mr. Havisham, "and I can bring a dozen others who will. Her father is a respectable sort of man, though he's low down in the world. Her mother was just like herself. She's dead, but he's alive, and he's honest enough to be ashamed of her. He'll tell you who she is, and whether she married me or not."

Then he clenched his hand suddenly and turned on her.

"Where's the child?" he demanded. "He's going with me! He is done with you, and so am I!"

And just as he finished saying the words, the door leading into the bedroom opened a little, and the boy, probably attracted by the sound of the loud voices, looked in. He was not a handsome boy, but he had rather a nice face, and he was quite like Ben, his father, as any one could see, and there was the three-cornered scar on his chin.

Ben walked up to him and took his hand, and his own was trembling.

"Yes," he said, "I could swear to him, too. Tom," he said to the little fellow, "I'm your father; I've come to take you away. Where's your hat?"

The boy pointed to where it lay on a chair. It evidently rather pleased him to hear that he was going away. He had been so accustomed to queer experiences that it did not surprise him to be told by a stranger that he was his father. He objected so much to the woman who had come a few months before to the place where he had lived since his babyhood, and who had suddenly announced that she was his mother, that he was quite ready for a change. Ben took up the hat and marched to the door.

"If you want me again," he said to Mr. Havisham, "you know where to find me."

He walked out of the room, holding the child's hand and not looking at the woman once. She was fairly raving with fury, and the Earl was calmly gazing at her through his eyeglasses, which he had quietly placed upon his aristocratic, eagle nose.

"Come, come, my young woman," said Mr. Havisham. "This won't do at all. If you don't want to be locked up, you really must behave yourself."

And there was something so very business-like in his tones that, probably feeling that the safest thing she could do would be to get out of the way, she gave him one savage look and dashed past him into the next room and slammed the door.

"We shall have no more trouble with her," said Mr. Havisham.

And he was right; for that very night she left the Dorincourt Arms and took the train to London, and was seen no more.

When the Earl left the room after the interview, he went at once to his carriage.

"To Court Lodge," he said to Thomas.

"To Court Lodge," said Thomas to the coachman as he mounted the box; "an' you may depend on it, things are taking a uniggspected turn."

When the carriage stopped at Court Lodge, Cedric was in the drawing-room with his mother.

The Earl came in without being announced. He looked an inch or so taller, and a great many years younger. His deep eyes flashed.

"Where," he said, "is Lord Fauntleroy?"

Mrs. Errol came forward, a flush rising to her cheek.

"Is it Lord Fauntleroy?" she asked. "Is it, indeed!"

127

The Earl put out his hand and grasped hers.

"Yes," he answered, "it is."

Then he put his other hand on Cedric's shoulder.

"Fauntleroy," he said in his unceremonious, authoritative way, "ask your mother when she will come to us at the Castle."

Fauntleroy flung his arms around his mother's neck.

"To live with us!" he cried. "To live with us always!"

The Earl looked at Mrs. Errol, and Mrs. Errol looked at the Earl.

His lordship was entirely in earnest. He had made up his mind to waste no time in arranging this matter. He had begun to think it would suit him to make friends with his heir's mother.

"Are you quite sure you want me?" said Mrs. Errol, with her soft, pretty smile.

"Quite sure," he said bluntly. "We have always wanted you, but we were not exactly aware of it. We hope you will come."

XV

Ben took his boy and went back to his cattle ranch in California, and he returned under very comfortable circumstances. Just before his going, Mr. Havisham had an interview with him in which the lawyer told him that the Earl of Dorincourt wished to do something for the boy who might have turned out to be Lord Fauntleroy, and so he had decided that it would be a good plan to invest in a cattle ranch of his own, and put Ben in charge of it on terms which would make it pay him very well, and which would lay a foundation for his son's future. And so when Ben went away, he went as the prospective master of a ranch which would be almost as good as his own, and might easily become his own in time, as indeed it did in the course of a few years; and Tom, the boy, grew up on it into a fine young man and was devotedly fond of his father; and they were so successful and happy that Ben used to say that Tom made up to him for all the troubles he had ever had.

But Dick and Mr. Hobbs—who had actually come over with the others to see that things were properly looked after—did not return for some time. It had been decided at the outset that the Earl would provide for Dick, and would see that he received a solid education; and Mr. Hobbs had decided that as he himself had left a reliable substitute in charge of his store, he could afford to wait to see the festivities which were to celebrate Lord Fauntleroy's eighth birthday. All the tenantry were invited, and there were to be feasting and dancing and games in the park, and bonfires and fire-works in the evening.

"Just like the Fourth of July!" said Lord Fauntleroy. "It seems a pity my birthday wasn't on the Fourth, doesn't it? For then we could keep them both together."

It must be confessed that at first the Earl and Mr. Hobbs were not as intimate as it might have been hoped they would become, in the interests of the British aristocracy. The fact was that the Earl had known very few grocery-men, and Mr. Hobbs had not had many very close acquaintances who were earls; and so in their rare interviews conversation did not flourish. It must also be owned that Mr. Hobbs had been rather overwhelmed by the splendors Fauntleroy felt it his duty to show him.

The entrance gate and the stone lions and the avenue impressed Mr. Hobbs somewhat at the beginning, and when he saw the Castle, and the flower-gardens, and the hot-houses, and the terraces, and the peacocks, and the dungeon, and the armor, and the great staircase, and the stables, and the liveried servants, he really was quite bewildered. But it was the picture gallery which seemed to be the finishing stroke.

"Somethin' in the manner of a museum?" he said to Fauntleroy, when he was led into the great, beautiful room.

"N—no—!" said Fauntleroy, rather doubtfully. "I don't THINK it's a museum. My grandfather says these are my ancestors."

"Your aunt's sisters!" ejaculated Mr. Hobbs. "ALL of 'em? Your great-uncle, he MUST have had a family! Did he raise 'em all?"

And he sank into a seat and looked around him with quite an agitated countenance, until with the greatest difficulty Lord Fauntleroy managed to explain that the walls were not lined entirely with the portraits of the progeny of his great-uncle.

He found it necessary, in fact, to call in the assistance of Mrs. Mellon, who knew all about the pictures, and could tell who painted them and when, and who added romantic stories of the lords and ladies who were the originals. When Mr. Hobbs once understood, and had heard some of these stories, he was very much fascinated and liked the picture gallery almost better than anything else; and he would often walk over from the village, where he staid at the Dorincourt Arms, and would spend half an hour or so wandering about the gallery, staring at the painted ladies and gentlemen, who also stared at him, and shaking his head nearly all the time.

"And they was all earls!" he would say, "er pretty nigh it! An' HE'S goin' to be one of 'em, an' own it all!"

Privately he was not nearly so much disgusted with earls and their mode of life as he had expected to be, and it is to be doubted whether his strictly republican principles were not shaken a little by a closer acquaintance with castles and ancestors and all the rest of it. At any rate, one day he uttered a very remarkable and unexpected sentiment:

"I wouldn't have minded bein' one of 'em myself!" he said— which was really a great concession.

What a grand day it was when little Lord Fauntleroy's birthday arrived, and how his young lordship enjoyed it! How beautiful the park looked, filled with the thronging people dressed in their gayest and best, and with the flags flying from the tents and the top of the Castle! Nobody had staid away who could possibly come, because everybody was really glad that little Lord Fauntleroy was to be little Lord Fauntleroy still, and some day was to be the master of everything. Every one wanted to have a look at him, and at his pretty, kind mother, who had made so many friends. And positively every one liked the Earl rather better, and felt more amiably toward him because the little boy loved and trusted him so, and because, also, he had now made friends with and behaved respectfully to his heir's mother. It was said that he was even beginning to be fond of her, too, and that between his young lordship and his young lordship's mother, the Earl might be changed in time into quite a well-behaved old nobleman, and everybody might be happier and better off.

What scores and scores of people there were under the trees, and in the tents, and on the lawns! Farmers and farmers' wives in their Sunday suits and bonnets and shawls; girls and their sweethearts; children frolicking and chasing about; and old dames in red cloaks gossiping together. At the Castle, there were ladies and gentlemen who had come to see the fun, and to congratulate the Earl, and to meet Mrs. Errol. Lady Lorredaile and Sir Harry were there, and Sir Thomas Asshe and his daughters, and Mr. Havisham, of course, and then beautiful Miss Vivian Herbert, with the loveliest white gown and lace parasol, and a circle of gentlemen to take care of her—though she evidently liked Fauntleroy better than all of them put together. And when he saw her and ran to her and put his arm around her neck, she put her arms around him, too, and kissed him as warmly as if he had been her own favorite little brother, and she said:

"Dear little Lord Fauntleroy! dear little boy! I am so glad! I am so glad!"

And afterward she walked about the grounds with him, and let him show her everything. And when he took her to where Mr. Hobbs and Dick were, and said to her, "This is my old, old friend Mr. Hobbs, Miss Herbert, and this is my other old friend Dick. I told them how pretty you were, and I told them they should see you if you came to my birthday,"—she shook hands with them both, and stood and talked to them in her prettiest way, asking them about America and their voyage and their life since they had been in England; while Fauntleroy stood by, looking up at her with adoring eyes, and his cheeks quite flushed with delight because he saw that Mr. Hobbs and Dick liked her so much.

"Well," said Dick solemnly, afterward, "she's the daisiest gal I ever saw! She's—well, she's just a daisy, that's what she is, 'n' no mistake!"

Everybody looked after her as she passed, and every one looked after little Lord Fauntleroy. And the sun shone and the flags fluttered and the games were played and the dances danced, and as the gayeties went on and the joyous afternoon passed, his little lordship was simply radiantly happy.

The whole world seemed beautiful to him.

There was some one else who was happy, too,—an old man, who, though he had been rich and noble all his life, had not often been very honestly happy. Perhaps, indeed, I shall tell you that I think it was because he was rather better than he had been that he was rather happier. He had not, indeed, suddenly become as good as Fauntleroy thought him; but, at least, he had begun to love something, and he had several times found a sort of pleasure in doing the kind things which the innocent, kind little heart of a child had suggested,—and that was a beginning. And every day he had been more pleased with his son's wife. It was true, as the people said, that he was beginning to like her too. He liked to hear her sweet voice and to see her sweet face; and as he sat in his arm-chair, he used to watch her and listen as she talked to her boy; and he heard loving, gentle words which were new to him, and he began to see why the little fellow who had lived in a New York side street and known grocery-men and made friends with boot-blacks, was still so well-bred and manly a little fellow that he made no one ashamed of him, even when fortune changed him into the heir to an English earldom, living in an English castle.

It was really a very simple thing, after all,—it was only that he had lived near a kind and gentle heart, and had been taught to think kind thoughts always and to care for others. It is a very little thing, perhaps, but it is the best thing of all. He knew nothing of earls and castles; he was quite ignorant of all grand and splendid things; but he was always lovable because he was simple and loving. To be so is like being born a king.

As the old Earl of Dorincourt looked at him that day, moving about the park among the people, talking to those he knew and making his ready little bow when any one greeted him, entertaining his friends Dick and Mr. Hobbs, or standing near his mother or Miss Herbert listening to their conversation, the old nobleman was very well satisfied with him. And he had never been better satisfied than he was when they went down to the biggest tent, where the more important tenants of the Dorincourt estate were sitting down to the grand collation of the day.

They were drinking toasts; and, after they had drunk the health of the Earl, with much more enthusiasm than his name had ever been greeted with before, they proposed the health of "Little Lord Fauntleroy." And if there had ever been any doubt at all as to whether his lordship was popular or not, it would have been settled that instant. Such a clamor of voices, and such a rattle of glasses and applause! They had begun to like him so much, those warm-hearted people, that they forgot to feel any restraint before the ladies and gentlemen from the castle, who had come to see them. They made quite a decent uproar, and one or two motherly women looked tenderly at the little fellow where he stood, with his mother on one side and the Earl on the other, and grew quite moist about the eyes, and said to one another:

"God bless him, the pretty little dear!"

Little Lord Fauntleroy was delighted. He stood and smiled, and made bows, and flushed rosy red with pleasure up to the roots of his bright hair.

"Is it because they like me, Dearest?" he said to his mother. "Is it, Dearest? I'm so glad!"

And then the Earl put his hand on the child's shoulder and said to him:

"Fauntleroy, say to them that you thank them for their kindness."

Fauntleroy gave a glance up at him and then at his mother.

"Must I?" he asked just a trifle shyly, and she smiled, and so did Miss Herbert, and they both nodded. And so he made a little step forward, and everybody looked at him—such a beautiful, innocent little fellow he was, too, with his brave, trustful face!—and he spoke as loudly as he could, his childish voice ringing out quite clear and strong.

"I'm ever so much obliged to you!" he said, "and—I hope you'll enjoy my birthday—because I've enjoyed it so much—and—I'm very glad I'm going to be an earl; I didn't think at first I should like it, but now I do—and I love this place so, and I think it is beautiful—and—and—and when I am an earl, I am going to try to be as good as my grandfather."

And amid the shouts and clamor of applause, he stepped back with a little sigh of relief, and put his hand into the Earl's and stood close to him, smiling and leaning against his side.

And that would be the very end of my story; but I must add one curious piece of information, which is that Mr. Hobbs became so fascinated with high life and was so reluctant to leave his young friend that he actually sold his corner store in New York, and settled in the English village of Erlesboro, where he opened a shop which was patronized by the Castle and consequently was a great success. And though he and the Earl never became very intimate, if you will believe me, that man Hobbs became in time more aristocratic than his lordship himself, and he read the Court news every morning, and followed all the doings of the House of Lords! And about ten years after, when Dick, who had finished his education and was going to visit his brother in California, asked the good grocer if he did not wish to return to America, he shook his head seriously.

"Not to live there," he said. "Not to live there; I want to be near HIM, an' sort o' look after him. It's a good enough country for them that's young an' stirrin'—but there's faults in it. There's not an auntsister among 'em—nor an earl!"

Criminal Procedure

Scottish Criminal Law and Practice Series

Series Editor

The Rt Hon The Lord McCluskey

Criminal Procedure

Albert V Sheehan MA, LLB
Sheriff of Tayside, Central and Fife at Falkirk

David Robert Hingston LLB, NP
Procurator Fiscal at Dingwall

Frank R Crowe LLB
Assistant Solicitor at the Crown Office

with a chapter on Fatal Accident Inquiries

David R Smith MA, LLB
Regional Procurator Fiscal for Tayside, Central and Fife

Robert Ferguson Lees LLB
Regional Procurator Fiscal for North Strathclyde

Butterworths
Law Society of Scotland

Edinburgh   1990

Law Society of Scotland
26 Drumsheugh Gardens, Edinburgh EH3 7YR

Butterworths

United Kingdom	Butterworth & Co (Publishers) Ltd, 88 Kingsway, LONDON WC2B 6AB and 4 Hill Street, EDINBURGH EH2 3JZ
Australia	Butterworths Pty Ltd, SYDNEY, MELBOURNE, BRISBANE, ADELAIDE, PERTH, CANBERRA and HOBART
Canada	Butterworth & Co (Canada) Ltd, TORONTO and VANCOUVER
Ireland	Butterworth (Ireland) Ltd, DUBLIN
Malaysia	Malayan Law Journal Sdn Bhd, KUALA LUMPUR
New Zealand	Butterworths of New Zealand Ltd, WELLINGTON and AUCKLAND
Puerto Rico	Equity de Puerto Rico, Inc, HATO REY
Singapore	Butterworth & Co (Asia) Pte Ltd, SINGAPORE
USA	Butterworth Legal Publishers, ST PAUL, Minnesota, SEATTLE, Washington, BOSTON, Massachusetts, AUSTIN, Texas and D & S Publishers, CLEARWATER, Florida

A CIP Catalogue record for this book is available from the British Library.

ISBN 0 406 121265

Printed in Great Britain by Thomson Litho Ltd, East Kilbride, Scotland

PREFACE

When the late Sir Thomas Smith, QC, invited me to write an article on criminal procedure for *The Laws of Scotland: Stair Memorial Encyclopaedia,* he asked me to make it compact yet sufficiently comprehensive and detailed for a practitioner who was perhaps unfamiliar with certain aspects of the criminal courts to find a general answer to a query, or at least a starting point for further researches.

In order to attempt this somewhat daunting task, I was fortunate to enlist the services of two collaborators, namely David Hingston, the Procurator Fiscal at Dingwall, and Frank Crowe, Assistant Solicitor at the Crown Office. As senior members of the procurator fiscal service, these two co-authors were able to bring to bear their extensive knowledge of criminal procedure and wide practical experience of the criminal courts.

In the first instance we divided the work between us. David Hingston wrote the sections dealing with general principles, pre-trial procedures, children and mental disorder, Frank Crowe wrote the part dealing with appeals, and I was responsible for the historical introduction, the parts dealing with trial and sentence and overall co-ordination of the article. Thereafter we each took the opportunity to comment on and suggest amendments to the work of the others so that in many respects the end result is one of common authorship. We would also like to acknowledge our indebtedness to Robert Black, QC, LLB, LLM, Professor of Scots law in the University of Edinburgh, who kindly undertook to edit our article before it was published in the *Stair Memorial Encyclopaedia,* although we as authors accept full responsibility for any errors or omissions.

After the article was published, it was suggested that it could also form the basis for the present book since its size would allow it to slip into the briefcase of the practitioner or law student who might consider using it as an outline to criminal procedure or as an initial point of reference. In this respect, we do not intend that it should act as a substitute for the *Encyclopaedia* or as a replacement for any other more extensive standard textbook, although it does contain matters which have not been published elsewhere. While the book is thus based on our article — and we would like to thank the Law Society of Scotland for readily agreeing to waive their rights of copyright in the *Encyclopaedia* — we have also taken the opportunity to make some amendments to the text and in particular to update it to state the law as at 1 May 1990.

The *Encyclopaedia* also contained an article on Fatal Accident Inquiries which was written by David Smith and Robert Lees. While fatal accident inquiries do not form part of criminal procedure, they may sometimes have an indirect relationship to criminal cases. More importantly, they form an integral part of the duties of the procurator fiscal about which the authors are particularly well qualified to write. It was therefore decided to include this chapter in the present book for the sake of completeness.

In conclusion, we would all like to thank the many people responsible for the typing and checking of manuscripts and the staff of Butterworth & Co (Publishers) Ltd, especially in Edinburgh, for their unfailing kindness, courtesy and co-operation.

Albert V Sheehan
September 1990

CONTENTS

3 Initial Steps 58

(a) Introduction 58
   (A) Detention 58
   (B) Arrest 60
   (c) Search, Fingerprinting and Identification Parades 63
   (D) The Person in Custody 66
(b) Preliminary Inquiries by the Procurator Fiscal 68
(c) Prosecutor's Duties at the end of the Preliminary Inquiries 71
(d) Plea Bargaining 74
(e) Bringing an Accused Before the Court 76
(f) Bail
(g) Solemn and Summary Procedure 83

4 Solemn Procedure

(a) Procedure at Appearances in Private 87
(b) Judicial Examination 90
(c) Early Plea of Guilty 93
(d) Preparation of the Defence 95
(e) Time Limits for Custody and Prosecution 98
(f) The Indictment 100
(g) Requirements on the Defence 103
(h) Special Defences 106
(i) Preliminary Diets and Issues 107
   (A) Preliminary Diets 107
   (B) Pleas to Competency and Relevancy 109
   (c) Pleas in Bar of Trial 110
   (D) Separating and Conjoining Charges and Trials 113

5 Summary Procedure 115

(a) Time Limits for Custody and Prosecution 115
(b) Preparation of the Defence 117
(c) The Complaint 120
(d) Requirements on the Defence 125
(e) Pre-trial Diets 126
   (A) Procedure at Pre-Trial Diet 126
   (B) Failure to Answer; Trial in Absence of Accused 127
   (c) Remit to Another Court 129
   (D) Continuation Without Plea 129
   (E) Postponement of Acceleration of Diet 130
   (F) Preliminary Pleas 130
   (G) Plea of Not Guilty
   (H) Plea of Guilty 132
   (I) Intermediate Diet 133

6 Trial 134

(a) The Trial Diet in Solemn Procedure 134
   (A) Calling the Diet; Presence of the Parties 134
   (B) Adjournment and Desertion 135
   (c) Misnomer and Misdescription 137
   (D) Pleading 138
   (E) Amendment of the Indictment 139

Table of Statutes

Table of Cases

A

References are to paragraphs

References are to paragraphs

References are to paragraphs

C

References are to paragraphs

D

References are to paragraphs

E

F

References are to paragraphs

References are to paragraphs

H

References are to paragraphs

References are to paragraphs

References are to paragraphs

M

References are to paragraphs

References are to paragraphs

References are to paragraphs

References are to paragraphs

References are to paragraphs

R

References are to paragraphs

References are to paragraphs

References are to paragraphs

References are to paragraphs

References are to paragraphs

1. HISTORICAL BACKGROUND

(a) Preliminary

1.01. Definition. In Scotland the terms 'crime' and 'criminal offence' can be defined as an act or omission punishable under common law or under statute law[1]. The means whereby criminal law is enforced is known as criminal procedure, which sets forth the rules relating to the investigation and prosecution of crimes and offences.

1 See G H Gordon *The Criminal Law of Scotland* (2nd edn, 1978) para 1.02.

1.02. Early history. Little is known about the maintenance of law and order in Scotland prior to the end of the eleventh century. The king and higher ranks of society such as earls and thanes enjoyed a 'peace' with the right to punish those who broke it. The modern crime of breach of the peace and the office of justice of the peace derive their terminology from this ancient use of the term 'peace'. There are no historical or legal records showing precisely how this early 'peace' was enforced, and it is likely that the application of the law varied widely from district to district. Geographic barriers and the absence of roads or other forms of access meant that large parts of Scotland, and in particular the Highlands and the Borders, were isolated and beyond the control of central government, with the consequence that in many instances 'men knew no measure of the law other than the length of their swords'[1].

The first effective attempt to impose a system of central control began towards the end of the eleventh century and continued throughout the twelfth and thirteenth centuries when the Scottish kings (and in particular David I, who reigned from 1124 to 1153) introduced the Norman feudal system and institutions of government. These reforms succeeded in establishing some limited uniformity of law enforcement, but unfortunately this development came to a halt in the early fourteenth century and did not resume until the seventeenth century. The main reasons for the decline lay in the troubled history of Scotland and the weakness of the monarchy during these intervening centuries. Frequent wars, internal and religious strife and the accession of children to the throne all contributed to deprive the country of a continuous strong central government. Disorder was rampant and crimes went unpunished; courts and legal officers became corrupt and inefficient; the administration of justice became localised to the detriment of the evolution of a national system; indeed, in the words of one writer, 'justice, outlawed, was in exile beyond the bounds of the kingdom'[2].

1 Camden, quoted in W C Dickinson *Scotland from the Earliest Times to 1963* (3rd edn, 1977 by A A M Duncan) p 8. See also D M Walker *A Legal History of Scotland* (1988) vol 1, ch 2.
2 *Chronicle of Moray* (1398), quoted in *Dickinson* p 201. See also p 200. See generally J Irvine Smith 'Criminal Procedure' in *An Introduction to Scottish Legal History* (Stair Soc vol 20, 1958), pp 426 ff, G H C Paton 'The Dark Ages' (Stair Soc vol 20) pp 18 ff, and D M Walker *The Scottish Legal System* (5th edn, 1981) ch 4.

1.03. The seventeenth century onwards. When times became relatively less troubled towards the end of the seventeenth century, the development of the law began to advance once more, but the real impetus for change occurred in the following century when the Scottish and English Parliaments were united in 1707 and the Scottish criminal courts were reorganised in 1748[1]. Although the Treaty of Union sought to ensure that Scots law retained its separate identity, the laws passed by the new Parliament of Great Britain were inevitably coloured by English law, and Scottish jurists became increasingly imbued with English legal principles and traditions[2]. Despite these external influences, Scottish criminal procedure continued to develop independently throughout the nineteenth and twentieth centuries, and today it remains distinct and different from that in England.

1 See the Heritable Jurisdictions (Scotland) Act 1746 (c 43).
2 See eg *Earl of Eglinton v Campbell* (1769) Maclaurin 505, where Lord Kames stated that if there was any doubt in the law of Scotland 'that of England would have weight'. See also J Irvine Smith 'Criminal Law' in *An Introduction to Scottish Legal History* (Stair Soc vol 20, 1958) p 281.

(b) The Development of the Scottish Criminal Courts

(A) INTRODUCTION

1.04. General. In modern Scotland the criminal courts of first instance are the High Court of Justiciary, the sheriff court and the district court[1]. In former times, in addition to the justiciary and sheriff courts, criminal cases were also heard in regality, barony, stewartry and bailiery courts (sometimes known collectively as the franchise courts) until such courts were abolished in 1748, and in burgh and justice of the peace courts (which were replaced by the district courts in 1975). Relatively minor criminal jurisdiction was also enjoyed by the admiralty, forestry and miners' courts, none of which has survived to modern times.

In the eleventh and twelfth centuries the Scottish kings sought to extend their royal authority throughout the whole country by introducing reforms based on the Norman system of government. Some parts of the country were placed under the control of royal officers appointed for this purpose and given wide administrative powers, including the right to hold courts. In general the royal officer was a sheriff, but where the land was owned by the king the officer was a stewart or a bailie. Courts of this nature were not, however, instituted in all parts of Scotland, as some of the feudal charters granted as a consequence of the contemporaneous introduction of the feudal system specifically entitled the holders to administer justice in courts known as regality or barony courts[2]. This period also saw the creation of burghs which held their own burgh courts with extensive powers[3]. Furthermore, it was during this time that the kings appointed justiciars with criminal jurisdiction throughout the whole country except for the regalities and stewartries[4].

1 As to these courts generally, see COURTS AND COMPETENCY, vol 6, paras 848 ff, 1022 ff, 1155 ff. See also paras 1.05 ff, 1.09 ff, 1.17, below.
2 See P McIntyre 'The Franchise Courts' in *An Introduction to Scottish Legal History* (Stair Soc vol 20, 1958) pp 374 ff, and see paras 1.20 ff below.
3 See G S Pryde 'The Burgh Courts and Allied Jurisdictions' in *An Introduction to Scottish Legal History* pp 384 ff. See also LOCAL GOVERNMENT, vol 14, para 13, and para 1.18 below.

4 See W C Dickinson 'The High Court of Justiciary' in *An Introduction to Scottish Legal History* pp 408 ff.

(B) THE HIGH COURT OF JUSTICIARY

1.05. Origin. The High Court of Justiciary[1] owes its origins to the office of Justiciar, the first recorded instance of which occurs in 1166[2]. While there is a passing reference in the early eleventh century to a justice and his '*clericus*', the Justiciar created by the Norman reforms superseded or altered this earlier office[3].

In these days the king could, and sometimes did, administer justice in person[4], and for this purpose he held a court known as the '*curia domini regis vel justiarii*' at which he was assisted by his Justiciar, his clerk, his deputies and his assessors. Even in the twelfth century however, it is clear that the king frequently delegated the task of holding the court to the Justiciar. Initially it appears that there was at least one Justiciar with jurisdiction throughout the whole country (with the exception of the regalities and stewartries), but by the early thirteenth century one Justiciar was appointed for the country north of the Forth and another for south of the Forth[5]. By the fifteenth century the office was known as that of the Justice General[6], and in the sixteenth century the two appointments were reunited and the office became hereditary until 1628 when it was resigned into the king's hands (with the exception of the office of Justiciar of Argyll and the Western Isles, which remained hereditary until the office was abolished in 1748)[7]. In 1836, on the death of James, 3rd Duke of Montrose, the office, which was now entitled the Lord Justice-General, was combined with that of the Lord President of the Court of Session, Scotland's supreme civil court[8].

1 See COURTS AND COMPETENCY, vol 6, paras 848 ff.
2 See W C Dickinson 'The High Court of Justiciary' in *An Introduction to Scottish Legal History* (Stair Soc vol 20, 1958) p 408.
3 The Citations Act 1555 (c 6) refers to persons being summoned to appear before 'the Justice, his Deputis or vtheris jugeis . . . having powar of Justiciarie in criminall causis'.
4 See further CONSTITUTIONAL LAW, vol 5, para 624; and D M Walker *A Legal History of Scotland* (1988) vol 1, p 212.
5 *Dickinson* p 408. For further details, see *Walker* pp 215–222.
6 See eg the Circuits Courts Act 1487 (Oct 1, c 2) (APS ii, 176).
7 *Dickinson* p 410; Heritable Jurisdictions (Scotland) Act 1746 (c 43).
8 Provision for this had been made by the Court of Session Act 1830 (c 69), s 18.

1.06. Personnel. Prior to 1836 the Justiciar did not require to be legally qualified and the Court of Session appointed assessors to sit in the Justiciary Court. In practice, much of the judicial work in the Justiciary Court was undertaken either by the Lord Justice-Clerk or by deputes appointed either by the Justiciar or by the king. The Lord Justice-Clerk was originally the clerk of the court, but after 1532 the office was generally held by a Senator of the College of Justice, and from at least 1663 onwards he not only acted as a judge in the Justiciary Court but also began to preside over it[1]. In 1808 the Lord Justice-Clerk was appointed to preside over the Second Division of the Court of Session, and in consequence it became compulsory for him to be a Senator of the College of Justice[2].

As a result of the volume of business in the court, it was not uncommon for the Justiciar to appoint deputes to act on his behalf, in addition to the Lord Justice-Clerk. Initially deputes did not require to have any legal expertise but by the sixteenth century they tended to be legally qualified, albeit that in many instances the deputes were relatively inexperienced advocates apart from occasions when a Court of Session judge was deputised. In 1672 the office of justice-depute was abolished and the High Court of Justiciary was established consisting of the Lord Justice-General, the Lord Justice-Clerk and five judges of the Court of Session[3], this number being increased in 1887 to include all the judges from that court[4].

1 This practice was recognised by an Act of the Scots Privy Council in 1663 and confirmed when the High Court of Justiciary was reconstituted by the Courts Act 1672 (c 40): see COURTS AND COMPETENCY, vol 6, paras 848, 857, 859 and 876; and W C Dickinson 'The High Court of Justiciary' in *An Introduction to Scottish Legal History* (Stair Soc vol 20, 1958) p 411.
2 See the Court of Session Act 1808 (c 151), s 2 (repealed) (now the Court of Session Act 1988 (c 36), s 2(2)).
3 Courts Act 1672 (c 40): see *Dickinson* p 411.
4 Criminal Procedure (Scotland) Act 1887 (c 35), s 44 (repealed).

1.07. Ayres and circuits. The early Justiciars went on circuits (known as 'ayres') from sheriffdom to sheriffdom[1], but in later times the circuits became irregular or even non-existent although the Justiciary Court did continue to sit in Edinburgh. In 1746 it was enacted that circuits should be held twice a year[2], and subsequent legislation provided for further circuits[3]. In 1925 the High Court of Justiciary was empowered to determine the number and location of its circuits[4] and circuit courts are now held wherever and whenever they are required by the volume of business[5].

1 See COURTS AND COMPETENCY, vol 6, paras 852, 853, and D M Walker *A Legal History of Scotland* (1988) vol 1, p 223.
2 Heritable Jurisdictions (Scotland) Act 1746 (c 43), s 31: see COURTS AND COMPETENCY, vol 6, para 858.
3 W C Dickinson 'The High Court of Justiciary' in *An Introduction to Scottish Legal History* (Stair Soc vol 20, 1958) pp 408, 411. For further details, see COURTS AND COMPETENCY, vol 6, para 858.
4 Circuit Courts and Criminal Procedure (Scotland) Act 1925 (c 81) (repealed).
5 *Dickinson* p 411; Criminal Procedure (Scotland) Act 1975 (c 21), s 114; COURTS AND COMPETENCY, vol 6, paras 858, 877.

1.08. Jurisdiction. The jurisdiction of the Justiciar was formerly both criminal and civil, but the civil jurisdiction gradually fell into desuetude after the foundation of the Court of Session in 1532[1], although the High Court of Justiciary continued to hear appeals in civil small debt cases until 1971[2]. In criminal matters, in addition to dealing with appeals from the sheriff court, the Justiciar held a court of first instance in criminal cases and in particular for those cases which were sufficiently serious to be designated 'pleas of the Crown'. Today the High Court of Justiciary is exclusively a criminal court.

1 W C Dickinson 'The High Court of Justiciary' in *An Introduction to Scottish Legal History* (Stair Soc vol 20, 1958) p 409.
2 Ie until the repeal of the Small Debt (Scotland) Act 1837 (c 41) by the Sheriff Courts (Scotland) Act 1971 (c 58), s 35(2). See also COURTS AND COMPETENCY, vol 6, para 858.

(C) THE SHERIFF COURT

1.09. Origin. The sheriff court originates from the powers given to the sheriff, an office which pre-dates Norman times. Prior to the eleventh century, England and parts of Scotland were divided for administrative purposes into districts known as shires[1]. The sheriff (or shire-reeve) was the officer appointed by the king to preside over the shire moots and to exercise military, financial, administrative and judicial functions on his behalf[2]. As part of these duties he was required to hold a sheriff (or shire-reeve) court which had both criminal and civil jurisdiction. The English Norman kings were more powerful than their predecessors, and in order to enforce their authority they retained the office of sheriff but used it to greater effect by giving the sheriff more extensive powers.

While it is possible that the earlier form of sheriff existed in Scotland before the Norman Conquest of England, there is little evidence to this effect, and with the introduction of Norman influence into Scotland towards the end of the eleventh century the Scottish sheriffs who were appointed thereafter were based on the Norman model[3]. During this era the Scottish kings embarked on a programme of building royal castles which were placed under the charge of sheriffs, and the surrounding area was known as a sheriffdom — although in later times it did not follow that every sheriff was based in a castle. The first known record of a Scottish sheriff occurred during the reign of Alexander I (1107–1124). Various charters of David I (1124–1153) referred to sheriffs, and by the time of Alexander III (1249–1286) there is evidence that there were twenty-two sheriffdoms. This number had increased to at least twenty-five by 1305. By the sixteenth century it is probable that shrieval jurisdictions extended to the whole of Scotland with the exception of those areas administered as regalities.

1 See D M Walker *A Legal History of Scotland* (1988) vol 1, pp 32 ff.
2 *Walker* p 226.
3 I A Milne 'The Sheriff Court before the Sixteenth Century' in *An Introduction to Scottish Legal History* (Stair Soc vol 20, 1958) p 350; COURTS AND COMPETENCY, vol 6, para 1022; *Walker* p 226.

1.10. Duties of the sheriff. As the representative of the king, the Scottish sheriff was given a wide range of duties. In military matters he was responsible for local defence and for ensuring that persons liable for military service were properly armed and trained. Since there was no other form of local government, general local administration devolved upon the sheriff and he was required to preserve the king's peace[1] (in which connection he could call out the muster or '*posse comitatus*')[2]. He made payments on behalf of the king and collected any royal taxes, rents or other dues together with the 'profits of justice'[3]. The latter constituted an important source of royal revenue since imprisonment as a punishment was largely unknown prior to 1800 and the courts commonly imposed financial penalties in the form of fines and forfeitures[4]. The sheriff received a proportion of these profits as part of his remuneration (and according to one authority he was also entitled to defray his expenses by imposing a local levy known as sheriff aid or amercements[5]).

1 I A Milne 'The Sheriff Court before the Sixteenth Century' in *An Introduction to Scottish Legal History* (Stair Soc vol 20, 1958) p 352; LOCAL GOVERNMENT, vol 14, para 26.
2 According to Erskine *Institute* I,4,4, 'The Sheriff was long the judge-ordinary to whom the preservation of the public peace was committed; and as such was, and is still, authorised to apprehend fugitives, rebels, and notorious offenders against the peace; and, if necessary, to call the *posse comitatus* to his assistance'. In an article in (1877) J Juris p 205 it is stated that 'There has ... been no statute taking away the Sheriff's powers in this respect'.
3 *Milne* p 352.
4 D M Walker *A Legal History of Scotland* (1988) vol 1, p 228.
5 See eg J Bond *A Compleat Guide for Justices of the Peace* (2nd edn, 1696) Pt I, p 245.

1.11. Judicial functions of the sheriff. The sheriff held a court with criminal and civil jurisdiction throughout the sheriffdom. In criminal matters this court was competent to hear all cases except pleas of the Crown, and its powers of punishment extended to the death penalty. The court could be presided over by the sheriff in person but, as most sheriffs normally regarded their other functions as more important, they frequently appointed deputes who in turn appointed substitutes for this purpose. By the end of the sixteenth century, deputes (although not substitutes) required to have legal qualifications[1].

In the early days, when the sheriff sat in court his main function was restricted to directing the court on points of law. The court itself was comprised of suitors who were the local barons, tenants, freeholders and representatives of religious institutions required to render suit (that is, to attend the court)[2] — although latterly this duty could apparently be discharged by sending proxies. Some of the suitors were selected to try each case, preference being given to those who had prior knowledge of the facts, and after they had been sworn ('*jurati*') this jury sat in judgment ('*assisa*' or 'assize') in order to ascertain the truth which they declared in the form of a verdict ('*veredictum*' or 'true-saying')[3]. The sheriff did not act as a judge in the modern sense until after an Act of 1540[4] and the falling into decline of this type of jury in the fifteenth and sixteenth centuries[5].

Originally there were two types of sheriff court, namely a head court which was supposed to sit every forty days to deal with more important cases, and a lower or intermediate court which sat as required in different parts of the sheriffdom to hear less important suits[6].

1 I A Milne 'The Sheriff Court before the Sixteenth Century' in *An Introduction to Scottish Legal History* (Stair Soc vol 20, 1958) pp 351, 353; C A Malcolm 'The Sheriff Court: Sixteenth Century and Later' in the same work, pp 360–362.
2 *Milne* p 353.
3 *Milne* p 354.
4 Civil Procedure Act 1540 (Dec 3, c 7); *Malcolm* p 360; D Maxwell 'Civil Procedure' (Stair Soc vol 20) p 419.
5 See para 1.42 below.
6 *Milne* pp 352, 353.

1.12. Defects in shrieval justice. By the fifteenth century shrieval justice had fallen into disrepute, largely because the office of sheriff was often allowed to become hereditary and, as a consequence, since sheriffs ceased to depend on individual selection and appointment by the king, they could not be controlled effectively by central government. Sheriffs became notoriously lax in regard to their judicial duties — indeed one authority cites a sheriff who sentenced and executed offenders, merely calling a jury later to homolgate his actions[1]. Delays were common and bribery was not unknown; judicial ignorance of the law and procedure gave rise to complaints from litigants; and sheriffs often allowed personal and political considerations to sway their judgment rather than enforcing the law in a fair and impartial manner[2].

These grievances, combined with the frequent failure to collect or forward royal dues, gave rise to various unsuccessful attempts in the fifteenth, sixteenth and seventeenth centuries to abolish hereditary sheriffdoms or alternatively to curb the worst of their evils. In 1455[3] and 1567[4] attempts were made to abolish hereditary sheriffs by means of statutes, but these were either ignored or not enforced. James VI compelled some hereditary sheriffs to resign, replacing them with sheriffs who were appointed on a yearly basis, but Charles II reverted to the former practice of appointment. By the eighteenth century the office of sheriff could be purchased, and in 1708 one sheriffdom was even sold at an auction sale[5]. Measures to compel sheriffs to perform their duties in a more conscientious manner met with similar failure. A statute of 1503[6] seeking to prevent sheriffs from making unjust awards or taking bribes proved to be ineffective. In 1597 sheriffs ceased to be responsible for the collection of royal taxes and dues[7]. In the seventeenth century sheriffs were required to attend circuit justiciary courts to answer any complaints against them. None of these measures had real or lasting effects.

1 J Cameron *Prisons and Punishment in Scotland* (1983) p 5.
2 C A Malcolm 'The Sheriff Court: Sixteenth Century and Later' in *An Introduction to Scottish Legal History* (Stair Soc vol 20, 1958) p 356.
3 Tenure of Office Act 1455 (c 5).
4 Act 1567 c 23 (APS iii, 39).
5 *Malcolm* pp 357–359.
6 Sheriff Court Expenses Act 1503 (c 11).
7 Supply Act 1597 (c 48).

1.13. Abolition of heritable jurisdictions. The Jacobite Rebellion in 1745 emphasised the influence which could be wielded by persons holding hereditary offices with wide administrative and judicial powers and the Heritable Jurisdictions (Scotland) Act 1746 abolished all heritable jurisdictions as from 25 March 1748. The preamble to the Act gives its purpose as

'remedying the inconveniences that have arisen . . . from the multiplicity and extent of heritable jurisdictions . . . , for restoring to the Crown the powers of jurisdiction originally and properly belonging thereto . . . and for extending the influence, benefit and protection of the King's laws and courts of justice to all his Majesty's subjects in Scotland'.

In place of the hereditary sheriffs, the Act provided for sheriffs who were to be appointed by the Crown for not more than one year[1]. Furthermore, sheriffs ceased to receive any share of the fines and forfeitures imposed by their courts, all of which were to go to the Crown[2].

1 Heritable Jurisdictions (Scotland) Act 1746 (c 43), ss 4, 5.
2 Ibid, s 43.

1.14. The sheriff, the sheriff depute and the sheriff principal. In the event, no sheriffs were ever appointed under the Heritable Jurisdictions (Scotland) Act 1746[1], and instead a sheriff depute was appointed to each shire immediately after the Act, although he was not in fact a depute to anyone. Sheriffs depute were paid by the Crown and were required to be advocates of at least three years' standing[2], a period which was later increased to ten years[3]. After 1828 the term 'depute' was dropped from the title[4], and later the office became known as 'sheriff principal', a title which was formalised in 1971[5]. The initial number of twenty-nine deputes was gradually reduced in the nineteenth and twentieth centuries by combining sheriffdoms, and the Sheriffdoms Reorganisation Order 1974 divided Scotland into its present six sheriffdoms, each with a full-time sheriff principal[6].

1 The power under the Heritable Jurisdictions (Scotland) Act 1746 (c 43), s 4, to appoint sheriffs was abolished by the Statute Law Revision Act 1892 (c 19), s 1, Schedule.
2 Heritable Jurisdictions (Scotland) Act 1746, s 29; C A Malcolm 'The Sheriff Court: Sixteenth Century and Later' in *An Introduction to Scottish Legal History* (Stair Soc vol 20, 1958) p 361.
3 See now the Sheriff Courts (Scotland) Act 1971 (c 58), s 5(1). For further details concerning the qualifications, tenure, powers and duties of sheriffs principal, see I D Macphail *Sheriff Court Practice* (1988) paras 1.07–1.13, and COURTS AND COMPETENCY, vol 6, para 1053.
4 Circuit Courts (Scotland) Act 1828 (c 29), s 22.
5 Sheriff Courts (Scotland) Act 1971, s 4(1): see COURTS AND COMPETENCY, vol 6, para 1028.
6 Further as to the Sheriffdoms Reorganisation Order 1974, SI 1974/2087, and modern sheriff court districts, see COURTS AND COMPETENCY, vol 6, paras 1025–1027.

1.15. Sheriff substitute. Sheriffs depute were supposed to reside in their sheriffdoms for at least four months in the year[1], but as they were permitted to retain their private legal practices most deputes ignored this condition and appointed substitutes to undertake the bulk of the work in the sheriff court. Many substitutes were lacking in legal qualifications, and if a complex case arose it was sent to the depute in Edinburgh. In civil cases a dissatisfied litigant sometimes asked for the depute's views, and in time this came to be regarded as an informal type of appeal. In 1838 and 1853 this appellate procedure in civil cases was recognised and formalised by statute[2]. The problems arising from the use of unqualified substitutes continued until 1825 when it was enacted that a substitute required to be an advocate or solicitor of at least three years' standing[3]. This was later increased to ten years[4].

In the first instance, substitutes were appointed by the depute[5] and could be dismissed by him. When the depute died or demitted office the substitute's appointment also fell. In 1787 the salaries of substitutes became payable by the Crown[6] and in 1832 the appointments became *aut vitam aut culpam*[7], although retiral later became compulsory on reaching the age of seventy-two years[8]. In 1838 the power to dismiss a substitute was transferred from the depute to the Lord President and the Lord Justice-Clerk[9] and after 1877 all appointments of substitutes were made by the Crown[10]. Finally in 1971 the term 'substitute' was dropped from the title, and the office is now known by the designation of 'sheriff'[11].

1 Heritable Jurisdictions (Scotland) Act 1746 (c 43), s 29. This requirement was abolished by the Sheriff Courts (Scotland) Act 1838 (c 119), s 1.
2 Ibid, s 20; Sheriff Courts (Scotland) Act 1853 (c 80), s 16: see COURTS AND COMPETENCY, vol 6, para 1029.
3 Sheriff Courts (Scotland) Act 1825 (c 23), s 9: see COURTS AND COMPETENCY, vol 6, para 1030.
4 Sheriff Courts (Scotland) Act 1971 (c 58), s 5.
5 Heritable Jurisdictions (Scotland) Act 1746, s 29.
6 Warrant of 9 October 1787.
7 C A Malcolm 'The Sheriff Court: Sixteenth Century and Later' in *An Introduction to Scottish Legal History* (Stair Soc vol 20, 1958) pp 361, 362.
8 Sheriff's Pensions (Scotland) Act 1961 (c 42), s 6.
9 Sheriff Courts (Scotland) Act 1838, s 3: see now the Sheriff Courts (Scotland) Act 1971, s 12, under which the Lord President and the Lord Justice-Clerk may make a report to the Secretary of State for Scotland, who may make an order by statutory instrument, subject to annulment by either House of Parliament, removing a sheriff principal or a sheriff from office on grounds of unfitness by reason of inability, neglect of duty or misbehaviour. In practice the Lord Advocate may suggest to a sheriff that he consider resigning to avoid recourse to the statutory procedure. Further as to the qualifications, tenure, powers and duties of sheriffs, see I D Macphail *Sheriff Court Practice* (1988) paras 1.14-1.17, and COURTS AND COMPETENCY, vol 6, para 1042.
10 Sheriff Courts (Scotland) Act 1877 (c 50), s 3.
11 Sheriff Courts (Scotland) Act 1971, s 4(1).

1.16. Criminal jurisdiction. The criminal jurisdiction of the sheriff court has always extended to all crimes and offences which were not excluded by their gravity or by statutory provision or by the sentence appropriate to them[1]. Treason has never been competent before the sheriff court, and breach of duty by magistrates and deforcement of messengers have long appeared in the same category. Similarly crimes known as pleas of the Crown have always fallen within the exclusive jurisdiction of the High Court of Justiciary. The law regarding 'pleas of the Crown' has changed over the years. Hume lists these crimes as murder, robbery, rape and fireraising[2], although at one time the sheriff could try cases of murder if the accused was caught red-handed[3], and today robbery and fireraising may be prosecuted in the sheriff court[4]. The High Court also has sole jurisdiction in certain statutory offences, two modern examples being contraventions of the Official Secrets Act 1911[5], and offences against the Geneva Conventions Act 1957 committed outside the United Kingdom[6].

A more important restriction on the sheriff court has resulted from the diminution of its powers of sentence. Much of Scots criminal law depends on common law which does not have fixed penalties, and consequently the choice of court in which a particular case is to be presented depends on the powers of punishment of that court. At one time the sheriff court had very wide powers of punishment including imposition of the death penalty[7]. Gradually cases meriting more serious penalties were taken in the High Court. By the eighteenth century sheriffs had ceased to hear cases involving the death penalty and according to Hume 'it was settled in the case of Duncan Kennedy[8], that to give doom of transportation is not within the commission of a Sheriff'[9]. When transportation was abolished it was replaced by penal servitude with a minimum sentence of three years[10], which could be imposed only by the High Court. In effect, the power of the sheriff court was thus restricted to a sentence of imprisonment of less than three years, and when penal servitude was abolished by the Criminal Justice (Scotland) Act 1949, the maximum sentence of the sheriff court was further restricted to two years' imprisonment[11]. However, recent legislation has restored to three years the maximum sentence of imprisonment that can be imposed by a sheriff in solemn proceedings[12].

1 Hume *Commentaries* II,60 ff.
2 *Hume* II,59.
3 *Hume* II,62,63.
4 Criminal Procedure (Scotland) Act 1975 (c 21), s 291(3) (amended by the Criminal Justice (Scotland) Act 1980 (c 62), s 38).
5 Official Secrets Act 1911 (c 28), s 10(3).
6 Geneva Conventions Act 1957 (c 52), s 1(3).
7 *Hume* II,58.
8 *Duncan Kennedy* (1767) MacLaurin Remarkable Cases no. 77.
9 *Hume* II,61.
10 Penal Servitude Act 1853 (c 99), ss 1–4; Penal Servitude Act 1857 (c 3), ss 1, 2; Penal Servitude Act 1891 (c 69), s 1.
11 Criminal Justice (Scotland) Act 1949 (c 94), s 16(1). See also the Criminal Procedure (Scotland) Act 1975, s 221(1) (as originally enacted).
12 Ibid, ss 2(2), 221(1) (amended by the Criminal Justice (Scotland) Act 1987 (c 41), s 58(1), (3)).

(D) THE DISTRICT COURT AND ITS PREDECESSORS

1.17. The district court. Prior to 1975 there was a range of courts with lesser powers than the sheriff court, namely the burgh, police and justice of the peace courts. These courts were all abolished by the District Courts (Scotland) Act 1975 which created the district court in their place[1]. In 1975 Scotland was divided into districts for the purpose of local government[2] and the Act empowered each local authority to determine where and when the district court should sit within the district[3]. The district court, which has only criminal jurisdiction, consists of one or more justices (who are not legally qualified) or a stipendiary magistrate (although the latter have been appointed only in Glasgow)[4].

1 District Courts (Scotland) Act 1975 (c 20), s 1(1). See further COURTS AND COMPETENCY, vol 6, paras 1155 ff.
2 Local Government (Scotland) Act 1973 (c 65), s 1(4).
3 District Courts (Scotland) Act 1975, s 2(1).
4 Ibid, s 2(2). See Z K Bonkowski, N R Hutton and J J McManus *Lay Justice?* (1987).

1.18. The burgh court and the police court. Burgh courts came into being in the twelfth century with the creation of burghs[1]. Just as 'new towns' were established in the twentieth century, David I (1124–1153) and his successors founded or approved new settlements for the purpose of fostering trade and manufacture in order to benefit the royal revenues. To prevent undue influence from feudal overlords, burghs were given a degree of autonomy and to an extent they were empowered to make their own laws. They were also permitted to have their own courts and magistrates called *Ballivi* or bailies. In the fifteenth and sixteenth centuries burghs were divided into royal burghs and lesser burghs (known as barony or regality burghs), but this differentiation ceased to have any real effect by the nineteenth century. A further categorisation began after 1833 when a distinction was made between parliamentary burghs which could elect their own members of Parliament[2], and police burghs which had full rights of local government, including the right to hold their own police courts[3].

The geographical jurisdiction of the burgh court was restricted to the bounds of the burgh, but within its area the criminal jurisdiction of the court was originally very extensive. Apart from pleas of the Crown, the early burgh courts could try all criminal cases, including murder where the accused was caught red-handed[4]. Until the seventeenth century the burgh court had the power of capital punishment, and it was not uncommon for thieves and adulterers to be hanged and for witches to be burnt — for example, the records of Ayr show that in 1589 it cost the burgh £7 3s 8d to burn a witch and in 1593 it cost £1 11s 4d to execute 'Jonet Smyth the hussie'. Other penalties included the jougs or stocks, the cuck-stool, scourging, branding, banishment from the burgh and the imposition of fines and forfeiture. Financial penalties were often favoured for lesser crimes since the 'profits of justice' were used to build or maintain roads, bridges or similar projects for the common good of the burgh[5]. If an indigent offender could not pay his fine he was often ordered to give several days free labour as a form of community service.

With the passage of time the burgh courts gradually ceased to deal with the more serious crimes. Most burghs regarded such trials as an onerous and expensive public duty which brought no financial profit, and as the sheriff and justiciary courts with concurrent jurisdiction became more common and more effective the burghs were not unwilling to cede the trial of serious cases to these courts[6]. By the eighteenth century the burgh courts in practice dealt only with minor criminal cases, and by the nineteenth century some burgh courts had virtually ceased to sit as all criminal cases were taken in the sheriff court. When the new police courts were created in 1833, the police magistrates were given the same powers as a sheriff substitute, but by 1908 the power of the burgh and police courts was restricted to a maximum sentence of sixty days' imprisonment or a fine of £10 and crimes such as theft by housebreaking and theft of an amount exceeding £10 were excluded from the competence of the court[7]. Despite these restrictions, the burgh and police courts continued to function in the twentieth century and, indeed, as an increasing volume of business gave rise to pressure in the sheriff court, there was a corresponding and substantial increase in the number of minor cases prosecuted in the burgh court. By the time the burgh and police courts were abolished in 1975[8], many of them — especially in the cities and larger burghs — were extremely busy courts with a considerable volume of criminal business[9].

1 G S Pryde 'The Burgh Courts and Allied Jurisdictions' in *An Introduction to Scottish Legal History* (Stair Soc vol 20, 1958) pp 384 ff; COURTS AND COMPETENCY, vol 6, paras 1155–1158; LOCAL GOVERNMENT, vol 14, paras 10 ff; D M Walker *A Legal History of Scotland* (1988) vol 1, ch 8.
2 Representation of the People (Scotland) Act 1832 (c 65), ss 7–11.
3 Burghs and Police (Scotland) Act 1833 (c 46), especially ss 135, 136; *Pryde* pp 384, 385, 390.
4 *Pryde* pp 386, 387; *Walker* p 205.
5 *Pryde* p 388; W C Dickinson *Scotland from the Earliest Times to 1603* (3rd edn, 1977 by A A M Duncan) p 297.
6 *Pryde* pp 388, 389.
7 See eg the Burgh Police (Scotland) Act 1892 (c 55), ss 454, 459, 490.
8 District Courts (Scotland) Act 1975 (c 20), s 1(1).
9 See further COURTS AND COMPETENCY, vol 6, para 1167.

1.19. The justice of the peace courts. The office of justice of the peace was introduced into Scotland in 1587 by James VI in an attempt to remedy some of the deficiences of the other criminal courts[1]. The intention was to appoint 'godlie, wise and vertuous gentilmen' in each shire to enforce the law and to report on the conduct of the sheriffs[2], but the system did not take root and in due course sheriffs became responsible for supervising the justices. The powers given to the justices were insufficient to allow them any degree of real authority, and the office was so widely disfavoured by the populace at large that in 1683 the Privy Council threatened to punish anyone who refused appointment. After 1707 various attempts were made to increase the prestige of the justices, and while their powers were always subordinate to those of the sheriffs, justices were appointed in each shire where they were given certain administrative functions and held courts with criminal and civil jurisdiction.

The territorial jurisdiction of the justice of the peace court was restricted to the shire, excluding any burghs which had burgh or police courts. The criminal jurisdiction of the justices' court more or less corresponded with that of the burgh courts and by 1908 their powers were identical. Until they were abolished in 1975[3], their history in the twentieth century paralleled that of the burgh courts and, with regard to their role as a criminal court, they were generally viewed as the county equivalent of the burgh courts.

1 Criminal Justice Act 1587 (c 57): see J Irvine Smith 'The Transition to the Modern Law 1532–1660' in *An Introduction to Scottish Legal History* (Stair Soc vol 20, 1958) p 40. For further details, see COURTS AND COMPETENCY, vol 6, para 1169.
2 Justices of the Peace Act 1609 (c 14).
3 District Courts (Scotland) Act 1975 (c 20), s 1(1).

(E) THE FRANCHISE COURTS

1.20. Introduction. The franchise courts came into being with the introduction of the feudal system into Scotland and remained until, with one minor exception, they were abolished in 1748. One of the essential concepts of the feudal system was that the king could issue charters giving grants of land together with certain rights over the tenants on their land. At the king's discretion, the grant might also include the right to hold courts for the purpose of enforcing the criminal law and deciding civil disputes, but the franchise to hold such courts was regarded as being distinct from the grant of the land itself. If the holder disposed of the land, he still retained his jurisdictional rights which passed from father to son. The extent of the jurisdiction depended on the nature of the grant and there were four types of franchise each with its own court, namely the regality, the barony, the stewartry and the bailiery[1].

1 P McIntyre 'The Franchise Courts' in *An Introduction to Scottish Legal History* (Stair Soc vol 20, 1958) pp 374 ff: see paras 1.21 ff below.

1.21. The regality court. The king's right to dispense justice formed part of his *regalia*, but from early times kings were wont to make grants *in liberam regalitatem* which included the right of 'haute justice', conferring on the holder a jurisdiction equivalent to that held by the king himself, with the exception of the right to try cases of treason. Initially these rights were usually granted by the king because he was not sufficiently powerful to exercise them on his own behalf and by this means he ensured that law and order would be enforced by someone who was able to do so. By the fourteenth century, however, rather than supplementing royal government, regalities were often wrested from weak kings and used by the holders to set up what was tantamount to an alternative system of government. In the fifteenth century, as central authority became more powerful, it was not uncommon for regalities to be given by the king without a grant of land, and such commissions were regarded as a means of delegating the royal authority[1].

The criminal jurisdiction of a regality court was equivalent to that of the royal court, and generally included the right to try pleas of the Crown. Apart from cases of treason, the king's writ did not run in the regality and the king's officers had no authority to enter its lands[2]. All forfeitures and fines imposed by the court accrued to the lord of regality. The regality court was usually presided over by a bailie (or his deputes), but if the regality encompassed a whole shire, the sheriff might become the head officer in the regality. The second officer of the regality was the Justiciar, who presided when the regality sat as a justiciary court to hear serious criminal cases. The procedure was similar to that in the sheriff court. Originally, the president only directed the court on matters of law and the verdict of the court was given by a jury selected from among the suitors, but in the sixteenth century the president assumed the functions of a judge in the modern sense. In theory an appeal could be taken from the regality court to Parliament, but it appears that, especially in criminal cases, this right was seldom exercised[3].

1 P McIntyre 'The Franchise Courts' in *An Introduction to Scottish Legal History* (Stair Soc vol 20, 1958) pp 377, 378.
2 See COURTS AND COMPETENCY, vol 6, para 854.
3 *McIntyre* pp 379, 380.

1.22. The barony court. A barony was a grant *in liberam baroniam* and conferred lesser rights and jurisdiction than a regality. In criminal matters, the barony court had the right of 'pit and gallows' and could try cases of murder if the accused was caught red-handed, theft where the thief was found in possession of the stolen goods, and other lesser crimes. The penalties included death and, according to one authority[1], the barony court could even sentence an 'unwanted general nuisance' to be hanged or drowned. All fines and forfeitures accrued to the baron. Where the barony court lay within a regality, appeals could be taken to the regality court; elsewhere an appeal could be taken to the sheriff, who was supposed to ensure that baronial justice was properly exercised. A dissatisfied litigant was entitled to claim that the decision (known as a 'doom') was 'false, stinking and rotten' and the sheriff in reviewing the decision would pronounce it as 'well said' (that is, the appeal failed) or 'evil given' (that is, the appeal succeeded). As a general rule it appears that appeals were normally restricted to civil cases and the sheriff seldom took any real interest in criminal matters. By the late sixteenth century the criminal jurisdiction of the barony courts had been greatly restricted by statute, and their importance declined as the authority of the sheriff court increased[2].

1 W C Dickinson *Scotland from the Earliest Times to 1603* (3rd edn, 1977 by A A M Duncan) p 84.
2 P McIntyre 'The Franchise Courts' in *An Introduction to Scottish Legal History* (Stair Soc vol 20, 1958) pp 374-377; D M Walker *A Legal History of Scotland* (1988) vol 1, pp 232-235; *Dickinson* pp 84, 85.

1.23. The stewartry and bailiery courts. Stewarts and bailies were royal officers appointed by the king to administer land owned directly by the king. The extent of their powers depended on the nature of the authority delegated to them. The stewartry court was given the same jurisdiction as the regality court whereas the bailiery court had equivalent jurisdiction to the sheriff who had no jurisdiction over anyone residing in a stewartry or bailiery[1]. In later years, however, while the land remained the property of the king, the offices of

stewart and bailie with their respective jurisdictions tended to become hereditary and passed from father to son independently of royal authority.

1 P McIntyre 'The Franchise Courts' in *An Introduction to Scottish Legal History* (Stair Soc vol 20,
    1958) pp 381, 382.

1.24. Replegiation. Replegiation or repledging was a process whereby a
franchise or sheriff court could exercise the right to try any person who was
normally subject to its jurisdiction and who had been cited to appear before
another court[1]. The locus of the crime was irrelevant; all that mattered was that
the person was normally subject to the jurisdiction of the court seeking to
exercise the right. In return that court required to grant a pledge or surety that
justice would be done[2], although in practice it was virtually impossible to
establish that the proceedings would be, or had been, fairly and properly
conducted. Even cases such as murder could be repledged from the justiciary
court to the regality court and, as this procedure was regularly used to protect
kinsmen, followers and the like, it constituted a gross abuse of the legal system
by allowing alleged perpetrators of crime to evade trial in the royal courts. In the
sixteenth and seventeenth centuries attempts were made to limit the right to
repledge, and after the High Court of Justiciary was established in 1672 replegiation to courts other than the regality court became largely ineffective.

1 J Irvine Smith 'Criminal Procedure' in *An Introduction to Scottish Legal History* (Stair Soc vol 20,
    1958) pp 430–432; COURTS AND COMPETENCY, vol 6, para 854.
2 The pledge was known as a 'culreach': Hume *Commentaries* II, 30.

1.25. Abolition of the franchise courts. The lack of control and supervision
over the franchise courts together with their power to repledge cases from the
royal courts was adverse to the development of a strong central government and
in particular to a uniform system of law enforcement. The person presiding over
the court seldom had any legal qualifications and the courts themselves were
notoriously corrupt and inefficient, with the result that they were unpopular
with the public, which lacked confidence in them. As the central courts gained
acceptance and authority, the use of the franchise courts began to diminish, but,
as in the case of hereditary sheriffs, it was the after-effects of the 1745 Jacobite
Rebellion which brought about their ultimate abolition. Under the Heritable
Jurisdictions (Scotland) Act 1746 the regality, stewartry and bailiery courts were
dissolved and their jurisdictions were vested in the High Court of Justiciary and
the sheriff court[1]. Barony courts were allowed to continue, but their powers of
punishment were restricted to a fine of twenty shillings or setting in the stocks
for three hours, and as a result barony courts soon fell into disuse[2].

1 Heritable Jurisdictions (Scotland) Act 1746 (c 43), s 1.
2 P McIntyre 'The Franchise Courts' in *An Introduction to Scottish Legal History* (Stair Soc vol 20,
    1958) p 382; COURTS AND COMPETENCY, vol 6, para 856.

(c) Title to Prosecute: The Public Prosecutor

(A) INTRODUCTION

1.26. Private and public prosecution. The responsibility for instituting
criminal proceedings formerly lay with the victim or his relatives. While admit-

tedly the state had a strong interest in the enforcement of the criminal law, it was generally considered that the prime function of the criminal courts was to provide a remedy to private parties seeking compensation or vengeance in respect of injuries or loss arising from the criminal actings of another. There were, however, various defects in this approach[1]. Powerful criminals escaped justice as weak victims were afraid to institute proceedings, while the wealthy purchased immunity from sentence[2]; certain crimes had no specific victim and hence no one had a title to prosecute; finally, failure to prosecute diminished the profits of justice to the detriment of the Treasury. As a consequence of these failings the concept of a public prosecutor began to emerge in the fifteenth century. In 1424 the Justice Clerk was required to prosecute cases of muirburn[3] (setting fire to a heath or muir); in 1436 the sheriff was empowered to prosecute certain criminals 'gif na partie follower appearis'[4]; and various local officials were given the right to prosecute certain minor offences[5]; but the real movement towards the establishment of a system of public prosecutions arose from the involvement of the Lord Advocate as public prosecutor.

1 J Irvine Smith 'Criminal Procedure' in *An Introduction to Scottish Legal History* (Stair Soc vol 20, 1958) pp 432–434.
2 As to pardons, see para 1.54 below.
3 Muirburn Act 1424 (c 21).
4 Pursuit by Sheriffs Act 1436 (c 4).
5 *Irvine Smith* p 434.

(B) THE LORD ADVOCATE

1.27. History of the office of Lord Advocate. During the fifteenth century the Crown was sometimes represented by an advocate in civil cases. In 1479 an unnamed advocate appears to have acted on behalf of the king in a treason trial[1] and in a similar trial in 1483 John Ross of Montgrennan was designed as 'advocat to his hienes'. The same person had been respectively described as the 'king's commissioner' and the 'king's procurator' in two previous civil cases in 1476 and 1477, and in 1478 he appeared in court in Edinburgh, designed as 'Advocate for the King'[2]. It is probable that at this period no single permanent officer held the post of King's Advocate, but rather that an advocate was appointed to act for the king on an *ad hoc* basis, initially in civil cases and thereafter in criminal cases. The use of the King's Advocate (or Lord Advocate as he was later known) in criminal cases gradually became more common, and in due course it became the practice for private parties to obtain his concurrence in private prosecutions. During the sixteenth century the volume of criminal business devolving on the Advocate increased, and in 1544 an Advocate Depute was appointed. From time to time the Privy Council gave a special warrant to the Lord Advocate to prosecute alone in specific serious cases, and in 1579 the Council directed the Advocate to prosecute criminals even when the victim or his relatives failed to do so. This measure did not meet with success, but an Act of the Scots Parliament of 1587 gave the Lord Advocate the right to prosecute 'slaughters and utheris crimes' even if 'the parties be silent or wald utherwayis privily agree'[3]. The effect of this Act was to recognise the status of the Lord Advocate as the public prosecutor with the right to prosecute alone and in his own interest. His pre-eminence over the private prosecutor was emphasised in the case of *Beaver*[4] in 1719, when the court held that the Advocate's title to prosecute was not extinguished by a pardon granted by the victim to the accused, and conversely in 1829 when the court decided that if the Lord Advocate granted an indemnity to the accused, it was not competent to institute a subsequent private prosecution[5].

1 Research paper by A L Murray (Scottish Record Office 1977). See generally J Irvine Smith 'Criminal Procedure' in *An Introduction to Scottish Legal History* (Stair Soc vol 20, 1958) pp 434, 435, and CONSTITUTIONAL LAW, vol 5, paras 509, 536.
2 See CONSTITUTIONAL LAW, vol 5, para 536.
3 Jurors Act 1587 (c 54).
4 *Beaver* (1719) Hume *Commentaries* II, 133.
5 *Hare v Wilson* (1829) Syme 373, where the mother of one of the victims of Burke and Hare had sought to bring a private prosecution against Hare, who had gained indemnity against prosecution by turning king's evidence at the trial of Burke.

1.28. Private prosecutors and the Lord Advocate. The right of the victim to institute proceedings by means of a bill of criminal letters did not disappear completely, and that right still exists today. However, it became the normal practice to obtain the concurrence of the public prosecutor and, according to MacLaurin, by 1723 it was essential in all cases involving the death penalty or other punishment[1]. Gradually it became the established rule that all private prosecutions required concurrence, and Hume, writing in 1797, stated that this requirement was in accordance with 'ancient and invariable style'[2]. The court nevertheless retained a discretion to dispense with concurrence on the application of the private party, and in certain restricted instances private prosecutions have been allowed to proceed in its absence. In the case of *J and P Coats Ltd v Brown*[3] the court in effect decided that where the victim established a prima facie case and the Lord Advocate did not show cause for his failure to concur, the court on the application of the victim could authorise the victim to institute proceedings without the Advocate's concurrence. In the *Sweeney* case[4] the court allowed the victim of an assault and rape to bring a private prosecution which the Lord Advocate did not oppose but in which he did not concur, he having twice instituted abortive proceedings against the accused persons and thereafter intimated to them that he did not intend to proceed further against them. Where, however, the victim has not suffered a personal wrong or where the wrong falls into the category of a public offence (such as perjury or attempting to pervert the course of justice), the courts will not permit a private prosecution without the concurrence of the public prosecutor[5]. While the victim therefore still retains some right to institute proceedings, private prosecutions by victims are virtually unknown and their demise may be traced to the Jurors Act 1587[6]. After that date the Lord Advocate began to assume the duty of prosecuting all serious crimes by way of indictment while private parties increasingly declined to take the responsibility of instituting criminal proceedings. There were various reasons for this change. In the trial of *James Connell* in 1599[7] the court held that the Lord Advocate could not be compelled to disclose the name of his informer, and as a result a private party could give information about a crime without fear of retribution by the offender. Likewise, while a private individual seeking to raise a prosecution could be subjected to pressure or coercion, the same considerations did not apply to a public prosecutor, who could proceed with the case regardless of the power or status of the offender. A further consideration was that by reporting the matter to the public prosecutor and leaving the prosecution to him, the private individual avoided the cost[8] and trouble of a private prosecution with the risk of an additional claim for expenses if the accused were acquitted. Finally, with the passage of time public confidence in the ability and impartiality of the public prosecutor grew and, moreover, as the investigation of crime became more sophisticated, it became difficult for a private individual to match the resources made available by the state for this purpose.

1 J MacLaurin *Arguments and Decisions in Remarkable Cases* (1774) p 68.

2 Hume *Commentaries* II, 125.
3 *J and P Coats Ltd v Brown* 1909 SC (J) 29, 6 Adam 19. See also COURTS AND COMPETENCY, vol 6, para 872.
4 *X v Sweeney* 1982 JC 70, 1982 SCCR 161, 1983 SLT 48.
5 *M'Bain v Crichton* 1961 JC 25, 1961 SLT 209; *Trapp v M, Trapp v Y* 1971 SLT (Notes) 30; *Meehan v Inglis* 1974 SLT (Notes) 61.
6 As to the Jurors Act 1587 (c 54), see para 1.27 above. In relation to the sheriff's summary court, see para 1.31 below, and for the district court, see para 1.38 below.
7 *James Connell* 1599 Fountainhall i, 136.
8 However, in *X v Sweeney* 1982 JC 70, 1982 SCCR 161, 1983 SLT 48, the private prosecutor was granted legal aid to conduct the prosecution.

1.29. Modern status of the office. The stature of the office of Lord Advocate grew as he became more and more involved in the prosecution process. By the sixteenth century he was an important constitutional figure in the Scottish government and was regarded as one of the great Officers of State. Before 1707 he was *ex officio* a member of the Scots Parliament, and since that date he has always been a member of the United Kingdom government in his capacity of chief law officer and legal adviser to the government in relation to Scotland[1]. He is appointed by the government of the day and demits office with it. As a member of the government he is answerable to Parliament, and while by constitutional convention he is not required to justify any decision to prosecute or not to prosecute, in the past, and in particular in the eighteenth and nineteenth centuries, it was not unknown for the Lord Advocate to be subjected to parliamentary attacks[2]. In present times, as a matter of concession, the Lord Advocate will frequently give information to Parliament, particularly if pressed to do so on some issue of public interest, but he still retains a discretion as to the amount of detail divulged, and if Parliament is not thereby satisfied, a tribunal of inquiry into the facts of the case may be set up[3]. In practice a victim (or any other person with a direct interest) who is aggrieved by a prosecutorial decision will usually complain in the first instance to the Lord Advocate in person, and in such cases the Lord Advocate may review the decision or possibly offer some explanation. Thereafter if the complainer remains dissatisfied it is still open to him to raise the matter in Parliament with the aid of his member of Parliament.

1 See generally CONSTITUTIONAL LAW, vol 5, paras 535 ff. See further para 2.15 below.
2 For further details and examples, see W G Normand 'The Public Prosecutor in Scotland' (1938) 54 LQR 345.
3 See CONSTITUTIONAL LAW, vol 5, para 535.

(C) THE PROCURATOR FISCAL

1.30. Origin and development of the office. The public prosecutor in the sheriff and district courts is the procurator fiscal. From the records now available it is impossible to trace the exact date when this office was first introduced into Scotland. Since the twelfth or thirteenth centuries the term 'procurator' was commonly applied to an agent appearing for a party in a civil suit. 'Fiscal' means pertaining to the public treasury, otherwise known as the 'fisk' or 'fisc'. The title 'procurator fiscal' was known in the early French feudal courts, where an official of this name acted as the 'man of business' for the local lord and, as part of his duties, collected fines and forfeitures from the local court. While he might therefore have had some financial interest in criminal proceedings, there is nothing to suggest that at this early period he took any active part in instituting or conducting them.

As the reforms to the Scottish legal system in the eleventh and twelfth centuries were based on the Norman model, it does not seem unreasonable to surmise, in the absence of contrary evidence[1], that the office of procurator fiscal first appeared at this time and that he was appointed by the sheriff to perform the same duties as his French feudal counterpart. Certainly from early times one of the most important functions of the Scottish procurator fiscal was to represent the fisk and collect the fines and financial penalties imposed in the sheriff court, and indeed this function remained with him until 1927 when it was transferred to the sheriff clerk[2]. Even today the procurator fiscal is required to check the sheriff clerk's record of fines and certify it as being accurate[3].

Before the sixteenth century the sheriff acted both as prosecutor and judge in his own court. The Pursuit by Sheriffs Act 1436 (c 4) gave statutory recognition to this practice and at the same time empowered sheriffs to institute criminal proceedings at their own instance in the absence of a private prosecutor. In the second half of the sixteenth century, as sheriffs adopted a judicial role similar to that of a modern judge (as a consequence of the Civil Procedure Act 1540 (Dec 3, c 7), it gradually came to be regarded as inconsistent for him to continue to act as prosecutor and he therefore began to delegate his prosecutorial duties to the procurator fiscal as one of his officers[4]. The change may also have been influenced by the obvious advantages which were seen to arise from the emergence of the Lord Advocate as the prosecutor in the Justiciary Court and a desire to adopt a similar prosecution system in the sheriff court.

The prosecuting duties of the procurator fiscal soon became so extensive that in the seventeenth century he was described by Sir George Mackenzie as 'the pursuer in place of his Majesty's Advocate' in the sheriff court[5], and it became common to obtain his concurrence in private prosecutions. His status as public prosecutor was recognised by the Criminal Procedure Act 1700 (c 6), and in 1818 the Third Report to Parliament by the Commissioners of the Courts of Justice designed him as 'the prosecutor for the public interest before the sheriff court'. A style for a libel in the Circuit Courts (Scotland) Act 1828[6] referred to the 'Procurator Fiscal of Court [*or other Party with his concurrence*]' as the prosecutor in the sheriff court, and in Barclay's *Digest*, published in 1853, the author states that 'the procurator fiscal is the public prosecutor appointed by the sheriff. Criminal prosecution must be at his instance or with his concourse'[7]. The Summary Procedure (Scotland) Act 1864 entitled him to prosecute at his own instance under all statutes which did not specifically name a prosecutor[8] and further provided that expenses could not be awarded against him in respect of sheriff court proceedings unless a particular statute authorised such an award[9].

1 According to another theory the office was only imported from France in the middle of the sixteenth century when Scotland had strong links with that country, which by then had a system of public prosecutors. This theory is largely based on the fact that the earliest written references to the procurator fiscal which have so far been traced relate to appointments of this officer to act as prosecutor in the courts of burghs which regularly traded with France. This does not explain why the Scots should select the title 'procurator fiscal' when the French prosecutors were known by this time as '*procureurs*'. It would also mean that the office must rapidly have spread from the burgh courts and extended to all the criminal courts in Scotland over the space of a few decades: see W Reid 'The Origins of the Procurator Fiscal in Scotland' 1965 JR 154.

2 This change was effected by an inter-departmental agreement when both officers became full-time civil servants as a result of the Sheriff Courts and Legal Officers (Scotland) Act 1927 (c 35). See para 1.36 below. Prior to 1927 fines were remitted to the Treasury at the end of each quarter, and by lodging the fines in a bank as soon as they were received the procurator fiscal commonly received the bank interest arising therefrom.

3 The fines are checked daily or at similar regular intervals except in the case of the larger courts where since 1 October 1986 officials in the Crown Office have undertaken this duty on behalf of procurators fiscal and now audit the figures relating to fines supplied by sheriff clerks to Scottish Courts Administration.

4 About the same time a *procurator fiscalis* prosecuted in the courts of Rome, Naples and Milan, and an officer known as the 'fiscal' was the prosecutor in the courts of the Holy Roman Empire.

5 G Mackenzie *The Laws and Customs of Scotland in Matters Criminal* (1678) p 212.
6 Circuit Courts (Scotland) Act 1828 (c 29), Sch C, no 1.
7 H Barclay *A Digest of the Law of Scotland on the Office and Duties of a Justice of the Peace* (1853) p 43.
8 Summary Procedure (Scotland) Act 1864 (c 53), s 4.
9 Ibid, s 30. Prior to this Act expenses could be awarded against a procurator fiscal: see eg Alison *Practice* (1833) p 93, where such awards are described as 'a practice perfectly familiar to the Court'. The exemption provided by the 1864 Act did not apply where the procurator fiscal was involved in proceedings in the High Court of Justiciary, such as bills of suspension (appeals).

1.31. Modern status of the office of procurator fiscal. Legislation in the nineteenth and twentieth centuries reinforced the position of the procurator fiscal as the public prosecutor in the sheriff court[1], and today, with a few minor exceptions, he may be regarded as the sole prosecutor there. One exception concerns public bodies which have a statutory right to prosecute certain offences and to appoint a qualified person to act as prosecutor in the public interest[2]. However, since all public bodies such as government departments, local authorities and the like now refer their cases to the procurator fiscal for prosecution, such cases are largely restricted to local authority prosecutions against parents who allow their children to truant from school and even these cases are frequently passed to the procurator fiscal. Another exception relates to private prosecutions by individuals who have been given express authority to prosecute by statutes relating to game and salmon fisheries[3]. While prosecutions under these statutes are not unknown, they are relatively uncommon[4]. Other private prosecutions are still theoretically competent in the sheriff court, presumably under the same conditions as apply to the bringing of a private prosecution in the High Court of Justiciary; but private prosecutions of this nature are now unknown and the matter is largely academic as it is highly improbable that an individual would take such pains in a case so trivial as to merit only summary proceedings[5].

1 See eg *M'Millan v Grant* 1924 JC 13 at 23, 1924 SLT 86 at 91, per Lord Sands; *Houston v MacDonald* 1988 SCCR 611, 1989 SLT 276.
2 This category of public prosecutor derives its authority from the definition of 'prosecutor' in the Summary Jurisdiction (Scotland) Act 1908 (c 65), s 2 (repealed), which is now incorporated in the definition of 'prosecutor' in the Criminal Procedure (Scotland) Act 1975 (c 21), s 462(1), and from *Templeton v King* 1933 JC 58, 1933 SLT 443.
3 See eg the Game (Scotland) Act 1772 (13 Geo 3 c 54), s 8, the Game (Scotland) Act 1832 (c 68), s 2, the Salmon Fisheries (Scotland) Act 1868 (c 123), s 30, and the Ground Game Act 1880 (c 47), s 7.
4 For a modern example of a private prosecution under the Salmon Fisheries (Scotland) Act 1868 (c 123), see *Fishmongers' Co v Bruce* 1980 SLT (Notes) 35.
5 Private prosecutions for common law crimes require the concurrence of the procurator fiscal, as do prosecutions for statutory offences (where imprisonment without the option of a fine is competent) unless the statute provides otherwise: Criminal Procedure (Scotland) Act 1975 (c 21), s 311(4); R W Renton and H H Brown *Criminal Procedure according to the Law of Scotland* (5th edn, 1983) para 13-19. As to private prosecutions in the High Court of Justiciary, see para 1.28 above. The concurrence of the public prosecutor is also required in civil cases for alleged breach of interdict: see *Gribben v Gribben* 1976 SLT 266.

(D) RELATIONSHIP BETWEEN THE LORD ADVOCATE AND THE PROCURATOR FISCAL

1.32. Appointment of procurator fiscal by sheriff. Despite his duties as a prosecutor, the procurator fiscal remained an officer of the sheriff until 1907. Certainly by the nineteenth century, and probably from a much earlier period, he received a formal commission from the sheriff and 'in the event of disobedience of his orders, whether the fiscal likes them or not, the sheriff had the power of dismissing the fiscal without explanation or apology'[1]. According to the Commissioners' Third Parliamentary Report in 1818 the procurator fiscal 'is usually, if not in all cases, one of the procurators or agents before the court', albeit that he did not require to be legally qualified and the post was usually held on a part-time basis in conjunction with some other office, or, where appropriate, with a private legal practice. While the prosecuting duties of the procurator fiscal and the Lord Advocate may have corresponded in their respective courts, each seems to have operated independently of the other until some time during the eighteenth century when a link began to be forged between them, partly because of the growing power of the Lord Advocate and partly, almost by accident, because of financial considerations.

1 This statement was made by the Lord Advocate (William Watson) in a debate in the House of Commons on 6 March 1877.

1.33. Income and expenditure. The procurator fiscal was formerly required to meet any expenditure (such as payments to deputes or clerical staff) out of his own pocket, and he recovered his outlays and derived his income from a variety of sources including awards of expenses in his favour and fees for various services (for example for concurring in private prosecutions). Prior to 1724 the extent to which he received a fee for each case he prosecuted is not clear, but such fees were paid to him after that year from a local fund known as 'rogue money' or the 'rogue fund'[1]. One of his most important sources of income 'according to ancient usage' was a proportion of the fines levied in the sheriff court[2]. In the first instance certain statutes provided that a specified proportion of the penalty was to be paid to him (for example an Act of 1581 stated that half the penalty was to be paid to the 'ordinar officiares' of the court[3]), but a greater part of his income came from a proportion of the share which the sheriff retained from all the fines and forfeitures imposed in the court. In this respect it is interesting to note from seventeenth century court records that criminal actions commonly concluded for two payments to be made by the offender, namely compensation to the victim and a sum to be paid to the fisk. The Heritable Jurisdictions (Scotland) Act 1746, which abolished hereditary sheriffs, also rescinded the sheriff's right to a share in the fines and revenues[4] and consequently the income of the procurator fiscal was correspondingly diminished[5].

1 Rogue money was a fund established by the Bail in Criminal Cases (Scotland) Act 1724 (c 26), s 12, as a consequence of the Jacobite Rebellion in 1715. Its proceeds were used for apprehending and prosecuting criminals and its income was derived from an annual levy imposed on all landowners and, later, from county funds.
2 *Third Report to Parliament by the Commissioners of the Courts of Justice* (1818).
3 Sumptuary Act 1581 (c 19).
4 Heritable Jurisdictions (Scotland) Act 1746 (c 43), s 43.
5 An Act of Adjournal of 1748 laid down the fee chargeable by the procurator fiscal for concurring in a private prosecution, but made no provision to compensate him for losing a share of the fines.

1.34. Links with the Lord Advocate. After the Heritable Jurisdictions (Scotland) Act 1746 (c 43) there was a considerable increase in the fees paid to procurators fiscal from the rogue fund, and in order to relieve the counties of some of this expenditure the Treasury agreed in 1776 to take responsibility for paying the fees due to the procurator fiscal in respect of certain aspects of his work including 'precognitions transmitted to the Lord Advocate' and framing indictments 'when ordered by the Lord Advocate'. Summary prosecutions and other matters not reported to the Lord Advocate continued to be paid by fees drawn on the rogue fund[1]. It is significant that the sole purpose of this ruling was to alter the method of paying the procurator fiscal and it did not seek to impose any new duties upon him. It therefore provides clear evidence that prior to 1776 a link had been established between the Lord Advocate and the procurator fiscal and that the fiscal was sending precognitions to and receiving orders from the Lord Advocate.

Further evidence of the link is to be found in the rules issued to sheriffs by the Lord Advocate in 1765 entitled 'Rules to be observed in taking Precognitions and making Presentments for Trial of Crimes before the Circuit Courts'[2]. The rules were revised in 1824, 1834 and 1839, and while they were intended initially for use by the sheriffs, they were also binding on the procurator fiscal, and when a further revision was made in 1868 they were specifically directed towards the procurator fiscal[3].

The importance of these rules is referred to in a minute lodged by the Lord Advocate in a case in 1895 in which the Lord Advocate stated:

'That it appears, from a comparison of the rules of 1765 with those of 1834, as well as from other sources of information[4], that, in the intervening period, the Lord Advocate had come to exercise a more general and direct authority over procurators-fiscal than formerly, and that it had become the practice for the Lord Advocate or his Deputes, not only to issue orders to procurators-fiscal as to whether any, and if any, what, proceedings should be taken with reference to cases reported to the Crown office, but also to give directions as to the course which procurators-fiscal should follow with reference to cases not so reported.

That since 1834, and probably from an earlier period, procurators-fiscal have been directly responsible to, and subject to the orders of, the Lord Advocate in all matters relating to the investigation of criminal charges, and the manner in which such charges should be tried or otherwise disposed of, as well as in making inquiries in regard to complaints and similar matters'[5].

In the first half of the nineteenth century the growing authority of the Lord Advocate over the procurator fiscal expanded to cover matters other than the prosecution of criminal cases. In 1839 the Lord Advocate instructed the procurator fiscal to report all suspicious, sudden or accidental deaths. Later the procurator fiscal was ordered to submit certain reports in relation to the Mines and Collieries Act 1842 (c 99) and the Poor Law (Scotland) Act 1845 (c 83); and in 1848 the procurator fiscal was required to send a return every four months narrating the sentence or other disposal of all cases reported to the Lord Advocate. For their part, the procurators fiscal do not appear to have opposed the growing assumption of authority over them by the Lord Advocate, possibly because, in terms of the 1776 Treasury agreement, they received a Treasury fee for all items transmitted to the Lord Advocate.

The development of the 1776 agreement in this manner had not been foreseen by the Treasury, which now found itself bound to pay a growing number of fees for business over which it had no means of control. In order to impose some limit on this expenditure, the Treasury issued a direction in 1851 that all procurators fiscal who received fees in excess of £400 per annum were to receive a Treasury salary in lieu of fees. In the first instance seventeen procurators fiscal were placed on individual salaries ranging from £410 to £1,500 per annum, and by 1877 this number had increased to forty-five, leaving only six procurators fiscal who were not in receipt of a salary. When this measure was first proposed by the Treasury in 1850, some of the county authorities, possibly because of their experience after the passing of the 1746 Act, were apprehensive that a salaried procurator fiscal might seek to increase the volume of work attracting fees from the rogue fund and they accordingly put pressure on the Treasury to take responsibility for rogue fund fees. In response to this demand, the Treasury agreed in 1851 to relieve the rogue fund of all expenses connected with criminal prosecutions where the case had proceeded to trial or at least where there was a warrant for committal by the sheriff[6]. This solution, however, failed to absolve the counties from responsibility for cases which did not fall into this category, and procurators fiscal continued to derive some income from rogue fund fees[7]. It is also of interest to note that the rules made by the Treasury in 1851 were followed by the Summary Procedure (Scotland) Act 1864, which provided that, unless authorised by statute, 'expenses shall not be awarded to or against any public prosecutor'[8].

1 The full table of fees may be found in the *Third Report to Parliament by the Commissioners of the Courts of Justice* (1818) p 52. After 1776, cases transmitted to the Lord Advocate became colloquially known as 'reported cases' and the remainder were known as 'unreported cases'. If the Lord Advocate instructed that no proceedings should be taken in a case reported to him, he had a discretion to authorise that any fees or outlays incurred should be borne by the Treasury. In due course procurators fiscal who had incurred expenses in cases which they had marked 'no proceedings' also began to report these cases to the Lord Advocate with a request that the Treasury should pay the outlays, and such cases became known as 'unreported no proceedings cases' — that is, they had not hitherto been reported.
2 The rules are set out in Hume *Commentaries* II, 535 (App X).
3 Eg the 1868 Rules state 'where the Procurator Fiscal is credibly informed of the commission of any crime . . . he ought to take prompt and immediate steps for apprehending the party accused. In doubtful cases, or when any unusual difficulty occurs, he may take the advice of Crown Counsel'.
4 The 'other information' may have included the Third Parliamentary Report (1818) which states 'Under the direction of the sheriff the [procurator fiscal] prepares and transmits to the Lord Advocate all the informations and precognitions respecting crimes which do not fall under the exclusive jurisdiction of the [sheriff court]'.
5 *Dumfries County Council v Phyn* (1895) 22 R 538 at 544.
6 1877 J Juris 557.
7 See the minute by the Lord Advocate in *Dumfries County Council v Phyn* (1895) 22 R 538 at 544. No accurate research has so far been undertaken to quantify the exact amount of these fees, but it is generally known that they were not regarded as inconsiderable.
8 Summary Procedure (Scotland) Act 1864 (c 53), s 22.

1.35. Control and removal from office. While the combined effect of all of the above measures meant that the Lord Advocate was in virtual control of the procurator fiscal, in law the procurator fiscal remained an officer of the sheriff, who continued to be responsible for his selection, appointment and dismissal. Consequently, should a procurator fail to perform his duties in a satisfactory manner, no real sanction was available to the Lord Advocate (or the Treasury) other than attempting to persuade the sheriff to revoke the procurator fiscal's commission. The first attempt to remedy this anomaly was made by the Sheriff Courts (Scotland) Act 1877, which enacted that the appointment of a procurator fiscal by the sheriff required the approval of one of his Majesty's Principal Secretaries of State[1] (later known as the Secretary of State for Scotland), who was also empowered to remove a procurator fiscal from office on the grounds of inability or misbehaviour, provided he had received a report from the Lord President of the Court of Session and the Lord Justice-Clerk[2].

Subsequent legislation continued to bind the Lord Advocate and the procurator fiscal closer together. The Criminal Procedure (Scotland) Act 1887 deprived the procurator fiscal of his discretion to prosecute cases before a sheriff and jury by way of a bill of criminal letters and stated that in future all such cases were to proceed on an indictment at the instance of and by the authority of the Lord Advocate[3]. Finally, the right of appointing the procurator fiscal was removed from the sheriff and vested in the Lord Advocate by the Sheriff Courts (Scotland) Act 1907[4], and since then all procurators fiscal have been appointed by receiving a commission from the Lord Advocate. The Lord Advocate was not, however, given the power to dismiss the procurator fiscal from office as the provisions of the 1877 Act regarding dismissal were re-enacted by the 1907 Act[5].

It was still not regarded as essential for the procurator fiscal to be legally qualified and, once appointed, he held office *ad vitam aut culpam* without any fixed retiral age. Most procurators fiscal took office 'relatively late in life'[6], and there was no unified procurator fiscal service with a career structure and avenues of promotion. His income continued to be derived from a Treasury salary determined on an individual basis, and from rogue money, concurrence and other fees, and since at the beginning of the present century only about one-third of the procurators fiscal were full-time; many of them had additional income from other sources. In return they were required to meet the expenses of running their own offices and paying for their deputes and other staff.

1 Sheriff Courts (Scotland) Act 1877 (c 50), s 6.
2 Ibid, s 5.
3 Criminal Procedure (Scotland) Act 1887 (c 35), s 2. Prior to this Act indictment procedure had been reserved for cases prosecuted by the Lord Advocate in the High Court of Justiciary.
4 Sheriff Courts (Scotland) Act 1907 (c 51), s 22 (repealed): see now the Sheriff Courts and Legal Officers (Scotland) Act 1927 (c 35), s 1(2).
5 Sheriff Courts (Scotland) Act 1907, s 23 (repealed): see now the Sheriff Courts and Legal Officers (Scotland) Act 1927, s 1(3).
6 *Report of the Departmental Committee on Procurators Fiscal, Sheriff-Clerks, The Commissary Clerk, the Sheriff-Clerk of Chancery and their Respective Staffs* (the 'Blackburn Report') (1921) p 16, para 34.

1.36. The procurator fiscal service. It was against this background that the office of procurator fiscal was subjected to further scrutiny by Lord Salvesen's Minor Legal Appointments Committee in 1910, by the Royal Commission on the Civil Service in 1915 and perhaps more importantly by Lord Blackburn's Departmental Committee in 1921[1] which gave rise to the Sheriff Courts and Legal Officers (Scotland) Act 1927 on which the modern procurator fiscal service[2] is based.

The 1927 Act, while confirming the Lord Advocate's right to appoint procurators fiscal[3], also transferred to him the power of removing them from office on receipt of a report from the Lord President of the Court of Session and the Lord Justice Clerk[4], and by a subsequent amendment to the Act the Lord Advocate was given the power to transfer a procurator fiscal from one district to the post of procurator fiscal or depute in another without the necessity of a report from the Lord President or the Lord Justice-Clerk[5]. The decisions as to the total number of procurators fiscal, the limits of their individual districts and which posts would be full-time were also placed within the determination of the Lord Advocate, subject to Treasury approval[6]. The holders of full-time posts were forbidden to engage in private legal practice or carry on any other employment 'of such a nature as will in the opinion of the ... Lord Advocate ... interfere with the due discharge' of the procurator fiscal's duties[7]. The Act also removed from the procurator fiscal the burden of paying for his own staff by empowering the Lord Advocate to appoint such procurator fiscal deputes and other staff as he considered necessary (with the proviso that he obtain Treasury consent as to numbers and salaries)[8]. The provision that all full-time procurators fiscal and staff should be 'deemed to be employed in the Civil Service'[9] had particularly important consequences. As civil servants, full-time procurators fiscal and their staff became entitled to salaries, pension rights, office facilities and all the benefits accorded to other civil servants, but in return they were bound by civil service conditions of employment including a retiral age of sixty-five years and payment to the Treasury of all fees, expenses and the like otherwise receivable by the procurator fiscal[10]. As regards future entrants to the procurator fiscal service, it was subsequently made a condition of civil service appointment that all applicants for the post of procurator fiscal or procurator fiscal depute required to be qualified either as a Scottish solicitor or advocate, and while the Lord Advocate was not debarred from giving a commission to an unqualified person, such a person would not be deemed to be a civil servant and thus he would not be entitled to the civil service salary appropriate for a procurator fiscal or depute[11].

Since the passing of the 1927 Act, the procurator fiscal service has become increasingly assimilated into the civil service, and apart from the fact that a procurator fiscal receives a commission from the Lord Advocate on appointment and that dismissal requires a judicial report, the service is now virtually indistinguishable from any other civil service department[12]. All legally-qualified staff receive salaries corresponding to those paid to other legal civil servants, all fiscals depute being placed on one of two lower salary scales and all procurators fiscal (with the exception of six Regional procurators fiscal)[13] being placed on one of two higher ones. As a result of the Act, all procurators fiscal appointed thereafter have been legally qualified and have tended to regard themselves as members of a unified procurator fiscal service rather than individually appointed and otherwise unrelated procurators fiscal. It is now normal practice for solicitors or advocates to make their careers in the service, first being appointed as a depute (often at a relatively young age and not long after qualifying) and later progressing by promotion to the more senior posts.

The procurator fiscal today is under the complete control of the Lord Advocate[14] who is politically responsible for the actings of the procurator fiscal, although he is not vicariously liable for any criminal act by the procurator fiscal[15]. The procurator fiscal is bound by regulations issued with the authority of the Lord Advocate which state that 'departure from the regulations ... will always require explanation and justification. Unjustified departure will be regarded as a breach of discipline[16]. The regulations further state 'Procurators fiscal are subject in the discharge of their duties to the instructions of the Lord Advocate ... [and] may be directed by the Lord Advocate as to the mode of prosecution in certain types of cases ... Summary cases proceed at the instance of the procurator fiscal, subject to any directions issued by the Lord Advocate'.

1 Report of the Departmental Committee on Procurators Fiscal, Sheriff-Clerks, The Commissary Clerk, the Sheriff-Clerk of Chancery and their Respective Staffs (the 'Blackburn Report') (1921).
2 The phrase 'procurator fiscal service' was first used in the Sheriff Courts and Legal Officers Act 1927 (c 35), s 4.
3 Ibid, s 1(2).
4 Ibid, s 1(2), (3). It is not necessary to receive such a report before removing a procurator fiscal depute from office.
5 Ibid, s 1(4)(b), (5) (added by the Law Reform (Miscellaneous Provisions) (Scotland) Act 1985 (c 73), s 47).
6 Sheriff Courts and Legal Officers Act 1927, ss 1(2), 3. Gradually all procurator fiscal posts became full-time appointments. The last part-time post was abolished in 1979.
7 Ibid, s 3. In practice the Lord Advocate has generally allowed procurators fiscal to hold only academic or honorary posts.
8 Ibid, ss 2, 5.
9 Ibid, s 6 (amended by the Superannuation Act 1972 (c 11), s 29(1), Sch 6, para 10).
10 The Sheriff Courts and Legal Officers Act 1927, s 12, provides that all awards of expenses to the procurator fiscal and all fines are to be paid to the Treasury.
11 The Blackburn committee recommended that all procurators fiscal and deputes should be legally qualified (Report, para 6). The Treasury (which controlled Civil Service conditions of employment) imposed a condition that any person appointed after 1927 to the post of procurator fiscal or depute required to be qualified as a Scottish solicitor or advocate as a condition of his employment as a civil servant. In practice, especially in remote districts, the Lord Advocate or the procurator fiscal with his consent may sometimes give an honorary deputation to an unqualified person or alternatively appoint a local solicitor as a part-time depute to deal with any emerg-

encies in the absence of the procurator fiscal. The former do not receive any remuneration for these duties and the latter do not receive civil service salaries.

12 The procurators fiscal in post at the time of the Sheriff Courts and Legal Officers Act 1927 were given the choice by s 7 of being bound by the terms of the Act or of continuing with their existing conditions of office. The majority accepted the terms of the Act, but a few did not. The last procurator fiscal to lack legal qualifications retired in 1962.

13 See para 1.40 below.

14 He is not 'the sheriff's advocate in the public interest': *Green v Smith* 1987 SCCR 686 at 689, 1988 SLT 175 at 177, 178.

15 *McDonald v Lord Advocate* 1988 SCCR 239 at 247, 1988 SLT 713 at 718.

16 *Procurator Fiscal Service Book of Regulations* (1984) Preface, reg 1.02.

(E) THE SOLICITOR GENERAL AND CROWN COUNSEL

1.37. The Lord Advocate's staff. While the Lord Advocate has overall responsibility for the prosecution of crime in Scotland, he is assisted by the Solicitor General for Scotland and by advocates depute, known collectively as 'Crown counsel'. The Solicitor General, despite his title, is an advocate and, like the Lord Advocate, he is a law officer appointed by the government with whom he also demits office[1]. He may discharge all the functions of the Lord Advocate if the office of Lord Advocate is vacant or if the Lord Advocate is unable to act because of absence or illness or if the Lord Advocate authorises him to do so in any particular case[2]. Should the Lord Advocate die or otherwise be removed from office, indictments may be brought in the name of the Solicitor General. Advocates depute are members of the Scottish bar appointed for this purpose, supposedly on a part-time basis, by the Lord Advocate and hold office at his pleasure, although since 1970 they have ceased to demit office with the Lord Advocate. They receive Treasury salaries in respect of their prosecution duties and, while they are debarred from defending criminal cases, they are permitted to continue their civil practices. Most cases sent to the Lord Advocate by the procurator fiscal are placed before Crown counsel who decide whether a prosecution should proceed and issue such instructions as are necessary to the procurator fiscal. As Crown counsel are deputising for the Lord Advocate, the procurator fiscal is bound by these instructions[3]. Crown counsel also conduct the prosecution of cases before the High Court of Justiciary, although in exceptional instances the prosecution may be presented by the Lord Advocate or Solicitor General in person.

1 Further as to the origins and office of Solicitor General, see CONSTITUTIONAL LAW, vol 5, para 543.

2 Law Officers Act 1944 (c 25), s 2(1).

3 Instructions in individual cases are given by Crown counsel, and anyone departing from Crown counsel's instructions may be called upon to justify his actions: *Procurator Fiscal Service Book of Regulations* (1984) reg 1.02.

(F) THE PUBLIC PROSECUTOR IN THE DISTRICT COURT

1.38. General. The public prosecutors in the burghs, police and justice of the peace courts were also known as procurators fiscal, but as they were appointed by the local authorities responsible for these courts, unlike the procurators fiscal in the sheriff court, they did not come under the control of the Lord Advocate. They did not require to be legally qualified and in the nineteenth century it was not unknown for a police officer to be appointed for this duty. By the twentieth century it had become the practice to appoint a local solicitor to act as a part-time procurator fiscal and this situation continued until 1975[1]. The District Courts (Scotland) Act 1975, which replaced all of these courts with the district court[2], also empowered the Lord Advocate to direct that 'all prosecutions ... shall proceed at the instance of a procurator fiscal appointed by him'[3], and in pursuance of this provision, the Lord Advocate subsequently directed that the procurator fiscal in the sheriff court in which district the district court is situated should also act as prosecutor at the district court.

1 See COURTS AND COMPETENCY, vol 6, para 1157.
2 District Courts (Scotland) Act 1971 (c 20), s 1(1).
3 Ibid, s 6(1). In applying this Act to 'all prosecutions', the title of any private prosecutor would appear to be expressly excluded unless he were 'appointed' by the Lord Advocate.

(G) THE CROWN AGENT AND THE CROWN OFFICE

1.39. Solicitors to the Lord Advocate. At the Scottish Bar an advocate must be instructed by a solicitor or, as he was more commonly known in former times, a law agent. The Lord Advocate is no exception to this rule, and the solicitor responsible for instructing him became known as the agent for the Crown, or Crown Agent[1]. It could be argued, however, that the Lord Advocate is not appearing as counsel instructed by a solicitor. Although the Crown Agent prepares the papers for the Lord Advocate's appearance in court, he does not 'instruct' the Lord Advocate who appears before the court in his own right. For at least three hundred years prior to 1945 the Lord Advocate appointed an Edinburgh solicitor to act as his agent, and the office changed hands as each Lord Advocate came to power. The Crown Agent performed his duties on a part-time basis and until 1900, when he was given a Treasury salary, he was paid a fee for each case. The Crown Agent conducted his business from his private legal office, but at the beginning of the nineteenth century he was given official office premises in Parliament Square, Edinburgh, later known as the Crown Office[2]. Initially the Advocates Depute continued to work from their own chambers and only the Lord Advocate and the Solicitor General occupied rooms in the Crown Office, which was staffed by two clerks appointed by the Crown Agent and two copy clerks appointed by the clerks to copy precognitions, correspondence and the like. In 1880, by which time the number of clerks had grown to six (in addition to the copy clerks), the head clerk and one of the others were given Civil Service salaries and in 1911 the remaining four clerks also became civil servants. As civil servants, the clerks, unlike the part-time Crown Agent, continued in post when the office of Lord Advocate changed hands and as a consequence, especially as the volume of work in the Crown Office expanded, an increasing amount of responsibility devolved upon the clerks and in particular upon the head clerk. To remedy this situation, it was decided in 1945 that the post of Crown Agent should be held by a solicitor employed as a full-time civil servant who would not change office with each Lord Advocate, and since that date all Crown Agents have been so employed.

1 See eg Rules to be observed in taking Precognitions and making Presentments for Trial of Crimes before the Circuit Courts (1765), rr X, XIII, XX, set out in Hume *Commentaries* II, 535 (App X).
2 These premises were probably acquired when Parliament Square was rebuilt after the fires of 1810 and 1820. The Crown Office is no longer situated in Parliament Square but at 5–7 Regent Rd, Edinburgh EH7 5BL (telephone 031–557 3800). For one of the earliest references to the Crown Office, see Alison *Practice* (1833) p xl.

1.40. Supervision of the procurator fiscal service. While the Crown Agent continues to act as instructing solicitor for the Lord Advocate, he has assumed since 1945 a growing authority over procurators fiscal. Prior to 1927 when procurators fiscal did not require to be legally qualified it was necessary for the Crown to have a solicitor in the person of the Crown Agent. After that date, when it became the rule for all procurators fiscal to be qualified, while they accepted that the Crown Agent was in charge of the Crown Office, they tended to regard him somewhat in the same way as a country solicitor regards his Edinburgh correspondent. In particular, as the procurator fiscal was appointed on commission by the Lord Advocate, he considered that it was the Lord Advocate, and not the Crown Agent, who had authority over him. Although both Crown Agent and fiscal may have been civil servants, the procurator fiscal did not look on the service as a Civil Service department with the Crown Agent as its head[1]. Moreover, the Crown Agent could not — and still cannot — issue directions to the procurator fiscal about the prosecution of any particular case. This situation began to change after the Crown Agent was made a civil servant in 1945 as the Treasury came to regard him as the link between it and the procurator fiscal on all matters concerning pay and conditions of service. Thereafter as the service gradually became indistinguishable from any other Civil Service department, the Crown Agent acquired the superior status and salary accorded to the head of a department and the Crown Office gained the description of the headquarters of the procurator fiscal service.

As the senior civil servant in the procurator fiscal service, the Crown Agent now has considerable authority over the procurator fiscal. Although only the Lord Advocate may appoint or transfer a procurator fiscal, he will normally take account of any recommendations made by the Crown Agent and in the case of a fiscal depute it is sufficient if the letter of appointment is signed by or on behalf of the Crown Agent. Likewise as the Crown Agent is responsible for the general administration and efficiency of the procurator fiscal service, he may issue instructions to procurators fiscal for this purpose[2]. In order to assist the Crown Agent with these duties the post of regional procurator fiscal was created in each of the six sheriffdoms in 1974. The regional procurator fiscal (in addition to acting as procurator fiscal in his own district) was also given the responsibility for ensuring that all the other procurators fiscal in his region (that is, sheriffdom) comply with Crown Office policies; he may advise procurators fiscal when he considers it appropriate; he may deploy staff; and, while he may not alter the decision which another procurator fiscal has made regarding a particular case, he may 'persuade' him to do so[3].

1 The Crown Agent received a lower salary than some senior procurators fiscal. Furthermore when procurators fiscal wished to improve their salaries or conditions of service, they did not apply to the Crown Agent, but submitted 'memorials' direct to the Lord Advocate who, if he decided to pursue the matter further, negotiated with the Treasury.
2 For example a procurator fiscal may not engage in any other form of remunerative employment without the prior approval of the Crown Agent, and if a procurator fiscal is charged with a criminal offence or becomes involved as a party in civil litigation, or becomes bankrupt, he must notify the Crown Agent immediately: *Crown Office Book of Regulations* (1984) regs 1.07, 1.10, 1.11. Similarly the Crown Agent may deploy staff from one district to another as he considers necessary.
3 *Crown Office Book of Regulations* (1984) reg 1.14.

(d) Development of Scottish Criminal Procedure

(A) INTRODUCTION

1.41. Mediaeval procedure. In mediaeval times Scottish criminal procedure, unlike certain other areas of Scots law, was relatively undeveloped. Today if certain procedures are not properly followed at the investigative stage of the proceedings or during the trial, any evidence obtained is unlikely to be admitted as proof. In early times such distinctions were largely unknown. When an offender was caught *in flagrante delicto*, justice was summarily given to him 'within that sun'[1], which was later defined as being within three days. Where the accused's guilt was not patently obvious, there were various means of resolving the issue, the most important being trial by ordeal, trial by combat, compurgation and trial by jury[2].

Trial by ordeal probably died out during the thirteenth century. The accused was required to undergo some form of ordeal such as carrying a red-hot iron for a distance of nine feet, or lifting a stone from a cauldron of boiling water. If his hand was uninjured after three days, he was declared innocent, otherwise he was found guilty. Trial by combat began to replace trial by ordeal during the twelfth century and although it was disapproved by the Lateran Council of 1215 it continued into the fourteenth century and possibly later. The last recorded instance of this procedure occurred in 1603 when the Earl of Moubray was challenged to combat and, although this form of trial has never been formally abolished, it was agreed in a case in 1985 that trial by combat had now fallen into desuetude and was no longer competent[3].

Trial by compurgation was known in pre-Norman times, and while it had virtually died out by the mid-fifteenth century, there is a reference to compurgation in the records of a barony court in 1622. The accused was brought before the court and made a simple denial or assertion under oath in which he was supported by a number of compurgators or oath helpers who swore a similar oath, not because they could give any corroborative evidence, but because they supported the credibility of the accused. If the accused was unable to find sufficient compurgators (for example, three were required for a denial of theft) or if any compurgator failed to take the oath in the approved form, the accused was convicted.

1 Murder Act 1432 (c 1) (APS ii, 20): see J Irvine Smith 'Criminal Procedure' in *An Introduction to Scottish Legal History* (Stair Soc vol 20, 1958) p 426.
2 See generally *Irvine Smith* p 426; D M Walker *A Legal History of Scotland* (1988) vol 1, pp 279–295.
3 *H M Advocate v Burnside* April 1985 (unreported): see *The Scotsman, The Glasgow Herald* and *The Times* 19, 23 April 1985; and H L MacQueen 'Desuetude, the *Cessante* Maxim and Trial by Combat in Scotland' (1986) 7 Journal of Legal History 90.

1.42. Development of trial by jury. The original form of a trial by jury consisted of trial before a jury empanelled from among the suitors who attended the court. In selecting the jury, preference was given to persons who had some knowledge of the accused or of the facts of the case, and since the total population of Scotland in the thirteenth century was estimated as 400,000, mostly living in small scattered communities, it was not difficult to find jurors with this qualification. In 1230 Acts of the Scots Parliament[1] gave the accused an option to elect for trial by jury or inquest, and this form of trial gradually replaced ordeal, combat and compurgation in all the criminal courts[2].

By the fifteenth or sixteenth centuries juries had ceased to base their verdicts on personal knowledge of the case or the accused[3] and their decisions were based on the testimony of witnesses speaking to the facts of the case. Important procedural reforms were introduced in 1587[4] whereby all evidence required to be produced in the presence of the accused and any questions which the jury wished to ask had to be asked in his presence; no one was allowed to contact the jury after it had retired; and if the Crown sought improperly to influence the verdict, the accused was entitled to an acquittal.

There appears to have been no limit on the number of persons cited for jury service (the jury itself being selected from those present), until 1579, when the number was restricted to forty-five[5]. The prosecutor was responsible for preparing the jury list until 1690 when by Act of Adjournal the duty devolved to the clerk of court and thereafter in 1825 to the sheriffs[6]. The size of the jury varied from thirteen to fifteen (although there are examples of juries numbering eleven or seventeen), and from 1535 an odd number became the rule. The verdict was always by a simple majority. The jury was selected by the judge[7], and as objection to a juror could be made only on cause shown, this power was sometimes abused by judges who selected jurors according to their political bias or support for the Crown — indeed, according to Lord Cockburn, this practice 'very nearly gave the judge the power of returning the verdict'. In 1822 the accused was allowed five peremptory challenges[8], and in 1825 it was enacted that jurors should be selected by ballot[9].

1 Acts 1230 cc 5, 6 (APS i, 399). It is possible that an earlier Act (c 5, APS i, 318) during the reign of David I (1124–1153) gave the accused the right to claim trial by his peers, but there is some doubt as to the authenticity and application of this Act: see D M Walker *A Legal History of Scotland* (1988) vol 1, p 232, and D M Walker *The Scottish Jurists* (1985) p 23. See also I D Willock *The Origins and Development of the Jury in Scotland* (Stair Soc vol 23, 1966) p 179.
2 See also D M Walker *A Legal History of Scotland* (1988) vol 1, p 231.
3 Hume (*Commentaries* II, 319) states that 'vestiges' of relying on jurors with personal knowledge were found as late as the seventeenth century.
4 Criminal Justice Act 1587 (c 57).
5 Officers at Arms Act 1579 (c 14).
6 Jurors (Scotland) Act 1825 (c 22), s 3.
7 Mackenzie also makes reference to jurors being selected by the Lord Advocate, but the Lord Advocate was a Senator of the College of Justice until the late seventeenth century.
8 Jurors in Criminal Trials (Scotland) Act 1822 (c 85), s 1.
9 Jurors (Scotland) Act 1825, ss 16, 17. See generally J Irvine Smith 'Criminal Procedure' in *An Introduction to Scottish Legal History* (Stair Soc vol 20, 1958) pp 441, 442.

(B) PRE-TRIAL PROCEDURE

1.43. Apprehension of the accused. There were various methods of arresting the accused and bringing him before the court. According to common law, an individual present at the commission of a crime has always been entitled to arrest the accused[1]; statutes passed in 1528, 1567 and 1661 empowered the lieges to pursue and arrest common criminals[2]. Sheriffs have always had a right of pursuit and arrest, and certainly by the end of the seventeenth century the oral authority of a sheriff or magistrate to whom an immediate complaint of a crime had been made entitled the informer or others to arrest and even kill an accused who resisted arrest[3]. When justices of the peace were introduced they were given the statutory right in 1617 to appoint constables with certain powers of arrest[4]. In the seventeenth and eighteenth centuries many towns had watchmen or guards to keep the peace and arrest persons seen committing offences, and after 1724 some counties used rogue money[5] to finance a similar system in country districts. Most of these measures were, however, ineffectual, and when necessary recourse was had to the army.

The concept of a police force in the modern sense was long resisted and distrusted on the ground that it would represent an intrusion into the rights of the individual, but in 1800 under the authority of a private Act of Parliament Scotland's first statutory police force was established in Glasgow. Various towns and cities followed this example, especially after public general legislation in the 1830s and 1840s facilitated the establishment of police forces in royal and other burghs. The Police (Scotland) Act 1857 required all counties to form police forces unless they had already done so, and by the end of the nineteenth century police forces existed in every part of Scotland. As a consequence most arrests nowadays are carried out by police constables[6].

1 Hume *Commentaries* II,76. For further detail, see J Irvine Smith 'Criminal Procedure' in *An Introduction to Scottish Legal History* (Stair Soc Vol 20, 1958) pp 426–428.
2 Coroner's Arrestments Act 1528 (c 1); Fire Raising Act 1567 (c 40); Homicide Act 1661 (c 217).
3 See Hume *Commentaries* II,75, referring to *Gillespie* 1694.
4 Justice of the Peace Act 1617 (c 8).
5 See para 1.33 above.
6 P Gordon *Policing Scotland* (1980) pp 11–29.

1.44. Pre-trial investigations. Rules for the pre-trial investigation of crime can be traced back to the fourteenth century[1]. A very early Scots statute stated that in a case of murder it was necessary to examine the body and hold an inquest[2], and further statutes were passed in 1398[3], 1438[4] and 1449[5] providing for accusations of crime to be given in writing to the sheriff. With the gradual demise of the private prosecutor and the growing practice of leaving prosecutions to the public prosecutor, it became necessary for someone other than the victim to take some responsibility for the pre-trial investigations[6]. In theory the sheriff became increasingly involved in such investigations, and this practice was recognised by the Circuit Courts (Scotland) Act 1709[7]. After the office of sheriff was reformed by the Heritable Jurisdictions (Scotland) Act 1746 (c 43), the sheriff was given the duty of making immediate inquiry into every crime committed within his jurisdiction as soon as a complaint was laid before him by the procurator fiscal or the injured party[8]. In practice, probably in the seventeenth century and certainly in the eighteenth century, the sheriff delegated most of the preliminary investigative work to his procurator fiscal.

1 See generally J Irvine Smith 'Criminal Procedure' in *An Introduction to Scottish Legal History* (Stair Soc vol 20, 1958) p 428.
2 APS i, 737 (c 2).
3 APS i, 573.
4 APS ii, 32 (c 2).
5 APS ii, 34 (c 8).
6 Justices of the peace were also given the duty of investigating breaches of certain statutes after that office was instituted in the late sixteenth century.
7 Circuit Courts (Scotland) Act 1709 (c 16), s 4.
8 Hume *Commentaries* II,26; *Irvine Smith* p 428.

1.45. Precognitions. In the fourteenth and fifteenth centuries various statutes made provision for accusations of crime to be given in writing before the sheriff or the lieutenant or his deputy[1], and in due course witnesses whose evidence was regarded as essential for the forthcoming trial were thereafter brought before the sheriff and examined, usually under oath, and their evidence was recorded in a formal statement known as a precognition. Prior to the Criminal Justice Act 1587 (c 57) it was competent for the only evidence at the trial to be the witness's assent to his precognition, but after that date witnesses were called to give evidence at the trial and the main purpose of the precognitions was confined to 'directing his Majesty's Advocate how to lay his libel and deduce his evidence'[2]. At one time the precognitions were obtained by the sheriff questioning the witness and reducing his deposition to writing, and although parties to the case were entitled to lodge interrogatories listing the points on which they wished the witnesses to be examined, the sheriff had a discretion as to whether any such matters should be put to the witness. Similarly, it was left to the sheriff to decide which witnesses should be precognosced[3]. During the eighteenth century, if not earlier, the duty of questioning the witnesses began to fall mainly upon the procurator fiscal, and the sheriff largely (though not exclusively) confined his task to dictating the precognitions to the sheriff clerk[4]. In due course the procurator fiscal sometimes took witness statements on his own behalf, which also became known as precognitions albeit that they had not been taken on oath before a sheriff, and this came to be regarded as the normal practice. Today precognitions on oath are only taken in exceptional instances[5].

Some time after the Circuit Courts (Scotland) Act 1709 (c 16) procurators fiscal began to present a petition[6] (known as an 'information and presentment') to the sheriff, with accompanying precognitions, in which they asked the sheriff to find that there was sufficient evidence to justify further proceedings and to transmit the case with the precognitions for such proceedings in the High Court of Justiciary. Until the nineteenth century procurators fiscal continued to present precognitions and the other evidence before the sheriff and sent the case to the Lord Advocate only after the sheriff had scrutinised them and decided to commit the accused for trial[7]. Towards the end of the nineteenth century, however, sheriffs gradually adopted the practice of committing the accused for trial 'on the procurator fiscal's responsibility' without examining the precognitions[8], and in due course this was adopted as the normal rule. Today precognitions are never shown to the sheriff, and indeed in most instances the procurator fiscal will rely on information he has been given by the police when he moves the sheriff to commit the accused for trial, only obtaining precognitions at some later stage before the case is sent to Crown counsel. In any event, under modern procedure committal for trial is not an essential prerequisite for further proceedings, and while the absence of committal will result in the release of an accused who is in custody, it does not affect the right of the Lord Advocate to indict him at a later stage[9].

1 Acts of 1398 (APS i, 573), 1438 (APS ii, 32 (c 2)) and 1449 (APS ii, 34 (c 8)).
2 J Irvine Smith 'Criminal Procedure' in *An Introduction to Scottish Legal History* (Stair Soc vol 20, 1958) pp 428, 429. See also Hume *Commentaries* II, 81.
3 It was also competent for the Lord Advocate to precognosce witnesses before a judge of the High Court of Justiciary or alternatively for such a judge to take the precognitions, but this practice seems to have died out towards the end of the seventeenth century: *Irvine Smith* pp 428, 429.
4 *The Third Report by the Commissioners of the Courts of Justice* (1818) lists fees payable to the procurator fiscal for 'attending' at and 'taking' precognitions and fees payable to sheriff clerks for 'writing' precognitions. See 1877 J Juris 250, where it is suggested that the practice began by the sheriff delegating the task of precognoscing 'unimportant cases' to the procurator fiscal. See also *Galbraith v Sawers* (1840) 3 D 52.
5 See *Low v MacNeill* 1981 SCCR 243 at 246, 247, Sh Ct. See also the rights given to the defence by the Criminal Justice (Scotland) Act 1980 (c 62), s 9 (citation of defence witness for precognition), and *Brady v Lockhart* 1985 SCCR 349.
6 For the style for this petition, see *Hume* II, 537.
7 1877 J Juris 321 refers to an undated letter from the Crown Agent to a procurator fiscal who had sent a case to the Lord Advocate before the sheriff had committed the accused for trial. The letter states that Crown counsel do not wish to know whether the fiscal considered it necessary to commit the accused, but rather whether the sheriff took this view. The letter continues, 'If the evidence is not laid before the sheriff with a view of his applying his mind to that question and of affording to Crown Counsel the benefit of his decision upon it, an irregularity has been committed'.
8 1877 J Juris 322. The author attributes this practice partly to financial reasons and partly because the precognitions required to be properly examined by Crown counsel before further proceedings could be taken at the instance of the Crown.
9 R W Renton and H H Brown *Criminal Procedure according to the Law of Scotland* (5th edn, 1983 by G H Gordon) para 5-70; *M'Vey v H M Advocate* 1911 SC (J) 94, 6 Adam 503; *Herron v A, B, C and D* 1977 SLT (Sh Ct) 24. See also *Low v MacNeill* 1981 SCCR 243 at 245, 247, Sh Ct, and *O'Reilly v HM Advocate* 1984 SCCR 352, 1985 SLT 99.

1.46. Judicial examination. Until the end of the nineteenth century, the accused was brought before the sheriff after his arrest and examined with regard to the facts of the case — indeed in this respect Scottish procedure tended to be inquisitorial rather than accusatorial[1]. The accused was not placed on oath, and the examination served various purposes. First, it gave the accused an opportunity to state his case and perhaps persuade the sheriff not to commit him. Secondly, it allowed the Crown to confront the accused with the evidence, discover in advance of the trial what the defence case was likely to be and possibly obtain a confession. Thirdly, since the accused could not give evidence at his trial prior to 1898[2], his judicial declaration was the only means whereby his statement could be introduced at the trial, even although it could only be used as evidence against him and not in his favour. In the course of the examination, the accused could be challenged with the various evidential factors incriminating him and asked for his reply. It therefore followed that the sheriff required a detailed knowledge of the other precognitions if he were to examine the accused properly. At the end of the preliminary examination the accused could be committed to prison for further examination, and thereafter he could be brought back before the sheriff for re-examination as often as the sheriff deemed necessary, perhaps as additional prosecution evidence came to light[3]. In theory the questions were put by the sheriff, but by the nineteenth century if not earlier it was the procurator fiscal who did so[4], and the sheriff's presence acted as a safeguard against unfair or oppressive questioning[5]. The exact nature of the examination may have varied at different periods of time and, according to a case decided in 1843, 'the examination should not turn into a long professional cross examination'[6].

For various reasons[7], judicial examination of this type declined towards the end of the nineteenth century and may now be regarded as largely obsolete[8]. In a case in 1887 it was said that the examination was to be held by and not merely before the sheriff and that the accused was entitled to refuse to answer questions at any time, thus bringing the examination to an end[9]. In the same year the Criminal Procedure (Scotland) Act 1887 gave the accused the right to a private interview with his solicitor before the examination and to have him present during it[10]. 'Judicial examination thereafter became increasingly a mere formality at which the accused acknowledged his name and said nothing further'[11]. The Criminal Evidence Act 1898 gave the accused the right to give evidence at his trial[12], and the declaration thus diminished in importance from the point of view of the accused. Finally, the Summary Jurisdiction (Scotland) Act 1908 made it competent to commit the accused for trial without taking a declaration from him if he intimated that he did not wish to make one[13]. For the prosecutor investigating the case and preparing for trial, the ending of this type of judicial examination meant that he had to change the emphasis of his investigation, and rather than concentrating on the accused with a view to ascertaining his defence or obtaining a confession, he now required to turn his attention to making a more extensive inquiry into his own case and hopefully preparing against any line of defence which he could now only surmise.

1 Prior to 1689 the accused could be — and sometimes was — examined under torture, especially in cases of witchcraft, but this practice ceased after the Claim of Right 1689 (c 28) and the Treason Act 1708 (c 21). See also J Irvine Smith 'Criminal Procedure' in *An Introduction to Scottish Legal History* (Stair Soc vol 20, 1958) p 429.
2 See the text and note 12 below.
3 If the accused was committed for further examination he could apply for bail, but if this was refused he had no right of appeal (which is still the position under current procedure: see the Criminal Procedure (Scotland) Act 1975 (c 21), ss 26(3), 27; R W Renton and H H Brown *Criminal Procedure according to the Law of Scotland* (3rd edn, 1983) para 5-75). For examples of the

procedure followed, see *HM Advocate v M'Leod* (1858) 3 Irv 79, and *HM Advocate v M'Lauchlan* (1862) 4 Irv 220.

4 The sheriff clerk wrote the actual declaration, if necessary, at the sheriff's dictation. *The Third Report of the Commissioners of the Courts of Justice* (1818) gives the fees then payable to the procurator fiscal for 'taking' declarations.

5 J H A Macdonald *The Criminal Law of Scotland* (3rd edn, 1894) p 265. However, any safeguard afforded by the presence of the sheriff may have been illusory rather than real: for example, in *Mackay* (1831) 3 SJ 302, Hume *Commentaries* II, Bell's Notes 242, it was held that the taking of a declaration was valid although the sheriff 'fell asleep at intervals'.

6 *HM Advocate v Kelly* (1843) 1 Broun 543.

7 For criticisms of the judicial examination procedure, see Hume *Commentaries* II, 325.

8 A modified form of judicial examination was reintroduced by the Criminal Justice (Scotland) Act 1980 (c 62), s 6: see paras 2.03, 2.06, below, and *The Operation of the Judicial Examination Procedure* (Scottish Office Central Unit Research Paper, 1986).

9 *HM Advocate v Brims* (1887) 1 White 462.

10 Criminal Procedure (Scotland) Act 1887 (c 35), s 17. See now the Criminal Procedure (Scotland) Act 1975, s 19, and para 3.16 below.

11 *Second Report by the Committee on Criminal Procedure in Scotland* (The Thompson Report) (Cmnd 6218) (1975) para 8.05.

12 Criminal Evidence Act 1898 (c 36), s 1. See now the Criminal Procedure (Scotland) Act 1975, ss 141–144.

13 Summary Jurisdiction (Scotland) Act 1908 (c 65), s 77(1). See now the Criminal Procedure (Scotland) Act 1975, s 20(1)–(3).

1.47. Police investigations. The modern police forces came into existence in the nineteenth century[1] against the background of a long established system of the investigation of crime by the sheriff and the procurator fiscal. Initially the principal function of the police in relation to criminal matters was restricted to keeping the peace and preventing crime. They were given no statutory power to investigate crime, and indeed some forces did not have a detective branch before 1939[2]. Even today the procurator fiscal retains the responsibility for investigating all criminal offences in his district, and the chief constable is required by statute to comply with any lawful instruction he receives from the procurator fiscal in relation to the investigation of crime[3]. In practice, however, all police forces now have a detective branch known as the Criminal Investigation Department which specialises in the investigation of crime and has a wide range of experts in all fields of crime detection. In addition to these resources, the volume of crime and the ease of access which the public has to the police have all resulted in the major burden of criminal investigations being moved from the procurator fiscal to the police. The role of the procurator fiscal is reserved to general supervision, and he will not normally become actively involved in any particular case until after the police have made the preliminary investigation and reported the case to him.[4] Thereafter it is the duty of the police 'to put before the procurator fiscal everything which may be relevant and material to the issue of whether the suspected party is innocent or guilty'[5]. Once the case is reported to him the procurator fiscal will decide on the basis of the police report whether or not he should prosecute the accused, he may instruct the police to make further inquiries, or he may make such inquiries himself[6]. If he decides upon the last course, or where he institutes proceedings which are likely to be prosecuted on indictment, the procurator fiscal will investigate the case further by precognoscing the witnesses and by calling upon the services of such experts and obtaining such further evidence as he considers necessary.

The growth of the investigative role of the police has thus brought about some change in the duties of the procurator fiscal in this area. Where the case is prosecuted on a summary complaint, it is unusual for the procurator fiscal to make further inquiries in person and he will normally rely on the police to make the pre-trial investigation. Even in more serious cases which the procurator fiscal is required to precognosce, he may occasionally treat certain statements taken by the police as if they were precognitions and will report the case to Crown counsel on that basis. In other instances he may also delegate to members of his staff (known as 'precognition officers'[7]) the task of precognoscing and investigating all or part of the case.

1 See para 1.43 above.
2 While the City of Glasgow Police claims that its first detective officer was appointed in 1819, he did not play an active role in criminal investigations. The Inspector of Constabulary for Scotland noted that it was only the 1939–45 war which encouraged some police forces to establish detective branches: P Gordon *Policing Scotland* (1980) p 24.
3 Police (Scotland) Act 1967 (c 77), s 17(3) proviso. The police are also subject to any instructions issued to them by the Lord Advocate with regard to the reporting of crimes for prosecution: Criminal Procedure (Scotland) Act 1975 (c 21), ss 9, 293.
4 This does not apply to cases investigated and reported by such government departments as the Customs and Excise and the Inland Revenue.
5 *Smith v HM Advocate* 1952 JC 66, 1952 SLT 286; *Stirling v Associated Newspapers Ltd* 1960 JC 5, 1960 SLT 5; *Hall v Associated Newspapers Ltd* 1979 JC 1, 1978 SLT 241. See also *Report of the Inquiry into the Murder of Mrs Rachel Ross* (The Hunter Report) (HC Paper (1981–82) no. 444).
6 The procurator fiscal will usually leave much of the subsequent inquiry to the police except in complex fraud, embezzlement or corruption cases or where it is considered preferable for some other reason that he should conduct the investigation in person.
7 Precognition officers have no legal qualifications.

1.48. Taking up dittay. In former times when the High Court of Justiciary went on circuit there was a pre-trial procedure known as 'taking up dittay' which did not apply when the court was sitting in Edinburgh[1]. Under this procedure, which can be traced to a statute of Alexander II (1214–1249)[2], the Justiciar ordered the head man and two or three other responsible persons in each town to make inquiries into all crimes which had recently been committed with a view to bringing the offenders before the next circuit court. The duty of making these inquiries soon passed to the sheriff, and it became the practice before the arrival of the circuit court in any particular town for the Justiciar to send a document known as a 'brieve of dittay' to the sheriff ordering him to summon the most reputable men in his sheriffdom before the justice clerk in order to give the justice clerk information regarding recent crimes, together with the evidence against the accused. On the basis of this information, the justice clerk compiled a listknown as the 'portuous roll and traistis' giving the names of the accused and the dittays or indictments libelled against them. The justice clerk thereafter arranged to bring the accused and the witnesses before the circuit court. Various amendments were later made to this procedure by statute. The Circuit Courts (Scotland) Act 1709 abolished the portuous roll, and in its place sheriffs were required to hold twice-yearly courts for the purpose of receiving information about crimes and thereafter to send abstracts of these crimes to the justice clerk forty days before the sitting of the circuit court[3]. This cumbrous procedure was finally abolished by the Circuit Courts (Scotland) Act 1828 which required all crimes to be brought to trial in the circuit courts in the same way as they were brought before the High Court of Justiciary in Edinburgh[4].

1 Likewise this procedure did not apply to sheriff and jury cases. For further details of this procedure, see Hume *Commentaries* II, 23; COURTS AND COMPETENCY, vol 6, para 853. The word 'dittay' is derived from the Old French *ditté* (Latin: *dictatum*).
2 APS i 403 (c 14).
3 Circuit Courts (Scotland) Act 1709 (c 16), ss 3, 4.
4 Circuit Courts (Scotland) Act 1828 (c 29), s 5. See generally J Irvine Smith 'Criminal Procedure' in *An Introduction to Scottish Legal History* (Stair Soc vol 20, 1958) pp 429, 430, and W C Dickinson 'The High Court of Justiciary' (Stair Soc vol 20) p 409.

(C) RIGHTS OF THE ACCUSED

1.49. General. In former times the accused was faced with a pre-trial procedure which was largely inquisitorial, a trial which might be fairly brief[1] and at which he had no right to give evidence before 1898[2], and, if convicted, a sentence which would be regarded as severe by modern standards. Scottish criminal procedure did, however, make some attempts to protect his rights.

1 See para 1.55 below.
2 See para 1.46 above.

1.50. Legal representation. By an Act of the Scots Parliament of 1587 the accused was given the right to be legally represented at his trial[1], although it seems he could only exercise that right if he was able to pay for the services of counsel. After the foundation of the High Court of Justiciary in 1672, the Faculty of Advocates took it upon itself as a public duty to provide free representation in the High Court for accused persons in indigent circumstances, although it was not until 1825 that a system known as the Poor's Roll was established giving poor persons the right to be represented free of charge by a solicitor in the sheriff court. This system later became subjected to some criticism in that while it ensured the accused was represented at his trial, there was no provision for detailed investigation and preparation of the defence case in advance of the trial[2]. Finally in 1964 a scheme of free legal aid was instituted for the preparation of the defence and the representation at the trial of all accused persons who were unable to meet this expenditure on their own behalf[3].

1 Parliament Act 1587 (c 16); Criminal Justice Act 1587 (c 57), on which a valuable commentary was made in *Graham v Cuthbert* 1951 JC 25, 1951 SLT 58. A system for providing free representation for poor litigants in civil cases was instituted by the Poor's Counsel Act 1424 (c 24).
2 See C N Stoddart *The Law and Practice of Legal Aid in Scotland* (2nd edn, 1985) para 1-12.
3 See the Legal Aid and Solicitors (Scotland) Act 1949 (c 63) (amended by the Criminal Justice (Scotland) Act 1963 (c 39), s 48, Sch 4). See now the Legal Aid (Scotland) Act 1986 (c 47), Pt I (ss 1–5), Pt IV (ss 21–25) and Pt VI (ss 29–46). Details of how the legal aid scheme is operated are to be found in *Stoddart*.

1.51. Bail. From the earliest times there has always been a system whereby an accused person awaiting trial could be released from custody on bail, which formerly meant that a sum of money was lodged as caution for his appearance at the trial. This procedure was necessitated by the fact that long delays, sometimes stretching to years, might elapse between the commission of the crime and the subsequent trial and because prison accommodation was either non-existent or unsuitable for the long and secure detention of prisoners. All crimes appear to have been bailable with the exception of treason and murder, bail for which required the special consent of the king, or later, of the Lord Advocate[1]. Following the Criminal Procedure Act 1700 (c 6) all crimes were bailable as a matter of right unless the crime was punishable by capital punishment, in which case the question of bail was left to the discretion of the High Court of Justiciary. That Act also imposed maximum sums of bail determinable in accordance with the accused's social position, thus preventing the ordering of exorbitant sums of bail. Some modification was made to the 1700 Act by the Criminal Procedure (Scotland) Act 1887 in relation to bail prior to committal[2], and the Act itself was replaced by the Bail (Scotland) Act 1888, which stated that all crimes except murder and treason were to be bailable[3] and that the grant or refusal of bail, and the amount of money (if bail were granted) were to be left to the discretion of the court[4]. The requirement for lodging sums of money for bail was abolished by

the Bail etc (Scotland) Act 1980[5], which, together with the Criminal Procedure
(Scotland) Act 1975[6], now regulates the conditions applicable to bail[7].

1 See the Murder Act 1471 (c3), the Crime Act 1540 (c38), the Murder Act 1555 (c4), and the
   King's Peace Act 1587 (c59). See also J Irvine Smith 'Criminal Procedure' in *An Introduction to
   Scottish Legal History* (Stair Soc vol 20, 1958) p 430.
2 Criminal Procedure (Scotland) Act 1887 (c35), s 18.
3 Bail (Scotland) Act 1888 (c36), s 2. Murder and treason are bailable at the discretion of the
   quorum of the High Court and the Lord Advocate: see R W Renton and H H Brown *Criminal
   Procedure according to the Law of Scotland* (5th edn, 1983) para 5-75.
4 Bail (Scotland) Act 1888, ss 2, 4.
5 Bail etc (Scotland) Act 1980 (c4), s 1(1).
6 Many of the relevant provisions scattered through the Criminal Procedure (Scotland) Act 1975
   (c21) were amended by the Bail etc (Scotland) Act 1980.
7 See paras 3.38 ff below.

1.52. Prevention of undue delay. One of the defects in Scottish criminal
procedure was the lack of any provision to prevent undue delay in bringing a
case to trial, especially where the accused was detained in custody[1]. This
omission was remedied by the Criminal Procedure Act 1700 (c6), which
allowed the accused to lodge a petition with the court calling upon the prosecutor to specify within the next sixty days when the diet of trial was to be held,
and if the prosecutor did not do so the accused was entitled to his release from
custody. His release did not, however, preclude a subsequent prosecution, but if
the accused was recommitted to prison on the same charge, the trial had to be
concluded within forty days, failing which the accused was released and was 'for
ever free' from further prosecution or punishment for that crime[2]. The provisions were modified by the Criminal Procedure (Scotland) Act 1887, which
enacted that an accused detained in custody for sixty days without an indictment
being served could give notice to the Lord Advocate requiring him to serve an
indictment within fourteen days or show cause to the High Court of Justiciary
why the accused should not be released[3]. Thereafter if the accused's period of
custody extended to eighty days (for example, if the High Court were satisfied
with the Lord Advocate's reasons for continuing the detention) and an indictment was served on him, then unless the trial was concluded within a period of
one hundred and ten days of his committal for trial, the accused was to be
forthwith 'set at liberty, and declared for ever free from all question or process
for the crime with which he was charged'[3]. Further changes to these rules were
implemented by the Criminal Procedure (Scotland) Act 1975 as amended by the
Criminal Justice (Scotland) Act 1980[4].

1 This was one of the grievances contained in the Claim of Right 1689 (c28).
2 See Hume *Commentaries* II,99 ff.
3 Criminal Procedure (Scotland) Act 1887 (c35), s 43.
4 Criminal Procedure (Scotland) Act 1975 (c21), s 101 (amended by the Criminal Justice (Scotland) Act 1980 (c62), s 14(1)).

1.53. Special defences. Under mediaeval procedure the accused could not
allege anything that directly contradicted the charge, on the ground that the
Crown witnesses, unlike the defence, never committed perjury[1]. Where the
accused's defence rested on insanity, alibi or self-defence the accused could
lodge a document known as a 'brieve' or 'precept of exculpation' which was
remitted to a preliminary hearing. If the defence was established, all further
proceedings were abandoned and the accused was usually given a pardon to
protect him against any action by the victim or his relatives. In the seventeenth
century the practice of holding preliminary hearings for this purpose ceased and
the accused was permitted to call witnesses at his trial in support of his defence[2].

While it is probable that the Crown would gain advance notice of such a defence when the accused was judicially examined, the Heritable Jurisdictions (Scotland) Act 1746 required the defence to give special notice of the defence on the day before the trial[3], and the Criminal Procedure (Scotland) Act 1887 stated that notice had to be given at the preliminary diet[4] which, until 1980 at least[5], was held at least nine days before the trial. The modern procedure is governed by the Criminal Procedure (Scotland) Act 1975[6].

1 See J Irvine Smith and Ian Macdonald 'Criminal Law' in *An Introduction to Scottish Legal History* (Stair Soc vol 20, 1958), and J Irvine Smith 'Criminal Procedure' (Stair Soc vol 20) pp 439, 440.
2 Courts Act 1672 (c 40). In the trial of *Macadam and Long* (1735) Hume II, 300, the Crown formally abandoned the preliminary trial procedure, but this merely recognised that the practice had fallen into disuse for some time. For a general discussion on special defences, see J *Irvine Smith* 439, 440; J Irvine Smith and Ian Macdonald 'Criminal Law' in Stair Soc vol 20, pp 292–296; and J Irvine Smith 'The Rise of Modern Scots Law' in Stair Soc vol 20, p 47.
3 Heritable Jurisdictions (Scotland) Act 1746 (c 43), s 41.
4 Criminal Procedure (Scotland) Act 1887 (c 35), s 36.
5 Preliminary diets were abolished by the Criminal Justice (Scotland) Act 1980 (c 62), s 12.
6 Criminal Procedure (Scotland) Act 1975 (c 21), ss 76, 82 (amended by the Criminal Justice (Scotland) Act 1980, ss 12, 13, Sch 4, paras 5, 10). See also paras 4.36–4.39 below.

1.54. Pardons. At one time the royal pardon (or 'remission' as it was sometimes called) was freely obtained both before and after conviction to allow an accused to escape the consequences of his crime 'in so far as these were exigible by the state'[1]. The pardon might be unconditional or might impose conditions such as banishment or forfeiture, and was usually only granted on making a payment (known as a 'composition') to the Crown, such payments being an important source of royal revenue.

A pardon did not absolve the accused from any action which the victim or his relatives might take to recover damages from him, and both statute and practice ensured that the rights of the victim were not adversely affected by a pardon[2]. Indeed, until the sixteenth century the civil aspect of a crime was almost as important as the criminal, and if the injured party and the offender agreed terms for compensation the victim might not be particularly interested in proceeding further with a criminal action, this being one of the reasons for the 1587 Act giving the Lord Advocate the right to prosecute even if 'the parties be silent or wald utherwayis privily agree'[3]. A fourteenth-century statute[4] enacted that a pardon would be null and void unless compensation were paid within a year and a day of the pardon being granted, and later statutes in the fifteenth and sixteenth centuries made the pardon conditional on the accused finding surety for compensation, failure to do so resulting in imposition of the original sentence[5]. In cases of homicide the accused could request a pardon only if he produced a document called 'letters of slaines' in which the next of kin of the victim stated that compensation had been paid, that they had forgiven the accused and that they concurred in the request for a pardon[6].

The frequency with which pardons were used, especially in the sixteenth and seventeenth centuries, meant that the royal pardon played a very important part in the administration of criminal justice, but the use of pardons in this way and for these purposes ceased at the beginning of the eighteenth century[7]. Today it remains part of the royal prerogative and is occasionally exercised when there is no other remedy for rectifying a miscarriage of justice.

1 See further J Irvine Smith and Ian Macdonald 'Criminal Law' in *An Introduction to Scottish Legal History* (Stair Soc vol 20, 1958) pp 297 ff; R Black 'A Historical Survey of Delictual Liability in Scotland for Personal Injuries and Death; Part I' (1975) 8 Comparative and International Law Journal of South Africa 46 at 58, 59, 65–70; C H W Gane 'The Effect of a Pardon in Scots Law' 1980 JR 18.

2 The victim could raise actions of assythment or spuilzie, depending on whether the damage arose from personal injury or other loss. In the nineteenth century both actions were in practice absorbed into the civil law of reparation. The action of assythment was formally abolished by the Damages (Scotland) Act 1976 (c 13), s 8. For the history of the action, see *Black* 52–70. Within the past few years a practice has evolved whereby a procurator fiscal in the exercise of his discretion may suggest to an accused person that if he pays suitable compensation to the victim no criminal proceedings will be taken. It is understood that this practice is confined to minor criminal cases. With regard to the court's powers to award compensation to the victim after the accused has been convicted, see paras 7.16, 7.20, below.

3 Jurors Act 1587 (c 54); para 1.27 above.

4 APS i, 499 (c 44), passed during the reign of David I (1329–1370).

5 See eg the Remissions Acts 1584 (c 12), 1592 (c 67) and 1593 (c 16).

6 See *Black* pp 58–60.

7 Another similar measure which was not so commonly used and which has also fallen into desuetude is the writ or precept of respite, whereby the king prohibited further proceedings in a criminal action: see *Irvine Smith and Macdonald* pp 298, 299. Pardon should not be confused with statutes (usually referred to as 'Acts of Indemnity') which gave an amnesty from prosecution to certain offenders after a period of rebellion or the like: *Irvine Smith and Macdonald* p 299; *Black* p 58.

(D) SOLEMN TRIAL PROCEDURE

1.55. Length of trial. Apart from a period lasting approximately from 1587 to 1746 jury trials tended to be of relatively short duration until the beginning of the twentieth century. For example, when the Justice Ayre went on circuit to Jedburgh in 1493 it disposed of 193 cases in six days, and in 1847 a Glasgow sitting of the High Court dealt with ninety-six cases (of which fifty-three went to trial) in nine days. By modern standards many of these cases were neither serious nor complex since, until the middle of the nineteenth century, only very trivial cases were tried by way of summary procedure[1]. The main reason for the business being conducted with such dispatch was, however, procedural. Prior to 1587 the accused was not required to be present throughout the trial[2], he was not entitled to legal representation[3], and while witnesses were called to give evidence, it sufficed if they merely assented to the precognitions which they had previously given[4]. Even when these rules were reversed by statute in 1587[5], the prolongation of jury trials which followed was due mainly to the style of indictment which permitted the accused, now represented by counsel, to engage in a lengthy debate in which technical objections could be taken to its relevancy[6]. This practice ceased when the Heritable Jurisdictions (Scotland) Act 1746 provided that the charge should be remitted to the jury only after the court had issued a preliminary interlocutor dismissing the plea to the relevancy, and that if the plea were sustained the proceedings came to a halt without the case coming before a jury[7]. After 1746 jury trials reverted to being of shorter length as many of the other procedural rules (some of which went back beyond 1587) were not altered until later.

1 Alison *Practice* (1833) pp 56, 57, states that theft in excess of £10, theft by housebreaking and assault resulting in the fracture of a bone all seem to require a jury. See also COURTS AND COMPETENCY, vol 6, para 858, and J Irvine Smith 'Criminal Procedure' in *An Introduction to Scottish Legal History* (Stair Soc vol 20, 1958) p 437.

2 See para 1.42 above.

3 See para 1.50 above.

4 See para 1.45 above.

5 Criminal Justice Act 1587 (c 57).

6 See *Irvine Smith* pp 438, 439, and para 1.59 below.

7 Heritable Jurisdictions (Scotland) Act 1746 (c 43), s 41. Lengthy pre-trial debates ended when the style of the indictment was simplified by the Criminal Procedure (Scotland) Act 1887 (c 35), ss 2, 4–15, Sch A.

1.56. Evidence and procedure. When the case was called and the accused wished to plead guilty, it was still necessary to proceed to a formal trial at which a jury was empanelled, the accused pleaded guilty and the jury thereafter returned a verdict of guilty, until this procedure was altered by the Circuit Courts (Scotland) Act 1828, which dispensed with the need for a jury in such cases[1]. If the accused pleaded not guilty, the onus of proving the charge lay upon the prosecution, but since the accused would have been previously questioned at length and confronted with the Crown evidence at his judicial examination, the Crown case could be based on a self-incriminating declaration by the accused with minimal corroboration[2]. Where alternatively the Crown relied on the oral evidence of witnesses, it required to produce corroborated evidence implicating the accused as the person who had committed the crime (in accordance with the rule *unus testis nullus testis*), but the number of witnesses whose evidence was admissible before the court was greatly reduced by rules which formerly disqualified certain persons such as relatives, convicted criminals and others from giving evidence[3]. Moreover, while the accused had the right to question the Crown witnesses, it was long held that he could not challenge their evidence on the ground that the Crown witnesses, unlike those for the defence, never committed perjury[4]. At the close of the Crown case, the accused could not give evidence on his own behalf prior to 1898[5], and although after the seventeenth century he could lead witnesses in support of a special defence such as alibi or self-defence, prior to that period a defence of this nature was decided at a preliminary hearing before the commencement of the jury trial[6].

1　Circuit Courts (Scotland) Act 1828 (c 29), s 14.
2　This practice ceased in the late nineteenth century: see para 1.46 above.
3　At one time women were precluded from giving evidence: see Hume *Commentaries* II, 339. For the full list of persons ineligible to give evidence, see *Hume* II, 339–377. 'After being sworn the witness has next to purge himself of the suspicion of malice and ill will to the pannel ... of all receipt or promise of good deed or reward for his evidence — and of all instruction how to depone': *Hume* II, 377. This was known as 'purging of malice and partial counsel'.
4　See para 1.53 above.
5　Criminal Evidence Act 1898 (c 36), s 1: para 1.46 above.
6　See para 1.53 above.

1.57. Speeches and charge to the jury. At the conclusion of all the evidence the prosecution and defence were entitled to address the jury, the defence having the last word[1], but, according to Alison, writing in 1833,

'As the pressure of business increases, the necessity of expedition and dispatch is more strongly felt by all parties: confessions[2] take place by advice of counsel in cases where resistance is hopeless, or is likely to render the pannel's case worse than it appears on the indictment; speeches are dispensed with on both sides, in those instances where nothing can be said against the evidence; and the weight of pleading and legal ability reserved for those more doubtful cases, where it is really called for by the interests of justice, and where it often interferes with decisive effect in favour of the innocent prisoner'[3].

Until the middle of the eighteenth century it does not seem to have been the practice of the judge to charge (that is, address) the jury after the prosecution and defence had been given an opportunity to do so — albeit that the judge's charge is an important part of the modern jury trial and it is now a common ground of appeal that the judge has misdirected the jury. In the case of *Katherine Nairn and Patrick Ogilvie*[4] who were convicted of murder in the High Court of Justiciary in 1765, Lord Kames, one of the judges, addressed the jury 'upon the whole case' after defence counsel had done so. After the jury returned a verdict of guilty, the defence entered a plea that judgment should be arrested on various grounds, one of which was that the address by Lord Kames had contravened the right of the defence to speak last in accordance with the Courts Act 1672. This ground and the others were dismissed 'in respect of the regularity and accuracy' with which the trial had been conducted. The right of the judge to charge the jury was subsequently given statutory recognition[5].

1 Courts Act 1672 (c 40): see now the Criminal Procedure (Scotland) Act 1975 (c 21), s 152, and para 6.29 below.
2 Ie pleas of guilty.
3 Alison *Practice* p 371. See also Sheriff D B Smith 'A Respectable Infusion of Dignified Crime' 1978 JR 1.
4 W Roughead *Twelve Scots Trials* (1913).
5 Justiciary and Circuit Courts (Scotland) Act 1783 (c 45), s 5.

1.58. Adjournments. After 1587 and until the middle of the nineteenth century, the trial was not adjourned for any purpose after the jury had been sworn, unless it was too difficult to hear all the evidence at one diet and if both parties in such circumstances consented to an adjournment[1]. As a result it was not unknown for the court to sit continuously for periods of over forty hours — for example in the case of *Katherine Nairn and Patrick Ogilvie*[2] the jury was empanelled at 7 am on Monday 12 August and the trial continued for forty-three consecutive hours without an adjournment or interruption until the jury retired at 2 am on Wednesday 14 August. The Lord Justice-Clerk and five other judges presided at that trial; the prosecution was conducted by the Lord Advocate, the Solicitor General and three other advocates; and each of the accused was represented by two advocates. Provided at least one counsel remained present for each party, it appears that it was not regarded as necessary for the others to remain in court throughout the entire period and there is a passing reference to the fact that at least one of them 'went out for a little air' from time to time. In all probability counsel would take it in turns to leave the court in protracted trials of this nature. The narrative of the *Nairn* case also reveals that the jury 'repeatedly dispersed into different corners of the house, eating and drinking as they pleased and talking to the Crown witnesses and the counsel for the prosecution' and that 'between three and five o'clock on Tuesday morning only one of the judges remained upon the bench, the rest retiring and conversing in private with sundry of the jury and others'. The court later repelled a defence plea that such behaviour was 'irregular'.

1 After the mid-nineteenth century, when it became the practice to adjourn the court and restrict its sitting to more reasonable hours, the jury required to be kept in seclusion until the Criminal Procedure (Scotland) Act 1887 (c 35), s 55, rendered this unnecessary in all but capital cases. See now the Criminal Procedure (Scotland) Act 1975 (c 21), s 153.
2 W Roughead *Twelve Scots Trials* (1913).

1.59. Verdicts. Until the seventeenth century the indictment was framed in fairly simple terms and the jury was merely asked to return a verdict of guilty (otherwise known as 'fylet', 'convickit' or culpable) or not guilty (sometimes recorded as 'clengit', 'free' or 'innocent'). In the second half of the seventeenth century it became the practice to draft indictments (or bills of criminal letters) in a complex and formal style where any minor error in form might result in the indictment being dismissed[1]. The indictment was written as a syllogism or logical argument in which the first part (known as the 'major premise') stated the name of the crime and that it was punishable by law; the second part (known as the 'minor premise') averred that the accused was guilty of the crime and narrated the evidence supporting the averment; the third part (or conclusion) said that if the accused was convicted, he should be punished.

Between 1660 and 1688, juries sometimes refused to convict persons prosecuted under certain unpopular statutes, and as a consequence a rule was introduced at the instigation of the Lord Advocate that 'in no case whatever, the jury had a right to exercise their judgment upon any point, except the evidence relating to the different facts charged in the indictment'[2] — in other words, the jury's function was restricted to assessing the evidence with a view to finding whether the facts libelled in the second part of the indictment had been proven (proved) or were not proven (not proved).

If the jury found the facts proven, the court then had the responsibility of disposing of the case in terms of the conclusion; if the jury held that the averments were not proven, the case came to an end. This practice continued until the case of *Samuel Hale and Carnegie of Finhaven* in 1728[3] when the jury, at the behest of the defence, reasserted its former power and returned a verdict of not guilty.

Since 1728 the jury has had a choice of verdicts, namely guilty, not guilty or not proven. It can be argued that a verdict of not proven leaves some stigma against the accused, or that strictly speaking it is appropriate only where there is some evidence against the accused although not enough to convict him (for example where the jury accepts the evidence of one Crown witness but finds that there is not sufficient reliable corroborative evidence)[4]. Modern judges do not, however, seek to distinguish between a verdict of not guilty and one of not proven when directing the jury, and either verdict results in the acquittal of the accused, who has no right of appeal against a not proven verdict.

1 This style was abolished by the Criminal Procedure (Scotland) Act 1887 (c 35), ss 2, 4–15, Sch A: see para 1.55 above.

2 J Irvine Smith 'Criminal Procedure' in *An Introduction to Scottish Legal History* (Stair Soc vol 20, 1958) p 442.

3 *Samuel Hale and Carnegie of Finhaven* (1728) Hume *Commentaries* II, 440.

4 See T B Smith *A Short Commentary on the Law of Scotland* (1962) p 227, and *Second Report by the Committee on Criminal Procedure in Scotland* (The Thompson Report) (Cmnd 6218) (1975) paras 51.02–51.05.

(E) SUMMARY PROCEDURE

1.60. Trial without jury in inferior courts. Apart from the High Court of Justiciary, it is clear from the earliest times that the other Scottish courts had an inherent power to punish minor offences in a summary way, reserving trial by jury for the more serious crimes. Little is known about the early forms of summary procedure[1]. In due course the procedure for the most trivial offences became akin to that of the civil procedure at the time. For slightly more serious cases there was a trial at which evidence was led, but until the eighteenth century, if the penalty for the offence was restricted to a fine, the issue could be resolved by means of an oath of verity by the accused who was placed on oath, and if he thereafter simply denied his guilt, this was regarded as conclusive and rendered all other evidence incompetent. Summary procedure in its modern form was not introduced until the nineteenth century. Some statutory provisions were contained in the Circuit Courts (Scotland) Act 1828[2], but a more important legislative measure was the Summary Procedure (Scotland) Act 1864[3]. Unfortunately separate procedural rules were later introduced by the Burgh Police (Scotland) Act 1892[4], and yet others were to be found in some of the local Police Acts for the large cities. This situation was remedied by the Summary Jurisdiction (Scotland) Act 1908 (c 65), which introduced uniform procedure for all summary courts. The 1908 Act was in turn superseded by various statutes in the twentieth century and the rules for summary procedure are now largely contained in the Criminal Procedure (Scotland) Act 1975[5].

1 Accounts of nineteenth-century summary procedure may be found in H J Moncrieff *The Law of Review in Criminal Cases* (1877) and J H A Macdonald *The Criminal Law of Scotland* (3rd edn, 1894) pp 515–530. See also COURTS AND COMPETENCY, vol 6, para 1058.
2 See the Circuit Courts (Scotland) Act 1828 (c 29), ss 18–20.
3 The Summary Procedure (Scotland) Act 1864 (c 53) provided for uniformity of process in summary criminal prosecutions and prosecutions for penalties in the inferior courts in Scotland.
4 See the Burgh Police (Scotland) Act 1892 (c 55), especially ss 477–516.
5 Criminal Procedure (Scotland) Act 1975 (c 21), Pt II (ss 283–457).

(F) SENTENCE

1.61. Penalties. Apart from detecting, apprehending and convicting the person who has committed a criminal act, in former times the rules of criminal procedure were framed mainly with a view to ensuring that the criminal paid compensation to the victim[1], and perhaps thereafter ridding the community of his presence (by banishment, transportation or death[2]), or to punishing him in such a way that he, or others tempted to commit crime, would be deterred from further offending. Indeed the old form of indictment concluded with the words that if the accused were convicted he 'ought to be punished with the pains of law to deter others from committing the like crimes in all times coming', and although such words are no longer required, they are still implied in all indictments[3]. While it was generally accepted that the king's peace should be preserved, little thought was given to the reformation or rehabilitation of the criminal until such concepts began to take root in the nineteenth century.

1 From this aim arose the frequent use of pardons: see para 1.54 above.
2 There were various forms of death penalty, including burning or strangling at the stake, drowning, beheading and hanging, the last mentioned being the most usual after the end of the seventeenth century. For further details of forms of sentences, see J Irvine Smith 'Criminal Procedure' in *An Introduction to Scottish Legal History* (Stair Soc vol 20, 1958) pp 444 ff, and J Cameron *Prisons and Punishment in Scotland* (1983).
3 See the Criminal Procedure (Scotland) Act 1887 (c 35), s 20, now the Criminal Procedure (Scotland) Act 1975 (c 21), s 47, and para 7.10 below.

1.62. Capital and non-capital punishment. Until 1834 there were almost fifty capital crimes in Scotland (as opposed to three hundred in England), but in that year and the years which followed the number was reduced by statute[1] and by practice and eventually the death penalty was restricted to cases of murder, attempted murder and treason[2]. The death penalty for murder was further restricted by the Homicide Act 1957[3] and finally abolished by the Murder (Abolition of Death Penalty) Act 1965[4]. Today, treason remains as the only capital crime in Scotland[5]. Banishment from Scotland or from a particular district was abolished by the Criminal Law (Scotland) Act 1830[6] and transportation beyond the seas was replaced by penal servitude by the Penal Servitude Act 1857[7]. At one time corporal punishment could be imposed. It took various forms including whipping, dismembering the hand, removing or boring the tongue, nailing the ear to the gallows, branding on the cheek or forehead, shaving the head, and exposure in the pillory or stocks[8]. All of these punishments gradually disappeared in the eighteenth century, although the birching of children under the age of fourteen was not finally abolished until the Criminal Justice Act 1948[9].

1 See the Forgery, Abolition of Punishment of Death Act 1832 (c 123), the Transportation Act 1834 (c 67), and the Capital Punishment Abolition Act 1835 (c 81).
2 Criminal Procedure (Scotland) Act 1887 (c 35), s 56.
3 Homicide Act 1957 (c 11), Pt IV (ss 13–15).

4 Murder (Abolition of Death Penalty) Act 1965 (c 71), s 1.
5 The death penalty for treason is inflicted by hanging. The former penalty of hanging, drawing
  and quartering was abolished by the Criminal Justice (Scotland) Act 1949 (c 94), s 14.
6 Criminal Law (Scotland) Act 1830 (c 37), s 10.
7 Penal Servitude Act 1857 (c 3), s 2.
8 See J Irvine Smith 'Criminal Procedure' in *An Introduction to Scottish Legal History* (Stair Soc
  vol 20, 1958) p 446, and J Cameron *Prisons and Punishment in Scotland* (1983) ch 1.
9 Criminal Justice Act 1948 (c 58), s 2.

1.63. Custodial and non-custodial penalties. In the nineteenth century, while sentencing retained its general purpose of deterrence, punishment and protecting society from the criminal, greater consideration was given to reforming him from his delinquent way of life. Prisons were built, and apart from minor offenders who were fined, the normal sentence was penal servitude or imprisonment. The former was introduced by the Penal Servitude Acts of 1853 and 1857[1] and had a minimum term of three years and a maximum of life. The prisoner was detained under a strict disciplined regime with hard work (in order to teach him the error of his ways), but as this rehabilitative element did not seem to meet with success, penal servitude was abolished by the Criminal Justice (Scotland) Act 1949 and replaced with imprisonment[2] for which the maximum sentence is now life. Until 1949 imprisonment had been regarded as a punishment for lesser crimes. In the eighteenth century few sentences exceeded twelve months, and prior to 1949 the maximum sentence could not normally exceed two years[3]. In addition the court had a discretion to impose a condition of hard labour, but this fell into disuse at the beginning of the twentieth century and was formally abolished by the 1949 Act[4]. The same Act and the Prisons (Scotland) Act 1952 also made provision for the remission of up to one-third of the sentence imposed by the court on any offender 'on the ground of his industry and good conduct' while the sentence is being served[5]. Furthermore, under the Criminal Justice Act 1967, the Parole Board may recommend the release on licence of any prisoner who has completed at least one-third of his sentence or a specified period, whichever is the longer[6]. The principle of rehabilitation was given further impetus in the twentieth century when courts began to defer sentence on an offender, with or without conditions as to his behaviour in the interim[7]; with the introduction of probation in 1907 whereby the accused was placed under the supervision and guidance of a probation officer[8]; and in 1978 when the courts were empowered to order an offender to undertake a number of hours of unpaid work known as 'community service'[9].

1 Penal Servitude Act 1853 (c 99), ss 2–4; Penal Servitude Act 1857 (c 3), ss 1, 2.
2 Criminal Justice (Scotland) Act 1949 (c 94), s 16(1).
3 Penal Servitude Act 1891 (c 69), s 1.
4 Criminal Justice (Scotland) Act 1949, s 16(2).
5 Ibid, s 56; Prisons (Scotland) Act 1952 (c 61), s 20.
6 Criminal Justice Act 1967 (c 80), s 60(1) (amended by the Criminal Justice Act 1972 (c 71),
  ss 35(1), 66(7)).
7 See para 7.20 below.
8 Probation of Offenders Act 1907 (c 17).
9 Community Service by Offenders (Scotland) Act 1978 (c 49). A similar form of sentence was not
  unknown in the mediaeval burgh courts: see para 1.18 above.

2. GENERAL PRINCIPLES

(a) Introduction

2.01. Accusatorial system. The modern Scottish system of criminal procedure is described as an accusatorial one as opposed to an inquisitorial system such as exists in European civil law jurisdictions such as France, Italy and elsewhere. The accusatorial system is, however, the one used most widely throughout the world from countries as diverse as the United States of America to the Union of Soviet Socialist Republics, involving as it does two sides presenting relevant evidence for the interpretation or judgment by the judge or by a judge and jury. The inquisitorial system on the other hand is one where an examining magistrate or judge makes inquiries into the facts before an accused is formally charged. Though the accusatorial system is the basis of our criminal prosecution system in Scotland, it was not always so[1], and in the past sheriffs in particular carried out some pre-trial inquiries. Traces of this inquisitorial system have not been completely excised in Scottish procedure, particularly when one considers judicial examination in cases on petition[2]. The accuser in Scotland is the Crown in the great majority of cases, albeit rarely other bodies may prosecute or have rights to prosecute[3]. In the High Court of Justiciary such prosecutions are taken on behalf of the Crown by one of the two Law Officers, namely the Lord Advocate or the Solicitor General, or one of the Advocates Depute[4], and in the lower courts by the procurator fiscal[5].

1 See para 1.44 above.
2 See paras 4.06 ff below.
3 See paras 2.22 ff below.
4 See para 2.16 below.
5 See para 2.18 below.

2.02. Burden and standard of proof. The fundamental principle of Scottish criminal procedure is that the onus of proof rests upon the prosecutor since an accused person is presumed to be innocent of the crime alleged until a case is established against him. The accused need take no step to establish his innocence even when he has lodged a special defence[1]. The prosecutor must establish his guilt; thus the onus or burden of proof is upon the prosecutor to prove the crime.

To establish the case against the accused the prosecutor must prove the necessary facts to found that case, and those facts must be believed by the court beyond reasonable doubt. This requirement is perhaps difficult to understand but if taken in context of a criminal trial may be more readily understood. Criminal acts are but a part of human behaviour which in turn is not controlled by mathematical principles or scientific formulae. It is not possible to be mathematically certain beyond any doubt whatsoever of facts that require to be proved to establish that a crime has been committed. To seek such would result in an inability to prosecute and convict any accused, with the resulting decay of society into anarchy. On the other hand a person's innocence, being a matter of such fundamental importance, should not be lightly taken away, and thus the facts have to be established to the high extent of being proved beyond reasonable doubt, rather than any doubt. It is to be noted and contrasted with the position in civil law where a lower extent of proof is involved, namely requiring to establish the case only on the balance of probability[2].

1 See paras 4.36 ff below.
2 See generally A B Wilkinson *The Scottish Law of Evidence* (1986) pp 211, 212.

2.03. Corroboration. Scottish criminal procedure requires that the essential facts to establish the case against the accused person be based on corroborated evidence, that is that the evidence relating to each and every essential fact is derived from more than one source[1]. The rule applies not only to the facts constituting the crime but equally importantly to the identification of the accused person as the perpetrator of that crime. By this requirement of corroboration an attempt is made to prevent conviction by biased evidence or even by a simple mistake by a witness. A single lying witness or a single mistaken witness would not provide the necessary two sources to corroborate the essential facts. Similarly, using the same conceptual argument it can be seen why it requires more than the simple confession of an accused person to convict him of that crime[2] because such an admission would emanate from only one source, the accused himself. In a case where there is an admission of the crime the prosecutor still requires to seek corroboration from some other source that the accused committed the crime as libelled before he can secure a conviction.

However, Scottish criminal procedure does not require all facts to be established by corroborated evidence, but only the essential facts. For example, simple procedural matters do not require corroborated evidence to support them[3]. Furthermore, the quality of the evidence required to corroborate and thereby establish any particular fact will vary depending upon the quality of the other source involved in establishing that particular fact. A helpful analogy perhaps can be drawn if one considers each piece of evidence as being strands in a rope ultimately to support or not the case brought by the prosecutor[4].

1 A B Wilkinson *The Scottish Law of Evidence* (1986) pp 203–208.
2 R W Renton and H H Brown *Criminal Procedure according to the Law of Scotland* (5th edn, 1983 by G H Gordon) paras 18-59, 18-60.
3 *Lees v Macdonald* (1893) 20 R (J) 55, 3 White 468; *MacLeod v Nicol* 1970 JC 58, 1970 SLT 304. In addition, certain statutory offences do not require proof by corroborated evidence, eg certain road traffic offences: see the Road Traffic Offenders Act 1988 (c 53), s 21.
4 See A G Walker and N M L Walker *The Law of Evidence in Scotland* (1964) p 9.

2.04. Competency and relevancy of evidence. Before evidence can be admitted to probation it has to be both competent and relevant. Whether evidence is competent or not principally depends on how it was obtained, with the rule that is used being the balance of fairness, that balance being between the prosecutor on the one hand and the rights of the accused on the other. Because it is a balance, as society develops and changes so will the factors and the weight given to those factors change in either of the balances. Torture is no longer an acceptable method of obtaining evidence in Scots law, albeit evidence so obtained was perfectly admissible in the sixteenth century. Many factors are thrown into the balance including the nature of the crime alleged, the capability or otherwise of the accused person, with different requirements for example for children as opposed to adults, the nature of the investigator, the need or otherwise for speed to avoid the destruction or possible destruction of evidence etc. At the end of the day the ruling question is, was the evidence fairly obtained, balancing the rights of the Crown to investigate and bring criminals to justice, and the rights of an accused individual facing the power of the Crown[1]?

However, evidence may be fairly obtained and yet still inadmissible in that it is not relevant. Also, it must relate specifically and directly to the allegations of the specific crime with which the accused person is charged. It is not, for example, relevant that an accused person has previous convictions which may even be analogous to the charge in question when the inquiry is whether or not that person has committed this particular crime[2].

1 A B Wilkinson *The Scottish Law of Evidence* (1986) pp 118–122.
2 *Wilkinson* pp 11–32. See also the Criminal Procedure (Scotland) Act 1975 (c 21), ss 141, 346.

2.05. Oral testimony. Another principle of Scottish criminal procedure is that the evidence in question has to be given orally in the witness box by the witness giving his evidence on oath. With certain statutory exceptions[1] there is no provision in Scottish criminal procedure for evidence to be given by way of written statement or depositions by witnesses. A very limited exception permits the evidence of a witness to be taken on commission where that witness resides outwith the United Kingdom, the Channel Islands or the Isle of Man, or is too ill or infirm to attend the trial[2]. Even this limited exception is itself further limited by the requirement that there should be no unfairness to the other party by the receiving of evidence in this form[3]. In practice, however, not all evidence is given orally, and evidence may be given by way of lodging a minute of admission of the facts stated therein, or a joint minute admitting the facts by the prosecutor and the accused, but only where the accused person is legally represented[4].

1 See eg the Criminal Justice (Scotland) Act 1980 (c 62), s 26, Sch 1 (amended by the Criminal Justice (Scotland) Act 1987 (c 41), s 70(1), Sch 1, para 18) (evidence of routine matters by certificate).
2 Criminal Justice (Scotland) Act 1980, s 32(1) (amended by the Criminal Justice (Scotland) Act 1987, s 61(2)).
3 Criminal Justice (Scotland) Act 1980, s 32(2)(b).
4 Criminal Procedure (Scotland) Act 1975 (c 21), ss 150, 354: see paras 6.24, 6.47, below.

2.06. Prescription of crime. As regards the prescription of crime, it is necessary to differentiate between common law crimes and statutory crimes. There is no common law rule or statute of limitation or similar legislation operating in Scotland barring the prosecution, after a given period, of a crime against the common law[1]. Thus in theory an accused person could be charged many years after the event with the commission of a crime against the common law of Scotland. The limitation here and protection of an accused person would be by invocation of a preliminary plea of *mora*, taciturnity and delay[2]. An effective prescription also occurs one year after an accused person has been placed on petition charging him with that common law crime[3], but in that case the time limit does not start until the accused person has been first committed in terms of that petition, which event could occur some considerable time after the commission of the crime.

As far as statutory crimes are concerned a difference has to be drawn between solemn procedure and summary procedure. There is no general rule prescribing time limits within which a prosecution for a statutory offence must be brought when the case is held under solemn procedure, that is before a judge and jury. On summary procedure, however, there is a general rule which prohibits the prosecutor from instituting proceedings more than six months after the commission of the statutory offence[4]. That, however, is only a general rule, and specific statutes may either increase[5] or reduce[6] that period. Although there is no general rule in solemn procedure equivalent to that in summary procedure, the specific statute invoked may itself contain a limitation or prescription of the crime[7].

Albeit these statutory prescriptions may prohibit the prosecutor from bringing a prosecution in terms of the specific statute, it may be that the prosecutor could bring an analogous charge under the common law. For example, there are many offences under statute relating to obtaining money by false pretences from various government departments, which offences have statutory time limits attached to them. There is no prescription, however, on a common law charge of fraud which could be framed to meet the same circumstances as contained in these statutory charges.

1 *Sugden v HM Advocate* 1934 JC 103, 1934 SLT 465.
2 See paras 4.52, 5.01, below. See also *Tudhope v McCarthy* 1985 SCCR 76, 1985 SLT 392, and *Philips v Tudhope* 1987 SCCR 80.
3 See para 4.23 below. The rule does not apply where a case originally brought on petition has been reduced to summary proceedings: *MacDougall v Russell* 1985 SCCR 441, 1986 SLT 403.
4 Criminal Procedure (Scotland) Act 1975 (c 21), s 331.
5 See eg the Customs and Excise Management Act 1979 (c 2), s 147(1) (three years), and the Social Security Act 1986 (c 50), s 56(2) (one year).
6 Eg where a sample has been obtained a prosecution must be initiated within two months under the Food and Drugs (Scotland) Act 1956 (c 30), s 41(3).
7 See eg the Customs and Excise Management Act 1979, s 147(1) (three years).

(b) Constitution and Powers of Criminal Courts

(A) THE HIGH COURT OF JUSTICIARY

2.07. Composition and territorial jurisdiction. The High Court of Justiciary is the supreme criminal court in Scotland while sitting in its appellate capacity[1]. No appeal lies from the High Court of Justiciary to the House of Lords[2], and decisions of the House of Lords in matters criminal are not binding upon the Scottish courts. The High Court of Justiciary is a collegiate court; no one judge outranks another within it and the decision of any one judge is not binding upon any of his brethren[3]. The High Court of Justiciary is the highest criminal court in Scotland dealing exclusively with criminal cases. The judges of the High Court are also the judges in the Court of Session, which is the equivalent court dealing with civil matters in Scotland. There are at present twenty-four judges[4], consisting of the Lord Justice-General, the Lord Justice-Clerk and twenty-two Lords Commissioners of Justiciary, one of whom is permanently seconded to the Scottish Law Commission as its chairman. The Lord Justice-General has important constitutional and administrative functions but has no overriding authority over the other judges and cannot overrule their decisions. The High Court sits in Edinburgh and in its capacity as a trial court also goes on circuit to the other principal towns of Scotland as required. The High Court, unlike the lower criminal courts, has no restriction on its territorial jurisdiction, having universal jurisdiction throughout Scotland. It can try at any place at which it is holding a sitting a crime that occurred anywhere in Scotland[5]. It is sometimes necessary to take cases from one part of Scotland to be heard before a High Court sitting in a far removed and different part of Scotland, usually to accommodate that trial within the terms of the limitations of time for keeping an accused person in custody[6].

1 See COURTS AND COMPETENCY, vol 6, paras 860, 861.

2 Criminal Procedure (Scotland) Act 1975 (c 21), ss 262, 281.
3 See SOURCES OF LAW (FORMAL), vol 22, paras 305–312, and especially para 312.
4 Court of Session Act 1988 (c 36), s 1(1).
5 Criminal Procedure (Scotland) Act 1975, s 112 (substituted by the Criminal Justice (Scotland) Act 1987 (c 41), s 57(1)).
6 As to these limitations, see paras 4.20 ff below.

2.08. Procedure and jurisdiction as to subject matter and sentence. All trials in the High Court of Justiciary are before a jury of fifteen persons and a single judge. On occasion more than one judge, normally either two or three, may sit in a case with the jury to decide an important or complex case at first instance[1]. This provision is rarely used, and is not to be confused with the situation where the judges are sitting in their appellate role[2].

The High Court has exclusive jurisdiction to deal with the crimes of treason, murder, rape, deforcement of messengers and breach of duty by magistrates[3]. In addition it can competently try any common law or statutory offence save those in which its jurisdiction has by statute been expressly (or by necessary implication) excluded. In practice it hears cases where in the opinion of the prosecutor, either because of the gravity of the crime or the previous convictions or history of the accused, a sentence in excess of three years' imprisonment would be merited[4].

In common law cases the High Court has unlimited power of sentence with no limit to the monetary penalties it can impose either by way of fine or compensation by offenders, and also no limit to the length of imprisonment that it can impose on convicted persons[5]. Its powers of imprisonment may be limited by statute when it is dealing with a statutory offence, depending upon the particular terms of the statute concerned.

1 Two or more judges may preside for the whole or any part of the trial in cases of difficulty or importance: Criminal Procedure (Scotland) Act 1975 (c 21), s 113(4) proviso (amended by the Criminal Justice (Scotland) Act 1980 (c 62), s 83(2), Sch 7, para 32, and the Criminal Justice (Scotland) Act 1987 (c 41), s 70(2), Sch 2).
2 See para 2.13 below.
3 Hume *Commentaries* II, 58, 59; J H A Macdonald *The Criminal Law of Scotland* (5th edn, 1948) p 193. On certain statutory offences also, exclusive jurisdiction is conferred on the High Court. If incest remains a crime at common law, the High Court will have exclusive jurisdiction.
4 Criminal Procedure (Scotland) Act 1975, s 2 (amended by the Criminal Justice (Scotland) Act 1987, s 58(1)).
5 R W Renton and H H Brown *Criminal Procedure according to the Law of Scotland* (5th edn, 1983) paras 17-01, 17-22.

(B) THE SHERIFF COURT

2.09. Personnel and territorial jurisdiction. The vast bulk of criminal prosecutions in Scotland are heard in the sheriff courts. Scotland is divided into six sheriffdoms, being Grampian, Highland and Islands; Tayside, Central and Fife; Lothian and Borders; Glasgow and Strathkelvin; North Strathclyde; and South Strathclyde, Dumfries and Galloway[1]. Each has a sheriff principal. Within each sheriffdom there are a number of sheriff court districts with the numbers of these districts depending upon the geographic area covered. Thus the sheriffdom of Glasgow and Strathkelvin has only one district and the sheriffdom of Grampian, Highland and Islands has sixteen sheriff court districts. Situated in each district there is a sheriff court. Each sheriff court district has one or more sheriffs permanently attached to it. Glasgow and Strathkelvin, for example, presently has twenty-three, while at the other extreme Dornoch sheriff court and Wick sheriff court share a single sheriff who acts in both districts. A sheriff has jurisdiction in all districts of the sheriffdom to which he is appointed[2], and it is probably the case that an offence committed in one sheriff court district can competently be tried in another district of the same sheriffdom[3].

The role of the sheriff principal as far as criminal procedure is concerned is an administrative one. He is able and entitled to sit as a sheriff hearing cases in any of the districts within his sheriffdom but has no appellate function in criminal matters.

1 See the Sheriffdoms Reorganisation Order 1974, SI 1974/2087, and COURTS AND COMPETENCY, vol 6, paras 1025, 1026.
2 Sheriff Courts (Scotland) Act 1971 (c 58), s 7.
3 R W Renton and H H Brown *Criminal Procedure according to the Law of Scotland* (5th edn, 1983) para 1-30. See *Kelso District Committee v Fairbairn* (1891) 3 White 94 at 99; *Tait v Johnston* (1891) 18 R 606.

2.10. Solemn and summary procedure. The sheriff court hears cases in summary procedure, that is a sheriff sitting alone, or in solemn procedure, that is a sheriff sitting with a jury. The sheriff is the only judge with this dual jurisdiction. His territorial jurisdiction is the same, whether sitting alone or with a jury. The difference between the two forms of procedure is the sentence that can be imposed after conviction. Sitting alone the sheriff can impose a fine of up to the prescribed sum upon an accused person, and imprison that person for a period not exceeding three months for a first offence[1]. For a second or subsequent offence inferring dishonesty or personal violence he may sentence to imprisonment for a period not exceeding six months[2]. When sitting with a jury in a solemn procedure the sheriff can impose an unlimited financial penalty by way of fine[3] and imprison for up to three years[4]. If, after conviction in solemn proceedings only, the sheriff is of the opinion that the offence in the circumstances merits a more severe sentence, he has the power to remit the case to the High Court of Justiciary for sentence, in which case it will be dealt with in the High Court as if originally tried there, that is under the same potential penalties as could be imposed in the High Court[5]. In such circumstances the High Court does not rehear the case but relies on a summary thereof given by the prosecution and defence together with any pleas or evidence in mitigation produced by the defence.

1 Criminal Procedure (Scotland) Act 1975 (c 21), s 289 (amended by the Criminal Law Act 1977 (c 45), s 63(1), Sch 11, para 4). The prescribed sum is £2,000 or such other sum as is for the time being substituted therefor by order: Criminal Procedure (Scotland) Act 1975, s 289B(6) (added by the Criminal Law Act 1977, Sch 11, para 5, substituted by the Criminal Justice Act 1982 (c 48), s 55(2), and amended by the Increase of Criminal Penalties etc (Scotland) Order 1984, SI 1984/526, art 3).
2 Criminal Procedure (Scotland) Act 1975, s 290.
3 Ibid, s 193A (added by the Criminal Law Act 1977, Sch 11, para 1, and amended by the Criminal Justice (Scotland) Act 1980 (c 62), s 83(2), Sch 7, para 37, and the Criminal Justice Act 1982, s 77, Sch 15, para 17).
4 Criminal Procedure (Scotland) Act 1975, s 2(2) (amended by the Criminal Justice (Scotland) Act 1987 (c 41), s 58(1)).
5 Criminal Procedure (Scotland) Act 1975, s 104 (substituted by the Criminal Justice (Scotland) Act 1980, s 12, Sch 4, para 15, and amended by the Criminal Justice (Scotland) Act 1987, s 58(2)).

(C) THE DISTRICT COURT

2.11. Constitution. The district court is the newest court in Scotland, having been brought into existence in terms of the District Courts (Scotland) Act 1975 to replace the minor courts that existed before, namely the burgh courts, the police courts and the justice of the peace courts[1]. Not only are the district courts the newest courts, they are also unique in that, with the exception of the stipendiary magistrates in Glasgow, the judges in these courts, that is the justices, are lay persons. The justices can either sit alone or more than one can sit at a time, though this is unusual. They have a qualified clerk of court and legal assessor instructed and paid for by the district council for the area of the court. The extent to which they are used varies considerably throughout the country, with extensive use of them being made in the cities but considerably less use being made of these courts in the country areas. There are no district courts in the Orkney and Shetland Islands. Provision is made for the disestablishment of any district court where there is insufficient business[2].

1 District Courts (Scotland) Act 1975 (c 20), s 1(1). See COURTS AND COMPETENCY, vol 6, paras 1160 ff, and Z K Bankowski, N R Hutton and J J McManus *Lay Justice?* (1987).
2 District Courts (Scotland) Act 1975, s 1A (added by the Law Reform (Miscellaneous Provisions) (Scotland) Act 1985 (c 73), s 33). See the Disestablishment of District Court (Orkney) Order 1986, SI 1986/1836.

2.12. Powers. The district court may impose imprisonment for a period not exceeding sixty days or a fine not exceeding level 4 on the standard scale unless the particular statute under which the prosecution is brought prescribes a different penalty[1]. Presently only in Glasgow does there exist a different form of district court which is presided over not by lay justices but by a stipendiary magistrate[2]. In this court the stipendiary magistrate is a qualified lawyer and has the summary criminal jurisdiction and powers of a sheriff. There is no provision, however, for a stipendiary magistrate, albeit he has the equivalent powers of a sheriff, to sit with a jury and deal with solemn proceedings.

1 Criminal Procedure (Scotland) Act 1975 (c 21), s 284 (amended by the Criminal Law Act 1977 (c 45), s 63(1), Sch 11, para 3, and the Criminal Justice Act 1982 (c 48), s 56(3), Sch 7, para 4); Criminal Justice (Scotland) Act 1980 (c 62), s 7(1) (amended by the Criminal Justice Act 1982, ss 56(3), 78, Schs 7, 16). 'The standard scale' means the scale set out in the Criminal Procedure (Scotland) Act 1975, s 289G(1) (added by the Criminal Justice Act 1982, s 54, and amended by the Increase of Criminal Penalties etc (Scotland) Order 1984, SI 1984/526, art 4): Interpretation Act 1978 (c 30), Sch 1 (amended by the Criminal Justice Act 1988 (c 33), s 170(1), Sch 15, para 58(a)). The standard scale is as follows:

level 1	£50
level 2	£100
level 3	£400
level 4	£1,000
level 5	£2,000

2 The District Courts (Scotland) Act 1975 (c 20), s 5, permits the adoption of a stipendiary magistrate's court anywhere in Scotland.

(D) CRIMINAL APPEALS

2.13. Appellate jurisdiction of the High Court. In Scotland the only court of appeal in criminal matters, whether summary or solemn, is the High Court of Justiciary sitting in appellate form[1]. There is no appeal from the district court to the sheriff court, nor from the sheriff to the sheriff principal, in criminal matters. There is no appeal in Scots criminal procedure to the House of Lords[2]. The High Court as a court of appeal sits in Edinburgh, and appeals may be taken there from any criminal court in Scotland, including the High Court itself. In its appellate capacity the High Court consists of three or more Lords Commissioners of Justiciary, normally presided over by either the Lord Justice-

General or the Lord Justice-Clerk. If an important question is raised or it is necessary to review earlier decisions of the High Court, then more than three judges may sit. The court does not retry the case.

1 Criminal Procedure (Scotland) Act 1975 (c 21), ss 228(1), 442(1) (respectively substituted by the Criminal Justice (Scotland) Act 1980 (c 62), ss 33, 34, Sch 2, para 1, Sch 3, para 1). Appeals in solemn proceedings are heard on the Criminal Appeal Roll, and appeals in summary proceedings are heard on the Justiciary Roll.
2 Criminal Procedure (Scotland) Act 1975, ss 262, 281.

(c) The Public Prosecutor

2.14. The principle of public prosecution. In Scotland the vast bulk of prosecutions are instituted and conducted by public officials, namely the procurator fiscal in the district court and sheriff court, and the law officers of the Crown and Crown Counsel in the High Court of Justiciary. The public prosecutor, deriving his title from the Lord Advocate, is master of the instance with an almost absolute right to decide who should be prosecuted and in which court the case should be tried. Almost all prosecutions in Scotland, in whatever court, are carried out at the instance of the public prosecutor[1].

1 For exceptions, see paras 2.22 ff below.

2.15. The Lord Advocate. The Lord Advocate is head of the prosecution service in Scotland and the minister responsible for the actions of the procurators fiscal[1]. He is a minister of the Crown, though usually not a member of the Cabinet. He is appointed by the Prime Minister and, his office being a political appointment, he changes office every time there is a change in government. He is the senior law officer of the Crown in Scotland, the other being the Solicitor General for Scotland, and as such has functions and responsibilities to government beyond the demands and requirements of being the public prosecutor. Thus he is also minister in charge of a second department, namely the Lord Advocate's Department, situated in London, which is a separate body from the Crown Agent and Crown Office and not connected with criminal procedure and prosecutions, and has joint responsibility with the Secretary of State for Scotland for a third department, the Scottish Courts Administration[2].

The Lord Advocate is the senior prosecutor, and all indictments run in his name, whether they are tried in the High Court or the sheriff court. He may himself appear to conduct a prosecution, but this is infrequent given the width of his other ministerial responsibilities. Like any other departmental minister he is responsible for the policy of the prosecution service, and lays down guidelines which all prosecutors must follow. He also lays down guidelines to the police which they too must follow[3]. He is also actively involved in certain aspects of the criminal prosecution process: for example, only the law officers decide whether or not a case should continue as a murder charge or should be reduced to one of culpable homicide or marked 'no proceedings'.

1 See CONSTITUTIONAL LAW, vol 5, para 509. See also paras 1.27–1.29 above.
2 See generally CONSTITUTIONAL LAW, vol 5, paras 535 ff.
3 See the Criminal Procedure (Scotland) Act 1975 (c 21), ss 9, 293, and *Dumfries County Council v Phyn* (1895) 22 R 538, 2 SLT 580.

2.16. The Solicitor General and Crown Counsel. The Solicitor General for Scotland is the junior of the law officers of the Crown and is subordinate to the

Lord Advocate. Like the Lord Advocate his is a political appointment: he is appointed by the Prime Minister and changes office every time there is a change of government[1]. It is usual for one of the law officers to be a member of the House of Commons and it has become increasingly common for the other to be created a peer and so become a member of the House of Lords[2]. The role of the Solicitor General is that of a junior minister to the Lord Advocate[3].

The Lord Advocate appoints a number of advocates to act on his behalf in taking the day-to-day decisions in matters referred to Crown Office for opinion, in giving advice and instruction to the procurators fiscal and in conducting trials in the High Court of Justiciary and appeals to that court. These advocates (of whom there are at present twelve) are called Advocates Depute. All are experienced counsel, some of whom are senior counsel (QCs) and some junior. It is no longer the practice that AdvocatesDepute demit office on the appointment of a new Lord Advocate. Advocates Depute are not prohibited from continuing to deal with civil cases and are therefore part-time appointments. The Lord Advocate, the Solicitor General and the Advocates Depute are referred to collectively as 'Crown Counsel'. Apart from conducting trials in the High Court and appeals before that court, the principal function of Crown Counsel is to consider the reports submitted to them, under instruction by the Lord Advocate, by the procurators fiscal. To some extent, therefore, they exercise a controlling or monitoring role in relation to the activities of the procurators fiscal. The Lord Advocate may direct any type of case or any individual case to be referred to Crown Counsel for instructions, and these instructions must be carried out by the procurator fiscal. Not only does this include all cases which the procurator fiscal would wish to proceed on indictment, but a great many other matters covering the whole spectrum of the responsibilities of the procurator fiscal. The instructions as to what type of cases require to be reported and considered by Crown Counsel vary from time to time.

1 See CONSTITUTIONAL LAW, vol 5, para 543. See also para 1.37 above.
2 See CONSTITUTIONAL LAW, vol 5, para 539.
3 Hume *Commentaries* II, 130.

2.17. The Crown Agent and the Crown Office. The Lord Advocate has a permanent staff known as the Crown Office situated in Edinburgh which is headed by the Crown Agent[1]. Appointments to the Crown Office are made from the procurator fiscal service. The function of the Crown Office is to administer the prosecution system and to provide advice and instruction to local procurators fiscal. The staff of the Crown Office also act as instructing solicitors to Crown Counsel. The staff, including the Crown Agent, are permanent civil servants and do not change with each Lord Advocate. The Crown Agent is the departmental head of the procurator fiscal service, the Civil Service head of department as opposed to the ministerial head who is the Lord Advocate. He has a depute and at present a legal staff of fourteen.

1 See also paras 1.39, 1.40, above.

2.18. The procurator fiscal. The procurator fiscal is the prosecutor in the sheriff court, both for solemn and summary proceedings, and in the district court, whether before a justice or a stipendiary magistrate. The procurator fiscal conducts over 99 per cent of the criminal prosecutions in Scotland. He is responsible within his area for investigating all crimes[1], not only those that he prosecutes himself but also those that are reported by him to Crown Counsel with a view to prosecution in the High Court of Justiciary. In a High Court trial he sits with, and acts as instructing solicitor to, Crown Counsel. Deriving his power as he does from the Lord Advocate, he too is master of the instance. This gives him an almost absolute discretion to decide who should be prosecuted and in which court for which crimes, unless there is legal provision to the contrary or specific instructions from the Lord Advocate which require to be followed. Albeit other persons have a concurrent right to institute criminal proceedings[2], it is the case that today the procurator fiscal conducts virtually all cases heard in those courts in which he is acting, from whatever source they emanate, for example from the police, from Customs and Excise, from the Health and Safety Executive, from the Department of Social Security and from local authority consumer protection departments. It is worth noting that the procurator fiscal continues to have the right in all cases referred to him, unless specifically directed by the Lord Advocate or Crown Counsel, to decide whether or not to institute proceedings, for what charges, and to bring the person accused before whatever court he considers appropriate, provided that there is no common law rule or statutory provision to the contrary.

1 See para 2.21 below.
2 See paras 2.22 ff below.

2.19. Other responsibilities of the procurator fiscal. The procurator fiscal has responsibilities other than with regard to prosecution. A principal one is to act as the equivalent of the English coroner in Scotland, conducting inquiries and investigations into sudden and unexpected deaths, and thereafter taking whatever steps are necessary, including if appropriate conducting a fatal accident inquiry before the sheriff[1]. Deaths which occur in a considerable variety of circumstances must be reported to the procurator fiscal by various bodies including the medical profession, the Health and Safety Executive and the registrars of births, deaths and marriages, as well as the police. Although in the great majority of cases the circumstances of the death do not give rise to criminal proceedings, this function of the procurator fiscal ensures that he is advised at an early stage of the circumstances of the death, and therefore controls the procedure thereafter so as not to interfere with possible criminal proceedings in appropriate cases, thereby excluding prejudicial publicity etc. The procurator fiscal also has other functions such as acting as agent for the Crown as *ultimus haeres*, and in dealing with treasure trove[2].

1 Ie in terms of the Fatal Accidents and Sudden Deaths Inquiries (Scotland) Act 1976 (c 14): see paras 11.01 ff below.
2 If the procurator fiscal raises an action in the civil court (eg an action of multiple poinding) the writ may be signed by him personally or by his depute: *Carmichael v Wingate* 1990 GWD 12–632.

2.20. Relationship of the prosecutor to the judiciary. The prosecutor, whether he be Lord Advocate, Solicitor General, Advocate Depute or procurator fiscal, is independent of the judiciary and no judge can compel him to bring or to abandon a prosecution or direct him as to what charge should be brought or how any case should be conducted. The prosecutor as master of the instance[1] is entirely responsible for the conduct of the prosecution. This includes the right to withdraw the case or to accept a plea of guilty to a lesser charge at any stage. In solemn cases, even after the conviction of the accused by a jury, the prosecutor can choose to decline to move the court for sentence. In that event the judge cannot proceed to impose sentence[2].

1 See J H A Macdonald *The Criminal Law of Scotland* (5th edn, 1948) p 212.
2 Hume *Commentaries* II,470, 471; *Macdonald* p 348.

2.21. Relationship of the prosecutor to the police. The police are bound to comply with any instructions that the Lord Advocate may from time to time issue to any chief constable[1]. In relation to the investigation of offences the chief constable, and through him his constables, must comply with the instructions of the procurator fiscal[2]. The ultimate responsibility for the investigation of criminal offences lies with the procurator fiscal and not with the police. He is completely independent of the police, who are subordinate to him and subject to his control. In serious crimes, such as murder, the procurator fiscal may attend personally at the scene of the crime to give direct instructions as to what inquiries are to be carried out. The police report cases to the procurator fiscal where in their view there is sufficient evidence to justify taking proceedings against a particular accused. The procurator fiscal may, however, instruct the police to report to him any case at any time. In other cases the procurator fiscal may in his discretion order that certain offences need not be reported, for example speeding cases where the amount by which the statutory speed limit is exceeded is not high.

The procurator fiscal is responsible for the investigation of all crimes, including allegations of crime committed by police officers, whether or not committed in the course of the officer's official duty. The procurator fiscal, however, is not responsible for investigating allegations of misconduct by police officers which are not criminal offences but which constitute breach of the disciplinary regulations, the latter being a matter for the appropriate Deputy Chief Constable. Allegations of criminal conduct by police officers on duty are referred in the first instance to the regional procurator fiscal[3], who may either investigate the allegation personally or delegate this task to the procurator fiscal of the district in which the alleged offence was committed. Thereafter if there is found to be any substance in the allegation the regional procurator fiscal submits a detailed report to the Crown Office for a decision as to whether or not criminal proceedings are to be initiated. This procedure ensures that a proper and independent decision is taken, particularly as the requirement to report is on the basis of there being 'any substance' in the allegation and not on the usual higher level of there being sufficient evidence to justify taking proceedings. Where the allegation of criminal conduct by a police officer arises not out of his official duties but out of his private life, such allegation is treated like any similar allegation against a member of the public, with the decision to prosecute or not being taken by the district procurator fiscal in the normal way.

1 Criminal Procedure (Scotland) Act 1975 (c 21), ss 9, 293; see eg *Dumfries County Council v Phyn* (1895) 22 R 538, 2 SLT 580.
2 Police (Scotland) Act 1967 (c 77), s 17(3) proviso.
3 See para 1.40 above.

(d) Institution of Proceedings by Persons other than the Procurator Fiscal

2.22. Proceedings by private individuals. Private prosecutions in summary courts for common law offences are virtually unknown. Private prosecutions for statutory offences still occur, the principal one being for trespassing in pursuit of game by day, prosecution for which may be conducted by the aggrieved landowner or by a person with a right to kill game on the land[1]. A complaint by a private prosecutor for an offence at common law or for a statutory offence where imprisonment without the option of a fine is competent, unless the statute provides to the contrary, requires the concurrence of the public prosecutor before it may be brought[2]. Thus in practice for common law offences the public prosecutor has a veto on prosecutions at summary level. There is no comparable veto in solemn proceedings, however, but instances of private prosecutions are exceedingly rare with only two cases having occurred this century[3]. The concurrence of the Lord Advocate, which failing consent of the High Court, is required[4]. The High Court is the only competent court in which a private prosecutor may bring indictment proceedings[4]. The prosecution is brought by way of criminal letters. The basis of it goes back to our early prosecution system; thus it is at the instance of a party wronged or injured by the crime, and he must show that the crime alleged is a wrong to himself[5]. He must also demonstrate to the court that he has applied to the Lord Advocate for concurrence in the prosecution[6] and the concurrence or otherwise of the Lord Advocate is a significant factor taken into account by the High Court when considering whether or not to grant the requested criminal letters. If the alleged crime does not affect the individual complainer directly but rather is a public wrong, then it is not a suitable case for the granting of criminal letters[7].

1 Game (Scotland) Act 1832 (c 68), s 2.
2 Criminal Procedure (Scotland) Act 1975 (c 21), s 311(4).
3 *J and P Coats Ltd v Brown* 1909 SC (J) 29, 6 Adam 19; *X v Sweeney* 1982 JC 70, 1982 SCCR 161, 1983 SLT 48.
4 R W Renton and H H Brown *Criminal Procedure according to the Law of Scotland* (5th edn, 1983) para 4–04. For an example where the Lord Advocate refused concurrence, see *McDonald v Lord Advocate* 1988 SCCR 239, 1988 SLT 713.
5 *J and P Coats Ltd v Brown* 1909 SC (J) 29 at 33, 34, 6 Adam 19 at 37, per Lord Justice-Clerk Macdonald.
6 *Robertson v HM Advocate* (1892) 3 White 230; *J and P Coats Ltd v Brown* 1909 SC (J) 29, 6 Adam 19.
7 *M'Bain v Crichton* 1961 JC 25, 1961 SLT 209; *Trapp v M, Trapp v Y* 1971 SLT (Notes) 30.

2.23. Proceedings by the court. All courts may *ex proprio motu* deal with parties before them for contempt of court[1]. The court does not require the concurrence of the prosecutor and there is no requirement for a complaint or indictment[2]. However, the circumstances of the offence may be such that they could form the basis of a charge to be brought by the public prosecutor. For example, should a witness refuse to answer questions, that could be contempt of court where both the court and the prosecutor would have a *locus* to prosecute[3]. Thus in practice the judge concerned would frequently seek the views of the prosecutor as to whether or not the prosecutor wished to bring separate proceedings and leave the matter to him if he so wished rather than deal with the matter *ex proprio motu*. However, the court is not bound so to inquire of the prosecutor and, having so inquired, is not bound by the prosecutor's view since the court itself has jurisdiction to deal immediately with these matters[4].

1 See CONTEMPT OF COURT, vol 6, paras 318 ff.
2 See eg *Muirhead v Douglas* 1979 SLT (Notes) 17; *McKinnon v Douglas* 1982 SCCR 80, 1982 SLT 375, and the Criminal Procedure (Scotland) Act 1975, s 344 (amended by the Criminal Justice (Scotland) Act 1980 (c 62), ss 46(1)(c), 83(2), Sch 7, para 55, and the Criminal Justice Act 1982 (c 48), s 56(3), Sch 7, para 8).
3 *HM Advocate v Airs* 1975 JC 64, 1975 SLT 177.
4 If a sheriff proceeds *ex proprio motu* he is not entitled to appoint the procurator fiscal 'the sheriff's advocate in the public interest': *Green v Smith* 1987 SCCR 686 at 689, 1988 SLT 175 at 177, 178.

2.24. Proceedings by public bodies and officials. By statute prosecutions for a number of offences may be instituted in Scotland by public bodies and officials, for example summary proceedings by officers of HM Customs and Excise[1] and by an education authority[2]. The right to institute proceedings is contained in the particular statute. In practice, however, these prosecutions are normally undertaken by the procurator fiscal notwithstanding the right of the public body or official to prosecute. Where the procurator fiscal is invited by the public body to prosecute, the case is dealt with by him just like any other case, with the fiscal exercising his right to refuse to prosecute if he deems it appropriate. Where the fiscal declines to prosecute, usually no proceedings would be taken by the public body.

1 Customs and Excise Management Act 1979 (c 2), ss 145(1)–(3), 175(1)(d).
2 Education (Scotland) Act 1980 (c 44), s 43(2).

(e) Criminal Jurisdiction

2.25. Original and appellate jurisdiction. All three Scottish criminal courts — the High Court of Justiciary, the sheriff court and the district court — have original jurisdiction, that is, the right to hear cases at first instance[1]. Appellate jurisdiction in respect of both solemn and summary proceedings is vested in the High Court of Justiciary alone[2].

1 R W Renton and H H Brown *Criminal Procedure according to the Law of Scotland* (5th edn, 1983) para 1–06.
2 *Renton and Brown* para 1–06. See paras 8.01 ff below.

2.26. Territorial jurisdiction. The principal circumstance which determines jurisdiction in criminal cases in Scotland is the *locus delicti*, the place where the crime was committed, though exceptions to this general rule are created by a small number of individual statutes[1] which confer jurisdiction on courts other than, and usually additional to, those of the *locus delicti*. In certain cases several courts may have jurisdiction to try the case either because the crime was committed on or near a boundary between two jurisdictions[2] or by virtue of the terms of a statute conferring concurrent jurisdiction[3] or because the crime itself was one which was capable of being and was committed in more than one place; thus, for example, a blackmail letter posted in one jurisdiction to an address in another jurisdiction would found jurisdiction in both courts[4]. The High Court of Justiciary has jurisdiction throughout the whole of Scotland, including its territorial waters[5]. The limits of the territorial jurisdiction of the sheriff and district courts are the boundaries of the sheriffdom and the justice of the peace commission area respectively[6].

1 See eg the Customs and Excise Management Act 1979 (c 2), s 148(1) (court of place where accused resides or is found, or where thing was detained or seized), and the Wildlife and Countryside Act 1981 (c 69), s 21(7) (court of place where the accused is found).
2 Criminal Procedure (Scotland) Act 1975 (c 21), ss 4, 287.
3 See eg ibid, s 288(4) (concurrent jurisdiction of sheriff with every other court in his sheriffdom).
4 Cf *Laird v HM Advocate* 1984 SCCR 469, 1985 SLT 298.
5 J H A Macdonald *The Criminal Law of Scotland* (5th edn, 1948) p 191; *Lewis v Blair* (1858) 3 Irv 16. Territorial waters extend to 12 nautical miles from the coast: Territorial Sea Act 1987 (c 49), s 1. Offshore installations in connection with oil or gas in the United Kingdom continental shelf outwith the 12-mile limit are included in the jurisdiction, as are incidents occurring within 500 metres of such an installation: Criminal Jurisdiction (Offshore Activities) Order 1987, SI 1987/2198.
6 See *Kelso District Committee v Fairbairn* (1891) 3 White 94; Criminal Procedure (Scotland) Act 1975, ss 3, 4, 287; District Courts (Scotland) Act 1975 (c 20), ss 2(1), 3(4).

2.27. Extra-territorial jurisdiction. In exceptional cases a court may have jurisdiction even if the crime took place outwith its own territorial limit. For example, in treason jurisdiction is founded not upon *locus delicti* but upon allegiance[1]. Where an offence under the law of Scotland is committed by any person aboard a British ship on the high seas or by a British subject aboard a British ship in a foreign port or harbour, or by a British subject on board a foreign ship to which he does not belong[2], the criminal courts of Scotland have jurisdiction to try the accused for that offence[3]. Where a person has in his possession in Scotland property which he has stolen in any other part of the United Kingdom, he may be dealt with for theft in Scotland, and similarly a person who receives in Scotland property stolen elsewhere in the United Kingdom may be dealt with for reset in Scotland[4]. At common law, however, there is generally no power to prosecute in a Scottish court for an offence committed outside Scotland, and thus if an accused commits fraud in England he cannot be tried for it in Scotland or vice versa. It is very much an exception to the general rule where extra-territorial jurisdiction can be used to take a case in a Scottish court. Such exceptions are usually statutory in origin and the scope and extent of, and any limitations on, the jurisdiction derive from the terms of the particular statute[5].

1 Hume *Commentaries* II, 50.
2 Passengers do not belong to the ship on which they are carried: see *R v Kelly* [1982] AC 665, [1981] 2 All ER 1098, HL.
3 Merchant Shipping Act 1894 (c 60), s 686. See also s 684.
4 Criminal Procedure (Scotland) Act 1975 (c 21), ss 7, 292.
5 See generally R W Renton and H H Brown *Criminal Procedure according to the Law of Scotland* (5th edn, 1983) paras 1-08–1-22.

2.28. Multiple jurisdiction. It is a fairly common occurrence that a person is alleged to have committed offences in a number of different territorial jurisdictions within Scotland. A court will have jurisdiction to try all of the offences or crimes providing it has jurisdiction to try one of them[1]. The requirement is that one of the offences appears on the complaint or indictment to have been committed within the territory of the court, and the court does not lose jurisdiction if the prosecutor fails to secure a conviction or withdraws the charge against the accused with regard to the only crime allegedly committed within the jurisdiction of the court[2]. In these circumstances the court may still sentence upon the crimes committed elsewhere provided they were either committed within Scotland or the court has extra-territorial jurisdiction to try the crime[3].

1 Criminal Procedure (Scotland) Act 1975 (c 21), ss 4, 5, 287(4) (s 5 being amended by the Criminal Justice (Scotland) Act 1987 (c 41), s 70(1), (2), Sch 1, para 4, Sch 2).
2 *Mackie v HM Advocate* 1979 JC 20, 1979 SLT 114.
3 See generally R W Renton and H H Brown *Criminal Procedure according to the Law of Scotland* (5th edn, 1983) paras 1-24–1-30.

2.29. Jurisdiction as to subject matter. Even if the particular court has territorial jurisdiction, that is the offence was committed within its boundaries, that does not necessarily mean that a case may be brought to that court. Charges of treason, murder, rape (and perhaps incest), deforcement of messengers and breach of duty by magistrates, can be heard only by the High Court of Justiciary, which has exclusive jurisdiction in these matters[1]. With these exceptions the sheriff court has jurisdiction to try any case. The sheriff has jurisdiction concurrent with the district court in regard to all offences competent for trial in the district court[2]. The district court, however, does not have jurisdiction to try all matters that can be heard before a sheriff court under summary procedure. Thus it may not try charges of wilful fireraising or attempt thereat, stouthrief, theft by housebreaking, housebreaking with intent to steal; theft, reset of theft, fraud or embezzlement to a value exceeding level 4 on the standard scale[3]; assault involving a fractured limb or with intent to ravish, or to the danger of life, or assault by stabbing; or uttering forged documents or bank or banker's notes, or offences under Acts relating to coinage[4], but where a stipendiary magistrate is sitting in the district court he has the powers of the sheriff acting summarily albeit that he is sitting in a district court[5].

1 See para 2.08 above.
2 Criminal Procedure (Scotland) Act 1975 (c 21), s 288(4).
3 As to the standard scale, see para 2.12, note 1, above.
4 Criminal Procedure (Scotland) Act 1975, s 285 (amended by the Criminal Justice (Scotland) Act 1980 (c 62), ss 7(3), 83(3), Sch 8, and the Criminal Justice Act 1982 (c 48), s 56(3), Sch 7, para 6).
5 See para 2.11 above.

3. INITIAL STEPS

(a) Introduction

(A) DETENTION

3.01. General. Neither detention nor arrest is an essential preliminary step for the initiation of a criminal prosecution. Clearly detention and arrest are not possible where the accused person is a legal person such as a firm or a company, and not an individual. Furthermore, there are many offences where the physical taking into custody of an accused person is totally inappropriate, for example simple speeding offences or failure to hold a television licence, or where the investigating officers (such as Department of Health and Social Security officials or factory inspectors) may have no powers of arrest or detention. But in the majority of more serious criminal prosecutions the accused will at some point have been detained or arrested or both. It is important to differentiate between detention and arrest.

3.02. Right to detain. Before 1981 the only method whereby the police could take a person into custody was to arrest him. Now the police also have powers of detention. Detention is a statutory power short of arrest accorded to the police[1] to take a person into custody to enable them to carry out further investigations[2]. Specific rules are laid down governing the questioning of the detainee, his rights of access to a solicitor or other person and the length of the period for which he may be detained[3]. Detention is not an essential precursor to arrest, and arrest may, and frequently does, take place without detention. Nor does detention necessarily lead to arrest[4]. For example, the further inquiries may show that there is insufficient evidence to charge the person detained with an offence and arrest him.

Before a constable may detain anybody he must have reasonable grounds for suspecting that that person has committed or is committing an offence punishable by imprisonment[5]. The two important factors are the need to have these reasonable grounds and the circumstance that the offence is punishable by imprisonment[5]. All common law crimes are by definition punishable by imprisonment, but many statutory offences are not. As the requirement is 'punishable by imprisonment', the fact that in a particular instance the accused is not ultimately imprisoned is irrelevant. The constable is entitled to detain a person meeting these criteria to enable him to carry out investigations into the offence and to determine whether criminal proceedings should be instigated against that person[5]. The constable must take him as quickly as is reasonably practicable to a police station or other premises[6].

Detention may not last more than six hours, and must be terminated before then either when the detainee is arrested or when there are no longer grounds to detain him for the purpose of investigating the offence or determining whether

58

criminal proceedings should be instigated against him[7]. Having been released from detention the person may not be detained again on the same grounds or on any grounds arising out of the same circumstances that resulted in his earlier detention[8].

At the time of the detention the constable must inform the detainee of his suspicion, of the general nature of the offence suspected and of the reason for the detention; and a record must be kept of various matters including the place where the detention begins, the police station to which the detainee is taken, the time of detention and of arrival at the police station, the time when the detainee was informed of his statutory rights[9] and when any requests by him for information regarding his detention to be supplied to other persons[10] were made and complied with, and the time when and method by which the detention came to an end[11].

While under detention the detainee may be questioned by the police about the suspected offence, but the fact that he has been detained does not affect the normal rules on admissibility of evidence with regard to the questioning of a suspect or potential suspect, as the detainee is[12]. However, he is under no obligation to answer any of the questions other than to give his name and address, and he must be so informed on his arrival at the police station or other premises[13]. While in detention he may be searched as if he were under arrest, and fingerprints, palmprints, nail scrapings, hair samples etc may be taken as if he were under arrest[14]. Contrary to the position where a person has been arrested, a detainee may not be put on an identification parade unless he consents. There are important safeguards with regard to a detainee's right to inform a solicitor and some other named person of his detention[15]. Somewhat different rules apply if the detainee is a child[16].

1 Similar powers of detention can now be exercised by customs and excise officers: see the Criminal Justice (Scotland) Act 1987 (c 41), ss 48–50.
2 Criminal Justice (Scotland) Act 1980 (c 62), s 2(1).
3 See ibid, s 2.
4 However, detention terminates if and when the detainee is arrested: ibid, s 2(2)(a).
5 Ibid, s 2(1).
6 Ibid, s 2(1). 'Premises' is not defined.
7 Ibid, s 2(2).
8 Ibid, s 2(3).
9 See the text to note 13 below.
10 See the text and note 15 below.
11 Criminal Justice (Scotland) Act 1980, s 2(4).
12 Ibid, s 2(5)(a). Detention for longer than six hours does not render evidence inadmissible if it is otherwise admissible: *Grant v HM Advocate* 1989 SCCR 618.
13 Ibid, s 2(7).
14 Ibid, s 2(5)(b), (c). Prints, impressions etc must be destroyed immediately if no proceedings are taken or if the detainee is prosecuted but acquitted: s 2(5)(c) proviso.
15 Ibid, s 3(1)(b): see para 3.16 below.
16 See ibid, s 3(3), (4), which concern parental access. 'Child' means a person under the age of sixteen, and 'parent' includes guardian: s 3(5).

3.03. Nature of detention. A person detained is in legal custody equally with someone who has been arrested. He is not free to leave the premises nor to communicate with whomever he chooses. The theoretical difference between the two positions is this: unless the police officer has reasonable grounds for believing that he is entitled to charge the accused, that is that there is a prima facie case against him, he should not arrest him but merely detain him, where all that need be demonstrated is that the officer has reasonable grounds for suspecting that he has committed an offence but has not as yet obtained sufficient information to show a prima facie case. Whether this is a realistic distinction in practice remains to be seen[1]. The period of detention has also been criticised both for being unnecessarily long and also for being unnecessarily short, and it is probably worth noting that the subsequent adoption of a similar procedure in England permitted detention for twenty-four hours[2]. There are at present no proposals for amending the Scottish limit of six hours.

1 See J Watson 'Police Powers: Detention or Arrest, a Legal Complication' (1988) 33 JLSS 29.
2 Police and Criminal Evidence Act 1984 (c 60), s 41(1).

(B) ARREST

3.04. Arrest without warrant by police officers. Detention is not a necessary prerequisite for arrest. A constable may arrest a person without warrant for either common law offences[1] or statutory offences[2]. A constable has a common law power to arrest an offender wherever this is necessary in the interests of justice[3]. He may be called upon to justify his action by the arrested person, who could sue him in the civil courts for damages for an unwarranted arrest[4]. Accordingly in practice someone committing a minor offence who has a known fixed abode, and who is unlikely to hinder the course of justice by interfering with witnesses or disposing of stolen property or other evidence, is unlikely to be arrested. As arrest itself is not an essential prerequisite for the initiation of criminal proceedings, which can and frequently are initiated by citation of the accused to attend court[5], its use should be limited and justifiable, as arrest and being kept in custody clearly are serious impositions upon an individual's rights. The controlling factor is that it requires to be in the interests of justice that the person be arrested, and there is a considerable variety of factors to be taken into account, including the nature of the crime and its seriousness[6], the character of the accused, his likelihood or ability to abscond, his likelihood of interfering with witnesses or evidence, and his likelihood of committing other offences if liberated[7].

1 R W Renton and H H Brown *Criminal Procedure according to the Law of Scotland* (5th edn, 1983) paras 5-18–5-21.
2 *Renton and Brown* paras 5-22, 5-23.
3 See eg Alison *Practice* p 371; *Peggie v Clark* (1868) 7 M 89.
4 See eg *Shields v Shearer* 1914 SC (HL) 33, 1914 1 SLT 360; *Robertson v Keith* 1936 SC 29, 1936 SLT 9; *McLeod v Shaw* 1981 SCCR 54, 1981 SLT (Notes) 93; *Dahl v Chief Constable, Central Scotland Police* 1983 SLT 420. The normal test for wrongful arrest is whether it was reasonable in the circumstances for the arresting officer to believe that it was justified: *McLeod v Shaw*.
5 See para 3.31 below.
6 See eg *Peggie v Clark* (1868) 7 M 89.
7 See generally *Renton and Brown* para 5-21.

3.05. Arrest without warrant by private citizens. A private citizen is entitled to arrest without warrant for a serious crime he has witnessed[1] and may also become involved in arresting someone if he himself does not have the right but is assisting someone who has such a right, albeit that person is another private citizen or a police constable[2]. Should the private citizen arrest anybody he must hand him over to a police constable as soon as possible[3] or else face the possibility of an action of damages for wrongful arrest. A private citizen does not have a right to arrest anyone for a statutory offence. The only parties who have such rights are police constables or other specified parties whose rights would be set out in the particular statute concerned.

1 Hume *Commentaries* II,76; Alison *Practice* p 119; J H A Macdonald *The Criminal Law of Scotland* (5th edn, 1948) p 197. See *Bryans v Guild* 1989 SCCR 569 and *Cardona v Cardle* 1989 SCCR 287.

2 *Hume* II,75,76; *Alison* pp 116, 117; *Macdonald* p 197. The owner, tenant or occupier of property in, upon or in respect of which offences of drunkenness and being on premises with intent to commit theft or having tools likely to be used for theft in terms of the Civic Government (Scotland) Act 1982 (c45), ss 50, 57, 58, are being committed, may apprehend the offender and detain him until he can be handed over to a constable: s 59(3).
3 *Mackenzie v Young* (1902) 10 SLT 231, OH; *John Lewis & Co Ltd v Tims* [1952] AC 676, [1952] 1 All ER 1203, HL.

3.06. Arrest without warrant for statutory offences. The same basic principle applies in statutory offences as applies in common law crimes for arrest without warrant. The arrest requires to be justified, and this involves showing that it was in the interests of justice that arrest was used instead of some other method of initiating criminal proceedings[1]. Some statutes contain special provisions allowing arrest without warrant, the more common of which relate to drink driving offences[2], the possession of offensive weapons[3] and the possession of dangerous drugs[4]. However, certain statutes themselves contain no specific provisions allowing arrest without warrant, but nevertheless arrests are commonly carried out in terms of them[5], though in such cases presumably it would be argued that the gravity of the offence or the likelihood of the party, if not arrested, committing a further offence is likely to be such that arrest is necessary in the interests of justice. It is generally implied in the statutes where there is a power to arrest someone committing an offence that the power should also extend to allowing the arrest of someone reasonably suspected of committing the offence[6]. A good example is the power to arrest someone who is driving while unfit through drink or drugs[7]. In practice he is arrested at the roadside and yet the evidence will be obtained in the police station when he is examined by the police surgeon in due course.

1 *Peggie v Clark* (1868) 7 M 89; *Leask v Burt* (1893) 21 R 32, 1 SLT 270.
2 Road Traffic Act 1988 (c52), s4(6).
3 Prevention of Crime Act 1953 (c14), s1 (amended by the Police and Criminal Evidence Act 1984 (c60), ss26(1), 119(2), Sch 7, Pt I).
4 Misuse of Drugs Act 1971 (c38), s5(2). See generally R W Renton and H H Brown *Criminal Procedure according to the Law of Scotland* (5th edn, 1983) para 5–93.
5 See eg the Police (Scotland) Act 1967, s41 (amended by the Criminal Law Act 1977 (c45), s63(1), Sch 11, para 13, and the Criminal Justice (Scotland) Act 1980 (c62), s57); and the Sexual Offences (Scotland) Act 1976, ss1–5, 7–14, and ss2A–2C (added by the Incest and Related Offences (Scotland) Act 1986 (c36), s1).
6 *Wiltshire v Barrett* [1966] 1 QB 312, [1965] 2 All ER 271, CA; *Nicol v Lowe* 1989 SCCR 675.
7 Ie in terms of the Road Traffic Act 1988, s4(6).

3.07. Consequences of unlawful arrest. Unlawful arrest does not vitiate the subsequent criminal proceedings[1]. Its only relevance is in relation to a civil claim for damages and the admissibility or otherwise of evidence obtained thereby, for example by search of the arrested person[2].

1 *Sinclair v HM Advocate* (1890) 17 R (J) 38, 2 White 481; *M'Hattie v Wyness* (1892) 19 R (J) 95, 3 White 289; *Lloyd v HM Advocate* (1899) 1 F (J) 31, 2 Adam 637. See also the Criminal Procedure (Scotland) Act 1975 (c21), s321(4).
2 For an example see *Nicol v Lowe* 1989 SCCR 675.

3.08. Arrest under warrant generally. A warrant for the arrest of an accused person may be issued by a court at the request of the prosecutor in either solemn or summary proceedings. The prosecutor may have a number of reasons for seeking a warrant to arrest an accused person albeit he has other means of bringing him to court, for example by citation. The more usual reasons will be that he has been unable to effect service of a citation upon the accused, or that he requires him to be arrested to enable him to be fingerprinted so that the fingerprints on arrest can be led in evidence to compare with fingerprints found at the scene of a crime. Another reason may be the seriousness of the crime, and this is the basic reason for taking a warrant to arrest in the petition which initiates solemn proceedings. Obviously the use of a warrant by a police officer in effecting arrest protects him from a claim of damages for wrongful arrest as he is acting under authority of the court which issued the warrant in the first place.

Because the date on which a warrant to apprehend is granted stops the running of a time bar in summary proceedings for statutory offences provided that the warrant is then executed without undue delay[1], it is important that the warrant should be executed as soon as possible and without undue delay. Failure so to execute it could render the proceedings time-barred as the taking of the warrant will have no effect on the running of the time bar if it is not enforced without delay. Frequently if a warrant is simply taken for evidential purposes, for example to obtain fingerprints, then the police may arrange with the accused that he attend at a certain time and place (normally a police station) to surrender to the warrant rather than arrest him thereon. His attendance is the equivalent of execution of the warrant when considering the question of time bar[2].

The arresting officer does not require to be in physical possession of the warrant itself but merely to be aware of its existence. However, the arrested person should be shown the warrant itself as soon as possible thereafter, though the officer should retain possession of it[3].

1 Criminal Procedure (Scotland) Act 1975 (c 21), s 331(3). See also *Farquharson v Whyte* (1886) 13 R (J) 29, 1 White 26.
2 *Spowart v Burr* (1895) 22 R (J) 30, 1 Adam 539; *Young v Smith* 1981 SCCR 85, 1981 SLT (Notes) 101.
3 Hume *Commentaries* II, 79; J H A Macdonald *The Criminal Law of Scotland* (5th edn, 1948) p 199.

3.09. Arrest under warrant furth of the jurisdiction. A person for whose arrest a warrant exists may be found and arrested elsewhere in Scotland outwith the jurisdiction of the court granting the warrant, or furth of Scotland. As the High Court of Justiciary has universal jurisdiction throughout Scotland a warrant issued by that court is valid throughout Scotland without further action being required, although these warrants in practice are limited to warrants to arrest a person who has failed to appear for trial or sentence, or for contempt of court proceedings, as all other procedure which would ultimately lead to a High Court appearance would normally otherwise commence in the sheriff court. A warrant issued by any sheriff is enforceable throughout Scotland and is warrant to have an accused physically arrested and brought before the sheriff court issuing the warrant[1]. There is no equivalent provision with regard to warrants issued by the district court, and theoretically a person arrested on such a warrant furth of the jurisdiction of the district court should be brought before a court in the jurisdiction in which he is arrested and the prosecutor then move to have him detained in custody and transferred to the jurisdiction of the issuing court. In practice this is not done as it could result in the party concerned being kept in custody for up to four days, which is not permitted[2]. As the ground of any objection to being taken straight to the district court issuing the warrant would be that the person concerned has been unlawfully detained, which is a matter for civil damages only, not vitiating the criminal process, no objection is taken in practice. Taking the prisoner directly to the issuing court effectively cuts down the time in custody which would inevitably otherwise arise if he were taken at first to a court of the jurisdiction of the arrest and thereafter transferred[2] to the court issuing the warrant. The procedure of bringing a person before a court with a view to remitting him elsewhere does, however, occasionally occur in practice, but normally only with regard to a warrant issued by a court martial or for an absconding serviceman.

1 Criminal Procedure (Scotland) Act 1975 (c21), ss 15, 327.
2 See ibid, s 286.

3.10. Arrest furth of Scotland. Different rules apply where the person to be arrested is furth of Scotland, either elsewhere within the United Kingdom or in any foreign country. Where the accused is in a foreign country extradition proceedings require to be initiated, involving application to the court of the jurisdiction in which the person is to be found for a warrant to be issued by that court to have him arrested and brought before the appropriate court of that country to determine whether or not he is to be extradited back to Scotland. The process is lengthy and cumbersome and very expensive. The crime has to be a crime in both countries and also of a non-political nature as defined by the country in which he is found. There has to be an extradition treaty in existence between the United Kingdom and the country concerned[1]. In these circumstances jurisdiction is rarely invoked and only for the most serious crimes.

More commonly, however, a person to be arrested is to be found in England, Wales or Northern Ireland[2]. An officer of the police force where the person is to be found may arrest him without having physical possession of the Scottish warrant, or any action being required with regard to that warrant by the court of the jurisdiction of the place in which the person is found. The arrested person is then detained by that officer and handed over to officers of the police force in Scotland of the area in which is situated the court issuing the warrant to bring the person back to that court. In other words, the warrant is given effect in just the same way as a warrant for arrest issued by the sheriff is executed in Scotland outwith his own territorial jurisdiction[3].

Specific rules apply to the Republic of Ireland which are part way between extradition and simple enforcement of a warrant outside Scotland[4]. The procedure here parallels the pre-1977 procedure for arresting someone in England under the warrant of a Scottish court. An officer of the police force of the area in which is situated the court in Scotland issuing the warrant witnesses the signature of the judge concerned on the warrant and then takes the warrant to the court of the part of the Republic of Ireland in which the accused person resides and swears there on oath that the signature is correct. Thereafter the court in Ireland may indorse the warrant and allow the officer to arrest the person and bring him back to Scotland without formal extradition. As indicated, this is a half-way house between formal extradition and normal arrest in that the arrested person has rights of appeal to the Irish courts with regard to the indorsement and his removal from Ireland which no person has within the United Kingdom. A further parallel with extradition is that the crime must be an offence in both jurisdictions and that the crime must not be of a political nature. A further restriction is that the crime must not be of a revenue nature, for example an offence under the enactments relating to taxes, duties or exchange control.

1 See R W Renton and H H Brown *Criminal Procedure according to the Law of Scotland* (5th edn, 1983) para 5-50.
2 Ibid, para 5-41.
3 Criminal Law Act 1977 (c45), s 38.
4 See the Backing of Warrants (Republic of Ireland) Act 1965 (c45), and *Renton and Brown* para 5-52.

(C) SEARCH, FINGERPRINTING AND IDENTIFICATION PARADES

3.11. General. Whether a person has been detained or arrested with or without a warrant, the same rules apply to searching his person and taking his fingerprints[1]. However, only a person who has been arrested may be placed on an identification parade unless he consents[2]. As far as searches of premises are concerned, a difference can be drawn between persons arrested under warrant and those either detained or arrested without a warrant[3].

1 See *Jackson v Stevenson* (1897) 24 R (J) 38, 2 Adam 255; *Adair v M'Garry* 1933 JC 72, 1933 SLT 482; *Bell v Leadbetter* 1934 JC 74, 1934 SLT 322 (arrest); Criminal Justice (Scotland) Act 1980 (c 62), s 2(5) (detention).
2 *Adair v M'Garry* 1933 JC 72, 1933 SLT 482 (arrest). There is no provision in the Criminal Justice (Scotland) Act 1980, s 2, permitting the placing of a detainee on an identification parade without his consent.
3 See para 3.15 below.

3.12. Search of the person. The person, clothing, pockets, handbag and other personal effects of someone who is in custody either under arrest or in detention may lawfully be searched. The power to search someone who has been arrested is a common law power[1]. The equivalent power is given by statute to search someone who has been detained[2]. The power of search does not extend to the taking of blood samples, having the subject medically examined for evidential purposes without his consent, taking impressions of his teeth or undertaking any other such invasion of the person's body. The power to carry out these particular procedures must either be found in statute, for example to obtain a blood sample where there is an allegation of drunk driving, or be granted in a specific warrant obtained from the sheriff[3]. The only exception to this is in case of urgency where there is no time to obtain a warrant to carry out this type of search without the evidence being destroyed in the interim[4]. Evidence obtained by an unlawful search will be inadmissible unless the court, in its discretion, excuses the irregularity and admits the evidence[5].

1 *Jackson v Stevenson* (1897) 24 R (J) 38, 2 Adam 255; *Adair v M'Garry* 1933 JC 72, 1933 SLT 482; *Bell v Leadbetter* 1934 JC 74, 1934 SLT 322.
2 Criminal Justice (Scotland) Act 1980 (c 62), s 2(5).
3 See eg *Hay v HM Advocate* 1968 JC 40, 1968 SLT 334, and *HM Advocate v Milford* 1973 SLT 12.
4 *Bell v Hogg* 1967 JC 49, 1967 SLT 290; *Hay v HM Advocate* 1968 JC 40, 1968 SLT 334.
5 See R W Renton and H H Brown *Criminal Procedure according to the Law of Scotland* (5th edn, 1983) para 18-100.

3.13. Fingerprinting. A person who has been arrested may have his fingerprints, palmprints, palm rubbings, nail scrapings etc taken as a matter of common law[1]. These fingerprints, palmprints and such other prints and impressions as may reasonably be considered appropriate with regard to the circumstances of the suspected offence may be taken from a person who has been detained[2]. As statute permits the same powers of search to be exercised upon a detainee as upon an arrestee[3], such things as nail scrapings may also be taken from a detainee.

1 R W Renton and H H Brown *Criminal Procedure according to the Law of Scotland* (5th edn, 1983) para 5-30. See *Lees v Weston* 1989 SCCR 177 for an example of a petition by the prosecutor to take fingerprints late on in proceedings after full committal. See als *McGlennan v Kelly* 1989 SCCR 355.
2 Criminal Justice (Scotland) Act 1980 (c 62), s 2(5)(c).
3 Ibid, s 2(5)(b).

3.14. Identification parades. A detainee is in a different position from an arrestee with regard to being placed on an identification parade. The rules regarding arrestees are determined by common law[1], whereas detainees are the creature of statute, and the statute contains no power to place a detainee against his will upon an identification parade. There would, however, be no wrong committed and the evidence would be admissible if the detainee agreed voluntarily to attend the identification parade (which might eliminate him from the inquiry for which he has been detained). Although common law would permit a person to be placed forcibly upon an identification parade once he has been arrested, the parade would be useless in practice as any witness attempting dispassionately to view the line-up of potential suspects would find one person being restrained by two policemen while the others were standing still, and any identification so made would be somewhat suspect. If a person refuses to take part in an identification parade, the police would in practice have to resort to some other method of identification such as showing a selection of photographs or allowing the witness to see the person sitting in a room, failing which they would require to dispense with such pre-trial identification. A new power has been given to the accused and his legal advisers since 1980 in that he can now call for an identification parade to be held when the Crown has not held one or is refusing to do so[2].

1 See eg *Adair v M'Garry* 1933 JC 72, 1933 SLT 482. In unusual circumstances the prosecutor may seek a court order to hold a parade, for example see *Currie v McGlennan* 1989 SCCR 466.
2 See the Criminal Justice (Scotland) Act 1980 (c 62), s 10, and para 4.15 below.

3.15. Search of premises. The terms of the warrant normally obtained, either on a summary complaint or on a petition, permit officers of the law to search the accused's dwelling house, repositories and any place where he may be found with a view to taking possession of articles relevant to the charge on the petition or complaint[1]. However, once they are carrying out that search they are entitled to take matters not relating to that specific charge if these articles themselves are suspicious or indicate other offences, and the finding of these items would be admissible evidence in any further proceedings[2]. What they are not permitted to do is to take away items, such as the books of a business, to see whether or not on further examination they would disclose offences of which at that time they had no specific knowledge[3]. Where they are arresting somebody without a warrant or are detaining him then they are relying on common law powers of search which would certainly permit them to search the place at which the accused was found but would not, unless the circumstances are of great urgency, permit a search of his home unless he was found there[4]. If the investigating officer, whether he is police officer or customs officer or whomsoever, wishes to search other places than that specified in a warrant, then the proper and safe course is to apply to the court for a specific warrant to search. Subject to specific statutory provisions to the contrary[5], such warrants may be granted by justices of the peace or sheriffs, and may be granted on the application of either an individual investigating officer or the procurator fiscal. Searches of premises are frequently carried out, without either arrest, detention or warrant, where the party having authority over the premises gives consent for the search. However, searches may be carried out even without authority or consent in cases of urgency[6] and the evidence obtained may be admissible, but that is a question of admissibility of evidence rather than a right to search[7].

Customs and excise officers may act under the writ of assistance, which is a general power to search premises at any time without specific reference to the premises or specific warrant being obtained therefor. This writ is issued by the Sovereign and lasts throughout the period of his or her reign.

1 See R W Renton and H H Brown *Criminal Procedure according to the Law of Scotland* (5th edn, 1983) para 5-34.
2 *HM Advocate v Hepper* 1958 JC 39, 1958 SLT 160; *Tierney v Allan* 1989 SCCR 344.
3 *HM Advocate v Turnbull* 1951 JC 96, 1951 SLT 409; *Innes v Jessop* 1989 SCCR 441, 1990 SLT 211.

4 *HM Advocate v M'Guigan* 1936 JC 16, 1936 SLT 161.
5 See R Black 'JPs, Sheriffs and Official Secrets' (1987) 32 JLSS 138, and 'JPs, Sheriffs and Official Secrets — Again' (1987) 32 JLSS 253.
6 *HM Advocate v M'Guigan* 1936 JC 16, 1936 SLT 161; A B Wilkinson *The Scottish Law of Evidence* (1986) pp 118–122.
7 See *Renton and Brown* para 18-100.

(D) THE PERSON IN CUSTODY

3.16. Rights of the person in custody. The most important right of a person in custody, whether arrested or detained, is to know why he is there. Accordingly a detainee must be told as soon as he is detained that he is suspected of having committed a crime, the general nature of the crime and the reason for the detention[1], and the fact that this and various other matters have been done must be recorded in the police station or other place to which the detainee has been taken[2]. As far as an arrested person is concerned, he must be charged as soon as possible after his arrest[3]. It is to be borne in mind that at this stage we are dealing with charging by police officers or some third party, such as customs officers, when dealing with detainees or arrested persons. The terms of the charges laid by these officers at the time of detention or arrest are not binding upon the public prosecutor when he comes to bring the case before a court, and this police charge must not be confused with the terms of the charges on the complaint or indictment which is served upon the accused in due course. As, however, it is the police or other officer who is keeping the person in custody, that person must be told why at least in the view of that officer he is being so kept.

The second important right of a detainee or arrestee is to have some third party informed without delay of the fact that he is now in custody, except where delay is necessary in the interest of the investigation or prevention of crime or the apprehension of offenders[4]. The person in custody, whether arrestee or detainee, must be informed of his right to have this third person informed immediately on his arrival at the police station or other place of custody or, if already there, immediately he is detained or arrested[4]. The right is not to have an interview with the person or speak to him, merely to have attempts made to inform him of the fact that the person is now in custody. Subject to the same safeguards as in the case of intimation to a third party, all persons in custody also have the right to have a solicitor informed without delay of the fact that they are in custody[5], and thereafter to have a consultation in private with that solicitor. If the person in custody does not have a solicitor of his own then the duty solicitor under the legal aid scheme is available to act for him, and the police would normally contact that solicitor. As it is the right of the solicitor concerned to choose whether or not to attend the police station to interview his client, it follows that the right of the person in custody is merely to have a solicitor informed, not to have an interview with a solicitor.

There is no right in Scotland for a person in custody himself to make a telephone call to anybody. All calls are made on his behalf by police officers. The officers are only under a duty to take reasonable steps to inform the person named and the solicitor of the fact that the arrestee or detainee is in custody, and their failure to make contact is no ground for vitiating any further proceedings.

1 Criminal Justice (Scotland) Act 1980 (c 62), s 2(4). This right and the other rights described in this paragraph may differ where the person is arrested or detained in connection with terrorism charges — for further detail see the Criminal Justice (Scotland) Act 1980 (c 62), ss 3A–3D (added by the Law Reform (Miscellaneous Provisions) (Scotland) Act 1985 (c 73), s 35) and *Forbes v HM Advocate* 1990 SCCR 69.
2 Ibid, s 2(4)(a)–(f).

3 *Chalmers v HM Advocate* 1954 JC 66, 1954 SLT 177.
4 Criminal Justice (Scotland) Act 1980, s 3(1).
5 Criminal Procedure (Scotland) Act 1975 (c 21), ss 19, 305 (respectively amended by the Criminal Justice (Scotland) Act 1980, s 83(2), Sch 7, paras 25, 52); Criminal Justice (Scotland) Act 1980, s 3(1).

3.17. Liberation by the police. A person who has been arrested may be liberated by the police without any order upon him to appear at any future court, with a view to his being cited to appear if the procurator fiscal thinks appropriate, or he may be liberated by the police on an undertaking to appear at a named court on a named date at a named time[1]. Alternatively the police may detain him in custody to appear in court from custody[1]. The course which is chosen is a matter of discretion for the police under general guidelines issued by the Lord Advocate and the procurator fiscal. A person liberated on an undertaking to appear at a subsequent court signs a form in the police station giving his undertaking to appear, and is provided with a copy of the undertaking, giving details of where and when he is to appear. This could be at any reasonable future date. Failure to attend court in terms of the undertaking is itself an offence[2]. Liberation in such terms in no way binds the procurator fiscal to take proceedings on the charges at that time or in that court, and the procurator fiscal may choose to cite the liberated person to another court or date, or to take no proceedings at all, as he deems appropriate.

1 Criminal Procedure (Scotland) Act 1975 (c 21), ss 18(2), 295(1) (respectively substituted by the Bail etc (Scotland) Act 1980 (c 4), ss 7(1), 8).
2 Criminal Procedure (Scotland) Act 1975, ss 18(3), 295(2) (as so substituted).

3.18. Appearance in court from custody. A person who has been arrested must either be liberated or brought before a court without delay, and in any event not later than the first lawful day after he has been taken into custody[1]. The day of his arrest does not count for this requirement. The next lawful day excludes Saturday, Sunday or a prescribed court holiday, but that does not exclude his being taken before a court on these days if a court is in fact sitting on such a day for the disposal of criminal business, albeit this is somewhat unusual[1]. Accordingly it is quite conceivable if somebody was arrested in the early hours of a Friday morning that he would not need to be taken before a court until the following Tuesday if there were a court holiday on the Monday intervening, as the requirement is not to bring him to court within twenty-four hours but by the next lawful day. Failure to do so or for the prosecutor to delay unreasonably in bringing him before the court does not vitiate criminal proceedings, but could give rise to an action of damages on the part of the arrestee. The question of the arrestee's liberty is in the hands of the police under direction of the procurator fiscal, there being no procedure available to the arrested person to apply to a court for his liberation at least until after the expiry of the next lawful day after his arrest.

Specific exceptional rules apply in cases of terrorism. These are derived from the statute creating the offence, which permits a person to be detained for up to forty-eight hours or, if the Secretary of State permits, up to five days, without being brought before a court[2].

1 R W Renton and H H Brown *Criminal Procedure according to the Law of Scotland* (5th edn, 1983) para 5-54; Criminal Procedure (Scotland) Act 1975 (c 21), s 19(3) and s 321(3) (amended by the Bail etc (Scotland) Act 1980 (c 3), s 12(2), (3), Sch 1, para 7, Sch 2).

2 Prevention of Terrorism (Temporary Provisions) Act 1984 (c 8), s 12(4)–(7). See also the Criminal Justice (Scotland) Act 1980 (c 62), ss 3A–3D (added by the Law Reform (Miscellaneous Provisions) (Scotland) Act 1985 (c 73), s 35).

(b) Preliminary Inquiries by the Procurator Fiscal

3.19. Sources of information. The procurator fiscal is responsible for making inquiries into allegations of crime of whatever nature occurring within the jurisdiction of the court to which he is attached. Obviously it is not practicable for him personally to inquire into all the circumstances of every allegation made, and he relies upon others, principally the police, to make these inquiries on his behalf. The theory, however, becomes practice in more serious crimes where the procurator fiscal will frequently be closely involved with the inquiry, for example attending at the scene of a murder and at the subsequent post mortem of the victim, and the police will keep him informed of developments and take his instructions as the inquiry proceeds. The majority of reports received by the procurator fiscal emanate from initial inquiry by the police, and frequently no further inquiries are required. However, any person or body[1] may bring matters to the attention of the procurator fiscal directly and the fiscal then has discretion whether to proceed further. The procurator fiscal may make inquiries as and where he sees fit in order to obtain information and evidence relevant to the alleged crime, subject only to very restricted exceptions.

The principal exception is that he may not question the accused or potential accused, as the basis of the Scottish criminal system is accusatorial not inquisitorial. However, where solemn procedure applies judicial examination may follow arrest[2]. The accused may or may not make a voluntary declaration concerning the charge[3]; and the prosecutor has the right to address questions directed towards eliciting from the accused any denial, explanations, justification or comment on the matters averred[4]. These questions are restricted to determining the category and nature of a proposed defence; eliciting comment on an extra-judicial confession; or elaborating on any declarations volunteered by the accused[4]. Failure to answer the prosecutor's questions may be commented on adversely at a subsequent trial by the prosecutor, the judge or a co-accused[5].

The limitations on the general right of the procurator fiscal to information are few. They may include confidentiality between a solicitor and a client[6] but not between a doctor and his patient or a journalist and his source of information. Should such confidentiality be claimed and the person concerned refuse to give to the procurator fiscal information relevant to the inquiry, the fiscal would be entitled to seek a warrant from the sheriff to have that person brought before the sheriff for precognition on oath[7]. That warrant would normally be granted without the person concerned being given an opportunity to object to it. The procedure at precognition on oath is in private and the defence has no right to attend.

Thus, generally speaking, the procurator fiscal is entitled to have inquiries made of whomsoever in his view has relevant information to provide with regard to the matter in hand and to require that person to provide him with documents, productions or otherwise relating to that question, and the person concerned has no statutory right to refuse. In Scotland there is no obligation upon individuals to provide information to the police. Failure to do so, with the exception of some statutory offences[8], does not constitute any offence[9].

1 Eg the Department of Social Security, HM Customs and Excise, the Post Office, the Companies Registration Office, and the Registrar of Births, Deaths and Marriages.

2 Criminal Procedure (Scotland) Act 1975 (c 21), ss 20, 20A (respectively amended and added by the Criminal Justice (Scotland) Act 1980 (c 62), s 6(1), (2)). See generally R W Renton and H H Brown *Criminal Procedure according to the Law of Scotland* (5th edn, 1983) paras 5-58–5-63. See also paras 4.06 ff below.

3 Criminal Procedure (Scotland) Act 1975, s 20 (as so amended).

4 Ibid, s 20A(1) (as added: see note 2 above).

5 Ibid, s 20A(5) (as so added).

6 A G Walker and N M L Walker *The Law of Evidence in Scotland* (1964) pp 414–416; *HM Advocate v Parker* 1944 JC 49, 1944 SLT 195.

7 Criminal Procedure (Scotland) Act 1975, ss 310, 315(3) (s 310 being amended by the Criminal Justice (Scotland) Act 1980, ss 83(2), (3), Sch 7, para 53, Sch 8). See eg *Coll* 1977 JC 29, 1977 SLT 58.

8 See eg the Road Traffic Act 1988 (c 52), s 172 (identification of driver), and the Criminal Justice (Scotland) Act 1980, s 1 (identification of suspect or potential witness).

9 See R Black 'A Question of Confidence' (1982) 27 JLSS 299 and 389.

3.20. Use of experts. No individual can be an expert in all matters, and the procurator fiscal is no exception. To enable him to fulfil his function in making proper inquiries he must be able to call upon the assistance of experts where appropriate. Some of these are readily and frequently available to him, such as forensic scientists employed by police authorities, experts in fingerprint comparison or handwriting, pathologists and police surgeons. There is no limit to the expert advice the procurator fiscal may choose to request, subject to any general directions from the Lord Advocate concerning the efficacy of such evidence, its weight and the cost to the public purse in obtaining it. As the procurator fiscal considers allegations of crimes reported to him by bodies other than the police, then frequently these other bodies themselves will have expertise available to the fiscal to enable him to complete his inquiries.

3.21. Post mortem dissections. At common law the procurator fiscal has the right to order a post mortem dissection upon a body found in his jurisdiction to enable him to complete or further his investigations into the circumstances of the death. The procurator fiscal not only has a role in investigating the possible criminal aspect of the death but he also acts as the equivalent of the coroner carrying out inquiries into sudden, unexpected or suspicious deaths. The right is an absolute one despite objections that may be held by next of kin or others, and the body may not be disposed of without the express consent of the procurator fiscal. Usually, however, a post mortem dissection on behalf of the procurator fiscal is carried out in terms of a warrant granted by the sheriff upon an application made by the procurator fiscal to have the post mortem conducted. The standard petition form for such a post mortem simply states that the procurator fiscal is of the opinion that the circumstances call for investigation and require a dissection of the body for a number of alternate reasons, two of which are simply that there are circumstances of suspicion or that there are allegations that the death was a result of criminal conduct by some other person. No question arises of there being a prima facie case to answer, nor is a considerable body of evidence required to support the petition. The petition simply reinforces the position of the procurator fiscal in his function and permits him to carry out his duty in fully investigating the circumstances of alleged or possible offences.

3.22. Productions. In the course of an inquiry the police may take possession of various items for their potential evidential value, and the procurator fiscal is responsible for the safe-keeping and production in court of these items. The first question which has to be decided is whether or not it is necessary to keep the particular item with a view to producing it subsequently in court as an essential element of the proof[1]. Various factors have to be taken into account, including whether it is practicable and convenient to produce the article in court[2] and also whether or not the item in question (for example food) is going to deteriorate. In some cases it might be appropriate to allow the defence an opportunity to examine an article before it is returned or destroyed, and failure to do so may result in evidence being held to be inadmissible by the court[3]. It is really a matter of the discretion of the fiscal as to what evidence will be necessary for the court proceedings, taking into account the interests of justice and the rights of the accused or potential accused. Similar requirements are involved when dealing with the release of human bodies which are all real evidence in cases where the manner of causing the death is an essential requirement of the specific charge envisaged, for example murder or causing death by reckless driving. The procurator fiscal will take all necessary steps to ensure that the cause of death is properly ascertained and capable of proof. Every effort is made to release the body to the executors or next of kin for burial as soon as possible. If there is an accused, the defence should be given an opportunity to carry out its own separate post mortem or examination before the body is returned to the executors for burial. To preserve possible evidence it is not uncommon in cases of alleged murder for the Crown to release the body for burial only, and not for cremation or removal furth of Scotland so that if necessary it can be exhumed for further examination. Where there is no person accused a balance has to be struck between the rights of a potential accused whose identity is unknown and may not be discovered for some time, and those of the next of kin seeking the return of the body of the deceased.

1 *Tudhope v Stewart* 1986 SCCR 384, 1986 SLT 659. Whether an article needs to be produced in evidence depends upon whether or not the article itself is essential for proving the case. For example, if the charge relates to taking salmon by unlawful means such as gill netting, then the fish themselves, bearing the marks of the net, would, if available, be essential evidence.
2 *Maciver v Mackenzie* 1942 JC 51, 1942 SLT 144; *MacLeod v Woodmuir Miners Welfare Society Social Club* 1961 JC 5, 1960 SLT 349.
3 *Anderson v Laverock* 1976 JC 9, 1976 SLT 62; *Miln v Maher* 1979 JC 58, 1979 SLT (Notes) 10; *Houston v HM Advocate* 1990 SCCR 4.

3.23. Instructions to the police or others. The procurator fiscal is the public investigator originally acting on behalf of the sheriff in his examining role. This function and power long pre-dated the inception of police forces, and accordingly, within the close working relationship between prosecutor and police, the police remain subject to the fiscal's control, statutorily bound to obey his instructions[1]. It is the duty of the police, where an offence has been committed, to take all such lawful measures and make such reports to the appropriate prosecutor as may be necessary for the purpose of bringing the offender with all due speed to justice[2]. In practice the police carry out most of the preliminary inquiries and frequently submit a report containing sufficient details so that no further inquiries are required. However, if the procurator fiscal is not satisfied with the evidence as presented to him he can and does instruct the appropriate additional inquiries.

Where persons other than the police report matters to the procurator fiscal there is no corresponding power to require them to carry out further inquiries on his behalf. However, as the procurator fiscal has the right to refuse to take proceedings, and would exercise that right in the absence of sufficient evidence, then a request by the procurator fiscal for further information from such a body would normally be met.

1 Police (Scotland) Act 1967 (c 77), s 17(3) proviso.
2 Ibid, s 17(1)(b).

3.24. Incidental applications to the court. Incidental applications to the court enabling the procurator fiscal to carry out certain aspects of his preliminary investigation may be made at any stage of the proceedings[1]. It may be necessary, for example, to have blood samples or teeth impressions taken or to search for stolen property. In summary procedure such an application is made in, or as near as may be to, the statutory form[2] and, where necessary, warrant to break open lockfast places is implied. Whether there is any intimation of the application to an accused person will depend upon the particular circumstances and the view of the court. In cases where no proceedings have yet been initiated by the prosecutor by way of petition, warrant or complaint it would be unusual to require intimation to a potential accused, thereby giving him an opportunity to destroy possible evidence. However, once criminal proceedings have been initiated by either of these methods then it would be a matter for the discretion of the court whether or not such an application by the prosecutor would be granted without at least hearing objections by the accused or his legal representative[3].

1   R W Renton and H H Brown *Criminal Procedure according to the Law of Scotland* (5th edn, 1983) para 14-32.
2   Criminal Procedure (Scotland) Act 1975 (c 21), s 310 (amended by the Criminal Justice (Scotland) Act 1980 (c 62), s 83(2), (3), Sch 7, para 53, Sch 8). For the form, see the Summary Jurisdiction (Scotland) Act 1954 (c 48), Sch 2, Pt I.
3   *Hay v HM Advocate* 1968 JC 40, 1968 SLT 334; *HM Advocate v Milford* 1973 SLT 12.

(c) Prosecutor's Duties at the end of the Preliminary Inquiries

3.25. Decision as to whether or not to prosecute. The procurator fiscal, having reached a conclusion that he has available to him all the evidence that can reasonably and lawfully be obtained relating to the allegation of a crime by a named accused, has first of all to consider whether or not that evidence would justify him in initiating criminal proceedings[1]. He has to be satisfied that the facts disclosed constitute a crime according to the law of Scotland and that there is sufficient legally admissible evidence to justify charging a named person with that crime. If he is not so satisfied and yet is of the view that no further evidence can usefully or reasonably be obtained, then he should take no proceedings on the matter. He must also be satisfied that there is no legal bar to instituting proceedings, such as lack of jurisdiction or, where the offence is statutory, the operation of a time bar[2]. Alternatively he may decide that the charge is more appropriately a question of civil right. Where out-of-date statutory regulations have been contravened he may decide, in the interests of good sense, not to proceed at all[3]. The next question he has to ask himself is whether in the interests of justice a prosecution is at all necessary or whether some alternative to prosecution should be used. Factors such as the triviality of the crime alleged and the criminal record of the party accused; his age or infirmity; the reliability of the source of information laid against him; the circumstances of the offence and any explanation offered which would suggest mitigating factors: these are all matters that would be considered. The factors cover the whole spectrum of human behaviour. For example, conduct which may be acceptable at a crowded football match would be unacceptable in a church meeting; a minor road accident that was caused by the frailty of the elderly driver involved who immediately thereafter has given up his driving licence and resolved to drive no more; the theft of a pint of milk from a doorstep by a sixteen-year-old homeless and penniless person desperate for food; factors such as these and others are taken into account by procurators fiscal and by Advocates Depute in deciding whether or not someone should be prosecuted and, if so, upon which charges and before which court. The decision as to the court of course affects the maximum penalty that can be imposed upon the accused in the event of his being found guilty of the crime alleged.

1 R W Renton and H H Brown *Criminal Procedure according to the Law of Scotland* (5th edn, 1983) para 3-01.
2 See eg the Road Traffic Offenders Act 1988 (c 53), s 1.
3 *Kirkland v Cairns* 1951 JC 61, 1951 SLT 324. Cf *Bego v Gardner* 1933 JC 23, 1932 SLT 110.

3.26. Discretion to order no further proceedings. The first consideration of the procurator fiscal is whether the accused should have no proceedings of any nature taken against him for the allegation concerned. The procurator fiscal has an absolute right in this matter, subject, as previously indicated, to general directions by the Lord Advocate. His decision not to proceed is not normally intimated to an accused person though there are a few exceptions. For example, where on his instructions a notice of intended prosecution has been sent to a driver[1] but no proceedings are to be taken thereafter, the procurator fiscal will advise him of that decision. For common law offences his right not to take proceedings is almost unchallengeable[2]. The views of the alleged victim are considered by, but are in no way binding upon, the procurator fiscal. Anyone aggrieved by the decision may raise the matter with the Lord Advocate, who may instruct a report from the procurator fiscal. Where further evidence comes to light the decision not to proceed may be reviewed[3].

1 Ie in terms of the Road Traffic Offenders Act 1988 (c 53), s 1.
2 See paras 2.14 ff, 2.22 ff, above.
3 See, however, *Thom v HM Advocate* 1976 JC 48, 1976 SLT 232.

3.27. Discretion to warn or take alternative action. If the procurator fiscal is of the view that the offence is not trivial or the circumstances are such that a decision to take no proceedings would be inappropriate, it is open to him to issue a warning to the accused that conduct of the nature alleged is unacceptable and if repeated is liable to result in prosecution. This warning is, of course, not a conviction and is not recorded as such. This has been criticised as implying that the person concerned has committed an offence, and therefore as contrary to the fundamental rule that a person is innocent until proved guilty. By issuing a warning the procurator fiscal is denying him a chance to insist upon his innocence. Because of this such a decision to warn an individual is confidential and is not revealed to third parties, including the complainer. To remove the warning system would result in more people being prosecuted in public court, and in practice few individuals receiving a warning would prefer that option. The procurator fiscal may issue the warning himself or in writing or by the hand of a senior police officer, as he sees fit. A total alternative, but one which is dependent on available resources, is to guide the accused away from the prosecution side altogether and, for example, with the co-operation of the social work services or Alcoholics Anonymous or whatever group is appropriate, arrange for treatment and assistance rather than taking criminal proceedings. If at the end of the day the sentence is likely to be probation it may be more appropriate, if the person concerned is willing to undergo supervision on a voluntary basis, not to take any criminal proceedings but to allow him to take this option instead.

3.28. Discretion to offer fixed penalty. Because of the pressure of work upon the courts and the costs involved in the summary prosecution of a large volume of minor offences, and also to some extent because of the feeling that many of the trivial matters that courts deal with from time to time are not suitable for inclusion in courts which at the same time may be dealing with serious assaults, a committee under Lord Stewart was set up to look at the alternatives to prosecution. Part of the recommendations of that committee[1] have been adopted with regard to minor road traffic offences[2] which either involve no mandatory penalty points being endorsed upon a driver's licence or alternatively no discretion in the points, that is, where a fixed number of points are to be imposed. In such cases it is open to the procurator fiscal to offer the person accused a chance to pay a fixed penalty with or without endorsement of his licence as appropriate rather than be prosecuted through the normal process[3]. This is merely one of the options available to the procurator fiscal, and he is not bound to take it. It may be inappropriate where, for example, a person is alleged to have committed a number of offences at the same time, some of which could be dealt with by fixed penalty, and others which, in terms of the relevant statute, could not. In such cases injustice would be done unless the whole picture was put before the court. In the event of the person to whom the conditional offer has been made declining to pay the fixed penalty, whether by actively refusing or by failing to pay within the appropriate period, then the procurator fiscal has the right to initiate criminal proceedings in the normal way. Thus a person who feels that he is innocent is not penalised by his failure to take up the fixed penalty offer[4].

1 *Reports of the Committee on Alternatives to Prosecution* (the Stewart Committee): *The Motorist and Fixed Penalties* (Cmnd 8027) (1980), and *Keeping Offenders out of Court: Further Alternatives to Prosecution* (Cmnd 8958) (1983).

2 Road Traffic Offenders Act 1988 (c 53), Pt III (ss 51–90), replacing the Transport Act 1982 (c 49), Pt III (ss 27–51) (repealed).

3 Road Traffic Offenders Act 1988, ss 75–77 (replacing eg the Transport Act 1982, s 42 (amended by the Law Reform (Miscellaneous Provisions) (Scotland) Act 1985 (c 73), s 59(1), Sch 2, para 26).

4 In 1986 another type of fixed penalty was introduced which is controlled by the police and not the procurator fiscal. Although it is derived from a United Kingdom statute, the Road Traffic Offenders Act 1988, Pt III (replacing the Transport Act 1982, Pt III), its use differs between Scotland and England. In Scotland the Lord Advocate has directed the police to use these fixed penalties only for non-endorsable stationary vehicle offences (in practice, parking offences and failure to display a tax disc), whereas in England there has been no such restriction and they are also used for example in speeding and driving licence offences. Furthermore, contrary to the position with the fixed penalty issued by the procurator fiscal, these police fixed penalties require the recipient actively to object and reject the penalty. His failure to do so properly and timeously will result in the penalty being treated as a fine imposed upon him recoverable in the normal way for fines, including imprisonment for non-payment.

3.29. Fiscal fines. The Stewart Committee[1] also proposed as an alternative to prosecution that in certain circumstances the procurator fiscal should be empowered to offer alleged offenders the opportunity to pay a fine. This proposal in a modified form was brought into effect in 1987 for offences which could competently be tried before a district court but excluding those which could be dealt with by a fixed penalty[2]. Like the fixed penalty, if the alleged offender declines to pay or wishes to deny the allegation, the procurator fiscal has the right to initiate criminal proceedings in the normal way. Payment of the fiscal fine is not a conviction, does not give rise to a criminal record and precludes further prosecution for the alleged offence. It is envisaged that fiscal fines will be a half-way house to be used in cases which merit more than simply a warning but yet do not merit the full paraphernalia of prosecution resulting in the offender having a criminal record.

1 As to the reports of this committee, see para 3.28, note 1, above.

2 Criminal Justice (Scotland) Act 1987 (c 41), s 56: see para 7.26 below.

3.30. Discretion as to the nature of the charge. The same set of circumstances could give rise to a number of different charges, for example a minor assault may constitute a breach of the peace or *vice versa*. The procurator fiscal has an absolute discretion as to the nature of the charge he proposes to ask an accused to answer. He is in no way bound by the terms of the charge with which the police have formerly cautioned and charged an accused person, or indeed the terms of the charge that any other body has placed before the procurator fiscal for his consideration. Equally he may name a new accused, either in addition or in substitution for the one designated by the police. Where the accused has previous convictions the procurator fiscal will decide which ones are to be libelled against him. The procurator fiscal is master of the instance and may decide in all the circumstances whether one charge in his view is more appropriate than another, and apart from direction by the Lord Advocate cannot be obliged to change the terms of the charge by any person, be it complainer, police officer or court, provided always that the charge is a lawful one in terms of competency and relevancy.

3.31. Discretion as to the form of proceedings in court. The procurator fiscal is master of the instance and has a right to decide whether the proceedings are to be summary or solemn[1], that is before a judge sitting alone in the district court or sheriff court or before a judge and jury in the sheriff court or the High Court of Justiciary. He also has an absolute discretion as to what court the proceedings are to be brought before, subject to the charge being competent in that court[2] and taking account of any statutory restriction requiring summary procedure. It is worth noting that unlike the situation in England and Wales the accused has no rights in this matter at all. The accused has no right to demand that his case be taken in any court other than that chosen by the procurator fiscal or to insist upon being heard by a jury rather than judge, or *vice versa*. Where the procurator fiscal decides to initiate solemn proceedings, placing a person on petition with a view to taking him before a jury in due course, the ultimate decision to keep that case before a jury is one for Crown Counsel. The vast majority of prosecutions are taken before a judge alone; solemn procedure would be considered where the sentencing powers of the summary court could not adequately match the gravity of the offence[3]. In the case of a statutory offence the Act creating the offence may provide that it must be prosecuted summarily; where no such provision is made, the choice of procedure is determined as for common law crimes[4].

1 *Clark and Bendall v Stuart* (1886) 13 R (J) 86 at 95, 1 White 191 at 208, 209, per Lord McLaren.
2 See paras 2.25 ff above.
3 *Second Report on Criminal Procedure in Scotland* (the Thomson Report) (Cmnd 6218) (1975) para 13.05.
4 Ibid, para 13.06.

(d) Plea bargaining

3.32. Introduction. The term 'plea bargaining', with its suggestions of trade-offs and concessions, is a misnomer when applied to Scottish procedure, and the process is better understood when referred to as 'plea adjustment' or 'plea negotiation'. The process involves negotiations between the prosecutor and the defence with a view to finding the partial plea most acceptable to both parties[1]. Inevitably it is therefore a plea to a lesser allegation than that contained in the indictment or summary complaint or in appropriate cases the proposed indictment. The reduction may be by way of reduction of the charge itself to a lesser one, by amendment of the wording of the charge, or by deletion of one or a number of charges. This process does not involve the judge and thus it is not in this respect a negotiation involving sentence[2]; however, if the defence can persuade the prosecutor to accept a plea of guilty to a lesser charge, it may reasonably anticipate that a correspondingly lower sentence might be imposed. There are no rules for the basis of this process of negotiation, and the circumstances will depend upon the individuals carrying out the negotiations and the circumstances of each case.

1 'There is no statutory authority for plea adjustment but it is accepted as proper practice for either the accused's legal adviser or the prosecutor to approach the other and negotiate the acceptance of a partial plea': *Second Report by the Committee on Criminal Procedure in Scotland* (the Thomson Report) (Cmnd 6218) (1975) p 97.
2 See A V Sheehan *Criminal Procedure in Scotland and France* (1975) p 120.

3.33. Factors to be considered. Although negotiations are between the procurator fiscal and a defence solicitor or between Crown counsel and defence counsel, the prosecutor may wish to give consideration to the views of the police or other reporting agency, or the victim. The prosecutor is, however, master of the instance with an absolute right and discretion in his prosecution, and thus the decision as to whether or not he accepts any offered plea will ultimately be his alone. Procurators fiscal are normally willing to discuss any relevant matters with defence solicitors, and this practice has been reinforced by instructions to them by the Lord Advocate[1]. Negotiations can take place at any time up to the leading of evidence at a trial or even during the trial, which may be adjourned for this purpose at the request of the parties. It should be borne in mind that at the time he makes the decision to institute criminal proceedings there is one principal source of evidence which is not available to the prosecutor, namely the evidence of the accused, and only if the accused makes a statement under caution or in answer to a charge may the prosecutor have any information as to the accused's position with regard to the charges against him. It therefore follows that if the full circumstances of the accused's position are made known to the prosecutor showing either that the accused has an absolute defence to the charges against him, or alternatively that the mitigating circumstances are such that it is no longer in the interests of justice to continue with the proceedings, the prosecutor might be persuaded to reduce or amend the charge or even to desert the charge completely[2].

1 See 1980 SLT (News) 42; (1980) 25 JLSS 132; (1982) 27 JLSS 534; (1983) 28 JLSS 77.
2 For a more detailed discussion of the circumstances in which a prosecutor may consider a reduced charge, see S R Moody and J Tombs *Prosecution in the Public Interest* (1982) pp 108, 109, 120 ff.

3.34. Position of the Crown and the defence. Since there are no formal rules regarding plea bargaining, the process depends on mutual trust between the parties. It is the duty of the Crown to put before the court ultimately, and therefore before the defence solicitor in negotiations at any earlier stage, all relevant information, including those matters which speak against the Crown case as much as those which favour it. The defence on the other hand has a duty to its client and is not required to give all the relevant information to the fiscal in the negotiations. Negotiations are treated as confidential by both parties and, where unsuccessful, information disclosed to an opponent should not be founded upon by either side at the subsequent trial. When considering what pleas should be tendered, the defence should also consider whether or not in appropriate cases a minute of disclaimer to any property should be given. If property relating directly or indirectly to any particular charge is retained as evidence, then if a plea of not guilty is to be accepted with regard to that charge, the question of the ownership of that property may require to be considered, and a minute by the accused disclaiming any interest in the property may avoid a subsequent dispute when the procurator fiscal comes to dispose of it[1].

1 The acceptance by the prosecutor of a not guilty plea or of a partial plea will affect the victim's rights to a compensation order under the Criminal Justice (Scotland) Act 1980 (c 62), Pt IV (ss 58–67), but not to a claim against the Criminal Injuries Compensation Board under the Criminal Justice Act 1988 (c 33), ss 108–117: see para 7.16 below.

3.35. Accelerated diet. If a plea negotiation is successful, both parties should consider whether or not it is in the interests of justice to accelerate the matter and have it disposed of at an early diet of court[1]. This is particularly relevant with regard to a trial diet which can then be freed for other court business if an early plea is tendered.

1 See the Criminal Procedure (Scotland) Act 1975 (c 21), s 314 (amended by the Criminal Justice (Scotland) Act 1980 (c 62), ss 11, 83(3), Sch 8), para 5.29 above and para 6.37 below.

3.36. Unrepresented accused. The system of negotiation as described above is in practice limited to cases where the accused is legally represented. It is not available to an unrepresented accused for the reasons referred to elsewhere[1].

1 See para 5.07 above.

(e) Bringing an Accused Before the Court

3.37. Bringing an accused before the court. An accused person may already be in custody or the procurator fiscal may wish to have him arrested, or alternatively an arrangement may be made to have him attend court at an agreed time and place. If the person is already in custody then the prosecutor must consider whether or not to bring him before court that day[1] or to liberate him without bringing him to court with a view either to making further inquiries and citing him to court later[2], or to use the alternatives to prosecution which are open to him. The two principal differences between someone being in custody and otherwise concern the questions of bail and legal representation. Clearly if a person is not in custody the question of bail is not really relevant until at least after conviction[3]. If he so chooses, a person in custody is entitled to be represented at no cost to himself by the duty solicitor under the legal aid scheme[4]. This right ceases once he is admitted to bail or committed for trial[5]. There is no corresponding right for a person appearing in court who is not in custody. With these two exceptions the procedure does not change whether or not a person is in custody. If a person is already in custody and is to be brought before the court that day he will be served either with a petition or a summary complaint, depending upon whether or not the prosecutor is considering initiating solemn or summary proceedings[6].

If a person is not already in custody and the prosecutor wishes him to be arrested, then he will seek from the court a warrant which can be either a petition warrant or a summary warrant, depending upon whether or not solemn or summary procedure is contemplated. If solemn procedure is to be initiated, arrest is always by way of warrant except against limited companies and partnerships, which, being legal rather than natural *personae*, cannot be arrested. On many occasions, however, the warrant will have been taken for evidential reasons or as a formality to initiate solemn proceedings and the accused person concerned would not actually be arrested but, by arrangement with the police or prosecutor, would surrender to the police at the court shortly before the time for the court, or as otherwise arranged. The person will appear in court from custody and be treated as if he were fully arrested, that is, he will be subject to searches and fingerprinting, with the full rights of a person in custody[7]. A person previously in custody but liberated on a signed undertaking given to the police that he would attend a specific court at a specific time[8] is treated as if he were in custody, retaining the right to representation by the duty solicitor under the legal aid scheme[9].

By far the majority of prosecutions are initiated by way of citation[10]. Thus a summary complaint is served upon the accused requiring him to attend to answer the charges in the complaint. In such cases the accused is not in custody and is not treated as such. He does not require to appear personally to answer the complaint and may do so either by writing or being represented by a solicitor. Appearance is, however, perfectly competent and many accused persons choose to attend personally[11]. Companies being legal and not natural persons cannot be arrested and brought before the court. Accordingly they require to be cited to appear[12]. It follows that since arrest is the normal process for initiating solemn proceedings, companies are an exception to that rule. In solemn cases companies are not placed on a petition. Proceedings against a company only would normally be initiated simply by service of the indictment[13]. As a matter of practice, before such service it would be normal for the prosecutor to have informed the company that he was considering proceedings against it thus enabling it to commence its preliminary inquiries in order to defend itself against the charges to be brought subsequently in terms of the indictment, in the same way as a natural person who had been arrested on petition.

1 Criminal Procedure (Scotland) Act 1975 (c 21), s 321(3) (amended by the Bail etc (Scotland) Act 1980 (c 4), s 12(2), (3), Sch 1, para 7, Sch 2).
2 Criminal Procedure (Scotland) Act 1975, s 295 (substituted by the Bail etc (Scotland) Act 1980, s 8).
3 See para 3.49 below.
4 A person who is liberated by the police on an undertaking (see para 3.17 above) and who appears in court in terms of that undertaking is treated as if he were in custody and is entitled to the free assistance of a duty solicitor.
5 Legal Aid (Scotland) Act 1986 (c 47), s 22.
6 See paras 3.50 ff below.
7 See paras 3.11–3.16 above.
8 See the Criminal Procedure (Scotland) Act 1975, s 295 (as substituted: see note 2 above), and para 3.17 above.
9 R W Renton and H H Brown *Criminal Procedure according to the Law of Scotland* (5th edn, 1983) para 5-55. See (1980) 25 JLSS 249.
10 As to citation, see the Criminal Procedure (Scotland) Act 1975, ss 315–319, and paras 5.16 ff below.
11 See para 5.23 below.
12 Criminal Procedure (Scotland) Act 1975, s 316(2)(c): see *Renton and Brown* paras 13-25, 13-26.
13 Ibid, s 74(7).

(f) Bail

3.38. General principles. It is a cardinal principle of law that an accused person is innocent until proven guilty, and the question of bail before conviction has nothing whatsoever to do with the accused's innocence or guilt of the charge against him. However, it is usual for a petition for bail on behalf of the accused to contain an averment that the accused is innocent of the charge libelled.

Furthermore, if an accused person on petition is committed, having given written intimation to the prosecutor of his intention to plead guilty, then the normal terms of that committal do not allow for the granting of bail[1]. Bail is an order of the court granted in terms of the Bail etc (Scotland) Act 1980 (c 4). It is to be distinguished from what is commonly referred to as 'police bail', which is in fact liberation under very different terms and conditions[2], and which is restricted to ordering the accused to attend at a court at a given place and time; no other conditions are attached and failure to attend is a separate offence. Bail granted by a court, however, has a number of conditions attached to it[3] the breach of any of which is an offence.

1 See para 3.43 below.
2 See para 2.13 above.
3 See para 3.40 below.

3.39. What crimes are bailable. All crimes except murder and treason are bailable[1]. Thus a person charged with any crime except murder and treason may legitimately apply to the court before which he is brought seeking an order to be liberated on bail. There is no legal impediment in applying for bail for a very serious offence other than murder or treason, though obviously, in the interests of justice, with which bail is concerned, the more serious the crime committed the more difficult it may be to obtain bail. At common law where the crime of murder or treason is concerned, the Lord Advocate or the High Court of Justiciary may, at his or its discretion, accept bail[2]. However, no single judge may order the liberation on bail of a person so charged; only a quorum of the High Court may allow bail for these crimes[3].

1 Criminal Procedure (Scotland) Act 1975 (c 21), ss 26(1), 28(3), 298(1).
2 Ibid, s 35; Hume *Commentaries* II,90; J H A Macdonald *The Criminal Law of Scotland* (5th edn, 1948) p 206; *McLaren v HM Advocate* 1967 SLT (Notes) 43.
3 *Milne v M'Nicol* 1944 JC 151, 1945 SLT 10.

3.40. Conditions of bail. There are four standard statutory conditions of bail, namely:
(1) that the accused appears at the appointed time at every diet relating to the offence with which he is charged of which he is given due notice;
(2) that he does not commit an offence while on bail;
(3) that he does not interfere with witnesses or otherwise obstruct the course of justice whether in relation to himself or any other person; and
(4) that he makes himself available for the purposes of enabling inquiries or a report to be made to assist the court in dealing with him for the offence with which he is charged[1].
The court may impose any other conditions it sees fit in addition to these four statutory conditions. These could include the lodging of money by the accused or on his behalf[2], though this is most unusual. A more common additional condition is that the accused person keeps away from a specific place or person: this condition is much used in matrimonial dispute cases or where children may be involved. It may well be in the interests of the accused in appropriate cases to offer to undertake some additional conditions when seeking release on bail rather than to wait for the court to impose what may be even more onerous a condition or refuse to grant bail at all. If the accused person refuses to accept any of the conditions then he is simply remanded in custody, albeit he has an appeal available to him against the imposition of any conditions[3].

1 Bail etc (Scotland) Act 1980 (c 4), s 1(2)(a)–(d). The standard conditions are mandatory, not discretionary: *MacNeill v Milne* 1984 SCCR 427.

2 Bail etc (Scotland) Act 1980, s 1(3).

3 See para 3.45 below.

3.41. Opposition to bail. It is for the court to decide whether or not bail should be granted in any case, and it may refuse to do so even if the prosecutor has no objections, though this would be unusual[1]. The decision and the responsibility remain those of the court and not the prosecutor, though the attitude of the prosecutor to bail is normally given careful consideration by the court. The prosecutor may object to the granting of bail on one of a number of grounds including the fact that his inquiries are incomplete and that freedom granted to the accused is likely to interfere with those inquiries; that the accused is likely to abscond if given his freedom[2]; that the accused is likely to reoffend if granted freedom; and that the nature of the offence is such that in the interests of justice or for the protection of the public bail should not be granted. The whole matter is a question of balance of the interests of justice on the one hand and of the rights of the accused on the other. It is not only competent but normal for the prosecutor to put before the court at this stage any previous convictions that the accused may have in an attempt to show that he is likely to abscond or reoffend[3]. The prosecutor is not obliged to give full details to the court of what inquiries he still wishes to conduct or in what manner specifically freedom granted to the accused is likely to interfere with those inquiries. Clearly there will be instances where this would not be in the interests of justice, for example where allegations of terrorism are involved. It may well be that the prosecutor would not wish the accused, with his ability to communicate the information, to know at that stage what other inquiries are in hand. However, if the court is not satisfied with the information provided by the prosecutor, then the remedy in the hands of the court is to grant bail to the accused. In reaching its decision as to whether or not to grant bail the court will, if appropriate, take into account a variety of factors: that the accused is presently on bail on other matters for example, or on deferred sentence, or on probation, or undertaking a community service order, or has been liberated without order to appear at another court, that is, he has been ordained to appear at another court on another matter. If any of these circumstances apply it is unlikely that the accused will be granted bail[4]. An application for bail should not be made when the accused is currently serving a prison sentence[5].

1 There would have to be a ground for refusing bail sufficient to justify the court in exercising its discretion to refuse bail: *G v Spiers* 1988 SCCR 517. The High Court has recently gone further and said that bail should be granted where the Crown does not object: *Maxwell v McGlennan* 1989 SCCR 117, *sub nom Spiers v Maxwell* 1989 SLT 282n.

2 See eg *HM Advocate v Docherty* 1958 SLT (Notes) 50.

3 Cf *MacDonald v Clifford* 1952 JC 22, *sub nom Clifford v MacDonald* 1952 SLT 31; *MacLeod v Wright* 1959 JC 12.

4 *Smith v M* 1982 JC 67, 1982 SCCR 115, 1982 SLT 421. See generally R W Renton and H H Brown *Criminal Procedure according to the Law of Scotland* (5th edn, 1983) paras 5-78, 5-79.

5 *Currie v HM Advocate* (1980) SCCR Supp 248.

3.42. Bail in solemn proceedings. It is competent to lodge a petition applying for bail at any stage in solemn proceedings although the two normal occasions occur when the accused appears first of all and is remanded in custody for further inquiries[1] and when he appears on a second occasion and is then fully committed on that petition. If no application is made at further examination stage it is competent to apply at full committal, and if no application is made at full committal it is competent to apply thereafter. If an application has been lodged at the first stage (further examination), and bail is refused, it is competent to apply at full committal as if it were a first application[2]. In any other circumstances, namely after full committal, once bail has been refused the proper procedure for applying thereafter for bail is either to appeal the decision or to apply for a review of bail[3]. Appeal before full committal is available only to the prosecutor[4]. In solemn proceedings, that is, when the accused is on petition, it is necessary to lodge a written petition applying for bail. In summary proceedings an oral application suffices. The application must be disposed of within twenty-four hours after its presentation to the sheriff for his consideration, failing which the accused is forthwith liberated[5]. It is to be noted that the twenty-four hours begins with the presentation of the application to the sheriff and not with lodging it with the sheriff clerk[6].

The prosecutor must be given an opportunity to be heard on the application prior to a decision being taken[7], though there is no penalty for a failure to give the prosecutor such an opportunity, and thus the granting of the bail would not be void. In such cases the prosecutor could appeal against the decision granting bail.

There are two principal differences between bail applications at the two stages, one legal and one practical. The legal difference is that the applicant has a right of appeal against refusal of bail or the terms and conditions upon which it is granted only after full committal. He has no right of appeal at earlier stages[8]. The practical difference is that when the Crown expresses opposition to the granting of bail at further examination stage, albeit the court continues to exercise its discretion whether or not to refuse bail, normally the court will follow the prosecutor's objection and refuse bail. On the other hand at full committal the court frequently disagrees with the prosecutor and allows bail despite his opposition. If bail has been granted at further examination stage the accused is not brought before the court again for full committal[9].

1 Criminal Procedure (Scotland) Act 1975 (c 21), s 26(2) (amended by the Bail etc (Scotland) Act 1980 (c 4), s 12(2), Sch 1, para 3).
2 Criminal Procedure (Scotland) Act 1975, s 27.
3 See paras 3.45, 3.48, below.
4 Criminal Procedure (Scotland) Act 1975, s 31(1), (2).
5 Ibid, s 28(2). 'Twenty-four hours' means twenty-four hours, and not twenty-four hours and twenty minutes: *Gibbons* 1988 SCCR 270.
6 *HM Advocate v Keegan* 1981 SLT (Notes) 35. See also *Tin Fan Lau* 1986 SCCR 140, 1986 SLT 535.
7 Criminal Procedure (Scotland) Act 1975, s 28(1).
8 Ibid, s 31(2).
9 Ibid, s 26(4). Should any indictment which is thereafter served on the accused be deserted *pro loco et tempore*, the original bail order will remain in force: *Jamieson v HM Advocate* 1990 SCCR 137 (unless, presumably, the accused lodges an incidental application craving the court to release him from the conditions of bail and the court grants the application).

3.43. Section 102 committal. If an accused person on petition indicates to the prosecutor in writing in terms of section 102 of the Criminal Procedure (Scotland) Act 1975 his intention to plead guilty[1] before committal either at further examination or at full committal stage, then he may be committed in terms of that letter. The normal style of warrant on the petition in such circumstances does not allow for the granting of bail. However, the provisions in the 1975 Act[2] permit such an application without limitation, and it must therefore be competent to apply for bail. Since the admission of guilt of the charges is a relevant factor for the court to consider when determining the question of bail, consideration should be given by those representing the accused as to whether or not to defer the delivery of the letter pleading guilty to the prosecutor until after committal has taken place.

1 For the Criminal Procedure (Scotland) Act 1975 (c 21), s 102, see paras 4.10 ff below.
2 Ibid, ss 26, 28.

3.44. Summary procedure. In summary proceedings bail applications are made orally and are not required to be in writing. While it is competent for bail to be required even though an accused person is not in custody[1], it is most unusual for bail even to be considered in such cases. Indeed it is difficult to envisage why the prosecutor may consider a person requires to be restricted by bail conditions when he was content to bring him to court by way of citation instead of having him arrested, which was within his discretion. As it is not competent to bring murder or treason charges on a summary complaint, all offences on a summary complaint are bailable and, as for solemn proceedings, must be heard within twenty-four hours of the application being presented to the judge, failing which the accused must be forthwith liberated, and the prosecutor must be given an opportunity to be heard thereon[2]. Normally the bail application would be made when the accused first appears to answer the complaint, but there is no restriction on when to apply and situations can arise where it could be later, for example when the accused is serving a prison sentence at the time of the first appearance but is liberated from that before the trial diet.

1 Criminal Procedure (Scotland) Act 1975 (c 21), s 298(1).
2 Ibid, s 298(2).

3.45. Appeals. With the exception of appeals in solemn procedure at committal for further examination stage[1], the position with regard to appeals is the same whether for solemn or summary proceedings and for prosecutor and accused alike. In all cases appeal is to a High Court judge in chambers, whether it be from the district court or the sheriff court[2]. In the event of the prosecutor appealing against the allowance of bail or its conditions the accused is detained in custody notwithstanding the granting of bail by the lower court[3]. Unlike an application for bail where a twenty-four-hour time limit applies, there is no time limit fixed with regard to a bail appeal; it is to be heard within such time as seems just. In the event of a prosecutor's appeal, whereby a person is kept in custody notwithstanding the grant of bail by the lower court, the appeal must be heard within seventy-two hours if the place of application is on the mainland or ninety-six hours if in the islands of the Outer Hebrides, Orkney or Shetland; otherwise the accused is liberated whether or not the appeal has been disposed of, unless the High Court orders to the contrary[4]. In computing these times neither Sundays nor public holidays, whether general or court holidays, are to be counted[4]. Written notice of appeal must be given immediately to the opposite party[5] and the appeal is disposed of after such inquiry and hearing of parties as the High Court deems just[6]. Once an appeal has been dealt with it is not competent to lodge another appeal thereafter, the proper procedure being to seek a review of the bail[7]. It is unusual for the accused to be personally present during the hearing of the bail appeal, normally being represented by counsel or, if during a court vacation, by a solicitor. The interlocutor of the High Court is transmitted to the clerk of the inferior court whose responsibility it is to arrange for the accused to be liberated on bail forthwith, if that is the decision of the High Court. The clerk must be satisfied that the accused is willing to fulfil any conditions imposed by the High Court. In most instances this is achieved by again bringing the accused before the inferior court; alternatively this may be arranged by telephone with the appropriate prison governor. Refusal by the accused to accept the conditions imposed by the High Court would simply result in the accused being detained in custody.

1 In solemn proceedings at further examination stage only the prosecutor has a right of appeal against the allowance of bail or the conditions on which it has been granted: Criminal Procedure (Scotland) Act 1975 (c 21), s 31(2).
2 Ibid, ss 31(4), 300(3).
3 Ibid, ss 31(2), 300(1).
4 Ibid, ss 31(1), 300(4).
5 Ibid, ss 31(3), 300(2).
6 Ibid, ss 31(4), 300(3).
7 See para 3.46 below.

3.46. Review of bail. The district court or sheriff court may review its decision on bail where it either originally refused bail or allowed bail on conditions which the accused has either refused or not been able to meet[1]. If however an appeal has been taken in respect of the earlier decision then the application for review should not be made to the lower court but to the High Court of Justiciary which dealt with the appeal[2]. An application for review of the court's decision may not be made before the fifth day after that decision, and an application for review of a subsequent decision may not be made until the fifteenth day after that latter decision[3]. It is, of course, competent to appeal against a decision of the reviewing court. An application for review of the original bail decision is unlikely to be entertained by the court unless there has been some change in the circumstances from the position as presented to the court by either the prosecutor or the applicant at the earlier hearing.

1 Criminal Procedure (Scotland) Act 1975 (c 21), ss 30(1), (2), 299(1), (2) (ss 30(2), 299(2) being respectively amended by the Bail etc (Scotland) Act 1980 (c 4), s 12(2), Sch 1, paras 4, 6).
2 *HM Advocate v Jones* 1964 SLT (Sh Ct) 50; *Ward v HM Advocate* 1972 SLT (Notes) 22.
3 Criminal Procedure (Scotland) Act 1975, ss 30(3), 299(3).

3.47. Bail offences. It is an offence to breach any of the bail conditions[1]: this is additional to the offence for which bail was granted. It is neither relevant nor material that the accused may subsequently have been acquitted of the charge on the original complaint, petition or indictment in respect of which the bail order has been made. Penalties for breach of the bail conditions may be imposed in addition to any other penalty which is competent for the court to impose with regard to the original offence, notwithstanding the total of penalties may exceed the maximum penalty which it is competent to impose in respect of the original offence. The result of this is that the court, when sentencing somebody for committing an original offence together with the subsequent offence with regard to breach of the bail conditions, could impose a total sentence in excess of its normal powers[2]. In solemn proceedings the charge relating to the bail offence can either be dealt with on a separate indictment or alternatively the original can be amended, at any time before the trial of the accused on the original offence, to include a charge relating to the bail offence. Which course of action will be taken depends upon what condition has been breached in the view of the prosecutor. If the condition breached is not itself a crime were it not for the bail order, then it is likely that the original indictment will be amended to include the bail charge. On the other hand if the alleged breach is the commission of further offences, then it is more likely that the breach of bail charge will be added to the new indictment. In summary proceedings a separate complaint from the original one is always required whether or not the breach involves a further offence.

Where a person has been arrested on the suspicion, based on reasonable grounds, that he has broken, is breaking or is likely to break his bail conditions[3], he is to be brought, if practicable, before the court which originally dealt with his bail application, not later than the first day after his arrest, Saturdays,

Sundays and court holidays excepted[4]. The court may recall the order granting bail or release the accused under the original bail order, or vary that order by imposing new bail conditions[5]. The same rights of appeal are available against any of these decisions as were available against the original order[6].

1 Bail etc (Scotland) Act 1980 (c 4), s 3(1). As to bail conditions, see para 3.40 above.
2 Ibid, s 3(5): see para 4.08, note 3, below. For penalties for bail offences, see s 3(2).
3 See ibid, s 3(7).
4 Ibid, s 3(8).
5 Ibid, s 3(9).
6 Ibid, s 3(10). As to appeals, see para 3.45 above.

3.48. Change of accused's address. It is worth noting that although it is an essential requirement of the bail provisions that the accused provides an address within the United Kingdom as his domicile of citation, it is not an offence for him to move from that address without informing the court. It is perfectly competent to provide as a domicile of citation an address at which he never intends to live, such as the office address of his solicitors. Should the accused wish to change his domicile of citation he should apply in writing to the court which granted bail[1]. Failure to do so constitutes no offence and will merely result in documents relating to the case being served at an address at which possibly he can no longer be reached; but yet he is deemed to have received the documents as duly and properly served upon him, whether or not he actually receives them.

1 Act of Adjournal (Consolidation) 1988, SI 1988/110, rr 4, 92.

3.49. Bail after conviction. All courts have power to adjourn cases after conviction but before sentence, and at such a stage may wish to consider whether or not the accused person should be liberated on bail or otherwise during the period of the adjournment[1]. Where the adjournment is for the purpose of obtaining a social inquiry report, the normal practice is to admit the accused person to bail unless there are good reasons for keeping him in custody[2]. In both solemn proceedings and summary proceedings bail is merely one of the options available, since the accused may either be remanded in custody, liberated on bail or ordained to appear at a subsequent hearing.

The only crime in Scotland carrying a mandatory sentence of imprisonment is murder, and accordingly it is always competent, except in a case of murder, for an accused person to be granted his liberty after conviction but pending sentence. As the Crown has no right to intervene in the court's decision with regard to sentence except where the proposed sentence is unlawful, neither has the Crown the right to intervene in the question whether or not the accused should be granted bail; nor does it have any right of appeal with regard to the decision. The accused, however, has the normal rights of appeal and review as if it were an order for bail before conviction[3].

1 Criminal Procedure (Scotland) Act 1975 (c 21), ss 179(1), 380(1) (both amended by the Bail etc (Scotland) Act 1980 (c 4), s 5, and amended respectively by the Criminal Justice (Scotland) Act 1980 (c 62), s 83(2), Sch 7, paras 36, 59).
2 *McGoldrick and Monaghan v Normand* 1988 SCCR 83, 1988 SLT 273n.
3 See also para 7.02 below.

(g) Solemn and Summary Procedure

3.50. Introduction. Although the preliminary steps are similar for solemn and summary procedure, once proceedings are initiated they thereafter take very different routes. It is important to understand the basic differences between the two systems. It is also necessary to appreciate that in solemn procedure there are very strict rules concerning what steps are to be taken and at what stage. Failure to adhere to these rules may be fatal to the prosecution or the defence. In summary procedure the rules are much more flexible. In this title reference to solemn procedure covers both the preliminary stages of appearance on petition and the trial diet. It is to be noted that it is not uncommon to find a charge starting on solemn procedure, whereas the ultimate trial takes place under summary procedure[1]. While it is permissible to initiate a summary complaint and then desert it, starting afresh under solemn procedure, this would be very unusual. It might happen where there was a marked change in the charge the accused was facing; for example a charge of assault to injury being raised to a charge of murder because the victim has subsequently died; or where the accused, having been liberated pending trial on a summary complaint, commits in the interim further offences justifying solemn proceedings[2].

1 Criminal Procedure (Scotland) Act 1975 (c21), s20(4).
2 It is competent for the court to refuse to entertain a petition which includes charges that have already appeared on a summary complaint but not been dealt with. Such a decision by the court would be very unusual. For an example, see *Normand v McQuillan* 1987 SCCR 440, Sh Ct, and the comments appended thereto.

3.51. Initial steps in solemn procedure. The initial stages in solemn procedure are taken by way of petition[1] at the instance of the prosecutor, although where the accused is a body corporate there is no preliminary procedure involved and the case can start with an indictment being served upon the company[2]. In modern practice solemn procedure is initiated only in the sheriff court[3]. Petition procedure is conducted before a sheriff even if the indictment is eventually to be heard before the High Court of Justiciary. The only matters of a preliminary nature going to the High Court would be by way of appeal with regard to the orders of the lower court[4] or by way of a preliminary diet where the indictment is to be called in the High Court[5]. Otherwise all preliminary matters are conducted before the sheriff, whichever court is involved. In solemn procedure the court must either remand the accused in custody or liberate him on bail[6], whereas in summary matters the accused can be simply ordered to appear at the later diet without bail[7]. The petition is an initiating step in procedure and is not a writ upon which objections can be taken to competency and relevancy[8]. The terms of the petition in no way bind the terms of the indictment that may follow, as can readily be understood if the concept and timing of the petition is considered. Solemn procedure is used either where a serious crime has been committed or alternatively where the prosecutor feels that the powers of sentence of the summary court are insufficient given the criminal record of the perpetrator. Frequently petition proceedings are taken where there is only preliminary information available to the prosecutor, a person is in custody and he has to be dealt with quickly[9]. As in any other prosecution initiated by him, the prosecutor has to be satisfied that there is a prima facie case against the accused. But it is likely that at this very early stage the facts of the case will not have been fully investigated and the prosecutor will have only limited information concerning the witnesses and evidence available. Therefore it may be that after he has had sufficient time to inquire into these circumstances the charges which finally appear on the indictment differ materially from those on the petition. It is not possible to plead guilty to a petition, except by letter in terms of section 102 of the Criminal Procedure (Scotland) Act 1975[10]. While providing time limits within which the trial must commence[11] or the indictment be served[12], solemn procedure, unlike summary procedure, does not fix the next diet for the case to call again in court. In solemn procedure the accused may make two appearances on the one petition, at which he may be committed for further examination and fully committed respectively. Rights to bail will vary depending upon which stage has been reached[13]. Only in solemn procedure does an accused person face judicial examination[14].

1 Criminal Procedure (Scotland) Act 1975 (c 21), s 12.
2 See ibid, s 74(1). It is competent, though unusual, for the Crown to indict an individual without first having placed him on petition: *O'Reilly v HM Advocate* 1984 SCCR 352, 1985 SLT 99.
3 See R W Renton and H H Brown *Criminal Procedure according to the Law of Scotland* (5th edn, 1983) para 5-02.
4 Eg bail appeal in terms of the Criminal Procedure (Scotland) Act 1975, s 31: see para 3.45 above.
5 Eg where the competency or relevancy of the indictment is challenged: see *Renton and Brown* paras 9-01 ff.
6 The Crown may, of course, liberate an accused without bail.
7 Criminal Procedure (Scotland) Act 1975, s 295 (substituted by the Bail etc (Scotland) Act 1980 (c 4), s 8): see para 3.17 above.
8 However, for an example of a plea to the competency of a petition, on the ground of oppression, see *Normand v McQuillan* 1987 SCCR 440, Sh Ct.
9 An undesirable effect of the one-year rule (as to which see para 4.33 below) occurs in practice in major white collar crime. Because of the time required to inquire into and prepare a case of this nature, a petition is not raised until late to avoid difficulties with the one-year rule. The position of the accused may be thereby prejudiced, as he may be unaware of the possibility of charges against him. The limited counter-plea of *mora* (see para 2.06 above) is of little help in such a case.
10 As to the Criminal Procedure (Scotland) Act 1975, s 102, see para 4.10 below.
11 See ibid, s 101(1) (substituted by the Criminal Justice (Scotland) Act 1980 (c 62), s 14 (1)), and para 4.23 below.
12 Criminal Procedure (Scotland) Act 1975, s 101(2) (as so substituted).
13 See para 3.43 above.
14 As to judicial examination, see paras 4.26 ff below.

3.52. Differences in documentation. The documentation served upon the accused varies considerably between summary and solemn procedure. In solemn procedure the papers begin with a petition, but that is not the document upon which the accused will ultimately stand trial. Thereafter he is served with an indictment[1] within the statutory time limit[2]. Attached is a copy of the list of witnesses and productions that the Crown propose to refer to when leading evidence at the forthcoming trial. It is competent for the Crown, with leave of the court, to call witnesses or refer to productions other than those on the list[3]. The accused is also served with a schedule of previous convictions[4], but there is no notice of penalties. This is to be contrasted with summary procedure where the document initiating the process, the summary complaint[5], which sets out the charges, is the document upon which the accused will face trial. There is no preliminary documentation equivalent to a petition. The complaint will not provide the accused with information as to the witnesses who may be called or the productions that are to be referred to. In practice the procurator fiscal will provide this information, as a courtesy, when applied for in writing. The accused will also receive a list of his previous convictions and a schedule showing the penalty that can be imposed upon him for any statutory offence on the complaint[6]. Without the penalty notice, no penalty can be imposed with regard to that offence[7]. In solemn proceedings there are requirements upon the defence to give written notice of any special defence and of lists of productions and witnesses[8]. With the limited exception of giving advance notice of a special defence of alibi or insanity[9] the defence is under no obligation in summary procedure to give information to the prosecutor of the line of defence that may be taken, the witnesses who may be called or the productions that may be referred to. Unlike solemn procedure, which initially is conducted in private at the petition stages, summary procedure, with rare exceptions relating to children or offences of a sexual nature, is always conducted in open court.

1 Criminal Procedure (Scotland) Act 1975 (c 21), s 70.
2 See paras 4.20 ff below.
3 Criminal Procedure (Scotland) Act 1975, s 81 (amended by the Criminal Justice (Scotland) Act 1980 (c 62), s 83(2), Sch 7, para 28).
4 Criminal Procedure (Scotland) Act 1975, s 68(2).
5 Ibid, s 311(1).
6 Ibid, s 311(5).
7 See generally R W Renton and H H Brown *Criminal Procedure according to the Law of Scotland* (5th edn, 1983) paras 13-60–13-65.
8 Criminal Procedure (Scotland) Act 1975, s 82(1) (substituted by the Criminal Justice (Scotland) Act 1980, s 13).
9 Criminal Procedure (Scotland) Act 1975, ss 339, 375(3). Cf *Adam v MacNeill* 1972 JC 1, 1971 SLT (Notes) 80.

3.53. Sentencing powers. In summary procedure the court has no power to remit a case to a higher court for sentence. In solemn procedure, however, the sheriff has the power at his own hand to remit a case to the High Court of Justiciary if it is his opinion at the conclusion of the trial diet, having heard the case, that his maximum powers of sentence are inadequate to deal with the matter before him[1]. Thus in summary proceedings the prosecutor, by choosing his court, sets a limit on the maximum sentence to be imposed. In solemn proceedings the matter is entirely in the hands of the court, always providing that the sentence does not exceed any relevant statutory limit. There is no maximum sentence of imprisonment or fine that may be imposed for any common law offence, from breach of the peace to culpable homicide.

1 Criminal Procedure (Scotland) Act 1975 (c 21), s 104(1) (substituted by the Criminal Justice (Scotland) Act 1980 (c 62), s 12, Sch 4, para 15).

4. SOLEMN PROCEDURE

(a) Procedure at Appearances in Private

4.01. Introduction. Solemn procedure today reflects the historical development of criminal investigation, and many of the steps of process clearly show those historical roots[1]. Accordingly the petition, the document initiating the procedure at the instance of the procurator fiscal, is framed in the third person. The petition informs the sheriff[2], who was the official historically charged with the duty to inquire into allegations of crime[3], of the nature of the allegations against the accused, referred to in solemn proceedings as the 'panel'. The accused is therefore not formally charged at this stage; this does not occur until he subsequently receives an indictment. Because he has not been charged, no objection can be taken to the relevancy of the charges on the petition[4]. Thus no objection can be taken if the petition contains charges which would not be permitted in the same form on the indictment, for example where one charge shows that the accused has previous convictions. An accused, unless he is a legal person such as a company[5], is always in custody, even if it is a matter of arrangement rather than physical arrest. Because he is in custody he is entitled to the services of a solicitor under the legal aid scheme before appearing in court[6]. Since the accused cannot apply for liberation on bail until after this appearance before the sheriff[7], it is important that the first examination occur as soon as possible after arrest[8]. The proceedings on petition are held in chambers and in private. The only persons present are the sheriff and sheriff clerk, the procurator fiscal, the accused, the defence solicitor and any police escort. Co-accused on the same petition are not present during the proceedings relating to the accused[9]. It is competent and within the power of the sheriff to delay the first examination for a period not exceeding forty-eight hours from the time of the person's arrest in order to allow for the attendance of a solicitor nominated by the accused[10]. Should the accused attend the examination without a solicitor, the sheriff is obliged to advise him of his right[11].

1 See paras 1.41 ff above.
2 Petitions may be presented only to the sheriff, not to the district court or the High Court of Justiciary.
3 See para 1.44 above.
4 See, however, *Normand v McQuillan* 1987 SCCR 440, Sh Ct, where a plea to the competency of a petition was upheld by the sheriff, who refused to commit the accused.
5 See para 3.37 above.
6 Legal Aid (Scotland) Act 1986 (c 47), s 22.
7 Criminal Procedure (Scotland) Act 1975 (c 21), s 26(2) (amended by the Bail etc (Scotland) Act 1980 (c 4), s 12(2), Sch 1, para 3).
8 R W Renton and H H Brown *Criminal Procedure according to the Law of Scotland* (5th edn, 1983) para 5-54.
9 Criminal Procedure (Scotland) Act 1975, s 20(3C) (added by the Criminal Justice (Scotland) Act 1980 (c 62), s 6(1)).

10 Criminal Procedure (Scotland) Act 1975, s 19(3).
11 *HM Advocate v Goodall* (1888) 15 R (J) 82, 2 White 1.

4.02. First examination. At the first appearance, which is referred to as appearance for examination on the charge or charges on the petition, the accused is judicially admonished[1] and then asked whether he tenders any plea or makes or emits any declaration. Normally he does neither of these. The plea referred to here does not concern his guilt or innocence of the charge, since it is not competent to tender such a plea to a petition[2]. A plea of guilty in terms of section 102 of the Criminal Procedure (Scotland) Act 1975, which must be made in writing, is a separate matter[3]. The plea referred to can only be to the competency of the proceedings[4] or relate to the sanity or sobriety[5] of the accused with regard to his ability to emit the declaration. As declarations themselves have almost fallen into disuse the phrase as it is classically used has become a meaningless formality.

The expression 'appearance for examination' is derived from the sheriff's original investigative role when he had to satisfy himself that there was a sufficiency of evidence against the accused to support the charge being made. Part of this examination involved his examining or questioning the accused, and this procedure later developed to include the accused making an unsworn statement or declaration as well as answering questions. In the eighteenth and nineteenth centuries this common law process of judicial examination was often very lengthy indeed. At that time[6] the accused had no right to give evidence at his own trial, and emitting a declaration was the only avenue open to him to present his own account in answer to the charge. He was, however, at a great disadvantage because the questioning was very wide and far-ranging, partly in the hope that he might confess or make damaging admissions[7]. Furthermore, while he was not bound to answer any question put to him, failure to do so would be noted and could be commented upon unfavourably at his trial. At his trial the declaration and judicial examination could be used against him but not, except at the discretion of the Crown, in his favour[8].

Given the extreme difficulty for an accused person and his legal representatives in the process of declaration and old-style judicial examination at common law, it is not surprising to find that while the right still remains to emit a declaration this is no longer a live part of modern criminal practice. Albeit the common law judicial examination may still be competent, as modern judicial examination[9] is much more restricted, it is likely that were a declaration to be emitted by an accused he would be judicially examined on it on the statutory basis only, or the common law judicial examination would be restricted simply to the sheriff asking any questions necessary to clarify any ambiguities in the declaration. Only the procurator fiscal can choose whether or not to subject the accused to a new-style judicial examination, and neither the accused nor the sheriff can force him to do so.

In such circumstances, however, it may be advantageous to the accused to have his version of events put on record at the earliest possible opportunity. This could be achieved by emitting a declaration. In the event of an accused wishing to emit a declaration, it is not taken on oath. The statement is taken before a sheriff and noted in longhand by the sheriff clerk. The declaration so emitted may be produced and founded upon by the prosecutor at the trial. Theoretically it cannot be insisted upon by the accused if the prosecutor refrains from producing it at the trial[10], although no prosecutor today would normally refuse such a defence request[11].

In practice the accused or his solicitor starts the petition procedure by stating that he makes no plea and emits no declaration. He may then be judicially examined under the new statutory procedure and will then be committed for further examination, or fully committed until liberated in due course of law.

1 A judicial caution is indispensable to the validity of a declaration: cf W G Dickson *The Law of Evidence in Scotland* (3rd edn, 1887 by P J Hamilton Grierson) paras 319, 320, and Act of Adjournal (Consolidation) 1988, SI 1988/110, r 15, Sch 1, Form 10.
2 See para 3.51 above.
3 As to the Criminal Procedure (Scotland) Act 1975 (c 21), s 102, see paras 4.10 ff below.
4 See paras 4.45 ff below, and *Normand v McQuillan* 1987 SCCR 440, Sh Ct, cited in para 4.01, note 4, above.
5 Alison *Practice* p 557; *Dickson* para 316.
6 Ie until the passing of the Criminal Evidence Act 1898 (c 36).
7 See generally G H Gordon 'Institution of Criminal Proceedings in Scotland' (1968) 19 NILQ 249 at 254–259.
8 *HM Advocate v Kennedy* (1842) 1 Broun 497.
9 See paras 4.06 ff below.
10 J H A Macdonald *The Criminal Law of Scotland* (3rd edn, 1894) p 329.
11 Since a modern judicial examination cannot take the place of an accused giving or calling evidence (see para 4.08 below), a prosecutor would be reluctant to permit a declaration, being simply an unsworn, untested statement, to be put before the court were the accused not to give or call evidence.

4.03. New-style judicial examination. The important new judicial examination procedure is discussed in detail below[1]. It is now a common but not necessary part of pre-trial solemn procedure and takes place, at the discretion of the procurator fiscal, either at the first appearance of the accused, or alternatively and more usually at the second diet, that is the diet of further examination, and before full committal[2]. At this stage the procurator fiscal should have sufficient information to be satisfied that the terms of the charge on the petition are relevant to the accused and that there is at least a prima facie case against him. The purpose of modern judicial examination is to allow the accused an early opportunity to state his defence to the charge which is likely to form the basis of an indictment, to give notice to the Crown of that defence, and to allow investigation of it. It is therefore important that the procurator fiscal is satisfied that the examination is on a charge relevant to an indictment to follow. The line taken by the defence at this stage is of vital importance to it in the subsequent trial, making credibility difficult to maintain if a defence other than that disclosed at judicial examination is later adopted[3].

Where a case has started on petition and is later reduced to summary proceedings, the judicial examination is admissible in those summary proceedings[4].

1 See paras 4.06 ff below.
2 It is competent though unusual for a judicial examination to be conducted at some other time if the accused makes an extra-judicial confession to or in the hearing of a police officer. This particular judicial examination would relate only to the confession and would only be permitted if there had been no earlier judicial examination about the same confession: see the Criminal Procedure (Scotland) Act 1975 (c 21), s 20(3A) (added by the Criminal Justice (Scotland) Act 1980 (c 62), s 6(1)).
3 If the procurator fiscal refuses to have the accused judicially examined and the accused or his agent considers it important to put on record a defence to the allegation in the petition, the accused could emit a declaration: see para 4.02 above.
4 See the Criminal Procedure (Scotland) Act 1975, s 352 (substituted by the Criminal Justice (Scotland) Act 1980, s 6(4)).

4.04. Further examination. At the conclusion of the first examination, the prosecutor has two options available to him. He may move to continue the case for further inquiries, that is, move for a committal for further examination, or alternatively he may move for committal of the accused to prison until liberated in due course of law, that is, full committal. The prosecutor may continue for further examination only once on any petition. If the accused is remanded for further examination he must be brought back before the court for full committal within nine days. If the prosecutor does not do so the sheriff would be entitled to refuse his subsequent motion for full committal[1]. Refusal by the sheriff to commit fully does not affect the Crown's right eventually to bring the accused on indictment before the court but results only in the accused being liberated without any order being made relating to bail or otherwise. Only the prosecutor has a right of appeal with regard to the granting of bail at committal for further examination[2]. If the accused is liberated on bail at further examination stage he does not require to be brought back for full committal since this liberation on bail is the equivalent of full committal[3].

1 *Herron v A, B, C and D* 1977 SLT (Sh Ct) 24; *Dunbar* 1986 SCCR 602.
2 See para 3.43 above.
3 Criminal Procedure (Scotland) Act 1975 (c 21), s 26(4).

4.05. Full committal. Since judicial examination takes place only at the discretion of the procurator fiscal he can move for full committal, if he so chooses, at the first appearance of the accused on the petition. Alternatively, if the accused has already been committed for further examination on the petition, he must be brought before a court within nine days and be fully committed with regard to that petition. At full committal stage both the accused and the Crown have a right of appeal concerning any bail order made by the court. In moving for full committal, the procurator fiscal is not required to produce any supportive evidence or otherwise justify his motion to the court; it is assumed that he has sufficient evidence to warrant committing the accused for trial. The sheriff, however, has a residual right to refuse[1].

1 *Herron v A, B, C and D* 1977 SLT (Sh Ct) 24; R W Renton and H H Brown *Criminal Procedure according to the Law of Scotland* (5th edn, 1983) para 5-70.

(b) Judicial Examination

4.06. The 1980 provisions. The old form of judicial examination at common law[1] has in practice been superseded by statutory provisions[2]. Since 1980 the procurator fiscal has been entitled to ask questions of the accused with a view to eliciting any denial, explanation, justification or comment the accused may have regarding matters averred in the charge or charges, provided such questioning is directed towards disclosing a category of defence and its nature and particulars[3]; the alleged making by the accused to, or in the hearing of, a police officer of an extrajudicial confession[4]; or what the accused said in any declaration emitted at the examination[5]. The accused is not on oath during this examination[6]. The procurator fiscal in framing his questions should not challenge the truth of anything said by the accused, should not reiterate a question that the accused has refused to answer, and should not ask leading questions[7]. It is the sheriff's duty to ensure that all questions are fairly put to the accused and understood by him[8]. The accused is entitled to have his solicitor with him and to consult with that solicitor before answering any question[9]. The solicitor may not answer any questions himself but he may, with the permission of the sheriff, ask questions of the accused in order to clarify any ambiguities in what has been said in reply to the fiscal's questions[10]. Should the accused be due to appear at the first examination without his solicitor, it is in the power of the sheriff to delay proceedings for up to forty-eight hours to allow for his attendance[11]. Where the same situation arises at further examinations, the equivalent time is a period not exceeding twenty-four hours[12].

The accused is first warned by the sheriff that he does not require to answer any question put to him but where he declines to answer and is subsequently tried, his having declined may be commented on by the prosecutor, the judge presiding at the trial, or any co-accused, in the event that either he or any witness on his behalf gives in evidence something which could have been stated appropriately in answer to the question that he declined to answer[13]. The effect of this is that if he does not state his defence to the charge at judicial examination, or at his trial wishes to change his line of defence from that intimated at judicial examination, it is very difficult for him to give or call evidence in support of the new position without having to overcome a large question of credibility as to its veracity. As the judicial examination takes place at a very early stage of the procedure, the accused and his agent have very little opportunity to inquire into the proposed line of defence they may wish to take at a subsequent trial and to prepare adequately for the judicial examination and its consequences. On the other hand an intimation at this early stage allows the Crown to inquire into the circumstances of the defence as intimated and, if appropriate, to amend the charges against the accused, or even to take no further proceedings. It also adds to the credibility of the accused if, at his trial, he gives evidence which accords with the judicial examination since he is able to say that his line of defence has always been consistent. The judicial examination is admissible evidence against the accused provided it has been lodged as a prosecution production[14]. Dealing with a statement which is exculpatory in whole or part is rather more complex. If, derived from parts of the Crown case, from the accused himself giving evidence or leading witnesses on his behalf, there is evidence capable of confirming his statement any exculpatory statement is admissible. It may demonstrate that his story has been consistent and enhance his credibility. Where there is no such supporting evidence and the statement is wholly exculpatory it is of no evidential value at all. It is not and cannot be admissible evidence of the truth of its contents nor can it enhance credibility as this cannot be in issue in such circumstances. Between these two positions and more commonly are statements which are partly incriminatory and partly exculpatory. In such cases the whole statement is admissible whether or not there is any other supporting exculpatory evidence and like any other evidence it would be for the jury to decide whether to accept all or part of the statement. Clearly it is more difficult to accept the exculpatory parts where no supporting evidence is led particularly as the trial judge would normally remind the jury that the exculpatory evidence taken from the statement was not taken under oath nor tested by cross examination[15].

1 See para 4.02 above.
2 See the Criminal Procedure (Scotland) Act 1975 (c 21), ss 20, 20A, 20B, and Act of Adjournal (Consolidation) 1988, SI 1988/110, rr 14–23.
3 Criminal Procedure (Scotland) Act 1975, s 20A(1)(a) (added by the Criminal Justice (Scotland) Act 1980 (c 62), s 6(2)).
4 Ibid, s 20A(1)(b) (as so added). For a judicial definition of 'confession', see *MacKenzie v HM Advocate* 1983 JC 13, 1982 SCCR 545, 1983 SLT 304; *Moran v HM Advocate* 1990 SCCR 40.
5 Criminal Procedure (Scotland) Act 1975, s 20A(1)(c) (as so added).
6 Act of Adjournal (Consolidation) 1988, r 18(3).
7 Criminal Procedure (Scotland) Act 1975, s 20A(2)(a)–(c) (as added: see note 3 above).
8 Ibid, s 20A(2) (as so added).
9 Ibid, s 20A(3) (as so added).
10 Ibid, s 20A(4) (as so added).
11 Ibid, s 19(3).
12 Ibid, s 20(3B) (added by the Criminal Justice (Scotland) Act 1980, s 6(1)).
13 Criminal Procedure (Scotland) Act 1975, s 20A(5) (as added: see note 3 above); Act of Adjournal (Consolidation) 1988, r 18(4).

14 Criminal Procedure (Scotland) Act 1975, s 78(2) (substituted by the Criminal Justice (Scotland) Act 1980, s 12, Sch 4, para 8). See *HM Advocate v Cafferty* 1984 SCCR 444, Sh Ct.
15 R W Renton and H H Brown *Criminal Procedure according to the Law of Scotland* (5th edn, 1983) para 18-21; *Morrison v HM Advocate* 1990 SCCR 235.

4.07. Record of the examination. A copy of the transcript of the examination is served upon the accused and his solicitor within fourteen days after the examination[1]. That record should be a verbatim record of the questions asked and the answers and declarations given[2], including refusal to answer. It includes the sheriff's warning[3] at the beginning explaining to the accused his right not to answer and to consult his solicitor but advising him of the consequences of declining to answer in the event of evidence being led by him or on his behalf at his trial[4]. The transcript should not include questions that have been put and disallowed, or the arguments concerning objections made whether or not the question was disallowed. Provision is made for the record to be made by a recognised court shorthand writer[5], and if such is used then no tape recording is required. In practice it is rare for a procurator fiscal to use a court shorthand writer, relying instead upon his own staff to act as secretaries taking shorthand, and in this case a tape-recorded record must be made of proceedings[6]. Two simultaneous recordings are taken, one of which is given to the procurator fiscal to enable the shorthand typist to compare notes with the contents of the tape recording, and the other is kept by the sheriff clerk[7]. The purpose of this tape kept by the sheriff clerk is to allow for rectification to be made to the terms of the transcript by comparison with an official copy of the recording of the proceedings.

1 Criminal Procedure (Scotland) Act 1975 (c 21), s 20B(3) (added by the Criminal Justice (Scotland) Act 1980 (c 62), s 6(2)). As to the record, see also Act of Adjournal (Consolidation) 1988, SI 1988/110, rr 15-18, Sch 1, Form 10.
2 Criminal Procedure (Scotland) Act 1975, s 20B(1) (as so added).
3 R W Renton and H H Brown *Criminal Procedure according to the Law of Scotland* (5th edn, 1983) para 5-61; I D Macphail 'Judicial Examination' (1982) 27 JLSS Workshop 296, note 20.
4 See the Criminal Procedure (Scotland) Act 1975, s 20A(3), (5) (as added: see note 1 above).
5 Ibid, s 20B(1) (as so added). Such a shorthand writer is one recognised for the purposes of ss 274, 276, or OCR r 73: Act of Adjournal (Consolidation) 1988, r 16(1).
6 Ibid, r 16(1).
7 Ibid, r 17.

4.08. Verification of the record. Once a transcript has been served upon the accused and his solicitor it is deemed to be accurate and complete unless notice is served in writing on the prosecutor within ten days of service of the transcript that it is inaccurate either because it contains an error or because it is incomplete[1]. The accused must apply to the sheriff within fourteen days of service of the transcript for the error or the incompleteness to be rectified[1]. The sheriff in turn must, within seven days of the application, hear both parties in chambers with regard to the rectification[1] unless the parties are agreed that such rectification is necessary[2]. The procurator fiscal has the same rights as the accused to correct errors or insert material missing from the transcript using the same procedure[3].

1 Criminal Procedure (Scotland) Act 1975 (c 21), s 20B(4) (added by the Criminal Justice (Scotland) Act 1980 (c 62), s 6(2)).
2 Criminal Procedure (Scotland) Act 1975, s 20B(4) proviso (as so added).
3 Ibid, s 20B(4) (as so added).

4.09. Deletion of extraneous matters. Since the judicial examination relates to the charges on the petition and reference is made, in the course of the examination, to all those charges, it follows that extraneous or indeed prejudicial matter which should not be put before a jury at a subsequent trial will often be contained in part at least of the recorded transcript. For example, the petition may refer to charges no longer on the indictment, or by implication may disclose that the accused has a criminal record where the petition charges relate to, for example, a number of road traffic offences including one of driving while disqualified. By the time the details of the indictment are worked out by the prosecutor it will be too late to have the transcript amended by way of rectification. Such a method would be inappropriate anyway as the record is accurate; the proper procedure is to seek a preliminary diet when an application to the court may be made to delete the extraneous material from the record of the judicial examination[1]. It is, however, competent at the trial diet on the application of either the accused or the prosecutor for the presiding judge to refuse to allow the transcript or part of it to be read to the jury, even if there has been no such preliminary diet to discuss and consider the matter.

1 Criminal Procedure (Scotland) Act 1975 (c 21), ss 76(1)(b), 151(2) (substituted by the Criminal Justice (Scotland) Act 1980 (c 62), ss 6(3), 12, Sch 4, para 5).

(c) Early Plea of Guilty

4.10. Section 102 indictment. It is not competent to plead guilty to the terms of a petition, only to an indictment[1]. It is therefore not competent to plead guilty at any of the preliminary stages of the petition procedure and have the case disposed of immediately. In order to plead guilty to a charge which the prosecutor intends to place on indictment the accused must tender a letter known as a 'section 102 letter' in terms of that section of the Criminal Procedure (Scotland) Act 1975. The letter, intimating a plea of guilty to the charge, charges or part of the charges, as appropriate, is addressed to the Crown Agent[2] and signed by the accused, not his solicitor. In practice it is handed to the procurator fiscal who has placed the accused on petition. The exact terms of the section 102 letter may arise as a result of plea bargaining[3] or simply represent a plea to all the charges. Where the letter is tendered before an indictment has been served the accused will receive a 'section 102 indictment' containing only those charges to which he proposes to plead guilty, and citing him to a 'section 102 diet'[4]. Where an ordinary indictment[5] has already been served and the letter then tendered, the accused will receive only a notice citing him to the accelerated trial diet[6], where he will plead to the terms of the original indictment.

1 See para 4.02 above.
2 Criminal Procedure (Scotland) Act 1975 (c 21), s 102(1) (substituted by the Criminal Justice (Scotland) Act 1980 (c 62), s 16).
3 See paras 3.32 ff below.
4 Act of Adjournal (Consolidation) 1988, SI 1988/110, r 12(1)(a), Sch 1, Form 6.
5 Ie one served under the Criminal Procedure (Scotland) Act 1975, s 75 (substituted by the Criminal Justice (Scotland) Act 1980, s 12, Sch 4, para 4).
6 Act of Adjournal (Consolidation) 1988, r 12(1)(b), Sch 1, Form 7.

4.11. Withdrawal of plea. The tendering of a section 102 letter is not binding upon the accused; he may withdraw it at any time before he signs the minute on the indictment indicating his plea of guilty. Where the plea was taken to an incompetent or irrelevant charge, or under substantial error or misconception, or under circumstances which tended to prejudice the accused, there would be grounds for its withdrawal[1]. The withdrawal may not be commented on adversely by the prosecutor in the subsequent proceedings before a jury, nor may any reference be made to the fact that the accused signed a section 102 letter. However, the accused may not use withdrawal of the plea as a device to force the prosecutor to exceed the time limit available to him to serve a normal indictment and proceed to trial. Where a guilty plea has been tendered and then withdrawn at the section 102 diet, that diet must be deserted *pro loco et tempore* and the accused may be reindicted[2]. Where an ordinary indictment is served and a section 102 letter tendered but subsequently withdrawn, the original trial diet may be postponed, but such postponement does not count in the calculation of any relevant time limit[3]. Furthermore the tendering of a section 102 letter and even the service of an indictment in terms of that letter is not binding upon the prosecutor, who is entitled to desert the diet *pro loco et tempore* at any stage prior to moving for sentence as a matter of common law[4].

1 See R W Renton and H H Brown *Criminal Procedure according to the Law of Scotland* (5th edn, 1983) para 8-09.
2 *Pattison v Stevenson* (1903) 5 F (J) 43, 4 Adam 124.
3 Criminal Procedure (Scotland) Act 1975 (c 21), s 102(3) (substituted by the Criminal Justice (Scotland) Act 1980 (c 62), s 16); Act of Adjournal (Consolidation) 1988, SI 1988/110, r 12(3).
4 Cf *Pattison v Stevenson* (1903) 5 F (J) 43, 4 Adam 124.

4.12. Form of section 102 indictment. The form of the indictment in terms of section 102 is materially different from that of the normal indictment in that it contains no list of witnesses or productions[1]. It may contain in the one indictment a cumulation of charges which would not be permissible were the matter to have proceeded before a jury; thus it may contain reference to charges which show that the accused has previous convictions as well as charges which do not. The indictment has a four-day *induciae*, that is it must be served upon the accused not less than four clear days prior to the calling of the indictment[1]. Service contrary to the terms of the *induciae* is not fatal to the proceedings, but the accused would have the right to object to the indictment at the time and to refuse to plead to it. If, notwithstanding the shorter *induciae*, he does plead, then the indictment and the procedure thereafter is competent. A schedule of previous convictions relating to the accused which the prosecutor proposes to place before the court is also served with the indictment[2]. At the same time a notice is served upon the accused calling him to appear at the diet for the section 102 indictment at the appropriate court[3], date and time. It is now competent to indict directly to the High Court[4] or to the sheriff court as the prosecutor sees fit and, as a consequence, it is not unknown for a solicitor to offer a restricted section 102 letter stating that the accused will plead guilty only if he is indicted in the sheriff court in the first instance. If the indictment is heard in the sheriff court and the sheriff is of the opinion that he has insufficient sentencing power to deal with the offence he may remit the matter to the High Court for sentence[5]. The indictment and the related notice and schedule of previous convictions are served upon the accused either personally or by recorded delivery at his domicile of citation if he is liberated on bail, or upon him personally in prison if he is in custody[6]. A copy is sent as a matter of courtesy to his solicitor, but this is not a legal prerequisite for further proceedings.

1 Criminal Procedure (Scotland) Act 1975 (c 21), s 102(1) (substituted by the Criminal Justice (Scotland) Act 1980 (c 62), s 16).
2 Criminal Procedure (Scotland) Act 1975, s 68(4). As to objections to the accuracy of the schedule of previous convictions, see s 68(4).
3 'Appropriate court' means (1) where no indictment had been served when the section 102 letter was given, either the High Court of Justiciary or the sheriff court; (2) in any other case, the court specified in the notice of trial diet under ibid, s 75: s 102(2) (as substituted: see note 1 above).
4 Ibid, s 102(2) (as so substituted).

5 Ibid, s 104(1) (substituted by the Criminal Justice (Scotland) Act 1980, s 12, Sch 4, para 15).
6 See R W Renton and H H Brown *Criminal Procedure according to the Law of Scotland* (5th edn, 1983) para 7–04.

4.13. Procedure in court. A section 102 indictment is heard before a judge alone and no jury is involved. The indictment is called by the clerk of court. The accused identifies himself and he or his legal representative intimates his plea of guilty in terms of the indictment. The accused then signs a minute admitting the charges on the indictment and that is then countersigned by the judge. The case may fall where this procedure is not strictly adhered to[1]. Up to this point the Crown remains master of the instance and can withdraw the indictment if so minded and have the diet deserted *pro loco et tempore*[2]. The prosecutor then moves for sentence. Without that motion the court may not impose sentence. The prosecutor lays the schedule of previous convictions before the court, if appropriate; this may be deemed to be the equivalent of moving for sentence[3]. The procedure then continues as for any plea: the prosecutor narrates the circumstances, the accused or his agent delivers the plea in mitigation, and the court then proceeds to sentence in the normal way.

As it is necessary on many occasions to obtain reports upon the accused before he can be sentenced, such as social inquiry reports[4] or psychiatric reports, and as neither the court nor the prosecutor has the right to order these before the section 102 plea is tendered and accepted in court, then sentence will have to be deferred to a later date to enable these reports to be obtained. It is, however, both competent and permissible for the reports to be obtained before the calling of the diet if the agent for the accused agrees to the reports being ordered before the plea is tendered, so that they are available for the court sitting. By using this procedure the court will have the necessary reports at the time the section 102 diet is called and will thus be able impose sentence without further delay.

1 *HM Advocate v Galloway* (1894) 1 Adam 375, 1 SLT 604.
2 *Pattison v Stevenson* (1903) 5 F (J) 43, 4 Adam 124.
3 *Noon v HM Advocate* 1960 JC 52, 1960 SLT (Notes) 51. Cf para 7.01 below.
4 See paras 7.01 ff below.

(d) Preparation of the Defence

4.14. Introduction. Once an accused person has been fully committed the defence must prepare its case to enable it to answer the indictment which will be produced in due course. In many cases the interval between the service of the indictment and the trial diet may not be sufficient for full preparation. Thus it is advisable, though not essential, to start preparations without waiting for the service of the indictment even though some effort may be wasted in investigating matters which do not form part of the ultimate charge.

4.15. Identification parades. The Crown has always had a right at common law to place an accused person upon an identification parade[1]. By statute the defence now has a limited right to seek an identification parade where none has been held by the Crown, with a view to showing at an early stage the inability of Crown witnesses to identify the accused as the perpetrator of the offence. The prosecutor's right is a common law one and he holds an identification parade without having to apply to the court for permission to do so. The defence does not have the same right and must apply to the sheriff for permission[2]. The accused or his solicitor petitions the court requesting the sheriff to order the prosecutor to hold an identification parade[3], and the prosecutor has a right to be heard on the application[4]. The order may be made only if the prosecutor himself has not held such a parade or, having received a request by the accused for one, has refused or is unreasonably delaying holding the parade; and in addition the defence has to show to the sheriff's satisfaction that an identification parade is a reasonable requirement in the circumstances[5]. In practice the procurator fiscal is likely to agree to a request by an accused for a parade, unless he considers the request frivolous or otherwise unreasonable, thereby obviating any need for an application to the court.

1 *Adair v M'Garry* 1933 JC 72, 1933 SLT 482.
2 Criminal Justice (Scotland) Act 1980 (c 62), s 10(1).
3 Ibid, s 10(3); Act of Adjournal (Consolidation) 1988, SI 1988/110, r 13, Sch 1, Forms 8, 9.
4 Criminal Justice (Scotland) Act 1980, s 10(2).
5 Ibid, s 10(2)(a)–(c).

4.16. Post mortems. As with identification parades, the right of the prosecutor to hold a post mortem arises at common law and no such equivalent right is held by the defence. In practice, however, in allegations of murder or culpable homicide for example, where an accused person may have been identified at an early stage in the proceedings, it is normal for the Crown, after the conclusion of its own post mortem, to allow the defence an opportunity to have the body examined by an appropriate expert. However, it would be unreasonable for the Crown to refuse to hand the body to the next of kin for disposal on the mere possibility that at some further date, as yet unspecified, a person may be arrested and charged with murder or culpable homicide and may wish to carry out a separate examination. In any case where the defence considers it necessary to hold a post mortem or examination of a body and the Crown has not given consent in the normal fashion it would be competent for the defence to apply to the court for a warrant.

4.17. Examination of Crown productions and witnesses. Before the service of the indictment upon the accused, the defence has no enforceable right to insist upon examining any productions held by the Crown relating to an allegation, nor does it have a right to information concerning the witnesses who may be called[1]. However, at the request of the defence the procurator fiscal will normally allow such examination as is reasonable, provided it does not interfere with his own inquiries. Similarly the procurator fiscal is likely to agree to providing a preliminary list of the witnesses he may call on the indictment. Indeed, he may be consulted by the defence solicitor at any stage of the inquiry[2], though he may not be prepared to give full details while inquiries are still pending. Once the indictment is served, information concerning witnesses and productions is immediately available to the defence from the annexed schedules[3].

1 *Slater v HM Advocate* 1928 JC 94, 1928 SLT 602; *Smith v HM Advocate* 1952 JC 66, 1952 SLT 286.
2 See 1980 SLT (News) 42 (Lord Advocate's instructions to procurators fiscal); (1980) 25 JLSS 132; (1982) 27 JLSS 534; (1983) 28 JLSS 77.
3 See para 4.26 below.

4.18. Recovery of documents. Where documents which are necessary for the preparation of the defence are in the hands of the Crown or of third parties, the accused person may petition the High Court of Justiciary for a commission and diligence for the recovery of the documents if the person having possession of them will not voluntarily make them available[1]. In relation to proceedings on indictment the only court with power to approve a specification of documents prepared by the defence and to grant such a commission and diligence is the

High Court, even though the trial itself is to be held in the sheriff court[2]. It is incompetent to grant a commission and diligence for the recovery of a witness's criminal record[2].

1 *Downie v HM Advocate* 1952 JC 37, 1952 SLT 159; *HM Advocate v Hasson* 1971 JC 35, 1971 SLT 199; *Davies* 1973 SLT (Notes) 36; *HM Advocate v Ashrif* 1988 SCCR 197, 1988 SLT 567.
2 *HM Advocate v Ashrif* 1988 SCCR 197, 1988 SLT 567.

4.19. Precognoscing witnesses. It is competent for the defence to procognosce witnesses who may have relevant evidence, whether or not the Crown has already done so. The names of these witnesses can be obtained from a number of sources. The terms of the charge on the petition may disclose obvious witnesses, such as a victim. The accused himself may be able to name persons as being potential witnesses, and the procurator fiscal might agree to release a preliminary list. Consultation with the procurator fiscal might indicate further those witnesses who are speaking to peripheral matters and who may not need to be precognosced at this early stage. The procurator fiscal has power at common law to make inquiries into any allegation of crime, and that includes the right to obtain statements from any witness with relevant evidence except the accused, or the few witnesses whose evidence may be subject to privilege[1]. In the event of any witness refusing to give a statement to the procurator fiscal, the fiscal is entitled to petition the court, without intimation to any other party, to precognosce that witness on oath. The defence has no right to object and does not even receive intimation of such an application. The defence may not attend a precognition on oath conducted by the procurator fiscal. The defence has no absolute right to insist upon a witness making a statement to it, but by statute it now has a limited right to precognition on oath which is analogous to the limited right to seek an identification parade. The sheriff may on the application of the accused grant warrant to cite a person (other than a co-accused) alleged to be a witness to appear before the sheriff for precognition on oath on behalf of the defence[2]. This right refers to any criminal proceedings, whether before the district court, the sheriff or the High Court of Justiciary. The accused or his solicitor petitions the sheriff for such an order and the sheriff is then required to order intimation of the application to be made to the procurator fiscal[3]. The procurator fiscal attends any hearing fixed by the sheriff to determine whether or not the application should be granted, but does not attend the diet at which the precognition is actually taken. This procedure is very new, and no guidelines have been laid down as to what factors the sheriff should take into account in allowing such precognition on oath[4]. It may be that the witness whose unwillingness necessitates the initiation of this procedure will later indicate his willingness to give a precognition to the defence, thus rendering the procedure unnecessary. It has been suggested that the order should be made only in those circumstances where the Crown would consider precognoscing a witness on oath[5]. Despite the wide powers of the Crown to precognosce on oath, in practice such cases are limited to those where it is felt likely that a witness will commit perjury or go back on his statement unless it is taken on oath.

1 See paras 3.19 ff above.
2 Criminal Justice (Scotland) Act 1980 (c 62), s 9(1). A person who, having been cited to attend for precognition fails to attends, refuses to give information or produce evidence or prevaricates in his evidence, commits an offence: s 9(2), (3). The procedure is regulated by Act of Adjournal (Consolidation) 1988, SI 1988/110, rr 5–9.
3 Ibid, r 5, Sch 1, Forms 1, 2.

4 *Low v MacNeill* 1981 SCCR 243, Sh Ct; *Cirignaco v Lockhart* 1985 SCCR 157, 1986 SLT (Sh Ct) 11; *Brady v Lockhart* 1985 SCCR 349.
5 *Low v MacNeill* 1981 SCCR 243, Sh Ct.

(e) Time Limits for Custody and Prosecution

4.20. Introduction. There is no time bar for the prosecution of common law offences in either solemn or summary proceedings[1]. It does not matter when the offence was allegedly committed; the accused can still be charged with the commission of that offence at any time thereafter without any limit imposed on the prosecutor bringing the charge[2]. The six-month time limit applicable to statutory offences relates only to summary procedure[3]; there is no equivalent time limit applicable in solemn proceedings. However, the statute relevant to the particular crime may itself set a time limit for the institution of proceedings. Solemn proceedings are instituted either on the date upon which a warrant to arrest the accused was sought by the procurator fiscal or the date upon which the accused was put before the court on a petition charging him with the offence, whichever date is the sooner[4]. Once proceedings have been intiated, however, there are very definite time limits within which an accused person must be brought to trial. The starting date for calculating the relevant period differs according to whether or not the accused is in custody with regard to that petition.

1 For the time limits in summary proceedings, see paras 5.01 ff below.
2 *Sugden v HM Advocate* 1934 JC 103, 1934 SLT 465, but see para 4.52 below.
3 Criminal Procedure (Scotland) Act 1975 (c 21), s 331(1).
4 *Hall v Associated Newspapers Ltd* 1979 JC 1, 1978 SLT 241.

4.21. The hundred-and-ten-day rule. Where an accused is in custody by virtue of a warrant on a petition committing him for trial for any offence, he may not be detained in terms of that warrant for a total period of more than one hundred and ten days without being brought to trial[1]. Unless the period has been extended[2], failure to start the trial within the one hundred and ten days results in the immediate liberation of the accused, who is thereafter to be free forever from all question or process for the offence for which he had been kept in custody[3]. The period to be counted towards the one hundred and ten days relates solely to that caused by his incarceration in terms of the warrant of committal. If that period is interrupted by, for example, a sentence of imprisonment being imposed in the interim, then the accused is no longer in custody by virtue of the warrant but there by virtue of the sentence of imprisonment, and the computation of the one hundred and ten days halts and does not run again until after he has completed his period of imprisonment[4]. It is also to be noted that the period starts from committal for trial (that is full committal) on the petition, not the earlier committal for further examination. A single High Court judge may grant an extension of the one-hundred-and-ten-day period where, for example, delay is the result of the illness of the accused or an essential witness, or for any other sufficient cause not attributable to the fault of the prosecutor[5].

1 Criminal Procedure (Scotland) Act 1975 (c 21), s 101(2)(b) (substituted by the Criminal Justice (Scotland) Act 1980 (c 62), s 14(1)).
2 See para 4.24 below.

3 Criminal Procedure (Scotland) Act 1975, s 101(2)(b) (as substituted: see note 1 above).
4 *Wallace v HM Advocate* 1959 JC 71, 1959 SLT 320. See R W Renton and H H Brown *Criminal Procedure according to the Law of Scotland* (5th edn, 1983) para 7-39, note 1.
5 *Renton and Brown* para 7-38; *MacDougall v Russell* 1985 SCCR 441, 1986 SLT 403.

4.22. The eighty-day rule. A subsidiary rule known as the eighty-day rule applies to a person detained in custody and awaiting service of the indictment. Like the one-hundred-and-ten-day rule the starting point for computation of the period is the date of full committal. The requirement is that within eighty days an indictment must be served upon the accused, and if it is not he must be liberated forthwith[1]. Unlike the one-hundred-and-ten-day rule, failure to observe this rule results in the accused being given his liberty, but does not free him from prosecution for the offence[2].

1 Criminal Procedure (Scotland) Act 1975 (c 21), s 101(2)(a) (substituted by the Criminal Justice (Scotland) Act 1980 (c 62), s 14(1)).
2 See, however, *HM Advocate v Walker* 1981 JC 102, 1981 SCCR 154, 1981 SLT (Notes) 111.

4.23. The one-year rule. The one-year rule applies to a person who is not in custody and, unlike the eighty- and one-hundred-and-ten-day rules, it starts from the date of the first appearance of the accused on a petition[1]. In terms of this rule the trial on indictment must be commenced within twelve months, which failing the accused must be discharged forthwith and be free forever from all question or process for the offence on indictment[1]. It does not, however, preclude the Crown from prosecuting outwith the one-year period on a summary complaint if that is competent for the charge[2]. Unlike the eighty- or one-hundred-and-ten-day rules the one-year rule applies even if in the interim the accused has been sentenced to a period of imprisonment on another matter.

1 Criminal Procedure (Scotland) Act 1975 (c 21), s 101(1) (substituted by the Criminal Justice (Scotland) Act 1980 (c 62), s 14(1)).
2 *MacDougall v Russell* 1985 SCCR 441, 1986 SLT 403.

4.24. Extension of the time limits. The eighty-day, the one-hundred-and-ten-day and the one-year periods may each be extended by application to the sheriff or, as appropriate, a single judge of the High Court of Justiciary[1], and the grant or refusal of any application to extend the period may be appealed against by note of appeal presented to the High Court[2]. These applications are not, however, readily granted to the Crown. The Crown has to show that there is sufficient cause for the delay for which the prosecutor is not responsible, for example that the accused has become insane in the interim[3].

However, where the application relates to the one-year rule extension may be granted on the wider ground of 'cause shown'[4]; fault of the prosecution will not automatically preclude an extension[5], but neither will the fact that the charges are serious justify one[6]. The complexity of the case being investigated by the Crown would not be a good reason for delay[7]. Nor would the subsequent discovery that a Crown witness who had been excused by the prosecutor was in fact an essential witness[8]. In the case of the one-year rule no effect is given to the rule if the period has been interrupted by the failure of the accused, for whose arrest a warrant has been granted, to appear at a diet in the case[9].

In the case of the one-hundred-and-ten-day rule, the application may be granted if the judge is satisfied that delay in commencing the trial is due to the illness of the accused or of a judge, the absence or illness of any necessary witness or any other sufficient cause not attributable to the prosecutor's fault[10].

In the case of the eighty-day rule, the application may be granted 'for any sufficient cause'[11], but the judge may not grant it if he is satisfied that, but for some fault on the part of the prosecution, the indictment could have been served within the eighty-day period[12].

1 Criminal Procedure (Scotland) Act 1975 (c 21), s 101(1) proviso (ii), (3), (4) (substituted by the Criminal Justice (Scotland) Act 1980 (c 62), s 14(1)).
2 Criminal Procedure (Scotland) Act 1975, s 101(5) (as so substituted).
3 *HM Advocate v Bickerstaff* 1926 JC 65, 1926 SLT 121.
4 Criminal Procedure (Scotland) Act 1975, s 101(1) proviso (ii) (as substituted: see note 1 above). See eg *Dobbie v HM Advocate* 1986 SCCR 72, 1986 SLT 648n; *Rudge v HM Advocate* 1989 SCCR 105.
5 *Mallison v HM Advocate* 1987 SCCR 320.
6 R W Renton and H H Brown *Criminal Procedure according to the Law of Scotland* (5th edn, 1983) para 7-41; *Watson v HM Advocate* 1983 SCCR 115, 1983 SLT 471; *HM Advocate v Swift* 1984 SCCR 216, 1985 SLT 26.
7 *HM Advocate v MacTavish* 1974 JC 19, 1974 SLT 246.
8 *Berry v HM Advocate* 1988 SCCR 458.
9 Criminal Procedure (Scotland) Act 1975, s 101(1) proviso (i) (as substituted: see note 1 above).
10 Ibid, s 101(4)(a)–(c) (as so substituted).
11 Ibid, s 101(3) (as so substituted).
12 Ibid, s 101(3) proviso (as so substituted).

(f) The Indictment

4.25. Introduction. In solemn proceedings both in the High Court of Justiciary and in the sheriff court the indictment is the crucial writ charging the accused with the crime or crimes upon which he is to face trial. This is the first writ he receives to which he may tender a plea of guilty or any preliminary pleas to the competency or relevancy of the proceedings. The petition he receives earlier is a preliminary writ which has frequently been drafted before the procurator fiscal has had an opportunity to investigate fully the allegations against the accused, and the charges contained on that petition may vary from those on the indictment[1]. The charges on the indictment require the prior approval of Crown Counsel before the indictment may be signed and served upon the accused. The indictment runs in the name of the Lord Advocate and is signed by him, exceptionally by the Solicitor General, or by an Advocate Depute if the case is to be heard in the High Court[2]. If the case is to be heard in the sheriff court the procurator fiscal signs, but prefixes his signature with the words 'by Authority of Her Majesty's Advocate'[2]. Indictments raised by or in the name of one Lord Advocate remain competent and effective notwithstanding his resignation, removal, promotion or death and the appointment of a different Lord Advocate before the case either calls in court or is finally disposed of[3]. Similarly, after the departure of one Lord Advocate indictments run in the name of the Solicitor General until such time as a new Lord Advocate is appointed, and these too continue as competent prosecutions[3].

1 See para 4.21 above.
2 Criminal Procedure (Scotland) Act 1975 (c 21), s 41.
3 Ibid, s 42.

4.26. Form of indictment. The indictment must be in a prescribed style[1] or as nearly as may be in such a form[2]. The indictment names an accused, giving his address either as his domicile of citation in terms of his bail order or the prison in which he is detained, and then proceeds to specify the charges which he is called upon to answer. The charges have to be both competent and relevant[3]. Contrary to the position in a section 102 indictment[4], the indictment may not contain a mixture of charges any one of which necessarily shows that the accused has previous convictions while other charges do not[5]. Each charge has to contain three elements: the date of the alleged offence, the place where it was committed and a statement of the *modus*. Failure adequately to specify these first two elements or failure in the third to specify sufficient facts to constitute a crime and infer guilt may result in the defence taking a plea to the relevancy of the charge[6].

There is, however, statutory provision giving implied latitude in statement both of time and place where exactness is not of the essence of the charge[7]. Specification of the *locus* in most cases determines the jurisdiction of the court, and accuracy in this respect is essential[8]. Exceptionally, however, statements of time and place may be made in broader terms where the circumstances of the case make such latitude reasonable.[9] Crucial to the indictment is specification of the mode of commission of the offence, of the facts and circumstances which will disclose an indictable common law crime, or contravention of an Act of Parliament applicable to Scotland, and from which the guilt of the accused may be inferred. The statutory prescribed forms apply to most ordinary offences. If the crime is a statutory offence there must also be reference to the statute concerned and to the section allegedly contravened, although the Act need not be quoted[10].

It is unnecessary to specify a *nomen juris*[11], or alternatives where two or more persons are charged[12], or any allegation that a person is 'guilty, actor or art and part'[13], or the words 'all which or part thereof'[14], or to use such qualifying words as 'wilfully', 'maliciously', 'wickedly and feloniously' or other words alleging intent or knowledge[15]; all these matters are implied.

1 See the Criminal Procedure (Scotland) Act 1887 (c 35), Sch A (amended by the Criminal Justice (Scotland) Act 1949 (c 94), s 79(3), Sch 12).
2 Criminal Procedure (Scotland) Act 1975 (c 21), s 41.
3 See para 4.35 below.
4 See para 4.10 above.
5 Criminal Procedure (Scotland) Act 1975, s 68(1).
6 See generally R W Renton and H H Brown *Criminal Procedure according to the Law of Scotland* (5th edn, 1983) paras 6-13-6-21.
7 Criminal Procedure (Scotland) Act 1975, s 50(1), (2). See for example *Hamilton v W* (otherwise reported as *W v Hamilton*) 1989 SCCR 42; *Hunter v Guild* 1990 GWD 2-74.
8 Hume *Commentaries* II,209; *M'Millan v Grant* 1924 JC 13, 1924 SLT 86.
9 Alison *Practice* p 256; *Ogg v HM Advocate* 1938 JC 152 at 154, per Lord Russell; *Murray v HM Advocate* 1987 SCCR 249.
10 Criminal Procedure (Scotland) Act 1975, s 49.
11 Ibid, s 44.
12 Ibid, s 45.
13 Ibid, s 46.
14 Ibid, s 47.
15 Ibid, s 48.

4.27. Lists of productions and witnesses. Annexed to the indictment is a list of the productions to which reference is to be made by the Crown witnesses in the course of the trial, and a list of the witnesses speaking to the evidence[1]. The list of productions itself may be in two parts, one relating to the documentary productions to be referred to[2] and one to the non-documentary productions, known as labels. The list of witnesses should show the names and addresses of the witnesses in order that they can be identified and traced by the defence to enable it to obtain statements and prepare its case. The addresses do not have to be the home addresses of the various witnesses, and places of employment are frequently given where the witness is speaking to matters related to that employment, such as a bank official or police officer. To avoid possible intimidation of a witness, or where a witness is frightened and unwilling to give an address publicly, it is permissible to provide for a witness an accommodation address, such as care of a specified police station. The significance of the lists is that these witnesses, together with those on the list provided by the defence, are the only witnesses who may be called to give evidence in the trial, except in a very limited situation of evidence in replication[3] or where a section 81 notice[4] has been lodged. Similarly the productions listed, both documentary and labelled, together with those on the defence list, are the only productions which may be referred to. Accordingly the Crown may not call some other party or have a witness bring with him productions which are not on the list, or take evidence from that production, with the exception of notes made by the witness at the time of the incident and used for refreshing his memory. If the Crown wishes to lead additional witnesses or refer to additional productions other than those on these lists, it must lodge a section 81 notice prior to the commencement of the trial.

1 Criminal Procedure (Scotland) Act 1975 (c 21), s 78(1) (substituted by the Criminal Justice (Scotland) Act 1980 (c 62), s 12, Sch 4, para 8).
2 The list of productions must include the record of proceedings at the examination of the accused (see para 4.07 above): Criminal Procedure (Scotland) Act 1975, s 78(2) (as so substituted).
3 See para 6.28 below.
4 As to the Criminal Procedure (Scotland) Act 1975, s 81, see para 4.29 below.

4.28. Service of indictment. The clerk of the appropriate court, that is the sheriff court or the High Court of Justiciary, grants a warrant to the prosecutor to cite the accused to the trial diet[1]. A copy of the indictment, including the lists of witnesses and productions, together with a notice to the accused intimating to him the place, date and time of the diet of the court, is then served upon him by an officer of law[2]. Although 'officer of law' includes macers, messengers-at-arms and sheriff officers, other persons having authority to execute a warrant of court, constables and prison officers[3], in practice in Scotland indictments are served by police officers or, where the person on whom service is effected is in prison, by a prison officer. The citation is signed by the serving officer and a witness[4]. The copy of the indictment must bear the signature of the prosecutor, namely the Advocate Depute or procurator fiscal as appropriate, at the end of the indictment and of each list[5]. At the same time a separate schedule of previous convictions, if any, is served upon the accused[6]. Where he is in custody he is served personally with the documentation. Where, however, he is liberated on bail, service of the documentation to the domicile of citation is all that is required[7]. Normally police officers will attempt to effect citation by leaving the documentation in the hands of somebody at that address, but if they can get no answer it is perfectly competent to leave the documentation pinned to the most obvious door and thereby effect proper citation[8]. Failure to serve an indictment properly is fatal to any subsequent proceedings and is not cured by the accused's appearance at the trial, unlike the position for summary proceedings[9]. The accused is required to object to the validity of the citation against him by way of a preliminary diet[10]. On the occasions where the accused is neither in custody nor on bail, because for example he was detained in custody for more than eighty days without service of the indictment, and liberated in terms of the eighty-day rule[11], it is advisable that service should be made upon him personally if he can be found. If the accused is a limited company the indictment is served by delivering a copy of it with the appropriate notices to the registered office or, if there is no registered office, or the registered office is not in the United Kingdom, at the principal place of business in the United Kingdom of that company. Such service can be effected either by officers of court or by sending a copy by registered or recorded delivery post[12].

1 Criminal Procedure (Scotland) Act 1975 (c 21), s 69 (amended by the Criminal Justice (Scotland) Act 1980 (c 62), s 12, Sch 4, para 2, and Act of Adjournal (Consolidation) 1988, SI 1988/110, r 10(2)). See Act of Adjournal (Consolidation) 1988, r 10(1), Sch 1, Form 3.
2 Criminal Procedure (Scotland) Act 1975, s 71.
3 Ibid, s 462(1).
4 Ibid, s 69 (as amended: see note 1 above); Act of Adjournal (Consolidation) 1988, r 10(1), Sch 1, Form 4.
5 Criminal Procedure (Scotland) Act 1975, s 41.
6 Ibid, s 68(2).
7 Bail etc (Scotland) Act 1980 (c 4), s 2(2), (3). Even if the accused is subsequently detained in prison in connection with some other matter it is sufficient to serve the indictment upon him at his domicile of citation if the bail order in respect of the original offence is still in force: *Jamieson v HM Advocate* 1990 SCCR 137.
8 *Welsh v HM Advocate* 1986 SCCR 233, 1986 SLT 664n.
9 *Hester v MacDonald* 1961 SC 370, 1961 SLT 414.
10 Criminal Procedure (Scotland) Act 1975, s 108 (amended by the Criminal Justice (Scotland) Act 1980, Sch 4, para 10, and the Law Reform (Miscellaneous Provisions) (Scotland) Act 1985 (c 73), s 59(1), Sch 2, para 18).
11 See para 4.22 above.
12 Criminal Procedure (Scotland) Act 1975, s 74(1).

4.29. Additional witnesses and productions. After the indictment has been served it is not competent to amend it by adding additional witnesses or productions[1]. The proper procedure is for the prosecutor to have given a written 'section 81 notice' to the defence of the name and address of the witness or details of the production not less than two clear days before the day on which the jury is sworn to try the case[2]. It also requires the leave of the court before the prosecutor can examine this additional witness[3]. The court might delay the trial to enable the defence to precognosce the witness or examine the productions.

1 See, however, the Bail etc (Scotland) Act 1980 (c 4), s 3(4), and para 6.13 below.
2 Criminal Procedure (Scotland) Act 1975 (c 21), s 81 (amended by the Criminal Justice (Scotland) Act 1980 (c 62), s 83(2), Sch 7, para 28), which is expressed to be subject to the Criminal Procedure (Scotland) Act 1975, s 82A (added by the Criminal Justice (Scotland) Act 1980, s 27), under which it is competent for either side to examine the other's witnesses or put in evidence any production included in any list or notice lodged by the other.
3 Criminal Procedure (Scotland) Act 1975, s 81.

4.30. Lodging of record copy of indictment etc. The record copy of the indictment, that is, the principal, should be lodged with the clerk of the trial court on or before the date of service of the indictment on the accused[1]. A copy of the lists of witnesses and of productions, including the record of proceedings at the judicial examination, must be lodged with the clerk of the trial court not less than ten clear days before the trial diet[1], though in practice those lists are lodged at the same time as the record copy indictment.

1 Criminal Procedure (Scotland) Act 1975 (c 21), s 78(1) (substituted by the Criminal Justice (Scotland) Act 1980 (c 62), s 12, Sch 4, para 8). See *HM Advocate v Graham* 1985 SCCR 169, 1985 SLT 498.

(g) Requirements on the Defence

4.31. Introduction. In solemn proceedings there are requirements placed upon the defence as a matter of law which have to be adhered to, and failure to do so could seriously affect the ability to lead a proper defence to the charge. More flexibility is given to the defence than to the Crown, partly because the defence may have less time to prepare the case. In theory it does not know the charges or the witnesses speaking to them until service of the indictment upon the accused, which can be on a minimum *induciae* of twenty-nine clear days[1]. Moreover, it is in the interests of justice that an accused is not prejudiced by the failure of his legal advisers to carry out steps properly. This does not mean that the defence may ignore the rules; in each case that it fails to adhere to them it will have to justify its position and seek the consent of the court in order to lead the evidence or carry out those steps which should have been taken at some other stage in the proceedings.

1 Criminal Procedure (Scotland) Act 1975 (c 21), s 75 (substituted by the Criminal Justice (Scotland) Act 1980 (c 62), s 12, Sch 4, para 4).

4.32. Lists of productions and witnesses. Just as the Crown is obliged to give the defence lists of productions and witnesses by attaching a copy to the indictment, so too is the defence obliged to lodge similar lists. Unlike the Crown list, which must contain all those who are likely to be giving evidence for the Crown, the defence list is more restricted. It has to submit only the additional witnesses and productions to which it wishes to refer and which are not included in the Crown list[1]. It does not have to repeat productions which or persons who already feature on the Crown lists. It is not necessary to include in the list the accused or any co-accused. The list must be given to the procurator fiscal of the appropriate court if the jury trial is to be held in the sheriff court, or to the Crown Agent if it is to be held in the High Court of Justiciary, at least three clear days before the day on which the jury is sworn to try the case[1]. There is no equivalent of a section 81 notice by the Crown[2]. This is because the Crown must lodge these lists with the indictment when it is served, whereas the defence lists require only three days' notice, and there should be no need for an additional list in those three days. In the event of additional witnesses or productions being required for which the three-day notice cannot be given, it is open to the defence to seek leave of the court to lead this evidence, if the request is made before the jury is sworn to try the case. It is too late after the jury is sworn to try to bring in an additional witness, for example half way through the trial. However, in such cases it is competent to lead the evidence if the prosecutor waives his right to object; but if he does not waive this right then there is no remedy available to the defence for its failure to give timeous notice[3].

1 Criminal Procedure (Scotland) Act 1975 (c 21), s 82(2) (amended by the Criminal Justice (Scotland) Act 1980 (c 62), s 12, Sch 4, para 10).
2 Ie a notice of additional witnesses and productions not included in the Crown list: see the Criminal Procedure (Scotland) Act 1975, s 81, and para 4.29 above.
3 *Lowson v HM Advocate* 1943 JC 141, 1944 SLT 74. But see also *HM Advocate v Higgins*, Stirling High Court, 11 June 1990 (unreported). See also para 6.27 below.

4.33. Preliminary pleas. There are a number of matters which the defence may plead only before the trial diet. Notice of its intention to do so must be given within the appropriate period[1], and failure to do so could result in this line of defence not being admissible at the trial diet.

These matters of which advance notice must be given include the special defences[2], incrimination[3], pleas to the competency and relevancy of the indictment[4], pleas in bar of trial[5] and pleas with regard to separation and conjunction of charges and trials[6], and other matters which could be resolved with advantage before the trial[7]. Advance notice must also be given of the defence's desire to amend the transcript of the judicial examination or to delete from it matters which should not be there[8], or to challenge the production of a transcript of the accused's tape-recorded interview with the police as evidence for the Crown[9].

1 As to the appropriate period, see notes 4–7 below.

2 See the Criminal Procedure (Scotland) Act 1975 (c21), s82(1) (substituted by the Criminal Justice (Scotland) Act 1980 (c62), s13); Act of Adjournal (Consolidation) 1988, SI 1988/110, r68, and para 4.36 below.

3 See the Criminal Procedure (Scotland) Act 1975, s82(1).

4 Ibid, s76(1)(a) (substituted by the Criminal Justice (Scotland) Act 1980, s12, Sch 4, para 5): see paras 4.40, 4.45, below. The appropriate period is fifteen clear days after service of the indictment: Criminal Procedure (Scotland) Act 1975, s76(7)(a) (as so substituted).

5 Ibid, s76(1)(b) (as so substituted): see paras 2.40, 2.46–2.53, below. The appropriate period is the period from the service of the indictment to ten clear days before the trial diet: s76(7)(b) (as so substituted).

6 Ibid, s76(1)(b) (as so substituted): see paras 4.40, 4.54, 4.55, below. The period is as stated in note 5 above.

7 Ibid, s76(1)(c) (as so substituted). The appropriate period is the period from the service of the indictment to the trial diet: s76(7)(c) (as so substituted).

8 See para 4.09 above.

9 Criminal Justice (Scotland) Act 1987 (c41), s60(1). Notice of intention to challenge must be given not less than six days before the trial: s60(2).

4.34. Examination and recovery of productions. The Crown documentary productions are usually lodged with the appropriate clerk of court along with the record copy indictment and at the same time, that is when the indictment is served[1]. It is not, however, the practice to lodge the labelled productions at that time, although the accused is entitled to see the productions before the trial and to see them in the office of the appropriate clerk of court[2]. The defence has an absolute right to examine these without let or hindrance and in cases of difficulty is entitled to apply to the trial court for a warrant to inspect and examine them and to subject them if appropriate to scientific examination[3]. Nevertheless there may be productions which the Crown is not lodging and yet are important for the defence case. In such circumstances where documents or other productions are in the possession of the Crown or a third party and are not available to the accused, he is entitled to petition the High Court to grant a commission and diligence for their recovery. It is established practice that the petition is to the High Court, notwithstanding that the trial may be taking place in a sheriff court[4]. The terms of the petition must give an indication in general terms of the relationship the productions bear to the charge the accused is facing and the proposed defence for which these are necessary[5].

1 The Criminal Procedure (Scotland) Act 1975 (c21), s83 (amended by the Criminal Justice (Scotland) Act 1980 (c62), s12, Sch 4, para 11), is derived from the Criminal Procedure (Scotland) Act 1887 (c35), s37, and refers to the 'existing law and practice'. Unlike the specific requirements as to the time for lodging the record copy indictment and the lists of witnesses and productions, there is no equivalent specific requirement as to when the productions themselves have to be lodged, and practice varies around Scotland.

2 Criminal Procedure (Scotland) Act 1975, s83 (as so amended); *Stark and Smith v HM Advocate* 1938 JC 170, 1938 SLT 516. See, however, *MacNeil v HM Advocate* 1986 SCCR 288 at 298–300.

3 *Davies* 1973 SLT (Notes) 36.

4 See para 4.18 above, and *HM Advocate v Ashrif* 1988 SCCR 197, 1988 SLT 567.

5 *Downie v HM Advocate* 1952 JC 37, 1952 SLT 159.

4.35. Objections to Crown witnesses. The Crown is required to list the witnesses it proposes to call in support of its case so that the defence may know their identity in advance of the trial diet and statements may be taken from them to ascertain what evidence they are able to give. If a witness has been wrongly identified by, for example, the wrong name or part of a name being given, or the wrong address, and the defence is unable to trace him, injustice would result unless objection could be taken to that witness. The important criterion is a failure to identify or trace, not a failure to obtain a statement from, the witness. Objection must be given in writing at least ten days before the commencement of the trial, otherwise the witness remains competent for the Crown unless the defence can show cause to the court for its failure to give proper intimation[1]. The written intimation must be to the court, the prosecutor and to any co-accused[1]. Where intimation is properly made or cause can be shown to allow the objection to be lodged late, the remedy given to the defence is by way of postponement, adjournment or otherwise as appears to the court to be appropriate to enable the defence to trace the witness in sufficient time to precognosce him before the trial commences[2].

1 Criminal Procedure (Scotland) Act 1975 (c 21), s 80(1) (substituted by the Criminal Justice (Scotland) Act 1980 (c 62), s 12, Sch 4, para 9).
2 Criminal Procedure (Scotland) Act 1975, s 80(2) (as so substituted).

(h) Special Defences

4.36. Lodging of special defences. One of the essential steps the defence has to take in solemn proceedings is to give notice of a special defence if one is available. Such a notice has to be lodged with the appropriate clerk of court at least ten days before the commencement of the trial[1]. If the defence is unable to do so timeously, it may apply to the court and show cause for lodging the notice late; but in any event it must be lodged before the oath is administered to the jury[2]. This requirement is vital since failure to give the proper notice or to obtain the consent of the court where the notice was late could result in the line of defence no longer being available and no evidence being led in support of it. The court may permit late lodging even if no reasonable cause is shown, if the Crown does not object.

1 Criminal Procedure (Scotland) Act 1975 (c 21), s 82(1)(a) (substituted by the Criminal Justice (Scotland) Act 1980 (c 62), s 13).
2 Criminal Procedure (Scotland) Act 1975, s 82(1)(b) (as so substituted).

4.37. Meaning of 'special defence'. The term 'special defence' is a precise one. It does not mean any possible defence to the charge or even the general line of defence but those circumstances which fall into the following categories: alibi[1]; insanity at the time of the act[2]; incrimination[3]; and self defence[4]. Evidence that the accused was asleep at the time when he committed the crime charged[5] may no longer constitute a special defence[6], but as a matter of practice it would be better to be intimated if the circumstances were applicable. It is to be noted that the list is not exhaustive of all defences and does not, for example, include coercion[7], necessity[8], diminished responsibility, provocation or any other plea of a mitigating nature.

1 *HM Advocate v Gairdner* (1838) 2 Swin 180; *HM Advocate v M'Lellan* (1843) 1 Broun 510.
2 Criminal Procedure (Scotland) Act 1975 (c 21), s 174(2); *HM Advocate v Mitchell* 1951 JC 53, 1951 SLT 200.
3 *HM Advocate v Robertson* (1859) 3 Irv 328; *HM Advocate v Laing* (1871) 2 Coup 23. A notice requires to be lodged even when it refers to the actings of a co-accused as the basis of this special defence: *Pike v HM Advocate* 1987 SCCR 163, but see also *McShane v HM Advocate* 1989 SCCR 687 and para 6.30, note 20 below.
4 *William Younger* (1828) Hume *Commentaries* II, Bell's Notes 236; *HM Advocate v M'Glone* 1955 JC 14, 1955 SLT 79.
5 *HM Advocate v Fraser* (1878) 4 Coup 70.
6 *HM Advocate v Cunningham* 1963 JC 80, 1963 SLT 345.
7 *Thomson v HM Advocate* 1983 JC 69, 1983 SLT 682, 1983 SCCR 368.
8 *Connorton v Annan* 1981 SCCR 307; *Tudhope v Grubb* 1983 SCCR 350, Sh Ct; *MacLeod v MacDougall* 1988 SCCR 519; *McNab v Guild* 1989 SCCR 138.

4.38. The requirement of fair notice. The sole purpose of a special defence is to give fair notice to the Crown of a line of evidence or a possible line of evidence that may be led on behalf of the defence[1]. With the exception of the special defence of insanity, it has no effect upon the onus of proof, which remains with the Crown to prove its case beyond reasonable doubt[2]. It does not imply that the defence must prove anything despite the inference in the style used in the written notice, which is to the effect that the accused 'pleads not guilty and specially without prejudice to said plea' etc, giving details of the special defence. It has been held that:

> 'The only purpose of the special defence is to give fair notice to the Crown and once such notice has been given the only issue for a jury is to decide, upon the whole evidence before them, whether the Crown has established the accused's guilt beyond reasonable doubt. When a special defence is pleaded. . . all that requires to be said of the special defence. . . is that if that evidence, whether from one or more witnesses, is believed, or creates in the minds of the jury reasonable doubt as to the guilt of the accused in the matters libelled, the Crown case must fail and that they must acquit'[3].

1 R W Renton and H H Brown *Criminal Procedure according to the Law of Scotland* (5th edn, 1983) para 7-21; *HM Advocate v Peters* (1969) 33 JCL 209; *Thomson v HM Advocate* 1983 JC 69, 1983 SCCR 368, 1983 SLT 682.
2 *Renton and Brown* para 18-02.
3 *Lambie v HM Advocate* 1973 JC 53 at 58, 59, 1973 SLT 219 at 222, per Lord Justice-General Emslie.

4.39. Withdrawal of special defence. Special defences should be pleaded with some care, as can be seen by a study of the case of *Williamson v HM Advocate*[1], where a special defence of self defence had been lodged but subsequently withdrawn prior to empanelling the jury, and the line that the defence then took at the trial was one of alibi. It was ruled to be competent for the Crown to question the accused upon the circumstances of his lodging the earlier special defence notwithstanding possible confidentiality between an accused and his legal adviser. The object of the cross-examination was to test the credibility of the accused in the light of the fact that he must have informed his advisers of a very different story earlier for the self defence plea to have been lodged.

1 *Williamson v HM Advocate* 1980 JC 22, 1978 SLT (Notes) 38.

(i) Preliminary Diets and Issues

(A) PRELIMINARY DIETS

4.40. Introduction. Prior to 1980 solemn proceedings had two diets, the first of which was known as the 'pleading diet' and the second the 'trial diet'. The principal purposes of the pleading diet were to discover whether the accused intended to plead guilty to the charges thus avoiding the unnecessary calling of witnesses and jurors, and to deal with preliminary matters before any jurors or witnesses had been cited to minimise inconvenience to them. Unfortunately this aim was not always achieved. For example, preliminary pleas with regard to a High Court trial could only be dealt with in the High Court even though the first or pleading diet was called in the sheriff court; the outcome of the preliminary plea was therefore not known until the trial diet. Accordingly the practice of holding a first diet was discontinued in 1980[1], and today we have simply one diet, the trial diet.

However, preliminary matters still require to be dealt with when the situation arises, and accordingly a preliminary diet will be held to deal with them[2]. These diets can either be mandatory or discretionary, depending upon the circumstances. A preliminary diet is mandatory to inquire into objections to the validity of the citation and matters of competency or relevancy of the indictment[3]. The discretionary preliminary diet relates to pleas in bar of trial, application for separation or conjunction of charges or trials[4], and any other matter which could in the opinion of the prosecutor or accused be resolved with advantage before the trial[5], such as amendment of the transcript of the judicial examination.

1 Criminal Justice (Scotland) Act 1980 (c 62), s 12.
2 As to the preliminary diet, see Act of Adjournal (Consolidation) 1988, SI 1988/110, rr 24–40.
3 Criminal Procedure (Scotland) Act 1975 (c 21), s 76(1)(a) (substituted by the Criminal Justice (Scotland) Act 1980, s 12, Sch 4, para 5): see para 4.45 below.
4 Criminal Procedure (Scotland) Act 1975, s 76(1)(b) (as so substituted): see paras 4.46–4.53 (pleas in bar of trial) and paras 4.54, 4.55 (separation and conjunction) below.
5 Ibid, s 76(1)(c) (as so substituted). See *McDonald v HM Advocate, Valentine v HM Advocate* 1989 SCCR 165.

4.41. Notice of preliminary diet. Whether mandatory or discretionary, preliminary diets are instituted upon written notice being given to the court and to the other parties by the person, normally the accused, making the application[1]. The other parties would include the prosecutor and co-accused, as appropriate. If a preliminary diet has been ordered on any particular notice then it is competent for the court to consider at that diet any other notice intimated to the court and to the other parties at least twenty-four hours before that preliminary diet[2].

1 Criminal Procedure (Scotland) Act 1975 (c 21), s 76(1) (substituted by the Criminal Justice (Scotland) Act 1980 (c 62), s 12, Sch 4, para 5); Act of Adjournal (Consolidation) 1988, SI 1988/110, rr 24, 25, Sch 1, Form 15. For the 'appropriate period' within which the notice is to be given, see para 4.33, notes 4–7, above.
2 Criminal Procedure (Scotland) Act 1975, s 76(3) (as so substituted).

4.42. Procedure at preliminary diet. The procedure at the preliminary diet is the same whether it is mandatory or discretionary. It is a diet of the court which the accused is required to attend[1], and failure to attend would be a breach of bail conditions if the accused is on bail. However, the court may permit the diet to proceed notwithstanding the absence of an accused, but this is unusual and should be avoided wherever possible. The diet is held before a judge of the court for which a trial diet was fixed, that is, before a sheriff, if it is a sheriff and jury trial, or a High Court judge if a High Court trial. The usual form of the diet is by way of debate without the leading of evidence, though witnesses may be called if, for example, the objection relates to non-timeous citation. The next stage in the proceedings depends upon the decision of the preliminary diet; the subject matter of the plea may either go to the root of the prosecution, such as competency (which if upheld would stop further proceedings), or to minor amendment (for example to the record of the judicial examination, which would have no effect upon further proceedings). If appropriate, therefore, at the end of the preliminary diet the accused is called upon to tender a plea to the charges, and if he pleads not guilty the case is continued to the trial diet originally fixed for the trial. If he pleads guilty the case is disposed of in the usual way. A record of the proceedings at the diet is kept[2].

1 Criminal Procedure (Scotland) Act 1975 (c 21), s 76(6) (substituted by the Criminal Justice (Scotland) Act 1980 (c 62), s 12, Sch 4, para 5).
2 Act of Adjournal (Consolidation) 1988, SI 1988/110, r 33(3).

4.43. Appeals from preliminary diet. As the purpose of the preliminary diet is to clear such matters away as to avoid disrupting the trial diet, provision has been made for a pre-trial appeal from the decision of the preliminary diet. This right of appeal is, however, without prejudice to the accused's right to appeal after conviction or indeed to the prosecutor's right to appeal by advocation. The interim appeal requires the leave of the court, which must be sought not later than two days after the original decision[1]. The appeal is taken to the High Court of Justiciary on note of appeal[2], and when an appeal is taken the High Court may postpone the trial diet[3]. The appeal can deal only with matters raised and decided at the preliminary diet[4].

1 Criminal Procedure (Scotland) Act 1975 (c 21), s 76A(1) (added by the Criminal Justice (Scotland) Act 1980 (c 62), s 12, Sch 4, para 5).
2 Criminal Procedure (Scotland) Act 1975, s 76A(1) (as so added); Act of Adjournal (Consolidation) 1988, SI 1988/110, rr 35, 36, Sch 1, Form 17.
3 Criminal Procedure (Scotland) Act 1975, s 76A(2) (as so added).
4 *Templeton v HM Advocate* 1987 SCCR 693, 1988 SLT 171n.

4.44. Postponement of trial diet. If a preliminary diet is ordered the court concerned may postpone the trial diet for a period not exceeding twenty-one days unless extended further by the High Court of Justiciary, and the postponement does not count towards any time limit applying in respect of the case[1]. This provision effectively extends the one-hundred-and-ten-day rule and the one-year rule in such cases[2]. A similar provision applies where there has been an appeal in connection with the preliminary diet, but because appeals may take longer there is no upper limit to the permissible period of postponement, although any period of postponement caused by the appeal does count towards time limits, unless the High Court directs otherwise[3].

1 Criminal Procedure (Scotland) Act 1975 (c 21), s 76(4) (substituted by the Criminal Justice (Scotland) Act 1980 (c 62), s 12, Sch 4, para 5).
2 As to these rules, see paras 4.21, 4.22, above.
3 Criminal Procedure (Scotland) Act 1975, s 76A(2) (added by the Criminal Justice (Scotland) Act 1980, Sch 4, para 5).

(B) PLEAS TO COMPETENCY AND RELEVANCY

4.45. Competency or relevancy. Pleas to the competency or relevancy of the indictment require the holding of a mandatory preliminary diet[1]. The two are not the same; an objection to competency strikes at the right to prosecute, whereas an objection to relevancy is on the basis that the libel as a whole is insufficient in law to justify the court in calling upon the person accused to plead to the charge, or alternatively is so lacking in specification that it is unjust that he be asked to plead to the charge. A plea to the competency, if upheld, stops the particular proceedings. A plea to the relevancy, if upheld, may be put right by amendment of the indictment and the proceedings can thereafter continue.

There are a number of possible objections to competency, but the principal grounds are that the particular court has no jurisdiction to try the crime charged[2]; that the judge has a particular interest in the accused or the circumstances[3]; that the proceedings are time-barred[4]; that the prosecutor has no title or interest to prosecute[5]; that the particular charge may not be tried in the form taken, for example that it is limited to summary prosecution only; or that there has been a breach of the one-hundred-and-ten-day rule or the one-year rule[6].

With regard to objections to relevancy, the important grounds are that the libel does not set forth facts which constitute either a crime at common law or a contravention of an Act of Parliament applicable to Scotland; that the libel is defective or ambiguous in specification[7]; that the libel in a statutory offence mentions inaccurately the Act of Parliament or the section contravened; or that the libel contains material errors in the designation of the accused etc[8]. The first objection to relevancy (that the libel does not constitute a crime known to the law of Scotland) is always subject to the declaratory power of the High Court to declare that the circumstances before it do indeed contravene the law of Scotland. There is no similar power vested in the sheriff court, and thus it may be that the same indictment could be held to be irrelevant in the sheriff court but relevant in the High Court using declaratory powers not available to the sheriff.

It is not a valid plea to the competency that the indictment was not preceded by a petition in relation to the same offence[9]. Similarly it is not a valid plea to the competency that the accused was not committed or validly committed for trial[10].

The effect of an objection to competency or relevancy being upheld will depend upon the particular circumstances of the case. If, for example, the competency objection has been on the basis that the particular court has no jurisdiction to try the case, then the indictment would be deserted *pro loco et tempore* and a new indictment with a new trial diet may be served upon the accused to call in the court which does have jurisdiction. If on the other hand the plea to the competency is that the one-hundred-and-ten-day rule has been contravened, then in terms of that rule the accused can never be brought to trial with regard to the allegations concerned, and that would be the end of the matter. As far as a plea to the relevancy is concerned, if the indictment can be amended to become relevant, that may be done either with an adjournment granted to the defence and the amended indictment then proceeding to trial, or alternatively the original indictment can be deserted *pro loco et tempore* and a new relevant indictment served for a new trial diet, all as the circumstances demand. When the indictment is *funditus* null it cannot be amended[11].

1 Criminal Procedure (Scotland) Act 1975 (c 21), s 76(1(a) (substituted by the Criminal Justice (Scotland) Act 1980 (c 62), s 12, Sch 4, para 5): see para 4.40 above.
2 As to jurisdiction, see paras 2.20–2.24 above.
3 *Bradford v McLeod* 1985 SCCR 379, 1986 SLT 244; *Harper of Oban (Engineering) Ltd v Henderson* 1988 SCCR 351, 1989 SLT 21.
4 As to time limits, see paras 4.20–4.24 above.
5 *HM Advocate v Hanna* 1975 SLT (Sh Ct) 24.
6 As to these rules, see paras 4.21, 4.23, above.
7 *Sayers v HM Advocate* 1982 JC 17, 1981 SCCR 312, 1982 SLT 220. For objections that the time span during which it is alleged that an offence was committed was too great, see *Lockhart v McKenzie* 1988 SCCR 421, Sh Ct, following *HM Advocate v Creighton* (1876) 3 Coup 254.
8 Cf *Keane v HM Advocate* 1986 SCCR 491, 1987 SLT 220n, where an indictment was amended to substitute the correct accused in respect of one charge on an indictment with a plurality of accused persons and charges.
9 *O'Reilly v HM Advocate* 1984 SCCR 352, 1985 SLT 99.
10 *M'Vey v HM Advocate* 1911 SC (J) 94, 6 Adam 503.
11 Cf G H Gordon 'Fundamental Nullity and the Power of Amendment' 1974 SLT (News) 154.

(C) PLEAS IN BAR OF TRIAL

4.46. Pleas in bar of trial generally. A plea in bar of trial gives rise to an application for a discretionary preliminary diet[1], and if sustained it stops further proceedings in the indictment, though it may be competent to raise a fresh one.

The pleas in bar of trial are nonage, insanity, *res judicata, socius criminis*, personal bar, *mora*, taciturnity and delay; and prejudicial publicity. They are discussed in the paragraphs which follow.

1 Criminal Procedure (Scotland) Act 1975 (c 21), s 76(1)(b) (substituted by the Criminal Justice (Scotland) Act 1980 (c 62), s 12, Sch 4, para 5): see para 4.40 above.

4.47. Nonage. The first plea in bar of trial is nonage: that the accused is under eight years of age. This is conclusive evidence that he cannot be found guilty of an offence[1].

1 Criminal Procedure (Scotland) Act 1975 (c 21), ss 170, 369. Cf Hume *Commentaries* I, 35.

4.48. Insanity at the time of trial. The second plea in bar of trial is insanity at the time of trial rendering the accused unfit to plead[1]. This is not to be confused with the special defence of insanity at the time of the offence[2].

1 See paras 10.01, 10.02, below.
2 See para 4.37 above.

4.49. Res judicata. The third plea in bar of trial is *res judicata* on the grounds either that a libel in the same form as the indictment, and founded on the same facts, has already been judged irrelevant or that the accused has tholed his assize. To thole his assize an accused must have been brought before a competent court and either have pled guilty or stood trial and been found guilty, not proven or not guilty on the specific offence set out in the indictment[1]. An alternative situation giving rise to the same plea is where a court has deserted the original matter *simpliciter* and its decision has not been reversed on appeal[2]. Two exceptions to the rule apply. The first is where an accused has been tried for assault with or without aggravation; should the victim thereafter die, it is competent to reindict on a charge of murder or culpable homicide[3]. The second exception arises under the statutory provisions whereby the High Court on appeal can order a new trial to take place; in such circumstances a plea of *res judicata* would not be heard[4]. It may be that it is competent to try an accused in the High Court on a libel which the sheriff has held to be irrelevant[5].

1 *Dunlop v HM Advocate* 1974 JC 59, *sub nom HM Advocate v Dunlop and Macklow* 1974 SLT 242. For summary proceedings, see *Milne v Guild* 1985 SCCR 464, 1986 SLT 431.
2 Criminal Procedure (Scotland) Act 1975 (c 21), s 127(1A) (added by the Criminal Justice (Scotland) Act 1980 (c 26), s 18(1)).
3 *HM Advocate v Stewart* (1866) 5 Irv 310; *HM Advocate v O'Connor* (1882) 10 R (J) 40, 5 Coup 206.
4 See the Criminal Procedure (Scotland) Act 1975, s 255(1) (substituted by the Criminal Justice (Scotland) Act 1980, s 33, Sch 2, para 19): see para 8.15 below.
5 *HM Advocate v Fleming* (1866) 5 Irv 289.

4.50. *Socius criminis*. The fourth plea in bar of trial relates to a *socius criminis*. Where an accused person has previously been called as a witness by the prosecutor and has given evidence on behalf of the prosecutor in the trial he cannot thereafter be charged with the offence in reference to which he gave that evidence[1]. The scope of this plea is further limited by the requirement that he must have been called by the prosecutor as a *socius criminis* in relation to the earlier matter, and he must have given evidence on behalf of the prosecutor[2]. If the prosecutor does not lead his evidence at the earlier trial but he is called by the defence, then the plea is not available to him even if he had been on the prosecutor's list of witnesses when called by the defence[3].

1 *M'Ginley v MacLeod* 1963 JC 11, 1963 SLT 2; *O'Neill v Wilson* 1983 JC 42, 1983 SCCR 265, 1983 SLT 573.

2 See C N Stoddart 'The Immunity Rule' (1983) 28 JLSS 453.
3 *M'Ginley v MacLeod* 1963 JC 11, 1963 SLT 2.

4.51. Personal bar. The fifth plea in bar of trial relates to personal bar upon the prosecutor where he has renounced his right to prosecute. The renunciation can be implied by, for example, a desertion *simpliciter*, or it can be specifically stated[1]. It is to be noted that a renunciation by the procurator fiscal binds the Lord Advocate[2]. However, renunciation by the public prosecutor does not constitute a bar to private prosecution[3].

1 See eg *Thom v HM Advocate* 1976 JC 48, 1976 SLT 232; *HM Advocate v Stewart* 1980 JC 84; *McConnachie v Scott* 1988 SCCR 176, 1988 SLT 480.
2 See *Thom v HM Advocate* 1976 JC 48, 1976 SLT 232.
3 *X v Sweeney* 1982 JC 70, 1982 SCCR 161, 1983 SLT 48.

4.52. *Mora*, taciturnity and delay. The sixth plea in bar of trial is *mora*, taciturnity and delay, that is, where the Crown has acted oppressively and has unreasonably delayed bringing the matter to court. Unlike the foregoing pleas in bar of trial this is a question of a balance in the interests of justice and very much depends upon the circumstances. These will vary from case to case, and account will be taken of factors such as the gravity of the charges, the notice given to the accused of the charges so that he can gather evidence for the defence timeously and before it is lost, the length of any period of delay and any explanation given for it. This can be shown by contrasting two cases, the first being a charge of assault taken on summary procedure two years after the event, where the accused was not charged with the assault at the time and accordingly thereby given no notice that an allegation was outstanding against him. In that case the plea of oppression was upheld and the complaint dismissed as incompetent[1]. On the other hand, in a case on indictment alleging fraud and embezzlement involving actings by solicitors which took place some four years before the service of a petition charging the various parties with some of the allegations, the matter ultimately calling for a trial a further four years later, the plea of oppression was repelled[2].

1 *Tudhope v McCarthy* 1985 SCCR 76, 1985 SLT 392. See also *Philips v Tudhope* 1987 SCCR 80, and *McFarlane v Jessop* 1988 SCCR 186, 1988 SLT 596; *McGeown v HM Advocate* 1989 SCCR 95; *Connachan v Douglas* 1990 SCCR 101.
2 *Leslie v HM Advocate* 31 January 1984, High Court of Justiciary (unreported), detailed in *Tudhope v McCarthy* 1985 SCCR 76 at 81–84 (Commentary). See also *HM Advocate v Stewart* 1980 JC 84, *Hamilton v W* (otherwise reported as *W v Hamilton*) 1989 SCCR 42; *Jessop v Nicholson* 1989 GWD 39–1795.

4.53. Prejudicial publicity. The final plea in bar of trial relates to prejudicial publicity, that is, publicity by way of media reporting prior to or in the course of a trial such that the accused cannot have a fair trial. Again, rather like oppression, this is a question of fact and depends upon the circumstances. It is, however, more difficult to sustain a plea of prejudicial publicity than it is to sustain a plea of oppression as it is a matter of presumption that a jury, given proper direction, will not be affected by extraneous material. For example, where a nurse was to stand trial on allegations involving assaulting a patient to the danger of her life, a television company put out on a national broadcast an item about euthanasia which made specific reference to the trial about to take place the following day; and it was held that these actions gave such grave prejudicial publicity that the Crown would not be able to proceed with the trial. The trial was deserted and no further indictment raised[1]. On the other hand, newspaper articles referring to horrific murders giving lurid details about the various acts and referring by name to the accused detailing his involvement, at least in part, were held not to be sufficient grounds for sustaining the plea and the trial proceeded to a conviction and imposition of a sentence of life imprisonment on the accused[2].

1 *Atkins v London Weekend Television Ltd* 1978 JC 48, 1978 SLT 76.
2 *Hall v Associated Newspapers Ltd* 1979 JC 1, 1978 SLT 241. See also *Sturman v HM Advocate* 1980 JC 111, 1980 SLT 182; *X v Sweeney* 1982 JC 70, 1982 SCCR 161, 1983 SLT 48; *Kilbane v HM Advocate* 1989 SCCR 313; *Spink v HM Advocate* 1989 SCCR 413.

(D) SEPARATING AND CONJOINING CHARGES AND TRIALS

4.54. Separation and conjunction of charges in trials. Whether or not charges or trials should be separated or conjoined is dealt with by a discretionary preliminary diet[1]. It is for the Crown to decide what charges are to be placed on any particular indictment, and the only remedy open to the accused if he considers that he has been unfairly prejudiced by the combination of charges or by being tried with a co-accused is to seek a separation of the charges or trials as appropriate. It may be that the charges are entirely dissimilar, such as housebreaking on one day at one place and rape on another date at a different place. It may even be that two accused persons are on the housebreaking charge and only one on the rape. The housebreaker not involved in the rape may feel that he is prejudiced by being linked with his co-accused in the minds of the jury if evidence of both charges is led at the same time. On the other hand the Crown frequently includes all charges that it is competent to put onto one indictment on the principle that an accused is entitled to have all outstanding charges against him dealt with at once. Indeed the Crown may be subject to criticism for not doing so[2]. The court is slow to interfere with the prosecutor's right to indict and will do so only where a material risk of real prejudice to the accused can be demonstrated[3]. A material risk of real prejudice does not arise merely because the charges in an indictment are of different kinds of crime committed at different times at different places and in different circumstances. Consideration may more frequently be given to separation of trials where two accused are alleged to have acted in the commission of the one crime and it is the intention of one to blame the other. However, since it is not possible for one accused to insist that another accused give evidence that might incriminate the latter, the plea is rarely sustained. If two accused are on the same indictment, one has no right to insist upon the other giving evidence, as both have independently the right not to give evidence. If they are charged separately then the one who has not yet been tried, though he can be called as a witness, is not obliged to answer any questions which might incriminate himself and thus cannot be forced to give evidence favourable to the co-accused.

1 Criminal Procedure (Scotland) Act 1975 (c 21), s 76(1)(b) (substituted by the Criminal Justice (Scotland) Act 1980 (c 62), s 12, Sch 4, para 5): see para 4.40 above.
2 *Kesson v Heatly* 1964 JC 40, 1964 SLT 157.
3 *Reid v HM Advocate* 1984 SCCR 153, 1984 SLT 391. See also U R Vass 'The Motion for Separation of Charges' 1987 SLT (News) 369.

4.55. Conjoining of trials. Where the Crown has not decided to charge all accused on the one indictment, it is competent to petition the court to conjoin the trials where it is felt that the defence of one may be prejudiced by the separation of the trials[1]. However, a more common and analogous situation arises where there are a number of co-accused on the one indictment and for some reason the Crown is unable to proceed against one of the accused, perhaps because he has fled or is too ill to stand trial, but yet wishes to continue with regard to the others or, conversely, does not wish to proceed to trial against the others despite their wish to proceed in the absence of the missing accused. Though the motion is not for a conjoining of trials, since there is only one trial, the basis of the plea to have the trial of the remaining accused adjourned is the same as that for conjoining trials. If it is known that one accused is going to be unavailable through, for example, illness then it would be competent either for the Crown or a co-accused to move for a preliminary diet to hear the arguments in favour of adjournment.

1　*HM Advocate v Clark* 1935 JC 51, 1935 SLT 143. See also *Mowbray v Robertson* 1990 GWD 10–531.

5. SUMMARY PROCEDURE

(a) Time Limits for Custody and Prosecution

5.01. Initiating common law proceedings. There is no time bar in summary proceedings for common law offences, and a prosecution can be initiated any time after the commission of the offence[1]. However, as in solemn proceedings, it is open to the accused to present a preliminary plea in bar of trial with regard to *mora*, taciturnity and delay[2] if the period appears to be too long between the incident and the prosecution. Since one of the factors to be considered by the courts in such a plea is the gravity of the offence, the fact that the charge is being taken on a summary complaint rather than on indictment may present the prosecutor with some difficulty in justifying the delay on this ground. Accordingly a shorter period of delay is likely to give rise to a successful plea in bar of trial than in solemn proceedings[3].

1 *Sugden v HM Advocate* 1934 JC 103, 1934 SLT 465.
2 *Tudhope v McCarthy* 1985 SCCR 76, 1985 SLT 392; *Tudhope v Clement* 1985 SCCR 252, Sh Ct; *Connachan v Douglas* 1990 SCCR 101. See also para 4.52 above.
3 *Tudhope v McCarthy* 1985 SCCR 76, 1985 SLT 392; *Philips v Tudhope* 1987 SCCR 80.

5.02. Initiating proceedings for statutory offences. Unlike solemn proceedings, there is a time bar for the institution of proceedings applicable in statutory offences in all cases. The Criminal Procedure (Scotland) Act 1975 fixes a period of six months after the date on which the contravention occurred, unless the particular statute or order contravened fixes another period which may be longer or shorter than six months[1]. Where the offence is of a continuous nature, then the six-month period referred to, or whatever period the particular statute fixes, starts from the end of the continuous contravention[1]. In respect of offences involving bodily injury to children under the age of seventeen and certain other statutory exceptions involving child victims[2] there is a further modification of this rule in that although it is not competent to convict of an offence committed more than six months before the commencement of the proceedings, evidence may be taken of acts constituting or contributing to the offence committed at any previous time[3]. Though not affecting the question of time bar it is important to consult the statute concerned in case some preliminary action requires to be taken by the prosecutor before he can institute proceedings at all[4].

1 Criminal Procedure (Scotland) Act 1975 (c 21), s 331(1).
2 Ie any offence under the Children and Young Persons (Scotland) Act 1937 (c 37), s 12, s 15, s 22 or s 23, one under the Sexual Offences (Scotland) Act 1976, or one under the Criminal Justice (Scotland) Act 1980 (c 62), s 80(7): see the Criminal Procedure (Scotland) Act 1975, Sch 1,

paras (a), (aa), (c), (d) (amended by the Sexual Offences (Scotland) Act 1976, s 21(1), (2), Schs 1, 2, and the Criminal Justice Act 1988 (c 33), s 170(1), Sch 15, para 50).

3 Criminal Procedure (Scotland) Act 1975, s 331(2), Sch 1, para (d) (amended by the Incest and Related Offences (Scotland) Act 1986, s 21(1), Sch 1, para 2).

4 See eg the requirements of the Road Traffic Offenders Act 1988 (c 53), s 1 (warning, service of complaint or notice of intended prosecution).

5.03. Computation of time. The computation of the period does not include the day of the offence itself but does include the date on which proceedings are commenced[1]. The majority of the problems with regard to time bar relate to the circumstances of the commencement of the proceedings. Summary proceedings are instituted either by citing an accused to appear at a given court on a given date and time[2], or alternatively by arresting him and bringing him before the court or by making arrangements to have him attend in terms of a warrant to arrest granted by the appropriate court[3]. Citation can be at the hand of the prosecutor, either by post[4] or by personal service or it can be in terms of a warrant to cite granted by the court[5]. The latter procedure is principally used to commence proceedings formally when there is a danger of the time limit expiring. In citation cases, proceedings commence with citation of the accused, not with the appearance of the accused in court. Thus it is possible to have a citation properly effected within six months from the date of the offence and yet the diet to which an accused is called in terms of that citation may be outwith the six months. In such a case the proceedings are not time-barred[6]. If the citation is defective, no proceedings have been commenced within the six months and the case is time-barred[7]. However, where an accused, or a solicitor appearing for him in his absence, appears in order to answer a complaint, it is not competent to plead want of due citation or informality in the citation or its execution[8]. In cases starting in terms of a warrant either to arrest or to cite, granted in terms of section 314 of the Criminal Procedure (Scotland) Act 1975[9], proceedings are deemed to be commenced on the date on which the warrant is granted and not the date upon which the accused is actually cited or arrested in terms of that warrant[10]. However, it is an important proviso to this that the warrant must be executed without undue delay[10]. In the case of postal citation execution of the warrant to cite occurs when the citation is posted, not when it is received[11]. But where it is returned 'Not known at this address' it is not executed[12]. So where an accused returns a citation 'Not known at this address' and then avoids personal service for the rest of the six months, it appears that he will avoid prosecution. If any delay is due to the fault of the accused, perhaps because he could not be found or was too ill to arrest and bring to court, then the case would not be time-barred[13]. However, the onus is on the prosecutor to show that there has not been undue delay[14].

1 *Frew v Morris* (1897) 24 R (J) 50, 2 Adam 267; *Tudhope v Lawson* 1983 SCCR 435, Sh Ct.

2 See the Criminal Procedure (Scotland) Act 1975 (c 21), ss 315–319.

3 See ibid, s 314(1)(b).

4 Where an accused does not receive the citation it would appear to be ineffective: *Keily v Tudhope* 1986 SCCR 251, 1987 SLT 99n; see R W Renton and H H Brown *Criminal Procedure according to the Law of Scotland* (5th edn, 1983) para 13-09.

5 Criminal Procedure (Scotland) Act 1975, s 331(3) (amended by the Criminal Justice (Scotland) Act 1980 (c 62), ss 11(b), 83(3), Sch 8). The warrant to cite refers to the court order pronounced under the Criminal Procedure (Scotland) Act 1975, s 314(1)(a), assigning a diet for the disposal of the case, to which the accused is then cited.

6 *Lockhart v Bradley* 1977 SLT 5.

7 *Orr v Lowdon* 1987 SCCR 515.

8 Criminal Procedure (Scotland) Act 1975, s 334(6). See, however, *Laird v Anderson* (1895) 23 R (J) 14, 2 Adam 18, and *Beattie v M'Kinnon* 1977 JC 64.

9 See eg *Tudhope v Buckner* 1985 SCCR 352, Sh Ct.
10 Criminal Procedure (Scotland) Act 1975, s 331(3) (as amended: see note 5 above). It does not require the arrest of the accused: *Young v Smith* 1981 SLT (N) 101.
11 Ibid, s 316(3). See *Lockhart v Bradley* 1977 SLT 5.
12 *Keily v Tudhope* 1986 SCCR 251 at 255, 1987 SLT 99n at 101, per Lord Justice-Clerk Ross: 'In the present case . . . there was no effective execution of the warrant; it cannot therefore be contended that the warrant was executed without undue delay'.
13 *Tudhope v Mathieson* 1981 SCCR 231 (but see *Keily v Tudhope* 1986 SCCR 251, 1987 SLT 99n).
14 *Smith v Peter Walker & Son (Edinburgh) Ltd* 1978 JC 44; *Carmichael v Sardar & Sons* 1983 SCCR 433, Sh Ct; *Beattie v Tudhope* 1984 SCCR 198, 1984 SLT 423n; *Stagecoach Ltd v MacPhail* 1986 SCCR 184; *Ross Inns Ltd v Smith* 1986 SCCR 409, 1987 SLT 121.

5.04. Time limits subsequent to taking proceedings. There is no equivalent in summary proceedings of the one-year rule under solemn proceedings[1], and theoretically a court could continue to adjourn a case without commencing a trial for a longer period in summary proceedings than under solemn proceedings. There is, however, an equivalent of the one-hundred-and-ten-day rule[2] with regard to persons kept in custody in that the trial has to be commenced within forty days of bringing the complaint in court[3]. As in the case of the one-hundred-and-ten-day rule the period of incarceration has to be in respect of the particular warrant for that summary trial. In other words, if the accused is imprisoned on another matter or detained on another warrant in the interim, then the forty days stops running until that other matter is completed. However, the running of the forty days is not interrupted by a period of detention for pre-sentencing reports on another charge[4]. Similarly there are provisions for an application to the court for an extension of the forty-day period where the delay is not attributable to the fault of the prosecutor, such application being made to the sheriff[5], not to the High Court. It may be noted that the one-hundred-and-ten-day rule in relation to solemn procedure does not start until the date of the accused's committal for trial, which may be some time after he was originally remanded in custody. The forty-day rule starts from the time the complaint is brought to court providing the accused is detained from that time onwards. Thus if the case is continued for further inquiry or for proof on a preliminary plea and the accused is remanded in custody, that period counts towards the computation of the forty days. If the trial is not commenced within forty days where an accused is in custody in that regard he is, just as in the one-hundred-and-ten-day rule for solemn proceedings, forever free from all question or process for that offence[6].

1 See para 4.23 above, and cf *MacDougall v Russell* 1985 SCCR 441, 1986 SLT 403.
2 See para 4.21 above.
3 Criminal Procedure (Scotland) Act 1975 (c 21), s 331A(1) (added by the Criminal Justice (Scotland) Act 1980 (c 62), s 14(2)). For these purposes a trial is to be taken to commence when the first witness is sworn: Criminal Procedure (Scotland) Act 1975, s 331A(4) (as so added).
4 *Lockhart v Robb* 1988 SCCR 381, Sh Ct.
5 Criminal Procedure (Scotland) Act 1975, s 331A(2) (as so added). Appeal from the grant or refusal of an extension lies to the High Court: s 331A(3); Act of Adjournal (Consolidation) 1988, SI 1988/110, r 100, Sch 1, Form 54.
6 Criminal Procedure (Scotland) Act 1975, s 331A(1) (as so added).

(b) Preparation of the Defence

5.05. Introduction. It is much easier to prepare to defend a summary prosecution than a solemn one because the initial document, the complaint[1], is the final writ upon which the accused will go to trial. In solemn procedure, on the other hand, the charges set down in the initial document, the petition, may vary considerably from those in the final document, the indictment[2]. Accordingly in summary proceedings right at the very beginning the defence knows the exact nature of the charge it has to answer. There is no judicial examination and committal[3], except where the case originally commenced on petition[4]. Notice need only be given of pleas of alibi or insanity in bar of trial[5], and there is no requirement to provide lists of witnesses, special defences etc as in solemn proceedings. The provisions relating to defence applications for identification parades[6] and the precognition of witnesses on oath by the defence[7] apply equally to summary and solemn proceedings. The time given to prepare the defence will depend to some extent upon whether or not an accused has been cited or arrested: in the first case citation will be for some future specified date, whereas the arrested person will be appearing in court no later than the next lawful day[8]. Indeed, although an arrested person will have knowledge of the police charge against him, he will not know the terms of the complaint until shortly before he is to be brought to court to answer it. In such a case there is very little time for any defence to be prepared.

The procedure is summary, and cases should be dealt with summarily. Indeed, when the accused pleads not guilty the court may proceed to trial at once unless either party moves for an adjournment, and the court must then judge whether or not it is expedient to grant that adjournment[9]. If the accused has been brought from custody he is entitled to an adjournment for not less than forty-eight hours before the trial proceeds[10]. It is, however, exceedingly unusual to proceed to trial instantly except in cases where, for example, a prosecution witness is about to leave the area or a seaman is about to return to sea, in which case the witness's evidence may be taken that day and the case thereafter adjourned to a much later date for the rest of the evidence to be heard. The same circumstances apply to the defence who may have a witness about to leave; it is permissible for that witness to be examined prior to the evidence for the prosecution having been concluded or even started[11].

1 Criminal Procedure (Scotland) Act 1975 (c 21), s 311(1).
2 See para 4.25 above.
3 As to judicial examination, see paras 4.06 ff above.
4 See the Criminal Procedure (Scotland) Act 1975, s 20(4).
5 See para 5.21 below.
6 Criminal Justice (Scotland) Act 1980 (c 62), s 10 (see para 4.15 above); Act of Adjournal (Consolidation) 1988, SI 1988/110, r 98, Sch 1, Form 52.
7 Criminal Justice (Scotland) Act 1980, s 9 (see para 4.19 above); Act of Adjournal (Consolidation) 1988, rr 93–97, Sch 1, Form 51.
8 Criminal Procedure (Scotland) Act 1975, s 321(3) (amended by the Bail etc (Scotland) Act 1980 (c 4), s 12(2), (3), Sch 1, para 7, Sch 2).
9 Criminal Procedure (Scotland) Act 1975, s 337(a) (amended by the Bail etc (Scotland) Act 1980, Sch 2).
10 Criminal Procedure (Scotland) Act 1975, s 337(c).
11 Ibid, s 337(h).

5.06. Recovery of documents. Where documents which are necessary for the defence are in the hands of the Crown or of third parties, the accused by petition may seek a commission and diligence for their recovery if the possessor will not voluntarily make them available[1]. In relation to summary proceedings, it would seem that the only court with power to approve a specification of documents prepared by the defence and to grant such a commission and diligence is the High Court of Justiciary, even though the trial itself is to be held in the sheriff court or the district court[2]. It is incompetent to grant a commission and diligence for the recovery of a witness's criminal record[2].

1 See para 4.18 above.
2 *HM Advocate v Ashrif* 1988 SCCR 197, 1988 SLT 567.

5.07. Witnesses. If the case is brought to court by way of citation, there is sufficient time for the defence solicitor to obtain from the accused information relevant to the allegation in the complaint and the details and the names and addresses of any supporting witnesses. There may also be time to consult the procurator fiscal about the Crown evidence and to obtain from him a provisional list of witnesses. Such a list can be only provisional since at that early stage the fiscal will probably be working from a summary of the circumstances provided to him by the police and he will not have detailed information of what each witness is likely to say. Accordingly the provisional list may include witnesses who may not be called at the trial, or may not include witnesses who after further inquiry are deemed by the fiscal to be necessary. Defence solicitors should use this list of witnesses with caution, and in the event of a witness being essential for the defence the defence should cite that witness for the trial diet rather than rely on the prosecutor to do so. Procurators fiscal have been instructed by the Lord Advocate to be prepared to discuss the evidence and the circumstances of any case with a defence solicitor at a mutually convenient time, and this of course includes the time after citation but before the case calls[1]. Indeed, a solicitor acting for a client who has been charged by the police but who has not yet received a summons may contact the fiscal with a view to discussing the case in the hope of persuading him not to institute proceedings.

An accused person who is not legally represented will not normally be issued with a list of Crown witnesses or be able to discuss the case with the procurator fiscal. Witnesses are not commonly aware that the defence is entitled to precognosce them with regard to their evidence and they might be distressed if approached by the accused in person attempting to discover their evidence before a trial. Where the accused approaches the procurator fiscal it is important that he is not prejudiced by any misunderstanding or improper disclosure on his part. Accordingly the fiscal will usually provide the accused with basic information only, and recommend strongly that he should approach a solicitor to act on his behalf in making further inquiries.

1 See the authorities cited in para 4.17, note 2, above.

5.08. Intermediate diets. To avoid unnecessary delay in bringing cases to trial or cases being put down for trial unnecessarily, the intermediate diet has been instituted to enable the court to inquire whether the accused intends to adhere to a not guilty plea and to ascertain the state of preparation of both parties to the case[1]. Furthermore, many defence solicitors who have had insufficient time to make preliminary inquiries consider it useful and mutually advantageous to ask for the case to be continued without plea at the first calling rather than plead not guilty immediately[2].

1 Criminal Procedure (Scotland) Act 1975 (c 21), s 337A(1) (added by the Criminal Justice (Scotland) Act 1980 (c 62), s 15): see para 5.33 below.
2 See para 5.28 below.

5.09. Preliminary pleas. It is essential for all defenders, whether they are individuals or agents acting for an accused person, to consider the question of preliminary pleas to competency, relevancy and special capacity as soon as they receive a complaint[1]. If these are not tendered before any other plea to the charge is made no objection can be taken later except with the leave of the court, and that only on cause shown[2]. A request to continue the case without plea does not contravene this requirement as no plea has been tendered.

1 As to preliminary pleas, see para 5.30 below. For particular preliminary pleas, see paras 4.45 ff above.
2 Criminal Procedure (Scotland) Act 1975 (c 21), s 334(1) (amended by the Criminal Justice (Scotland) Act 1980 (c 62), s 83(2), Sch 7, para 54(a)).

(c) The Complaint

5.10. Introduction. The complaint is the principal writ in summary proceedings. It is the first document served upon the accused and contains the charge or charges which ultimately he will be asked to answer. In summary procedure there is no comparable preliminary writ to the petition in solemn procedure. If the crime is a statutory one a notice of penalties will be served with the complaint[1], but there is no such notice if it is a common law crime. A list of the accused's previous convictions that the prosecutor would wish to refer to at the conclusion of the trial or after a plea of guilty will also be served at the same time[2]. Unlike solemn proceedings, no list of witnesses to be called by the Crown or list of productions to be referred to by Crown witnesses accompanies the complaint. Similarly the productions do not require to be lodged in the court before the trial.

1 Criminal Procedure (Scotland) Act 1975 (c 21), s 311(5); Act of Adjournal (Consolidation) 1988, SI 1988/110, r 87(2), Sch 1, Form 46.
2 Criminal Procedure (Scotland) Act 1975, s 357(1)(a); Act of Adjournal (Consolidation) 1988, r 87(4), Sch 1, Form 48.

5.11. Heading of complaint. All summary proceedings, whether in the name of the public prosecutor or of a private prosecutor, are instituted by way of complaint[1]. The complaint, if by the procurator fiscal, is simply headed 'The complaint of the procurator fiscal against . . .' and thereafter the details of the accused are inserted. A complaint does not run in the name of the Lord Advocate even if the case started by way of petition. If the complaint is at the instance of a private prosecutor it is normal to name and design him to show his interest in raising the proceedings. In the case of a statutory offence it is not required to add the particular Act under which the charge is brought in the heading. Nor is it necessary to refer to any Act conferring jurisdiction[2].

The complaint requires to be signed by the prosecutor to be a competent writ[3]. The signature must be on the principal complaint and need not appear on the copy of the complaint served upon the accused which can be 'signed' by way of facsimile signature. A complaint at the instance of a private prosecutor for an offence at common law, or for a statutory offence when imprisonment without the option of a fine is competent, requires, unless the statute provides to the contrary, the concurrence of the public prosecutor of the court in which the complaint is brought, and that concurrence is indorsed upon the complaint by the prosecutor, without which the complaint is incompetent[4]. Where the consent or authority of some official has been obtained, this fact should appear in the complaint[5]. Persons prosecuting in the public interest do not require to obtain the concurrence of the procurator fiscal in a complaint at their instance[6].

1 Criminal Procedure (Scotland) Act 1975 (c 21), s 311(1).
2 *M'Laren v Macleod* 1913 SC (J) 61, 7 Adam 102; R W Renton and H H Brown *Criminal Procedure according to the Law of Scotland* (5th edn, 1983) para 13-29.
3 Criminal Procedure (Scotland) Act 1975, s 311(2); *Lowe v Bee* 1989 SCCR 476. In the case of a private prosecution the prosecutor's solicitor signs the complaint: s 311(2).
4 Ibid, s 311(4); *Lundie v MacBrayne* (1894) 21 R (J) 33, 1 Adam 342.
5 *Stevenson v Roger* 1915 SC (J) 24, 7 Adam 571.

6 *Templeton v King* 1933 JC 58, 1933 SLT 443. See also the definition of 'prosecutor' in the Criminal
   Procedure (Scotland) Act 1975, s 462(1).

5.12. Form of complaint. The form of the complaint itself, and of the notice
of penalties and schedule of previous convictions, is prescribed by Act of
Adjournal[1], whereas the form of the charge in the complaint is controlled by Act
of Parliament[2]. The statute makes provision for latitude, when setting out the
charge, in time[3], place and quantities; for the implication of certain aspects of
criminal intent, such as 'wilfully', 'maliciously', 'culpably and recklessly' etc,
without requiring a specific statement; for conviction of a charge without the
aggravation where only the aggravated charge is libelled (for example conviction for theft on a charge of robbery), including the power to convict of an
offence without the aggravation even if that offence was committed outside the
jurisdiction of the court, provided that the aggravated crime was committed
within the court's jurisdiction; and for the conviction of a common law offence
where the charge on the complaint is a statutory one[4]. The statute also provides
that in a charge alleged to be committed by somebody in a special capacity, the
accused will be held to admit that he possesses that special capacity unless he
makes a challenge as a preliminary objection prior to tendering a plea[5]. The
description of a statutory offence in the words of the statute contravened, or in
similar words, is sufficient[6] provided it gives fair notice of the charge which the
accused has to meet[7].

1 Criminal Procedure (Scotland) Act 1975 (c 21), ss 311(1), (5), 357(1)(a); Act of Adjournal
   (Consolidation) 1988, SI 1988/110, r 87(1), (2), (4), Sch 1, Forms 45, 46, 48.
2 Criminal Procedure (Scotland) Act 1975, s 312 (amended by the Criminal Justice (Scotland) Act
   1980 (c 62), s 46(1)(b), and the Criminal Justice Act 1982 (c 48), s 56(3), Sch 7, para 7).
3 For an example of latitude in time see *Hamilton v W* (otherwise reported as *W v Hamilton*) 1989
   SCCR 42.
4 Criminal Procedure (Scotland) Act 1975, s 312(e)–(g), (m), (n), (t). See *Buchanan v Hamilton* 1989
   SCCR 398, 1990 SLT 244.
5 Ibid, s 312(x): see para 5.30 below.
6 Ibid, s 312(p).
7 *Blair v Keane* 1981 JC 19, 1981 SLT (Notes) 4; *Walkingshaw v Robison and Davidson Ltd* 1988
   SCCR 318, 1989 SLT 17.

5.13. Amendment of complaint. It is competent at any time prior to the
determination of a summary prosecution, unless the court sees just cause to the
contrary, to amend the complaint[1], provided that the amendment does not
change the character of the offence charged[2]. Accordingly minor mistakes in the
designation of the accused or the details of the charges do not vitiate the
proceedings and can be rectified quite simply without requiring a new complaint to be raised. It may be the case, however, that a radically defective
complaint cannot be transformed by such amendment into a relevant one: 'to
remedy a defect does not mean to transform into a libel what never was a libel'[3].

1 Criminal Procedure (Scotland) Act 1975 (c 21), s 335(1).
2 Ibid, s 355(2). See eg *MacArthur v MacNeill* 1986 SCCR 552, 1987 SLT 299n.
3 *Macintosh v Metcalfe* (1886) 13 R (J) 96 at 98, 1 White 218 at 226, per Lord McLaren. See generally
   R W Renton and H H Brown *Criminal Procedure according to the Law of Scotland* (5th edn, 1983)
   paras 14-66, 14-67, and 'The Amendment of Summary Complaints' 1988 SCOLAG 9. See,
   however, *Duffy v Ingram* 1987 SCCR 286, 1988 SLT 226n, where it was held that the statutory
   power of amendment was wide enough to cover the curing of such a radical defect as the absence
   from the complaint of a date for the commission of the offences.

5.14. Penalty notices and schedules of previous convictions. No penalty
notice is served in relation to a common law charge. If the charge or one of the

charges on the complaint is a statutory one then a notice of penalty applicable to that charge has to be served at the same time as the complaint is served upon the accused[1]. Failure to serve a penalty notice or a failure to set out the relevant penalties adequately and unambiguously means that no penalty can be imposed with regard to that charge by the court[2]. However, at any time prior to the determination of the summary prosecution, it is competent to amend a penalty notice by deletion, alteration or addition so as to cure any error or defect it may contain[3]. The penalty notice served upon the accused is not signed by the prosecutor[4].

A copy of the list of previous convictions which the prosecutor intends to refer to in the event of the accused being found guilty or pleading guilty to any of the charges on the complaint should be served on the accused at the same time as the complaint[5]. If such a list has not been served upon the accused it is not competent for the prosecutor to make reference to any conviction when addressing the court prior to the accused being sentenced. It is competent to amend the list of convictions if there are any errors or defects therein[6]. The list of convictions does not require to be signed by the prosecutor[7].

If there are errors in the schedule of previous convictions or penalty notices these are not dealt with by way of a preliminary plea or diet, as are errors on the complaint. Objections to the terms of the penalty notices or list of previous convictions are not made until after the accused has been found guilty or pled guilty and the prosecutor tenders the appropriate list or notice to the court before sentence. At that point objections are intimated orally by the defence and the court hears the parties thereon[8]. In practice a difference can be drawn between penalty notices and schedules of previous convictions. In the latter case it is normal to draw the attention of the prosecutor to the error or alleged error at an early stage to enable him to have the matter checked, and to amend accordingly, before the list of convictions is placed before the court, thereby avoiding unnecessary delay. No prejudice is suffered by the accused in such circumstances. However, with regard to the penalty notice, it may be that the error contained in it is of such a nature that it is not competent to amend at the stage when the notice is to be placed before the court[9]. If there is no competent penalty notice before the court no penalty can be imposed for that charge[10]. If, however, prior notice is given to the prosecutor, it may be that he would be able to desert the case *pro loco et tempore* and start afresh with a corrected penalty notice.

1   Criminal Procedure (Scotland) Act 1975 (c 21), s 311(5). The notice is to be in the form as nearly as may be to Act of Adjournal (Consolidation) 1988, SI 1988/110, Sch 1, Form 46: r 87(2). The notice must be served on the accused; it does not suffice to serve it on his solicitor: *Geddes v Hamilton* 1986 SCCR 165, 1986 SLT 536. As to proof of service, see *Muir v Carmichael* 1988 SCCR 79. This notice is a prerequisite to sentence: see para 7.01 below.

2   See eg *Jackson v Stevenson* (1897) 24 R (J) 38, 2 Adam 255; *Scott v Annan* 1981 SCCR 172, 1982 SLT 90. See also para 7.01 below, and R W Renton and H H Brown *Criminal Procedure according to the Law of Scotland* (5th edn, 1983) para 13-60.

3   Criminal Procedure (Scotland) Act 1975, s 335(1). See *Cochrane v West Calder Co-operative Society* 1978 SLT (Notes) 22; *Donnachie v Smith* 1989 SCCR 144.

4   Act of Adjournal (Consolidation) 1988, Sch 1, Form 46.

5   Criminal Procedure (Scotland) Act 1975, s 357(1)(a). The schedule is to be as nearly as may be to Act of Adjournal 1988, Sch 1, Form 48: r 87(4).

6   Criminal Procedure (Scotland) Act 1975, s 335(1).

7   Act of Adjournal 1988, Sch 1, Form 48.

8   See *Cochrane v West Calder Co-operative Society* 1978 SLT (Notes) 22.

9   See eg *Tudhope v Eadie* 1984 JC 6, 1983 SCCR 464, 1984 SLT 178, and *Miller v Allan* 1984 SCCR 28, 1984 SLT 280.

10 See also para 7.01 below. Where a penalty notice has been served upon the accused but the prosecutor is unable immediately to produce a copy of the notice to the court, the court may permit an adjournment for the Crown to prepare a fresh copy of the penalty notice previously served.

5.15. Service of documents. Where an accused is brought before a court by way of arrest he will normally have had the complaint served upon him and, if appropriate, a penalty notice for statutory offences and a list of previous convictions. Where the accused is cited to appear, he is also served with a number of other documents: a citation[1], and a form on which to state whether he intends to appear personally or be represented by a solicitor, with a space for him to complete the name of the solicitor representing him, and a form enabling him to tender his plea in writing whether it be of guilty or not guilty[2]. If he is pleading guilty, then he is invited to place an explanation before the court with regard to the offence. He also receives a form on which to state his means, his income, his spouse's income where appropriate, and details of his expenditure to enable the court to impose a fine commensurate with his ability to pay, and to allow him time to pay it[3]. Where the procurator fiscal has chosen this method of bringing the accused to court the citation is a mandatory document which must be sent, and without which he is not called to answer the complaint. The other forms are for the benefit of the accused and failure to send or use them does not vitiate proceedings.

1 As to the citation, see para 5.16 below.
2 Act of Adjournal (Consolidation) 1988, SI 1988/110, r 88(a), Sch 1, Form 49.
3 Ibid, r 88(b), Sch 1, Form 50.

5.16. Citation of accused. The Criminal Procedure (Scotland) Act 1975 is a sufficient warrant for the citation of the accused in a summary prosecution to any ordinary sitting of the court or to any special diet fixed by the court or any adjournment thereof[1]. The citation is in a form prescribed by Act of Adjournal[2]. It gives the accused directions as to how to answer the complaint, informs him of the availability of legal aid, and is signed by the prosecutor. The citation proceeds on an *induciae* of at least forty-eight hours unless in the special circumstances of the case the court fixes a shorter *induciae*[3] or where certain statutes prescribe their own *induciae*. The decision in *Dunlop v Goudie*[4] is probably no longer the law. It was there held that a complaint served and an appearance made on an *induciae* shorter than that set down by statute rendered the proceedings null and void[5]. Indeed the Act does not require a complaint to be served on an accused at all in those circumstances where he is present at the first calling and he has legal assistance in his defence[6], or even where he has no legal assistance but the complaint, or the substance of it, has been read over to him[7]. In these situations, or where the complaint has been served on him[8], he will be asked to plead in common form[9]. These situations will occur only where the offence is non-statutory and where previous convictions are not to be relied on since it is required that notices of penalties and of previous convictions be served with the complaint before the first calling of the case[10]. It is not competent for any person appearing to answer a complaint or for a solicitor appearing for the accused in his defence to plead want of due citation or informality therein or the execution thereof[11]. It may be that the only significance of the forty-eight-hour *induciae* is that a failure to allow this by the prosecutor would not entitle him to move for a warrant for the arrest of the accused in the event of the accused failing to answer that citation, rather than rendering the proceedings null and void.

1 Criminal Procedure (Scotland) Act 1975 (c 21), s 315(1).
2 Ibid, s 315(2); Act of Adjournal (Consolidation) 1988, SI 1988/110, r 87(3), Sch 1, Form 47.
3 Criminal Procedure (Scotland) Act 1975, s 315(2).
4 *Dunlop v Goudie* (1895) 22 R (J) 34, 1 Adam 554.
5 See now the Criminal Procedure (Scotland) Act 1975, s 454(1), and R W Renton and H H Brown *Criminal Procedure according to the Law of Scotland* (5th edn, 1983) para 13-75.
6 Criminal Procedure (Scotland) Act 1975, s 334(1)(c); cf *Kelly v Rae* 1917 JC 12, 1916 2 SLT 246.

7 Criminal Procedure (Scotland) Act 1975, s 334(1)(b); see *Renton and Brown* para 13-78.
8 Criminal Procedure (Scotland) Act 1975, s 334(1)(a).
9 Ibid, s 334(1).
10 Ibid, ss 311(5), 357(1)(a).
11 Ibid, s 334(6).

5.17. Manner of citation. Citation may be effected by serving the documents either personally or postally[1]. Personal citation has a wider interpretation than simply handing the documents to the accused himself, in that the citation can be left for him at his home or place of business in the care of somebody either residing in that house or employed at his business or, where he has no known home or place of business, at any other place in which he may at the time be resident[2]. Thus, for example, it could be handed to a child in his home and the child fail to hand the documents thereafter to the adult, and yet full citation is deemed to have occurred. Personal service is also effected upon a master seaman or person employed in a vessel if the citation is simply left with a person on board the vessel who is connected with that vessel[3]. Personal citation is usually effected by a police officer on behalf of the prosecutor, and is used where it is felt essential to prove the fact of citation either to prevent the running of the time bar[4] or where, because of the nature of the crime or the personal circumstances of the accused, the prosecutor wishes to have proof of service to enable him to obtain a warrant for the arrest of the accused should he fail to attend court in answer to the citation, and the prosecutor considers it a real possibility that the accused may so fail. Personal citation is required before a warrant can be taken for the apprehension of a non-appearing accused because if the alternative method of citation is used, that is postal citation, no warrant can be obtained unless it can be proved to the court that the accused received the citation or that the contents came to his knowledge[5]. There is no similar proviso with regard to personal service. Indeed if the accused does not in fact receive the citation in personal service because, for example, it is delivered to some other occupant of the house who fails to pass it on to him, he is deemed to have received it and can be arrested for failing to answer it. Postal service on an accused person can be by way of recorded delivery or by registered post to his home or place of business or to any other place in which he at the time may be resident[5].

The time of the citation may be significant with regard to preventing the imposition of a time bar. In personal service cases the accused is deemed to be cited on the day that the personal service is carried out, whereas in postal service he is deemed (at least for the purpose of reckoning the *induciae*) to be cited twenty-four hours after the letter is posted[6], even if in fact he does not receive it for a considerable time thereafter[7].

Citation of juristic persons is effected if the citation is left at their ordinary place of business with a partner, director, secretary or other official, or alternatively if they are cited in the same manner as if the proceedings were in a civil court[8]. Thus it is competent to serve postally upon these bodies at their principal place of business or registered office as appropriate. Where the accused are a body of trustees, citation is effected if left with any one of them who is resident in Scotland or with their known solicitor in Scotland[9].

1 Criminal Procedure (Scotland) Act 1975 (c 21), s 316(1)–(3).
2 Ibid, s 316(2)(a).
3 Ibid, s 316(2)(b).
4 See paras 5.01 ff above.
5 Criminal Procedure (Scotland) Act 1975, s 316(3).
6 Ibid, s 319(1); Interpretation Act 1978 (c 30), s 7.
7 *Lockhart v Bradley* 1977 SLT 5; *Keily v Tudhope* 1986 SCCR 251, 1987 SLT 99n.
8 Criminal Procedure (Scotland) Act 1975, s 316(2)(c).
9 Ibid, s 316(2)(d).

5.18. Citation furth of Scotland. As far as accused persons resident in parts of the United Kingdom furth of Scotland are concerned, citation may be effected in like manner as in Scotland, that is either personally by officers of law or postally using the recorded delivery or registered post system[1]. There is no system for citing accused persons who are outwith the United Kingdom.

1 Criminal Law Act 1977 (c 45), s 39(3) (amended by the Criminal Justice (Scotland) Act 1980 (c 62), s 83(2), Sch 7, para 79); see Act of Adjournal (Consolidation) 1988, SI 1988/110, r 91.

(d) Requirements on the Defence

5.19. Introduction. Unlike the position in solemn procedure, there are very few requirements upon the defence in summary procedure. There are no lists of witnesses or productions to be lodged. In practice there are three matters which have to be considered, those relating to pleas to the competency and relevancy[1] including, where appropriate, special capacity offences and objections to citation[1]; pleas in bar of trial[2]; and the provision requiring notice to be given of a plea of alibi or insanity[3].

1 See para 5.30 below.
2 See paras 4.46 ff above.
3 See para 5.21 below.

5.20. Rights of the defence. While the requirements on the defence are very limited in summary proceedings, the same rights exist as in solemn proceedings to make inquiries, to recover documents[1], to precognosce witnesses, to seek a warrant to precognosce witnesses on oath[2], to apply for an identification parade[3] and to consult the procurator fiscal. Unlike solemn proceedings where a list of witnesses provided by the Crown is annexed to the indictment giving notice to the defence of the witnesses to be called and upon whichthe defence can rely as being called, it is essential in summary procedure that the defence cites any witness whom it thinks will be necessary to the conduct of the defence rather than relying upon the prosecutor to do so. In particular it is important that the defence does not view the receipt of a preliminary list of witnesses from the procurator fiscal as an indication that those witnesses will be cited to the trial.

1 See paras 4.18, 5.06, above.
2 See paras 4.19, 5.07, above, the Criminal Justice (Scotland) Act 1980 (c 62), s 9, and Act of Adjournal (Consolidation) 1988, SI 1988/110, rr 93–97, Sch 1, Form 51.
3 See paras 4.15, 5.04, above, the Criminal Justice (Scotland) Act 1980, s 10, and Act of Adjournal 1988, r 98, Sch 1, Form 52.

5.21. Special defences. All the special defences[1] available in solemn proceedings are also available in summary proceedings, and the effect of pleading them is the same in both types of procedure. However, with the exception of the pleas of alibi[2] and of insanity in bar of trial[3], no prior notice requires to be given of these in summary proceedings. Where the above exceptions apply, notice only requires to be given before the examination of the first Crown witness. The notice should give particulars of, for example, the time and place of an alibi and of the witnesses to be called in support of it. It is, however, preferable to provide this information to the procurator fiscal before the trial starts as he is entitled to an adjournment of the case to inquire into either of the pleas if he has not had sufficient notice of them[3].

1 Criminal Procedure (Scotland) Act 1975 (c 21), s 339.
2 Ibid, s 375(3).
3 Ibid, ss 339, 375(3).

(e) Pre-trial Diets

(A) PROCEDURE AT PRE-TRIAL DIET

5.22. Calling the case. The prosecutor is master of the instance, and having prepared the complaint it is for him to decide when the case should be called. If the accused is not in custody the procurator fiscal chooses a date for the first calling, or pleading diet, to which the accused is cited to answer the complaint. Alternatively the accused is brought before the court as a custody case or, having been arrested and then liberated by the police on an undertaking[1], he appears by arrangement. Similarly, where a warrant has been obtained for his arrest, the accused may remain at liberty on an undertaking until the calling of his case. Neither the court nor the accused can insist that the case be called on the day specified in the citation, and if the prosecutor does not do so then the instance simply falls. This does not give rise to a preliminary plea in bar of trial of *res judicata*[2] since the accused has not tholed his assize. The prosecutor is free to start proceedings again by citing the accused to a new diet, assuming that this is not time-barred[3] by his failure to call it at the earlier diet. Similarly if the accused is in custody and is not brought before the court on the next lawful day[4] he is entitled to be liberated from custody, there being no authority to detain him further. As with a cited case, the accused has not tholed his assize and can be dealt with subsequently for the offence for which he was in custody. As it is for the prosecutor to determine whether or not a case is called, a case cannot be called in his absence. It is also for the prosecutor alone to determine in what order cases are to be called where there is more than one to be put before a court.

1 Criminal Procedure (Scotland) Act 1975 (c 21), s 295(1) (substituted by the Bail etc (Scotland) Act 1980 (c 3), s 8).
2 Cf para 4.49 above.
3 See paras 5.01 ff above.
4 See the Criminal Procedure (Scotland) Act 1975, s 321(3) (amended by the Bail etc (Scotland) Act 1980, s 12(2), (3), Sch 1, para 7, Sch 2).

5.23. Answering the complaint. Where the accused appears from custody to answer the charges, a copy of the complaint, with appropriate notices[1], is normally served upon him[2]. The case is called by the clerk of court calling out the name of the accused, who is then placed in the dock and his name and address confirmed. An accused in custody has the right to be represented by a solicitor under the legal aid scheme and would normally be so represented. In such cases the solicitor indicates to the court that he represents the accused and indicates on his behalf a plea of guilty or not guilty. A plea of guilty must be confirmed by the accused himself[3]. If the accused has chosen not to be represented he is normally asked if he has received a copy of the complaint, if he understands the charge or charges, and whether he pleads guilty or not guilty to them. It is competent, but unusual, to require an accused to plead to the terms of the complaint when it has not been served upon, but simply read to, him or he has legal assistance in his defence[4].

In cited cases the accused may appear to answer the complaint either personally, with or without a solicitor; or by being represented by a solicitor or by some other person authorised by him[5]; or by tendering a written plea[6]. Forms are normally served with the complaint which allow the cited accused to tender a plea in written form[7]. If these forms are properly completed this is an adequate method of pleading to the charges. The written plea is sent either to the prosecutor or to the clerk of the court before the day of the relevant diet and when the case calls it is placed before the court as the plea of the accused. Written intimation does not require to be made by the accused himself but can be made by anyone authorised by him provided that that is clear from the terms of the plea[8]. Alternatively a solicitor or some other person who satisfies the court that he is authorised by the accused may appear on behalf of the accused and tender a plea in his absence[9].

1 See para 5.14 above.
2 See para 5.16 above.
3 See para 6.40 below.
4 Criminal Procedure (Scotland) Act 1975 (c 21), s 334(1)(b), (c): see para 5.16 above.
5 Ibid, s 334(3)(b).
6 Ibid, s 334(3)(a).
7 See para 5.15 above.
8 Criminal Procedure (Scotland) Act 1975, s 334(3)(a).
9 Ibid, s 334(3)(b).

5.24. Bail etc. If the case is not disposed of at the first calling but continued for whatever purpose to a future diet, then consideration has to be given to the question of the accused's liberty in the interim. There are four options open to the court: to remand the accused in custody to the continued diet; to liberate him on bail[1]; to ordain him to appear at the continued diet; or, where the accused has pled guilty, to dispense with his further appearance and proceed to sentence him or continue the case to a later diet for sentence. In summary proceedings alone the court may ordain the accused to appear at the next diet without making any requirement as to bail; in this case he is liberated without any of the conditions imposed under bail on the simple order to appear at the next diet[2]. Failure to appear at the subsequent diet is both a statutory offence[3] and a common law offence of contempt of court[4]. The fourth option open to the court is to continue the case without requiring a personal appearance, and this frequently occurs in minor cases, or where the accused is represented by a solicitor, and it is unlikely that sentences of imprisonment or disqualification from driving will be imposed at the later diet[5].

1 As to bail, see paras 3.38 ff above. As to rights of appeal and review, see the Criminal Procedure (Scotland) Act 1975 (c 21), ss 299, 300, and paras 3.45, 3.46, above.
2 In solemn proceedings the accused must be either remanded in custody or liberated on bail before conviction. After conviction he may be released and ordained to appear at a later diet.
3 Criminal Procedure (Scotland) Act 1975, s 338(2) (added by the Criminal Justice (Scotland) Act 1980 (c 62), s 17).
4 See para 5.25 below.
5 If such sentences are in contemplation the accused will be ordained to appear personally at a later diet.

(B) FAILURE TO ANSWER; TRIAL IN ABSENCE OF ACCUSED

5.25. Failure to answer. Since failure to appear by a person who has been cited may arise not only out of deliberate neglect or default on his part but quite simply because he has not received the complaint, or because his written plea has been delayed in the post and not received timeously, care has to be exercised by a prosecutor as to what step he takes next. To some extent this will be governed by the manner of citation[1]. If citation has been effected by post it is not competent for the prosecutor to seek a warrant to arrest the accused unless he proves to the court that the accused received the citation or that the contents came to his knowledge[2]. Where there has been personal citation the prosecutor may forthwith move for a warrant for the arrest of the accused on his failure to answer the complaint at the appointed diet[3]. More usually, however, even if personal citation has been effected, the prosecutor will move the court to continue the case without plea and intimate the new diet to the accused[4]. If the accused still fails to answer the complaint the position adopted by the prosecutor will depend upon whether or not the case would be time-barred by his deserting the complaint *pro loco et tempore*[5] and starting afresh. If no such question arises, it is likely that the prosecutor would start a new prosecution by seeking a warrant on the new complaint for the arrest of the accused and thereafter having him brought in custody to answer the complaint. If, however, questions of potential time-bar arise, then provided the prosecutor can satisfy the court that the accused received the citation or that the contents came to his knowledge by the terms of a subsequent intimation, then a warrant would be sought for the arrest of the accused on the original complaint[6]. While failure by the accused to answer a diet of which he has been given notice constitutes a statutory offence[7] in addition to contempt of court, it is unusual for this offence to be prosecuted. On the other hand it may well constitute a reason either for requiring bail to be imposed upon the accused or indeed for opposing the grant of bail when the accused finally appears to answer the charges. However, it is not uncommon for the court *ex proprio motu* to impose a penalty upon the accused for contempt of court with regard to his failure to attend the earlier diet. Any penalty for this, or for breach of a bail condition, may be added to any other sentence imposed with regard to the offences on the complaint, even if the effect is that the total sentence exceeds the maximum penalty which would otherwise be competent[8].

1 See para 5.17 above.
2 Criminal Procedure (Scotland) Act 1975 (c 21), s 316(3) proviso.
3 Ibid, s 338(1)(c).
4 Ibid, s 338(1)(a).
5 Ibid, s 338A(1) (added by the Criminal Justice (Scotland) Act 1980 (c 62), s 18(2)).
6 Criminal Procedure (Scotland) Act 1975, s 338(1)(c).
7 Ibid, s 338(2) (added by the Criminal Justice (Scotland) Act 1980, s 17).
8 Bail etc (Scotland) Act 1980 (c 3), s 3(5): see para 7.08, note 3, below. See also the Criminal Procedure (Scotland) Act 1975, ss 294(4), 295(3), 296(5) (respectively added, substituted and added by the Bail etc (Scotland) Act 1980, ss 7(2), 8, 9(b)).

5.26. Trial in absence of accused. Where an accused is charged with a statutory offence for which a sentence of imprisonment cannot be imposed in the first instance, but only as an alternative to non-payment of a fine, or where the statute founded on or conferring jurisdiction authorises procedure in the absence of the accused, it is competent to lead the evidence against the accused in his absence and to have the case disposed of by the court, provided the prosecutor can prove that the accused has been cited to or received intimation of the diet which he had failed to attend[1]. Unless a statute founded on authorises conviction in default of appearance, evidence must be led[1]. Though this power exists, it is rarely invoked where the accused is a natural person. It may be used in practice where the accused is a juristic person such as a limited company which cannot be arrested and brought to court to answer the complaint.

1 Criminal Procedure (Scotland) Act 1975 (c 21), s 338(1)(b): see para 6.36 below.

(C) REMIT TO ANOTHER COURT

5.27. Remit to another court. Since 1975 the procurator fiscal has been the prosecutor in both the district court (inaugurated in 1975) and the sheriff court. Accordingly, because complaints in both courts are at his instance and because he can determine in which court a case is to be prosecuted, it is not necessary for the prosecutor to invoke the statutory powers which permit transfer of a summary criminal case from a lower court to a higher one[1]. The origins of this statutory procedure are to be found in the Burgh Police (Scotland) Act 1892[2], which was enacted at a time when there were several minor courts each with their own prosecutor and where by error a summary criminal case might be brought in a lower court lacking jurisdiction and accordingly the matter required to be remitted to a higher court (namely the sheriff court). Although the power remains in the modern legislation, it is difficult to justify its use on behalf of a prosecutor who finds that he has inadvertently brought a case before the wrong court; in this situation he should desert the case *pro loco et tempore* and serve a fresh complaint upon the accused, to be heard immediately in the other court, without requiring him to be detained in custody *ad interim*. The current statutory provision also contains a power for the court itself to remit the proceedings to a higher court without any definition or limitation[3], even though the 1892 Act prescribed remits to the sheriff court alone[4]. In practice the modern provision is simply not used in normal criminal prosecutions[5].

1 Criminal Procedure (Scotland) Act 1975 (c 21), s 286.
2 See the Burgh Police (Scotland) Act 1892 (c 55), s 459 (repealed).
3 Criminal Procedure (Scotland) Act 1975, s 286.
4 As the High Court of Justiciary does not hear cases under summary procedure, it would appear that the sheriff court could not remit a summary case to a higher court, except, possibly, in very exceptional circumstances, to a court-martial.
5 See generally R W Renton and H H Brown *Criminal Procedure according to the Law of Scotland* (5th edn, 1983) para 12-20. The power to remit is used when the other court is one where the procurator fiscal has no jurisdiction, eg a military court-martial. It could also be used in cases where the mental health of the accused is questioned, but at a time when it is too late to desert the original complaint and bring fresh proceedings in the sheriff court. See para 10.04 below.

(D) CONTINUATION WITHOUT PLEA

5.28. Continuation or adjournment without plea. In summary proceedings there are provisions available to both the prosecutor and the defence to ask the court to adjourn a case without a plea being tendered. Cases are continued without plea for many reasons, including the failure of the accused to answer the complaint, without explanation being given, and to allow time for him to do so; to allow time for the defence to investigate the circumstances of the charge; to allow time for the prosecutor to investigate any information provided to him by the defence; or to allow time for the accused to seek legal advice or to appear personally at a later diet when he is unable to appear at an earlier one. A case may also be continued without plea where there has been a preliminary plea to the competency or relevancy of the complaint[1]. Where a case is continued without plea, it may be continued only for such reasonable time as may in the circumstances be necessary, not exceeding in all a period of seven days, or on special cause shown twenty-one days from the date of apprehension of the accused[2]. During such continuation, the accused may be remanded in custody, liberated with or without bail or ordained to appear[3]. It has been suggested that if he is to be remanded in custody, the period of the remand should not exceed seven days[4]. Where, however, a longer continuation is required, the court has a discretion (which it may exercise either *ex proprio motu* or on the motion of one of the parties) to adjourn the case for such longer period as is necessary, although in such circumstances the accused could not be remanded in custody[5].

1 See para 5.30 below.
2 Criminal Procedure (Scotland) Act 1975 (c 21), s 328.
3 Ibid, s 328 (amended by the Criminal Justice (Scotland) Act 1987 (c 41), s 62(1)). No judge may allow bail or ordain a person to appear in a case which he is not competent to try: Criminal Procedure (Scotland) Act 1975, s 328 proviso (as so amended).
4 R W Renton and H H Brown *Criminal Procedure according to the Law of Scotland* (5th edn, 1983) para 14-04.
5 The court's power to adjourn is derived from its inherent common law power: see also para 6.37 below. It cannot involve the accused being remanded in custody for longer than twenty-one days because of the terms of the Criminal Procedure (Scotland) Act 1975, s 328.

(E) POSTPONEMENT OF ACCELERATION OF DIET

5.29. Postponement or acceleration of diet. Where the court has fixed a diet for the case to proceed, and both or either of the parties wish that diet to be discharged and an earlier or later diet to be fixed in lieu thereof, the procedure is as follows. Where both parties seek an earlier diet, they may make a joint application in writing requesting the court to fix an earlier diet[1]. Where both parties seek a later diet, they may make a joint written or oral application which the court must grant unless the court considers it should not do so because there has been unnecessary delay on the part of one or more of the parties[2]. Where only one of the parties wishes an earlier or later diet and the other has refused to make a joint application after receiving intimation of the request, the party seeking the earlier or later diet may apply to the court for a hearing to consider his request, and after hearing both parties thereon, the court will either grant or refuse the request[3]. The need to postpone or accelerate a diet may arise for a number of reasons including the unavailability of essential witnesses at the original diet, the accused's desire to change a plea of not guilty to guilty and have the case disposed of quickly, or a change in the demands upon the court diary, for example a need to hold a jury trial or a fatal accident inquiry on days which had otherwise been allocated for summary business.

1 Criminal Procedure (Scotland) Act 1975 (c 21), s 314(3) (amended by the Criminal Justice (Scotland) Act 1980 (c 62), ss 11(b), 83(3), Sch 8).
2 Criminal Procedure (Scotland) Act 1975, s 314(4) (added by the Criminal Justice (Scotland) Act 1980, s 11(c)); Act of Adjournal (Consolidation) 1988, SI 1988/110, r 99(1).
3 Criminal Procedure (Scotland) Act 1975, s 314(5), (6) (as so added); Act of Adjournal (Consolidation) 1988, r 99(2), Sch 1, Form 53.

(F) PRELIMINARY PLEAS

5.30. Preliminary pleas. A preliminary plea to the competency or relevancy of the complaint or the proceedings including pleas in bar of trial must be stated before any other plea, normally at the first calling[1]. Failure to meet this requirement could result in serious prejudice to an accused since the objection may not be stated later except with the leave of the court on cause shown[2]. Equally, a denial that the accused is in a special capacity specified on the complaint and necessary to form the charge should be stated as a preliminary plea. Failure to do so before a plea is tendered at the first calling will result in the accused being deemed to be in that special capacity, and no proof may be heard on that point subsequently[3]. A preliminary plea to the competency, relevancy or to special capacity as appropriate[4] is intimated when the case is called and details of the plea are given. The prosecutor must then be asked if he accepts or opposes the plea[5]. If he accepts that the complaint is incompetent it falls. If he accepts that it is irrelevant he may either move to amend the complaint[6] to render it relevant or desert *pro loco et tempore* and start afresh with a new relevant complaint. If, however, he rejects the plea he is called upon to rebut it either immediately if possible or more usually at a later hearing, and the case is continued without plea to a new diet for that purpose. After it has heard submissions from both parties on the plea, the court will either hold the complaint competent or incompetent, relevant or irrelevant, as the case may be[7]. At that stage it is competent to appeal the decision of the court to the High Court of Justiciary[8]. However, the appeal must be taken not later than two days after the decision of the lower court and requires the leave of the lower court[8]. If the case is appealed to the High Court the trial diet may be postponed if necessary and any period taken up with the appeal may in the discretion of the High Court be taken not to count towards any time limit applying in respect of the case[9] including the forty-day rule[10].

1 Criminal Procedure (Scotland) Act 1975 (c21), s334(1) (amended by the Criminal Justice (Scotland) Act 1980 (c62), s83(2), Sch 7, para 54(a)). Where a case has been continued without plea (see para 5.28 above), no plea has been tendered and it is quite competent to state the preliminary plea at the next calling of the case.
2 Criminal Procedure (Scotland) Act 1975, s334(1). See eg *Henderson v Ingram* 1982 SCCR 135. However, it is permissible at an appeal for the High Court to consider a plea to the competency even though no such plea was tendered to the lower court. In practice such a plea to the competency will usually be heard by the lower court even if not made timeously. No similar provision applies for pleas to the relevancy, which may not be heard on appeal if not made to the lower court at the appropriate time.
3 Criminal Procedure (Scotland) Act 1975, s312(x).
4 See para 4.45 above.
5 *Waugh v Paterson* 1924 JC 52, 1924 SLT 432.
6 Criminal Procedure (Scotland) Act 1975, s335.
7 Where both a plea as to competency and a plea as to relevancy are made, the court should deal with both, and not decide on one and find it unnecessary to deal with the other: see *Walkingshaw v Robison and Davidson Ltd* 1988 SCCR 318, 1989 SLT 17.
8 Criminal Procedure (Scotland) Act 1975, s334(2A) (added by the Criminal Justice (Scotland) Act 1980, s36).
9 Criminal Procedure (Scotland) Act 1975, s334(2B) (as so added).
10 As to this rule, see ibid, s331A (added by the Criminal Justice (Scotland) Act 1980, s14(2)), and para 5.04 above.

(G) PLEA OF NOT GUILTY

5.31. Plea of not guilty. A plea of not guilty arises either because of a specific plea to that effect or because a plea of guilty has been tendered and not accepted by the prosecutor. A plea of guilty not accepted is deemed to be a plea of not guilty[1]. The prosecutor, being master of the instance, has the right at common law not to accept any pleas tendered[2]. This may arise not only where the plea is unacceptable, being simply a partial plea, but also where, by acceptance of a plea to one charge, the prosecutor would not be permitted to lead evidence relating to that charge which he feels may be of assistance to him with regard to other charges on the complaint. Indeed the prosecutor is not even bound to accept a plea of guilty to the whole of a complaint[3], though it is a little difficult to see in what circumstance this would arise today since a co-accused, once he has pled guilty or been acquitted, is a competent witness for the prosecution[4]. The equivalent of a plea of not guilty also arises in limited circumstances where an accused is charged with a statutory offence for which a sentence of imprisonment cannot be imposed in the first instance or where the statute founded on or conferring jurisdiction authorises procedure in the absence of the accused, and the accused fails to answer the complaint. In such circumstances the prosecutor can lead evidence[5] as if a plea of not guilty had been tendered. If a plea of not guilty is tendered the court may proceed to trial at once[6], though this is exceedingly unusual since the prosecutor is unlikely to have his witnesses present. If the accused is in custody he is entitled to an adjournment of the case for not less than forty-eight hours before the trial commences, unless it is necessary to start the trial immediately because witnesses would not otherwise be available if it were delayed[7]. Normally the diet is adjourned to a future date, either directly to a trial diet or to both a trial diet and an intermediate diet[8]. At that point the question of the liberation of the accused arises and a decision must be made whether he is to be liberated on bail, ordained to appear or remanded in custody[9].

1 Criminal Procedure (Scotland) Act 1975 (c 21), s 334(5) proviso.
2 *HM Advocate v Peter* (1840) 2 Swin 492.
3 *Kirkwood v Coalburn District Co-operative Society* 1930 JC 38, 1930 SLT 707. A plea of guilty to part only of the charge counts as a plea of guilty: Criminal Procedure (Scotland) Act 1975, s 334(5).
4 Ibid, s 346(3) (amended by the Criminal Justice (Scotland) Act 1987 (c 41), s 70(1), Sch 1, para 8).
5 See para 5.26 above.
6 Criminal Procedure (Scotland) Act 1975, s 337(a) (amended by the Bail etc (Scotland) Act 1980 (c 3), s 12(3), Sch 2).
7 Criminal Procedure (Scotland) Act 1975, s 337(c).
8 See para 5.33 below.
9 See para 5.24 above.

(H) PLEA OF GUILTY

5.32. Plea of guilty. Where the accused pleads guilty to the charge or part of it and that plea is accepted by the prosecutor it is recorded and signed by either the judge or the clerk of the court[1]. The prosecutor then places before the court the previous convictions and penalty notices as appropriate. If the case involves endorsement of a driving licence, the licence should be placed before the court at this stage. Thereafter the prosecutor narrates the circumstances of the offence and the defence follows with a plea of mitigation. The judge then imposes sentence[2]. Once this sentence is recorded the plea cannot be withdrawn[3]; the accused's only remedy is to appeal to the High Court of Justiciary[4]. The prosecutor is not bound to accept a plea of guilty either to the whole of the complaint or to part thereof. If the plea is not accepted, it should be recorded, but may not be used against the accused[5]. The prosecutor remains master of the instance and no party, including the court, can insist that he accepts a plea tendered, or reject his decision to accept a modified plea. In other words if a plea to a lesser charge is tendered, and accepted by the prosecutor, the court cannot insist that the matter proceed to proof on the major charge instead. If a plea of guilty has been made and accepted to a charge or part of a charge it is not necessary for the prosecutor to establish that charge or part of the charge[6].

1 Criminal Procedure (Scotland) Act 1975 (c 21), s 336; see para 6.40 below and *Skeen v Sullivan* 1980 SLT (Notes) 11. The plea having been tendered and accepted, the prosecutor may not thereafter desert *pro loco et tempore* and attempt to start afresh without being met with a successful plea of *res judicata*. The court does not require to have sentenced the accused on the earlier complaint: see *Milne v Guild* 1985 SCCR 464, 1986 SLT 431.

2 See paras 7.01 ff below.
3 Before sentence a guilty plea may be withdrawn at the discretion of the court. For example, where an unrepresented accused pleads guilty and the case is continued for reports, it may be discovered during the adjournment that the accused has a colourable defence. In these circumstances he may be permitted to withdraw his plea of guilty. Where, however, a similar attempt is made on hearing a heavier sentence than expected being pronounced, the motion to withdraw the plea would probably be refused. See *M'Clung v Cruickshank* 1964 JC 64; *Tudhope v Campbell* 1979 JC 24, *sub nom Tudhope v Colbert* 1978 SLT (Notes) 57; *Smith v Carmichael* 1987 SCCR 735.
4 *MacNeill v MacGregor* 1975 JC 55, 1975 SLT (Notes) 46; *MacGregor v MacNeill* 1975 JC 57, 1975 SLT (Notes) 54. See generally R W Renton and H H Brown *Criminal Procedure according to the Law of Scotland* (5th edn, 1983) paras 14-28–14-31.
5 *Strathern v Sloan* 1937 JC 76, 1937 SLT 503.
6 Criminal Procedure (Scotland) Act 1975, s 337(g).

(I) INTERMEDIATE DIET

5.33. Intermediate diet. In 1980 a provision was introduced to allow the court to fix an intermediate diet in an attempt to minimise the waste of court time and inconvenience to witnesses caused by late intimation of changes of plea from not guilty to guilty[1]. The court[2] may at any time before the trial diet (not only at the diet when the plea of not guilty is tendered, but at any subsequent time) fix an intermediate diet for the purpose of ascertaining the state of preparation of the prosecutor and of the accused with respect to their cases and whether the accused intends to adhere to the plea of not guilty[3]. The intermediate diet should be close enough to the trial diet to allow those representing the accused sufficient time to prepare their case and make all necessary inquiries, and then advise the accused on the question whether or not to adhere to the plea of not guilty. On the other hand it should not be so close to the trial diet that it does not allow sufficient time either for witnesses to be cited, or for the court diary to be rearranged in the event of a guilty plea being tendered at the intermediate diet. If the accused is cited to, or receives intimation of, the intermediate diet he is required to attend[4], and failure to do so could result in a warrant being granted for his arrest[5]; it would also be a breach of the standard bail conditions[6] if bail had been imposed. Failure to attend or call an intermediate diet does not result in the trial diet falling, since the accused is ordered to attend both diets.

1 Criminal Procedure (Scotland) Act 1975 (c 21), s 337A (added by the Criminal Justice (Scotland) Act 1980 (c 62), s 15).
2 It is also available to the prosecutor to request an intermediate diet, in terms of the Criminal Procedure (Scotland) Act 1975, s 310 (amended by the Criminal Justice (Scotland) Act 1980, s 83(2), (3), Sch 7, para 53, Sch 8).
3 Criminal Procedure (Scotland) Act 1975, s 337A(1) (as added: see note 1 above). At the intermediate diet the court may ask the prosecutor and the accused any questions for these purposes: s 337A(2) (as so added).
4 Ibid, s 337A(3) (as so added).
5 Ibid, s 338(1)(c).
6 See the Bail etc (Scotland) Act 1980 (c 4), s 1(2), and para 3.40 above.

6. TRIAL

(a) The Trial Diet in Solemn Procedure

6.01. Calling the diet. The trial diet, like all criminal diets, is peremptory, and the instance will fall if the indictment is not called for trial either on the date specified in the notice served on the accused with the indictment or within the period during which a sitting of the court is to take place, or on a date substituted therefore by the court[1]. The falling of the instance bars the prosecutor from proceeding further on that particular indictment (although he may proceed later with a fresh indictment) unless within nine days he gives notice to the accused on another copy of the indictment that he is to appear at a further diet[2]. The calling of the indictment comprises the clerk of court saying 'Call the indictment, Her Majesty's Advocate against A B' and having the accused identify himself.

1 *Hull v HM Advocate* 1945 JC 83, 1945 SLT 202; *McDonald v HM Advocate* 1988 SCCR 298, 1988 SLT 693; Hume *Commentaries* II,263,264; Alison *Practice* pp 343, 344. Prior to the trial diet the court may substitute a diet under the Criminal Procedure (Scotland) Act 1975 (c 21), s 20B(5)(b), s 76, s 76A or s 102(3), or postpone it under s 77A (respectively added by the Criminal Justice (Scotland) Act 1980 (c 62), s 6(2), substituted and added by s 12, Sch 4, para 5, substituted by s 16, and added by Sch 4, para 7).
2 Criminal Procedure (Scotland) Act 1975, s 127 (amended by the Criminal Justice (Scotland) Act 1980, Sch 4, para 27).

6.02. The presence of the parties. The prosecutor must be personally present in court throughout the entire proceedings[1]. As a general rule, the accused must be present when the indictment is called and remain present at all times, as must his advocate or solicitor if he is legally represented[2]. The prosecutor is responsible for arranging that an accused who is in custody is brought to court[3]. The accused may conduct his case personally or may have an advocate (in the High Court of Justiciary) or an advocate or solicitor or both (in the sheriff court) to represent him[4]. If he is under the age of sixteen he may be accompanied by a parent or some other adult, and if he is deaf or dumb or does not understand English an interpreter should be engaged as an officer of the court[5].

1 In an emergency the court may appoint someone to act for the prosecutor in an interim capacity: *Macrae v Cooper* (1882) 9 R (J) 11, 4 Coup 561; *Walker v Emslie* (1899) 2 F (J) 18, 3 Adam 102. In *Skeen v Summerhill* (1975) 39 JCL 59, a sentence pronounced in the absence of the prosecutor was quashed as being incompetent.
2 Criminal Procedure (Scotland) Act 1975 (c 21), s 145(1); *Walker v Emslie* (1899) 2 F (J) 18, 3 Adam 102; *Jackson v HM Advocate* 1982 JC 117, sub nom *McAvoy v HM Advocate* 1982 SCCR 263, 1983 SLT 16; *Cunningham v HM Advocate* 1984 JC 37, 1984 SCCR 40, 1984 SLT 249. See, however, para 6.03 below, and *Gardiner v HM Advocate* (1976) SCCR Supp 159, quoted in R W Renton and H H Brown *Criminal Procedure according to the Law of Scotland* (5th edn, 1983) paras 10-05, 10-06,

and *Anderson v McLeod* 1987 SCCR 566. If the accused's legal representative is absent, it may be oppressive to refuse an adjournment: *Fraser v MacKinnon* 1981 SCCR 91; *McKinnon v Douglas* 1982 SCCR 80, 1982 SLT 375; *Kane v Tudhope* 1986 SCCR 161, 1986 SLT 649; *Benson v Tudhope* 1986 SCCR 422, 1987 SLT 312n. Information from a social worker should be given in open court rather than at a private interview with the judge: *W v HM Advocate* 1989 SCCR 461, although it was held that there was no miscarriage of justice where a sheriff interviewed the accused's previous solicitor in private in order to confirm the accuracy of his (the sheriff's) notes: *Young v Douglas* 1989 SCCR 112.

3 *Renton and Brown* para 10–07.

4 He may not be represented by any other person: *AB v CD* (1834) 12 S 504; *Equity and Law Life Assurance Society v Tritonia Ltd* 1943 SC (HL) 88, 1944 SLT 24; *Kennedy v O* 1975 SLT 235.

5 *HM Advocate v Olsson* 1941 JC 63, 1941 SLT 402; *Liszewski v Thomson* 1942 JC 55, 1942 SLT 147. A Gaelic speaker whose first language is English is not entitled to have his trial conducted in Gaelic: *Taylor v Haughney* 1982 SCCR 360. The interpreter takes an oath to undertake his duties truly and faithfully.

6.03. Absence of the accused. Where the accused fails to answer to the indictment and the prosecutor can produce evidence of service, the court will normally grant a warrant to arrest him on the motion of the prosecutor[1]. Similarly a warrant will be granted if the accused fails to appear after any adjournment for lunch or overnight. In certain circumstances, however, proceedings are competent in the absence of the accused. An accused who is mentally ill may be absent during the hearing of a plea in bar of trial[2]. An accused who disrupts the proceedings may be removed from the court while the trial continues in his absence[3]. If the accused fails to attend at a continued diet (for example where he pleaded guilty and the case is continued to a later date for sentence) the case may be further continued in his absence[4]. It is also sometimes competent to adjourn or desert the case in the absence of the accused[5].

1 R W Renton and H H Brown *Criminal Procedure according to the Law of Scotland* (5th edn, 1983) para 10–06.

2 *Renton and Brown* para 10–04.

3 Criminal Procedure (Scotland) Act 1975 (c 21), s 145(1) proviso, which does not extend to summary proceedings. If the accused is not represented, the court must appoint counsel or a solicitor to act for him in his absence: s 145(1) proviso.

4 *Gardiner v HM Advocate* (1976) SCCR Supp 159.

5 See para 6.05, below.

6.04. Accused body corporate. Where the accused is a body corporate, it may be represented by one of its officers or servants for the purposes of objecting to competency or relevancy, or tendering a plea of guilty or not guilty, or making a statement in mitigation of sentence[1]. If it fails to appear for trial, it is deemed to have pleaded not guilty[2] and the court must proceed to trial in the absence of the accused if moved to do so by the prosecutor, provided it is satisfied that the indictment has been properly served[3].

1 Criminal Procedure (Scotland) Act 1975 (c 21), s 74(2), (8).

2 R W Renton and H H Brown *Criminal Procedure according to the Law of Scotland* (5th edn, 1983) para 10–09.

3 Criminal Procedure (Scotland) Act 1975, s 74(4) (amended by the Criminal Justice (Scotland) Act 1980 (c 62), s 12, Sch 4, para 3).

(B) ADJOURNMENT AND DESERTION

6.05. Adjournment of the trial diet. Where an indictment is not brought to trial at the trial diet, the court may adjourn it to a subsequent sitting of the court for which a warrant has been issued (provided that the sitting is within two months in the case of the High Court or one month in the case of the sheriff court), and if the prosecutor requires the indictment to be called and makes a competent motion to this effect, the court must grant it[1]. It is not necessary for the accused to be present when the motion is made, but if he is absent he must be given intimation of the adjourned diet in the prescribed form[2].

The court also has a general power to adjourn the trial either immediately after it is called or at any stage in the proceedings if it 'shall see cause' to do so[3], the criterion being whether the adjournment is necessary in the interests of justice[4], for example where a material witness is absent or where new and important facts have been discovered or where the defence wishes an opportunity to inspect Crown productions which were not timeously lodged[5]. An adjournment of this nature will be 'over a day or days'[6] and will be kept to a minimum, with a view to saving expense and inconvenience to jurors and witnesses (unlike summary procedure where lengthy adjournments are not unknown).

Unless the trial is adjourned as above described, it must proceed from day to day until concluded[7], except for any brief adjournment until later in the day, over lunch, overnight or at weekends. If, during a brief interruption of this nature, the court deals with some other business, then unless the interrupted trial has been formally adjourned, the instance falls[8]. Such short adjournments need not be formally minuted but all other adjournments must be to a specified time and place and must be recorded in a written interlocutor which is duly signed[9]. Failure to observe this rule will render all further proceedings null[10].

1 Criminal Procedure (Scotland) Act 1975 (c 21), s 77 (substituted by the Criminal Justice (Scotland) Act 1980 (c 62), s 12, Sch 4, para 6); Act of Adjournal (Consolidation) 1988, SI 1988/110, r 41. See also R W Renton and H H Brown *Criminal Procedure according to the Law of Scotland* (5th edn, 1983) para 10-21. See also *McDonald v HM Advocate* 1988 SCCR 298, 1988 SLT 693.
2 Act of Adjournal (Consolidation) 1988, r 41(4), Sch 1, Form 19.
3 Criminal Procedure (Scotland) Act 1975, s 136.
4 *Vetters v HM Advocate* 1943 JC 138, 1944 SLT 85; J H A Macdonald *The Criminal Law of Scotland* (5th edn, 1948) p 279.
5 For further details, see *Renton and Brown* para 10-14. See also *Skeen v McLaren* 1976 SLT (Notes) 14, and *Tudhope v Lawrie* 1979 JC 44, 1979 SLT (Notes) 13.
6 Criminal Procedure (Scotland) Act 1975, s 136.
7 Ibid, s 136; *Kyle v HM Advocate* 1987 SCCR 116, 1988 SLT 601.
8 See *Renton and Brown* para 10-13, discussing *Law v HM Advocate* 1973 SLT (Notes) 14, and *Barr v Ingram* 1977 SLT 173.
9 Criminal Procedure (Scotland) Act 1975, s 77 (as substituted: see note 1 above); Act of Adjournal (Consolidation) 1988, r 41(5).
10 *Hull v HM Advocate* 1945 JC 83, 1945 SLT 202; *Law v HM Advocate* 1973 SLT (Notes) 14; Hume *Commentaries* II, 263; Alison *Practice* pp 343, 344. But see also *Kiely v HM Advocate* 1990 SCCR 151.

6.06. Desertion *pro loco et tempore*. Before the jury is sworn (or if the accused pleads guilty, before he is sentenced), the prosecutor may move the court to desert the diet *pro loco et tempore* without giving any reasons for his motion[1]. While the granting of the motion lies within the discretion of the court, it will normally accede to it unless it is opposed and the granting would result in injustice to the accused[2]. After the jury is sworn the court may desert the diet *pro loco et tempore* at any time either on the motion of the prosecutor or *ex proprio motu* if the trial is unable to proceed or if continuing with the trial would result in a miscarriage of justice[3]. Should the prosecutor wish to proceed further with a case which has been deserted *pro loco et tempore*, he may do so by means of a fresh indictment[4], or within nine days he may give notice to the accused on another copy of the original indictment that he is to appear at a further diet[5], or he may move the court to adjourn the case for a fresh diet of trial at a subsequent sitting of the court (provided a sitting has been arranged within two months, in the case of the High Court, or one month in the case of the sheriff court)[6].

1 *HM Advocate v Ross* (1848) Arkley 481; *HM Advocate v Martin* (1858) 3 Irv 177; *Dunlop v HM Advocate* 1974 JC 59, *sub nom HM Advocate v Dunlop and Marklow* 1974 SLT 242. See also earlier authorities cited in R W Renton and H H Brown *Criminal Procedure according to the Law of Scotland* (5th edn, 1983) para 10-15, note 3; Alison *Practice* pp 98, 355, 356; Hume *Commentaries* II,276. If the accused is on bail he will remain on bail even if the indictment is deserted *pro loco et tempore: Jamieson v HM Advocate* 1990 SCCR 137 (unless presumably he craves the court in an incidental application to release him from the conditions of bail either at the time the diet is deserted or on a subsequent date, and the court grants the application).

2 *HM Advocate v M'Atamney* (1867) 5 Irv 363; *Tudhope v Gough* 1982 SCCR 157.

3 *HM Advocate v Brown and Foss* 1966 SLT 341, where the court deserted *ex proprio motu* when the accused became ill in the course of the trial; *Farrell v HM Advocate* 1984 SCCR 301, 1985 SLT 58, where the court deserted the diet on the prosecutor's motion when an essential witness became ill whilst giving evidence; *HM Advocate v Cafferty* 1984 SCCR 444, Sh Ct, where the sheriff deserted the diet *ex proprio motu* to avoid injustice; *Mallison v HM Advocate* 1987 SCCR 320. See also the opinion of Lord Hunter in *Binks v HM Advocate* 1984 JC 108 at 113, 114, 1984 SCCR 335 at 345, 1985 SLT 59 at 64.

4 *Collins v Lang* (1887) 15 R (J) 7, 1 White 482.

5 Criminal Procedure (Scotland) Act 1975 (c 21), s 127(1) (amended by the Criminal Justice (Scotland) Act 1980 (c 62), s 12, Sch 4, para 27).

6 Criminal Procedure (Scotland) Act 1975, s 77 (substituted by the Criminal Justice (Scotland) Act 1980, Sch 4, para 6); *Renton and Brown* para 10-15; see para 6.05 above.

6.07. Desertion *simpliciter*. The court may desert the diet *simpliciter* either on the motion of the prosecutor or *ex proprio motu*[1], but in the latter instance the prosecutor may appeal against the decision of the court by way of advocation. The effect of desertion *simpliciter* is that no further procedure can take place on the indictment and no fresh libel can be raised against the accused by the same prosecutor on the same grounds[2], although he is still liable to prosecution should proceedings exceptionally be raised by a private prosecutor[3].

1 Criminal Procedure (Scotland) Act 1975 (c 21), s 127(1A) (added by the Criminal Justice (Scotland) Act 1980 (c 62), s 12, Sch 4, para 27); *Mackenzie v Maclean* 1980 JC 89, 1981 SLT 2.

2 *HM Advocate v Hall* (1881) 8 R (J) 52, 4 Coup 500; *Collins v Lang* (1887) 15 R (J) 7, 1 White 482.

3 *X v Sweeney* 1982 JC 70, 1982 SCCR 161, 1983 SLT 48.

6.08. Death or illness of the judge. Where the court is unable to proceed because of the death or illness of the presiding judge and no evidence has been led, the clerk of court may adjourn the diet to a later sitting of the court[1]. If evidence has been led, the clerk may desert the case *pro loco et tempore* and discharge the jury[2], in which case the Lord Advocate may subsequently proceed by way of a fresh indictment[3].

1 Criminal Procedure (Scotland) Act 1975 (c 21), s 128(1)(a), (b). See further R W Renton and H H Brown *Criminal Procedure according to the Law of Scotland* (5th edn, 1983) para 10-19.

2 Criminal Procedure (Scotland) Act 1975, s 128(1)(c).

3 Ibid, s 128(2).

(C) MISNOMER AND MISDESCRIPTION

6.09. Misnomers and misdescriptions. Any objection in respect of a misnomer or misdescription of any person named in the indictment or on the list of witnesses is usually stated after the indictment is called and before the jury is sworn[1]. Unless the accused has given written notice of his objection to the prosecutor and any co-accused ten days before the trial diet, the court will not admit the objection except on cause shown[2]. Where the court hears the objection and is satisfied that the accused has not been given sufficient information to identify the person named in the indictment or to find the witness in time to precognosce him, it may postpone or adjourn the diet or grant such other remedy as appears appropriate[3].

1 R W Renton and H H Brown *Criminal Procedure according to the Law of Scotland* (5th edn, 1983) para 10-11. But see also *Healy v HM Advocate* 1990 GWD 9-472.
2 Criminal Procedure (Scotland) Act 1975 (c 21), s 80(1) (substituted by the Criminal Justice (Scotland) Act 1980 (c 62), s 12, Sch 4, para 9).
3 Criminal Procedure (Scotland) Act 1975, s 80(2) (as so substituted).

(D) PLEADING

6.10. Pleading. If the parties are present and the diet is neither adjourned nor deserted, the next step is for the accused to intimate whether he is pleading guilty or not guilty to the charge or charges in the indictment. Where he pleads guilty, a written copy of the plea must be signed by him (if he can write) and countersigned by the judge[1]. He may also plead guilty to any other crime of which he could competently be convicted, even if there is no charge relating to the other crime (for example, he may plead guilty to reset if he is charged with theft), or he may plead guilty to part of the charge, or, where there is more than one charge, he may plead guilty to one or more but not to others. Whether the plea is to the whole indictment as libelled or is only a partial plea, the prosecutor has a discretion to accept or reject it, and if he accepts it, his acceptance is normally endorsed on the record beside the written plea[2]. His refusal to accept a plea is also recorded, but if he proceeds to trial and in the course of the trial decides to accept a plea of guilty, he cannot do so unless the accused of new tenders a guilty plea[3]. If the accused pleads guilty to one of a number of charges, that plea may not be used as evidence in support of the remaining charges[4], and where the plea is made before the jury is empanelled, that charge will not be read to the jury, nor will it be asked to return a verdict on it.

When there is a plea to one or more charges, the prosecutor may proceed to trial on the remainder and the court will defer sentence on the guilty plea until the conclusion of the trial; alternatively the prosecutor may accept the plea of not guilty to the remaining charges, or he may desert them, in which case the court will pass sentence on the charge or charges to which the guilty plea relates. Similarly where there is more than one accused and one (or more) plead guilty while others plead not guilty, the court will normally defer sentence on the guilty accused until the conclusion of the trial of the co-accused unless the prosecutor accepts the not guilty plea or pleas or makes a successful motion to adjourn the trial against the co-accused or to desert the case against them *pro loco et tempore*[5].

1 Criminal Procedure (Scotland) Act 1975 (c 21), s 103(1) (substituted by the Criminal Justice (Scotland) Act 1980 (c 62), s 12, Sch 4, para 14). A plea of guilty by or on behalf of a company does not require to be signed: Criminal Procedure (Scotland) Act 1975, s 103(4) (as so substituted). See also s 124. Where the plea of guilty, though tendered and signed by the accused, is based on a misunderstanding, the High Court of Justiciary on appeal may set aside the verdict and grant authority to the Crown to raise a fresh prosecution: *Slater v HM Advocate* 1987 SCCR 745. But see also *Healy v HM Advocate* 1990 GWD 9-472.
2 The prosecutor has the right to insist on the case going for trial. For example, the Crown will seldom accept a plea of guilty on a murder charge. In other instances it may refuse a partial plea for evidential reasons where it wishes to lead evidence about these matters during the remainder

of the trial. See also *HM Advocate v Peter* (1840) 2 Swin 492, and *Strathern v Sloan* 1937 JC 76, 1937 SLT 503.

3 *Strathern v Sloan* 1937 JC 76, 1937 SLT 503.
4 *Walsh v HM Advocate* 1961 JC 51, 1961 SLT 137; *McColl v Skeen* 1980 SLT (Notes) 53.
5 For example, the prosecutor may wish to consider what bearing the guilty plea will have in relation to his case against the remaining accused and/or he may wish to precognosce the accused who has pleaded guilty with a view to leading him as a witness at the subsequent trial of the co-accused.

6.11. Refusal to plead. If the accused refuses to plead, or remains silent, or makes a statement which is not a direct and unambiguous admission of guilt, or makes a statement inconsistent with a plea of guilty, or if there is reason to believe that he does not understand the proceedings, the plea is recorded as not guilty[1].

1 J H A Macdonald *The Criminal Law of Scotland* (5th edn, 1948) p 278; *Dawes v Cardle* 1987 SCCR 135.

6.12. Plea of not guilty. When the accused pleads not guilty, the court has a discretion to allow him to intimate a special defence or a defence of incrimination if it is satisfied that there is good reason for not intimating it timeously[1]. Should the granting of this motion result in prejudice to the prosecutor, he may move to desert the case *pro loco et tempore* or the court may adjourn it *ex proprio motu*. In making this motion, it is not uncommon for the defence to state that the failure to make timeous intimation is due to the fault of the accused's legal advisers rather than the accused personally and that refusal to grant it would be unfair to him. Refusal of the motion precludes the defence from leading evidence of the special defence, and should the accused give evidence he may not be asked questions with a view to eliciting such evidence. If, notwithstanding this prohibition, the accused in the course of his evidence says, for example, that he was elsewhere at the time of the crime, or that he acted in self-defence, the jury must be told to disregard this evidence. To avoid the artificiality of this situation or unfairness to the accused, the prosecutor will sometimes refrain from opposing the motion but will move that the case be deserted or adjourned where the granting of the motion would prejudice the Crown. The court also has a discretion to permit the defence to lodge lists of witnesses or productions on cause being shown for the failure to lodge them timeously, and if it allows the defence to do so the prosecutor is entitled to an adjournment or postponement or such other remedy as seems just[2].

1 Criminal Procedure (Scotland) Act 1975 (c 21), s 82(1) (substituted by the Criminal Justice (Scotland) Act 1980 (c 62), s 13). In relation to incrimination, the Act only refers to incrimination of a co-accused, but where a third person is incriminated it may be that the court will apply this provision if refusal would result in prejudice or a miscarriage of justice. The Act of Adjournal (Consolidation) 1988, SI 1988/110, r 68, requires the accused to lodge a notice of a special defence with the clerk of court and to send a copy to the prosecutor and any co-accused.
2 Criminal Procedure (Scotland) Act 1975, s 82(2) (amended by the Criminal Justice (Scotland) Act 1980, s 12, Sch 4, para 10). There is no duty on the prosecutor to refrain from objecting to the late lodging of a list of witnesses or productions: *Manley v HM Advocate* 11 February 1947, High Court (unreported); *HM Advocate v Young* August 1966, High Court, Glasgow (unreported).

(E) AMENDMENT OF THE INDICTMENT

6.13. Amendment of the indictment. Before the jury is empanelled, or at any time thereafter before the determination of the case, it is competent, unless the court sees just cause to the contrary, to amend the indictment by deletion, alteration or addition in order to cure any error or defect, or to meet any objection or to cure any discrepancy or variance between the indictment and the evidence[1]. The indictment may also be altered at the trial diet to add a charge of breach of bail conditions[2]. Any amendment should be authenticated by the clerk of court[3].

An indictment which is fundamentally null can not be cured by amendment[4]; nor will an amendment be allowed if it changes the character of the offence[5]. It has also been held to be incompetent to amend the list of productions (and presumably the list of witnesses) if this would result in an otherwise unlisted production (or witness) being adduced as evidence[6]. If the court, in allowing an amendment, considers that the accused has been prejudiced thereby, it may grant him an adjournment or such other remedy as seems just[7].

1 Criminal Procedure (Scotland) Act 1975 (c 21), s 123(2); *Herron v Gemmell* 1975 SLT (Notes) 93; *Tudhope v Usher* 1976 SLT (Notes) 49; *Keane v HM Advocate* 1986 SCCR 491, 1987 SLT 220n. No trial is to fail or the ends of justice be allowed to be defeated by reason of any discrepancy or variation between the indictment and the evidence: Criminal Procedure (Scotland) Act 1975, s 123(1).

2 Bail etc (Scotland) Act 1980 (c 4), s 3(4), which also allows the addition of witnesses or productions for this purpose. As to bail conditions, see para 3.40 above.

3 Criminal Procedure (Scotland) Act 1975, s 123(4).

4 *HM Advocate v Hanna* 1975 SLT (Sh Ct) 24. See also R W Renton and H H Brown *Criminal Procedure according to the Law of Scotland* (5th edn, 1983) paras 14-66, 14-67, and J H A Macdonald *The Criminal Law of Scotland* (5th edn, 1948) pp 250, 251.

5 Criminal Procedure (Scotland) Act 1975, s 123(3).

6 *HM Advocate v Swift* 1984 JC 83, 1983 SCCR 204.

7 Criminal Procedure (Scotland) Act 1975, s 123(3). In *HM Advocate v Brown* 1983 SLT 136 the trial was adjourned for a day.

(F) THE JURY

6.14. Empanelling the jury. Before the judge comes onto the bench, the clerk of court will have checked that all the jurors who have been cited to attend (in accordance with the list of assize prepared by him) are present in court unless they have been excused[1]. If any juror is absent and has not been excused, his name will be called again after the court has convened and if he does not then appear he is liable to a fine not exceeding level 3 on the standard scale[2]. A copy of the list of assize is given to the defence and prosecution and each of the names on the list is also written on a separate piece of paper and put in a glass bowl or urn. In the presence of the accused, the clerk then ballots the jury by drawing fifteen names at random from the bowl, each juror taking a seat in the jury box as his or her name is called.

As each juror is balloted, but not thereafter, he may be challenged by the prosecutor or the persons accused, each of whom has three peremptory challenges[3]. No further challenges are permissible unless on cause shown[4] — such as insanity, deafness, dumbness, blindness, minority, relationship, enmity, close connection with a party or witness, or personal connection with, or knowledge of, the facts of the case on the part of a juror[5]. It is not sufficient cause that a juror is of any particular race, creed, political view or occupation, or that he might feel some prejudice towards the crime charged or the background of its commission[6]; nor is it sufficient cause that there has been considerable pre-trial publicity about the case[7]. There can be no general questioning of jurors by the judge or by any of the parties to the case, the vetting of jurors being a system 'against which the law of Scotland has steadfastly closed its doors'[8]. The court has power to excuse a juror from serving, but the grounds of excuse must be stated in open court[9].

Where there is more than one trial at a sitting, the jury at one trial may also serve at a subsequent trial with the consent of the prosecutor and the defence[10]. In such circumstances it is not necessary to have a ballot at the subsequent trial as the whole jury must be taken, but the jury must be sworn for each trial.

After the jury of fifteen has been balloted, the clerk informs them of the charge against the accused, usually by reading it to them, but in a complex indictment he may confine this to a summary approved by the judge[11]. While it is not necessary to give the jury copies of the indictment, copies are normally given if the judge thinks fit[11]. The copies will not have a list of productions or witnesses appended[11] and should not contain charges to which the accused has pleaded guilty before the jury was empanelled[12]. The clerk of court then administers the oath by asking the jury to stand and hold up their right hands and asking them, 'Do you swear by Almighty God that you will well and truly try the accused and give a true verdict according to the evidence?', to which the jurors reply, 'I do'[13]. A juror who objects to being sworn may make a solemn affirmation by repeating after the clerk, 'I, A B, do solemnly, sincerely and truly declare and affirm that I will well and truly try the accused and give a true verdict according to the evidence'[14]. The jurors resume their seats and the clerk will then read to them any special defence, although failure to do so does not necessarily amount to a miscarriage of justice[15]. At this stage it is still competent to excuse a juror or jurors and replace him or them with a juror or jurors balloted from the unempanelled jurors, provided this procedure is followed before any evidence is led[16]. As a consequence the judge should discharge the unempanelled jurors only after the first witness for the Crown has entered the witness box and taken the oath[16].

1 For further details about the preparation of the list of assize and the citation of jurors, see R W Renton and H H Brown *Criminal Procedure according to the Law of Scotland* (5th edn, 1983) paras 7-26, 7-35, and the Law Reform (Miscellaneous Provisions) (Scotland) Act 1985 (c 73), s 23, and *HM Advocate v Leslie* 1985 SCCR 1. The method of balloting the jury is prescribed by the Criminal Procedure (Scotland) Act 1975 (c 21), s 129 (amended by the Criminal Justice (Scotland) Act 1987 (c 41), s 70(1), Sch 1, para 7).

2 Criminal Procedure (Scotland) Act 1975, s 99(1) (amended by the Law Reform (Miscellaneous Provisions) (Scotland) Act 1980 (c 55), s 2(3), and the Criminal Procedure (Scotland) Act 1975, s 289G(2) (added by the Criminal Justice Act 1982 (c 48), s 54)). As to the standard scale, see para 2.12, note 1, above.

3 Criminal Procedure (Scotland) Act 1975, s 130(1), (2) (amended by the Criminal Justice (Scotland) Act 1980 (c 62), s 23); *Dawson v M'Lennan* (1863) 4 Irv 357. In practice the Crown seldom challenges a juror. The challenge must be made when the juror's name is called: *Mitchell v HM Advocate* 1971 SLT (Notes) 82.

4 Criminal Procedure (Scotland) Act 1975, s 130(4).

5 *Renton and Brown* para 10-31. Since at the time the jury is balloted the jurors will have no knowledge of the charge or the nature of the evidence, it can sometimes happen that in the course of the trial it is discovered that a juror has a personal connection with the case or is related to a witness. Such a circumstance should be brought to the judge's attention, and he will consider whether or not the juror should be discharged: see para 6.16 below. For the procedure to be followed where the judge has any personal interest in or knowledge of the case, see paras 6.41, 6.44, below.

6 *M v HM Advocate* 1974 SLT (Notes) 25. See also HM *Advocate v Devine* (1962) 78 Sh Ct Rep 173, where the court repelled a challenge based on the fact that the juror had served on an earlier jury dealing with an incident which had occurred about the same time and at the same place.

7 *Stuurman v HM Advocate* 1980 JC 111, 1980 SLT 182; *X v Sweeney* 1982 JC 70, 1982 SCCR 161, 1983 SLT 48; *Spink v HM Advocate* 1989 SCCR 415; *Kilbane v HM Advocate* 1989 SCCR 313, but see also para 6.17, note 2 below.

8 *McCadden v HM Advocate* 1985 SCCR 282, 1986 SLT 138. See also *Spink v HM Advocate* 1989 SCCR 413 where the Lord Justice General (Emslie) added, 'What would be perfectly appropri-

ate... is to ask jurors at the appropriate time if there are any reasons known to them which would make it desireable that they should not take part in the particular trial'.

9 Criminal Procedure (Scotland) Act 1975, s 133; Law Reform (Miscellaneous Provisions) (Scotland) Act 1980, s 1(6). The degree to which the grounds are specified in open court lies within the discretion of the judge — for example it might suffice to state that the juror was excused because information had reached him which meant that it was not appropriate or suitable for him to continue as a juror: *Hughes, Petitioner* 1990 SLT 142, 1989 SCCR 490.

10 Criminal Procedure (Scotland) Act 1975, s 132(1). If consent is given by the accused's legal representatives outwith his presence, the accused may withdraw the consent before the jury is sworn: *Lamont v HM Advocate* 1943 JC 21, 1943 SLT 125.

11 Criminal Procedure (Scotland) Act 1975, s 135.

12 See para 6.10 above.

13 Criminal Procedure (Scotland) Act 1975, s 135; Act of Adjournal (Consolidation) 1988, SI 1988/110, r 69(1), Sch 1, Form 33, Pt 1.

14 Ibid, r 69(2), Sch 1, Form 33, Pt 2. Where it is not reasonably practicable to swear a juror in a manner appropriate to his religious beliefs without inconvenience and delay, he must affirm: Oaths Act 1978 (c 19), s 5.

15 *Moar v HM Advocate* 1949 JC 31, 1949 SLT 106; *Sandlan v HM Advocate* 1983 JC 22, 1983 SCCR 71, 1983 SLT 519; *Thomson v HM Advocate* 1983 JC 69, 1983 SCCR 368, 1983 SLT 682. See also *Mullen v HM Advocate* 1978 SLT (Notes) 33, which suggests that consideration be given to discontinuing the practice. There is no requirement to read out a notice by the accused that he intends to incriminate a third party: *McShane v HM Advocate* 1989 SCCR 687.

16 Criminal Procedure (Scotland) Act 1975, s 129 (amended by the Criminal Justice (Scotland) Act 1987, Sch 1, para 7); *Practice Note* by the Lord Justice-General dated *22 January 1988*. Section 129 empowers the judge to discharge the entire jury and empanel a fresh one and, if insufficient unempanelled jurors are present for this purpose, the trial may be adjourned in terms of s 136 to allow further unempanelled jurors to be brought to court: *Hughes, Petitioner* 1990 SLT 142, 1989 SCCR 490.

6.15. Verdict once case remitted to jury. Once the case has thus been remitted to the jury, only the jury can return a verdict on the indictment, except where the judge upholds a defence submission that there is no case to answer at the close of the Crown case, in which instance the judge returns a verdict of acquittal[1]. Hence if the accused changes his plea to guilty in the course of the trial after the jury is empanelled, the jury is required, albeit on the direction of the judge, to return an immediate unanimous verdict of guilty[2]. If the plea does not relate to all the charges on the indictment, the trial will continue in respect of the remaining charges. Failure to take such a verdict from the jury renders any subsequent procedure incompetent, and no sentence can lawfully be passed on the charges to which the plea of guilty relates[2], but the absence of a verdict means that the accused has not tholed his assize and he may be reindicted[3]. Likewise, if the Crown abandons all or some of the charges after the jury has been empanelled, the jury must return an immediate unanimous verdict of not guilty on the direction of the judge, and if the abandonment relates to the whole indictment, the accused will be discharged. If the not guilty verdict is not taken from the jury or recorded, the Crown is personally barred from reindicting the accused and is taken to have renounced its right to prosecute[4], although in exceptional cases the accused might still risk prosecution by a private prosecutor[5]. Another consequence of remitting the case to the jury is that the whole evidence must be taken in its presence[6], but where a question of law (including objections to the relevancy of the indictment, or objections to the admissibility or relevancy of evidence) is to be debated, the debate is held outwith the presence of the jury, which requires to retire until the debate is concluded[7].

1 As to submissions of no case to answer, see para 6.25 below.

2 R W Renton and H H Brown *Criminal Procedure according to the Law of Scotland* (5th edn, 1983) para 10-51.

3 *Dunlop v HM Advocate* 1974 JC 59, *sub nom HM Advocate v Dunlop and Marklow* 1974 SLT 242. See also *Renton and Brown* para 9-27 .

4 *Thom v HM Advocate* 1976 JC 48, 1976 SLT 232. See also *Renton and Brown* paras 9-32, 10-49.

5 *X v Sweeney* 1982 JC 70, 1982 SCCR 161, 1983 SLT 48.
6 Hume *Commentaries* II,404,405; Alison *Practice* p 548.
7 See *Renton and Brown* para 18-44, which also discusses the procedure known as a 'trial within a trial' for deciding such evidential matters.

6.16. Management of the jury. In the course of the trial, if a juror becomes unfit to serve 'through illness or for any other reason' the court on the motion of either party may excuse the juror and direct that the trial proceed before the remainder provided that there are not less than twelve remaining jurors[1]. The phrase 'for any other reason' may be widely interpreted and will include the situation where there has been improper communication with a juror or where a juror has behaved improperly. There must be no communication on the subject of the trial between a juror and any other person after the jury is sworn, and if this rule is breached it will depend on the circumstances whether the defect can be cured by declaring the juror to be unfit and excusing him. If the infringement is minor it may not be necessary to excuse the juror and it may be possible to proceed with the trial provided the judge gives a proper direction to the jury about the infringement. In more serious cases, where there is a risk that the whole jury might be prejudiced by the breach, it may be necessary to desert the diet *pro loco et tempore*. A trivial remark to a juror may be ignored and cured by a satisfactory direction by the judge[2]; an attempt to bribe or threaten a juror in the course of the trial is likely to render him unfit, but provided the other jurors have not been prejudiced it may be possible to excuse the juror and proceed with the trial[3].

> 'Where the improper conduct of the juror comes to light during the trial... the matter can be investigated by the trial judge on the spot, including, inter alia, an interview with the juror, and an instant decision can be reached with a view to preventing a damaging result, either by dismissing the juror... or... discharging pro loco et tempore... In particular, in an inquiry during the trial, it would appear that the juror and his co-jurors could be questioned by the trial judge under the provisions of section 8(2) of the Contempt of Court Act 1981[4] not only about the matters complained of, but about the extent, if any, to which the allegedly offending juror had influenced or sought to influence the other members of the jury on the issues of the case'[5].

If the trial is adjourned overnight, it is not necessary to seclude the jury during the adjournment unless the court, either *ex proprio motu* or on the motion of one of the parties, directs to the contrary. In such an exceptional case the jury is accommodated overnight in strict seclusion under the charge of court officials, and if a juror requires to make any communication in regard to his private affairs he must do so through the clerk of court[6].

1 Criminal Procedure (Scotland) Act 1975 (c 21), s 134. See also R W Renton and H H Brown *Criminal Procedure according to the Law of Scotland* (5th edn, 1983) para 10–35, and *Farrell v HM Advocate* 1985 SCCR 23, 1985 SLT 324.
2 *Smart v HM Advocate* 1938 JC 148, 1938 SLT 511; *Hamilton v HM Advocate* 1986 SCCR 227, 1986 SLT 663.
3 *Stewart v HM Advocate* 1980 JC 103, 1980 SLT 245; *Hamilton v HM Advocate* 1986 SCCR 227, 1986 SLT 663.
4 It is generally a contempt of court to breach the confidentiality of a jury's deliberations (Contempt of Court Act 1981 (c 49), s 8(1)), but under s 8(2) disclosure may be made where necessary to enable the jury to reach its verdict: see para 6.31 below.
5 *McCadden v HM Advocate* 1985 SCCR 282 at 285, 1986 SLT 138 at 140, per Lord Justice-Clerk Wheatley; *Pike v HM Advocate* 1986 SCCR 633, 1987 SLT 488n; *Vass v HM Advocate* 1988 GWD 1–7.
6 *Renton and Brown* para 10-34.

(G) PUBLIC ACCESS TO COURTS; PUBLICITY

6.17. Public access to the court. Since justice should not only be done, but should be seen to be done, it is a cardinal principle of Scots law that the court must be open to the public (which in this connection includes representatives of the press) unless there is some provision to the contrary[1]. This rule does not apply to any pre-trial proceedings which are not held in open court, such as the appearance of the accused in private on petition or his judicial examination. While the press may not publish any details of the judicial examination, it may publish certain restricted information about the petition; but in general the press must take care that prior to the trial it does not publish anything 'which creates a substantial risk that the course of justice in the proceedings . . . will be seriously impeded or prejudiced'[2].

During a criminal trial the judge has a common law power to exclude the public if failure to do so would be prejudicial to national security (for example where the trial concerns a breach of the Official Secrets Acts 1911 (c 28) and 1920 (c 75)), and he may also order the court to be cleared if there is, or is likely to be, a disturbance or demonstration. An individual member of the public who interrupts or disrupts the proceedings may also be excluded and, if necessary, punished[3]. A child under the age of fourteen years (except for an infant in arms) is not permitted to be present in court unless his presence is required as a witness or 'for the purposes of justice'[4]. In a trial for rape 'or the like', or where the court is hearing an application to lead evidence attacking the morals or character of the victim of a sexual offence, the judge has a discretion to clear the court of all persons except the accused, counsel, solicitors[5], the jury, court officials and the police officers escorting the accused[6]. Strictly speaking an order to clear the court also applies to the press, but in practice reporters are allowed to remain on the understanding that they exercise discretion by refraining from publishing details of what has taken place when the court was closed[7]. Should a child be called as a witness in a case relating to an offence against, or any conduct contrary to, decency or morality, the judge has a discretion to clear the court of all persons except for officers of the court, parties, counsel, solicitors, persons otherwise directly concerned in the case and bona fide representatives of a newspaper or news agency[8].

1 This principle is based mainly on common law, but the Evidence Act 1686 (c 30) provides that there must be 'publication of the testimonies of witnesses'. See also COURTS AND COMPETENCY, vol 6, para 873.

2 Contempt of Court Act 1981 (c 49), s 2(2). Publication of such information may constitute contempt of court: see CONTEMPT OF COURT, vol 6, paras 305 ff. For further details, see the 1981 Act; *Atkins v London Weekend Television Ltd* 1978 JC 48, 1978 SLT 76; *Hall v Associated Newspapers Ltd* 1979 JC 1, 1978 SLT 241; and *Adams* 1987 SCCR 650. Prejudicial pre-trial publicity may, however, be founded on as a plea in bar of trial: *Stuurman v HM Advocate* 1980 JC 111, 1980 SLT 182; *X v Sweeney* 1982 JC 70, 1982 SCCR 161, 1983 SLT 48; *Kilbane v HM Advocate* 1989 SCCR 313; *Spink v HM Advocate* 1989 SCCR 413: see para 4.53 above. See also A J Bonnington 'Contempt of Court: A Practitioner's Viewpoint' 1988 SLT (News) 33.

3 Criminal Procedure (Scotland) Act 1975 (c 21), s 145(4), under which the offender is liable to imprisonment or a fine or both.

4 Ibid, s 165.

5 Ibid, s 145(3). For details of the nature of the evidence and offences to which the provision applies, see ss 141B, 346B (respectively added by the Law Reform (Miscellaneous Provisions) (Scotland) Act 1985 (c 73), s 36(1), (2)). In order to give psychological benefit, reassurance and support to the principal witnesses in trials involving rape or sexual assault, the judge should sufficiently advise them that the court has been cleared of all persons other than those directly involved: Recommendation of the Standing Committee on Criminal Procedure approved by the Lord Justice-General on 29 September 1987.

6 R W Renton and H H Brown *Criminal Procedure according to the Law of Scotland* (5th edn, 1983) para 10-37.

7 This practice is based on an informal agreement made by the Lord Justice-General and other High Court judges in 1973 whereby the press would be allowed to remain in court if it honoured the judge's intention of excluding the public in order to protect the witness. If the press was to dishonour this agreement it could, of course, be excluded like the rest of the public. Lord Avonside referred to this practice in *X v Sweeney* 1982 JC 70 at 92, 93, 1982 SCCR 161 at 177, 1983 SLT 48 at 61.

8 Criminal Procedure (Scotland) Act 1975, ss 166, 362.

6.18. Prohibition on press publicity. The press is sometimes prohibited from publishing certain matters despite their disclosure in open court in the presence of the public. Where a person under the age of sixteen is either the accused or the victim of the offence, the press may not reveal his name, address or school, or publish any picture, or give any other particulars calculated to lead to his identification, unless the court considers that such a prohibition would not be in the national interest[1]. The judge may also extend this prohibition to include witnesses under the age of sixteen years[2]. In the course of an application for bail prior to the trial, if particulars of the accused's previous convictions are given in open court, the publication of such information would almost certainly be considered as impeding or prejudicing the course of justice at the subsequent trial. In a trial involving sexual offences the press customarily refrains from publishing explicit details even where such evidence is given in open court. The court may also order that publication of part or all of any legal proceedings should be postponed if such an order is necessary to avoid a substantial risk of prejudice to the administration of justice in those proceedings or in any other pending or imminent proceedings[3].

Any press report of the trial must be fair and accurate[4] and it must not undermine the dignity of the court or ridicule the judge[5]. In order to ensure accuracy, there is nothing to prevent the press or any member of the public from taking notes during the trial, but it is contempt of court to use, or bring into court for use, any sound-recording instrument without leave of the court[6]. Where such leave is given, the court may impose such conditions as it thinks proper regarding the use of any recording which is made[7]. It is also contempt of court to publish any unauthorised recording, or any recording derived therefrom, by playing it in public or disposing of it with a view to such publication[8].

1 Criminal Procedure (Scotland) Act 1975 (c 21), ss 169(1), 374(1) (both substituted by the Criminal Justice (Scotland) Act 1980 (c 62), s 22). After the trial the Secretary of State may allow publication of such details if he considers it to be in the public interest: Criminal Procedure (Scotland) Act 1975, ss 169(1) proviso (iii), 374(1) proviso (iii) (as so substituted).

2 Ibid, ss 169(1) proviso (i), 374(1) proviso (i) (as so substituted). A witness not in this category may be given some degree of anonymity if the prosecutor allows him to use an accommodation address, such as that of a police station. This course is sometimes followed for rape victims or if a witness fears reprisals or has some other valid reason for not disclosing his home address.

3 Contempt of Court Act 1981 (c 49), s 4(2); *Keane v HM Advocate* 1986 SCCR 491, 1987 SLT 220n.

4 Contempt of Court Act 1981, s 4(1).

5 Under the Judges Act 1540 (c 22) this was known as 'murmuring of judges'. That Act was repealed by the Statute Law (Repeals) Act 1973 (c 39), but a report of this nature would now be considered as a contempt of court.

6 Contempt of Court Act 1981, s 9(1)(a). Section 9 does not apply to sound recordings made for the purpose of official transcripts: s 9(4).

7 Ibid, s 9(2). The use of a recording in contravention of these conditions is a contempt: s 9(1)(c).

8 Ibid, s 9(1)(b).

(H) PROSECUTION WITNESSES AND EVIDENCE

6.19. Preliminary matters. After the jury has been sworn, there are no opening speeches (as in English procedure) before leading the evidence, although at this stage in the proceedings some judges warn the jury of the impropriety of communications with a third party about the subject matter of the trial and at the same time give the jurors a brief general outline of the form the trial may take[1]. It is also necessary to administer the oath to the shorthand writer who, as an officer of the court, must note the evidence[2]. The shorthand notes are not normally extended (typed) unless they are required in whole or in part at a subsequent appeal but in exceptional cases, especially where the trial is long or complex, arrangements may be made to extend the notes on a daily basis so that a transcript may be available to the judge and the parties (but not the jury) in the course of the trial. The notes are also extended if an accused convicted of murder is later considered for parole. Extended notes require to be certified as correct, but the court does not require to accept them as accurate[3].

1 For example the jury might be told that the trial is expected to last two days, and that there will be no opening speeches. If such remarks are made, they should be brief and general, as the jury will be given more specific directions by the judge immediately before it retires to consider its verdict.
2 Should the shorthand writer change in the course of the trial the new writer must be sworn. As to the shorthand note, see further the Criminal Procedure (Scotland) Act 1975 (c 21), ss 274–276, and R W Renton and H H Brown *Criminal Procedure according to the Law of Scotland* (5th edn, 1983) para 10–88. A presiding sheriff is required by the Criminal Procedure (Scotland) Act 1975, s 146, to take a note of the evidence, and while there is no corresponding provision for a High Court judge, a High Court judge will also, in practice, note the evidence.
3 *Kyle v HM Advocate* 1987 SCCR 116, 1988 SLT 601; *McArthur v HM Advocate* 1989 SCCR 646.

6.20. Examination of witnesses for the Crown. As the Crown is the accuser and has the onus of proving the guilt of the accused beyond reasonable doubt, the evidence commences by the prosecutor calling his witnesses in whichever order he deems appropriate. Each witness enters the witness box, stands, raises his right hand and repeats after the judge (who also stands and raises his right hand), 'I swear by Almighty God that I will tell the truth, the whole truth and nothing but the truth' or, if he wishes to affirm, commences with the words 'I solemnly, sincerely and truly declare and affirm . . .'[1]. After taking the oath the witness usually remains standing throughout his evidence unless he is invited to sit by the court. Refusal to swear the oath or to affirm may be regarded as contempt of court[2]. A witness who is deaf, dumb or who does not understand English should be examined through a sworn interpreter[3].

The admissibility and competency of evidence and witnesses (including spouses and co-accused) are matters which are more properly discussed as part of the law of evidence[4] rather than procedure, and the following brief references to the rules relating to children and mentally disordered witnesses are only given because of the procedural difficulties which sometimes arise. A child is a competent witness provided the judge examines him and is satisfied that he has sufficient intelligence to understand the obligation to tell the truth[5]. There is no age limit which precludes a child from giving evidence, and a child under the age of twelve is admonished to tell the truth rather than being placed on oath; a child between the ages of twelve and fourteen may be placed on oath if the judge is satisfied the child understands the nature of the oath; a child of fourteen years or older is placed on oath[6]. A witness who suffers from mental disorder or who is prevented by weakness of intellect from understanding and taking the oath may be disqualified from giving evidence, although there have been instances where an insane person has been permitted to testify and in one case the opinion was expressed that an imbecile or weakminded person who was unable to understand the taking of the oath might be examined if 'shown to be capable of making a correct and truthful statement respecting facts as to which he or she is not likely to be mistaken'[7]. Where a witness is objected to on the ground of mental incapacity, the party seeking to call him may lead medical evidence to prove that the witness is capable of testifying and the other party may call medical evidence to prove the reverse. Medical evidence of this nature is competent even where the medical witnesses and productions are not contained in the lists attached to the indictment.

The prosecutor examines each of his witnesses in chief and should not ask improper prejudicial questions[8], nor should he ask leading questions except in relation to preliminary or incidental matters or facts which are not in dispute or unless the witness is hostile or is reluctant to answer questions or, in certain circumstances, gives evidence which differs from an earlier statement which he has made[9]. After the witness has been examined by the prosecutor, the defence may cross-examine him and also examine him *in causa* as he may not be called at a later stage as a defence witness[10]. Failure to challenge a witness's evidence by cross-examination is not necessarily fatal, nor does it necessarily mean that the evidence is accepted as true, but such failure may later be subject to comment and it may affect the weight given to the evidence[11]. Where there are several accused, each may cross-examine the witness in turn, usually in the order in which they appear on the indictment, but the order may be changed by the judge to avoid unfairness[12]. If a witness has been cross-examined by one accused and subsequently gives evidence incriminating him when being cross-examined by another accused, the incriminated accused may cross-examine the witness further[13]. At the conclusion of the cross-examination, the witness may be re-examined by the prosecutor on any matters arising from the cross-examination. Thereafter no further questions may be put to the witness by the parties except with leave of the court.

1 Act of Adjournal (Consolidation) 1988, SI 1988/110, r 70, Sch 1, Form 33, Pts 3, 4. Where it is not reasonably practicable to administer an oath appropriate to the witness's religious beliefs without inconvenience or delay, the witness must affirm: Oaths Act 1978 (c 19), s 5. An affirming witness need not raise his right hand.
2 In *Wylie v HM Advocate* 1966 SLT 149 witnesses who refused to take the oath in the High Court were sentenced to three years' imprisonment.
3 R W Renton and H H Brown *Criminal Procedure according to the Law of Scotland* (5th edn, 1983) para 18-81; A G Walker and N M L Walker *The Law of Evidence in Scotland* (1964) para 351.
4 The judge may be open to criticism if he disallows evidence to which no objection has been taken: *Kelso v HM Advocate* 1990 SCCR 9.
5 For example, see *Rees v Lowe* 1989 SCCR 664. See generally *The Evidence of Children and Other Potentially Vulnerable Witnesses* (Scot Law Com Discussion Paper no. 75) (June 1988).
6 For further details, see *Renton and Brown* para 18-82, and *Walker and Walker* para 349. In *HM Advocate v Thomson* (1857) 2 Irv 747 the evidence of a three-year-old child was rejected; in *HM Advocate v Miller* (1870) 1 Coup 430 the evidence of a three-and-a-half-year-old child was admitted.
7 *HM Advocate v Skene Black* (1887) 1 White 365; *HM Advocate v Stott* (1894) 1 Adam 386. See further *Renton and Brown* para 18-80, and *Walker and Walker* para 350. For a comparison with English law, see *R v Bellamy* [1986] Crim LR 54, CA.
8 *HM Advocate v Sinclair* 1986 SCCR 439, 1987 SLT 161.
9 See the Criminal Procedure (Scotland) Act 1975 (c 21), s 147. These matters relate to the law of evidence rather than procedure. For further details, see W G Dickson *The Law of Evidence in Scotland* (3rd edn, 1887) II, paras 1771, 1772, and *Walker and Walker* paras 339, 341.
10 Criminal Procedure (Scotland) Act 1975, s 148. However, in certain circumstances a witness may be recalled: see para 6.22 below.
11 *Young v Guild* 1984 SCCR 477, 1985 SLT 358.
12 *Sandlan v HM Advocate* 1983 JC 22, 1983 SCCR 71, 1983 SLT 519.
13 *Sandlan v HM Advocate* 1983 JC 22, 1983 SCCR 71, 1983 SLT 519; *Todd v HM Advocate* 1984 JC 13, 1983 SCCR 472, 1984 SLT 123.

6.21. Questioning by the judge or jury. It is competent for the judge to question the witness on any matter he considers relevant or important, but he should usually confine his questions to clarifying any ambiguities and must exercise discretion and restraint. He should not take over the role of counsel nor ask an excessive number of questions, and he must be careful that he does not give any impression that he has formed a personal view of the case or the credibility of the witness[1]. It is preferable that the judge should put any questions at the end of the witness's evidence, but if he elicits any new matter he must allow any party adversely affected thereby to examine the witness further[2]. A juror may also put a question to the witness, and while this seldom happens, the question, if allowed by the judge, should be put through him[3]. It also appears that the judge may have authority to require a party to provide copies of productions which are important as evidence but he should exercise that authority reasonably[4].

1 *Bergson v HM Advocate* 1972 SLT 242; *Livingstone v HM Advocate* (1974) SCCR Supp 68; *Nisbet v HM Advocate* 1979 SLT (Notes) 5; *Tallis v HM Advocate* 1982 SCCR 91; *Elliot v Tudhope* 1987 SCCR 85.
2 *M'Leod v HM Advocate* 1939 JC 68, 1939 SLT 556; J H A Macdonald *The Criminal Law of Scotland* (5th edn, 1948) p 299.
3 See also the Criminal Procedure (Scotland) Act 1975 (c 21), s 153(1), and para 6.30, note 31, below.
4 *Wilson v Caldwell* 1989 SCCR 273 in which the commentator also opines that if the judge orders a party to produce copies the cost must fall on that party.

6.22. Recall of witnesses. After a witness has concluded his evidence, he may be excused further attendance by leave of the court, failing which he should remain in court until the conclusion of the trial. He may, however, be recalled to give further evidence. At the conclusion of all the evidence for the party who called him, the judge has a common law power to recall a witness to clarify any ambiguities[1], and it may be that a witness who prevaricated when giving his evidence may be recalled to allow him to purge his contempt of court[2]. A witness may also be recalled by either party with leave of the court[3], and in such circumstances any further questions need not be limited to resolving ambiguities[4]. It is also competent to recall a witness where the court allows either party to lead additional evidence[5], or allows the prosecutor to lead evidence in replication[6].

1 *M'Neilie v HM Advocate* 1929 JC 50, 1929 SLT 145; *Davidson v M'Fadyean* 1942 JC 95, 1943 SLT 47; *Todd v MacDonald* 1960 JC 93, 1960 SLT (Notes) 53; *Lindie v HM Advocate* 1974 JC 1, 1974 SLT 208. See also *Brown v Smith* 1981 SCCR 206, 1982 SLT 301 (a summary case), which confirmed that a judge may recall a witness only to clarify ambiguities.
2 *Daniel Thomson v HM Advocate* 1988 SCCR 354, 1989 SLT 22n; R W Renton and H H Brown *Criminal Procedure according to the Law of Scotland* (5th edn, 1983) para 18-73. See also para 6.23 below.
3 Criminal Procedure (Scotland) Act 1975 (c 21), s 148A (added by the Criminal Justice Act 1982 (c 48), s 73(1)).
4 *Todd v MacDonald* 1960 JC 93, 1960 SLT (Notes) 53; *Daniel Thomson v HM Advocate* 1988 SCCR 354, 1989 SLT 22n. See *Renton and Brown* para 18-73.
5 Criminal Procedure (Scotland) Act 1975, s 149 (substituted by the Criminal Justice (Scotland) Act 1980 (c 62), s 30(1), and amended by the Criminal Justice (Scotland) Act 1987 (c 41), s 70(1), Sch 1, para 9). See also para 6.27 below.
6 Criminal Procedure (Scotland) Act 1975, s 149A (added by the Criminal Justice (Scotland) Act 1980, s 30(1), and amended by the Law Reform (Miscellaneous Provisions) (Scotland) Act 1985 (c 73), s 37). See also para 6.28 below.

6.23. Contempt or prevarication by witness. A witness who wilfully fails to attend court or who appears in a state of intoxication may be found guilty of contempt of court[1]. When the witness attends court he will normally be asked to wait in a witness room, and he should not enter the court room before he is called to give evidence, although an exception may be made in the case of an expert witness[2] or any other witness who is permitted by the court, on the application of one of the parties, to be present before giving evidence[3]. If a witness is approached by a third party while he is waiting to give evidence, or during a break in his evidence, the reliability of the witness may be put in question or his evidence may even be rendered inadmissible[4]. When giving his evidence, a witness must not use defiant or insulting language to the judge[5] and, while he is not bound to answer any question which is merely intended to insult or annoy him[6], failure to answer a competent and relevant question allowed by the judge may be considered as contempt of court[7]. A witness who prevaricates may be guilty of contempt[8]. Prevarication is:

> 'a loose and indefinite term which may mean many different things short of perjury; the general idea which it conveys is manifest unwillingness candidly to tell the whole truth, fencing with questions in such a manner as to show reluctance to disclose the truth and a disposition to conceal or withhold it'[9].

Neither the judge nor the prosecutor should say or do anything in the presence of the jury to indicate their views on the behaviour of the prevaricating witness, such as asking or ordering him to be detained until the end of the trial or suggesting that charges will be brought against him[10], and any order for the witness's detention must therefore be made outwith the presence of the jury[11]. At the discretion of the judge a witness so detained may be recalled and given an opportunity to purge his contempt by giving evidence without prevarication[12]. A witness who deliberately tells lies under oath is guilty of perjury.

1 Every court has power at common law to punish summarily acts in contempt of its authority: Hume *Commentaries* II, 138; *Orr v Annan* 1987 SCCR 242, 1988 SLT 251n. In summary proceedings certain types of contempt are governed by the Criminal Procedure (Scotland) Act 1975 (c 21), s 344 (amended by the Criminal Justice (Scotland) Act 1980 (c 62), ss 46(1)(c), 83(2), Sch 7, para 55, and the Criminal Justice Act 1982 (c 48), s 56(3), Sch 7, para 8). See further R W Renton and H H Brown *Criminal Procedure according to the Law of Scotland* (5th edn, 1983) paras 18-104, 18-105. See also the Contempt of Court Act 1981 (c 49), and CONTEMPT OF COURT, vol 6, paras 305 ff. Where there has been a preliminary diet (see paras 680 ff above) the judge has an implied power to excuse a witness from complying with his citation if the witness cannot give evidence which is relevant or competent to the indictment: *McDonald v HM Advocate, Valentine v HM Advocate* 1989 SCCR 165. If a witness has absconded (or means to abscond) either party may apply to the court for a warrant to arrest him and thereafter commit him to prison until the date of the trial unless the court allows him to find caution for his appearance: Alison *Principles and Practice* II, 398; Hume II, 375; *HM Advocate v Bell* 1936 JC 89; *Stallworth v HM Advocate* 1978 SLT 93; *Gerrard, Petitioner* 1984 SLT 108; *Renton and Brown* para 7-45. For an example of a case involving caution see *Sargeant, Petitioner* 1990 SLT 286, 1989 SCCR 448. For the corresponding provisions in summary procedure see para 5.46, note 9 below. In certain circumstances a witness who failed to answer his citation might also be prosecuted for attempting to pervert the course of justice — see for example *Nisbet v HM Advocate* 1989 GWD 32–1473 (where a witness convicted of this crime was sentenced to two years imprisonment).
2 Failure to observe this rule may preclude the witness from giving evidence: see *Renton and Brown* paras 18-79, 18-87.
3 Criminal Procedure (Scotland) Act 1975, ss 139A, 342A (added by the Criminal Justice (Scotland) Act 1987 (c 41), s 63), which further provide that the presence of the witness must not be contrary to the interests of justice.
4 *Renton and Brown* para 18-88.
5 Such behaviour may be considered as contempt of court.
6 *Renton and Brown* para 18-84.
7 *HM Advocate v Airs* 1975 JC 64, 1975 SLT 177; *Green v Smith* 1987 SCCR 686, 1988 SLT 175; *Smith* 1987 SCCR 726. However, see also the Contempt of Court Act 1981, s 10, which provides that it is not contempt of court for a witness to refuse to answer a question where the answer means disclosing the source of information in a publication for which he is responsible unless disclosure is necessary in the interests of justice or national security or for the prevention of disorder or crime: see CONTEMPT OF COURT, vol 6, para 316. For summary cases, see the Criminal Procedure (Scotland) Act 1975, s 344 (as amended: see note 1 above).
8 This is governed by common law in solemn proceedings (see *Renton and Brown* para 18-105), and by the Criminal Procedure (Scotland) Act 1975, s 344 (as so amended) in summary proceedings.
9 *Macleod v Speirs* (1884) 11 R (J) 26, 5 Coup 387.

10 *McAllister v HM Advocate* (1975) SCCR Supp 98; *Hutchison v HM Advocate* 1983 SCCR 504, 1984 SLT 233.

11 Cf however *McKenzie v HM Advocate* 1986 SCCR 94, 1986 SLT 389n.

12 *Renton and Brown* para 18-105; *Anderson v McLeod* 1987 SCCR 566; *Daniel Thomson v HM Advocate* 1988 SCCR 354, 1989 SLT 22n.

6.24. Evidence on commission and record of judicial examination. In addition to leading witnesses and lodging productions, the prosecutor before closing his case may lodge a record of any evidence taken on commission and request the clerk of court to read it to the jury. He must also lodge the record of any judicial examination of the accused[1], and if he does not request that it be read to the jury, the defence has the right to do so[2], although either party may ask the court to order that the record, or part of it, should not be read to the jury[3]. The purpose of this provision is to enable the judge to exclude from the jury any part of the examination which is prejudicial or unfair to the accused or any replies which were obtained in breach of the rules relating to the conduct of judicial examinations. In this latter connection, the defence, but not the prosecutor, may adduce as witnesses the persons who were present during the examination, even although they are not on the list of witnesses[4]. The defence interest in such an application is obvious, but the prosecutor's interest may be equally as great. Should the record at one part disclose a damaging admission by the accused and at another contain inadmissible, prejudicial evidence (for example evidence that the accused has previous convictions), the prosecutor may wish to have the former read to the jury while excluding the latter. Where a prosecutor does not take care to ensure that inadmissible prejudicial evidence (of which he is aware) is withheld from the jury, this could give rise to a miscarriage of justice with the consequence that the proceedings might be deserted or that any subsequent conviction might be quashed on appeal[5]. Finally, the prosecutor may request the clerk to read any minute of admissions concerning evidence which the parties have agreed should be admitted without further proof[6]. The prosecutor then intimates to the court that he has closed his case.

1 *HM Advocate v Cafferty* 1984 SCCR 444, Sh Ct; Criminal Procedure (Scotland) Act 1975 (c 21), s 78(2) (substituted by the Criminal Justice (Scotland) Act 1980 (c 62), s 12, Sch 4, para 8). As to judicial examination, see paras 4.06 ff above.

2 Criminal Procedure (Scotland) Act 1975, s 82A (added by the Criminal Justice (Scotland) Act 1980, s 27).

3 Criminal Procedure (Scotland) Act 1975, s 151(2) (substituted by the Criminal Justice (Scotland) Act 1980, s 6(3)). The request may be made at a preliminary diet prior to the trial or at any stage during the trial before the record is read: R W Renton and H H Brown *Criminal Procedure according to the Law of Scotland* (5th edn, 1983) para 9-05. See also *Moran v HM Advocate* 1990 SCCR 40.

4 Criminal Procedure (Scotland) Act 1975, s 151(1), (2) (as so substituted).

5 For further detail see para 4.06 above. this more properly falls within the law relating to evidence, as does the effect of disclosing that the accused has previous convictions. See *Renton and Brown* paras 10-42–10-46a.

6 See the Criminal Procedure (Scotland) Act 1975, s 150.

(1) NO CASE TO ANSWER

6.25. No case to answer. Immediately after the close of the prosecution case the accused may make a submission that there is no case for him to answer[1], and the judge is obliged to hear both parties (or at least the accused) in argument, even if it is clear that the submission is without merit[2]. The submission is heard by the judge outwith the presence of the jury[3], and if it succeeds the judge (and not the jury) will acquit the accused[4], but if it is rejected, the trial will proceed as if the submission had not been made[5]. Where there are a number of charges and the submission is made only or is upheld only in respect of some of them, the trial will proceed on the remainder[6]. In order to succeed, the submission must relate not only to the offence charged on the indictment, but also to any other offence of which the accused might be convicted[7] (for example if the charge is one of theft, the accused can be convicted of reset even if reset is not charged). Similarly, the submission will be rejected if the accused can be convicted of part of the charge libelled (for example on some parts of a charge of assault, or theft of some of the articles libelled in the charge)[8]. In considering the submission, the judge's views as to the credibility or reliability of the evidence are irrelevant, the test being whether there is evidence which, if accepted, would be sufficient in law for conviction[9].

If no submission is made, the judge has a common law power (which he may exercise *ex proprio motu* or on a motion by the defence) to hold that there is not sufficient evidence to allow the case (or one or more of the charges) to proceed to the jury for conviction. The prosecutor is entitled to insist that the judge defer consideration of this issue until after the prosecutor has addressed the jury[10]. Where the judge makes such a ruling, he can not acquit the accused, but must direct the jury to return a verdict of not guilty in respect of the charge or charges to which the ruling relates[11].

1 Criminal Procedure (Scotland) Act 1975 (c21), s 140A(1)(a) (added by the Criminal Justice (Scotland) Act 1980 (c62), s 19(1)).
2 *Taylor v Douglas* 1983 SCCR 323, 1984 SLT 69.
3 Criminal Procedure (Scotland) Act 1975, s 140A(2) (as added: see note 1 above).
4 Ibid, s 140A(3) (as so added). Where the sustaining of the submission results in the acquittal of the accused on one charge but where the trial continues in respect of other charges, the prosecutor should not make improper comment about the acquittal: *Dudgeon v HM Advocate* 1988 SCCR 147, 1988 SLT 476.
5 Criminal Procedure (Scotland) Act 1975, s 140A(4) (as so added).
6 Ibid, s 140A(3) (as so added).
7 Ibid, s 140A(1)(b) (as so added).
8 See ibid, ss 47, 61; *Myers v HM Advocate* 1936 JC 1, 1936 SLT 39; and R W Renton and H H Brown *Criminal Procedure according to the Law of Scotland* (5th edn, 1983) paras 10-48, 10-60.
9 *Williamson v Wither* 1981 SCCR 214. The law is unsettled as to the position where the judge wrongly rejects a submission and evidence is then led which proves to be sufficient for a conviction: see *Little v HM Advocate* 1983 JC 16, 1983 SCCR 56, 1983 SLT 489; *Stobbs v HM Advocate* 1983 SCCR 190; *Todd v HM Advocate* 1984 JC 13, 1983 SCCR 472, 1984 SLT 123.
10 See *Renton and Brown* para 10-50, and *Kent v HM Advocate* 1950 JC 38, 1950 SLT 130.
11 *Kent v HM Advocate* 1950 JC 38, 1950 SLT 130.

(J) DEFENCE WITNESSES AND EVIDENCE

6.26. Evidence for the accused. The accused has the right to lead evidence in exculpation, although he is not required to prove his innocence, which is presumed until he is proved to be guilty. Defence evidence is led in the same way as evidence for the prosecution, and while the accused may call his witnesses in any order he pleases, if he is giving evidence in person it is normal for him to do so before any of his witnesses. Where there is more than one accused, they will lead evidence in the order in which they appear on the indictment. The prosecutor will normally cross-examine the accused[1] and any other defence witness whose evidence contradicts the prosecution case, and while failure to do so is not a bar to a conviction, it may pose certain difficulties for the prosecutor[2]. Evidence given by or on behalf of one accused is evidence for or against a co-accused, and any accused may therefore cross-examine a witness called by the other and may further cross-examine him for a second time if the witness incriminates him in the course of a subsequent cross-examination[3]. Any cross-examination by a co-accused takes place before cross-examination by the prosecutor. After the witness has been cross-examined, he may be re-examined by the party leading him. In addition to leading witnesses, the accused may lodge a record of any evidence taken on commission on behalf of the defence and request the clerk of court to read it to the jury. He may also request that all or part of the record of his judicial examination be read to the jury if this has not already been done[4]. The accused then intimates to the court that he has closed his case; alternatively an intimation by the accused that he is not leading any evidence has the same effect.

1 If the judge intervenes while the accused is giving evidence, he should take care that he does not cross-examine the accused, especially if this affects credibility: *Dobbins v HM Advocate* (1980) SCCR Supp 253.
2 *Young v Guild* 1984 SCCR 477, 1985 SLT 358. See also para 6.21 above.
3 *Todd v HM Advocate* 1984 JC 13, 1983 SCCR 472, 1984 SLT 123. See also para 6.20 above.
4 This matter is fully discussed in para 6.24 above.

(K) ADDITIONAL EVIDENCE; EVIDENCE IN REPLICATION

6.27. Additional evidence. After a party has closed his case he may, before the commencement of speeches to the jury, make a motion requesting permission to lead additional evidence[1]. The court may grant such permission only where the judge considers the evidence to be prima facie material and in addition accepts that at the time the jury was sworn, either the additional evidence was not and could not reasonably have been made available, or its materiality could not have been reasonably foreseen by the party[2]. If the motion is allowed, witnesses and productions not included in the lists may be adduced as evidence and a witness who has previously given evidence may be recalled[3], but the judge, in granting the motion, may adjourn or postpone the trial before allowing the additional evidence to be led[4]. While there is no corresponding statutory power to allow an adjournment after the evidence has been led, such an adjournment is competent in pursuance of the court's common law powers[5].

1 Criminal Procedure (Scotland) Act 1975 (c 21), s 149(1) (substituted by the Criminal Justice (Scotland) Act 1980 (c 62), s 30(1)). Corresponding provision in respect of summary proceedings is made by the Criminal Procedure (Scotland) Act 1975, s 350 (substituted by the Criminal Justice (Scotland) Act 1980, s 30(2)).
2 Criminal Procedure (Scotland) Act 1975, s 149(1)(a), (b) (as so substituted, and amended by the Criminal Justice (Scotland) Act 1987 (c 41), s 70(1), Sch 1, para 9); *Brown v Smith* 1981 SCCR 206, 1982 SLT 301. See, however, *Campbell v Allan* 1988 SCCR 47.
3 Criminal Procedure (Scotland) Act 1975, s 149(2) (as so substituted).
4 Ibid, s 149(3) (as so substituted).
5 See para 6.05 above.

6.28. Evidence in replication. Apart from the provisions relating to additional evidence, the prosecutor may ask the court for permission to lead evidence in replication, provided the motion is made after the close of the defence evidence and before the commencement of the speeches[1]. The motion may be granted only where the prosecutor wishes to lead such evidence either for the purpose of contradicting evidence (given by any defence witness) which he could not reasonably have anticipated, or of proving that, on a specified occasion, a witness has made a statement which differs from the evidence given by him at the trial[2]. If evidence in replication is allowed, the accused is entitled to ask permission to lead additional evidence to counter it[3]. The rules regarding the adducing of witnesses and productions not on the lists, the recall of witnesses and the granting of adjournments and postponements are identical to those relating to the leading of additional evidence[4].

1 Criminal Procedure (Scotland) Act 1975 (c 21), s 149A(1) (added by the Criminal Justice (Scotland) Act 1980 (c 62), s 30(1), and amended by the Law Reform (Miscellaneous Provisions) (Scotland) Act 1985 (c 73), s 37). Corresponding provision in respect of summary proceedings is made by the Criminal Procedure (Scotland) Act 1975, s 350A (added by the Criminal Justice (Scotland) Act 1980, s 30(2), and amended as mentioned above).
2 Criminal Procedure (Scotland) Act 1975, s 149A(1) (as so added and amended). Evidence given by a defence witness includes evidence given by him in the course of cross-examination: *Sandlan v HM Advocate* 1983 JC 22, 1983 SCCR 71, 1983 SLT 519. The prosecutor may not call a witness in replication in order to contradict a Crown witness: *Campbell v Allan* 1988 SCCR 47. The proper course is to seek to recall the witness before the close of the Crown case under the Criminal Procedure (Scotland) Act 1975, s 148A (see para 6.22 above) or, in summary proceedings, under s 349A (respectively added by the Criminal Justice Act 1982 (c 48), s 73(1), (2)).
3 *Sandlan v HM Advocate* 1983 JC 22, 1983 SCCR 71, 1983 SLT 519.
4 Criminal Procedure (Scotland) Act 1975, s 149A(2), (3) (as added: see note 1 above); see para 6.27 above.

(L) SPEECHES

6.29. Addresses to the jury. After all the evidence has been led, the prosecutor and then the defence may address the jury, the defence always being entitled to the last word[1]. Where there is more than one accused, they address the jury in the order in which they appear on the indictment. It is customary for each party to seek to persuade the jury to give a verdict in his favour, and few rules govern the content of these speeches. The prosecutor should not make allegations against the accused which are irrelevant or unsupported by evidence[2]; and he must not comment on the failure of the accused[3] or his spouse[4] to give evidence[5]. Should he breach this latter rule, it is the duty of the judge to check him and to tell the jury to disregard the comment, failing which the conviction may be overturned on appeal unless the comment did not influence the result of the case[6]. Where the accused or any of his witnesses gave evidence about some matter on which the accused could have answered questions at his judicial examination but refused to do so, his refusal may be subject to comment by the prosecutor[7]. Unlike the prosecutor, an accused may comment on the failure of a co-accused to give evidence[8], but he must not refer to the failure of the spouse of a co-accused to give evidence[9]. He has the same right as the prosecutor to comment on the refusal of a co-accused to answer questions at his judicial examination[10].

1 Criminal Procedure (Scotland) Act 1975 (c 21), s 152.
2 *Martin v Boyd* 1908 SC (J) 52, 5 Adam 528; *Slater v HM Advocate* 1928 JC 94, 1928 SLT 602.
3 Criminal Procedure (Scotland) Act 1975, s 141(1)(b) (amended by the Criminal Justice (Scotland) Act 1980 (c 62), ss 28, 82(2), (3), Sch 7, para 33, Sch 8). The corresponding provision for summary proceedings is the Criminal Procedure (Scotland) Act 1975, s 346(1)(b) (amended by the Criminal Justice (Scotland) Act 1980, s 28, Sch 7, para 56, Sch 8).
4 Criminal Procedure (Scotland) Act 1975, s 143(3) (substituted by the Criminal Justice (Scotland) Act 1980, s 29). The corresponding provision for summary proceedings is the Criminal Procedure (Scotland) Act 1975, s 348(3) (as so substituted).
5 *Clark v HM Advocate* (1977) SCCR Supp 162; *Upton v HM Advocate* 1986 SCCR 188, 1986 SLT 594.
6 *Ross v Boyd* (1903) 5 F (J) 64, 4 Adam 184; *M'Attee v Hogg* (1903) 5 F (J) 67, 4 Adam 190; *M'Hugh v HM Advocate* 1978 JC 12.
7 Criminal Procedure (Scotland) Act 1975, s 20A(5) (added by the Criminal Justice (Scotland) Act 1980, s 6(2)).
8 The Criminal Procedure (Scotland) Act 1975, ss 141(1)(b), 346(1)(b), refer only to the prosecutor and not to the defence.

9 Ibid, ss 143(3), 348(3) (as substituted: see note 4 above).
10 Ibid, s 20A(5) (as added: see note 7 above).

(M) JUDGE'S CHARGE

6.30. Judge's charge. At the conclusion of the speeches by the prosecution and defence the judge addresses the jury, this address being known as the judge's charge[1]. The function of the jury is to determine the facts by assessing the reliability and credibility of the witnesses[2] and deciding what conclusions and inferences are to be drawn from the evidence and thereafter, by applying the law as defined and directed by the judge, to reach a verdict. The judge alone is responsible for directing the jury as to the law, and the jury must accept and follow any directions in law which he gives it. A misdirection in law by the judge may later be founded on as a ground of appeal[3], although it can sometimes be cured by a correct direction later in the charge[4]. The duty of the trial judge is:

> 'to explain to the jury the legal framework within which the evidence has to be considered, and, in so far as he considers it necessary, to put the evidence within that framework in such a way as to make clear to the jury the nature of the issue or issues which they have to decide'[5].

His primary duty is, therefore,

> 'to direct the jury upon the law applicable to the case . . . But it is a matter very much in his discretion whether he can help the jury by resuming the evidence on any particular aspect of the case'[6].

He

> 'does not give a summing up . . . by rehearsing all the evidence. All that the judge is required to do is to make reference to such of the evidence as is necessary for the determination of the issues . . . in an even-handed fashion so as not to give an advantage one way or the other'[7].

He should clearly focus the issues, especially where there has been confusing or conflicting evidence[8]; he should not present something as clearly proved without referring to evidence to the contrary[9]; and his directions to the jury should be free of contradiction and confusion[10]. If he refers to the evidence, he must be careful to avoid giving his own views or impressions, or in any way trespassing on the jury's province as masters of the facts[11].

Apart from making sure that the jury is properly directed as to the distinction between matters of fact and matters of law, there are several other directions which the judge should include in his charge in all jury trials. He must direct that the onus of proof lies upon the Crown[12] and that the standard of proof is beyond reasonable doubt[13]. The jury must also be given proper directions as to the need for corroboration of the Crown evidence[14] and be told which facts require corroboration[15]. As regards the defence, the judge should direct the jury that there is no onus on the accused[16], who is entitled to the presumption of innocence until he is proved guilty; and while the judge may draw the attention of the jury to the fact that the accused or his spouse failed to give evidence he should do so with restraint and only where necessary[17]. He should further direct the jury that where the defence has led evidence, it does not require to be corroborated and that the jury must acquit the accused if the defence has raised a reasonable doubt in its mind[18]. In relation to the charge on the indictment, the judge should define the law and the various elements the Crown must prove if it is to secure a conviction[19], and he should also define the legal requirements of any special defence[20].

Depending on the circumstances of the case, the judge may also be required to give directions on any aspect of the law relating to procedure or evidence which may arise, including, for example, the law relating to concert[21], and the rules that evidence led to discredit a witness is not evidence against the accused[22], that a statement made by one accused outwith the presence of another is not evidence against that other[23], and that incompetent or irrelevant evidence prejudicial to the accused should be disregarded[24].

With regard to the verdict, the jury must be directed that three verdicts are open to it, namely guilty, not guilty and not proven[25], and that it will be required to return a separate verdict in respect of each charge on the indictment. In addition, the judge should normally draw the jury's attention to all possible verdicts which are in issue, and the courses it should adopt on the various views of the evidence open to it: for example, depending on how it views the evidence, it might be competent for it to convict of culpable homicide rather than murder[26]. The jury must also be told that its verdict may be unanimous or by majority, but that if it is a majority verdict, it may not return a verdict of guilty unless at least eight of its number are in favour of such a decision[27]. The rule regarding a minimum of eight votes for a guilty verdict applies where the number of jurors has been reduced to less than fifteen[28]. At the conclusion of his charge, the judge should not ask the parties if they wish any other or further directions to be given[29] before inviting the jury to retire to consider its verdict[30]. After the jury has retired, it may request further directions from the judge or the judge may give it further directions *ex proprio motu*[31]. In either case, the directions must be given in open court in the presence of the accused[32]. The jury should not be asked to retire late in the day, especially after a long and difficult trial[33].

1 Justiciary and Circuit Courts (Scotland) Act 1783 (c 45), s 5 (repealed).
2 *Macmillan v HM Advocate* 1927 JC 62, 1927 SLT 425. The jurors are often referred to as the 'masters of the facts'.
3 R W Renton and H H Brown *Criminal Procedure according to the Law of Scotland* (5th edn, 1983) para 11-38. See also *Kyle v HM Advocate* 1987 SCCR 116, 1988 SLT 601; *Steven v HM Advocate* 1987 GWD 23-837.
4 *Moffat v HM Advocate* 1983 SCCR 121; *Dorrens v HM Advocate* 1983 SCCR 407; *Burns v HM Advocate* 1983 SLT 38.
5 *Rubin v HM Advocate* 1984 SCCR 96 at 112, per Lord Grieve.
6 *Hamilton v HM Advocate* 1938 JC 134 at 144, 1938 SLT 333 at 337, per Lord Justice-General Normand. See also *MacNeil v HM Advocate* 1986 SCCR 288.
7 *King v HM Advocate* 1985 SCCR 322 at 328, per Lord Justice-Clerk Wheatley. In being 'even-handed', he must ensure that he puts the defence case properly to the jury, although he need not cover it in every detail: see *Scott v HM Advocate* 1946 JC 90, 1946 SLT 140; *Fraser v HM Advocate* 1982 SCCR 458; *Gilmour v HM Advocate* 1982 SCCR 590; *Meek v HM Advocate* 1982 SCCR 613, 1983 SLT 280; *Rubin v HM Advocate* 1984 SCCR 96, 1984 SLT 369.
8 *Tonge v HM Advocate* 1982 SCCR 313, 1982 SLT 506.
9 *Mills v HM Advocate* 1935 JC 77; 1935 SLT 532.
10 *Greig v HM Advocate* 1949 SLT (Notes) 5..
11 *Simpson v HM Advocate* 1952 JC 1, *sub nom HM Advocate v Simpson* 1952 SLT 85; *McMillan v HM Advocate* 1979 SLT (Notes) 68; *Tallis v HM Advocate* 1982 SCCR 91; *Brady v HM Advocate* 1986 SCCR 191, 1986 SLT 686; *Cooney v HM Advocate* 1987 SCCR 60; *Larkin v HM Advocate* 1988 SCCR 30; *McArthur v HM Advocate* 1989 SCCR 646; *Crowe v HM Advocate* 1989 SCCR 681.
12 *Slater v HM Advocate* 1928 JC 94, 1928 SLT 602; *Lennie v HM Advocate* 1946 JC 79, 1946 SLT 212; *Owens v HM Advocate* 1946 JC 119, 1946 SLT 227; *M'Kenzie v HM Advocate* 1959 JC 32; *Earnshaw v HM Advocate* 1981 SCCR 279, 1982 SLT 179.
13 *M'Kenzie v HM Advocate* 1959 JC 32. Judges should adhere to the traditional formula when directing juries about reasonable doubt: *Shewan v HM Advocate* 1989 SCCR 364.
14 *Lockwood v Walker* 1910 SC (J) 3, 6 Adam 124; *Harrison v Mackenzie* 1923 JC 61, 1923 SLT 565; *Townsend v Strathern* 1923 JC 66, 1923 SLT 644; *Morton v HM Advocate* 1938 JC 50, 1938 SLT 27; *Wilson v HM Advocate* (1976) SCCR Supp 126.
15 *Dorrens v HM Advocate* 1983 SCCR 407. Not all facts require to be corroborated, but this relates to the law of evidence rather than of procedure: see Hume *Commentaries* II, 384–386; Alison

Practice p 551; *Scott v Jameson* 1914 SC (J) 187, 7 Adam 529; *Gillespie v Macmillan* 1957 JC 31, 1957 SLT 31; and *Renton and Brown* paras 18-52-18-64.

16 In certain circumstances there may be an onus on the accused, and in such cases the judge should direct the jury accordingly: see *Renton and Brown* para 18-02, but see also *McDonald v HM Advocate* 1989 GWD 38-1979..

17 *Brown v Macpherson* 1918 JC 3, 1917 2 SLT 134; *Costello v Macpherson* 1922 JC 9, 1922 SLT 35; *HM Advocate v Hardy* 1938 JC 144, 1938 SLT 412; *Scott v HM Advocate* 1946 JC 90, 1946 SLT 140; *Knowles v HM Advocate* 1975 JC 6; *Stewart v HM Advocate* 1980 JC 103, 1980 SLT 245; *Brady v HM Advocate* 1986 SCCR 191, 1986 SLT 686; *McShane v HM Advocate* 1989 SCCR 687. With regard to the failure by the accused to answer questions at his judicial examination, see the Criminal Procedure (Scotland) Act 1975 (c 21), s 20A(5) (added by the Criminal Justice (Scotland) Act 1980 (c 62), s 6(2)); *Alexander v HM Advocate* 1988 SCCR 542, 1989 SLT 193n.

18 *Hillan v HM Advocate* 1937 JC 53, 1937 SLT 396; *M'Cann v HM Advocate* 1960 JC 36, 1961 SLT 73; *Lambie v HM Advocate* 1973 JC 53, 1973 SLT 219; *Donnelly v HM Advocate* 1977 SLT 147; *Mullen v HM Advocate* 1978 SLT (Notes) 33; *King v HM Advocate* 1985 SCCR 322. However, see also *Dunn v HM Advocate* 1986 SCCR 340, 1987 SLT 295.

19 *M'Kenzie v HM Advocate* 1959 JC 32; *Black v HM Advocate* 1974 JC 43, 1974 SLT 247; *HM Advocate v McTavish* 1975 SLT (Notes) 27; *Spiers v HM Advocate* 1980 JC 36; *McIntyre v HM Advocate* 1981 SCCR 117; *Martin v HM Advocate* 1989 SCCR 546.

20 *Owens v HM Advocate* 1946 JC 119, 1946 SLT 227; *Elliott v HM Advocate* 1987 SCCR 278; *Ferris v HM Advocate* 1987 SCCR 722; *Jones v HM Advocate* 1989 SCCR 726. A notice of intention to lead evidence incriminating a co-accused is different from a special defence and does not require to be read out or referred to in the judge's charge: *McShane v HM Advocate* 1989 SCCR 687.

21 *Tobin v HM Advocate* 1934 JC 60, 1934 SLT 325; *Docherty v HM Advocate* 1945 JC 89, 1945 SLT 247; *Greig v HM Advocate* 1949 SLT (Notes) 5; *Shaw v HM Advocate* 1953 JC 51, 1953 SLT 179; *M'Phelim v HM Advocate* 1960 JC 17, 1960 SLT 214; *Burns v HM Advocate* 1983 SLT 38.

22 *Paterson v HM Advocate* 1974 JC 35, *sub nom HM Advocate v Paterson* 1974 SLT 53 .

23 *Black v HM Advocate* 1974 JC 43, 1974 SLT 247. See, however, *HM Advocate v Docherty* 1980 SLT (Notes) 33.

24 *Paterson v HM Advocate* 1974 JC 35, *sub nom HM Advocate v Paterson* 1974 SLT 53; *Smith v HM Advocate* 1975 SLT (Notes) 89; *Gemmill v HM Advocate* 1980 JC 16, 1979 SLT 217; *Jones v HM Advocate* 1981 SCCR 192.

25 *MacDiarmid v HM Advocate, Neill v HM Advocate* 1948 JC 12, 1948 SLT 202 ; *M'Nicol v HM Advocate* 1964 JC 25, 1964 SLT 151; *Hasson v HM Advocate* (1971) 35 JCL 271; *Bergson v HM Advocate* 1972 SLT 242. The judge should not attempt to explain the difference between a not proven and a not guilty verdict: *McDonald v HM Advocate* 1989 SCCR 29; 1989 SLT 298; *Fay v HM Advocate* 1989 SCCR 373; *McRae v HM Advocate* 1989 GWD 37-1747.

26 *Muir v HM Advocate* 1933 JC 46, 1933 SLT 403; *Docherty v HM Advocate* 1945 JC 89, 1945 SLT 247; *HM Advocate v Woods* 1972 SLT (Notes) 77. However, see also *Kilna v HM Advocate* 1960 JC 23; *Templeton v HM Advocate* 1961 JC 62, 1961 SLT 328; and *M'Hugh v HM Advocate* 1978 JC 12. For the full list of alternative verdicts, see *Renton and Brown* paras 10-61-10-63, the Criminal Procedure (Scotland) Act 1975 (c 21), ss 60-64, and s 216 (amended by the Criminal Justice (Scotland) Act 1987 (c 41), s 64(1)), the Sexual Offences (Scotland) Act 1976 (c 67), s 15, and *Sweeney v X* 1982 SCCR 509. See also *Buchanan v Hamilton* 1989 SCCR 398.

27 *M'Phelim v HM Advocate* 1960 JC 1, 1960 SLT 214; *Affleck v HM Advocate* 1987 SCCR 150; *Glen v HM Advocate* 1988 SCCR 37, 1988 SLT 369; *Heaney v HM Advocate* 1990 GWD 6-301. It is not necessary to direct the jury as to the majority required for a verdict of acquittal: *Mackay v HM Advocate* 1944 JC 153, 1945 SLT 97. The judge should not direct the jury that they should spend a reasonable time trying to reach a unanimous verdict before bringing in a majority verdict: *Crowe v HM Advocate* 1989 SCCR 681.

28 Criminal Procedure (Scotland) Act 1975, s 134. See also para 6.16 above.

29 *Alexander Thomson v HM Advocate* 1988 SCCR 534, 1989 SLT 170. However, in practice the omission of an essential direction in the charge may be brought to the attention of the judge by one of the parties, either directly or through the clerk of court.

30 The jury may return a verdict without retiring (Criminal Procedure (Scotland) Act 1975, s 155), but in practice this never happens. It emanates from the Criminal Justice Act 1587 (c 57) (repealed), which predates the modern charge to the jury.

31 Criminal Procedure (Scotland) Act 1975, s 153(3) (substituted by the Criminal Justice (Scotland) Act 1980 (c 62), s 24(1)). If any of the jurors has any doubt which he would like resolved, he must raise it in the presence of the accused in court before the jury retires: Criminal Procedure (Scotland) Act 1975, s 153(1).

32 *Cunningham v HM Advocate* 1984 JC 37, 1984 SCCR 40, 1984 SLT 249; *McColl v HM Advocate* 1989 SCCR 229.

33 *Aitken v HM Advocate* 1984 SCCR 81.

(N) VERDICT

6.31. Deliberations of the jury. When the jury retires, the clerk of court encloses the jurors in a room by themselves, and neither he nor any other person may be present with them after they are enclosed[1]. The judge may give such instructions as he considers appropriate for meals, refreshments, overnight accommodation (if required), the communication of any personal or business message (unconnected with the trial), or medical treatment[2]. Apart from communications in connection with such matters, no person may visit the jury room, nor may any juror leave the room, except where further directions are sought or given or where the jury asks to examine any productions[3]. Should the prosecutor or any other person contravene these rules, the accused 'shall be acquitted'[4]. The judge has a discretion to grant or refuse a request by the jury to see productions[5]. The jurors should not be shown documents which include matters which were not adduced as evidence at the trial or which were held to be inadmissible as evidence[6]; nor should they be given productions for the purpose of making a private examination of them[7]. Where the jury asks to see a production, a practice has grown whereby the judge may seek the views of the parties in chambers to see if there is any agreement as to whether the request should be granted or refused, but strictly speaking, and particularly if there is any dispute, this matter should be debated in open court in the presence of the accused[8].

It is contempt of court for anyone to obtain, disclose or solicit any particulars of statements made, opinions expressed, arguments advanced or votes cast by members of the jury in the course of their deliberations[9]. This provision does not apply to any disclosure made for the purpose of enabling the jury to arrive at, or in connection with the delivery of, its verdict, nor does it apply to a disclosure which is given in evidence in subsequent proceedings for an offence alleged to have been committed in relation to the jury in the earlier proceedings[10]. A disclosure made in the course of inquiries by the judge into alleged improper conduct of a juror would also be excluded[11].

1 Criminal Procedure (Scotland) Act 1975 (c 21), s 153(2) (amended by the Criminal Justice (Scotland) Act 1980 (c 62), s 24(1)).
2 Criminal Procedure (Scotland) Act 1975, s 153(3A) (added by the Criminal Justice (Scotland) Act 1980, s 24(1)); *Sayers v HM Advocate* 1982 JC 17, 1981 SCCR 312, 1982 SLT 220; *McKenzie v HM Advocate* 1986 SCCR 94, 1986 SLT 389n.
3 Criminal Procedure (Scotland) Act 1975, s 153(3) (substituted by the Criminal Justice (Scotland) Act 1980, s 24(1)). This provision does not prohibit the clerk of court asking the jury if it has understood the judge's directions (*Brownlie v HM Advocate* (1966) SCCR Supp 14); nor does it prohibit the judge recalling the jury *ex proprio motu* to give it further directions (*McBeth v HM Advocate* (1976) SCCR Supp 123). In *Matthewson v HM Advocate* 1989 SCCR 101 it was held that there was no breach of s 153(1) where at the request of the jury which had retired, the judge with the consent of the parties authorised someone on his behalf to demonstrate to a juror in the presence of the clerk of court how to operate a video machine.
4 Criminal Procedure (Scotland) Act 1975, s 153(4). This provision owes its origins to the Criminal Justice Act 1587 (c 57) (repealed).
5 *Paterson v HM Advocate* (1901) 4 F (J) 77, 3 Adam 490; *Hamilton v HM Advocate* 1980 JC 66; *Sandells v HM Advocate* 1980 SLT (Notes) 45; *McMurdo v HM Advocate* 1987 SCCR 343, 1988 SLT 234n.
6 *Grant v HM Advocate* 1938 JC 7, 1938 SLT 113; *Hamilton v HM Advocate* 1980 JC 66.
7 Eg to see if a stolen article was too heavy for one man to lift (*Sandells v HM Advocate* 1980 SLT (Notes) 45), or to determine whether documents were genuine or of common origin (*HM Advocate v Robertson* (1849) J Shaw 186; *HM Advocate v M'Gall* (1849) J Shaw 194).
8 *Hamilton v HM Advocate* 1980 JC 66; *Martin v HM Advocate* 1989 SCCR 546.
9 Contempt of Court Act 1981 (c 49), s 8(1).
10 Ibid, s 8(2).

11 *McCadden v HM Advocate* 1985 SCCR 282 at 285, 1986 SLT 138 at 140, per Lord Justice-Clerk
    Wheatley. See para 6.16 above.

6.32. Delivery and recording of verdict. When the jury returns after considering its verdict, the clerk of court asks who speaks for it, and when the foreman or chancellor rises he is asked by the clerk whether the jury has reached a verdict and, if so, to pronounce the verdict. The foreman then pronounces the jury's verdict and must also say (or must be asked) whether the verdict is unanimous or by majority, as this requires to be recorded[1]. Where the verdict is by majority, it is not customary to request the jury's voting figures, although there is no statutory provision which prevents such information being disclosed[2]. If the size of the jury has been reduced because a juror or jurors have been excused[3], a majority verdict of guilty still requires eight votes, and should the remaining jurors inform the court that fewer than eight of their number are in favour of a guilty verdict and that there is a not a majority in favour of any other verdict, the jury is deemed to have returned a not guilty verdict[4]. After the verdict is pronounced, but before it is recorded, the judge may ask the jury, if necessary, whether it wishes to give any explanation or make any amendment to the verdict[5], since this may not be done after the verdict is recorded[6]. The clerk of court then records the verdict, reads the record to the jury and asks it if the record is accurate[7].

The choice of verdicts open to the jury is not guilty, not proven[8] or guilty. A verdict of not guilty or not proven acquits the accused, with the consequence that he is assoilzied *simpliciter*, dismissed from the bar and, if he is in custody, immediately released. The accused has no right of appeal against a not proven verdict. The verdict must be in express terms, unambiguous[9] and consistent with the indictment[10]. It must dispose of all the charges and accused on the indictment[11], and if it does not do so it will be held that the jury has returned a verdict of not guilty in respect of any charges or accused omitted from the verdict[12]. Where the verdict is one of guilty, it must find that sufficient facts are proved to constitute a relevant charge[13], and if it fails to do so the judge may properly ask the jury to reconsider its verdict[14].

1 Criminal Procedure (Scotland) Act 1975 (c 21), s 154 proviso (amended by the Criminal Justice
   (Scotland) Act 1980 (c 62), s 24(2)). The Criminal Procedure (Scotland) Act 1975, s 154, provides
   that the verdict is to be returned orally unless the court directs that a written verdict is to be
   returned, but in practice courts no longer require written verdicts.
2 *McCadden v HM Advocate* 1985 SCCR 282, 1986 SLT 138. Despite this custom, in *Lord Advocate v
   Nicholson* 1958 SLT (Sh Ct) 17 the judge inquired as to the size of the majority.
3 See para 6.16 above.
4 Criminal Procedure (Scotland) Act 1975, s 134 proviso.
5 *Alexander* (1823) Shaw Just 99; *G and R Wilson* (1826) Syme 38; *William Hardie* (1831) Hume II,
   Bell's Notes 296; *HM Advocate v Waiters* (1836) 1 Swin 273.
6 *Janet Anderson or Darling* (1830) Hume II, Bell's Notes 295; *HM Advocate v Hunter* (1838) 2 Swin 1;
   M'Garry v HM Advocate 1959 JC 30; *Ralston v HM Advocate* 1989 GWD 33–1504.
7 While the recorded verdict should be read to the jury, failure to do so does not necessarily render
   the proceedings null: *Torri v HM Advocate* 1923 JC 52, 1923 SLT 553.
8 For the origins of the not proven verdict, see para 1.59 above.
9 *Brodie v Johnston* (1845) 2 Broun 559; *Lloyd v HM Advocate* (1899) 1 F (J) 31, 2 Adam 637; *Paterson
   v HM Advocate* (1901) 4 F (J) 7, 3 Adam 490; *Townsend v HM Advocate* 1914 SC (J) 85, 7 Adam
   378; *Hamilton v HM Advocate* 1938 JC 134, 1938 SLT 333; *Hancock v HM Advocate* 1981 JC 74,
   1981 SCCR 32; *Slater v HM Advocate* 1987 SCCR 745; *Watkin v HM Advocate* 1988 SCCR 443,
   1989 SLT 24.
10 *Macmillan v HM Advocate* (1888) 1 White 572; *Donald v Hart* (1892) 19 R (J) 88, 3 White 274; *Angus
   v HM Advocate* (1905) 8 F (J) 10, 4 Adam 640; *Gold v Neilson* 1908 SC (J) 5, 5 Adam 423; *Myers v
   HM Advocate* 1936 JC 1, 1936 SLT 39; *Blair v HM Advocate* 1989 SCCR 79, 1989 SLT 459 (in
   which it was held that where the words of the libel had not been amended before the jury retired
   to consider its verdict, the jury had no discretion to alter the wording of the libel by deleting the
   word 'pulling' and substituting the word 'removing').

11 *Young v HM Advocate* 1932 JC 63, 1932 SLT 465, but see also *White v HM Advocate* 1989 SCCR 553.
12 R W Renton and H H Brown *Criminal Procedure according to the Law of Scotland* (5th edn, 1983) para 10-60.
13 This situation may arise where the jury has deleted part of a charge: see *Kenny v HM Advocate* 1951 JC 104, 1951 SLT 363; *Sayers v HM Advocate* 1982 JC 17, 1981 SCCR 312, 1982 SLT 220; *Took v HM Advocate* 1988 SCCR 495, 1989 SLT 425. See, however, *Watkin v HM Advocate* 1988 SCCR 443, 1989 SLT 24.
14 *Took v HM Advocate* 1988 SCCR 495, 1989 SLT 425.

(O) RECORD OF PROCEEDINGS

6.33. Documentation. A record of the proceedings requires to be kept. The record should include the indictment, together with particulars of the judge, the accused, counsel or solicitors, the names of the jurors and witnesses, the plea, the verdict, and previous convictions which have been libelled and the sentence[1]. All interlocutors and all continuations or postponements also require to be minuted[2]. In the High Court of Justiciary the minutes are signed by the clerk of court and the record copy of the indictment and all printed proceedings are kept in the books of adjournal[3]; in the sheriff court the minutes are signed by the sheriff[4] and the record copy of the indictment is kept in the record book of the sheriff court[5].

A record of the proceedings or an extract of the sentence or order may be corrected if it is erroneous or incomplete[6]. The clerk of court may make the correction before the sentence or order is executed or, if there is an appeal, before the proceedings are sent to the Clerk of Justiciary[7]. After any of these steps has been taken, the entry may be corrected only by the authority of the court which passed the sentence (or made the order)[8], and such authority requires to be recorded[9]. All corrections must be authenticated by the signature of the clerk of court[9] and should be made openly, with no attempt to erase or change any words[10]. A correction made after the sentence or order is executed must be intimated to the prosecutor, the accused and his solicitor[11].

1 The record does not include the notes of evidence: see para 6.19 above.
2 Criminal Procedure (Scotland) Act 1975 (c 21), s 225.
3 Ibid, ss 225, 226.
4 R W Renton and H H Brown *Criminal Procedure according to the Law of Scotland* (5th edn, 1983) para 10-85.
5 Criminal Procedure (Scotland) Act 1975, s 227.
6 Ibid, s 227A(1) (added by the Criminal Justice (Scotland) Act 1980 (c 62), s 20).
7 Criminal Procedure (Scotland) Act 1975, s 227A(2)(a) (as so added).
8 Ibid, s 227A(2)(b), (c) (as so added).
9 Ibid, s 227A(5) (as so added).
10 See further *Renton and Brown* para 10-87.
11 Criminal Procedure (Scotland) Act 1975, s 227A(3) (as added: see note 6 above).

(b) The Trial Diet in Summary Procedure

(A) CALLING THE DIET; PRESENCE OF THE PARTIES

6.34. Calling the diet. When an accused person tenders a plea of not guilty at the first calling of a summary complaint, the court may proceed to trial forthwith, without adjourning to a trial diet[1]. In theory, therefore, should the court adjourn the case for trial, it is merely continuing the first diet. In practice, however, the case is always adjourned for trial and the trial diet is treated as a separate entity rather than a continuation of the first diet[2]. The trial diet, like all criminal diets, is peremptory, andif the complaint is not called the instance will fall[3], although the prosecutor may proceed by way of a fresh complaint[4] unless he is time-barred from doing so in the case of a statutory offence[5]. The diet is called, at the request of the procurator fiscal, by the clerk of court calling the accused's name[6]. In many courts it is the practice to start the day's business by calling all the complaints set down for trial that day in order to ascertain which cases are actually proceeding to trial and which,if any, are not (for example because the accused is pleading guilty, or because an essential witness is missing). This procedure, which is informally known as 'call-over', is usually followed by an adjournment of a few minutes during which the prosecutor will decide the order of the trials, and the parties may complete any final plea-bargaining and check that their respective witnesses are present.

1 Criminal Procedure (Scotland) Act 1975 (c 21), s 337(a) (amended by the Bail etc (Scotland) Act 1980 (c 4), s 12(3), Sch 2). Court business is arranged on the basis that this course will never be followed unless special arrangements are made to the contrary, eg where the accused or a witness is due to leave the country in the immediate future: see R W Renton and H H Brown *Criminal Procedure according to the Law of Scotland* (5th edn, 1983) para 14-01.
2 *Handley v Pirie* 1976 JC 65, 1977 SLT 30; *English v Smith* 1981 SCCR 143, 1981 SLT (Notes) 113; Criminal Procedure (Scotland) Act 1975, s 337(b). The trial diet may be accelerated by a motion of the parties: see s 314(3), (5), (6) (added by the Criminal Justice (Scotland) Act 1980 (c 62), s 11).
3 *Smith v Bernard* 1980 SLT (Notes) 81; *Renton and Brown* paras 14-02, 14-55.
4 *Cochran v Walker* (1900) 2 F (J) 52, 3 Adam 165.
5 Criminal Procedure (Scotland) Act 1975, s 331. This provision does not apply to common law crimes: *Sugden v HM Advocate* 1934 JC 103, 1934 SLT 465.
6 As master of the instance, the procurator fiscal may decide the order in which the complaints are to be called, or may instruct that a complaint is not to be called.

6.35. Presence of the parties. As in solemn proceedings, the prosecutor must be personally present in court throughout the entire proceedings[1]. As a general rule the accused must also be present when the complaint is called and at all times thereafter, as must his counsel or solicitor, if he is legally represented[2]. Where the accused is in custody, the prosecutor is responsible for arranging his attendance[3]. Should the accused fail to appear at the trial diet, the court may, if it is satisfied he received intimation of the diet, adjourn the diet to a later date or alternatively issue a warrant to apprehend the accused[4]. When the accused subsequently appears and does not give a reasonable excuse for his failure to attend the trial diet, he is liable to a fine not exceeding level 3 on the standard scale and three months' imprisonment (in the sheriff court) or sixty days' imprisonment (in the district court)[5]. At the subsequent appearance the trial may either proceed or, especially if the witnesses have not been cited, be further adjourned.

1 See para 6.02 above.
2 *Aitken v Wood* 1921 JC 84, 1921 2 SLT 124. In *Winning v Adair* 1949 JC 91, 1949 SLT 212, and *M'Cann v Adair* 1951 JC 127, 1951 SLT 326, convictions were quashed where the sheriff examined books outwith the presence of the accused. Cf however *Anderson v McLeod* 1987 SCCR 566. The rules relating to persons who may represent the accused at the trial, or who may accompany him or interpret for him, are the same as in solemn proceedings: see para 6.02 above. The court should not proceed to trial in the absence of the defence solicitor if he is likely to appear later in the day: *Fraser v MacKinnon* 1981 SCCR 91; *Kane v Tudhope* 1986 SCCR 161, 1986 SLT 649; *Benson v Tudhope* 1986 SCCR 422, 1987 SLT 312n. See also *W v HM Advocate* 1988 SCCR 461 and *Young v Douglas* 1989 SCCR 112 referred to more fully in para 6.02, note 2 above.
3 R W Renton and H H Brown *Criminal Procedure according to the Law of Scotland* (5th edn, 1983) para 10-07.
4 Criminal Procedure (Scotland) Act 1975 (c 21), s 338(1)(a), (c). Where the diet is adjourned, intimation must be made to the accused in terms of s 338(1)(a). If he pleads guilty by letter after a

warrant has been granted, the prosecutor may apply to the court to withdraw the warrant and dispose of the case at a convenient diet: *Renton and Brown* para 14-14.

5 Criminal Procedure (Scotland) Act 1975, s 338(2) (added by the Criminal Justice (Scotland) Act 1980 (c 62), s 17, and amended by the Criminal Procedure (Scotland) Act 1975, s 289G (added by the Criminal Justice Act 1982 (c 48), s 54)). As to the standard scale, see para 2.12, note 1, above. The penalty may be in addition to the penalty imposed upon conviction, even if it thereby exceeds the maximum powers of the court: Criminal Procedure (Scotland) Act 1975, s 338(3). In practice the prosecutor may give the accused an opportunity to attend on a specified date, and if he does so the warrant will then be formally enforced, failing which the warrant will be executed in the normal way.

6.36. Absence of the accused. In certain circumstances the case may proceed in the absence of the accused[1]. Where an accused person is not required to attend as a condition of bail, he may plead guilty in absence either by way of his solicitor (or any other person who satisfies the court that he has been authorised by the accused) or by sending a letter to that effect to the prosecutor. Provided the prosecutor accepts the plea, the court may hear and dispose of the case in the absence of the accused[2], unless it requires to adjourn the case and order his attendance in order to impose a custodial sentence[3] or to disqualify him from driving[4] or to place him on probation[5] or order him to perform community service[6]. It is also competent to proceed to trial in the absence of the accused where the proceedings relate to a statutory offence which is not punishable by imprisonment[7]. Before pursuing this course, which is very seldom followed, the court must be satisfied that the accused has received due intimation of the diet.

1 There is no provision in summary procedure for removing an accused who disrupts the proceedings: see para 6.03 above.
2 Criminal Procedure (Scotland) Act 1975 (c 21), s 334(3), (5).
3 Ibid, s 334(4). A custodial sentence may not be imposed in the absence of the accused. See eg *Campbell v Jessop* 1987 SCCR 670, 1988 SLT 160n.
4 *Trotter v Burnet* 1947 JC 151, 1948 SLT 57; *Sopwith v Cruickshank* 1959 JC 78; *Stephens v Gibb* 1984 SCCR 195; *Graham v MacDougall* 1988 GWD 9–384. See also para 6.02 below.
5 Criminal Procedure (Scotland) Act 1975, s 384. See also para 6.19 below.
6 See para 6.18 below.
7 Criminal Procedure (Scotland) Act 1975, s 338(1)(b); see eg *McCandless v MacDougall* 1987 SCCR 206. The court may allow a solicitor to appear on behalf of the accused. For further details, see R W Renton and H H Brown *Criminal Procedure according to the Law of Scotland* (5th edn, 1983) para 14-46. The prosecutor may find it difficult to identify the accused who is tried in absence.

(B) POSTPONEMENT, ADJOURNMENT AND DESERTION OF DIET

6.37. Postponement and adjournment of trial diet. When all the parties to the case make a joint oral or written application to have the trial postponed, the court must discharge the diet and fix a later one unless it considers that there has been unnecessary delay on the part of one or more of the parties[1]. If one of the parties applies for a postponement and another (that is, an opponent or a co-accused) refuses to concur, the court has a discretionary power to grant or refuse the application[2]. The trial diet may also be postponed by the High Court of Justiciary where there is a preliminary appeal in relation to an objection (for example to the competency or relevancy of the complaint)[3]. Apart from postponement, the court has a discretion at any stage in the proceedings (including when the trial is called, or during the course of the trial) to grant an adjournment either *ex proprio motu* or on the motion of one of the parties. This discretion may be based on the statutory power of the court to adjourn when 'necessary for the proper conduct of the case'[4], or on its inherent common law power to adjourn, or refuse to adjourn, any case where it is in the interests of justice to do so[5].

Before refusing an application for postponement or a motion for adjournment, the court must take account of the consequences of its decision not only for the parties but also for the public interest, and should refuse the request only 'after the most careful consideration, on weighty grounds and with due and accurate regard to the interests which will be affected or prejudiced'[6]. When considering the public interest, the court may have regard to the seriousness or triviality of the charge[7], but it must also ensure that there is no unfairness to the accused[8] — for example if he wishes the adjournment to prepare his case properly or to obtain an essential witness[9], or because his solicitor is not present[10]. Where the accused moves for an adjournment when the trial diet is called, the court may sometimes defer consideration of the motion until the close of the prosecution case in order to avoid unnecessary inconvenience or expense to prosecution witnesses who have been cited and are present to give evidence, and if the defence motion is thereafter granted, the trial will be adjourned part heard to a later date[11]. A prosecutor who intends moving for an adjournment should not normally cancel the attendance of his witnesses in anticipation of his motion being granted, since this, in effect, seeks to usurp the function of the court[12].

Unlike solemn procedure, there is no rule that the trial must proceed from day to day until concluded[13], and accordingly a summary trial may be adjourned over a period of days, weeks or months[14] unless the accused is in custody, in which case the adjournment will be limited to a few days, failing which he will be released. Except where the adjournment is to a later time on the same day, any adjourned proceedings will be fundamentally null unless the adjournment is to a specified time and place[15] and is properly recorded in a minute[16] which is signed on the day the adjournment is granted[17]. The decision to grant or refuse a postponement or adjournment may be appealed by an aggrieved party by way of advocation[18]. If the court refuses to adjourn the trial on the motion of the prosecutor (or to desert the case *pro loco et tempore*) and the prosecutor is unable or unwilling to proceed with the trial, the court must desert the diet *simpliciter*[19].

1 Criminal Procedure (Scotland) Act 1975 (c 21), s 314(4) (added by the Criminal Justice (Scotland) Act 1980 (c 62), s 11). Where there is more than one accused, all must concur in the application. There is no prescribed form.
2 Criminal Procedure (Scotland) Act 1975, s 314(5), (6) (as so added). The party seeking the postponement must intimate his intention to the others. If the application is made before the trial diet, the prosecutor should proceed by way of an incidental application under s 310 (amended by the Criminal Justice (Scotland) Act 1980, s 83(2), (3), Sch 7, para 53, Sch 8), whereas application by the accused should be made in terms of the Act of Adjournal (Consolidation) 1988, SI 1988/110, r 99(2), Sch 1, Form 53.
3 Criminal Procedure (Scotland) Act 1975, s 334(2B) (added by the Criminal Justice (Scotland) Act 1980, s 36). An appeal of this nature requires leave of the court and a party may only apply for leave after stating how he pleads to the charge. The application for leave must be dealt with immediately and if granted, the case can not immediately proceed to trial: see Criminal Procedure (Scotland) Act 1975, ss 334(2A) and 334(2C) (added by the Criminal Justice (Scotland) Act 1980, s 36; Act of Adjournal (Consolidation) 1988, SI 1988/110 rr 128(1) and 128(2) and *Lafferty v Jessop* 1989 SCCR 451, 1989 SLT 846.
4 Criminal Procedure (Scotland) Act 1975, s 337(f).
5 *Bruce v Linton and M'Dougall* (1860) 23 D 85; *Robertson v Duke of Atholl* (1869) 8 M 57, 1 Coup 348; *Vetters v HM Advocate* 1943 JC 138, 1944 SLT 85; *Platt v Lockhart* 1988 SCCR 308, 1988 SLT 845.
6 *Tudhope v Lawrie* 1979 JC 44 at 49, 1979 SLT (Notes) 13 at 14, per Lord Cameron. See also *Skeen v Skerret* 1976 SLT (Notes) 6; *Skeen v McLaren* 1976 SLT (Notes) 14; *Mackenzie v Maclean* 1980 JC 89, 1981 SLT 2; *Tudhope v Mitchell* 1986 SCCR 45; R W Renton and H H Brown *Criminal Procedure according to the Law of Scotland* (5th edn, 1983) para 14-57.

7 *Tudhope v Lawrie* 1979 JC 44, 1979 SLT (Notes) 13; *McNaughton v McPherson* 1980 SLT (Notes) 97.
8 *Tudhope v Gough* 1982 SCCR 157.
9 *Ferguson v M'Nab* (1884) 11 R (J) 63, 5 Coup 471; *MacKellar v Dickson* (1898) 25 R (J) 63, 2 Adam 504. See, however, *Haining v Milroy* (1893) 1 Adam 86; *Turnbull v HM Advocate* 1948 SN 19, 1948 SLT (Notes) 12; *Bingham v HM Advocate* 1961 SLT (Notes) 77; *Sim v Tudhope* 1987 SCCR 482; *Kerr v Tudhope* 1987 GWD 6–172. See also *Meechan v Jessop* 1989 SCCR 668 (where an adjournment was refused).
10 *Fraser v MacKinnon* 1981 SCCR 91.
11 *Renton and Brown* para 14-58.
12 *Renton and Brown* para 14-57. In exceptional cases he may be justified in cancelling his witnesses in order to avoid inconvenience to the public: *Skeen v Evans* 1979 SLT (Notes) 55.
13 See para 6.05 above.
14 *Renton and Brown* para 14-59.
15 *Barr v Ingram* 1977 SLT 173; *Jessop v First National Securities Ltd* 1988 SCCR 1, Sh Ct; *Lafferty v Jessop* 1989 SCCR 451, 1989 SLT 846.
16 *Hull v HM Advocate* 1945 JC 83, 1945 SLT 202; *Law v HM Advocate* 1973 SLT (Notes) 14.
17 *Taylor v Sempill* (1906) 8 F (J) 74, 5 Adam 114. However, see also *Furnheim v Watson* 1946 JC 99, 1946 SLT 297; *Pettigrew v Ingram* 1982 SCCR 259, 1982 SLT 435; and *Anderson v McLeod* 1987 SCCR 566.
18 *Skeen v Skerret* 1976 SLT (Notes) 6; *Skeen v McLaren* 1976 SLT (Notes) 14; *Tudhope v Lawrie* 1979 JC 44, 1979 SLT (Notes) 13; *Mackenzie v Maclean* 1980 JC 89, 1981 SLT 2; *Durant v Lockhart* 1985 SCCR 72, 1985 SLT 394.
19 Criminal Procedure (Scotland) Act 1975, s 338A(2) (added by the Criminal Justice (Scotland) Act 1980, s 18(2)). The prosecutor is entitled to move to desert *pro loco et tempore* if an adjournment is refused: *Tudhope v Gough* 1982 SCCR 157. For the effects of desertion *pro loco et tempore* and *simpliciter*, see paras 5.38, 5.39, below. In *Carmichael v Hutton* 1990 GWD 6–299 the decision of the sheriff to desert *simpliciter* after refusing an adjournment was overturned on appeal.

6.38. Desertion *pro loco et tempore*. If the case is not adjourned or if the prosecutor does not wish to proceed for some other reason, he may move the court to desert *pro loco et tempore*, provided he does so before the first witness is sworn[1], or, if the accused pleads guilty and no evidence has been led, before the notice of penalties is laid before the court[2] or sentence is passed[3]. While the court has a discretion to refuse this motion, it should not normally do so unless it is convinced, after balancing the interests of the parties and the interest of the public in the administration of justice, that a refusal is appropriate[4]. The prosecutor may appeal against a refusal by way of advocation. If the motion is refused and the prosecutor is thereafter unwilling or unable to proceed further, the court must desert the case *simpliciter*[5]. When the case is deserted *pro loco et tempore* the complaint falls and, if the accused is in custody, he is released. The prosecutor may, however, recommence proceedings on the same libel by way of a fresh complaint unless in the case of statutory offence such proceedings would be time-barred[6]. The court also has a common law power, as in solemn proceedings[7], to desert the diet and continue the proceedings on the same complaint, either on the motion of the prosecutor or *ex proprio motu*, if continuing the trial would result in a miscarriage of justice or in injustice to one of the parties. Such a situation would arise if, during the course of the trial, the judge, the prosecutor or the accused's legal representative died[8], or alternatively if any of them or the accused or an essential witness became ill, although in this latter instance it might be possible to resolve the difficulty by adjourning to a later date.

1 Criminal Procedure (Scotland) Act 1975 (c 21), s 338A(1) (added by the Criminal Justice (Scotland) Act 1980 (c 62), s 18(2)).
2 *Pirie v Rivard* 1976 SLT (Sh Ct) 59.
3 *MacPhail v McCabe* 1984 SCCR 146.
4 *Mackenzie v Maclean* 1980 JC 89, 1981 SLT 2; *Jessop v D* 1986 SCCR 716, 1987 SLT (Sh Ct) 115.
5 Criminal Procedure (Scotland) Act 1975, s 338A(2) (as added: see note 1 above).

6 Ibid, s 331.
7 See para 6.06 above.
8 *Lockhart v Platt* 1988 SCCR 68, Sh Ct; *Platt v Lockhart* 1988 SCCR 308, 1988 SLT 845 (High Court of Justiciary).

6.39. Desertion *simpliciter*. The court may desert the diet *simpliciter* either *ex proprio motu* (for example where it has refused to desert *pro loco et tempore* or adjourn and the prosecutor is unwilling or unable to proceed[1]) or on the motion of the prosecutor, if he does not wish to continue further with the case. The effect of desertion *simpliciter* is that no further proceedings can be taken in relation to the complaint and no fresh libel can be raised against the accused on the same grounds by the same prosecutor[2]. If the accused has been detained in custody awaiting the trial, he will be released immediately. Where the court has deserted the diet *simpliciter ex proprio motu*, the prosecutor may appeal against the decision by way of advocation[3] or by stated case[4].

1 See the Criminal Procedure (Scotland) Act 1975 (c 21), s 338A(2), and para 6.38 above.
2 *Collins v Lang* (1887) 15 R (J) 7, 1 White 482; *HM Advocate v Hall* (1881) 8 R (J) 52, 4 Coup 500. In theory the accused could still be prosecuted by a private prosecutor, but, unlike solemn proceedings, private prosecutions in summary courts are now unknown.
3 *Mackenzie v Maclean* 1980 JC 89, 1981 SLT 2.
4 'Desertion *simpliciter* is, however, a final determination in terms of section 444 of the 1975 Act... in the same way as an acquittal, and so appealable by stated case': G H Gordon *The Criminal Justice (Scotland) Act 1980* (1981) p 37. The Criminal Procedure (Scotland) Act 1975, s 444, relates to the manner of appeals by stated case: see paras 8.27 ff below.

(C) PLEADING

6.40. Pleading. If the parties are present and the diet is neither postponed nor adjourned, the next step is for the accused to intimate whether he is adhering to his plea of not guilty, as tendered at the first diet, or whether he now wishes to plead guilty to all or part of the complaint. Where his plea was given at the call-over and minuted, it is not necessary to minute it again[1]. It may be argued that the taking and recording of the plea might have some additional significance in that it might be held to constitute the commencement of the trial[2], although it is also arguable that the trial does not commence until the first witness is sworn[3]. Any plea tendered must be recorded, and failure to do so may be fatal to a conviction[4]. If the plea is one of guilty and it is accepted by the prosecutor, the plea must be authenticated by the signature of the judge or the clerk of court[5]. A guilty plea, whether to all or part of the complaint, which is intimated by the accused's legal representative must be confirmed by the accused personally, if he is present[6].

As in solemn procedure[7], the accused may plead guilty to any other crime of which he could competently be convicted on the charge libelled[8]. Where alternative charges are libelled, he may plead guilty to one of the alternatives. Where more than one charge is libelled, he may plead guilty to one or more, but not to others. He may also plead guilty to part of a charge (provided that that part constitutes a crime or offence). Whether the plea is to the whole complaint as libelled, or is only a partial plea, the prosecutor has a discretion to accept or reject it, but if he rejects it and proceeds to trial, he cannot thereafter accept the plea previously tendered by the accused unless it is renewed[9]. Where the accused pleads guilty to one or more charges, or where there are several accused and one or more plead guilty while others do not, and the pleas are accepted by the prosecutor, he may accept the remaining pleas of not guilty or he may proceed to trial on them, in which case the court will normally defer sentence on the guilty plea or pleas until the conclusion of the trial. During the trial of the remaining charges, no reference may be made to the charge or charges to which the plea of guilty has been accepted except that the guilty plea may be taken into account if it involves an admission relevant to the proof of another charge on the same complaint[10]. A guilty plea which was not accepted cannot be founded on by the prosecutor or used against the accused[11]. The prosecutor may also ask for an adjournment or move to desert the remainder of the complaint *pro loco et tempore*[12] where there is a partial plea or where one accused pleads guilty and others do not, especially if he wishes to consider the effect of the guilty plea on the remainder of this case. The court also has a discretion to allow the withdrawal of a guilty plea which has been accepted, if the plea was given as a result of trickery, coercion or a genuine misunderstanding[13]. This discretion may be exercised at any time before conviction and sentence have been recorded[14], and if any prejudice is thereby suffered by the prosecutor, the court will normally grant his motion for an adjournment or to desert *pro loco et tempore*.

1 R W Renton and H H Brown *Criminal Procedure according to the Law of Scotland* (5th edn, 1983) para 14-48. As to the call-over, see para 6.34 above.
2 *Handley v Pirie* 1976 JC 65, 1977 SLT 30. It may be important to determine the point at which the trial commences if the prosecutor is seeking to rely on documents or certificates which require to be served on the accused within a specified number of days before his trial, in terms of the Criminal Justice (Scotland) Act 1980 (c 62), s 26.
3 *Renton and Brown* para 14-47. The Criminal Procedure (Scotland) Act 1975 (c 21), s 331A(1) (added by the Criminal Justice (Scotland) Act 1980, s 14(2)), provides that where the accused is detained in custody his trial must commence within forty days, and that 'for the purposes of this section a trial shall be taken to commence when the first witness is sworn': see para 5.04 above.
4 *Millar v Brown* 1941 JC 12, 1941 SLT 53.
5 Criminal Procedure (Scotland) Act 1975, s 336. See also *Mackay v Patrick* (1882) 10 R (J) 10, 5 Coup 132. In practice the clerk of court authenticates the plea.
6 Act of Adjournal (Consolidation) 1988, SI 1988/110, r 119.
7 See para 6.10 above.
8 For example, he may plead guilty to reset if he is charged with theft; but unless it is separately libelled he may not plead guilty to an alternative charge of which he could not be convicted on the charge as it stands. Thus he may not plead guilty to malicious mischief if he is charged with housebreaking unless the former is specifically charged as an alternative on the complaint. For the full list of competent alternative pleas, see the Criminal Procedure (Scotland) Act 1975, ss 60–64, and s 216 (amended by the Criminal Justice (Scotland) Act 1987 (c 41), s 64(1)), and *Renton and Brown* paras 10-61–10-63.
9 *Strathern v Sloan* 1937 JC 76, 1937 SLT 503.
10 *Walsh v HM Advocate* 1961 JC 51, 1961 SLT 137; *McColl v Skeen* 1980 SLT (Notes) 53; Criminal Procedure (Scotland) Act 1975, s 337(g).
11 *Cochran v Ferguson* (1882) 10 R (J) 18, 5 Coup 169; *Brown v Macpherson* 1918 JC 3, 1917 2 SLT 134; *Strathern v Sloan* 1937 JC 76, 1937 SLT 503.
12 See para 6.38 above.
13 *Williams v Linton* (1878) 6 R (J) 12; *Spowart v Burr* (1895) 22 R (J) 30, 1 Adam 539; *Sarna v Adair* 1945 JC 141, 1945 SLT 306; *Smith v Carmichael* 1987 SCCR 735; *Crosbie v Hamilton* 1989 SCCR 499, but see also *Donaldson v Lees* 1989 SCCR 484 and *Healy v HM Advocate* 1990 SCCR 10, 1990 GWD 9–472 where leave to withdraw a guilty plea was refused. See further *Renton and Brown* para 8-09.
14 *Tudhope v Campbell* 1979 JC 24, *sub nom Tudhope v Colbert* 1978 SLT (Notes) 57 .

6.41. Plea of not guilty. When the accused pleads not guilty, the case will normally proceed to trial, except in very unusual circumstances where it may be improper for the judge to preside at the trial and preferable that the case should be placed before another judge[1]. The court has a discretion at this stage to allow the accused to make any denial or plea to the competency or relevancy of the complaint, provided the accused can show cause as to why he did not do so at the first diet and why he should be allowed to do so now[2]. If the accused intends to rely on a plea of insanity in bar of trial, he must give the prosecutor oral or written notice of the plea together with the witnesses who will substantiate it, before the first prosecution witness is examined[3] — although in practice this plea is usually lodged at the first diet and resolved at a hearing fixed specially for this purpose[4]. Similarly, where the accused's defence is based on a special defence of alibi, he must give notice to the prosecutor of the particulars of the alibi and the witnesses who will be called to support it, before the examination of the first prosecution witness[5]. This rule does not apply to other special defences[6]. Where notice of a defence of insanity or alibi is given at the trial diet, the prosecutor is entitled to an adjournment if he so desires[7], although, in the case of alibi, he may sometimes defer moving for an adjournment until the close of the prosecution case[8].

1 See para 6.44 below.
2 Criminal Procedure (Scotland) Act 1975 (c 21), s 334(1) (amended by the Criminal Justice (Scotland) Act 1980 (c 62), s 83(2), Sch 7, para 54(a)); *Henderson v Ingram* 1982 SCCR 135; *Sillars v Smith* 1982 SCCR 367, 1982 SLT 539. See also R W Renton and H H Brown *Criminal Procedure according to the Law of Scotland* (5th edn, 1983) para 14-15. Where the accused enters a plea to both the relevancy and the competency of the complaint, the judge should deal with both pleas: *Walkingshaw v Robison and Davidson Ltd* 1988 SCCR 318, 1989 SLT 17.
3 Criminal Procedure (Scotland) Act 1975, s 375(3).
4 *Renton and Brown* para 14-49.
5 Criminal Procedure (Scotland) Act 1975, s 339.
6 *Adam v MacNeill* 1972 JC 1, 1971 SLT (Notes) 80.
7 Criminal Procedure (Scotland) Act 1975, ss 339, 375(3).
8 In *Renton and Brown* para 14-51, the authors postulate that if notice of alibi is not timeously given, the court might allow the accused to give such notice at a later stage in the proceedings and at the same time allow the prosecutor to call additional evidence.

(D) AMENDMENT OF THE COMPLAINT

6.42. Amendment of the complaint. At any time before the determination of the prosecution the court has a statutory discretion, unless it sees just cause to the contrary, to allow the complaint, or any notices of penalty or previous convictions, to be amended by deletion, alteration or addition in order to cure any error or defect, or to meet any objections or to cure any discrepancy or variance between the complaint and the evidence[1]. There is no statutory definition of the phrase 'determination of the prosecution', and consequently some confusion has arisen as to the exact meaning of these words. In one instance it was held that it was too late to amend when the sheriff had started to give his judgment and had indicated his verdict[2], and conversely it has also been decided that the laying of previous convictions or a notice of penalties before the court after the verdict has been given does not constitute the determination of the prosecution[3].

The proposed amendment is incompetent if it changes the character of the offence[4] or if its purpose is to remedy a defect (such as omitting to libel the *locus* of the offence[5] or failing to sign the complaint[6]) which has rendered the complaint fundamentally null[7]. An amendment seeking to change the identity of the accused has been refused[8], although it may be allowed if it merely changes the capacity in which he had been charged[9]. A complaint which is not relevantly libelled, but which is otherwise competent, may be cured by way of amendment[10]. Unlike solemn procedure, it is not competent to amend a complaint in order to add a charge of contravening the Bail etc (Scotland) Act 1980[11], and if the prosecutor wishes to pursue such a charge he must either do so on a separate complaint or by deserting the original complaint and substituting a fresh one to which the further charge has been added[12].

If the court considers that the amendment is in any way prejudicial to the merits of the defence, it must 'grant such remedy to the accused by adjournment or otherwise as it shall think just'[13]. Although amendment of the complaint is allowable only at the discretion of the judge, if his decision is appealed the appeal court will not lightly interfere with the exercise of his discretion unless it is shown that the public interest or the interest of the accused has been affected[14]. The amendment should be engrossed on the complaint at the time it is allowed[15] and, while it is sufficiently authenticated by the initials of the clerk of court[16], it is possible that lack of authentication may not be fatal[17].

1 Criminal Procedure (Scotland) Act 1975 (c 21), s 335(1).
2 *Henderson v Callender* (1878) 6 R (J) 1, 4 Coup 120. The judge may also, in delivering his verdict, convict the accused subject to deletion of words from or addition of words to the charge, provided that his verdict is one which could competently be returned on the original complaint. This does not amount to amendment: *Simpson v Tudhope* 1987 SCCR 348, 1988 SLT 297.
3 *Cochrane v West Calder Co-operative Society* 1978 SLT (Notes) 22. See also R W Renton and H H Brown *Criminal Procedure according to the Law of Scotland* (5th edn, 1983) paras 14-66, 14-67. In *Tudhope v Campbell* 1979 JC 24, *sub nom Tudhope v Colbert* 1978 SLT (Notes) 57, the High Court of Justiciary held that determination occurs when the court's decision is formally entered into the record of the proceedings — hence if the court convicts the accused but continues the case for sentence, the entry of the conviction in the record will 'determine' the case *quoad* conviction, but that sentence will not be 'determined' until the subsequent disposal is also recorded. The statute refers only to the determination of the 'prosecution'.
4 Criminal Procedure (Scotland) Act 1975, s 335(2); *MacArthur v MacNeill* 1986 SCCR 552, 1987 SLT 299n.
5 *Macintosh v Metcalfe* 1886 13 R (J) 96, 1 White 218. However, if the *locus* is libelled it may be amended (*Ross v Boyd* (1903) 5 F (J) 64, 4 Adam 184; *Herron v Gemmell* 1975 SLT (Notes) 93), and an additional *locus* may be added (*Craig v Keane* 1981 SCCR 166, 1982 SLT 198; *Tudhope v Fulton* 1986 SCCR 567, 1987 SLT 419n; *Brown v McLeod* 1986 SCCR 615). But see also *Duffy v Ingram* 1987 SCCR 286, 1988 SLT 226n, where the prosecutor was allowed to amend a complaint which failed to libel the date on which the alleged offences were committed.
6 *Lowe v Bee* 1989 SCCR 476.
7 *Stevenson v M'Levy* (1879) 6 R (J) 33, 4 Coup 196; *Macintosh v Metcalfe* (1886) 13 R (J) 96, 1 White 218; *M'Millan v Grant* 1924 JC 13, 1924 SLT 86; *Lockhart v British School of Motoring* 1982 SCCR 188, 1983 SLT (Sh Ct) 73; *MacNeill v Robertson* 1982 SCCR 468; *Skinner v Patience* 1982 SLT (Sh Ct) 81; *Sterling-Winthrop Group Ltd v Allan* 1987 SCCR 25, 1987 SLT 652n. See also *Renton and Brown* paras 14-66, 14-67.
8 *Valentine v Thistle Leisure Ltd* 1983 SCCR 515, Sh Ct.
9 *Tudhope v Chung* 1985 SCCR 139.
10 *Aitchison v Tudhope* 1981 JC 65, 1981 SCCR 1, 1981 SLT 231; *Mackenzie v Brougham* 1984 SCCR 434, 1985 SLT 276; *Cook v Jessop* 1990 GWD 11-577.
11 Bail etc (Scotland) Act 1980 (c 4), s 3(4).
12 The latter course will not be competent if the complaint relates to statutory charges which would thus become time-barred in terms of the Criminal Procedure (Scotland) Act 1975, s 331.
13 Ibid, s 335(2).
14 *Cumming v Frame* 1909 SC (J) 56, 6 Adam 57. See also *Matheson v Ross* (1885) 12 R (J) 40, 5 Coup 582, where the prosecutor was allowed to amend the date of the offence as there was no prejudice to the accused, who declined an adjournment.
15 *Owens v Calderwood* (1869) 1 Coup 217.
16 Criminal Procedure (Scotland) Act 1975, s 335(3).
17 No conviction, sentence, judgment, order of the court or other proceedings whatsoever are to be quashed for want of form: ibid, s 454(1). See *Silk v Middleton* 1921 JC 69, 1921 1 SLT 278; *Sutherland v Shiach* 1928 JC 49, 1928 SLT 440; *Millar v Brown* 1941 JC 12, 1941 SLT 53; *Furnheim v Watson* 1946 JC 99, 1946 SLT 297; *Wilson v Brown* 1947 JC 81, 1947 SLT 276; *Pettigrew v Ingram* 1982 SCCR 259, 1982 SLT 435.

(E) PUBLIC ACCESS TO COURTS; PUBLICITY

6.43. Public access to court; publicity. The rules rating to public access to the courts and publicity of summary proceedings are identical to those for solemn proceedings[1], except that a person who interrupts or disrupts the proceedings is liable to be punished for contempt of court under the common law power of the court rather than under statute[2].

1 See paras 6.17, 6.18 above, and the Criminal Procedure (Scotland) Act 1975 (c21), ss 346B, 361, 374 (the first added by the Law Reform (Miscellaneous Provisions) (Scotland) Act 1985 (c73), s 36(2), and the last substituted by the Criminal Justice (Scotland) Act 1980 (c62), s 22, and amended by the Cable and Broadcasting Act 1984 (c46), s 57(1), Sch 5, para 30). See COURTS AND COMPETENCY, vol 6, para 873.

2 In solemn proceedings provision for the punishment of such behaviour is made by the Criminal Procedure (Scotland) Act 1975, s 145(4).

(F) THE CONDUCT OF THE TRIAL

6.44. Introduction. The conduct of the trial in summary proceedings follows the same basic pattern as in solemn proceedings except, of course, that there is no jury and there is no shorthand writer to note the evidence[1]. However, just as a juror may be challenged on cause shown[2], it is competent for the accused, and presumably for the prosecutor, to move that the sheriff should decline to take the trial or disqualify himself from hearing it, provided that cause can be shown for such a motion — for example if the sheriff has a personal interest in the circumstances of the case, or if he was present at the time and place the crime was allegedly committed[3] or where 'there are circumstances so affecting [him] as to be calculated to create in the mind of a reasonable man a suspicion of [his] impartiality, those circumstances are themselves sufficient to disqualify although in fact no bias exists'[4]. This is in keeping with the rule that justice must not only be done, but be seen to be done.

As previously stated[5], all proceedings must be conducted in the presence of the parties, and if it is necessary for the court to adjourn to some particular place, for example to examine the *locus* or a bulky production or to visit a witness who is too infirm to attend court, the entire court, including the judge, the clerk of court, the prosecutor, the accused and his legal representative must all adjourn to that place[6]. Adjournments of this nature are very uncommon and are dependent on the discretion of the court, which may be exercised *ex proprio motu* or on the motion of one of the parties. On arrival at the place the trial continues as if it were still in court, except that if the prosecutor examines a witness, the defence should be allowed to cross-examine him then and there and the prosecutor may thereafter continue his examination when the parties return to court and the witness re-enters the witness box.

1 See para 6.51 below.

2 See para 6.14 above.

3 *McDervitt v McLeod* 1982 SCCR 282; *Tennant v Houston* 1986 SCCR 556, 1987 SLT 317n; *Mowbray v Lowe* 1990 GWD 10–529.

4 *Bradford v McLeod* 1985 SCCR 379 at 382, 1986 SLT 244 at 247, per Lord Justice-Clerk Ross (quoting Eve J in *Law v Chartered Institute of Patent Agents* [1919] 2 Ch 276 at 289); *Harper of Oban (Engineering) Ltd v Henderson* 1988 SCCR 351, 1989 SLT 21. See also *Robertson v MacPhail* 1989 SCCR 693.

5 See para 6.35 above.

6 The procedure also applies to solemn proceedings, but as the jury will also require to adjourn to the place, such a course is avoided wherever possible. The power to adjourn to another place is referred to in the Criminal Justice (Scotland) Act 1980 (c62), s 32(6).

6.45. Objections to the evidence. In the course of the trial, should either party object to the competency or admissibility of evidence, the objection must be noted in the record if the party so requests[1], although failure to do so is not necessarily fatal to a conviction[2]. The objection is usually noted by the clerk of court. Failure to make an objection timeously may prevent it being raised later on appeal unless it can be shown that the evidence is so incompetent that it nullifies the whole proceedings[3]. The court should hear evidence to which objection has been taken under reservation as to its competency and relevancy, since failure to do so would preclude it being placed before the appeal court[4] and may result in the appeal court remitting the case back to the sheriff to hear the evidence[5].

1 Criminal Procedure (Scotland) Act 1975 (c 21), s 359 proviso. See, however, *Frame v Fyfe* 1948 JC 140, 1949 SLT 62, where it is suggested that it is not necessary to note objections at the request of the successful party.
2 *Cameron v Waugh* 1937 JC 5, 1937 SLT 53; *M'Donalds Ltd v Adair* 1944 JC 119, 1944 SLT 336.
3 Criminal Procedure (Scotland) Act 1975, s 454(1); *Robertson v Aitchison* 1981 SCCR 149, 1981 SLT (Notes) 127.
4 *Clark v Stuart* 1950 JC 8, 1949 SLT 461; *Copeland v Gillies* 1973 SLT 74.
5 *Aitchison v Rizza* 1985 SCCR 297.

(G) PROSECUTION WITNESSES AND EVIDENCE

6.46. The Crown case. As in solemn proceedings, the onus is on the Crown to prove the guilt of the accused beyond reasonable doubt, and as there are no opening speeches, the evidence commences by the prosecutor calling his witnesses in whichever order he deems appropriate[1]. Unlike an indictment, a summary complaint does not have a list of witnesses or productions appended to it, and there is no requirement on either party to notify the other of his witnesses or productions in advance of the trial (or even during it)[2]. In practice, however, the prosecutor will normally give a list of his witnesses to the accused in advance of the trial, or permit the accused to examine any productions if requested to do so on the understanding that the accused will give a reciprocal list of defence witnesses[3]. This practice does not restrict either party to calling only the witnesses who are specified on the informal list, and either may, without notice, call witnesses who are not on the list, or may decide not to cite witnesses who are listed. Co-operation before the trial has an obvious advantage since a party who is taken by surprise by some piece of evidence may seek to persuade the court to grant an adjournment if it can be shown that there has been prejudice or unfairness.

The presentation of the prosecution case follows the same lines as in solemn procedure[4], except that the court has a discretion to interrupt it and allow defence witnesses to be called, if it considers it expedient to do so[5]. This practice is most commonly used where the trial requires to be adjourned part heard and a defence witness will not be available on the later date. Otherwise, each witness is examined, cross-examined[6] and re-examined. The proceedings are conducted *viva voce*[7]. Where a witness has been present in court without permission during the proceedings and before giving evidence, the court has a discretion to allow him to give evidence if satisfied that his presence was not attributable to culpable negligence or criminal intent, that the witness has not been 'unduly instructed or influenced' by what took place during his presence and that no injustice will result[8]. Since difficulties of this nature can sometimes arise where the accused is not legally represented, it is common practice for the judge or one of the court officials to ensure that all witnesses have left the courtroom before the start of the trial. If a witness wilfully fails to attend (after being duly cited)[9], or unlawfully refuses to be sworn, or (after being sworn) refuses to answer any question which the court allows[10], or refuses to produce documents in his possession when required to do so by the court[11], or prevaricates when giving evidence[12], he may be summarily punished forthwith for contempt of court with a fine not exceeding level 3 on the standard scale or sentenced to imprisonment not exceeding twenty-one days[13]. Where the court does not deal summarily with such contempt, it is open to the prosecutor to institute proceedings at a later date[14].

1 The prosecutor may commence his case by laying certain documents or certificates before the court, but this is more properly considered as part of the law of evidence, not procedure.

2 An exception is where the accused intends to reply on a defence of alibi or insanity: see para 6.41 above. It appears that the judge may have authority to require a party to provide copies of productions which are important as evidence but he should exercise that authority reasonably: *Wilson v Caldwell* 1989 SCCR 273 (in which the commentator opines that if the judge does order a party to provide copies, the cost must fall on that party).

3 As this is only a courtesy arrangement it is not legally enforceable, and should a particular solicitor persistently fail to supply lists of defence witnesses after receiving lists of prosecution witnesses, it is open to the prosecutor to decline to give that solicitor lists of witnesses in future cases.

4 See paras 6.20–6.23 above, and the Criminal Procedure (Scotland) Act 1975 (c 21), s 340 (examination of witnesses).

5 Ibid, s 337(h).

6 A refusal by the judge to allow competent cross-examination of a prosecution witness will be fatal to a conviction: *Mackenzie v Jinks* 1934 JC 48, 1934 SLT 344.

7 Criminal Procedure (Scotland) Act 1975, s 359.

8 Ibid, s 343. This rule does not apply where a witness (usually an expert) is given permission to remain in court while other evidence is being given, or where the court is satisfied that it will not be contrary to the interests of justice to allow a witness to be present on the application of one of the parties: s 342A (added by the Criminal Justice (Scotland) Act 1987 (c 41), s 63).

9 *Orr v Annan* 1987 SCCR 242, 1988 SLT 251n. If a duly cited witness fails to attend, or if the court is satisfied by evidence on oath that a witness is not likely to attend, the court may grant a warrant in terms of the Criminal Procedure (Scotland) Act 1975, ss 320 and 321(5) for his arrest and detention in a police station, police cell or other convenient place until the date of the trial unless security is found to the amount fixed in the warrant for his appearance at all future diets. For an example of a case involving caution see *Sargeant, Petitioner* 1989 SCCR 448, 1990 SLT 286. In certain circumstances the witness might also risk prosecution for attempting to pervert the course of justice — see for example *Nisbet v HM Advocate* 1989 GWD 32–1473. See para 6.23, note 1 above and for further detail R W Renton and H H Brown *Criminal Procedure according to the Law of Scotland* (5th edn, 1983) paras 13–88 to 13–90.

10 See eg *Green v Smith* 1987 SCCR 686, 1988 SLT 175; *Smith* 1987 SCCR 726.

11 Unlike the position in solemn proceedings, productions are not lodged before the trial and it is competent to cite a witness to attend and produce any document which is required. Although the Criminal Procedure (Scotland) Act 1975, s 344(1), refers only to documents, it is likely that this provision would be extended to other articles.

12 See eg *Anderson v McLeod* 1987 SCCR 566.

13 Criminal Procedure (Scotland) Act 1975, s 344(1) (amended by the Criminal Justice (Scotland) Act 1980 (c 62), s 46(1)(c), and the Criminal Justice Act 1982 (c 48), s 56(3), Sch 7, para 8). As to the standard scale, see para 1.75, note 1, above. The clerk of court must record the act constituting the contempt or the statement forming the prevarication: Criminal Procedure (Scotland) Act 1975, s 344(2). For the meaning of 'prevarication', see para 6.23 above. The court may also grant a warrant for the apprehension of a witness who fails to attend, if satisfied that he has been duly cited: ss 320, 321. See also s 326(1).

14 Ibid, s 344(3). If the prosecutor institutes proceedings, it may be that the maximum penalty is a fine not exceeding level 4 on the standard scale or three months' imprisonment: see the Contempt of Court Act 1981 (c 49), s 15(2), and R W Renton and H H Brown *Criminal Procedure according to the Law of Scotland* (5th edn, 1983) para 18-15.

(H) NO CASE TO ANSWER

6.47. Close of the Crown case; no case to answer. In addition to oral and other evidence, the prosecutor, before closing his case, may found on the record of any judicial examination of the accused[1] (where the proceedings have commenced on petition and been reduced to a summary complaint) or, provided the accused is legally represented, on any facts which are admitted or agreed by all the parties[2], or, in the sheriff court, on evidence taken on commission[3].

Immediately after the close of the prosecution case the accused is entitled to make a submission that there is no case for him to answer which, if it is upheld, will result in his acquittal[4]. In considering the submission, the court is bound by the same rules as apply to solemn proceedings[5].

1 Criminal Procedure (Scotland) Act 1975 (c 21), s 352(1) (substituted by the Criminal Justice (Scotland) Act 1980 (c 62), s 6(4)). The rules relating to admissibility are the same as in solemn proceedings: see para 5.24 above. As there is no jury, it is not necessary to read the record aloud.
2 Criminal Procedure (Scotland) Act 1975, s 354(1). Admissions 'may' be made by minute of admissions (s 354(2)), in contrast with the position in solemn proceedings, where admissions 'shall' be made by way of such a minute (s 150(2)). It would therefore seem that in summary proceedings a verbal admission by all parties may suffice, although such an admission should be recorded in case there is a subsequent appeal. But see *Jessop v Kerr* 1989 SCCR 418, Sh Ct where a sheriff interpreted s 354(1) as meaning that a written minute was required and repelled a submission that verbal admissions would suffice.
3 Criminal Justice (Scotland) Act 1980, s 32.
4 Criminal Procedure (Scotland) Act 1975, s 345A (added by the Criminal Justice (Scotland) Act 1980, s 19(2)).
5 See para 6.25 above.

(i) DEFENCE WITNESSES AND EVIDENCE

6.48. The defence case. The accused has the right to lead evidence in exculpation if he wishes to do so, although he is not required to prove his innocence, which is presumed until he is proved to be guilty, and if he is not given an opportunity by the court to lead evidence, the court must return a verdict of not guilty[1]. He may not make an unsworn statement from the dock[2]. Where the accused is unrepresented, the judge will normally explain his rights and the procedure to him, but in doing so, must make it clear that the court cannot represent or look after his interests[3]. The accused may call his witnesses in any order he pleases, but if he is giving evidence himself[4] it is normal for him to do so before any of his witnesses in order to avoid adverse comment on his credibility and reliability. Where there is more than one accused, the order in which they may give evidence and examine witnesses is the same as in solemn proceedings[5]. While the accused is responsible for citing his own witnesses (and defraying their expenses[6]), if the prosecutor has witnesses present whom he has not called, he may, as a matter of courtesy, tender them to be called by the defence before they are released. Similarly, should the accused have difficulty in tracing or serving a citation on a witness, some prosecutors, as a matter of courtesy, may occasionally agree to cite the witness as if he were a prosecution witness, although in such circumstances it will be left to the accused to call the witness to the witness box to give evidence (and to defray his expenses)[7]. After the close of the defence case, the rights of the parties to call additional evidence and the right of the prosecutor to lead evidence in replication, while governed by separate statutory provisions[8], follow the same rules as in solemn proceedings[9].

1 *McArthur v Grosset* 1952 JC 12, 1952 SLT 88.
2 *Gilmour v HM Advocate* 1965 JC 45, *sub nom HM Advocate v Gilmour* 1966 SLT 198 . However, if he is convicted he is entitled to make such a statement in mitigation of sentence: *Falconer v Jessop* 1975 SLT (Notes) 78.
3 *Johannesson v Robertson* 1945 JC 146, 1945 SLT 328.

4 As to evidence by the accused, see the Criminal Procedure (Scotland) Act 1975 (c 21), ss 346(1), 347 (s 346(1) being amended by the Criminal Evidence Act 1979 (c 16), s 1, and the Criminal Justice (Scotland) Act 1980 (c 62), ss 28, 83(2), (3), Sch 7, para 56, Sch 8). See also para 5.26 above. The Criminal Procedure (Scotland) Act 1975, s 346(1), also makes provision for the questions which an accused may be asked.

5 See para 6.26 above, and ibid, s 346(2) (amended by the Criminal Justice (Scotland) Act 1987 (c 41), s 70(1), Sch 1, para 8).

6 Where the accused is on legal aid, defence witnesses will be recompensed at the same rates as prosecution witnesses. Payment of prosecution witnesses is governed by Treasury regulations and is made by the procurator fiscal.

7 This course has the advantage that the citation will be served by the police. As to witnesses who fail to attend, or who are unlikely to attend, or who go into hiding to avoid giving evidence, see the Criminal Procedure (Scotland) Act 1975, s 320, and *HM Advocate v Mannion* 1961 JC 79.

8 Criminal Procedure (Scotland) Act 1975, ss 349A, 350, 350A (respectively added by the Criminal Justice Act 1982 (c 48), s 73(2); and substituted by the Criminal Justice (Scotland) Act 1980, s 30(2); and added by s 30(2) and amended by the Law Reform (Miscellaneous Provisions) (Scotland) Act 1985 (c 73), s 37). The prosecutor may not call a witness in replication to contradict the evidence of a Crown witness (*Campbell v Allan* 1988 SCCR 47), but the judge may recall a witness to clear up an ambiguity (*Rollo v Wilson* 1988 SCCR 312, 1988 SLT 659).

9 See paras 6.27, 6.28, above.

(J) SPEECHES

6.49. Speeches. After all the evidence has been led, the prosecutor and then the defence may address the court, the defence always being entitled to the last word[1]. As there is no jury present, the speeches tend to be much briefer than in solemn proceedings, although their general content follows the same lines. The prosecutor must not comment on the failure of the accused[2] or his spouse[3] to give evidence and, if he does so, the court will disregard such comment. An accused may comment on the failure of a co-accused to give evidence[4], but he may not comment on the failure of the spouse of a co-accused to do so[5].

1 Criminal Procedure (Scotland) Act 1975 (c 21), s 351.
2 Ibid, s 346(1) proviso (b) (amended by the Criminal Justice (Scotland) Act 1980 (c 62), s 83(2), (3), Sch 7, para 56, Sch 8).
3 Criminal Procedure (Scotland) Act 1975, s 348(3) (substituted by the Criminal Justice (Scotland) Act 1980, s 29).
4 The Criminal Procedure (Scotland) Act 1975, s 346(1) proviso (b), is restricted to comment by the prosecutor.
5 Ibid, s 348(3) (as substituted: see note 3 above).

(K) VERDICT

6.50. Verdict. At the conclusion of the speeches the court will normally give its verdict immediately, although it may adjourn briefly or for a few days before doing so, especially if the issues are complex, or if the trial has been lengthy, or if for any other reason the judge decides that he wishes more time to consider his verdict. In reaching his verdict the judge must privately direct himself as to the law in the same manner in which he would address a jury and if he misdirects himself (that is, misapplies the law), his verdict may be appealed. Thereafter he must form a view as to the credibility and reliability of the evidence, giving the accused the benefit of any reasonable doubt. Although he is not required to give reasons for his verdict, in the event of an appeal he should be prepared to state which evidence he accepted and which he rejected. In the district court, if there is more than one judge and if the judges are equally divided in opinion as to the guilt of the accused, the verdict must be not guilty[1]. In any summary proceedings the verdict may be guilty, not guilty or not proven, and a conviction of part of the charge or charges implies an acquittal of the remainder[2]. As in solemn proceedings, the verdict must be in express terms, unambiguous, consistent with the complaint, and, if a conviction of part of the charge, it must constitute a relevant charge[3]. A verdict of not guilty or not proven acquits the accused with the consequence that he is dismissed from the bar and, if he is in custody, immediately released. He has no right of appeal against a verdict of not proven.

1 Criminal Procedure (Scotland) Act 1975 (c 21), s 355.
2 Ibid, s 427.
3 See para 6.32 above. As to alternative verdicts, see para 6.30 above, and in particular note 26.

(L) RECORD OF PROCEEDINGS

6.51. Record of proceedings. The record of the proceedings must include the complaint, the plea[1], a note of any documentary evidence produced[2], the conviction, the sentence or any other order of the court[3], any notice of penalties[4] and any notice of previous convictions[5]. In addition, at the request of one of the parties, it must record any objection to the competency or relevancy of the complaint or the evidence[6]. The record may be written, printed, or partly written and partly printed[7], and as nearly as possible it should follow the statutory form[8]. The minutes of procedure should be signed by the clerk of court or by the judge[9], preferably at the time and before any sentence or order is executed, although signature at a later time is not necessarily fatal if there has been no prejudice to the accused[10]. The rules for correcting an error in the record are identical to the corresponding rules in solemn proceedings[11].

Apart from the above requirements, no other record of the proceedings needs to be kept[12]. As there is no shorthand writer, there is no record of the evidence, but in practice the judge will usually take some notes of the evidence, bearing in mind that if there is an appeal by way of stated case he will require to state the facts of the case. Similarly, should there be a subsequent prosecution for perjury, or if for any other reason the judge is required to give evidence as to what took place at the trial, he may wish to refresh his memory from notes taken at the time.

1 Failure to record the plea may be fatal to a conviction: *Millar v Brown* 1941 JC 12, 1941 SLT 53. See also para 6.40 above.
2 For further details, see R W Renton and H H Brown *Criminal Procedure according to the Law of Scotland* (5th edn, 1983) para 14-75. Failure to note such evidence is not necessarily fatal unless it has prejudiced the accused and resulted in a miscarriage of justice: *Ogilvy v Mitchell* (1903) 5 F (J) 92, 4 Adam 237; *Silk v Middleton* 1921 JC 69, 1921 1 SLT 278; *Aldred v Miller* 1925 JC 21, 1925 SLT 33; *Cameron v Waugh* 1937 JC 5, 1937 SLT 53; *Millar v Brown* 1941 JC 12, 1941 SLT 53; *M'Donalds Ltd v Adair* 1944 JC 119, 1944 SLT 336; *Pennington v Mackenzie* 1946 JC 12, 1946 SLT 52; *Browning v Farrell* 1969 JC 64.
3 Criminal Procedure (Scotland) Act 1975 (c 21), s 359.
4 Ibid, s 357(1)(f).
5 Ibid, s 311(5).
6 Ibid, s 359 proviso: see para 6.45 above.
7 Ibid, s 360.
8 Ibid, ss 309(1), 430(1); Summary Jurisdiction (Scotland) Act 1954 (c 48), Sch 2, Pt V.
9 See the Criminal Procedure (Scotland) Act 1975, ss 309(2), 336, 341.
10 *Furnheim v Watson* 1946 JC 99, 1946 SLT 297; *Pettigrew v Ingram* 1982 SCCR 259, 1982 SLT 435.
11 Criminal Procedure (Scotland) Act 1975, s 439 (substituted by the Criminal Justice (Scotland) Act 1980, s 20). See also para 6.33 above.
12 Criminal Procedure (Scotland) Act 1975, s 359.

7. SENTENCE

(a) General

7.01. Preliminary procedure. Where an accused person pleads guilty or is found guilty, the court may proceed to sentence him provided that there is a formal or implied motion for sentence by the prosecutor and that it is competent for the court to impose sentence. In solemn proceedings the prosecutor should make an express motion for sentence, although such a motion may be implied if he lays previous convictions before the court[1]. In summary proceedings the prosecutor does not normally make a formal motion, but his motion for sentence is implied[2]. The prosecutor therefore has some discretion in this matter, and if there is no express or implied motion for sentence, or where the prosecutor specifically states that he is not moving for sentence either in relation to the whole indictment or complaint, or in relation to one of the charges, the court may not pass sentence thereon[3]. The accused may make a plea in bar of sentence if it relates to the sufficiency of the verdict or the powers of the court[4]. In summary cases, if the charge is based on statute rather than common law, a notice of the statutory penalties must have been served on the accused with the complaint[5], and the prosecutor must lay a copy of the notice before the judge at the time when the implied or express motion for sentence is made. Failure to observe either of these conditions precludes the court from imposing sentence, although if the prosecutor is unable to place before the court a copy of the notice served on the accused, the court may allow an adjournment to enable him to prepare a copy[6]. He may also rectify any errors in the notice by way of amendment[7]. The rules relating to notices of penalty do not apply to solemn cases. If the court for any reason does not pass sentence on the accused, it merely makes no further order and this is noted in the record of the proceedings. Where the court proceeds to sentence, the sentence must be consistent with the charge, within the law, and free from ambiguity[8].

1 *Noon v HM Advocate* 1960 JC 52, 1960 SLT (Notes) 51.
2 *Skeen v Sullivan* 1980 SLT (Notes) 11. See also the Criminal Procedure (Scotland) Act 1975 (c 21), s 336.
3 J H A Macdonald *The Criminal Law of Scotland* (5th edn, 1948) p 348; Hume *Commentaries* II, 470, 471, and Bell's Notes p 300; Alison *Practice* p 653. However once the prosecutor has moved for sentence expressly or by implication 'the matter moves entirely from the Crown to the court and it is desirable for good reasons of public policy that the Crown should not be involved in the process of sentencing in any way: *HM Advocate v McKenzie* 1989 SCCR 587.
4 It is not competent to base a plea in bar of sentence on objections to the libel or the evidence: *Macdonald* p 349; *Hume* II, 467; *Alison* p 651.
5 See para 5.14 above.
6 See the Criminal Procedure (Scotland) Act 1975, s 311(5); *Pirie v Rivard* 1976 SLT (Sh Ct) 59; *Smith v Moffat* 1981 SCCR 291, Sh Ct.

7 Criminal Procedure (Scotland) Act 1975, s 335(1). See also *Cochrane v West Calder Co-operative Society* 1978 SLT (Notes) 22; *Donnachie v Smith* 1989 SCCR 144.
8 *Macdonald* pp 350, 351. For example a sentence of imprisonment which does not state the date from which the sentence is to run, and an order for forfeiture which does not clearly describe the article to be forfeited, are fundamentally null: *Grant v Grant* (1885) 2 Irv 277; *Rankin v Wright* (1901) 4 F (J) 5, 3 Adam 483.

(B) ADJOURNMENT AND DEFERMENT

7.02. Adjournment prior to sentence. The court is entitled to adjourn the case before passing sentence or to defer sentence to a later date. Statute empowers the court to adjourn for any single period of up to three weeks to enable inquiries to be made or in order to determine the most suitable method of dealing with the case, and during the period of the adjournment the accused may be remanded in custody, released on bail or ordained to appear[1]. It is competent to have several adjournments of this nature, provided none exceeds three weeks, but where the accused is remanded in custody it is desirable that the case be dealt with as quickly as possible, and the accused has a right of appeal to the High Court of Justiciary against a refusal of bail[2]. The court may also adjourn the case in terms to make inquiry into the physical or mental condition of the accused[3]. In some instances the court may have no option but to adjourn the case, for example where it requires to obtain reports before imposing a custodial sentence[4], or where the accused is not present and the court intends either to impose a custodial sentence[5] (which cannot be pronounced in the absence of the accused[6]) or to disqualify him from driving[7]. In other instances the adjournment may be discretionary to allow the court to obtain such information or reports as it considers necessary for the proper disposal of the case.

Where the case is adjourned for reports or other information, the court has a discretion as to whether or not the accused is remanded in custody or released, with or without bail. Circumstances will vary from case to case but, in general, first offenders facing a minor charge where imprisonment or detention is not anticipated will normally not be remanded[8]. Children under the age of sixteen years may be detained by committing them to the care of the local authority[9].

1 Criminal Procedure (Scotland) Act 1975 (c 21), ss 179(1), 380(1) (amended by the Bail etc (Scotland) Act 1980 (c 4), s 5, and the Criminal Justice (Scotland) Act 1980 (c 62), s 83(2), Sch 7, paras 36, 59). The accused should normally be released on bail unless good reasons are noted for detaining him in custody: *McGoldrick and Monaghan v Normand* 1988 SCCR 83, 1988 SLT 273n.
2 Criminal Procedure (Scotland) Act 1975, ss 179(2), 380(2) (added by the Bail (Scotland) Act 1980, s 5, and amended by the Criminal Justice (Scotland) Act 1980, Sch 7, paras 36, 59); *Long v HM Advocate* 1984 SCCR 161. As to the effect of a remand in custody on the ultimate sentence, see para 7.13, text and note 18, below.
3 Criminal Procedure (Scotland) Act 1975, ss 180(1), 381(1).
4 See para 7.13 below.
5 Criminal Procedure (Scotland) Act 1975, ss 334(3), (4), 338(1)(b), and s 398(1) (amended by the Criminal Justice (Scotland) Act 1980, Sch 7, para 61).
6 *Campbell v Jessop* 1987 SCCR 670, 1988 SLT 160n.
7 The accused may have pleaded guilty by letter and thus not be present when the case calls in court. Disqualification should not be imposed without giving the accused an opportunity to appear in person and address the court in mitigation: *Stephens v Gibb* 1984 SCCR 195. An offender may not be placed on probation without consenting to the terms of the probation order: see para 7.13 below.
8 *Morrison v Clark* 1962 SLT 113; *McGoldrick and Monaghan v Normand* 1988 SCCR 83, 1988 SLT 273n; C G B Nicholson *The Law and Practice of Sentencing in Scotland* (1981) para 8-11.
9 *Nicholson* paras 8-12, 8-13 (amended by Supplement (1985)).

7.03. Deferment of sentence. As an alternative to an adjournment, the court may defer sentence after conviction[1]. There is no limit to the number of times that sentence may be deferred or to the length of the deferment. If sentence is deferred for more than three weeks the accused cannot be detained in custody, and should he fail to attend the subsequent diet the court must continue the case to a further diet unless it is prepared or empowered to grant a warrant for his arrest[2]. The purpose of the deferment may be to impose certain conditions on the accused[3], or to await the outcome of other proceedings against him and thus enable the court to dispose of all charges against him at the same time, or to allow the accused to be sentenced contemporaneously with other persons accused of the same charge[4]. Where there are several charges on the same complaint it is inappropriate to sentence the accused on some and defer sentence on others[5].

There is an important distinction between adjournment and deferment in that sentence may be deferred only 'after conviction', which means that the accused cannot seek thereafter to withdraw his plea of guilty, but he has the right to appeal against his conviction. On the other hand, where the case is adjourned, the court has not, strictly speaking, convicted the accused, and it may ultimately dispose of the case by way of probation or an absolute discharge, without proceeding to conviction[6].

1 Criminal Procedure (Scotland) Act 1975 (c 21), ss 219, 432 (amended by the Criminal Justice (Scotland) Act 1980 (c 62), s 54).
2 *Skeen v Sullivan* 1980 SLT (Notes) 11.
3 See para 7.20 below.
4 *Thom v Smith* 1979 SLT (Notes) 25; R W Renton and H H Brown *Criminal Procedure according to the Law of Scotland* (5th edn, 1983) para 15-14.
5 *Lennon v Copland* 1972 SLT (Notes) 68.
6 *Tudhope v McCauley* (1980), Sh Ct (reported as an annex to *Tudhope v Cullen* 1982 SCCR 276, Sh Ct); *Renton and Brown* para 15-17. In summary cases this situation can be avoided if the court adjourns under the Criminal Procedure (Scotland) Act 1975, s 337(f), rather than under s 432.

7.04. Interruption of proceedings for sentence. The court is permitted to interrupt either solemn or summary proceedings against an accused to sentence him in relation to some other case against him which is pending before the court[1]. Immediately thereafter, the court may sentence him on the case which has been interrupted, thus allowing both cases to be sentenced at the same time[2].

1 Act of Adjournal (Consolidation) 1988, SI 1988/110, ss 74, 123.
2 R W Renton and H H Brown *Criminal Procedure according to the Law of Scotland* (5th edn, 1983) para 10-76; C G B Nicholson *The Law and Practice of Sentencing in Scotland* (1981) para 8–33.

(C) PRONOUNCING AND RECORDING OF SENTENCE

7.05. Pronouncing and recording the sentence. The sentence must be pronounced orally by the judge in open court, and while the accused must be present in solemn proceedings, he may, where provision is made for it, be sentenced in absence in a summary case (for example where he has pleaded guilty by letter)[1]. A record of the sentence must be entered in the proceedings, and for summary cases the record must be in the appropriate statutory form[2]. Once the record is signed by the clerk of court it acts as a full warrant and authority for execution of the sentence[3]. A sentence of imprisonment will take effect from the date on which it is pronounced unless it is backdated or ordered to run from the expiry of a prison sentence which the accused is currently serving; similarly, fines and other monetary penalties are immediately payable unless time is allowed for payment[4]; and disposals such as probation, community service, disqualification from driving and the like also take immediate effect.

1 Criminal Procedure (Scotland) Act 1975, ss 217(1), 433; R W Renton and H H Brown *Criminal Procedure according to the Law of Scotland* (5th edn, 1983) para 15-21; *Watson v Argo* 1936 JC 87, 1936 SLT 427. See also para 7.02, note 7, above.
2 Criminal Procedure (Scotland) Act 1975, ss 217(2), 430(1). For the form, see the Summary Jurisdiction (Scotland) Act 1954 (c 48), Sch 2, Pt V.
3 Criminal Procedure (Scotland) Act 1975, ss 217(2), 430(1); *Paterson v MacLennan* 1914 SC (J) 123, 7 Adam 428; *Pettigrew v Ingram* 1982 SCCR 259, 1982 SLT 435,
4 See para 7.15 below.

7.06. Alteration of sentence. The clerk of court may correct any incomplete or erroneously recorded sentence, but the authority of the court to do so is required if the sentence has been executed[1]. If the correction is made after execution it must be intimated to the prosecutor and the accused or his solicitor[2]. The error must be corrected openly and properly authenticated, and no attempt should be made to erase or change the words[3]. With regard to summary proceedings, the court may alter or modify any sentence except where the accused has been sentenced to imprisonment and has started to serve his sentence[4]. This power may be exercised without the accused being present, but the court may not impose a higher sentence[5]. Where, however, the original sentence is incompetent the court may substitute a competent sentence even if it is of greater severity since the second sentence is not an alteration of a void sentence, but a proper imposition of sentence[6].

1 Criminal Procedure (Scotland) Act 1975 (c 21), ss 227A(1), (2), 439(1), (2) (respectively added and substituted by the Criminal Justice (Scotland) Act 1980 (c 62), s 20). See also *Ingram v Morgan* 1990 GWD 3–152.
2 Criminal Procedure (Scotland) Act 1975, ss 227A(3), 439(3) (as so added and substituted).
3 See R W Renton and H H Brown *Criminal Procedure according to the Law of Scotland* (5th edn, 1983) para 10-87 and the authorities there cited.
4 Criminal Procedure (Scotland) Act 1975, s 434(1). Where the accused has started to serve his sentence, the court is debarred from altering or modifying any auxiliary part of the sentence such as disqualification from driving: *Skeen v Sim* (1975) 39 JCL 277.
5 Criminal Procedure (Scotland) Act 1975, s 434(1), (3) (amended by the Criminal Justice (Scotland) Act 1980, s 83(3), Sch 8).
6 *Patrick v Copeland* 1969 JC 42, 1970 SLT 71; *McCallum v HM Advocate* 1988 GWD 15–655.

7.07. Cumulo penalties. It is competent to impose a cumulo penalty when there are several charges on the same indictment or complaint[1]. The cumulo penalty must not exceed the overall powers of the court, but within these limits the fine may exceed the maximum permissible on any individual charge[2]. It is not competent to impose a cumulo sentence of imprisonment if one of the charges cannot be disposed of in this way[3]. If one of the charges is later successfully appealed, difficulties may arise in determining the sentence appropriate for the remaining charges, and for this reason a cumulo penalty should be avoided if the charges are dissimilar or disparate[4].

1 Criminal Procedure (Scotland) Act 1975 (c 21), s 430(3). Strictly speaking, s 430(3), which relates to summary complaints, follows the wording of the Summary Jurisdiction (Scotland) Act 1954 (c 48), s 56(3) (repealed), and refers to 'a cumulo fine'. The 1954 Act was a consolidating Act, and this provision was based on the Summary Jurisdiction (Scotland) Act 1908 (c 65), s 53 (repealed), which refers to 'a cumulo penalty', which therefore includes imprisonment. See C G B Nicholson *The Law and Practice of Sentencing in Scotland* (1981) para 8-36.
2 *Wann v Macmillan* 1957 JC 20, 1956 SLT 369.
3 *M'Lauchlan v Davidson* 1921 JC 45, 1921 1 SLT 65.
4 *Paisley Ice Rink Ltd v Hill* 1944 JC 158, 1945 SLT 14; *Seaton v Allan* 1973 JC 24, 1974 SLT 234; *Caringi v HM Advocate* 1989 SCCR 223.

(D) CONSECUTIVE SENTENCES

7.08. Consecutive sentences. A sentence of imprisonment may be ordered to commence after the expiry of any prison sentence which the accused is currently serving in Scotland or England[1]. Where there are several charges on the same indictment or complaint[2], the court may impose a separate and consecutive sentence on each charge provided that the total sentence does not exceed the jurisdictional powers of sentence of the court: for example the district court (which has a maximum limit of sixty days' imprisonment) cannot impose consecutive sentences if the aggregate amounts to more than sixty days[3]. Should the accused appear and be sentenced on several different complaints on the same day, the court's power to impose an aggregate of consecutive sentences in excess of its normal powers will depend on the test of fairness to the accused and to the public interest. Where all the charges could have been included in the same complaint, or where their separation is due to some technical reason (such as libelling a charge of driving while disqualified[4]), the aggregate should not exceed the total powers of the court[5]. The limit may, however, be exceeded if the accused would otherwise be afforded an undue advantage (for example where the accused committed a further offence while on deferred sentence and appeared for sentence on both complaints on the same day, or where the accused had failed to appear on one complaint and was only sentenced on it on the same day as he was sentenced on a further complaint[6]).

1 J H A Macdonald *The Criminal Law of Scotland* (1948) p 357; *HM Advocate v Graham* (1842) 1 Broun 445; *Grey v HM Advocate* 1958 SLT 147; Criminal Procedure (Scotland) Act 1975 (c 21), s 430(4). Where the accused has been sentenced to life imprisonment, it is not appropriate to impose another sentence of imprisonment to run consecutively: *McRae v HM Advocate* 1987 SCCR 36. See also *Rankin v Lees* 1990 GWD 7–364. In *Proudfoot v Wither* 1990 SCCR 96 the accused was sentenced to imprisonment, appealed against sentence and while the appeal was pending he was sentenced to another term of imprisonment in another case. He then abandoned his appeal and when the original sentence was re-imposed it was held to be contrary to natural justice to order that sentence to run consecutively to the intervening sentence without giving the accused an opportunity to be heard on the matter. A consecutive sentence should be expressed as 'consecutive to the total period of imprisonment to which the prisoner is already subject' or as taking effect 'on the expiry of all sentences previously imposed': *Moore v MacPhail* 1986 SCCR 669. See also C G B Nicholson *The Law and Practice of Sentencing in Scotland* (1981) paras 8-41–8-48, and R W Renton and H H Brown *Criminal Procedure according to the Law of Scotland* (5th edn, 1983) paras 15-32–15-38.

2 See eg *McGuigan v Taylor Wilson* 1988 SCCR 474. Where a charge contains a number of sub-charges, the sub-charges may not be treated as separate charges for the purpose of sentence: *Beattie v HM Advocate* 1986 SCCR 605.

3 *Wishart v Heatly* 1953 JC 42, 1953 SLT 184. The Bail (Scotland) Act 1980 (c 4), s 3(5), allows a penalty for breach of bail conditions to be imposed in addition to any penalty imposed for the original offence notwithstanding that the total of penalties exceeds the penalty which is competent for the original offence: see para 3.47 above. For examples of consecutive penalties for breaches of bail conditions, see *Allan v Lockhart* 1986 SCCR 395, *Montgomery v HM Advocate* 1987 SCCR 264, and *Whyte v Normand* 1988 SCCR 792. But see also *Balderstone v HM Advocate* 1989 GWD 30–1373 where the commission of one offence having given rise to a breach of two bail orders, the High Court upheld a fine of £100 for one breach but reduced a fine and substituted an admonition for the other on the grounds that the second breach was effectively duplicating the first.

4 Ie contrary to the Road Traffic Act 1988 (c 52), s 103.

5 *Maguiness v MacDonald* 1953 JC 31, 1953 SLT 158; *Kesson v Heatly* 1964 JC 40, 1964 SLT 157; *Williamson v Farrell* 1975 SLT (Notes) 92; *Allan v Lockhart* 1986 SCCR 395; *Ross v McLeod* 1987 SCCR 525; *Moore v HM Advocate* 1989 SCCR 298. However, see also *HM Advocate v Logan* (1972) SCCR Supp 26.

6 *Thomson v Smith, Morgan v Smith* 1982 SCCR 57, 1982 SLT 546; *Haggerty v Tudhope* 1985 SCCR 121; *O'Lone v Tudhope* 1987 SCCR 211. However, see *Noble v Guild* 1987 SCCR 518; *Gilchrist v HM Advocate* 1988 GWD 3–105; and *Cartledge v McLeod* 1988 SCCR 129, 1988 SLT 389n. The

limit may also be exceeded if one of the sentences relates to contempt of court: *Young v Procurator Fiscal Kilmarnock* 5 April 1990, High Court (unreported).

(E) THE COURT'S DISCRETION; FACTORS AFFECTING SENTENCE

7.09. Introduction. Apart from murder (for which there is a fixed penalty) the court is given a wide discretion to determine the sentence within certain maximum limits[1]. Even where the penalty is fixed by statute, the court may impose a lesser sentence and is empowered to reduce any period of imprisonment, or to substitute a fine for imprisonment (which in the case of a summary prosecution is a maximum fine of £1,000 or £2,000, depending on whether the offence is only triable summarily or is also triable on indictment[2]), or to reduce the amount of any statutory fine, or to impose caution for good behaviour, or to dispense with the finding of caution[3].

Numerous factors have a bearing on how the discretion will be exercised[4]. In all cases there are certain matters which the court must take into account, such as previous convictions against the accused, the plea in mitigation on his behalf and, where appropriate, that he was subjected to provocation. Certain sentences require the court to consider a background report about the accused, or any time spent in custody awaiting disposal[5], or his means and ability to pay a financial penalty[6]. The court may also require to have regard to any sentence passed on a co-accused convicted of the same charge, although such a sentence is not necessarily binding[7]. In certain instances, possibly because of the gravity of the crime, the court may wish to pass a sentence which will act as a deterrent to the accused and, by implication, all indictments conclude with the words that the accused 'ought to be punished with the pains of law to deter others from committing the like crimes in all times coming'[8]. Closely allied to deterrence, and sometimes indistinguishable from it, is the question of prevalence of the offence, which may properly influence the court when considering sentence[9]. It may be relevant to consider the harm done to the victim[10] and the possibility of ordering the accused to make some form of restitution[11]. A sentence may be determined with a view to rehabilitating the accused (for example by probation or community service or requiring him to undergo some form of treatment or to comply with some other condition[12]), or conversely the over-riding consideration may be the public interest and the necessity to protect society from the criminal activities of the accused[13]. In many instances the court will require to strike a balance between some of these conflicting factors when deciding upon the appropriate sentence. The court must not, however, allow itself to be influenced by improper considerations (such as an improper interpretation of the evidence or incomplete local knowledge[14], or the fact that the accused tendered a guilty plea at an early stage in the proceedings[15] or that the accused had breached a civil interdict[16]), and if it does so, or if it imposes an excessive sentence, that sentence may be reduced on appeal[17]. Where a sentence is appealed, the judge is required to submit a report to the High Court of Justiciary in which he will usually give some explanation for his particular choice of sentence; but with that exception, the only occasions on which a judge is required to give his reasons and have them noted in the record of proceedings[18] are when a young offender is sentenced to detention[19], where a person is sentenced to imprisonment or detention for the first time[20], or where no time is allowed for payment of a fine[21].

1 The maximum powers of the different criminal courts are considered in paras 2.07–2.12 above. Unless there are exceptional circumstances, a court should not impose the maximum sentence for a first offence: *Baird v Lockhart* 1986 SCCR 514; *Kerr v Taylor-Wilson* 1987 GWD 15–563; *Kelly v Webster* 1989 GWD 38–1777.

2 Criminal Procedure (Scotland) Act 1975 (c 21), s 394 (amended by the Criminal Law Act 1977 (c 45), s 63(1), Sch 11, para 7, and the Criminal Justice Act 1982 (c 48), s 56(3), Sch 7, para 10), read with the Criminal Procedure (Scotland) Act 1975, s 289B (added by the Criminal Law Act 1977, Sch 11, para 5, substituted by the Criminal Justice Act 1982, s 55(2), and amended by the Criminal Justice (Scotland) Act 1987 (c 41), s 70(1), (2), Sch 1, para 15, Sch 2).

3 Criminal Procedure (Scotland) Act 1975, s 193 (amended by the Criminal Justice (Scotland) Act 1980 (c 62), s 83(3), Sch 8), and the Criminal Procedure (Scotland) Act 1975, s 394 (as amended: see note 2 above). See also *Lambie v Mearns* (1903) 5 F (J) 82, 4 Adam 207. The court may not exercise this power if a convention, treaty or agreement with a foreign state stipulates a minimum fine, or if proceedings are taken under a statute relating to the armed forces: ss 193, 394.

4 There is no tariff system for sentences, as in England. See further C G B Nicholson *The Law and Practice of Sentencing in Scotland* (1981) ch 10. It is impossible to give an exhaustive list of all the factors which might be taken into account — for example, courts have taken the following matters into consideration:—

(a) Age — *G v HM Advocate* 1989 GWD 30–1382; *Fitzpatrick v HM Advocate* 1989 GWD 32–1470.

(b) Lack of remorse — *G v HM Advocate* 1989 GWD 30–1382; *McGowan v HM Advocate* 1990 GWD 4–206.

(c) Motive — *McGill v HM Advocate* 1989 GWD 30–1384.

(d) Recovery of proceeds — *McGarth v HM Advocate* 1989 GWD 36–1664; *Halliday v Scott* 1989 GWD 39–1811; *Mungall v HM Advocate* 1990 GWD 4–201, although see also *Sjoberg v HM Advocate* 1990 GWD 12–611.

(e) Damage caused — *Wason v Douglas* 1990 GWD 3–133.

(f) Employment — *Walker v HM Advocate* 1989 GWD 32–1477; *McConnach v McNaughten* 1989 GWD 32–1486; *Boyle v Docherty* 1989 GWD 33–1510; *McPhail v Ingram* 1989 GWD 33–1517; *Nicholas v McNaughton* 1989 GWD 33–1534; *Sutcliffe v Lowe* 1989 GWD 33–1537; *Strickland v Annan* 1989 GWD 36–1654; *Etherson v Lees* 1989 GWD 37–1700; *Kellas v Colley* 1989 GWD 37–1716; *McLean v MacDougall* 1989 GWD 39–1832; *Russell v Scott* 1989 GWD 39–1835; *Miller v Jessop* 1989 GWD 39–1836; *Bell v Lowe* 1989 GWD 40–1861; *Gibson v HM Advocate* 1990 GWD 6–311; *Bardgett v Walkinshaw* 1990 GWD 7–394 — but see conversely *Ulhap v Jessop* 1989 GWD 33–1546; *Gibson v MacDougall* 1989 GWD 33–1547; *Smith v Annan* 1989 GWD 34–1572; *Newman v Carnegie* 1989 GWD 36–1680; *Smith v Walkinshaw* 1989 GWD 37–1732; *Morrison v Annan* 1990 GWD 1–33; *Tait v MacDougall* 1990 GWD 3–114; *Campbell v Douglas* 1990 GWD 3–145.

5 See para 7.18 below.

6 See paras 7.15, 7.16, below. The court should not impose a custodial sentence merely because the accused has insufficient means to pay a substantial fine: *Milligan v Jessop* 1988 SCCR 137.

7 This is called the 'comparative principle'. For examples, see *Davidson v HM Advocate* 1981 SCCR 371; *Lambert v Tudhope* 1982 SCCR 144; *Brodie v HM Advocate* 1982 SCCR 243; *Skilling v McLeod* 1987 SCCR 245; *Purves v Allan* 1987 GWD 2–61; *Smart v HM Advocate* 1987 GWD 10–322; *McCarrol v HM Advocate* 1987 GWD 10–328; *Kelly v Valentine* 1987 GWD 12–416; *Ferguson v Ingram* 1987 GWD 18–675; *Chapman v Jessop* 1987 GWD 19–727; *Doyle v Allan* 1987 GWD 39–1431; *Middlemass v Whitelaw* 1988 GWD 17–731; *Beauly v HM Advocate* 1988 GWD 17–740; *Morton v HM Advocate* 1988 GWD 17–741; *Colquhoun v Jessop* 1988 GWD 19–825; *Turnbull v Hamilton* 1988 GWD 20–862; *Bates v HM Advocate* 1989 SCCR 338; *Smaill v McGlennan* 1989 GWD 34–1562; *Blyth v Wilson* 1989 GWD 34–1573; *Brown v Annan* 1989 GWD 34–1574; *Traynor v Carmichael* 1989 GWD 34–1575; *Murray HM Advocate* 1989 GWD 37–1703; *Williamson v O'Brien* 1989 GWD 38–1757; *Rhind v Houston* 1989 GWD 40–1854; *Haggerty v HM Advocate* 1989 GWD 40–1863; *Halliday v Lowe* 1990 GWD 3–112; *Bell v McGlennan* 1990 GWD 3–113; *Scott v Lowe* 1990 SCCR 15. However, see also *Simpkins v HM Advocate* 1985 SCCR 30, where the court departed from the comparative principle as in *Lam v HM Advocate* 1988 SCCR 347, where the two accused were sentenced by the same judge, and in *Forrest v HM Advocate* 1988 SCCR 481, where they were sentenced by different judges.

8 The implication arises from the Criminal Procedure (Scotland) Act 1975, s 47, which replaced the Criminal Procedure (Scotland) Act 1887 (c 35), s 20 (repealed). See also para 1.61 above. For an example of deterrence in a summary case, see *Blues v MacPhail* 1982 SCCR 247; *Wagstaff v Wilson* 1989 SCCR 322; *Munro v McPhail* 1989 GWD 33–1545; but see also *Ruddy v Taylor Wilson* 1988 SCCR 193.

9 *Blair v Hawthorn* 1945 JC 17, 1945 SLT 141; *Campbell v Johnston* 1981 SCCR 179; *Paterson v MacNeill* 1982 SCCR 141; *O'Reilly v Smith* 28 May 1985 (unreported).

10 See eg, in relation to victims of assault, *Penman v MacPhail* 1987 SCCR 563; *Anderson v McLeod* 1987 SCCR 566; *Baillie v Walkingshaw* 1987 GWD 1–10; *Mahmood v MacKinnon* 1987 GWD 3–84; *Newman v HM Advocate* 1987 GWD 5–143; *McLean v Lockhart* 1987 GWD 16–592; *Keenan v Allan*

1987 GWD 38–1356; *Singh v HM Advocate* 1988 GWD 1–25; *Reid v Mackinnon* 1988 GWD 8–315; *Dougal v HM Advocate* 1988 GWD 12–509; *Mack v HM Advocate* 1988 GWD 13–553; *Jackson v HM Advocate* 1988 GWD 13–556; *Mitchell v HM Advocate* 1988 GWD 18–792; *Smith v HM Advocate* 1989 GWD 38–1760; *Scott v O'Brien* 1989 GWD 40–1855; *McManus v HM Advocate* 1990 GWD 1–21; *Robertson v HM Advocate* 1990 GWD 1–23; *Corns v HM Advocate* 1990 GWD 5–250; *Lumsden v Lowe* 1990; GWD 7–359; *Thomson v HM Advocate* 1990 GWD 10–538. However, in relation to victims of road traffic offences, see *McCallum v Hamilton* 1985 SCCR 368, 1986 SLT 156; *Sharp v HM Advocate* 1987 SCCR 179; *Ireland v Lockhart* 1987 GWD 1–38; *McCrone v Normand* 1988 SCCR 551, 1989 SLT 332. The court should not seek the views of the victim as to the sentence which the court should impose: *HM Advocate v McKenzie* 1989 SCCR 587.

11 See eg *Dolan v HM Advocate* 1986 SCCR 564; *White v HM Advocate* 1987 SCCR 73; and paras 7.16, 7.20, below.
12 See paras 7.18–7.20 below.
13 See eg *Walker v HM Advocate* 1987 SCCR 345; *Robertson v HM Advocate* 1987 SCCR 385; *McArthur v HM Advocate* 1987 GWD 2–52; *Bollan v Lockhart* 1987 GWD 9–283; *Austin v HM Advocate* 1987 GWD 29–1106; *Tooley v HM Advocate* 1987 GWD 37–1318; *Wood v HM Advocate* 1987 GWD 39–1426; *Singh v HM Advocate* 1988 GWD 1–25; *Sheekey v HM Advocate* 1988 GWD 17–737.
14 *Dorrens v HM Advocate* 1983 SCCR 407; *Harbert v Lockhart* 1 October 1982 (unreported); *Crawford v HM Advocate* 1989 GWD 32–1469; *Deuchar v Wilson* 1989 GWD 33–1533; *Brown v Jessop* 1989 GWD 33–1542; *W v HM Advocate* 1989 SCCR 461; *Ferries v HM Advocate* 1989 GWD 36–1663; *Bulloch v Carmichael* 1990 GWD 9–483; *Reid v HM Advocate* 1990 SCCR 83.
15 *Strawhorn v McLeod* 1987 SCCR 413. However, see also *Daniel Campbell v HM Advocate* 1986 SCCR 403, and *Inglis v Carmichael* 1987 GWD 25–930.
16 *Friend v Normand* 1988 SCCR 232.
17 See paras 8.54ff below.
18 If the reasons are not entered in the record this may not necessarily be fatal if they are given orally in court: *Binnie v Farrell* 1972 JC 49, 1972 SLT 212.
19 Criminal Procedure (Scotland) Act 1975, s 207(3) (substituted by the Criminal Justice (Scotland) Act 1980, s 45(1)). Except in the High Court, the reasons must be entered in the record: Criminal Procedure (Scotland) Act 1975, s 207(3).
20 Criminal Justice (Scotland) Act 1980, s 42(2).
21 Criminal Procedure (Scotland) Act 1975, s 396(2), (3); *Sullivan v McLeod* 1980 SLT (Notes) 99.

7.10. Previous convictions. The court may have regard to any previous conviction against the accused provided it is contained in a notice which the prosecutor has prepared and served on him[1]. The previous conviction must be dated prior to the current offence[2] and may not be libelled if it is under appeal[3]. While the prosecutor should not refer to convictions which are not in the notice[4], this practice is often ignored, and it is not uncommon for the prosecutor or defence to advise the court that the accused has subsequently been placed on probation or sent to prison[5]. The court may also take account of convictions mentioned in a social inquiry report, even if they are not libelled by the prosecutor[6]. In relation to road traffic offences, the court may take cognisance of any convictions endorsed on the accused's driving licence[7]. The court may only look at the conviction and sentence as recorded and should not consider the details or circumstances of the offence[8].

The prosecutor must lay the notice of previous convictions before the court at (but not before) the time of the express or implied motion for sentence[9], and he has a total discretion as to which, if any, of the previous convictions he chooses to libel. Where the court sees a notice of previous convictions at an earlier stage in the trial, this may not necessarily result in nullity of the proceedings if it happened by accident and not because of a deliberate act by the prosecutor[10]. Should there be an error or defect in the notice, the prosecutor may amend the notice with leave of the court, unless such an amendment would prejudice the accused[11].

In solemn procedure, a conviction libelled in the notice is held to apply to the accused unless he gives prior written notice that he objects to it[12]. In summary procedure, the accused must be asked if he admits the previous conviction unless he pleads guilty by letter, in which case he is deemed to admit any conviction in the notice unless he expressly denies it in the letter by which his plea was tendered[13]. In both solemn and summary procedure, if the accused does not admit a previous conviction the prosecutor may either withdraw it or lead evidence to prove it by means of an extract of the conviction, by witnesses and by fingerprint evidence[14].

1 Criminal Procedure (Scotland) Act 1975 (c 21), ss 159(2), 356(2). See also ss 68, 161, 357 (ss 68, 357 being amended respectively by the Criminal Justice (Scotland) Act 1980 (c 62), ss 12, 83(3), Sch 4, para 1, Sch 8, and by s 40). Prosecutors are instructed to libel only convictions from criminal courts in the United Kingdom, excluding Northern Ireland and courts-martial: Book of Regulations 6.57.

2 HM Advocate v Graham (1842) 1 Broun 445. Where there are several offences on the same indictment or complaint, the previous convictions should be dated prior to the date of the latest offence libelled.

3 M'Call v Mitchell 1911 SC (J) 1, 6 Adam 303.

4 Ramsay v HM Advocate 1959 JC 86, 1959 SLT 324; Adair v Hill 1943 JC 9, 1943 SLT 190.

5 C G B Nicholson The Law and Practice of Sentencing in Scotland (1981) para 8-05.

6 Sharp v Stevenson 1948 SLT (Notes) 79; Sillars v Copeland 1966 JC 8, 1966 SLT 89.

7 Road Traffic Offenders Act 1988 (c 53), s 31(1), which has effect notwithstanding the provisions of the Criminal Justice (Scotland) Act 1975, ss 311(5), 357(1), as to notices of penalties and previous convictions: Road Traffic Offenders Act 1988, s 31(2). In certain circumstances the court may also have regard to previous convictions for road traffic offences recorded in a computer printout provided by DVLC (which keeps a record of such convictions): McCallum v Scott 1986 SCCR 645, 1987 SLT 491n. However, see also Anderson v Allan 1985 SCCR 262.

8 Connell v Mitchell 1909 SC (J) 13, 5 Adam 641; Baker v M'Fadyean 1952 SLT (Notes) 69.

9 Criminal Procedure (Scotland) Act 1975, ss 161(1), 357(1)(b).

10 Johnston v Allan 1983 SCCR 500, 1984 SLT 261; O'Neill v Tudhope 1984 SCCR 276, 1984 SLT 424. In the course of the trial the prosecutor may make reference to the previous convictions of the accused where the character of the accused is in issue and the prosecutor is seeking permission from the judge to cross-examine the accused about his character: Leggate v HM Advocate 1988 SCCR 391, 1988 SLT 665. Where the prosecutor is not the person responsible for referring to the accused's record the judge has a discretion as to whether it is appropriate to give the jury any direction on the matter: Fyfe v HM Advocate 1989 SCCR 429.

11 Criminal Procedure (Scotland) Act 1975, s 161(2) (solemn proceedings). There is no specific statutory reference for amending a notice in summary proceedings, but in practice such amendments are frequently allowed on the same principle.

12 Criminal Procedure (Scotland) Act 1975, s 68(2). Where the case is proceeding to trial the accused must give five days' prior notice, but where he is pleading guilty the period of notice is two days: s 68(3) (as amended: see note 1 above).

13 Ibid, s 357(1) (as amended: see note 1 above).

14 If necessary, the prosecutor may be allowed an adjournment to adduce such evidence. For details as to the methods of proof, see ibid, ss 162–164, 357, 358.

7.11. Plea in mitigation. The accused must always be given an opportunity to address the court in mitigation of sentence[1]. While it is competent for the accused to call witnesses to speak to his character or to some medical condition, it is more common to rely on an *ex parte* statement together with any written references, letters or certificates which the accused cares to produce. Should he attempt to set up a false character, the prosecutor can probably lead evidence in rebuttal[2]. Further information concerning the accused's background may also be found in a social inquiry report, and the court will give such weight as it thinks proper to the accused's personal circumstances[3]. If the accused claims that there are special reasons for not being disqualified for driving, he must lead evidence to this effect unless the prosecution accepts the facts[4].

As regards the facts of the case, mitigating circumstances may have emerged in the course of the trial, or alternatively what is said in mitigation may not be disputed by the prosecution. Where the accused has tendered a plea of guilty, he cannot deny any part of the prosecution's narrative of the facts which constitutes an essential element of the offence, and should he seek to do so his proper course is to seek to withdraw his plea[5]. Should he deny other circumstances relative to the offence or advance some mitigating factor (for example provocation), and should such matters continue to remain in dispute between the parties, the court must either ignore them or allow evidence to be led on oath to resolve the dispute[6].

1 *Graham v M'Lennan* 1911 SC (J) 16, 6 Adam 315; *Ewart v Strathern* 1924 JC 45, 1924 SLT 359; *Falconer v Jessop* 1975 SLT (Notes) 78.
2 *HM Advocate v Nimmo* (1839) 2 Swin 338.
3 See C G B Nicholson *The Law and Practice of Sentencing in Scotland* (1981) paras 10-31, 10-32. The accused must be given a copy of any social inquiry report: Criminal Procedure (Scotland) Act 1975 (c 21), ss 192, 393.
4 R W Renton and H H Brown *Criminal Procedure according to the Law of Scotland* (5th edn, 1983) para 15-12; *McLeod v Scoular* 1974 JC 28, 1974 SLT (Notes) 44.
5 *Renton and Brown* para 15-11.
6 *Galloway v Adair* 1947 JC 7, 1947 SLT 23; *Forbes v HM Advocate* 1963 JC 68; *Barn v Smith* 1978 JC 17, 1978 SLT (Notes) 3; *Renton and Brown* para 10-71.

(b) Competent Sentences

(A) DEATH PENALTY

7.12. Death penalty. The death penalty is competent only in cases of treason[1]. Unless the sentence were commuted to life imprisonment, the death penalty would be executed by hanging[2]. After the execution it would be necessary to hold a formal inquiry under the Fatal Accidents and Sudden Deaths Inquiry (Scotland) Act 1976[3].

1 The death penalty for murder was initially abolished by the Murder (Abolition of Death Penalty) Act 1965 (c 71) for a period of five years. This was made permanent by a resolution of Parliament on 31 December 1969. No capital sentence is competent under the Criminal Procedure (Scotland) Act 1975 (c 21): s 220. The death penalty has not been abolished for treason, for which the substantive law is English, although if treason were to be prosecuted in Scotland the procedure and rules of evidence would be the same as those applicable under Scots law for murder: Criminal Justice (Scotland) Act 1980 (c 62), s 39.
2 The death sentence is pronounced as follows: 'A B, the sentence of the Court is that you be taken from this place to the Prison of . . . . [thence to be forthwith transmitted to the Prison of . . . .] therein to be detained until the . . . day of . . . . and upon that day within the said prison of . . . . between the hours of eight and ten o'clock forenoon you suffer death by hanging which is pronounced for Doom': Act of Adjournal (Consolidation) 1988, SI 1988/110, r 75, Sch 1, Form 34.
3 See the Fatal Accidents and Sudden Deaths Inquiry (Scotland) Act 1976 (c 14), s 1(1)(a)(ii).

(B) IMPRISONMENT

7.13. Imprisonment. The only custodial disposal for persons aged twenty-one or over is imprisonment[1]. A person convicted of murder must be sentenced to life imprisonment, and the judge may make a recommendation as to the minimum period which should elapse before the Secretary of State releases the accused on licence[2]. There is no upper limit on the power of the High Court of Justiciary in relation to common law offences, and it may impose a sentence of imprisonment for any fixed period or for life. Where the accused is convicted of a statutory offence, the power of the High Court is limited to the penalty provided by that statute.

The maximum period of imprisonment on indictment in the sheriff court is three years[3], but if the sheriff holds that such a sentence is inadequate, he may remit the accused to the High Court for sentence, giving his reasons for so doing[4]. Where there are two or more accused on the same indictment and the sheriff considers that only one or more should be remitted, he should nevertheless remit all the accused to the High Court[5]. If the accused appears on two separate indictments and the maximum penalty on one of them is within the sheriff's competence, he should sentence the accused on that indictment and remit only the other to the High Court[6].

A sheriff sitting summarily may impose a sentence not exceeding three months for a common law offence, but this period is increased to six months if the accused is convicted of (1) a second or subsequent offence inferring dishonest appropriation of property, or attempt thereat, or (2) a second or subsequent offence inferring personal violence (breach of the peace involving threats of violence not being an offence inferring personal violence for this purpose)[7]. As regards statutory offences,

(a) if the maximum fixed by the statute is less than three months, the court is limited to the statutory maximum;

(b) if the statute states that the offence may be tried either summarily or on indictment and no specific penalty is given for summary prosecution, the maximum is three months[8];

(c) if the statute expressly provides a maximum penalty in excess of three months in summary proceedings the court is limited to the statutory maximum[9];

(d) if the statute provides a different maximum on a first and on a second or subsequent conviction for an offence which is triable only summarily, the maximum penalty is the maximum available on any conviction[10].

The district court may not impose a sentence of imprisonment in excess of sixty days[11] for common law offences and in relation to statutory offences it is not competent to try any statutory offence where the maximum penalty exceeds imprisonment for sixty days or a fine at level 4 on the standard scale[12].

A summary court may not impose imprisonment for less than five days[13], although it may sentence the accused to be detained in legalised police cells, where available, for not more than four days or may order him to be detained in the court or in a police station until 8 pm on the day on which he was convicted[14].

If the accused has not been sentenced to imprisonment or detention on a previous occasion, the court may not pass such a sentence upon him unless, after obtaining a social inquiry report, it considers that no other disposal is appropriate (and in summary cases states and records its reasons for the sentence)[15]. This provision does not apply in cases of murder or where imprisonment is imposed in default of payment of a fine and no time is allowed for payment, or where the accused is convicted of contempt of court[16]. Similarly, a person who has not previously been convicted may not be given a custodial disposal unless he is legally represented or he has applied for and been refused legal aid on financial grounds or has been given an opportunity to apply for legal aid and has refused to do so[17].

In determining the period of imprisonment the court must have regard to any period of time which the accused has spent in custody while awaiting trial or sentence and may order that the sentence is to run from a prior date, such as the date when the accused was first taken into custody[18]. Once the accused has started to serve his sentence he will become entitled to remission of one-third of the period 'with a view to encouraging industry and good conduct', but this period, or part of it, may be forfeited for any breach of prison discipline[19]. When the court is considering the length of the sentence, it is improper to take remission into account[20]. A prisoner may also be released on parole after he has served twelve months (or such shorter period as the Secretary of State may prescribe) or one-third of his sentence, whichever is the longer[21]. The parole licence remains in force until the date when the prisoner would have been released on remission and until that date he is subject to recall[22]. A person sentenced to life imprisonment may be released on parole at any time by the Secretary of State, on the recommendation of the Parole Board for Scotland and after consulting the Lord Justice-General and the trial judge, if available, but he will remain on licence for the rest of his life[23]. Where a person on parole is convicted by the High Court or by the sheriff court (either summarily or on indictment) of an offence punishable on indictment with imprisonment, it may revoke the parole licence whether or not it passes any other sentence[24]. A person whose parole is revoked by a court may not be released on further parole for a further year or a third of the period for which the licence would have remained in force, whichever is the longer[25].

1 Any Act conferring power to pass a sentence of penal servitude or imprisonment with hard labour is to be read as conferring power to pass a sentence of imprisonment: Criminal Procedure (Scotland) Act 1975 (c 21), s 221(1).

2 Ibid, ss 205(1), 205A(1) (substituted and added by the Criminal Justice (Scotland) Act 1980 (c 62), s 43). As to persons under twenty-one convicted of murder, see para 7.14 below. A recommendation as to a minimum period is not binding on the Secretary of State but will be taken into account by him and by the Parole Board for Scotland. The judge must give his reasons for his recommendation, which can be appealed: Criminal Procedure (Scotland) Act 1975, s 205A(2), (3) (as so added).

3 Ibid, ss 2(2), 221(1) proviso (amended by the Criminal Justice (Scotland) Act 1987 (c 41), s 58(1), (3)). Although the amendment increasing the maximum sentence from two to three years came into effect on 1 January 1988, where the offence was committed before that date but sentence is passed after it, a sentence of three years imprisonment is competent: Gillies v HM Advocate 1988 SCCR 345, 1988 SLT 646n.

4 Criminal Procedure (Scotland) Act 1975, s 104(1), (1A) (substituted and added by the Criminal Justice (Scotland) Act 1980, s 12, Sch 4, para 15, and amended by the Criminal Justice (Scotland) Act 1987, s 58(2)). The procedure set out in the Criminal Procedure (Scotland) Act 1975, s 104, must be strictly adhered to: HM Advocate v Galloway (1894) 1 Adam 375, 1 SLT 604; HM Advocate v M'Donald (1896) 3 SLT 317. See further C G B Nicholson The Law and Practice of Sentencing in Scotland (1981) para 8-28.

5 HM Advocate v Clark 1955 JC 88, 1955 SLT 413.

6 HM Advocate v Anderson 1946 JC 81, 1946 SLT 201; HM Advocate v Stern 1974 JC 10, 1974 SLT 2.

7 Criminal Procedure (Scotland) Act 1975, s 209; Adair v Morton 1972 SLT (Notes) 70. In Jackson v McLeod 1987 GWD 16-602 (where the accused presumably had previous convictions for dishonesty) it was held that wasting police time by making a false report was not an offence of dishonesty for this purpose; but in Bradshaw v Jessop 1988 GWD 11-460, where an accused with a bad record for dishonesty gave a false name in order to conceal his identity and was charged with attempting to pervert the course of justice, the High Court upheld a sentence of six months' imprisonment although the maximum sentence for this offence on summary complaint is three months.

8 Criminal Procedure (Scotland) Act 1975, s 289B(1) (added by the Criminal Law Act 1977 (c 45), s 63(1), and substituted by the Criminal Justice Act 1982 (c 48), s 55(2)). For a more detailed discussion, see R W Renton and H H Brown Criminal Procedure according to the Law of Scotland (5th edn, 1983) para 17-03a.

9 Criminal Procedure (Scotland) Act 1975, s 289B(1) (as so added and substituted). Thus, for example, under the Post Office Act 1953 (c 36), s 58(1), the maximum penalty in the sheriff court on summary conviction is two years' imprisonment.

10 Criminal Procedure (Scotland) Act 1975, s 289E (added by the Criminal Justice Act 1982, s 54). Thus, for example, where the Police (Scotland) Act 1967 (c 77), s 41, provides a maximum penalty of three months' imprisonment for a first conviction and nine months for a second, the effect is that the maximum sentence for the first or any subsequent offence is nine months. Similarly the maximum sentence for a contravention of the Criminal Justice (Scotland) Act 1980, s 78 (vandalism), is now six months.

11 Criminal Procedure (Scotland) Act 1975, s 284(a).

12 Criminal Justice (Scotland) Act 1980, s 7(1) (amended by the Criminal Justice Act 1982, s 56(3), Sch 7, para 13).

13 Criminal Procedure (Scotland) Act 1975, s 425(1). As a general rule the imposition of a short sentence of imprisonment is discouraged: see eg *McKenzie v Lockhart* 1986 SCCR 663 (fourteen-day sentence quashed); *Kinney v Tudhope* 1985 SCCR 393 (twenty-one-day sentence quashed); and *Rowlands v Carnegie* 1986 GWD 4–64 and *Anderson v Hilary* 1987 GWD 26–998 (thirty-day sentences quashed). See also C G B Nicholson *The Law and Practice of Sentencing in Scotland* (1981) paras 3–06, 3–07.

14 Criminal Procedure (Scotland) Act 1975, s 424 (amended by the Criminal Justice (Scotland) Act 1980, s 83(2), Sch 7, para 68). Females may not be detained unless supervised by female officers.

15 Ibid, s 42(1), (2). See also *Binnie v Farrell* 1972 JC 49, 1972 SLT 212; *Crilley v MacDougall* 1986 SCCR 587; *Logan v Douglas* 1986 SCCR 590; *McMeckan v Annan* 1989 GWD 33–1515; *Perrie v Valentine* 1990 GWD 10–537. Information supplied by the prosecution or defence may not be used as alternative to a social inquiry report: *Auld v Herron* 1969 JC 4. For the rule regarding murder and a definition of a previous sentence of imprisonment or detention, see the Criminal Justice (Scotland) Act 1980, s 41(2), (3), applied by s 42(3), and *Renton and Brown* para 17–08. While the court must consider the social inquiry report it is not obliged to follow its recommendations: *Kyle v Cruickshank* 1961 JC 1; *Scott v MacDonald* 1961 SLT 257; *Hogg v Heatlie* 1962 SLT 39.

16 See the definition of 'sentence' in the Criminal Procedure (Scotland) Act 1975, s 462(1) (substituted by the Criminal Justice (Scotland) Act 1980, Sch 7, para 76(c)). See also *Sullivan v McLeod* 1980 SLT (Notes) 99.

17 Criminal Justice (Scotland) Act 1980, s 41(1).

18 Criminal Procedure (Scotland) Act 1975, ss 218, 431 (amended by the Criminal Justice (Scotland) Act 1980, s 83(2), (3), Sch 7, paras 40, 70, Sch 8). Although the court is obliged to have regard to time spent on remand, it is not obliged to backdate the sentence: *Lawther v HM Advocate* 1989 GWD 36–1653. In *Morrison v Scott* 1987 SCCR 376 and *McLaughlin v Jessop* 1989 GWD 39–1805 it was held that where the imposition of sentence is postponed because of the necessity of obtaining a report and the accused is meantime detained in custody and the sentence eventually imposed is the maximum, the sentence ought to be backdated to the date of the conclusion of the trial (ie the date of conviction). However, see also *Inglis v Carmichael* 1987 GWD 25–930, where the maximum sentence was imposed and was not backdated after a six-week remand, and *Hepburn v Jessop* 1987 GWD 36–1276, where the court imposed, but did not backdate, the maximum sentence after taking account of the time spent on remand. In *Johnstone v Carmichael* 1990 GWD 3–118 it was held that the sheriff was entitled not to backdate a custodial sentence to take account of two weeks' custody on remand. In *Neilson v HM Advocate* 1989 SCCR 527 it was stated that where the court decides to backdate the sentence on an accused who has been detained in custody and who has granted a s 102 letter, the sentence should be backdated to the date of the letter, whereas in *Killoran v Lees* 1989 GWD 30–1376 it was held that the court was entitled not to backdate a sentence where the accused could have pleaded guilty at an earlier date (although see para 6.09 and the cases in note 15 thereto above). The appeal court will not entertain an argument for backdating where this has not been made a ground of appeal: *Aitchison v HM Advocate* 1989 GWD 38–1753.

19 Prisons (Scotland) Act 1952 (c 61), s 20(1); Prison (Scotland) Rules 1952, SI 1952/565, r 37 (amended by SI 1981/1222). See also *Nicholson* paras 11–17, 11–19.

20 *Nicholson* para 8–40; *Waddell v HM Advocate* 1988 GWD 24–1022.

21 Criminal Justice Act 1967 (c 80), s 60(1), (1A) (amended and added by the Criminal Justice Act 1982, s 33(a)). Further as to parole, see *Renton and Brown* paras 17–12, 17–13, and *Nicholson* paras 11–23–11–34, and the annual reports of the Parole Board for Scotland.

22 Criminal Justice Act 1967, s 60(6) (amended by the Criminal Law Act 1977, s 65(4), Sch 12, para 7(4)).

23 Criminal Justice Act 1967, s 61(1), (4) (amended by the Criminal Justice (Scotland) Act 1980, Sch 7, para 18, and the Criminal Justice Act 1982, s 77, Sch 14, para 19).

24 Criminal Procedure (Scotland) Act 1975, ss 213(1), 422(1). This power is not given to the district court.

25 Criminal Justice Act 1967, s 62(10).

(C) DETENTION

7.14. Detention. It is not competent to impose a sentence of imprisonment on a person under twenty-one years of age[1], and the only custodial sentence for a person who is not less than sixteen but under twenty-one is a sentence of detention[2]. The period of detention must not exceed the maximum period of imprisonment which might otherwise have been imposed[2]. An accused convicted of murder will be sentenced to detention for life if he is aged eighteen but less than twenty-one; if he is under eighteen he will be sentenced to detention without limit of time in such place and under such conditions as the Secretary of State may direct[3].

The rule regarding legal representation is the same as for persons who are sentenced to imprisonment, as are the rules regarding the obtaining of social inquiry reports, with the exception that a social inquiry report must always be obtained before imposing detention, whether or not the accused has previously been sentenced to a custodial sentence[4]. The court must also take account of any information concerning the offender's character and physical and mental condition[4]. Any sentence of detention will be served in a young offenders institution[5].

The rules regarding remission of sentence[6] and parole[7] are the same as for imprisonment, except that the licence continues for the full period of the sentence and not just until the remission date; in addition, an offender sentenced to eighteen months or more may be released on licence rather than on remission or on parole[8], and any person sentenced to more than six months' detention may be placed under supervision after his release for a specified period[9]. Where an accused on supervision is convicted of an offence punishable with imprisonment, the court may order his recall[10].

Where the accused is under the age of sixteen (or is under the age of eighteen but is subject to a supervision requirement imposed by a children's hearing), his case will normally be dealt with by a children's hearing. Should he be prosecuted in the sheriff court or the High Court, the court may call for the advice of a children's hearing as to disposal and must do so if the child is already under supervision[11]. If the court thereafter decides to impose a custodial sentence, the child will be ordered to be detained for a specified period in such place and on such conditions as the Secretary of State may direct[12], and should the child be prosecuted on a summary complaint, the sheriff may order him to be so detained for any period not exceeding one year in local authority residential care[13]. When a child is released from detention he may be placed under supervision for a specified period[14].

1 Criminal Procedure (Scotland) Act 1975 (c 21), ss 207(1), 415(1) (substituted by the Criminal Justice (Scotland) Act 1980 (c 62), s 45(1)).
2 Criminal Procedure (Scotland) Act 1975, ss 207(2), 415(2) (as so substituted).
3 Criminal Procedure (Scotland) Act 1975, s 205(2), (3) (substituted by the Criminal Justice (Scotland) Act 1980, s 43). A person detained in a young offenders institution may be transferred to prison when he becomes twenty-one, and must be so transferred before he is twenty-three: Criminal Justice (Scotland) Act 1963 (c 39), s 10 (amended by the Criminal Procedure (Scotland) Act 1975, s 461(1), Sch 9, para 33, and the Criminal Justice (Scotland) Act 1980, s 45(2), Sch 5, para 1).
4 See para 7.13 above, and the Criminal Procedure (Scotland) Act 1975, ss 207(3), (4), 415(3), (4) (as substituted: see note 1 above).
5 Ibid, s 207(5), 415(5) (substituted by the Criminal Justice Act 1988 (c 33), s 124(1)). See also C G B Nicholson The Law and Practice of Sentencing in Scotland (1981) para 3-15. See further note 3 above.
6 Young Offenders (Scotland) Rules 1965, SI 1965/195, r 35; Detention Centre (Scotland) (Amendment) Rules 1983, SI 1983/1739. See also R W Renton and H H Brown Criminal Procedure according to the Law of Scotland (5th edn, 1983) paras 7-14-7-16.
7 Criminal Justice Act 1967 (c 80), s 60(8)(b).
8 Ibid, s 60(3)(b), (8)(b), applied by the Criminal Procedure (Scotland) Act 1975, ss 207(11), 415(11).
9 For further details, see the Criminal Justice (Scotland) Act 1963, s 12 (substituted by the Criminal Justice (Scotland) Act 1980, Sch 5, para 2, and amended by the Law Reform (Miscellaneous Provisions) (Scotland) Act 1985 (c 73), s 45(2)), and Renton and Brown paras 17-15, 17-16.

10 Criminal Procedure (Scotland) Act 1975, ss 212, 421 (the former amended by the Criminal Justice (Scotland) Act 1980, s 83(2), Sch 7, para 38, and the Criminal Justice (Scotland) Act 1987 (c 41), s 70(1), Sch 1, para 11, and the latter amended by the Criminal Justice (Scotland) Act 1980, Sch 7, para 67, and the Criminal Justice Act 1982 (c 48), ss 77, 78, Sch 15, para 18, Sch 16)).

11 Criminal Procedure (Scotland) Act 1975, ss 173, 372 (s 173 being amended by the Criminal Justice (Scotland) Act 1980, Sch 7, para 35). For a definition of 'child', see the Social Work (Scotland) Act 1968 (c 49), s 30, applied by the Criminal Procedure (Scotland) Act 1975, s 462(1). For further details about children, see *Nicholson* ch 5, and *Renton and Brown* ch 19. The court may also ask for advice from a children's hearing in respect of any person aged under seventeen and a half who is not under supervision: s 373; *Renton and Brown* para 19-23.

12 Criminal Procedure (Scotland) Act 1975, s 206(1) (substituted by the Criminal Justice (Scotland) Act 1980, s 44).

13 Criminal Procedure (Scotland) Act 1975, s 413(1) (substituted by the Criminal Justice (Scotland) Act 1987, s 59(1)).

14 Criminal Procedure (Scotland) Act 1975, s 206A (added by the Law Reform (Miscellaneous Provisions) (Scotland) Act 1985, s 45(1)).

(D) FINE

7.15. Fines. There is no maximum limit to the amount of a fine which may be imposed on conviction on indictment in the High Court of Justiciary or the sheriff court, even where the conviction is for a statutory offence for which a maximum fine is provided[1]. Where a common law offence is prosecuted summarily in the sheriff court the maximum fine[2] is the prescribed sum[3], and where such an offence is prosecuted in the district court the maximum fine is level 4 on the standard scale[4]. The maximum fines for statutory offences tried summarily in the sheriff court or tried in the district court are limited either by the statute creating the offence or by the Criminal Procedure (Scotland) Act 1975[5].

When the court is determining the amount of a fine it must take account of the means of the offender so far as known[6], and while in certain circumstances it may restrict the fine to a sum which the offender can pay within a reasonable time[7], in others it may order him to pay it over a lengthy period in order to 'extend the period over which he has to face up to his responsibilities to one which is commensurate with the seriousness of the offence'[8]. A court of summary jurisdiction may also order that the offender be searched and any money in his possession applied towards payment of the fine unless the court is satisfied that the money does not belong to him or that its loss would be more injurious to his family than his imprisonment or detention[9].

Fines imposed in the High Court are payable to HM Exchequer[10], and all other fines are paid to the clerk of court[11] (including fines initially paid to a police constable or governor of a prison). A fine may be paid at the bar of the court at the time when it is imposed. A court may refuse time to pay the fine if the offender appears to have sufficient means to pay forthwith or he does not ask for time to pay or he fails to satisfy the court that he has a fixed abode or if the court is satisfied for any other special reason that no time should be allowed[12]. If time to pay is refused and the offender fails to pay the fine, the court may impose an alternative period of imprisonment (or detention)[13] unless the offender is not legally represented and has not previously been sentenced to imprisonment or detention[14]. Unless there is a specific reason for refusing time to pay, the court must normally give the offender time to pay or allow him to pay by instalments and allow seven days to pay the fine or the first instalment[15]. Should the offender apply either orally or in writing for further time to pay, the court must grant such an extension unless it is satisfied that the failure to pay was wilful or that there is no reasonable prospect of payment if an extension of time is granted[16]. The court may also reduce the amount of any instalments or order them to be paid at longer intervals than originally fixed[17].

Where the offender is allowed time to pay the fine or is ordered to pay by instalments, the court must not, at the same time as imposing the fine, impose imprisonment in the event of a future default unless the offender is present and the court decides, having regard to the gravity of the offence[18] or the character of the offender or other special reason, that it is expedient to imprison on default without further inquiry; the court must state its reasons for such a decision and in summary cases the reasons must be entered in the record[19]. An offender allowed time to pay (or ordered to pay by instalments) may be placed under supervision at the time when the fine is imposed, or on a subsequent occasion, until the fine is paid, and such supervision is compulsory before the court may impose detention (for default) on an offender aged under twenty-one[20]. Unless imprisonment for default is imposed at the same time as the fine, the court may not impose imprisonment or detention until at some future diet (known as the means inquiry court) it has inquired in the offender's presence into the reason why the fine has not been paid[21]. The offender may be brought before the court by citation or by warrant[22]. It is not necessary to make such an inquiry if the accused is in prison. Where the accused has previously been placed under supervision the court may not impose imprisonment or detention without considering a written or oral report from the supervisor[23].

The court may order that the fine be recovered by way of civil diligence[24], and this is the only means of recovery where the accused is a company, association, incorporation or body of trustees[25]. It may also be used in the first instance where the accused is an individual and the court thinks it expedient, and if it is unsuccessful, imprisonment remains competent thereafter[26].

A fine may be remitted in whole or in part at any time by the court which is at that time responsible for its enforcement (which is the sheriff court when the fine is imposed by the High Court)[27]. The accused does not require to be present when the fine is remitted[28], and where he has been committed to prison for non-payment of the fine, he will be released if the whole fine is remitted or, where part of the fine is remitted, his period of imprisonment will be reduced by the same proportion[29].

1 Criminal Procedure (Scotland) Act 1975 (c 21), s 193A (added by the Criminal Law Act 1977 (c 45), s 63(1), Sch 11, para 1, and amended by the Criminal Justice (Scotland) Act 1980 (c 62), s 83(2), Sch 7, para 37, and the Criminal Justice Act 1982 (c 48), s 77, Sch 15, para 17).
2 Where the accused is a first offender the maximum penalty should be imposed only in exceptional circumstances: *McCandless v MacDougall* 1987 SCCR 206.
3 Criminal Procedure (Scotland) Act 1975, s 289(a) (amended by the Criminal Law Act 1977, Sch 11, para 4). As to the prescribed sum, see para 2.10, note 1, above.
4 Criminal Procedure (Scotland) Act 1975, s 284(b) (amended by the Criminal Law Act 1977, Sch 11, para 3(1), and the Criminal Justice Act 1982, s 56(3), Sch 7, para 4). As to the standard scale, see para 2.12, note 1, above.
5 The provisions relating to fines for statutory offences prosecuted in a summary court are somewhat complex. For further details, see R W Renton and H H Brown *Criminal Procedure according to the Law of Scotland* (5th edn, 1983) paras 17-22a–17-22d, and C G B Nicholson *The Law and Practice of Sentencing in Scotland* (1981) paras 2-74, 2-75, 2-75a. In the case of certain minor road traffic offences a fixed penalty may be imposed in lieu of a fine determined by the court: see para 7.26 below.
6 Criminal Procedure (Scotland) Act 1975, s 395(1) (applied to solemn procedure by s 194 (substituted by the Criminal Justice (Scotland) Act 1980, s 47)); R Black 'Fine Tuning' 1986 SLT (News) 185. See *Barbour v Robertson, Ram v Robertson* 1943 JC 46, 1943 SLT 215; *Kilpatrick v Allan* 28 May 1985 (unreported). See also eg *Brown v Carmichael* 1987 SCCR 183; *Hamilton v Scott* 1987 SCCR 188; *Thomson v Allan* 1987 SCCR 201; *Wilson v HM Advocate* 1987 GWD 40–1479; *Mallin v Normand* 1988 GWD 6–229; *Neilson v MacPhail* 1988 GWD 9–351; *Grenfell v Carmichael* 1988 GWD 17–739; *Budge v Hingston* 1988 GWD 17–742; *Miller v Normand* 1988 GWD 17–765; *Milligan v Jessop* 1988 SCCR 137; *Currys Ltd v Jessop* 1988 SCCR 447; *Gray v Wilson* 1989 GWD 34–1585; *Scott v Lowe* 1990 SCCR 15 — but see also *Buchan v McNaughton* 1990 SCCR 13.

7 A reasonable time may exceed twelve months: *Johnston v Lockhart* 1987 SCCR 337; *Blyth v McGlennan* 1989 GWD 28–1263. But three years is excessive: *Watt v McLeod* 1988 GWD 9–361. See also note 8 below.

8 *Lambert v Tudhope* 1982 SCCR 144; *Glen v McLeod* 1982 SCCR 449. See also *Mohammed v Allan* 1987 GWD 6–181, where it was held that a period of sixty weeks would act as a deterrent, *Allison v Allan* 1987 GWD 39–1361, where it was held that a period of two years would act as a reminder to the accused, and *Taylor v Cardle* 1988 SCCR 450, where the High Court upheld a fine of £280 but ordered that it be paid at £3 per week.

9 Criminal Procedure (Scotland) Act 1975, s 395(2) (amended by the Criminal Justice (Scotland) Act 1980, Sch 7, para 60). This provision does not apply on indictment.

10 Criminal Procedure (Scotland) Act 1975, s 203.

11 Ibid, s 412. Where the offender lives outwith the jurisdiction of the court, enforcement of payment may be transferred to the court having jurisdiction over his place of residence: s 403. See further *Renton and Brown* 17–36, and *Nicholson* paras 2–97–2–99.

12 Ibid, s 396(2) (as applied: see note 6 above). The court must state its reasons for refusing time to pay: s 396(3). See also *Sullivan v McLeod* 1980 SLT (Notes) 99 and *Robertson v Jessop* 1989 SCCR 387. The reason must be entered in the record: Criminal Procedure (Scotland) Act 1975, s 401(1). However, see also *Bruce v Hogg* 1966 JC 33, 1966 SLT (Notes) 77. The nature of the offence may not be considered as a special reason: *Barbour v Robertson, Ram v Robertson* 1943 JC 46, 1943 SLT 215.

13 Criminal Procedure (Scotland) Act 1975, s 396(2) (as so applied). The maximum period of imprisonment (or detention) which may be imposed for non-payment of a fine is as follows:

AMOUNT OF FINE	MAXIMUM PERIOD
Not exceeding £50.	7 days
Exceeding £50 but not exceeding £100.	14 days
Exceeding £100 but not exceeding £400.	30 days
Exceeding £400 but not exceeding £1,000.	60 days
Exceeding £1,000 but not exceeding £2,000.	90 days
Exceeding £2,000 but not exceeding £5,000.	6 months
Exceeding £5,000 but not exceeding £10,000.	9 months
Exceeding £10,000 but not exceeding £20,000.	12 months
Exceeding £20,000 but not exceeding £50,000.	18 months
Exceeding £50,000 but not exceeding £100,000.	2 years
Exceeding £100,000 but not exceeding £250,000.	3 years
Exceeding £250,000 but not exceeding £1m.	5 years
Exceeding £1m.	10 years

These periods are fixed by s 407(1A) (added by the Criminal Justice (Scotland) Act 1980, s 50, and amended by the Increase of Criminal Penalties etc (Scotland) Order 1984, SI 1984/526, art 5, the Law Reform (Miscellaneous Provisions) (Scotland) Act 1985 (c 73), s 40, and the Criminal Justice (Scotland) Act 1987 (c 41), s 67(1)). For a child under the age of sixteen the maximum period is one month's detention in a place chosen by the local authority: Criminal Procedure (Scotland) Act 1975, s 406 (as so applied). A period of imprisonment or detention imposed for non-payment of a fine or compensation order is not a sentence within the meaning of s 462(1) (amended by the Criminal Justice (Scotland) Act 1980, Sch 7, para 76(c)), and it may be ordered to run consecutively to any other sentence imposed upon the offender at the same time (*Beattie v HM Advocate* 1986 SCCR 605; *Cartledge v McLeod* 1988 SCCR 129, 1988 SLT 389 (Notes); *Young v Procurator Fiscal Kilmarnock* 5 April 1990, High Court (unreported)) unless by doing so the sentence would exceed the limits on the court's sentencing powers (*Kesson v Heatly* 1964 JC 40; *Fraser v Herron* 1968 JC 1, 1968 SLT 149). An order that the sentence is to run consecutively may not be made in the absence of the offender: *Campbell v Jessop* 1987 SCCR 670, 1988 SLT 160 (Notes). The sentence may not be ordered to run consecutively to a sentence which is currently being served (ie to a sentence imposed on a previous occasion: *Cain v Procurator Fiscal Kilmarnock* 5 April 1990, High Court (unreported)). Similarly since imprisonment or detention in default is not a 'sentence', if a sentence of imprisonment or detention is imposed for some other offence at a subsequent date, it cannot be ordered to run consecutively to the period being served for default: *Picken v McGlennan* 1990 GWD 12–604.

Where a number of fines are imposed on the same day, whether on the same complaint or on separate complaints, the fines are aggregated for the purpose of determining the alternative: Criminal Procedure (Scotland) Act 1975, s 407(1B) (as so added). See also *Renton and Brown* para 15–38 and *Nicholson* para 2–103, who disagree on the interpretation of this provision. Where part of the fine is paid, the period of imprisonment is proportionate to the part of the fine remaining unpaid: Criminal Procedure (Scotland) Act 1975, s 407(1D) (as so added). Where the offender is committed to prison for non-payment he may pay all or part of his fine to the governor, in which case he will be released or his period of imprisonment will be proportionately reduced: s 409 (amended by the Criminal Justice (Scotland) Act 1980, Sch 7, para 65, and applied: see note 6 above). A person aged seventeen or over against whom an extract conviction is issued for imprisonment for non-payment may be arrested in any part of the United Kingdom and may serve his imprisonment in the part of the United Kingdom in which he was arrested: Criminal Law Act 1977, s 38A (added by the Criminal Justice (Scotland) Act 1980, s 51, and amended by the Criminal Justice Act 1982, s 77, Sch 14, para 39).

14 Criminal Justice (Scotland) Act 1980, s 41. Section 42 and the Criminal Procedure (Scotland) Act 1975, ss 207 and 415 (see para 7.14 above), do not apply.

15 Ibid, s 396(1) (as applied: see note 6 above). The court may allow time to pay even where the accused does not request it: *Fraser v Herron* 1968 JC 1, 1968 SLT 149.

16 Criminal Procedure (Scotland) Act 1975, s 397 (amended by the Criminal Law Act 1977, Sch 11, para 8, and applied: see note 6 above). Before granting an extension the court should give the prosecutor an opportunity to be heard, although in practice this rule is ignored: see *Nicholson* para 2-87.

17 Criminal Procedure (Scotland) Act 1975, s 399 (amended by the Criminal Justice (Scotland) Act 1980, s 83(2), (3), Sch 7, para 62, Sch 8, and as applied: see note 6 above).

18 As to the gravity of the offence, see *Finnie v McLeod* 1983 SCCR 387, and *Dunlop v Allan* 1984 SCCR 329.

19 Criminal Procedure (Scotland) Act 1975, ss 396(4), 401(1) (as applied: see note 6 above). See *Buchanan v Hamilton* 1988 SCCR 379, where it was held that the nature of the offence was not a valid reason for imposing imprisonment on default without further inquiry.

20 Criminal Procedure (Scotland) Act 1975, s 400(1)–(5) (as so applied). The supervision will be by 'such person as the court may from time to time appoint': s 400(1). In most instances the supervision will be by the local social work department, but this is not essential and in some courts supervision is undertaken by court officials known as 'fines enforcement officers'. The supervision may be terminated at any time at the discretion of the court or if payment of the fine is transferred to another court: s 400(3). An offender under the age of twenty-one need not be placed on supervision if the court is satisfied that it is impracticable to do so: s 400(4). See also *Nicholson* paras 2-91, 2-92.

21 Ibid, s 398(1) (amended by the Criminal Justice (Scotland) Act 1980, Sch 7, para 61, and as applied: see note 6 above). The prosecutor is not usually present at the means inquiry court, and it is not common for the accused to be legally represented. When the offender appears before the Means Enquiry Court, the court may impose an immediate term of imprisonment in default of payment (see note 13 above) or may allow further time to pay, but if it adopts the latter course it may not at the same time impose an alternative period of imprisonment in the event of any future further default: *Stevenson v McGlennan* 1989 SCCR 711; *Craig v Procurator Fiscal Dundee* 5 April 1990, High Court (unreported). In the event of such further default the offender would require to be brought before a subsequent Means Enquiry Court which could impose an immediate term of imprisonment in default (unless it allowed even more time to pay). See further *Renton and Brown* para 17-29 and *Nicholson* para 2-89.

22 Criminal Procedure (Scotland) Act 1975, s 398(2).

23 Ibid, s 400(6).

24 Ibid, s 396(6), and s 411(1) (amended by the Criminal Justice (Scotland) Act 1980, s 52, Sch 7, para 66, Sch 8) (both as applied: see note 6 above).

25 Criminal Procedure (Scotland) Act 1975, s 333(a).

26 Criminal Justice (Scotland) Act 1980, s 52. See further *Renton and Brown* para 17-33 and *Nicholson* paras 2-109–2-111.

27 Criminal Procedure (Scotland) Act 1975, s 395A(1) (added by the Criminal Justice (Scotland) Act 1980, s 49, and as applied: see note 6 above).

28 Criminal Procedure (Scotland) Act 1975, s 395A(3) (as so added and applied).

29 Ibid, s 395A(2) (as so added and applied).

(E) COMPENSATION ORDER

7.16. Compensation orders. Where the accused is convicted and the court is not disposing of the case by way of an absolute discharge or probation, or is not deferring sentence to a later date, it may order the accused to pay compensation in addition to or instead of dealing with him in some other way[1]. The maximum amount of compensation for each offence is the same amount as the court can impose as a fine for a common law offence, which means that there is no limit when the accused is convicted on indictment; in the sheriff summary court, the limit is the prescribed sum, and in the district court the limit is level 4 on the standard scale[2]. These maxima apply to each offence, regardless of the number of offences on any particular indictment or complaint, and may be imposed in addition to a fine[3].

A compensation order may not be made in respect of loss suffered in consequence of the death of any person, or injury, loss or damage arising out of a road accident (except for damage to, but not loss of, a dishonestly taken vehicle)[4]. Apart from these exceptions, compensation may be ordered 'for any personal injury, loss or damage caused (whether directly or indirectly) by the acts which constituted the offence'[5]. The victim does not require to lodge a formal claim. The amount is not limited to physical damage and may allow for inconvenience caused to the victim; the damage need not be capable of precise valuation and does not require to be proved by corroborated evidence[6]. The scope for compensation is therefore very wide; it may be paid to anyone who has sustained loss or injury[7], although it may have a bearing on any subsequent award of damages in a civil case[8]. Where the court orders compensation to be paid to more than one person, it may determine the order in which each is to be paid[9].

When considering whether to make a compensation order and the amount to be paid under it, the court must have regard to the means of the offender, and if he is serving or is about to serve a custodial sentence it may not take account of earnings contingent on his obtaining employment after his release[10]. Should the means of the offender preclude payment of both a fine and a compensation order, the court 'should prefer a compensation order'[11]. Where the court imposes both a fine and a compensation order, any payments by the accused are first applied in satisfaction of the order[12]. Payment of the order is made to the clerk of court who will thereafter forward the money to the victim[13], who has no right to enforce the order[14]. Compensation orders are enforced in the same way as if they were fines and are governed by the same provisions regarding time for payment, payment by instalments, imprisonment in default, remission and transfer of enforcement to another court, except that on the occasion when the court makes the compensation order, it may not impose imprisonment for non-payment at the same time and can only do so at a subsequent means inquiry court[15]. It is competent to impose imprisonment in respect of a fine and not in respect of a compensation order but not *vice versa*, and where imprisonment is imposed on both (at a means inquiry court) the amounts are aggregated for the purpose of calculating the period of imprisonment[16]. Where the accused is imprisoned for default, his liability to pay the order is extinguished although the victim's civil remedies will remain[17].

1 Criminal Justice (Scotland) Act 1980 (c 62), s 58(1). A compensation order cannot be made along with an absolute discharge or probation, both of which are made without proceeding to conviction (Criminal Procedure (Scotland) Act 1975 (c 21), ss 383, 384(1)): Criminal Justice (Scotland) Act 1980, s 58(1) proviso (a), (b). Compensation or restitution (but not a formal compensation order) can still be made a condition of probation or deferred sentence. A compensation order may also be made at the end of a period of deferred sentence: s 58(1) proviso (c). In *Gibson v Lockhart* 11 May 1983 (unreported) a compensation order was imposed in the sheriff court, and on appeal the High Court of Justiciary deferred sentence to see if it would be paid: see C G B Nicholson *The Law and Practice of Sentencing in Scotland* (1981) para 10-75 (supplement). Compensation orders should not be confused with compensation assessed and awarded by the Criminal Injuries Compensation Board and paid by the state to a victim of a crime of violence regardless of whether the offender is convicted or even prosecuted. See, however, note 5 below. Details of the Criminal Injuries Compensation Board scheme (for which see the Criminal Justice Act 1988 (c 33), ss 108–117, Sch 7) are obtainable at any police office or by writing to the CICB, Blythswood House, 200 West Regent Street, Glasgow G2 4SW) (tel 041–221 0945). The Board will not consider a claim which amounts to less than £750.

2 Criminal Justice (Scotland) Act 1980, s 59(2), (3) (amended by the Criminal Justice Act 1982
   (c 48), s 56(3), Sch 7, para 16). As to the prescribed sum and the standard scale, see respectively
   para 2.10, note 1, and para 2.12, note 1, above.
3 Criminal Justice (Scotland) Act 1980, s 58(1); R W Renton and H H Brown *Criminal Procedure
   according to the Law of Scotland* (5th edn, 1983) para 17-39.
4 Criminal Justice (Scotland) Act 1980, s 58(2), (3); see the annotated edition of the Act in *Scottish
   Current Law Statutes*. See also *Renton and Brown* para 17-38. Conversely, if the accused is
   convicted of unlawful killing, he is precluded by the Forfeiture Act 1982 (c 34) from deriving any
   financial benefit (such as from life insurances) from his own crime, although he may petition the
   court to modify this rule: see ss 1, 2; *Cross* 1987 SCLR 356, 1987 SLT 384, OH; *Gilchrist, Petitioner*
   1989 GWD 40–1902.
5 Criminal Justice (Scotland) Act 1980, s 58(1). A compensation order should not be made if the
   victim's conduct would have prevented him from recovering compensation from the Criminal
   Injuries Compensation Board: *Brown v Normand* 1988 SCCR 229.
6 *Stewart v HM Advocate* 1982 SCCR 203; *Goodhall v Carmichael* 1984 SCCR 247; *Carmichael v
   Siddique* 1985 SCCR 145, Sh Ct; *Murphy v Carmichael* 1988 GWD 6–237; *Kane v Docherty* 1989
   GWD 28–1276, but see also *Lawrie v O'Brien* 1990 GWD 2–85; *Mackay v Lowe* 1990 GWD 3–121
   and *Smillie v Wilson* 1990 SCCR 133, 1990 GWD 9–478 where amounts awarded by compensation orders were reduced or disallowed on appeal.
7 *Tudhope v Furphy* 1982 SCCR 575 at 581, 1984 SLT (Sh Ct) 33 at 36, per Sheriff Kearney: '...
   section 60(1) of the 1980 Act [see below] can properly be read as empowering the sheriff clerk to
   pay out any compensation gathered in to the person who, on the best information available to
   him, is entitled to that fund . . . and to seek legal guidance from the sheriff [who may], after such
   inquiry as he considers appropriate and reasonable . . . issue appropriate directions to the sheriff
   clerk as to how the fund should be distributed and as to whose receipt should constitute a valid
   and sufficient discharge'.
8 See the Criminal Justice (Scotland) Act 1980, s 67.
9 Act of Adjournal (Consolidation) 1988, SI 1988/110, rr 78(d), 125(2)(d).
10 Criminal Justice (Scotland) Act 1980, s 59; *Watt v McLeod* 1988 GWD 9–361; *Clark v Cardle* 1989
   SCCR 92. See also para 7.15, note 6, above.
11 Criminal Justice (Scotland) Act 1980, s 61.
12 Ibid, s 62.
13 Ibid, s 60(1). Where imprisonment or detention is imposed for non-payment, payment may also
   be made to a police constable or prison governor under the Criminal Procedure (Scotland) Act
   1975, s 401(3) or s 409(1) (respectively added by the Criminal Justice (Scotland) Act 1980, s 83(2),
   Sch 7, para 62, and amended by Sch 7, para 65).
14 Only the court may enforce payment of the order: ibid, s 60(2). If the victim is under a legal
   disability the money is administered in the same way as money paid into court in respect of civil
   damages to such a person: Act of Adjournal (Consolidation) 1988, rr 82, 125(10).
15 Criminal Justice (Scotland) Act 1980, s 66(1), (2), applying to compensation orders the fines
   enforcement provisions of the Criminal Procedure (Scotland) Act 1975, excluding that part of
   s 396(4), (5), which empowers the court in certain circumstances to impose imprisonment for
   default at the same time as imposing the fine.
16 Criminal Justice (Scotland) Act 1980, s 66(2) proviso.
17 Ibid, s 67, which deals generally with the effect of a compensation order on a subsequent award
   of damages.

(F) CAUTION

7.17. Caution. The court can order the accused to lodge a sum of money
known as caution for his good behaviour for a period not exceeding the ensuing
twelve months in the sheriff court or six months in the district court[1]. While
presumably there is no limit to the maximum sum which may be ordered on
indictment[2], the maxima in summary proceedings in the sheriff court and in the
district court are respectively the amounts of the prescribed sum and of level 4
on the standard scale[3]. Caution may be ordered in addition to or in lieu of
imprisonment or a fine[3]. In summary procedure caution may be found by
consignation of the amount with the clerk of court or alternatively by a bond of
caution. In the case of consignation, the provisions relating to the payment of
fines and the imposition of imprisonment in default apply equally to caution,

except that it cannot be paid by instalments and the accused cannot be placed under supervision pending payment[4].

'Good behaviour' is not defined and, in practice, the court will order forfeiture of the caution only if the accused is convicted of a subsequent offence. Forfeiture is granted on the motion of the prosecutor, who normally presents a summary application for this purpose. Where the court orders forfeiture following a bond of caution, it may grant time for payment, or order recovery by civil diligence or order the accused to be imprisoned for the maximum periods prescribed[5] if he fails to pay the amount due under the bond within six days of receiving a charge to that effect[6].

1 Criminal Procedure (Scotland) Act 1975 (c 21), ss 284(c), 289(b). See also s 193 (amended by the Criminal Justice (Scotland) Act 1980 (c 62), ss 46(2), 83(3), Sch 8).
2 See R W Renton and H H Brown *Criminal Procedure according to the Law of Scotland* (5th edn, 1983) para 17-37.
3 Criminal Procedure (Scotland) Act 1975, ss 284(c), 289(b) (amended by the Criminal Law Act 1977 (c 45), s 63(1), Sch 11, paras 3, 4, and the Criminal Justice Act 1982 (c 48), s 56(3), Sch 7, para 5).
4 See the Criminal Procedure (Scotland) Act 1975, ss 396(1), 398(1), 407(1A), (2) (as variously amended). Section 397, which allows fines to be paid by instalments, and s 400, which deals with supervision pending payment of a fine, make no mention of compensation. Where imprisonment in default is not imposed at the same time as caution is ordered, s 398(1) does not provide for the accused to be brought before a means inquiry court, although in practice this is done.
5 See para 7.15, note 13, above.
6 Criminal Procedure (Scotland) Act 1975, s 303(1), and s 411 (amended by the Criminal Justice (Scotland) Act 1980, ss 52, 83(2), (3), Sch 7, para 66, Sch 8). No provision is made for solemn procedure.

(G) COMMUNITY SERVICE

7.18. Community service. The Community Service by Offenders (Scotland) Act 1978 empowers the court to dispose of the case of an offender aged sixteen years or over convicted of an offence punishable by imprisonment (other than murder) by ordering him to perform not less than forty and not more than two hundred and forty hours of unpaid work known as 'community service'[1]. Such an order may be accompanied by disqualification from driving, caution, forfeiture or a compensation order where appropriate, but otherwise it cannot be imposed with any other sentence[2]. The sentence can be given only if the court has been notified by the Secretary of State that there are arrangements for community service in the locality of the offender's residence[3]. Before making the order, the court must obtain a report from a local authority officer about the offender and be satisfied that he is suitable for such work and that provision has been made for him to perform it[4]. The offender or his solicitor is entitled to a copy of the report[5]. The court is also required to explain the purpose and effect of the order to the offender and obtain his consent to it[6]. An order may be made concurrently with or consecutive to another community service order, provided the total number of hours does not exceed two hundred and forty[7].

After the order is made, the offender must report to the local authority officer and tell him without delay of any change of address or times at which he usually works[8]. He must perform such work at such times as the officer instructs for the number of hours specified in the order, and must do so within twelve months (subject to the power of the court to review or amend the order)[9]. The officer must arrange enforcement of the order in such a way that, so far as practicable, it does not conflict with the offender's religious beliefs or interfere with his normal hours of work or attendance at any educational establishment[10].

Should the offender fail to perform the work satisfactorily or otherwise fail to obtemper the order, the local authority officer may appear before the court and give evidence to that effect, whereupon the court may issue a warrant to arrest or cite the offender[11]. When the offender subsequently appears before the court, he will be asked whether he admits or denies breaching the order. If he denies doing so a hearing will be fixed, if necessary, to determine the issue unless it can be determined then and there. No formal procedure is laid down for a hearing, but in normal practice the officer and such other witnesses as are necessary give evidence on oath and may be cross-examined by the offender, who is also afforded an opportunity to lead evidence[12]. If it is proved that the offender has failed without reasonable excuse to comply with any requirement of the order, the court may impose a fine not exceeding level 3 on the standard scale and continue the order, or revoke the order and sentence him as if the order had not been made, or vary the number of hours (within the specified minimum and maximum limits)[13].

The court may alter or revoke an order on the application of the offender or the officer if it appears in the interests of justice to do so[14]. In pursuance of this power, the court may extend the period of twelve months[15] or vary the number of hours or revoke the order and impose some other sentence provided the offender has made an application to this effect or, where the application is made by the officer, the offender has been cited to appear before the court[16]. If he fails to answer the citation, a warrant for his arrest may be issued. The attendance of the offender is not necessary if the court merely wishes to revoke the order and make no further order or sentence. Should the offender wish to move to another locality where there are arrangements and provisions for him to perform community service, the court has a discretion to transfer the order to that locality[17].

1 Community Service by Offenders (Scotland) Act 1978 (c 49), s 1(1).
2 Ibid, s 1(7); Criminal Justice (Scotland) Act 1980 (c 62), s 58(1). As to unpaid work as a condition of probation, see para 7.19, note 16, below. Where there is more than one complaint or charge the court may competently impose community service on one and impose a different sentence (eg detention) on the other: *McQueen v Lockhart* 1986 SCCR 20. This contrasts with the rules relating to probation and to deferred sentences, which may not be imposed where the accused is imprisoned on another charge or complaint: see para 6.19 below and *Downie v Irvine* 1964 JC 52, 1964 SLT 205 (probation); and para 7.20 below and *Lennon v Copland* 1972 SLT (Notes) 68 (deferred sentence).
3 Community Service by Offenders (Scotland) Act 1978, s 1(2)(b). As to the position where the offender resides elsewhere in the United Kingdom, see s 6 (amended by the Criminal Justice Act 1982 (c 48), s 78, Sch 16), and R W Renton and H H Brown *Criminal Procedure according to the Law of Scotland* (5th edn, 1983) para 17-21.
4 Community Service by Offenders (Scotland) Act 1978, s 1(2)(c). See also *Gray v McGlennan* 1990 GWD 4-190 where it was held that 200 hours' community service was not practical for an offender who was a full-time nurse.
5 Ibid, s 1(3).
6 Ibid, s 1(2)(a), (4). The accused does not have to show contrition or remorse as a prerequisite to the making of a community service order: *McCusker v HM Advocate* 1988 SCCR 235.
7 Community Service by Offenders (Scotland) Act 1978, s 2(2).
8 Ibid, s 3(1)(a).
9 Ibid, s 3(1)(b), (2).
10 Ibid, s 3(3).
11 Ibid, s 4(1). In practice the officer will often submit a brief written report to the court, narrating the details of the breach and asking for instructions. If the court orders further proceedings the officer will appear in chambers, after which the court may issue a warrant.
12 C G B Nicholson *The Law and Practice of Sentencing in Scotland* (1981) para 2-64 postulates that 'Once again procurators fiscal will no doubt come to the rescue'. The standard of proof is likely to be the same as for breach of probation: see para 7.19, note 32, below.

13 Community Service by Offenders (Scotland) Act 1978, s 4(2) (amended by the Criminal Justice
   Act 1982, s 56(3), Sch 7, para 12): see eg *McKay v Guild* 1988 GWD 20–861. As to the standard
   scale, see para 2.12, note 1, above.
14 Community Service by Offenders (Scotland) Act 1978, s 5.
15 The period may be extended only by order of the court. The community service officer has no
   power to do so: *HM Advocate v Hood* 1987 SCCR 63.
16 Community Service by Offenders (Scotland) Act 1978, s 5(1), (3).
17 Ibid, s 5(2).

(H) PROBATION

7.19. Probation. In solemn and summary proceedings, where the court considers it expedient in view of the circumstances of the case (including the nature
of the offence and the character of the offender) and where the sentence is not
fixed by law (for example murder), the court may make a probation order
requiring the offender to be under supervision for a specified period of not less
than six months and not more than three years[1]. In solemn proceedings, the
order may be made after conviction; in summary proceedings, the order may be
made without proceeding to conviction if the court is satisfied that the offender
committed the offence[2]. Despite the absence of a conviction, a summary court
in appropriate cases may also order that the offender's driving licence be
endorsed, or that he be disqualified from holding or obtaining a licence[3], or that
he is to forfeit any tools or other objects used or intended for use in the
commission of theft[4], or that he be deported[5]. Where there is more than one
charge, the offender should not be imprisoned on one and placed on probation
on the other[6].

Before making a probation order, the court must obtain a report, known as a
social inquiry report, about the circumstances and the offender's character[7], and
may adjourn the case for this purpose. A copy of the report must be given to the
offender or his solicitor or, in the case of an unrepresented offender under the
age of sixteen, to his parent or guardian[8]. The court is required to explain to the
offender the effect of the order and the consequences of failing to comply with it,
and to ensure that he is willing to obtemper it[9]. After an order is made, the clerk
of court must give a copy to the offender, to the local authority officer who is to
supervise him and to the person in charge of any institution or place in which the
offender may be required by the order to reside[10].

A probation order must be in the form prescribed by Act of Adjournal; it
must name the local authority area in which the offender resides or is to reside;
and it must order the offender to be of good behaviour, to conform to the
directions of the local authority officer and to inform that officer of any change
of address or employment[11]. In addition, the court has a discretionary power to
order the offender 'to comply ... with such requirements as the court ...
considers ... necessary for securing the good conduct of the offender or for
preventing a repetition by him of the offence or the commission of other
offences'[12]. This provision gives the court considerable latitude: for example, it
can order the offender to refrain from certain conduct or to behave in any
specific way which the court considers 'necessary'. The offender may be
required to give security for his good behaviour[13] or to reside in a particular
place[14], or to perform not less than forty and not more two hundred and forty
hours unpaid work[15]. Where the court is satisfied on the evidence of a registered
medical practitioner that the offender has a mental condition which requires and
is susceptible to treatment, it may impose as a condition of probation a requirement that the offender submit himself to treatment for a period not exceeding
twelve months[16].

The court can also require the offender to make restitution or pay compensation. Restitution differs from compensation and would apply where, for example, the court imposed a condition that the offender return stolen property to its lawful owner or personally repair damage he had caused, regardless of the value of the property or the cost of the damage. A condition of compensation requires the offender to pay a sum of money in a lump sum or by instalments to compensate the victim for his loss[17], but the sum awarded may not exceed the limits which apply to compensation orders[18], and the imposition of the condition is limited to the same types of case in which a compensation order may be made[19]. The compensation must be paid within eighteen months or not later than two months before the end of the period of probation, whichever first occurs[20], but the court may vary the condition of compensation on the application of the offender or his supervisory officer[21]. The money is paid by the offender to the clerk of court[22], and where the offender has been fined in respect of different offences in the same proceedings, any payment by him is first applied in satisfaction of the compensation[23]. The enforcement provisions relating to failure to pay compensation orders do not apply to a compensation condition[24], but failure to obtemper a condition of compensation may be considered to be a breach of probation[25]. Compensation awarded as a condition of probation has the same effect as a compensation order on any subsequent award of damages in civil proceedings[26].

Officers of the social work department of the local authority are responsible for supervising the offender and ensuring that he complies with the conditions of probation[27]. Such an officer may apply to the court to have the order discharged[28], and either he or the offender may apply to have it amended by cancelling any of the discretionary requirements or by inserting additional or substituted requirements[29]. Where the court proposes to amend the order it must cite the offender to appear and ensure that he is willing to comply with the amendment except when the application to amend is made by him, or where the purpose of the amendment is to cancel a requirement, to reduce the period of a requirement or to substitute a new local authority area[30].

If it appears to the court from information given to it on oath by the supervising officer that the offender has failed to comply with any requirement of a probation order, the court may cite the offender to appear or may issue a warrant for his arrest[31]. When the offender subsequently appears he must be asked whether he admits or denies the failure; should he deny it, a hearing will be held either then or on a subsequent occasion at which evidence may be led by both parties[32]. This procedure is competent even if the offender does not appear until after the expiry of the order[33]. Where it is proved to the satisfaction of the court that the offender has failed to comply with a requirement of the order, the court may allow the order to continue and impose a fine (not exceeding level 3 on the standard scale) or community service (where there are provisions and arrangements available) or may vary any of the requirements of the order (apart from extending it beyond the three-year period)[34]. Alternatively, the court may proceed to convict the offender of the offence for which he was placed on probation (unless, of course, he has already been so convicted — for example on indictment) and sentence him as if he had not been placed on probation, in which case the probation order will cease to have effect[35].

While one of the compulsory conditions of probation is that the offender should be of good behaviour, if he is subsequently convicted of an offence committed while he is on probation, he is not liable to be dealt with for failing to comply with a condition of probation[36]. Where it appears to the court responsible for the probation order that the offender has been convicted for such an offence, it may cite him to appear or issue a warrant for his arrest, and thereafter when the offender appears before the court and the court is satisfied that he has been so convicted, the court, if it thinks fit, may convict him of the offence for which he was placed on probation (unless he has already been convicted of it) and sentence him for that offence[37].

1 Criminal Procedure (Scotland) Act 1975 (c 21), ss 183(1), 384(1) (amended by the Criminal Justice (Scotland) Act 1987 (c 41), s 70(1), Sch 1, para 10).

2 Criminal Procedure (Scotland) Act 1975, ss 183(1), 384(1). In summary proceedings the minute should expressly state that the court did not proceed to conviction: *McPherson v Henderson* 1984 SCCR 294.

3 Road Traffic Offenders Act 1988 (c 53), s 46(3).

4 Civic Government (Scotland) Act 1982 (c 45), s 58(3), which is expressed to apply only where a convicted thief is found in possession of the tools.

5 See para 7.25 below.

6 *Downie v Irvine* 1964 JC 52, 1964 SLT 205.

7 Criminal Procedure (Scotland) Act 1975, ss 183(1), 384(1) (as amended: see note 1 above); *Jamieson v Heatly* 1959 JC 22, 1959 SLT 263.

8 Criminal Procedure (Scotland) Act 1975, ss 192, 393.

9 Ibid, ss 183(6), 384(6) (amended by the Community Service by Offenders (Scotland) Act 1978 (c 49), s 7, and the Criminal Justice Act 1982 (c 48), s 68(2), Sch 13, para 3).

10 Criminal Procedure (Scotland) Act 1975, ss 183(7), 384(7).

11 Ibid, ss 183(2), 384(2); Act of Adjournal (Consolidation) 1988, SI 1988/110, rr 76, 126, Sch 1, Form 36. For the procedure where the offender lives outwith the jurisdiction of the court, see R W Renton and H H Brown *Criminal Procedure according to the Law of Scotland* (5th edn, 1983) paras 17-48, 17-70–17-73.

12 Criminal Procedure (Scotland) Act 1975, ss 183(4), 384(4) (amended by the Community Service by Offenders (Scotland) Act 1978, s 7).

13 Criminal Procedure (Scotland) Act 1975, ss 190(1), (2), 391(1), (2). See also C G B Nicholson *The Law and Practice of Sentencing in Scotland* (1981) para 2-12.

14 A court may impose a residence condition only in accordance with the Criminal Procedure (Scotland) Act 1975, s 183(5) or s 384(5).

15 Ibid, ss 183(5A), 384(5A) (added by the Community Service by Offenders (Scotland) Act 1978, s 7, and amended by the Criminal Justice Act 1982, Sch 13, para 3), under which a condition requiring unpaid work can be imposed only where the Secretary of State has notified the court that arrangements exist for such work to be performed as a condition of probation. The offender must be aged sixteen years or over and have committed an offence punishable with imprisonment. There must be provision for the offender to perform the work. Unlike community service, failure to perform the work will result in a breach of probation. See further *Renton and Brown* para 17-56 and *Nicholson* paras 2-20–2-22.

16 Criminal Procedure (Scotland) Act 1975, ss 184, 385 (amended by the Mental Health (Amendment) (Scotland) Act 1983 (c 39), s 36(1)–(3), 39(3), Sch 3, and the Mental Health (Scotland) Act 1984 (c 36), s 127(1), Sch 3, paras 29, 36), which impose various requirements which must be met before a court can impose a condition of treatment. See further *Renton and Brown* paras 17-53–17-55, and *Nicholson* paras 2-14–2-19.

17 Criminal Procedure (Scotland) Act 1975, ss 183(4), (5B), (5C), (6), 186(2)(a), 384(4), (5B), (5C), (6), 387(2)(a) (all amended, and ss 183(5B), (5C), 384(5B), (5C) added, by the Criminal Justice (Scotland) Act 1987, s 65).

18 Criminal Procedure (Scotland) Act 1975, ss 183(5B), 384(5B) (as so added), applying the Criminal Justice (Scotland) Act 1980 (c 62), s 59, for which see para 7.16 above.

19 Criminal Procedure (Scotland) Act 1975, ss 183(5B), 384(5B) (as so added), applying the Criminal Justice (Scotland) Act 1980, s 58(2), (3), for which see para 7.16 above.

20 Criminal Procedure (Scotland) Act 1975, ss 183(5C)(a), 384(5C)(a) (as so added).

21 Ibid, ss 183(5C)(b), 384(5C)(b) (as so added).

22 Ibid, ss 183(5B), 384(5B) (as so added), applying the Criminal Justice (Scotland) Act 1980, s 60, for which see para 7.16 above.

23 Criminal Procedure (Scotland) Act 1975, ss 183(5B), 384(5B) (as so added), applying the Criminal Justice (Scotland) Act 1980, s 62, for which see para 7.16 above.

24 Ibid, s 66, which relates to the enforcement of compensation orders (see para 7.16 above), is not applied to compensation as a breach of probation.

25 Criminal Procedure (Scotland) Act 1975, ss 183(5C)(c), 384(5C)(c) (as added: see note 17 above), also state that a certificate from the clerk of court that the compensation, or an instalment of it, has not been paid is sufficient evidence of the breach.

26 Ibid, ss 183(5B), 384(5B) (as so added), applying the Criminal Justice (Scotland) Act 1980, s 67, for which see para 7.16 above.

27 Social Work (Scotland) Act 1968 (c 49), s 27 (amended by the Community Service by Offenders (Scotland) Act 1978, s 14, Sch 2, para 1).

28 Criminal Procedure (Scotland) Act 1975, ss 185(1), 386(1), Sch 5, para 1. In practice an application for discharge is usually confined to cases where the offender has completed part of his period of probation and the officer considers that further continuance of the order is unnecessary. The court has a discretion in deciding whether or not to grant the application.

29 Ibid, Sch 5, para 3. The court may not reduce the probation period or extend it beyond three years from the date of the original order: Sch 5, para 3 proviso (a). For further limits on the court's discretion to amend the order and the procedure to be followed, see Sch 5, para 3 provisos (b), (c), and *Renton and Brown* paras 17-58–17-62 and *Nicholson* paras 2-28–2-31.

30 Criminal Procedure (Scotland) Act 1975, Sch 5, para 5.

31 Ibid, ss 186(1), 387(1). The officer normally appears in chambers to give his information on oath (this being known colloquially as 'swearing to a breach of probation'), and the correct procedure must be followed: *Roy v Cruickshank* 1954 SLT 217.

32 No fixed procedure is laid down: see *Nicholson* para 2-34, where it is also suggested that the standard of proof should be the same as in criminal trials. See also *Valentine v Kennedy* 1987 SCCR 47 (Sh Ct), where it was held that the standard of proof in criminal trials should be followed. Reasonable refusal to undergo surgical, electrical or other treatment for a mental condition will not constitute a failure to comply: Criminal Procedure (Scotland) Act 1975, ss 186(4), 387(4).

33 See the definition of 'probationer' in ibid, s 462 (amended by the Criminal Justice (Scotland) Act 1980, s 25(b): 'a person who is under supervision by virtue of a probation order or who was under such supervision at the time of the commission of any relevant offence or failure to comply with such order'.

34 Criminal Procedure (Scotland) Act 1975, ss 186(2), 387(2) (amended by the Community Service by Offenders (Scotland) Act 1978, s 8, the Criminal Justice (Scotland) Act 1980, s 46(1), the Criminal Justice Act 1982, s 56(3), Sch 7, paras 3, 9 and the Criminal Justice (Scotland) Act 1987, s 65(5)).

35 Criminal Procedure (Scotland) Act 1975, ss 185(2), 186(2), 386(2), 387(2).

36 *Roy v Cruickshank* 1954 SLT 217.

37 Criminal Procedure (Scotland) Act 1975, ss 187(1), 388(1). Where the court making the subsequent conviction is the same court which imposed the earlier probation, it may deal with the offender there and then rather than citing him or issuing a warrant for his appearance at a later date: ss 187(2), 388(2). See further *Renton and Brown* paras 17-67–17-69 and *Nicholson* paras 2-37–2-39.

(I) DEFERRED SENTENCE

7.20. Deferred sentence. In either solemn or summary proceedings, when the accused is convicted, the court may defer its decision as to the appropriate sentence until a later specified date[1]. There is no limit to the period of such a deferment, and sentence may be deferred on more than one occasion. Furthermore, during the deferment, the accused may be subject to 'such conditions as the court may determine'[1]. At the deferred diet, the court has the same sentencing powers as it had at the time of conviction, and when considering the question of sentence it will take into account and make allowance for the extent to which the accused has complied with any conditions imposed upon him. The court may not sentence the accused before the expiry of the deferment, even where he is in breach of one of the conditions except where he is convicted, while on deferment, of an offence committed during the period of deferment. In such a case, where the subsequent conviction is in the same court, the court may pass sentence on both offences at the same time even if this is before the deferred date for the original offence; similarly, if the accused is subsequently convicted of such an offence in another court, the original court may cite him or issue a warrant for his arrest and, as soon as he appears, the court may sentence him for the original offence even although the period of deferment has not expired[2].

Where there is more than one charge on the indictment or complaint, the court should not impose a custodial sentence on one and defer sentence on another[3]. There are few if any restrictions on the conditions which the court may impose during the period of deferment[4]. While it may not impose a compensation order at the same time as deferring sentence, it can require the accused to recompense a victim or make good any other loss (regardless of the amount), and should the accused make no attempt to do so, the court can take this into account when he subsequently appears for sentence, and on that occasion, if appropriate, the court may impose a compensation order[5]. Normally the accused is required to be of good behaviour, and at the end of the period of deferment the court will usually receive a report from the social work department (if requested) or from the procurator fiscal. Where he has been of good behaviour, this should be reflected in the sentence[6]. Where the report is not favourable, whether or not the offender has committed any subsequent offences, the court may likewise take this into account when determining sentence[7].

1 Criminal Procedure (Scotland) Act 1975 (c 21), ss 219(1), 432(1). The accused does not require to wait until the end of the period of deferment before appealing against conviction: see ss 228, 442, 451 (respectively substituted by the Criminal Justice (Scotland) Act 1980 (c 62), ss 33, 34, Sch 2, para 1, Sch 3, paras 1, 10). The sheriff should not specify in advance the sentence he will impose at the end of the period of deferment: *Cassidy v Wilson* 1989 SCCR 6. When deferring sentence it is advisable that the judge should minute his reasons for doing so and at the end of the period of deferment the case should call before the same judge unless precluded from doing so by the exigencies of business: *Islam v HM Advocate* 1989 SCCR 109; *Main v Jessop* 1989 SCCR 437.
2 Criminal Procedure (Scotland) Act 1975, ss 219(2), (3), 432(2), (3) (added by the Criminal Justice (Scotland) Act 1980, s 54). See R W Renton and H H Brown *Criminal Procedure according to the Law of Scotland* (5th edn, 1983) para 17-80, and C G B Nicholson *The Law and Practice of Sentencing in Scotland)* (1981) paras 8-50, 8-51.
3 *Lennon v Copland* 1972 SLT (Notes) 68.
4 For further discussion on the aims and purposes of deferred sentences, see *Nicholson* paras 10-40–10-50, and A D Smith 'Deferred Sentences in Scotland' 1968 SLT (News) 153.
5 Criminal Justice (Scotland) Act 1980, s 58(1).
6 *Herron v Carmichael* 2 May 1984 (unreported); *McPherson v HM Advocate* 1986 SCCR 278; *Anderson v Guild* 1989 GWD 28–1269; *Carvil v Jessop* 1989 GWD 36–1667 although the court retains its discretion as to the appropriate sentence to impose: *Linton v Ingram* 1989 SCCR 487.
7 *Colquhoun v HM Advocate* 1985 SCCR 396; *Graham v HM Advocate* 1987 GWD 18–678; *Swanson v Guild* 1989 GWD 15-638.

(J) ADMONITION

7.21. Admonition. Any court may, if it appears to meet the justice of the case, dismiss with an admonition any person convicted of any offence[1]. In appropriate cases it may be accompanied by an order to endorse the accused's driving licence, or to disqualify him from driving or to forfeit items used in commission of the offence[2]. An admonition may be libelled as a previous conviction if the accused is subsequently convicted of another offence.

1 Criminal Procedure (Scotland) Act 1975 (c 21), ss 181, 382.
2 See para 7.23 below.

(K) ABSOLUTE DISCHARGE

7.22. Absolute discharge. Where an accused is convicted on indictment or where the court is satisfied in summary proceedings that he committed the offence charged, it may make an order discharging him absolutely if it is of the opinion that it is inexpedient to inflict punishment or inappropriate to make a probation order in view of the circumstances of the case, including the nature of the offence and the character of the accused[1]. Such an order may not, however, be made in cases such as murder where the sentence is fixed by law[1].

At the same time as granting an absolute discharge the court is also empowered in appropriate cases to order that the accused's driving licence is to be endorsed or that he is to be disqualified for driving[2], or that he is to be excluded from specified licensed premises[3], or that tools and implements for use in theft are to be forfeited[4], or may recommend that he be deported[5]. The accused has a right of appeal against the order (as well as against any of the ancillary orders)[6], and an absolute discharge may be libelled as a previous conviction in any subsequent proceedings[7].

1 Criminal Procedure (Scotland) Act 1975 (c 21), ss 182, 383. In summary proceedings the court makes the order without proceeding to conviction: s 383. See also *Walker v MacGillivray* (1980) SCCR Supp 244.
2 Road Traffic Offenders Act 1988 (c 53), s 46(3).
3 Licensed Premises (Exclusion of Certain Persons) Act 1980 (c 32), s 1(1), (2). See also para 7.24 below.
4 Civic Government (Scotland) Act 1982 (c 45), s 58(3).
5 Immigration Act 1971 (c 77), ss 3(6), 6: see also para 7.25 below.
6 Criminal Procedure (Scotland) Act 1975, s 392(4).
7 Ibid, ss 191(1), 392(1) (amended by the Criminal Justice (Scotland) Act 1980, s 83(3), Sch 8). It may not be used in evidence in civil proceedings under the Civil Evidence Act 1968 (c 64), s 11: Law Reform (Miscellaneous Provisions) (Scotland) Act 1968 (c 70), s 10(1), (5).

(L) FORFEITURE

7.23. Forfeiture. Where an accused is convicted in solemn or summary proceedings (except in summary proceedings if he is placed on probation or granted an absolute discharge[1]), the court may order forfeiture of any property in his possession or control at the time of his apprehension, provided the court is satisfied that it has been used or was intended by him to be used for the purpose of committing or facilitating the commission of any offence[2]. Facilitating the commission of the offence includes taking any steps after its commission for the purpose of disposing of property to which it relates or of avoiding apprehension or detection[3]. The use or intended use relates to any offence and is not restricted to the offence of which the accused is convicted[4]. Moreover, it does not matter if the use of the article was by someone other than the accused[5].

This general power applies to all crimes and offences, but in addition certain statutes creating offences contain specific provision for forfeiture in the event of conviction[6]. The powers of forfeiture given by such statutes may differ from the general power of forfeiture[7], and in the case of an offence where both apply the court will have an option to proceed under one rather than the other[8]. In summary proceedings, the court may not order forfeiture under one of these specific statutes unless the notice of penalties refers to liability to forfeiture and correctly describes the property[9], whereas if forfeiture is made under the general power of the court, no such reference is required in the notice of penalties. There also appears to be another important distinction where the property belongs to a third person rather than the accused. Where the court's power of forfeiture depends on a specific statute, it may not forfeit property which belongs to a third person[10]. Where, however, forfeiture is ordered in terms of the court's general power, property belonging to a third person may be forfeited provided the court bears in mind any interest which that third person may have in the property[11].

In practice many courts will not make a forfeiture order unless the article is produced in court or is otherwise in safe custody, and the forfeiture provisions of some statutes specifically preclude such an order unless the article is produced[12]. Where, however, a competent forfeiture order is made and the article is neither produced nor in safe custody, the court or a justice may issue a warrant to search for the article if satisfied by information on oath that it is believed with reasonable cause to be in any place or premises to which admission has been or is likely to be refused[13]. When the forfeited article is produced or seized, it is to be 'disposed of as the court may direct'[14]. The court may order the property to be destroyed (for example in the case of drugs, obscene literature or weapons) or may order it to be sold by or at the instance of the sheriff clerk and, in the absence of any directions to the contrary, the proceeds will be paid to HM Exchequer[15].

1 In summary proceedings the court may make a probation order or grant an absolute discharge without proceeding to conviction: Criminal Procedure (Scotland) Act 1975 (c 21), ss 383, 384(1); see R W Renton and H H Brown *Criminal Procedure according to the Law of Scotland* (5th edn, 1983) para 17-44, and C G B Nicholson *The Law and Practice of Sentencing in Scotland* (1981) paras 2-02, 7-02. See, however, *Wilson v Houston* 1988 GWD 13-566, where the accused was placed on probation and ordered to forfeit his car. See also the Civic Government (Scotland) Act 1982 (c 45), s 58(3), which permits the court, when granting an absolute discharge or making a probation order, to order the forfeiture of tools and implements for use in theft. Where the accused appeals against conviction or sentence the court may suspend forfeiture pending the determination of the appeal: Criminal Procedure (Scotland) Act 1975, ss 264(3), 443A (both added by the Criminal Justice (Scotland) Act 1987 (c 41), s 68).
2 Criminal Procedure (Scotland) Act 1975, s 223(1), and s 436(1) (substituted by the Criminal Justice (Scotland) Act 1980 (c 62), s 83(2), Sch 7, para 71). See eg *Carruthers v MacKinnon* 1986 SCCR 643; *Walsh v Taylor-Wilson* 1987 GWD 6-182; *McDuff v Carmichael* 1987 GWD 26-996; *Smith v Guild* 1989 GWD 33-1519; *Thomson v McNaugton* 1989 GWD 38-1750. However, see also *Hall v Carmichael* 1988 GWD 14-606, where a forfeiture order was quashed where the accused's only part in the offence was to act as driver and he was otherwise of relatively good character.
3 Criminal Procedure (Scotland) Act 1975, s 223(2), and s 436(2) (as so substituted).
4 *Donnelly v HM Advocate* 1984 SCCR 93.
5 *Renton and Brown* para 17-44. See eg *Bain v Taylor Wilson* 1987 SCCR 270.
6 See eg the Wireless Telegraphy Act 1949 (c 54), s 14(3) (substituted by the Telecommunications Act 1984 (c 12), s 82); the Salmon and Freshwater Fisheries (Protection) (Scotland) Act 1951 (c 26), s 19 (amended by the Salmon Act 1986 (c 62), s 41(1), (2), Sch 4, para 10, Sch 5); the Prevention of Crime Act 1953 (c 14), s 1(2); the Betting, Gaming and Lotteries Act 1963 (c 2), s 52(4); the Betting, Gaming and Lotteries Act 1964 (c 78), s 3(2), (3); the Misuse of Drugs Act 1971 (c 38), s 27; and the Civic Government (Scotland) Act 1982 (c 45), s 58(3).
7 See eg ibid, s 58(3), and note 1 above. See also *Simpson v Fraser* 1948 JC 1, 1948 SLT 124. The Criminal Justice (Scotland) Act 1987, Pt I (ss 1-47), gives the High Court of Justiciary powers analogous to forfeiture to make confiscation, restraint and sequestration orders in relation to the proceeds of drug trafficking.
8 Conversely, the wording of a statute creating a specific power of forfeiture may exclude the general power of forfeiture under the Criminal Procedure (Scotland) Act 1975 ss 223(1) and 436(1): *Aitken v Lockhart* 1989 SCCR 368.
9 Criminal Procedure (Scotland) Act 1975, s 311(5); *Rankin v Wright* (1901) 4 F (J) 5, 3 Adam 483.
10 *Loch Lomond Sailings Ltd v Hawthorn* 1962 JC 8, 1962 SLT 6; *J W Semple & Sons v MacDonald* 1963 JC 90, 1963 SLT 295.
11 *Lloyds and Scottish Finance Ltd v HM Advocate* 1974 JC 24, 1974 SLT 3.
13 See eg the Betting, Gaming and Lotteries Act 1963, s 52(4). See also *Shandon Supply Co Ltd v McLeod* Crown Office Circular A6/65.
13 Criminal Procedure (Scotland) Act 1975, ss 224, 437.
14 Ibid, ss 223(1), 436(1).
15 *Lloyds and Scottish Finance Ltd v HM Advocate* 1974 JC 24, 1974 SLT 3.

(M) DISQUALIFICATIONS AND INCAPACITIES

7.24. Disqualifications and incapacities. Various statutes provide that the court, in addition to any other penalty, may make an order disqualifying the offender from holding certain licences or permits or declaring him to be incapable of holding certain offices[1]. The most common example is to be found in the legislation dealing with traffic offences under which the court is either required or has a discretion to order that the offender be disqualified for holding or obtaining a licence to drive or that the conviction is to be endorsed upon his driving licence[2]. The offences to which these provisions apply are those specified in the Road Traffic Offenders Act 1988 and include the common law crime of theft or attempted theft of a motor vehicle[3]. The Criminal Justice Act 1972 allows the court also to disqualify from driving any person convicted on indictment of an offence in which a motor vehicle was used by anyone to facilitate the offence[4].

Other statutory examples include the Public Bodies Corrupt Practices Act 1889, whereby an offender may be ordered to forfeit any office held by him and declared incapable of holding any public office for a specified period[5]; the Protection of Animals (Amendment) Act 1954 and other legislation dealing with animal welfare, whereby an offender may be disqualified from keeping an animal[6]; the Betting, Gaming and Lotteries Act 1963, whereby an offender may be ordered to forfeit a bookmaker's or betting agency permit and be disqualified for holding such a permit for a specified time[7]; and the Licensing (Scotland) Act 1976, whereby an offender may be disqualified for holding a licence for a specified period and premises may be disqualified for use as licensed premises[8]. Analogous to such disqualifications is the power given to the court by the Licensed Premises (Exclusion of Certain Persons) Act 1980 to order that an offender be prohibited from entering particular licensed premises for a specified period if the court is satisfied that in committing the offence on these premises he resorted to, or offered or threatened to resort to violence[9].

1 If the accused appeals against conviction or sentence the court may suspend the order pending the determination of the appeal: Criminal Procedure (Scotland) Act 1975 (c 21), ss 264(3), 443A (both added by the Criminal Justice (Scotland) Act 1987 (c 41), s 68).

2 The provisions of the road traffic legislation relating to disqualification and endorsement are complex: see further C G B Nicholson *The Law and Practice of Sentencing in Scotland* (1981, with Supplement 1985).

3 See the Road Traffic Offenders Act 1988 (c 53), ss 9, 34, 44, Sch 2. In summary cases the notice of penalties under the Criminal Procedure (Scotland) Act 1975, s 311(5), refers to disqualifications and/or endorsement, although no such notice is required in cases of theft or attempted theft of a motor vehicle which is not a statutory charge.

4 Criminal Justice Act 1972 (c 71), s 24 (amended by the Powers of Criminal Courts Act 1973 (c 62), s 56(1), Sch 5, para 46). Facilitating the offence is defined in the same way as in the provisions relating to forfeiture: see para 6.23 above. See also the Criminal Justice Act 1972, s 24(4) (substituted by the Criminal Procedure (Scotland) Act 1975, s 461(1), Sch 9, para 48).

5 Public Bodies Corrupt Practices Act 1889 (c 69), s 2(c) (amended by the Representation of the People Act 1948 (c 65), s 52(7)).

6 Protection of Animals (Cruelty to Dogs) (Scotland) Act 1934 (c 25), s 1; Protection of Animals (Amendment) Act 1954 (c 40), s 1 — see for example *Gilchrist v Guild* 1989 GWD 38–1748; *Douglas v Walkinshaw* 1989 GWD 38–1749.

7 Betting, Gaming and Lotteries Act 1963 (c 2), s 11.

8 Licensing (Scotland) Act 1976 (c 66), s 67, Sch 5. For an example of disqualification under this Act see *Canavan v Carmichael* 1989 SCCR 480.

9 Licensed Premises (Exclusion of Certain Persons) Act 1980 (c 32), s 1(1). For further details, see the Act and R W Renton and H H Brown *Criminal Procedure according to the Law of Scotland* (5th edn, 1983) paras 7-26–7-32. An accused who contravenes the order is guilty of an offence for which he may be prosecuted.

(N) DEPORTATION

7.25. Deportation. The court has a discretion to recommend the deportation from the United Kingdom of any offender who is not a British citizen and who is convicted after he attains the age of seventeen years of an offence punishable with imprisonment (or who is found to have committed such an offence, notwithstanding that the court does not proceed to conviction)[1]. No regard is to be had to any enactment which restricts the imprisonment of young offenders or persons who have not previously been sentenced to imprisonment[2]. The recommendation may be made by the sheriff or High Court of Justiciary, but it must be made by the court which passes sentence; if the High Court passes sentence on an appeal, it can make such a recommendation only where the appeal is against conviction or sentence on indictment[3]. Before a recommendation is made, the offender must be given seven days' written notice of his liability for deportation and, where necessary, the court may adjourn the case to allow time for such a notice to be given[4].

A recommendation for deportation is a severe penalty and, apart from illegal immigrants, it should be made only where the offender is guilty of a serious offence, the test at the end of the day being 'whether to allow the offender to remain in this country would be contrary to the national interest'[5]. A recommendation may be appealed to the High Court in the same way as any other sentence[6]. When a recommendation is made, the Home Office should be notified as soon as possible and the offender must be detained in custody unless the court or the Home Secretary directs otherwise[7]. The recommendation is not binding on the Home Secretary who requires 'to decide in each case whether an offender's return to his country of origin would have consequences which would make his compulsory return unduly harsh[8]'.

1 Immigration Act 1971 (c 77), ss 3(6), 6(3) (the former amended by the British Nationality Act 1981 (c 61), s 39(6), Sch 4, para 2; the latter by the Criminal Justice Act 1982 (c 48), s 77, Sch 15, para 15). As to the position of Commonwealth and Irish citizens, see the Immigration Act 1971, ss 2, 7, and R W Renton and H H Brown *Criminal Procedure according to the Law of Scotland* (5th edn, 1983) para 17-84.
2 Immigration Act 1971, s 6(3)(b) (as so amended).
3 Ibid, s 6(1) proviso. Where the sheriff court remits an accused on indictment to the High Court for sentence, only the High Court may recommend deportation.
4 See ibid, s 6(2) (amended by the Criminal Procedure (Scotland) Act 1975 (c 21), s 461(1), Sch 9, para 47, and the British Nationality Act 1981, Sch 4, para 2). See *Renton and Brown* para 17-86. As to adjournment, see the Criminal Procedure (Scotland) Act 1975, ss 179, 380 (amended by the Bail etc (Scotland) Act 1980 (c 4), s 5, and the Criminal Justice (Scotland) Act 1980 (c 62), s 83(2), Sch 7, paras 36, 59), and para 7.02 above.
5 *Willms v Smith* 1981 SCCR 257, 1982 SLT 163. See also *Faboro v HM Advocate* 1982 SCCR 22; *Salehi v Smith* 1982 SCCR 552; and *Racine v Allan* 1988 GWD 16-707.
6 Immigration Act 1971, s 6(5) (amended by the Criminal Justice (Scotland) Act 1980, s 83(3), Sch 8, and the Criminal Justice Act 1982, ss 77, 78, Sch 15, para 15, Sch 16).
7 C G B Nicholson *The Law and Practice of Sentencing in Scotland* (1981) paras 7-24, 7-25 (Supplement). Nicholson suggests that the court should apply 'the normal considerations applicable to a grant or refusal of bail'.
8 *R v Nazari* [1980] 3 All ER 880 at 885, [1980] 1 WLR 1366 at 1373, 1374, CA, which is also quoted as a footnote to *Willms v Smith* 1981 SCCR 257.

(O) FIXED PENALTY

7.26. Fixed penalties. The Road Traffic Offenders Act 1988 provides for fixed penalties to be paid by an offender as an alternative to prosecution in and sentence by the court. Under the Act, the procurator fiscal may send a notice (known as a 'conditional offer') giving persons who have allegedly committed certain minor road traffic offences an opportunity to pay a fixed penalty as an alternative to prosecution[1]. The offences to which this provision apply are listed in the Act[2] and include offences such as speeding, failing to comply with traffic signs and the like. The fixed penalty is £32 if the offence requires obligatory endorsement of the offender's licence or £16 in all other cases[3]. If the procurator fiscal considers the offence to be too serious for a fixed penalty or where the offender is liable to be disqualified, the procurator fiscal retains an option to prosecute the offender in the district or sheriff court in the usual way[4]. An offender who opts to pay the fixed penalty must send it within twenty-eight days (or such longer time as the procurator fiscal may allow) to the clerk of the district court, together with his licence if the offence involves obligatory endorsement[5]. An offender who is given the option of a fixed penalty but who fails to pay it may be prosecuted in the usual way and, if convicted, he will be liable for the full penalty provided by the statute and not merely the restricted fixed penalty[6]. Such prosecutions are normally conducted in the district court.

Under a different fixed penalty system, for certain types of parking offences, a police constable or traffic warden may give a fixed penalty notice to a person on the spot or attach one to a motor vehicle[7].

If the offender fails to pay the fixed penalty to the clerk of court[8], he may be reported to the procurator fiscal for prosecution in the normal way and, if convicted, he will be liable for the full statutory penalty[9].

The Criminal Justice (Scotland) Act 1987 introduced another form of conditional offer (known colloquially as 'fiscal fines') applicable to any offence (other than certain road traffic offences) which can competently be tried in the district court[10]. The fixed penalty in this instance is £25[11], which is payable within twenty-eight days from the issue of the offer or by five fortnightly payments of £5[12]. Provided the procurator fiscal considers he has sufficient evidence to justify instituting proceedings, he may exercise his discretion and send a conditional offer to the accused, giving him an opportunity to pay the penalty instead of being prosecuted in the district court. If the accused pays the penalty, or the first instalment of it, timeously he cannot thereafter be prosecuted for the offence and his acceptance of the offer may not be recorded as a previous conviction against him[13]. If he does not accept the offer and if he fails to pay the penalty or the first instalment timeously, he may be prosecuted in the normal manner, and if he is convicted he will be liable for the full range of penalties applicable to the offence. Should he accept the offer and pay the first instalment but default on the remainder, payment of the balance is enforced by civil diligence[14]. As this procedure may be applied to any offence which may competently be prosecuted in the district court, and as the procurator fiscal has a wide discretion as to when he should use the procedure, variations in practice may arise as a result of local conditions or the views of the individual procurator fiscal. In general terms he will restrict the use of conditional offers to cases which in his view merit a fine of £25, and it follows that he will not make an offer if he considers that the case merits a lesser penalty, or that it merits a greater one, perhaps because of the gravity of the offence or its prevalence or public concern in his particular locality or because of the accused's record. He is unlikely to make a conditional offer if he considers that the offence should attract an ancillary or different type of penalty[15].

1 Road Traffic Offenders Act 1988 (c 53), s 75(2)–(4). The procedure was introduced by the Transport Act 1982 (c 49), s 42 (repealed).
2 Road Traffic Offenders Act 1988, ss 51, 75(3), Schs 3, 5. Further offences were added by the Fixed Penalty Offences (Scotland) Order 1990, SI 1990/466.
3 Ibid, s 53(2) and the Fixed Penalty (Increase) (Scotland) Order 1990, SI 1990/467.
4 See ibid, ss 75(6), (7), 76(2), (5), (6).

5 See ibid, s 75(6), (7).
6 See further ibid, ss 51–53, 58, 75–77; C G B Nicholson *The Law and Practice of Sentencing in Scotland* (1981) (1985 Supplement) p 34. About 87 per cent of offenders offered a fixed penalty opt to pay it: 1985 SLT (News) 83.
7 Road Traffic Offenders Act 1988, ss 54–68, 86(2).
8 Ibid, s 69(1).
9 The statutory penalty may well be in excess of the fixed penalty.
10 Criminal Justice (Scotland) Act 1987 (c 41), s 56(1), (2). This does not apply to a fixed penalty offence under the Road Traffic Offenders Act 1988, s 51, nor any other offence in respect of which a conditional offer may be sent under ss 75–77: Criminal Justice (Scotland) Act 1987, s 56(2) (amended by the Road Traffic (Consequential Provisions) Act 1988 (c 54), s 4, Sch 3, para 34).
11 Criminal Justice (Scotland) Act 1987 Fixed Penalty Order 1987, SI 1987/2025, art 2.
12 Criminal Justice (Scotland) Act 1987, s 56(3)(c); Criminal Justice (Scotland) Act 1987 Fixed Penalty Order 1987, art 3.
13 Criminal Justice (Scotland) Act 1987, s 56(2)(e), (6).
14 Ibid, s 56(9)(a), and s 56(9)(b), which disapplies the Criminal Procedure (Scotland) Act 1975 (c 21), ss 395(1), 395A(2), 396(1)–(6), 403(6), 406, 407(1)(a), (1A)–(1D), (2)–(4), 408, 409, 411(3), and the Criminal Justice (Scotland) Act 1980 (c 62), s 52.
15 Eg compensation, forfeiture, disqualification for keeping animals or exclusion from licensed premises under the Licensed Premises (Exclusion of Certain Persons) Act 1980 (c 32) (see generally para 7.24 above).

(P) EXPENSES

7.27. Expenses. As a general rule, no expenses are awarded in criminal proceedings apart from appeals and private prosecutions. As regards appeals, where a summary case is appealed to the High Court of Justiciary, that court has a discretion to award expenses at the conclusion of the appeal, but it has no power to do so in relation to solemn proceedings[1].

In the very rare case of a private prosecution by way of solemn proceedings, expenses may be awarded against the private prosecutor[2]. There are statutory rules regarding expenses in private prosecutions by way of summary proceedings. Briefly, if an award of expenses is competent in a private prosecution, the prosecutor's costs are restricted to set fees and may be recovered from the accused by way of civil diligence, or, in certain instances, out of any fine imposed upon him[3]. If expenses are awarded against a private prosecutor, the accused's costs are not restricted in the same manner, but his account may be remitted for taxation[4].

1 *HM Advocate v Aldred* 1922 JC 13, 1922 SLT 51; Criminal Procedure (Scotland) Act 1975 (c 21), ss 266, 267. In practice, if expenses are awarded in a summary appeal they are usually restricted to a fairly nominal sum. See further R W Renton and H H Brown *Criminal Procedure according to the Law of Scotland* (5th edn, 1983) para 17–90.
2 Hume *Commentaries* II, 127; Alison *Practice* p 113.
3 See the Criminal Procedure (Scotland) Act 1975, s 435 (amended by the Criminal Justice (Scotland) Act 1980 (c 62), s 46(1)(e), and the Increase of Criminal Penalties etc (Scotland) Order 1984, SI 1984/526, art 6. Civil diligence can be protracted and costly; consequently, where expenses are recoverable from a fine, the court may prefer this course in view of the provisions for enforcing payment of a fine. See further *Renton and Brown* para 17–89.
4 *J and G Cox Ltd v Lindsay* 1907 SC 96, 14 SLT 450.

(c) Rehabilitation of the Offender

7.28. Rehabilitation of the offender; spent convictions. In certain instances, if the offender is not reconvicted within a specified period, he is treated as rehabilitated and 'for all purposes in law, as a person who has not committed or been charged with or been prosecuted for or convicted of or sentenced for the offence or offences' of which he was convicted[1]. The conviction itself becomes spent and, unless the Rehabilitation of Offenders Act 1974 provides to the contrary, in any subsequent court proceedings evidence of the conviction is inadmissible and the offender may not be asked or compelled to answer questions which would involve acknowledging that he has such a conviction[2]. Spent convictions will not normally be libelled as previous convictions by the prosecutor[3]. In other circumstances, for example if the offender is applying for employment, in the absence of provision to the contrary[4], questions relating to previous convictions 'shall be treated as not relating to spent convictions' and the offender cannot be subjected to any liability or prejudice or to dismissal if he fails to disclose or acknowledge a spent conviction[5].

These rules do not apply to convictions whereby the offender was sentenced to imprisonment or detention or custody for life, or to detention during Her Majesty's pleasure, or to a term of imprisonment, youth custody or detention in excess of thirty months[6]. As regards other convictions, the period of time which must pass before the conviction becomes spent commences with the date of conviction and depends on the nature of the conviction, for example as follows[7]:

(1) absolute discharge, or discharge by a children's hearing: six months;
(2) probation, or supervision under the social work legislation: one year, or the period of probation or supervision, whichever is the longer;
(3) detention not exceeding six months: three years;
(4) detention exceeding six months but not exceeding thirty months, or any fine: five years;
(5) imprisonment or youth custody not exceeding six months: seven years;
(6) imprisonment or youth custody exceeding six months but not exceeding thirty months: ten years.

1 Rehabilitation of Offenders Act 1974 (c 53), ss 1(1), 4(1).
2 Ibid, s 4(1)(a). Proceedings which are excluded from this provision include those relating to adoption, marriage, the custody of children etc: s 7(2)(c). The full list and further details are to be found in ss 7, 8. Unauthorised disclosure of a spent conviction may constitute a criminal offence: see s 9.
3 Strictly speaking, the prosecutor may libel a spent conviction as a previous conviction: see ibid, s 7(2)(a). However, when the Act was being passed, it was conceded in Parliament that the spirit of the Act would be complied with and as a consequence prosecutors do not normally libel spent convictions unless they are particularly relevant or there is good reason for doing so.
4 Ibid, s 4(4), empowers the Secretary of State to exclude or modify the application of this rule. Under the Rehabilitation of Offenders Act 1974 (Exceptions) Order 1975, SI 1975/1023, persons excluded from the provisions of this part of the Act include, inter alia, advocates, solicitors, persons concerned in law enforcement, medical practitioners, registered teachers and persons employed in teaching, youth, community work and social services.
5 Rehabilitation of Offenders Act 1974, s 4(2).
6 See ibid, s 5(1) (amended by the Armed Forces Act 1976 (c 52), s 22(5), Sch 9, para 20(4); the Criminal Justice (Scotland) Act 1980 (c 62), s 83(2), Sch 7, para 24; and the Criminal Justice Act 1982 (c 48), s 77, Sch 14, para 36).
7 For full details, see the Rehabilitation of Offenders Act 1974, ss 5(2)–(11), 6 (amended by the Armed Forces Act 1976, Sch 9, para 21; the Criminal Justice (Scotland) Act 1980, Sch 7, para 24; the Armed Forces Act 1981 (c 55), s 28(1), Sch 4, para 2(2); the Criminal Justice Act 1982, Sch 14, para 37; the Mental Health (Amendment) Act 1982 (c 51), ss 65(1), 69(6), Sch 3, Pt I, para 49, Sch 5, para 1; the Mental Health Act 1983 (c 20), s 148, Sch 4, para 39; and the Mental Health (Scotland) Act 1984 (c 36), s 127(1), Sch 3, para 22). If the offender is ordered to be disqualified for driving, or made subject to some other disqualification, disability or the like, the period of rehabilitation may be extended to the date when the order ceases to have effect: Rehabilitation of Offenders Act 1974, s 5(8).

8. APPEALS

(a) General

8.01. Introduction. The law relating to appeals in respect of criminal cases is governed by the Criminal Procedure (Scotland) Act 1975[1]. Prior to the Criminal Appeal (Scotland) Act 1926 (c 15) there was no appeal in respect of convictions imposed in the High Court of Justiciary, but in certain circumstances an accused could appeal against conviction in the inferior courts by way of bill of suspension or advocation[2]. In summary proceedings appeal by stated case was introduced by the Summary Prosecutions Appeals (Scotland) Act 1875 (c 62). Summary appeals procedures were codified in the Summary Jurisdiction (Scotland) Act 1908 (c 65), and in turn these provisions were repealed and re-enacted in the Criminal Procedure (Scotland) Act 1975.

Following consideration by the Thomson Committee on Criminal Procedure[3], both solemn and summary appeals provisions were radically amended by the Criminal Justice (Scotland) Act 1980[4].

1 For solemn appeals, see the Criminal Procedure (Scotland) Act 1975 (c 21), ss 228–282 (amended by the Criminal Justice (Scotland) Act 1980 (c 62), s 33, Sch 2), and R W Renton and H H Brown *Criminal Procedure according to the Law of Scotland* (5th edn, 1983) ch 11. For summary appeals, see the Criminal Procedure (Scotland) Act 1975, ss 442–455 (amended by the Criminal Justice (Scotland) Act 1980, s 34, Sch 3, and *Renton and Brown* ch 16).
2 *Renton and Brown* para 11–01. See further paras 8.54 ff, 8.59 ff, below, and 1 *Encyclopaedia of the Laws of Scotland* (ed Lord Dunedin and J Wark) (1926) paras 1017–1080.
3 *Third Report on Criminal Appeals in Scotland* (the Thomson Report) (Cmnd 7005) (1977).
4 See note 1 above.

8.02. The High Court of Justiciary. The High Court of Justiciary is the final court of appeal in Scotland; there is no right of appeal to the House of Lords in criminal matters[1]. There is, of course, a right for accused persons convicted at a sitting of the High Court as a court of first instance to appeal to the High Court sitting as a court of appeal. Its decision on appeal is final, subject only to the exercise of the royal prerogative of mercy and to the power of the Secretary of State for Scotland to refer a case to the High Court whether or not there has been a previous appeal against conviction or sentence[2]. Where questions of interpretation of European Community law are the subject of appeal, the High Court may refer the proceedings to the Court of Justice of the European Communities[3].

A person sentenced for contempt in civil proceedings has no right of appeal to the High Court[4]. The prosecutor cannot appeal against the verdict of a jury in criminal proceedings[5]. In addition to advocation, suspension and the statutory modes of appeal provided for in the Criminal Procedure (Scotland) Act 1975, an appeal may be made to the *nobile officium* of the High Court where there is no other right of appeal, provided such a review is not expressly excluded by statute.

1 *Mackintosh v Lord Advocate* (1876) 3 R (HL) 34; Criminal Procedure (Scotland) Act 1975 (c 21), ss 262, 281. See also A J MacLean 'The House of Lords and Appeals from the High Court of Justiciary 1707–1887' 1985 JR 192, and Lord Fraser of Tullybelton 'The House of Lords as a Court of Last Resort for the United Kingdom' 1986 SLT (News) 33.
2 See the Criminal Procedure (Scotland) Act 1975, s 263, and para 8.21 below.
3 EEC Treaty, art 177; Euratom Treaty, art 150; ECSC Treaty, art 41; Act of Adjournal (Consolidation) 1988, SI 1988/110, rr 63–67, 113–118, Sch 1, Forms 31, 32. See R W Renton and H H Brown *Criminal Procedure according to the Law of Scotland* (5th edn, 1983) paras 11-53, 11-54, 16-184–16-191.
4 *Cordiner* 1973 JC 16, 1973 SLT 125.
5 See, however, the Criminal Procedure (Scotland) Act 1975, s 263A (added by the Criminal Justice (Scotland) Act 1980 (c 62), s 37), and para 8.18 below.

8.03. Quorum of judges. Three judges of the High Court of Justiciary form a quorum for hearing appeals and other related proceedings[1]. High Court judges sitting outside Edinburgh may certify points of law or preliminary matters for decision by the High Court sitting as a court of appeal[2]. In cases where the trial judge is assisted by other judges during the trial proceedings[3], appeals against conviction will in practice be heard by a greater number of judges than comprised the court which made the decision appealed against[4]. A full bench of the High Court can overrule the decision of a smaller full bench of judges[5].

1 Criminal Procedure (Scotland) Act 1975 (c 21), s 245(1) (amended by the Criminal Justice (Scotland) Act 1987 (c 41), s 70(1), Sch 1, para 13(1)).
2 R W Renton and H H Brown *Criminal Procedure according to the Law of Scotland* (5th edn, 1983) para 11-03.
3 Criminal Procedure (Scotland) Act 1975, s 113(4) proviso (amended by the Criminal Justice (Scotland) Act 1980 (c 62), s 83(2), Sch 7, para 32, and the Criminal Justice (Scotland) Act 1987, s 70(2), Sch 2); *Renton and Brown* para 11-04.
4 *Renton and Brown* para 11-04.
5 See eg *Brennan v HM Advocate* 1977 JC 38, 1977 SLT 151; and *Leggate v HM Advocate* 1988 SCCR 391, 1988 SLT 665 (seven judges), overruling *Templeton v McLeod* 1985 SCCR 357, 1986 SLT 149 (five judges).

8.04. Legal aid. Where an accused person wishes to appeal against conviction or sentence in solemn or summary proceedings and instructs his legal representative accordingly, fresh application for legal aid must be made. Application for a legal aid certificate must include a statement from the nominated solicitor as to his willingness to act and, where the nominated solicitor is of the opinion that there are substantial grounds for taking an appeal, a statement as to the nature of those grounds[1]. The application is made to the Scottish Legal Aid Board, which must be satisfied inter alia that it is in the interests of justice that legal aid should be made available[2].

1 Legal Aid (Scotland) Act 1986 (c 47), s 25; Criminal Legal Aid (Scotland) Regulations 1987, SI 1987/307, reg 13(1).
2 Ibid, regs 11(2), 13(2).

(b) Appeals arising from Solemn Procedure

(A) APPEAL FROM PRELIMINARY DIET

8.05. General. Either party has a right of appeal against the decision of a preliminary diet[1]. This right is in addition to the right of the accused person to appeal against any subsequent conviction or the prosecutor's right of advocation. Application for leave to appeal against the decisions of the court at a preliminary diet must be made immediately by the accused after tendering pleas to the charges[2], and the court must decide forthwith whether to grant or refuse the application[3]. A note of appeal must be lodged by the party appealing to the clerk of court not later than two days after the preliminary diet[4]. In sheriff court cases the sheriff must send a report on his decision to the Clerk of Justiciary and the Clerk of Justiciary on receipt of the proceedings sends a copy of the sheriff's report to the parties and fixes an appeal hearing[5]. Such appeals are given priority and may be held before the diet fixed for trial. The High Court, however, does have power to postpone the trial diet and direct that all or any part of this time is not to count towards any time limits[6]. In such cases the Clerk of Justiciary must send a copy of the High Court order to the sheriff clerk, all parties and the governor of the prison or institution in which the accused is detained, if relevant[7].

The High Court may uphold the decisions of judges of first instance or remit the case back with directions which may include directions regarding the fixing of a new diet[8]. An appeal against the decision of a preliminary diet may be abandoned at any time before the hearing by lodging a minute of abandonment with the Clerk of Justiciary[9]. No issue can be raised at such an appeal which was not an issue at the preliminary diet[10].

1 Criminal Procedure (Scotland) Act 1975 (c 21), s 76A(1) (added by the Criminal Justice (Scotland) Act 1980 (c 62), s 12, Sch 4, para 5); *Walkingshaw v Robinson & Davidson Ltd* 1989 GWD 26–1136.
2 See *Lafferty v Jessop* 1989 SCCR 451, 1989 GWD 32–1466 and Act of Adjournal (Consolidation) 1988 r 128(1).
3 Criminal Procedure (Scotland) Act 1975, s 76A(1) (as so added); Act of Adjournal (Consolidation) 1988, SI 1988/110, r 34; R W Renton and H H Brown *Criminal Procedure according to the Law of Scotland* (5th edn, 1983) para 9-14. See eg *Reid v HM Advocate* 1984 SCCR 153, 1984 SLT 391. The Crown does not need to seek leave immediately, but can do so not later than two days after the diet: see *Houston v MacDonald* 1988 SCCR 611 at 615, 1989 SLT 276 at 277, 278.
4 Criminal Procedure (Scotland) Act 1975, s 76A(1) (as so added); Act of Adjournal (Consolidation) 1988, r 35, Sch 1, Form 17.
5 Ibid, rr 36, 37.
6 Criminal Procedure (Scotland) Act 1975, s 76A(2) (as added: see note 1 above).
7 Act of Adjournal (Consolidation) 1988, r 38.
8 Criminal Procedure (Scotland) Act 1975, s 76A(3) (as added: see note 1 above).
9 Act of Adjournal (Consolidation) 1988, r 40.
10 *Templeton v HM Advocate* 1987 SCCR 693, 1988 SLT 171n; *Booth v Brien* 1989 GWD 10–422.

(B) APPEAL AGAINST CONVICTION AND AGAINST CONVICTION AND SENTENCE

(i) Introduction

8.06. Bringing the appeal. Where an accused convicted on indictment wishes to appeal to the High Court of Justiciary against conviction[1] or against both conviction and sentence[2], written intimation of intention to appeal must be lodged within two weeks of the final determination of the proceedings with the Clerk of Justiciary and a copy sent to the Crown Agent[3]. An appeal against conviction may be taken within two weeks of sentence first being deferred by the court[4]. Bail may be applied for at the appeal stage[5], and if necessary an appeal made to the High Court against refusal of interim liberation.

Within six weeks of lodging an intimation of intention to appeal a written note of appeal must be lodged with the Clerk of Justiciary who will copy it to the trial judge and the Crown Agent[6]. The note of appeal must contain a full statement and proper specification of all of the grounds of appeal[7] and must be signed by the appellant, his solicitor or counsel[8].

The two-week and six-week periods referred to above may be extended by the High Court following an application at any time[9]. Such extensions will be granted only where there are good reasons for non-compliance with the time limits[10]. The High Court has power to grant leave to the appellant to found on grounds not contained in the note of appeal[11], but this power is rarely exercised. The appeal may be refused if grounds are not adequately specified[12]. The appellant is entitled to see a transcript of the judge's charge to the jury before framing grounds of appeal, and this may result in the need to extend the time limit or to lodge supplementary grounds or substitute new reasons for those already notified[13].

1 The right of appeal arises under the Criminal Procedure (Scotland) Act 1975 (c 21), s 228(1)(a) (substituted by the Criminal Justice (Scotland) Act 1980 (c 62), s 33, Sch 2, para 1). An appeal against conviction is unlikely to succeed if the application concerns essential jury matters: *Pyne v HM Advocate* 1989 GWD 26–1134.

2 The right of appeal arises under the Criminal Procedure (Scotland) Act 1975, s 228(1)(c) (as so substituted).

3 Ibid, s 231(1) (substituted by the Criminal Justice (Scotland) Act 1980, Sch 2, para 3). The notice should follow the style laid down in Act of Adjournal (Consolidation) 1988, SI 1988/110, r 84, Sch 1, Form 37.

4 Criminal Procedure (Scotland) Act 1975, s 231(4) (as so substituted). As to deferred sentences, see s 219, and para 7.20 above.

5 Ibid, s 238 (amended by the Criminal Justice (Scotland) Act 1980, ss 33, 83(3), Sch 2, para 10, Sch 8).

6 Criminal Procedure (Scotland) Act 1975, s 233(1) (substituted by the Criminal Justice (Scotland) Act 1980, Sch 2, para 5).

7 Criminal Procedure (Scotland) Act 1975, s 233(2) (as so substituted); Act of Adjournal (Consolidation) 1988, r 84, Sch 1, Form 38; High Court of Justiciary Practice Note 'Appeals in Solemn Procedure etc' 1985 SLT (News) 120.

8 Criminal Procedure (Scotland) Act 1975, s 236c (added by the Criminal Justice (Scotland) Act 1980, Sch 2, para 8).

9 Criminal Procedure (Scotland) Act 1975, s 236B(2) (as so added); Act of Adjournal (Consolidation) 1988, r 84, Sch 1, Form 39.

10 See R W Renton and H H Brown *Criminal Procedure according to the Law of Scotland* (5th edn, 1983) para 11-14.

11 Criminal Procedure (Scotland) Act 1975, s 233(3) (as substituted: see note 6 above).

12 *Leighton v HM Advocate* 1931 JC 1, 1931 SLT 69; *Boyd v HM Advocate* 1939 JC 6; 1939 SLT 60; *Baxter v HM Advocate* 1989 GWD 1–6.

13 *Renton and Brown* para 11-17.

8.07. Abandonment of appeal. An appeal may be abandoned at any time prior to the hearing by lodging a notice of abandonment with the Clerk of Justiciary[1]. The appellant is deemed to have abandoned his appeal if he fails to appear at the hearing[2]. However, once the case has been called at the hearing the court is not obliged to consent to abandonment[3].

1 Criminal Procedure (Scotland) Act 1975 (c 21), s 244 (substituted by the Criminal Justice (Scotland) Act 1980 (c 62), s 33, Sch 2, para 13); Act of Adjournal (Consolidation) 1988, SI 1988/110, r 84, Sch 1, Form 41.

2 Criminal Procedure (Scotland) Act 1975, s 257 (amended by the Criminal Justice (Scotland) Act 1980, ss 33, 83(3), Sch 2, para 21, Sch 8); *Cosgrove v HM Advocate* 1946 SN 60.

3 *Ferguson v HM Advocate* 1980 JC 27, 1980 SLT 21.

(ii) The Appeal

8.08. Hearing of appeal. The date of hearing for the appeal is intimated by the Clerk of Justiciary to the Crown Agent and to the accused's solicitor or direct to the accused if he is unrepresented[1]. Three typed or printed copies of the appeal must thereupon be lodged with the High Court of Justiciary by the appellant[1].

It is competent, though unusual, for the appellant to present his case in writing rather than orally[2]. A copy of his written submission must be sent to the Clerk of Justiciary and the Crown Agent four days before the hearing[2], and the appellant may not then make oral submissions unless the court grants leave[3]. In such proceedings the respondent does not reply in writing but makes oral submissions at the appeal hearing in the normal way[4].

The accused is normally present at the hearing although he need not be where the appeal concerns questions of law only. Conversely the court can deal with appeals in the absence of the accused if he chooses and can sentence him in his absence[5].

The judge of first instance can be called upon to produce his notes[6]. Such notes are rarely requested as the judge is now required to send a written report to the Clerk of Justiciary as soon as reasonably practicable after receipt by the judge of the copy note of appeal[7]. This report is sent by the Clerk of Justiciary to the appellant or his solicitor and the Crown Agent[7]. Any productions and documents lodged in connection with the trial which forms the basis of the appeal proceedings are retained for use at the appeal hearing[8]. The High Court may order the extension of shorthand notes taken at the trial to facilitate consideration of the appeal[9]. The accused, the prosecutor and any person named in, or immediately affected by, any order made by the trial court may obtain transcripts[10].

The High Court has a variety of powers to which it may have recourse in considering appeals[11]. It may order production of documents and labelled productions relevant to the proceedings or may hear additional evidence or remit to any fit person to inquire and report on aspects of the case or, where necessary, appoint an expert assessor to assist in determining the appeal[12]. In certain circumstances the court may take account of factors not before the trial judge[13].

1 Criminal Procedure (Scotland) Act 1975, s 239(1) (amended by the Criminal Justice (Scotland) Act 1980 (c 62), s 33, Sch 2, para 11).
2 Criminal Procedure (Scotland) Act 1975, s 234(1) (amended by the Criminal Justice (Scotland) Act 1980, ss 33, 83(3), Sch 2, para 6, Sch 8).
3 Criminal Procedure (Scotland) Act 1975, s 234(3) (as so amended).
4 Ibid, s 234(2).
5 Ibid, s 258.
6 Ibid, s 146, and s 237 (substituted by the Criminal Justice (Scotland) Act 1980, Sch 2, para 9).
7 Criminal Procedure (Scotland) Act 1975, s 236A (added by the Criminal Justice (Scotland) Act 1980, Sch 2, para 8).
8 R W Renton and H H Brown *Criminal Procedure according to the Law of Scotland* (5th edn, 1983) para 11-07.
9 Criminal Procedure (Scotland) Act 1975, s 274(1) (amended by the Criminal Justice (Scotland) Act 1980, Sch 2, para 30, Sch 8). Cf *Raiker v HM Advocate* 1989 GWD 13-540.
10 Criminal Procedure (Scotland) Act 1975, s 275(3), (5).
11 *Renton and Brown* para 11-32.
12 Criminal Procedure (Scotland) Act 1975, s 252(a), (b), (d), (e) (substituted by the Criminal Justice (Scotland) Act 1980, Sch 2, para 16).
13 Criminal Procedure (Scotland) Act 1975, s 252(c) (as so substituted); see *Renton and Brown* para 11-32. This power may be limited to appeals against sentence: *Rubin v HM Advocate* 1984 SCCR 96 at 108, 1984 SLT 369 at 372, 373 (see also Sheriff Gordon's commentary at 1984 SCCR 112).

8.09. Determination of appeal. The Criminal Justice (Scotland) Act 1980 amended the powers of the High Court of Justiciary in determining appeals, and replaced the previous criteria with the single task of reviewing any alleged miscarriage of justice[1]. Previously the court could allow an appeal where it considered that the verdict was unreasonable and unsupportable on the evidence, or that there had been an erroneous decision on a point of law by the trial judge, or that there had been a miscarriage of justice[2].

However, the court has held that it need not allow an appeal in every case where a miscarriage of justice is established[3]. 'Miscarriage of justice' is not defined in the Criminal Procedure (Scotland) Act 1975. It is therefore worth while looking at the grounds of appeal provided in the previous legislation[4], as the High Court effectively may allow an appeal if these criteria are made out[5].

1 Criminal Procedure (Scotland) Act 1975 (c 21), s 228(2) (substituted by the Criminal Justice (Scotland) Act 1980 (c 62), s 33, Sch 2, para 1).
2 See the Criminal Appeal (Scotland) Act 1926 (c 15), s 2 (repealed), and the Criminal Procedure (Scotland) Act 1975, s 254 (as originally enacted). See also R W Renton and H H Brown *Criminal Procedure according to the Law of Scotland* (5th edn, 1983) para 11-33.
3 *McCuaig v HM Advocate* 1982 SCCR 125, 1982 SLT 383; *Jackson v HM Advocate* 1982 JC 117, *sub nom McAvoy v HM Advocate* 1982 SCCR 263, 1983 SLT 16.
4 See paras 8.10–8.13 below.
5 *Reilly v HM Advocate* 1981 SCCR 201.

(iii) Grounds of Appeal

8.10. Unreasonable verdict. The High Court has always interpreted strictly its power to allow an appeal on the ground that the verdict was unreasonable or unsupportable on the evidence, and will interfere with a verdict only if it is thought self-contradictory or perverse[1]. Thus the court has set aside convictions obtained only where the evidence was insufficient to support the verdict or the case lacked corroboration[2]. A weak case, conflicting evidence or questions as to the credibility of witnesses are not sufficient by themselves to cause the High Court to interfere with a verdict[3].

1 *Hamilton v HM Advocate* 1938 JC 134, 1938 SLT 333; *Hancock v HM Advocate* 1981 JC 74, 1981 SCCR 32; *Rubin v HM Advocate* 1984 SCCR 96, 1984 SLT 369; *White v HM Advocate* 1989 SCCR 553, 1989 GWD 38–1746; *Blair v HM Advocate* 1989 SCCR 79, 1989 SLT 459; *Watkins v HM Advocate* 1988 SCCR 443, 1989 SLT 24.
2 *Morton v HM Advocate* 1938 JC 50, 1938 SLT 27; *Kent v HM Advocate* 1950 JC 38, 1950 SLT 130; *Kenny v HM Advocate* 1951 JC 104, 1951 SLT 363.
3 *Macmillan v HM Advocate* 1927 JC 62, 1927 SLT 425; *Webb v HM Advocate* 1927 JC 92, 1927 SLT 631; *Dow v MacKnight* 1949 JC 38, 1949 SLT 95; *Rubin v HM Advocate* 1984 SCCR 96, 1984 SLT 369.

8.11. Error in law. Where a conviction flows from an incompetent or irrelevant indictment the conviction falls to be quashed. If the defect in the indictment is such as to render the charge fundamentally null the conviction will be quashed even though no objection has been taken at an earlier stage of the proceedings[1]. Similar results will follow if the court of first instance is shown to have acted in excess of its jurisdiction or the diet was not properly constituted[2]. The High Court may also quash the conviction if a wrong decision was made in the court of first instance to admit or reject evidence or allow a witness to be called or recalled or to refuse to allow parties to re-examine or cross-examine a witness[3]. Other errors in law which may be fatal to the conviction obtained arise where the trial judge incorrectly withdraws a line of defence which ought to have been left open to the jury or where he withdraws the right to convict the accused of a lesser charge[4]. There are, however, occasions where the judge should not direct the jury that alternative lesser verdicts are open to it[5].

1 *Sangster v HM Advocate* (1896) 24 R (J) 3, 2 Adam 182.

2 *Gallagher v HM Advocate* 1937 JC 27, 1937 SLT 75; *Hull v HM Advocate* 1945 JC 83, 1945 SLT 202.
3 *M'Neilie v HM Advocate* 1929 JC 50, 1929 SLT 145; *M'Leod v HM Advocate* 1939 JC 68, 1939 SLT 556; *McPherson v Copeland* 1961 JC 74, 1961 SLT 373; *Sandlan v HM Advocate* 1983 JC 22, 1983 SCCR 71, 1983 SLT 519; *Bates v HM Advocate* 1989 SCCR 338.
4 *Hillan v HM Advocate* 1937 JC 53; 1937 SLT 396; *Mackenzie v HM Advocate* 1982 SCCR 499, 1983 SLT 220.
5 *Kilna v HM Advocate* 1960 JC 23; *Templeton v HM Advocate* 1961 JC 62, 1961 SLT 328; *M'Hugh v HM Advocate* 1978 JC 12.

8.12. Misdirection by the trial judge. Misdirections may arise because the trial judge has incorrectly stated the position in law or in respect of fact to the jury or has omitted or given incorrect or ambiguous directions to the jury[1]. The approach of the High Court in such questions is to consider the judge's charge as a whole in the context of the trial which took place rather than to analyse aspects of the summing up in isolation[2]. Provided the judge's charge is considered to have been clear to the jury the High Court will not allow an appeal simply because the directions were not in a precise legal form[3]. There are, however, a variety of situations where the judge can be held to have misdirected the jury. The following list gives examples:
(1) incorrectly defining the crimes charged;
(2) incorrectly defining the requirements of any specific defence raised in the case[4];
(3) failing to direct that the onus of proof rests on the Crown and the nature of any onus which rests on the defence[5];
(4) failing in appropriate cases to warn regarding the evidence of an accomplice[6] or giving such a warning in the case of the evidence of a co-accused[7];
(5) incorrectly stating the value and weight of evidence[8];
(6) failing to state correctly the law relating to concert[9];
(7) failing to explain the verdicts open to the jury and the majority necessary for guilty[10].
    Even where counsel allude to an issue in their speeches, if the judge fails to direct the jury on an important point this may be fatal to the conviction[11]. It will be regarded as a misdirection where the judge stresses his own view of the evidence to the jury or fails to state the defence case properly[12] (although he need not cover it in detail), or omits to mention evidence to the contrary when dealing with factual matters[13]. The judge need not summarise or rehearse the whole of the evidence[14].

1 *Scott v HM Advocate* 1946 JC 90, 1946 SLT 140; *Greig v HM Advocate* 1949 SLT (Notes) 5; *Rubin v HM Advocate* 1984 SCCR 96, 1984 SLT 369; *Larkin v HM Advocate* 1988 SCCR 30; cf *White v HM Advocate* 1989 SCCR 553, 1989 GWD 38–1740.
2 *Muir v HM Advocate* 1933 JC 46, 1933 SLT 403; *M'Phelim v HM Advocate* 1960 JC 17, 1960 SLT 214; *Gemmill v HM Advocate* 1980 JC 16, 1979 SLT 217.
3 *Tobin v HM Advocate* 1934 JC 60, 1934 SLT 325; *Docherty v HM Advocate* 1945 JC 89, 1945 SLT 247; *M'Phelim v HM Advocate* 1960 JC 17, 1960 SLT 214.
4 *Owens v HM Advocate* 1946 JC 119, 1946 SLT 227; *Lambie v HM Advocate* 1973 JC 53, 1973 SLT 219.
5 *Hillan v HM Advocate* 1937 JC 53, 1937 SLT 396; *M'Kenzie v HM Advocate* 1959 JC 32; *M'Cann v HM Advocate* 1960 JC 36, 1961 SLT 73; *Donnelly v HM Advocate* 1977 SLT 147; *Mullen v HM Advocate* 1978 SLT (Notes) 33.
6 *Docherty v HM Advocate* 1987 SCCR 418, 1987 SLT 784 (nine judges).
7 *Slowey v HM Advocate* 1965 SLT 309; *McCourt v HM Advocate* 1977 SLT (Notes) 22.
8 *Morton v HM Advocate* 1938 JC 50, 1938 SLT 27; *Wilkie v HM Advocate* 1938 JC 128, 1938 SLT 366.
9 *Tobin v HM Advocate* 1934 JC 60, 1934 SLT 325; *Docherty v HM Advocate* 1945 JC 89, 1945 SLT 247; *Greig v HM Advocate* 1949 SLT (Notes) 5; *Burns v HM Advocate* 1983 SLT 38.
10 *McNichol v HM Advocate* 1964 JC 25, 1964 SLT 151; *Affleck v HM Advocate* 1987 SCCR 150; *Macdonald v HM Advocate* 1989 SCCR 29, 1989 SLT 298; *Fay v HM Advocate* 1989 SCCR 373.

11 *Muir v HM Advocate* 1933 JC 46, 1933 SLT 403. See, however, *Kilna v HM Advocate* 1960 JC 23.
12 *Fraser v HM Advocate* 1982 SCCR 458; *Meek v HM Advocate* 1982 SCCR 613, 1983 SLT 280; *Rubin v HM Advocate* 1984 SCCR 96, 1984 SLT 369.
13 *Mills v HM Advocate* 1935 JC 77, 1935 SLT 532; *Simpson v HM Advocate* 1952 JC 1, *sub nom HM Advocate v Simpson* 1952 SLT 85; *McMillan v HM Advocate* 1979 SLT (Notes) 68; *Tallis v HM Advocate* 1982 SCCR 91.
14 *MacNeil v HM Advocate* 1986 SCCR 288; *Brady v HM Advocate* 1986 SCCR 191, 1986 SLT 686.

8.13. Miscarriage of justice. In the past appeals have been taken on the ground of miscarriage of justice regarding irregularities in trial procedure and unfairness on the part of the judge or the Crown in relation to the conduct of the trial[1]. Examples of this type of miscarriage include conversations between witnesses and jurors, malpractice by a juror, failure to read a special defence to the jury, disclosing to the jury that an accused has pleaded guilty to part of the indictment and excessive questioning and cross-examination of witnesses by the trial judge[2].

Compensation may now be awarded by the Secretary of State where an appeal has been allowed on this ground[3].

1 *Smith v HM Advocate* 1952 JC 66, 1952 SLT 286; *Bergson v HM Advocate* (1970) 34 JCL 270; *Hutchison v HM Advocate* 1983 SCCR 504, 1984 SLT 233.
2 *Smart v HM Advocate* 1938 JC 148, 1938 SLT 511; *Moar v HM Advocate* 1949 JC 31, 1949 SLT 106; *Walsh v HM Advocate* 1961 JC 51, 1961 SLT 137; *Livingstone v HM Advocate* (1974) SCCR Supp 68; *Nisbet v HM Advocate* 1979 SLT (Notes) 5; *McCadden v HM Advocate* 1985 SCCR 282, 1986 SLT 138; *McColl v HM Advocate* 1989 SCCR 229, 1989 GWD 18–760.
3 See the Criminal Justice Act 1988 (c 33), s 133, and para 8.24 below.

8.14. Additional evidence. Since the passing of the Criminal Appeal (Scotland) Act 1926 (c 15) the High Court of Justiciary has had power to hear additional evidence and dispose of an appeal in the light of that evidence. This power has been exercised sparingly, and appeals will succeed only where the court is satisfied that had the jury heard the evidence an acquittal would have followed or alternatively, in view of the additional evidence, the jury's original verdict is seen as perverse or unreasonable[1]. Since the Criminal Justice (Scotland) Act 1980 amended the law on appeals[2], the High Court has held that additional evidence will be entertained where the court is satisfied that there may have been a miscarriage of justice[3], or where the court is satisfied that the jury would have acquitted if it had heard the new evidence[4]. The High Court will not entertain evidence which could have been made available at the trial in this context[5].

In appeals of this type the note of appeal should have attached precognitions of the witnesses sought to be adduced and their names and addresses. The court must be satisfied that the additional evidence placed before it is sufficiently substantial, convincing and trustworthy to warrant an inquiry[6]. When the court decides to hear additional evidence it may be heard by any High Court judge or person appointed by the court[7]. A diet of proof is fixed, and evidence is adduced in the usual manner by parties examining and cross-examining witnesses[8].

1 *Gallacher v HM Advocate* 1951 JC 38, 1951 SLT 158; *Higgins v HM Advocate* 1956 JC 69, 1956 SLT 307; *Lindie v HM Advocate* 1974 JC 1, 1974 SLT 208; *Preece v HM Advocate* [1981] Crim LR 783; *Courtney v MacKinnon* 1986 SCCR 545.
2 See para 8.01 above.
3 *Green v HM Advocate* 1983 SCCR 42; *Morland v HM Advocate* 1985 SCCR 316; cf *Moffat v HM Advocate* 1983 SCCR 121; *Mitchell v HM Advocate* 1989 SCCR 502.
4 *Cameron v HM Advocate* 1987 SCCR 608, 1988 SLT 169n.
5 *Jones v HM Advocate* 1989 SCCR 726; *Cameron v Lowe* 1989 GWD 1406.
6 *McCadden v HM Advocate* 1985 SCCR 282, 1986 SLT 138; *Morland v HM Advocate* 1985 SCCR 316; *Allison v HM Advocate* 1985 SCCR 408; *Thomas v HM Advocate* 1990 GWD 1–10.

7 Criminal Procedure (Scotland) Act 1975 (c 21), s 252(b) (substituted by the Criminal Justice (Scotland) Act 1980 (c 62), s 33, Sch 2, para 16).
8 Criminal Procedure (Scotland) Act 1975, s 253(1).

(iv) The Court's Powers

8.15. Disposal of appeals. The normal course is for the High Court of Justiciary either to refuse the appeal and affirm the jury's verdict or allow the appeal, set aside the verdict and quash the conviction[1]. The court may in certain circumstances substitute an amended verdict to a lesser charge, if such a course would have been competent at the trial and substitute another (but not more severe) sentence[1]. If the court decides that the appellant committed the act charged but was insane at the time, an acquittal by reason of insanity will be substituted for the conviction and a hospital order substituted[2]. The High Court does have a discretion to refuse an appeal even where there has been a miscarriage of justice where it is not considered sufficiently material to merit quashing the conviction[3].

Since 1980 the High Court has had power to dispose of the appeal by setting aside the conviction and granting authority to bring a new prosecution[4]. A new prosecution may be instituted by charging the accused with the same or similar offences arising out of the same facts, and the accused is not liable to any greater punishment than he faced in the earlier indictment[5]. Any such proceedings must be commenced within two months of the date on which the authority is given[6]. Proceedings are deemed to commence when a warrant to arrest or cite the accused is obtained, provided any such warrant is enforced without unreasonable delay[6]. If no proceedings are taken within the time limit the High Court's decision in relation to the appeal has the effect of an acquittal[7].

1 Criminal Procedure (Scotland) Act 1975 (c 21), s 254(1), (2) (substituted by the Criminal Justice (Scotland) Act 1980 (c 62), s 33, Sch 2, para 18); *Jamieson v HM Advocate* 1987 SCCR 484.
2 Criminal Procedure (Scotland) Act 1975, s 254(4) (as so substituted).
3 *McCuaig v HM Advocate* 1982 SCCR 125, 1982 SLT 383; *Jackson v HM Advocate* 1982 JC 117, *sub nom McAvoy v HM Advocate* 1982 SCCR 263, 1983 SLT 16.
4 Criminal Procedure (Scotland) Act 1975, s 254(1)(c) (as substituted: see note 1 above); *Mackenzie v HM Advocate* 1982 SCCR 449, 1983 SLT 220; *Cunningham v HM Advocate* 1984 JC 37, 1984 SCCR 40, 1984 SLT 249; *Mitchell v HM Advocate* 1989 SCCR 502; cf *McColl v HM Advocate* 1989 SCCR 229.
5 Criminal Procedure (Scotland) Act 1975, s 255(1) (substituted by the Criminal Justice (Scotland) Act 1980, Sch 2, para 19).
6 Criminal Procedure (Scotland) Act 1975, s 255(3) (as so substituted).
7 Ibid, s 255(4) (as so substituted).

(C) APPEAL AGAINST SENTENCE ALONE

8.16. General. Where an appeal is brought against sentence only a written note of appeal must be lodged with the Clerk of Justiciary within two weeks of sentence being passed[1]. The provisions relating to computation and extension of time limits, statements of grounds of appeal, the judge's report and the power to hear additional evidence also apply to appeals against sentence alone[2].

1 Criminal Procedure (Scotland) Act 1975 (c 21), s 233(1) (substituted by the Criminal Justice (Scotland) Act 1980 (c 62), s 33, Sch 2, para 8).
2 See paras 8.06 ff above, and R W Renton and H H Brown *Criminal Procedure according to the Law of Scotland* (5th edn, 1983) para 11-46.

8.17. Disposal of appeal. In refusing an appeal against sentence the High Court of Justiciary may affirm the sentence imposed by the court of first instance or increase it[1]. On the other hand, if the appeal is successful the court will impose whatever lesser sentence it deems appropriate[1]. Sentence, including a sentence of imprisonment, may be imposed in the absence of the appellant[2]. The court may hear additional evidence in determining an appeal[3]. The appeal criterion is alleged miscarriage of justice, but normally this centres upon whether the sentence imposed was excessive or inappropriate having regard to the circumstances of the case and the appellant's background and circumstances[4]. All facets of sentencing are appealable, including recommendations for a minimum period of imprisonment under a sentence of life imprisonment, hospital orders and interim hospital orders, disqualification for holding or obtaining a driving licence, compensation orders, recommendations for deportation and deferred sentences[5].

1 Criminal Procedure (Scotland) Act 1975 (c 21), s 254(3) (substituted by the Criminal Justice (Scotland) Act 1980 (c 62), s 33, Sch 2, para 18); *Boyle v HM Advocate* 1949 SLT (Notes) 40; *Connelly v HM Advocate* 1954 JC 90, 1954 SLT 259; *Grant v HM Advocate* 1985 SCCR 431; *Donnelly v HM Advocate* 1988 SCCR 386.
2 Criminal Procedure (Scotland) Act 1975, s 258.
3 Ibid, s 228(2) (substituted by the Criminal Justice (Scotland) Act 1980, Sch 2, para 1).
4 R W Renton and H H Brown *Criminal Procedure according to the Law of Scotland* (5th edn, 1983) para 11-47.
5 *Renton and Brown* para 11-49; C G B Nicholson *The Law and Practice of Sentencing in Scotland* (1981) para 2-07.

(D) OTHER MODES AND FORMS OF APPEAL

8.18. Lord Advocate's references. Procedure by way of Lord Advocate's reference was introduced in 1980 to enable the Crown to obtain a ruling in relation to any point of law which arose in respect of a charge on which an accused was acquitted[1]. Where the Lord Advocate refers such a matter to the High Court of Justiciary, the Clerk of Justiciary is obliged to intimate to the accused and his agent[1]. The accused may intimate not less than seven days prior to the hearing fixed whether he will be present or legally represented[2]. Failing such intimation of legal representation the High Court will appoint counsel to act as *amicus curiae* [3]. Any opinion on such a reference does not affect the acquittal in the trial[4].

1 Criminal Procedure (Scotland) Act 1975 (c 21), s 263A(1) (added by the Criminal Justice (Scotland) Act 1980 (c 62), s 37).
2 Criminal Procedure (Scotland) Act 1975, s 263A(2) (as so added).
3 Ibid, s 263A(3) (as so added).
4 Ibid, s 263A(5). See *Lord Advocate's Reference No 1 of 1983* 1984 JC 52, 1984 SCCR 62, 1984 SLT 337, and *Lord Advocate's Reference No 1 of 1985* 1986 SCCR 329, 1987 SLT 187.

8.19. Advocation. The remedy of advocation is available to the prosecutor where an indictment is dismissed on some preliminary ground or proceedings are terminated at some early stage of the proceedings. Historically it was not possible to advocate a decision of the High Court of Justiciary, but the procedure was extended in 1980[1]. Where the prosecutor is successful he has the power to serve a fresh indictment in the same terms as the original[2]. The prosecutor can advocate after the accused has pled to the charges but before being sentenced[3].

1 See the Criminal Procedure (Scotland) Act 1975, s 280A (added by the Criminal Justice (Scotland) Act 1980 (c 62), s 35). The topic is more fully discussed in paras 8.68 ff below.

2 Criminal Procedure (Scotland) Act 1975, s 280A(2) (as so added). See eg *HM Advocate v Sinclair* 1986 SCCR 439, 1987 SLT 161.
3 *HM Advocate v McKenzie* 1989 SCCR 587.

8.20. Appeals against references to the European Court of Justice. Where a trial court makes an order referring a case for a preliminary ruling to the Court of Justice of the European Community[1], either party may within fourteen days appeal against the order[2]. The High Court of Justiciary may dismiss the appeal and transmit the reference or sustain the appeal and remit the case back to the court of first instance to proceed as accords[3]. If a question of European law is raised the High Court sitting as an appeal court is obliged to make a reference[4].

1 Ie under the EEC Treaty, art 177, the Euratom Treaty, art 150, or the ECSC Treaty, art 41: see para 8.72 below.
2 Act of Adjournal (Consolidation) 1988, SI 1988/110, r 67(1), (2), Sch 1, Form 32. *Wither v Cowie* (1990) The Scotsman, 22 August, High Ct.
3 Ibid, r 67(4).
4 R W Renton and H H Brown *Criminal Procedure according to the Law of Scotland* (5th edn, 1983) paras 11-53, 11-54.

(E) MISCELLANEOUS PROVISIONS AS TO SOLEMN APPEALS

8.21. The prerogative of mercy. The statutory provisions relating to appeals in solemn proceedings do not affect the exercise of the royal prerogative of mercy[1]. Furthermore, the Secretary of State has power to refer a case after conviction to the High Court of Justiciary for appellate consideration, whether or not the case has been before the court on appeal previously[1]. This power of reference is exercisable whether or not the person convicted has petitioned for the exercise of Her Majesty's mercy[2].

1 Criminal Procedure (Scotland) Act 1975 (c 21), s 263(1) (amended by the Criminal Justice (Scotland) Act 1980, ss 33, 83(3), Sch 2, para 22, Sch 8).
2 Criminal Procedure (Scotland) Act 1975, s 263(2).

8.22. Expenses. No expenses are allowed on either side in relation to appeal proceedings[1].

1 See the Criminal Procedure (Scotland) Act 1975 (c 21), ss 266, 267.

8.23. Correction of errors. If an error in the record of proceedings or extract sentence is noticed during the course of appeal proceedings the High Court of Justiciary has power to deal with the case as if the entry had been corrected[1]. The High Court may then remit the case to the court of first instance for the entry to be corrected by the clerk of court, who authenticates the correction and records the names of the High Court judges authorising such a correction[2]. Any such correction is thereafter intimated to the parties[3]

1 Criminal Procedure (Scotland) Act 1975 (c 21), s 227A(4)(a) (added by the Criminal Justice (Scotland) Act 1980 (c 62), s 20).
2 Criminal Procedure (Scotland) Act 1975, s 227A(4)(b), (5) (as so added).
3 Ibid, s 227A(3) (as so added).

8.24. Compensation for miscarriage of justice. When a person has been convicted of a criminal offence, and when subsequently his conviction has been reversed[1] or he has been pardoned on the ground that a new or newly discovered fact shows beyond reasonable doubt that there has been a miscarriage of justice, the Secretary of State may on application pay compensation for the miscarriage of justice to the person who has suffered punishment as a result of the conviction or, if he has died, to his personal representatives, unless the non-disclosure of the unknown fact was wholly or partly attributable to the person convicted[2]. The question whether there is a right to such compensation is to be determined by the Secretary of State[3], and the amount of the compensation is to be assessed by an assessor appointed by the Secretary of State[4].

1 'Reversed' refers to a conviction quashed on an appeal out of time, or on a reference under the Criminal Procedure (Scotland) Act 1975 (c 21), s 263 (see para 6.21 above): Criminal Justice Act 1988 (c 33), s 133(5).
2 Ibid, s 133(1), (2).
3 Ibid, s 133(3).
4 Ibid, s 133(4). The assessor must be a practising advocate or solicitor, a person who holds or has held judicial office or a member of the Criminal Injuries Compensation Board: s 133(7), Sch 12, para 1.

(c) Appeals arising from Summary Procedure

(A) INTRODUCTION

8.25. Methods of appeal. Nowadays summary proceedings in inferior courts may be reviewed by the High Court of Justiciary by means of:
(1) appeal against decisions as to the competency or relevancy of proceedings[1];
(2) stated case where the accused appeals against conviction or conviction and sentence, or where the prosecutor appeals against an acquittal or an incompetent sentence[2];
(3) note of appeal, where the accused appeals against sentence alone[3];
(4) bill of suspension[4];
(5) bill of advocation[5];
(6) application to the *nobile officium*[6].
In addition, application may be made for a reference to the Court of Justice of the European Communities[7].

1 See para 8.26 below.
2 See paras 8.27 ff below. The prosecutor may appeal on a point of law only, but the accused has a wider right of appeal: see the Criminal Procedure (Scotland) Act 1975 (c 21), s 442(1)(a), (b) (substituted by the Criminal Justice (Scotland) Act 1980 (c 62), s 34, Sch 3, para 1).
3 See paras 8.54 ff below.
4 See paras 8.59 ff below.
5 See paras 8.68 ff below.
6 See para 8.71 below.
7 See para 8.72 below.

(B) COMPETENCY AND RELEVANCY

8.26. Appeal from preliminary diet. Either party may, with leave of the inferior court granted either on motion or *ex proprio motu*, appeal to the High Court of Justiciary against any decision taken following an objection at the preliminary diet to the competency or relevancy of the complaint or denial that the accused is the person charged by the police with the offence, provided that the appeal is marked within two days of the court's decision[1].

An application for leave to appeal should be made to the court immediately following upon the decision in order that the court can if appropriate fix a trial diet sufficiently far ahead for an appeal to be dealt with[2]. When leave to appeal is granted a written note of appeal must be lodged with the clerk of the inferior court within two days of the decision[3]. The clerk of the court sends a copy of the note to the respondent or his agent[4]. He requests a report from the judge, sends a copy of it to the parties and then transmits the proceedings to the Clerk of Justiciary[4]. The appellant may abandon the appeal at any time by lodging a minute of abandonment with the Clerk of Justiciary, who notifies the inferior court of the result of proceedings[5]. If, however, the appeal is pursued, the High Court may affirm the decision of the lower court or remit the case back with appropriate directions and, if necessary, may direct the inferior court to fix a trial diet where it has overturned a decision to dismiss a complaint[6].

Priority is given to appeals of this type in order that further proceedings are not unduly delayed[7]; but if necessary the High Court may postpone the trial diet[8]. Such a postponement may be ordered not to count towards any time limit applying to the proceedings[9].

1 Criminal Procedure (Scotland) Act 1975 (c 21), s 334(2A) (added by the Criminal Justice (Scotland) Act 1980 (c 62), s 36); *Walkingshaw v Robison and Davidson Ltd* 1989 SCCR 359.
2 See the Criminal Procedure (Scotland) Act 1975, s 334(2C) (as so added); Act of Adjournal (Consolidation) 1988, SI 1988/110, r 128(1), (2). The accused must plead to the charges before he can seek leave to appeal: see *Lafferty v Jessop* 1989 SCCR 451, 1989 GWD 32–1466 and the Act of Adjournal (Consolidation) 1988 r 128(1).
3 Ibid, r 128(4), (5), Sch 1, Form 78.
4 Ibid, r 128(6).
5 Ibid, r 128(10)–(12), Sch 1, Form 79.
6 Criminal Procedure (Scotland) Act 1975, s 334(2D) (as added: see note 1 above).
7 Act of Adjournal (Consolidation) 1988, r 128(8).
8 Criminal Procedure (Scotland) Act 1975, s 334(2B) (as added: see note 1 above). The Clerk of Justiciary must intimate the postponement to the clerk of the inferior court, any co-accused or their agents and the governor of any institution detaining the accused: Act of Adjournal (Consolidation) 1988, r 128(9).
9 Criminal Procedure (Scotland) Act 1975, s 334(2B) (as so added).

(C) APPEAL AGAINST CONVICTION OR CONVICTION AND SENTENCE OR BY PROSECUTOR

(i) Appeal by Stated Case generally

8.27. Introduction. Appeal to the High Court of Justiciary by stated case is the proper method of appeal in summary proceedings by an accused person seeking to have his conviction or both conviction and sentence reviewed or by the prosecutor seeking to have the court's decision to acquit reviewed or wishing to challenge the competency of any sentence imposed[1]. The High Court will not entertain appeals on questions of credibility alone[2].

Stated case is not an appropriate method of appealing against an order dismissing a complaint as incompetent or irrelevant[3]. Save in respect of a prosecutor's challenge to the competency of sentence, appeal by stated case is not the proper mode of appeal against an order of the court of acquittal, conviction or sentence which was incompetently made in the lower court[4]. However, where it is sought to challenge the conviction on its merits appeal by stated case is the correct mode of appeal in order that the High Court may consider the views of the trial judge as well as the argument of parties at the appeal hearing[5].

1 Criminal Procedure (Scotland) Act 1975 (c 21), ss 442(1), 444(1) (s 442(1) being substituted by the Criminal Justice (Scotland) Act 1980 (c 62), s 34, Sch 3, para 1).
2 *Montague v Carmichael* 1989 GWD 25–1075; *Wallace v Smith* 1990 GWD 3–109.
3 *Tudhope v Mathieson* 1981 SCCR 231. See para 8.26 above.
4 *MacNeill v MacGregor* 1975 JC 55, 1975 SLT (Notes) 46.
5 *Handley v Pirie* 1976 JC 65, 1977 SLT 30.

8.28. Legal aid for appeals. Legal aid must be applied for anew for appeal proceedings[1]. The application must be made in writing to the Scottish Legal Aid Board and be signed by the applicant; it must include a statement by the nominated solicitor of his willingness to act and, where that solicitor is of opinion that there are substantial grounds of appeal, must include a statement of the nature of those grounds[2]. If the board is satisfied that the applicant has substantial grounds for making the appeal and that it is reasonable that legal aid should be made available to him, the board will grant a legal aid certificate[3]. If the applicant had legal aid for the proceedings at first instance, his financial circumstances are not considered in determining his entitlement to legal aid for the appeal, but otherwise they are[4]. If the application for legal aid is successful, the appeal certificate will normally cover the appellant until the appeal is disposed of. Where the prosecutor has applied for a stated case the accused will normally receive legal aid[5].

1 Criminal Legal Aid (Scotland) Regulations 1987, SI 1987/307, reg 4(1)(f).
2 Legal Aid (Scotland) Act 1986 (c 47), s 25(1), (2); Criminal Legal Aid (Scotland) Regulations 1987, reg 13(1); R W Renton and H H Brown *Criminal Procedure according to the Law of Scotland* (5th edn, 1983) para 16–08.
3 Legal Aid (Scotland) Act 1986. s 25(2)(b).
4 Ibid, s 25(2)(a), (4).
5 See the Criminal Legal Aid (Scotland) Regulations 1987, reg 13(1)(c).

8.29. Bail. Where the appellant has been sentenced to a term of detention or imprisonment or remanded in custody he may apply for bail when marking a stated case appeal[1]. An application for bail must be dealt with by the inferior court within twenty-four hours of receipt[2]. If the application is unsuccessful or if bail conditions are unacceptable an appeal may be made to the High Court of Justiciary provided this is done within twenty-four hours[3].

1 Criminal Procedure (Scotland) Act 1975 (c 21), s 446(1) (substituted by the Criminal Justice (Scotland) Act 1980 (c 62), s 34, Sch 3, para 5).
2 Criminal Procedure (Scotland) Act 1975, s 446(2) (amended by the Bail etc (Scotland) Act 1980 (c 4), s 12(2), Sch 1, para 11); *HM Advocate v Keegan* 1981 SLT (Notes) 35; R W Renton and H H Brown *Criminal Procedure according to the Law of Scotland* (5th edn, 1983) para 16–67.
3 Criminal Procedure (Scotland) Act 1975, s 446(2) (as so amended); *Fenton* 1981 SCCR 288, 1982 SLT 164.

8.30. Form of stated case. Appeal by stated case was introduced by the Summary Prosecutions Appeals (Scotland) Act 1875 (c 62), the provisions of which were codified by the Summary Jurisdiction (Scotland) Act 1908 (c 65) and then re-enacted by the Criminal Procedure (Scotland) Act 1975. Further amendments have been made to the procedure by the Criminal Justice (Scotland) Act 1980 (c 62). The basic principle remains that where parties wish to appeal against the judge's determination in an inferior court in summary proceedings, the judge states the case by setting forth the facts and grounds of his determination for the opinion of the High Court of Justiciary. The judge advises the High Court of the history of the case and the nature of the charge and then lists the facts proved or admitted, sets forth the details of matters competent for review which the appellant wishes the High Court to consider, any points of law relevant thereto and the grounds of the original decision[1].

1 Criminal Procedure (Scotland) Act 1975 (c 21), s 447(2). For the prescribed style, see Act of Adjournal (Consolidation) 1988, SI 1988/10, r 127, Sch 1, Form 72.

(ii) Grounds of Appeal

8.31. Restrictions on stated case appeal procedure. The prosecutor may appeal against acquittal or sentence only on a point of law, but the accused may appeal against conviction or conviction and sentence on the general ground of miscarriage of justice[1]. Prior to the passing of the Criminal Justice (Scotland) Act 1980 the decision of the inferior judge as to the facts held proved in a case was final, and both accused and prosecutor were restricted to appeals on points of law[2]. Since 1980, however, the High Court of Justiciary has been able to consider whether the findings in fact were warranted by the evidence, and has on occasion looked closely at descriptions of evidence alleged to be inadequate and has considered the assessment by the inferior judge of the credibility of witnesses when shown to be based on mistaken beliefs[3].

On the other hand pre-1980 decisions are of relevance when considering stated case appeals taken by the prosecutor or where the accused appeals specifically on a point of law. A further distinction also requires to be drawn between findings in fact which are inferences drawn from other facts and basic or primary facts. The former have never been binding on the High Court, since incorrect inferences may have been drawn[4]. Another significant change made by the 1980 Act is that where parties disagree on facts stated by the judge in his draft case this must be recorded in the minute of proceedings of the adjustment hearing[5].

An appeal by stated case will not succeed if it is sought to review decisions on relevancy or competency unless objections to such decisions were timeously stated at the trial[6].

1 Criminal Procedure (Scotland) Act 1975 (c 21), s 442(1), (2) (substituted by the Criminal Justice (Scotland) Act 1980 (c 62), s 34, Sch 3, para 1).
2 Criminal Justice (Scotland) Act 1975, s 442 (as originally enacted); *Cromwell v Renton* 1911 SC (J) 86, 6 Adam 498; *Sommerville v Langmuir* 1932 JC 55, 1932 SLT 265.
3 *Wilson v Carmichael* 1982 SCCR 528; *Ballantyne v MacKinnon* 1983 SCCR 97. See also *Begg v Tudhope* 1983 SCCR 32; *Marshall v Smith* 1983 SCCR 156; and *Jordan v Lowe* 1989 GWD 17-715. In *Marshall v MacDougall* 1986 SCCR 376, 1987 SLT 123, the case was remitted back to the sheriff to investigate and hear evidence on remarks made after the trial by a witness which appeared to have a bearing on his credibility.
4 *Fraser v Anderson* (1899) 1 F (J) 60, 2 Adam 705.
5 Criminal Procedure (Scotland) Act 1975, s 448(2c) (added by the Criminal Justice (Scotland) Act 1980, Sch 3, para 7(a), and amended by the Law Reform (Miscellaneous Provisions) (Scotland) Act 1985 (c 73), s 59(2), Sch 4).
6 Criminal Procedure (Scotland) Act 1975, s 454(1); *Skeen v Murphy* 1978 SLT (Notes) 2. See also *Courtney v MacKinnon* 1986 SCCR 545, where a motion to hear fresh evidence was refused as no attempt had been made to adjourn the case to take the evidence at the trial.

8.32. Defects in form and objections to evidence. Proceedings will not be invalidated because of mere technical defects which do not go to the substance of the matter or prejudice the accused[1]. However, the admission of evidence by the inferior court which the High Court of Justiciary regards as incompetent may be fatal to the proceedings[2]. Where objections have been taken during the inferior court proceedings that have not been minuted, this may jeopardise the proceedings[3]. It is, of course, vital that objections are made at the appropriate time, that is at the first calling of the case, if the objections are to competency and relevancy of the proceedings or at the time where it is sought to challenge evidence being led[4]. Where it is shown that the proceedings are fundamentally null, objection can be taken at any time[5].

1 *Paterson v MacLennan* 1914 SC (J) 123, 7 Adam 428. See R W Renton and H H Brown *Criminal Procedure according to the Law of Scotland* (5th edn, 1983) para 16-21 and the other cases referred to therein.
2 *Handley v Pirie* 1976 JC 65, 1977 SLT 30.
3 *Connell v Mitchell* 1913 SC (J) 13, 7 Adam 23. See, however, *Cameron v Waugh* 1937 JC 5, 1937 SLT 53, and *M'Donalds Ltd v Adair* 1944 JC 119, 1944 SLT 336, where the objections had been noted by the judge and references appeared in the stated case.
4 Criminal Procedure (Scotland) Act 1975 (c 21), s 334(1), (2) (amended by the Criminal Justice (Scotland) Act 1980 (c 62), s 83(2), Sch 7, para 54(a), (b)); *Skeen v Murphy* 1978 SLT (Notes) 2; *Aitchison v Tudhope* 1981 JC 65, 1981 SCCR 1, 1981 SLT 231.
5 *Mitchell v Dean* 1979 JC 62, 1979 SLT (Notes) 12; *Robertson v Aitchison* 1981 SCCR 149, 1981 SLT (Notes) 127 and the authorities referred to therein; *Moffat v Smith* 1983 SCCR 392.

8.33. Miscarriage of justice. Miscarriage of justice is now the sole ground of appeal in a stated case taken by an accused[1]. It has been defined as being a substantial injustice to the accused[2]. Such a miscarriage may arise as a result of a mistake, irregularity, unfairness, or prejudice to the accused in the proceedings as well as where it can actually be shown that the accused did not commit the crime. If the improprieties founded upon are considered capable of having influenced the trial judge to the prejudice of the accused, the conviction is likely to be quashed[3]. Other areas of miscarriage may arise in relation to evidence wrongly excluded by the trial judge[4], instances where part of the trial is conducted outwith the accused's presence[5], and failure to grant adjournments[6] or to provide an interpreter in the case of a foreign accused with a poor command of English[7].

1 Criminal Procedure (Scotland) Act 1975 (c 21), s 442(2) (substituted by the Criminal Justice (Scotland) Act 1980 (c 62), s 34, Sch 3, para 1).
2 *Winning v Jeans* 1909 SC (J) 26 at 28, 6 Adam 1 at 6, per Lord Pearson.
3 *Falconer v Brown* (1893) 21 R (J) 1 at 3, 1 Adam 96 at 101, per Lord McLaren.
4 *Winning v Torrance* 1928 JC 79, 1928 SLT 544.
5 *Aitken v Wood* 1921 JC 84, 1921 2 SLT 124; *Watson v Argo* 1936 JC 87, 1936 SLT 427.
6 *MacKellar v Dickson* (1898) 25 R (J) 63, 2 Adam 504.
7 *Liszewski v Thomson* 1942 JC 55, 1942 SLT 147.

8.34. Incompetency, corruption and malice. The pre-1980 grounds of appeal of incompetency, corruption and malice are still of relevance, inasmuch as the presence of any of these factors would almost certainly be accepted as giving rise to a miscarriage of justice[1].

'Incompetency' has been defined as being an inability in the court to deal with the matter in hand, and as embracing any case with which the court had no power to deal[2]. Failure to note documentary evidence may amount to incompetency[3], and absence from the complaint of sufficient specification of the *locus* to show the jurisdiction of the inferior court has been held to amount to incompetency[4]. In a singular case[5] following on a plea of guilty, a conviction and sentence were purportedly recalled by the sheriff and the accused was permitted to tender a plea of not guilty. When after trial the court acquitted the accused, the prosecutor appealed by stated case against the court's decision to acquit the accused. The High Court of Justiciary held that the court's action in recalling the conviction was incompetent but that the stated case was also incompetent since the acquittal which it sought to have reviewed was *ultra vires*. From the above examples it will be clear that this is a very narrow ground of appeal. It is likely that where incompetence is an issue the proper mode of appeal will be by way of bill of suspension[6] rather than stated case.

Corruption and malice are also grounds which, if established by the appellant, would doubtless lead to a successful appeal since it would be necessary to show evidence of bribery or wickedness or capriciousness on the part of the judge[7].

1 See R W Renton and H H Brown *Criminal Procedure according to the Law of Scotland* (5th edn, 1983) paras 16-31–16-34.
2 *Robson v Menzies* 1913 SC (J) 90 at 93, 7 Adam 156 at 161, per Lord Justice-General Dunedin, approved in *Silk v Middleton* 1921 JC 69 at 74, 1921 1 SLT 278 at 280, per Lord Justice-Clerk Scott Dickson.
3 This was held not to be the case in *Silk v Middleton* 1921 JC 69, 1921 1 SLT 278; but see *Sutherland v Shiach* 1928 JC 49, 1928 SLT 440, and *Binnie v Farrell* 1972 JC 49 at 58, 1972 SLT 212 at 217, per Lord Cameron.
4 *Hefferan v Wright* 1911 SC (J) 20, 6 Adam 321; *M'Millan v Grant* 1924 JC 13, 1924 SLT 86.
5 *MacNeill v MacGregor* 1975 JC 55, 1975 SLT (Notes) 46.
6 As to bills of suspension, see paras 8.59 ff below.
7 *Adams v Great North of Scotland Rly Co* (1890) 18 R (HL) 1 at 9, 10; *Robson v Menzies* 1913 SC (J) 90 at 94, 98, 7 Adam 156 at 162, 169; *Bradford v McLeod* 1985 SCCR 379, 1986 SLT 244.

8.35. Oppression. Oppression can take a variety of forms, but occurs when the accused is treated unfairly by the court to such an extent that he is entitled to gain relief[1]. It may arise accidentally or as a result of an abuse of powers by the court or over-zealousness on the part of the judge[2]. An accused who is brought before the court from custody and pleads not guilty is normally entitled to an adjournment of at least forty-eight hours before trial and must be informed of this right[3]. Failure to inform an accused of this right may amount to oppression[4]. Any prejudice that is caused to the accused as a result of a breach in the court's statutory duty to grant an adjournment is likely to prove fatal to any conviction obtained[5]. Where no statutory provision applies, the judge in the inferior court must balance the interests of the Crown, the accused and the public in deciding whether to grant an adjournment[6]. The form of complaint itself may be held to be oppressive if it does not give fair notice to the accused of the crime alleged; but normally such a defect will be the subject of a preliminary plea to the relevancy based on the contention that the complaint was lacking in specification[7]. With limited exceptions[8] proceedings must be conducted in the presence of the accused, and if any proceedings are taken in his absence they are likely to be held to be oppressive, if not null and void[9]. If proceedings are taken outwith the presence of the accused's solicitor this may be held to be oppressive[10]. Similarly a refusal to hear proper competent evidence, the following of incompetent procedures by the judge or the refusal to hear reasons in support of a motion to withdraw a plea of guilty are likely to be held to amount to oppression[11], and a reference to previous convictions is oppressive if it can be shown that it created a risk of prejudice to the accused[12]. Unrepresented accused should be made aware of their rights at trial to cross-examine, lead evidence, and to make submissions to the court on evidence or in mitigation[13]. The presence of the judge at the incident featured in the charge is likely to prove fatal to any conviction and sentence imposed unless it can be shown that such presence at or near the incident could not have affected the judge's decision[14].

1 *Gordon v Mulholland* (1891) 18 R (J) 18 at 19, 2 White 576 at 580.
2 *M'Kenzie v M'Phee* (1889) 16 R (J) 53, 2 White 188; *Robson v Menzies* 1913 SC (J) 90, 7 Adam 156.
3 Criminal Procedure (Scotland) Act 1975 (c 21), s 337(c).
4 R W Renton and H H Brown *Criminal Procedure according to the Law of Scotland* (5th edn, 1983) para 16-37.
5 *Ferguson v M'Nab* (1884) 11 R (J) 63, 5 Coup 471; *MacKellar v Dickson* (1898) 25 R (J) 63, 2 Adam 504; *Renton and Brown* paras 16-38–16-40.
6 See para 6.37 above.
7 *Walker v Bonnar* (1894) 22 R (J) 22, 1 Adam 523. See para 8.26 above.
8 Criminal Procedure (Scotland) Act 1975, s 338(1)(b) (trial in absence). Section 145(1) proviso (added by the Criminal Justice (Scotland) Act 1980 (c 62), s 21), enabling the court to continue the trial in the absence of the accused if he misconducts himself, applies to solemn proceedings only (see para 6.03 above).
9 *Kelly v Rowan* (1897) 25 R (J) 3, 2 Adam 357.
10 *Williams v Linton* (1878) 6 R (J) 12; *Fraser v MacKinnon* 1981 SCCR 91.

11 *Laird v Neilson* (1905) 4 Adam 537, 12 SLT 858; *M'Clung v Cruickshank* 1964 JC 64; *Brown v Smith* 1981 SCCR 206, 1982 SLT 301; *Niven v Tudhope* 1982 SCCR 365.

12 *Boustead v M'Leod* 1979 JC 70, 1979 SLT (Notes) 48; *Robertson v Aitchison* 1981 SCCR 149, 1981 SLT (Notes) 127; *Moffat v Smith* 1983 SCCR 392; *Johnston v Allan* 1983 SCCR 500, 1984 SLT 261; *O'Neill v Tudhope* 1984 SCCR 276, 1984 SLT 424.

13 *Graham v M'Lennan* 1911 SC (J) 16, 6 Adam 315.

14 *McDervitt v McLeod* 1982 SCCR 282.

8.36. No case to answer. An incorrect decision in upholding a submission of no case to answer may result in a successful appeal by the prosecutor[1] and a remit by the High Court of Justiciary back to the inferior court to proceed further with the case. If an appeal against a decision of this type is taken by the accused following an unsuccessful submission, it still remains to be resolved by the High Court whether defence evidence led thereafter will be taken into account in determining the sufficiency of evidence[2]. There is, however, English authority to the effect that evidence subsequent to the submission given by a co-accused should not be taken into account in determining the appeal[3]. In that case the conviction was quashed. It is likely that this view would be taken by the High Court should the matter be raised on appeal[4]. But in another English case the appeal court regarded itself as entitled to consider the whole of the evidence (including that led for the defence) in determining whether to allow an appeal against conviction[5]. Normally parties will be heard in support of the submission, but the judge may dispense with hearing the prosecutor when he is satisfied there is sufficient material for the case to proceed and it has been held not to be oppressive to refuse to hear argument where the submission of no case to answer appears to be utterly without merit[6].

1 *Ingram v Macari* 1982 JC 1, 1981 SCCR 184, 1982 SLT 92; *Galt v Goodsir* 1981 SCCR 225, 1982 SLT 94; *Candle v Wilkinson* 1982 SCCR 33, 1982 SLT 315; *Smith v Paterson* 1982 SCCR 295, 1982 SLT 437. See also *Williamson v Wither* 1981 SCCR 214, which sets forth the criteria for deciding whether to accept or reject the submission, and paras 6.25, 6.47, above.

2 *Little v HM Advocate* 1983 JC 16, 1983 SCCR 56, 1983 SLT 489.

3 *R v Abbott* [1955] 2 QB 497, [1955] 2 All ER 899, CA.

4 *Little v HM Advocate* 1983 JC 16, 1983 SCCR 56, 1983 SLT 489; R W Renton and H H Brown *Criminal Procedure according to the Law of Scotland* (5th edn, 1983) para 16-45.

5 *R v Power* [1919] 1 KB 572, CCA.

6 *Taylor v Douglas* 1983 SCCR 323, 1984 SLT 69.

8.37. Additional evidence. Since 1980 it has been competent in summary procedure to seek to lead additional evidence at the appeal stage[1]. Any additional evidence so offered must not have been available or must be such that it could not reasonably have been made available or known of at the time of the trial[2]. Where the additional evidence raises the possibility that the trial judge might have reached a different view on credibility where credibility was the critical issue, an appeal is likely to succeed on this basis[3].

1 Criminal Procedure (Scotland) Act 1975 (c 21), s 452(4)(b) (added by the Criminal Justice (Scotland) Act 1980 (c 62), s 34, Sch 3, para 11).

2 *McKenzie v HM Advocate* 3 November 1983, HCJ (unreported); see R W Renton and H H Brown *Criminal Procedure according to the Law of Scotland* (5th edn, 1983) para 16-45a; cf *Cameron v Lowe* 1989 GWD 31-1406.

3 *Marshall v Smith* 1983 SCCR 156; see para 8.14 above.

(iii) Appeal against Sentence by Prosecutor

8.38. Appeals against sentence by the prosecutor. The law and procedure relating to appeals against sentence taken by the accused are discussed below[1].

Unlike appeals at the instance of the accused, for which the test is whether there has been a miscarriage of justice as a result of an excessive or inappropriate sentence, appeals against sentence by the prosecutor can be brought only on points of law[2]. For example it is competent for the prosecutor to appeal by stated case against a sentence of one year's disqualification imposed by the sheriff in a drink-driving case where a mandatory three-year minimum disqualification falls to be imposed because the accused has within the past ten years an analogous previous conviction or convictions or where the sheriff fails to disqualify in such a case where there are no special reasons for not disqualifying[3].

1 See paras 8.54 ff below.
2 Criminal Procedure (Scotland) Act 1975 (c 21), s 442(1)(b)(ii) (substituted by the Criminal Justice (Scotland) Act 1980 (c 62), s 34, Sch 3, para 1).
3 See the Road Traffic Offenders Act 1988 (c 53), s 34(3).

(iv) Procedure on Stated Case

8.39. Application for stated case. An application for a stated case must be lodged with the clerk of court within one week of the final determination of the proceedings[1]. It must contain a full statement of the matters which the appellant desires to bring under review and, where the appeal relates to sentence, a statement of that fact[2]. The application should be signed by the appellant or his solicitor and lodged with the clerk of court and a copy sent to the respondent or his solicitor within the one-week period[3]. Final determination of the proceedings occurs on the day on which sentence is passed in open court or the date on which sentence is deferred for a period[4]. However, an appeal against both conviction and sentence may be taken in the latter case where sentence is ultimately passed in open court after the period of deferment[5].

The application should be made in writing, preferably in the prescribed form[6], and where appropriate should contain a crave for bail or suspension of disqualification or of any other order imposed[7].

Where the application is made outwith the one-week period, application may be made to the High Court through the Clerk of Justiciary to extend the period for lodging the application[8]. Reasons for the lateness of the application must be given, and the application will be dealt with by a single judge with or without a hearing[9]. At any time within the three-week adjustment period or any longer period allowed by the court[10] the application may be amended, provided the amendments are lodged with the clerk of court and intimated to the respondent or his solicitor[11].

1 Criminal Procedure (Scotland) Act 1975 (c 21), s 444(1)(a) (substituted by the Criminal Justice (Scotland) Act 1980 (c 62), s 34, Sch 3, para 3); *Elliot* 1984 JC 63, 1984 SCCR 125, 1984 SLT 294; *Dickson v Valentine* 1988 SCCR 325, 1989 SLT 19. See also M Christie 'Applying for a Stated Case' (1984) 29 JLSS 457. See also *Burnside v Carmichael* 1989 GWD 1600 (High Court stated that the time limits were directory, not mandatory) and *McFadyen v Tudhope* 1986 SCCR 712.
2 Criminal Procedure (Scotland) Act 1975, s 444(1)(b) (as so substituted); *Galloway v Hillary* 1983 SCCR 119; High Court of Justiciary *Practice Note* 29 March 1985, 1985 SLT (News) 120. See also *Smith v HM Advocate* 1983 SCCR 30; *Durant v Lockhart* 1986 SCCR 23, 1986 SLT 312n; *Singh* 1986 SCCR 215, 1987 SLT 63n; and cf *Macdougall* 1986 SCCR 128. The requirement to state all the matters which the appellant desires to be brought under review must be strictly complied with: *Dickson v Valentine* 1988 SCCR 325, 1989 SLT 19. The grounds must be relevant: see *McQuarrie v Carmichael* 1989 SCCR 371.
3 Criminal Procedure (Scotland) Act 1975, s 444(1)(c) (as so substituted).
4 Ibid, s 451(3) (substituted by the Criminal Justice (Scotland) Act 1980, Sch 3, para 10). This final determination takes into account cases where sentence is deferred for good behaviour or other conditions are imposed in terms of the Criminal Procedure (Scotland) Act 1975, s 432 (see para 7.20 above).

5 See R W Renton and H H Brown *Criminal Procedure according to the Law of Scotland* (5th edn, 1983) para 16-60.
6 *Smith v Gray* 1925 JC 8 at 11, 1924 SLT 812 at 814; Act of Adjournal (Consolidation) 1988, SI 1988/110, r 127, Sch 1, Form 71.
7 *Renton and Brown* para 16-63.
8 Criminal Procedure (Scotland) Act 1975, s 444(3), (4), and see note 1 above.
9 Ibid, s 444(3)–(5) (amended by the Bail etc (Scotland) Act 1980 (c 4), s 12(2), Sch 1, para 10, and the Criminal Justice (Scotland) Act 1980, Sch 3, para 3). See *Elliot* 1984 JC 63, 1984 SCCR 125, 1984 SLT 294, where the Lord Justice-Clerk remitted an application of this type to a quorum of three judges to hear. See also *Berry* 1985 SCCR 106, where an unsuccessful attempt was made to invoke the *nobile officium* following an unsuccessful attempt to obtain an extension of time for lodging an application for a stated case.
10 Criminal Procedure (Scotland) Act 1975, s 448(1), (6) (amended by the Criminal Justice (Scotland) Act 1980, Sch 3, para 7(a), (c)). See para 8.45 below.
11 Criminal Procedure (Scotland) Act 1975, s 444(1B) (added by the Criminal Justice (Scotland) Act 1980, Sch 3, para 3).

8.40. Appellant in custody. Where the appellant is in custody the court may grant bail at the time the appeal is marked, grant a sist of execution or make any other interim order[1]. A bail application must be disposed of within twenty-four hours of its being presented to the court[2]. Any appeal against the decision of the inferior court in this context must be made within a further twenty-four hours[3]. Where the appellant is granted bail and then abandons his appeal the prosecutor may apply to the court for a warrant to apprehend and imprison the appellant for the unexpired portion of the sentence[4]. The court may order the sentence to run consecutively to any sentence subsequently imposed in situations where the appellant has been convicted of offences whilst on bail pending the appeal[5].

1 Criminal Procedure (Scotland) Act 1975 (c 21), s 446(1) (substituted by the Criminal Justice (Scotland) Act 1980 (c 62), s 34, Sch 3, para 5).
2 Criminal Procedure (Scotland) Act 1975, s 446(2) (amended by the Bail etc (Scotland) Act 1980 (c 4), s 12(2), Sch 1, para 10); R W Renton and H H Brown *Criminal Procedure according to the Law of Scotland* (5th edn, 1983) para 16-67.
3 Criminal Procedure (Scotland) Act 1975, s 446(2) (as so amended); *Fenton* 1981 SCCR 288, 1982 SLT 164; *Long v HM Advocate* 1984 SCCR 161.
4 Criminal Procedure (Scotland) Act 1975, s 446(4) (as so amended). The incidental application is made under s 310 in a petition following the style set out in the Summary Jurisdiction (Scotland) Act 1954 (c 48), Sch 2, Pt I.
5 Criminal Procedure (Scotland) Act 1975, s 446(5) (as so amended).

8.41. Consent to setting aside conviction. Where the accused appeals against conviction and the prosecutor is not prepared to maintain the judgment appealed against, he may lodge a minute with the clerk of court consenting to set aside the conviction and setting forth his reasons[1]. The minute should be copied to the appellant or his solicitor, and the clerk of court ascertains if the appellant still wishes to be heard by the High Court[2]. The proceedings are then transmitted to the Clerk of Justiciary and laid before a High Court judge who may set aside the conviction in whole or in part without hearing parties; or he may refuse so to do, in which case the matter is referred back to the inferior court to proceed as a normal appeal[3]. The prosecutor can only exercise this power within two weeks of receipt of the draft stated case or bill of suspension[4]. Lord Justice-General Cooper stated that the proper time for the prosecutor to lodge his minute is when the appeal is intimated to him and that it is an improper practice for prosecutors to defer lodging the minute until they have had an opportunity to peruse the draft stated case[5]. However, it is likely that the prosecution will wish to obtain Crown Counsel's instructions before lodging such a minute, and it is likely that the draft stated case will then be available when a minute is lodged. The prosecutor can embark on this course only when there is some fatal flaw in the proceedings or new facts have come to the prosecutor's knowledge[6]. Where questions of law are raised by the appeal it is likely that the High Court will wish to hear argument and will not simply agree to the conviction being set aside[7]. A maximum of £40 expenses may be awarded to the appellant if the conviction is set aside[8].

1 Criminal Procedure (Scotland) Act 1975 (c 21), s 453(1) (amended by the Criminal Justice (Scotland) Act 1980 (c 62), s 34, Sch 3, para 12).
2 Criminal Procedure (Scotland) Act 1975, s 453(2) (as so amended).
3 Ibid, s 453(3).
4 Ibid, s 453(5) (as amended: see note 1 above).
5 *O'Brien v Adair* 1947 JC 180 at 181, 1948 SLT 112 at 112, 113; R W Renton and H H Brown *Criminal Procedure according to the Law of Scotland* (5th edn, 1983) para 16-72.
6 *O'Brien v Adair* 1947 JC 180, 1948 SLT 112.
7 *Jensen v Wilson* 1912 SC (J) 3, 6 Adam 535.
8 Criminal Procedure (Scotland) Act 1975, s 453(3) (amended by the Criminal Justice (Scotland) Act 1980, s 46(1)(f)).

8.42. Draft stated case. Within three weeks of the final determination of the proceedings[1] the draft stated case must be prepared and copies issued by the clerk of court to the appellant and respondent or their solicitors[2]. The draft case is prepared by the sheriff or, if the appeal arises from district court proceedings, the clerk of court[3], and should be set out in the prescribed form, giving the nature of the case, the facts admitted or proved, the grounds for the decision reached and any other matters necessary for the proper understanding of the case by the High Court of Justiciary[4]. The sheriff principal of the sheriffdom in which the judgment was pronounced may extend the three-week period for issuing the stated case if the judge is temporarily absent from duty[5].

1 As to the final determination of proceedings, see para 8.39, text to note 4, above.
2 Criminal Procedure (Scotland) Act 1975 (c 21), s 447(1) (substituted by the Criminal Justice (Scotland) Act 1980 (c 62), s 34, Sch 3, para 6).
3 Criminal Procedure (Scotland) Act 1975, s 447(1) (as so substituted, and amended by the Law Reform (Miscellaneous Provisions) (Scotland) Act 1985 (c 73), s 59(1), Sch 2, para 20). Previously in the district court the justice prepared the draft case with such help from the clerk of court as was required, but the form of the stated cases so prepared was frequently the subject of criticism from the High Court: see eg *White v Allan* 1985 SCCR, 1985 SLT 396.
4 Criminal Procedure (Scotland) Act 1975, s 447(2) (amended by the Criminal Justice (Scotland) Act 1980, s 83(3), Sch 8); Act of Adjournal (Consolidation) 1988, SI 1988/110, r 127, Sch 1, Form 72.
5 Criminal Procedure (Scotland) Act 1975, s 451(2) (substituted by the Criminal Justice (Scotland) Act 1980, Sch 3, para 10). See *Renfrew District Council* 1987 SCCR 522.

8.43. Content of stated case. The stated case should state concisely and authoritatively the background to the case, the facts admitted or proved, any point of law decided and the reasons for the decision, and include sufficient detail for the High Court properly to consider the matter and hear argument thereon[1]. Where the appeal is against sentence also, the stated case will require to include any facts relevant to sentence and details of why the particular sentence was imposed[2]. Prior to 1980 it was held necessary to set out comprehensively the facts proved, even where the issue was confined to a narrow point[3]. However, the requirement on the appellant to specify the grounds of appeal effectively and precisely[4] now means that the stated case can be restricted to these matters, subject to any additional grounds that are lodged during the adjustment period. The judge should not normally narrate what the witnesses stated at trial but should form a view of the evidence and record it in the stated case accordingly[5]. Nevertheless, where the appeal has been taken by the prosecutor against a finding of no case to answer, the stated case should record the evidence led in order that the High Court may see how the decision was reached[6]. The defence submissions of no case to answer which were upheld should be specified in the stated case[7]. The stated case should be a comprehensive document without referring to annexations[8]. It must conclude with a question or questions in law for the opinion of the High Court[9].

1 Criminal Procedure (Scotland) Act 1975 (21), s 447(2) (amended by the Criminal Justice (Scotland) Act 1980 (c 62), s 83(3), Sch 8); Act of Adjournal (Consolidation) 1988, SI 1988/110, r 127, Sch 1, Form 72; *Mitchell v Smith* Crown Office circular A2/81.
2 *Industrial Distributions (Central Scotland) Ltd v Quinn* 1984 SCCR 5, 1984 SLT 240.
3 *Waddell v Kinnaird* 1922 JC 40, 1922 SLT 344.
4 Criminal Procedure (Scotland) Act 1975, s 444(1)(b) (substituted by the Criminal Justice (Scotland) Act 1980, s 34, Sch 3, para 3); *Singh* 1986 SCCR 215, 1987 SLT 63n; *Durant v Lockhart* 1986 SCCR 23, 1986 SLT 312n; cf *Henry v Docherty* 1989 SCCR 426, 1989 GWD 32–1465.
5 *Gordon v Hansen* 1914 SC (J) 131, 7 Adam 441; *Pert v Robinson* 1956 SLT 23; *Gordon v Allan* 1987 SLT 400n; *Mowbray v Guild* 1989 SCCR 535, 1989 GWD 36–1684; *Jordan v Allan* 1989 SCCR 202; *Petrovich v Jessop* 1990 SCCR 1.
6 *Galt v Goodsir* 1981 SCCR 225, 1982 SLT 94; *Carmichael v Gillooly* 1982 SCCR 119; *Smith v Paterson* 1982 SCCR 295, 1982 SLT 437; *Keane v Bathgate* 1983 SCCR 251, 1983 SLT 651; *Smith v Brown* 1987 SCCR 592, 1988 SLT 150; *McIntosh v Jessop* 1989 GWD 37–1695. The whole evidence led must be summarised in findings: *Bowman v Jessop* 1989 SCCR 547.
7 *Cardle v Wilkinson* 1982 SCCR 33 at 38, 1982 SLT 315 at 316.
8 *Mackenna v Dunn* 1918 SLT 66; *Cockburn v Gordon* 1928 JC 87, 1928 SLT 548. The exception to this rule is that the judge must append a note of any proposed adjustment rejected, the reasons for the rejection and a note of the evidence upon which that decision was taken: Criminal Procedure (Scotland) Act 1975, s 448(2D) (added by the Criminal Justice (Scotland) Act 1980, Sch 3, para 7(a)). The High Court cannot look behind the stated case if no question has been asked on a matter and the judge's note does not cover this aspect: *Began v Jessop* 1989 GWD 3–122.
9 *Needes v McLeod* 7 November 1984, HCJ (unreported); see R W Renton and H H Brown *Criminal Procedure according to the Law of Scotland* (5th edn, 1983) para 16-83.

8.44. Questions of law. As indicated above[1], the accused has an extensive right of appeal under the general heading of miscarriage of justice, whereas the prosecutor may appeal solely on a question of law. Frequently the appellant will wish to raise the question of whether there was sufficient evidence to support the conviction. This is a question of law. Care must be taken in framing the question[2]. Where it is desired to raise a specific legal issue the appellant must frame his application for a stated case in such a way as to focus the point; otherwise there is a danger that the High Court of Justiciary may consider that the matter has not been properly brought to the attention of the judge stating the case[3], unless the issue raised in the High Court is one of fundamental nullity in the proceedings[4]. If the appellant wishes to dispute a finding of fact, then there should be a specific question, if necessary added at the adjustment stage, addressed to whether there was sufficient evidence to warrant the finding[5]. Similarly, if a finding of fact is based upon evidence that was allegedly admitted or rejected improperly, a specific question must be asked if this decision is in issue[6]. In an appeal against conviction and sentence it will be necessary to add a question whether the sentence imposed was excessive or inappropriate[7].

1 See para 8.31 above.
2 *Jenkinson v Neilson Bros* (1899) 2 F (J) 13, 3 Adam 88; *Todd v Cochrane* (1901) 3 Adam 357, 9 SLT 59. See R W Renton and H H Brown *Criminal Procedure according to the Law of Scotland* (5th edn, 1983) para 16-85.
3 *Drummond v Hunter* 1948 JC 109, 1948 SLT 526; *Boyd v Lewis* 1959 SLT (Notes) 27; *McLeod v Campbell* 1986 SCCR 132. See, however, *O'Hara v Tudhope* 1986 SCCR 283, 1987 SLT 67n, where argument was allowed on a matter not covered by a question since the sheriff had refused to insert the question; *Little v Whitelaw* 1989 GWD 10–423; *Shields v Cardle* 1990 GWD 5–245.

4 *Christie v Barclay* 1974 JC 68; *Shaw v Smith* 1979 JC 51; *Robertson v Aitchison* 1981 SCCR 149, 1981 SLT (Notes) 127.
5 *Rattray v Paterson* 1954 SLT 107; *Prentice v Skeen* 1977 SLT (Notes) 21; *Cameron v Smith* 1982 SCCR 53 at 56, 1982 SLT 398n at 399.
6 *Falconer v Brown* (1893) 21 R (J) 1, 1 Adam 96; *Waddell v Kinnaird* 1922 JC 40, 1922 SLT 344; *MacLeod v Woodmuir Miners Welfare Society Social Club* 1961 JC 5, 1960 SLT 349; *Miln v Cullen* 1967 JC 21, 1967 SLT 35; *Bell v Hogg* 1967 JC 49, 1967 SLT 290.
7 Criminal Procedure (Scotland) Act 1975 (c 21), ss 452A(2), 453C(1) (respectively added by the Criminal Justice (Scotland) Act 1980 (c 62), s 34, Sch 3, paras 11, 13).

8.45. Adjustments and hearings. Within three weeks of the issue of the draft stated case, the appellant and respondent must intimate any proposed adjustments to the clerk of court and other parties or intimate that no adjustments are proposed[1]. Adjustments may be proposed to any part of the draft case including findings in fact and the trial judge's note of evidence[2]. If the appellant fails to intimate adjustments or that no adjustments are proposed he will be deemed to have abandoned his appeal, and if granted bail will be liable to arrest and imprisonment to serve the unexpired portion of his sentence[3]. The High Court of Justiciary may, however, extend the period for lodging adjustments[4]. If any adjustments are proposed or if the judge wishes to alter his draft, a hearing must take place within one week of the expiry of the adjustment period unless the sheriff principal grants an extension[5] or the High Court has granted an extension of the adjustment period, in which case the hearing should take place within one week of expiry of the extended period[6]. Even if parties are agreeable to the proposed adjustments or amendments, a hearing must be held, although the parties need not attend[7]. At the hearing any disputed finding in fact must be challenged[8], either orally at the hearing or in a proposed adjustment, but preferably by both modes. Any adjustment which is not withdrawn by the party proposing it and which is rejected by the judge or any amendment to the draft case made by the judge and not accepted by the parties must be referred to in the minute of proceedings relating to the hearing[9]. The High Court will refuse to hear at the appeal a point which could have been raised and taken account of at the adjustment stage but was not[10].

1 Criminal Procedure (Scotland) Act 1975 (c 21), s 448(1) (substituted by the Criminal Justice (Scotland) Act 1980 (c 62), s 34, Sch 3, para 7(a)).
2 *Wilson v Carmichael* 1982 SCCR 528. See also the cases cited in para 8.44, note 5, above, and *Ballantyne v MacKinnon* 1983 SCCR 97.
3 Criminal Procedure (Scotland) Act 1975, s 448(2) (as substituted: see note 1 above), applying s 446(4) (amended by the Bail etc (Scotland) Act 1980 (c 4), s 12(2), Sch 1, para 10).
4 Criminal Procedure (Scotland) Act 1975, s 448(6) (amended by the Criminal Justice (Scotland) Act 1980, Sch 3, para 7(c)). For the procedure followed by the High Court in such cases, see para 8.39 above.
5 Criminal Procedure (Scotland) Act 1975, ss 448(2A), 451(2) (respectively added and substituted by the Criminal Justice (Scotland) Act 1980, Sch 3, paras 7(a), 10).
6 Criminal Procedure (Scotland) Act 1975, s 448(2A) (as so added).
7 Ibid, s 448(2B) (as so added); *Campbell v Mackenzie* 1981 SCCR 341, 1982 SLT 250, referred to in R W Renton and H H Brown *Criminal Procedure according to the Law of Scotland* (5th edn, 1983) para 16-90, note 11.
8 Criminal Procedure (Scotland) Act 1975, s 448(2D)(b) (as so added); cf *McIntosh v Jessop* 1989 GWD 37-1695.
9 Ibid, s 448(2C) (as so added, and amended by the Law Reform (Miscellaneous Provisions) (Scotland) Act 1985 (c 73), s 59(2), Sch 4).
10 *Muir v McLeod* 1989 GWD 16-668.

8.46. Final stated case. Assuming the appeal is not subsequently abandoned, the judge must state and sign the stated case and must add as an appendix any adjustment proposed which was rejected, a note of the evidence alleged to support the adjustment and the reasons for rejection and a note of the evidence upon which any challenged finding in fact is based[1]. The case must be stated within two weeks of the hearing or within two weeks of the last date for adjustments if no hearing is required[1]. If the judge is absent from duty the sheriff principal may extend this period[2]. Where the judge is unable to sign a completed stated case (for example by reason of illness or death), it is competent to appeal instead by suspension or advocation[3].

1 Criminal Procedure (Scotland) Act 1975 (c 21), s 448(2D)(a), (b) (added by the Criminal Justice (Scotland) Act 1980 (c 62), s 34, Sch 3, para 7(a)).
2 Criminal Procedure (Scotland) Act 1975, s 451(2) (substituted by the Criminal Justice (Scotland) Act 1980, Sch 3, para 10).
3 See the Criminal Procedure (Scotland) Act 1975, s 444(2), and s 453A (added by the Criminal Justice (Scotland) Act 1980, Sch 3, para 13); and R W Renton and H H Brown *Criminal Procedure according to the Law of Scotland* (5th edn, 1983) para 16-117. As to bills of suspension and advocation, see paras 8.59ff, 8.68ff, below.

8.47. Transmission and lodgment of proceedings.

The clerk of court sends the stated case which has been signed by the judge to the appellant or his solicitor and a copy to the respondent or his solicitor and must transmit the complaint, minutes, productions and any other proceedings to the Clerk of Justiciary[1]. Thereafter the appellant or his agent must lodge the case with the Clerk of Justiciary within one week of receipt, failing which the appeal will be deemed abandoned[2]. Parties must instruct Edinburgh solicitors to act for them unless unrepresented[3]. The Crown Agent acts for procurators fiscal. The case should be lodged within the one-week period, although posting within the period has been held to suffice[4]. The date of receipt of the case by the appellant or his solicitor is not counted in computing the one-week period[5].

1 Criminal Procedure (Scotland) Act 1975 (c 21), s 448(3) (substituted by the Criminal Justice (Scotland) Act 1980 (c 62), s 34, Sch 3, para 7(b)). See also *Downie v Thomson* (1901) 9 SLT 251.
2 Criminal Procedure (Scotland) Act 1975, s 448(4), (5) (as so substituted).
3 Act of Adjournal (Consolidation) 1988, SI 1988/110, r 135.
4 *Smith v Gray* 1925 JC 8, 1924 SLT 812; but see *Elliot* 1984 JC 63, 1984 SCCR 125, 1984 SLT 294, and *Berry* 1985 SCCR 106. The safer course seems to be to lodge the case within the one-week period.
5 *Cameron v Macdonald* 1961 JC 11, 1961 SLT 10.

8.48. Extension of time.

Where the appellant has failed to comply with the statutory time limits he may apply in writing to the Clerk of Justiciary for an extension, stating the reasons for the application[1]. A judge of the High Court may dispose of the matter with or without a hearing[2]. The result of the application is conveyed by the Clerk of Justiciary to the clerk of the inferior court[2], who in turn advises the parties. There is no appeal against the decision of the High Court[3].

1 Criminal Procedure (Scotland) Act 1975 (c 21), s 448(6), (7) (the former amended by the Criminal Justice (Scotland) Act 1980 (c 62), s 34, Sch 3, para 7(c)).
2 Criminal Procedure (Scotland) Act 1975, s 448(8) (amended by the Bail etc (Scotland) Act 1980 (c 4), s 12(2), Sch 1, para 12, and the Criminal Justice (Scotland) Act 1980, Sch 3, para 7(d)).
3 *Berry* 1985 SCCR 106.

8.49. Abandonment of appeal.

The appellant may at any time abandon the appeal by lodging a signed minute of abandonment with the Clerk of Justiciary and sending a copy to the respondent or his solicitor[1]. Such abandonment does not preclude further appeal proceedings by way of suspension or advocation[2], but a petition to the *nobile officium* into the merits of the conviction would not be competent[3]. It is competent to abandon an appeal against sentence and maintain the appeal against conviction only or *vice versa*[4].

1 Criminal Procedure (Scotland) Act 1975 (c 21), s 449(1) (amended by the Criminal Justice (Scotland) Act 1980 (c 62), s 34, Sch 3, para 8(a)); Act of Adjournal (Consolidation) 1988, SI 1988/110, r 127, Sch 1, Form 70.
2 Criminal Procedure (Scotland) Act 1975, s 449(1) (as so amended).
3 *Anderson v HM Advocate* 1974 SLT 239.
4 See further para 8.53 below.

8.50. Printing. The appellant is charged with the duty of uplifting the case and proceedings from the Clerk of Justiciary and arranging for copies to be printed prior to the hearing[1]. Not later than seven days before the hearing the case and the proceedings must be returned together with six copies of the print for use by the High Court and five copies sent to the Edinburgh solicitor of the respondent or Crown Office if the respondent is the procurator fiscal. If for any reason these requirements are not complied with, application may be made to the Clerk of Justiciary asking for the case to be postponed to a later hearing in order that the requirements may be met[2].

1 Act of Adjournal (Consolidation) 1988, SI 1988/110, r 136(1).
2 Ibid, r 136(2), (3).

(v) The Court's Powers

8.51. Hearing of appeal. After consultation with the Lord Justice-General and the Lord Justice-Clerk, the Clerk of Justiciary fixes the hearings of appeals and issues a list of appeals with the dates of hearing on the Justiciary Roll, giving the appellants' Edinburgh solicitors at least fourteen days' notice of the dates fixed for the hearings[1]. Where the appellant has been granted bail he must attend the hearing in person, otherwise the appeal will be deemed abandoned unless cause can be shown for the appeal to proceed in his absence[2]. Unless leave of the High Court is given it is not competent for an appellant to found on matters not contained in the application for a stated case (if appropriate as amended)[3]. Any objections to the competency of the appeal should be raised before the merits of the appeal are argued[4]. In disposing of appeals the High Court may (1) order the production of relevant documents or articles, (2) hear additional relevant evidence or appoint a judge to hear such evidence, (3) take into account any relevant circumstances not before the trial judge, (4) remit the case to any fit person for inquiry and report, (5) appoint an expert assessor to assist it in its deliberations, (6) take account of any matter contained in a rejected adjustment, or (7) take account of any evidence contained in a note of the evidence supporting such rejected adjustments[5].

1 Criminal Procedure (Scotland) Act 1975 (c 21), s 452(1) (substituted by the Criminal Justice (Scotland) Act 1980 (c 62), s 34, Sch 3, para 11); Act of Adjournal (Consolidation) 1988, SI 1988/110, r 137.
2 Criminal Procedure (Scotland) Act 1975, s 453E (added by the Criminal Justice (Scotland) Act 1980, Sch 3, para 13).
3 Criminal Procedure (Scotland) Act 1975, s 452(3) (as substituted: see note 1 above). Fundamental nullities may, of course, be raised: *Sutherland v Shiach* 1928 JC 49, 1928 SLT 440.
4 *Thom v Caledonian Rly Co* (1886) 14 R (J) 5, 1 White 248.
5 Criminal Procedure (Scotland) Act 1975, s 452(4)(a)–(g) (as substituted: see note 1 above); R W Renton and H H Brown *Criminal Procedure according to the Law of Scotland* (5th edn, 1983) para 16-105.

8.52. Remit to the court of first instance. In addition to the above-mentioned powers[1] the High Court of Justiciary may remit the stated case back to the inferior court to amend it by clarifying facts or questions of law[2]. A motion for a remit of this type will be granted only if the party making the motion can specify the additional matters which should be sought from the inferior court and show that such material could result in a reversal of the judgment of that court[3].

1 See para 8.51 above.
2 Criminal Procedure (Scotland) Act 1975 (c 21), s 452(5) (substituted by the Criminal Justice (Scotland) Act 1980 (c 62), s 34, Sch 3, para 11). See also R W Renton and H H Brown *Criminal Procedure according to the Law of Scotland* (5th edn, 1983) para 16-106, note 1, where examples of such remits are given.
3 *Rogers v Howman* 1918 JC 88, at 96, *sub nom Howman v Rogers* 1918 2 SLT 78 at 83; cf *Neil v Wilson* 1989 GWD 35–1595; *Morrison v O'Brien* 1989 GWD 39–1793.

8.53. Disposal of appeal. The High Court of Justiciary, in disposing of a stated case appeal, may (1) remit the case back to the inferior court to proceed further in light of its opinion and any direction thereon; (2) affirm the verdict of the lower court; (3) quash the conviction and substitute an amended verdict of guilty which could have been returned by the inferior court; or (4) set aside the decision of the lower court and grant authority to the Crown to raise a fresh prosecution[1]. It need not issue a written opinion. The High Court may not increase sentence beyond the competent maximum of the inferior court[2]. Expenses may be awarded as the court thinks fit[3]. Where the High Court considers that the appellant was insane at the time of the offence it may quash the conviction and substitute a hospital order[4]. Any new proceedings authorised by the High Court must commence within two months of the grant of authority[5]. The appeal may be abandoned at any time prior to the hearing by lodging a minute of abandonment with the Clerk of Justiciary with a copy to all other parties[6]. Where the appeal is against both conviction and sentence the appellant may abandon the appeal against conviction and proceed only with the appeal against sentence[7].

1 Criminal Procedure (Scotland) Act 1975 (c 21), s 452A(1)(a)–(d) (added by the Criminal Justice (Scotland) Act 1980 (c 62), s 34, Sch 3, para 11).
2 Criminal Procedure (Scotland) Act 1975, s 452A(4) (as so added).
3 Ibid, s 452A(5) (as so added).
4 Ibid, s 453D(1) (added by the Criminal Justice (Scotland) Act 1980, Sch 3, para 13).
5 Criminal Procedure (Scotland) Act 1975, s 452B(3) (added by the Criminal Justice (Scotland) Act 1980, Sch 3, para 11).
6 Criminal Procedure (Scotland) Act 1975, s 449(1) (amended by the Criminal Justice (Scotland) Act 1980, Sch 3, para 8(a)); Act of Adjournal (Consolidation) 1988, SI 1988/110, r 127, Sch 1, Form 70.
7 Criminal Procedure (Scotland) Act 1975, s 442A(2) (added by the Criminal Justice (Scotland) Act 1980, Sch 3, para 1); Act of Adjournal (Consolidation) 1988, r 139.

(D) APPEAL AGAINST SENTENCE ALONE

8.54. Introduction. As stated above[1], the prosecutor may appeal against sentence only on a point of law, and must do so by stated case. However, an accused person who appeals against sentence alone may do so by a shortened form of procedure known as a 'note of appeal'.

1 See para 8.27 above.

8.55. Ground of appeal against sentence. The criterion for appeal against sentence is miscarriage of justice on the basis that the sentence imposed was either excessive or inappropriate[1]. Prior to 1980 the test applied was whether the sentence was 'harsh and oppressive', and a sentence merely alleged to be excessive would not necessarily be reduced by the High Court[2]. The older authorities are still, however, of value in determining whether a sentence imposed constitutes a miscarriage of justice[3]. 'Oppression' has been defined as being

> 'a disregard of the essentials of justice and the infliction of a penalty which is not properly related to the crime . . . but is either to be regarded as merely vindictive or as having proceeded upon some improper or irregular consideration or . . . upon some misleading statement of facts'[4].

A very heavy penalty imposed in the absence of aggravating factors will probably be regarded as a miscarriage of justice[5]. Any fine imposed upon an accused person must take into account the offender's means and fix a suitable figure which can be repaid within a reasonable period[6]. In certain situations it may be appropriate to pass an exemplary sentence, and the High Court will not interfere with this course if there are good reasons such as the prevalence of the offence in the locality[7]. But such a sentence may be held to be a miscarriage of justice if substantial mitigating factors present in the case have been ignored[8]. Miscarriage of justice will arise if the judge in passing sentence takes into account allegations made by the prosecution following a plea of guilty which are denied by the defence[9]. Similarly a failure to take into account mitigating factors such as provocation, or the consideration of previous convictions which are not properly before the court, will amount to miscarriage of justice[10]. Sentences which do not result in comparative justice for co-accused may be struck down on appeal[11]. The public interest may be pled as a reason for reducing the sentence, but in some cases this factor may equally militate in favour of refusing an appeal on this ground[12]. A recommendation for deportation will be upheld only in respect of a serious offence or a series of offences where it would be in the national interest to deport the accused[13].

1 Criminal Procedure (Scotland) Act 1975 (c 21), s 442(2) (substituted by the Criminal Justice (Scotland) Act 1980 (c 62), s 34, Sch 3, para 1). See also *Addison v MacKinnon* 1983 SCCR 52, and *Donaldson v HM Advocate* 1983 SCCR 216.

2 *Edward & Son v M'Kinnon* 1943 JC 156, 1944 SLT 120; *Henry v Docherty* 1989 SCCR 426; *Baxter v HM Advocate* 1989 GWD 1–6.

3 *Stewart v Cormack* 1941 JC 73, 1942 SLT 12; *W and A W Henderson Ltd v Forster* 1944 JC 91; *W v Muir* 1944 JC 128, 1944 SLT 334; *Blair v Hawthorn* 1945 JC 17, 1945 SLT 141; *Smith v Adair* 1945 JC 103, 1945 SLT 253; *Steven v Mackenzie* 1952 SLT (Notes) 17; *Fleming v MacDonald* 1958 JC 1, 1958 SLT 108; *Sopwith v Cruickshank* 1959 JC 78.

4 *Stewart v Cormack* 1941 JC 73 at 77, 1942 SLT 12 at 14, per Lord Justice-General Normand. See also *Galloway v Adair* 1947 JC 7, 1947 SLT 23.

5 *Edward & Son v M'Kinnon* 1943 JC 156, 1944 SLT 120; *Hoy v McLeod* 1983 SCCR 149.

6 *Glen v McLeod* 1982 SCCR 449; *Ketchen v Smith* 1982 SCCR 492. See, however, *Lambert v Tudhope* 1982 SCCR 144, where the High Court quashed a sentence of imprisonment and substituted a fine to be paid over two years 'to extend the period of which [the accused] has to face up to his responsibilities to one which is commensurate with the seriousness of the offence'. See also R Black 'Fine Tuning' 1986 SLT (News) 185.

7 *Campbell v Johnston* 1981 SCCR 179.

8 *Paterson v MacNeill* 1982 SCCR 141; *Blues v MacPhail* 1982 SCCR 247; *Norman v Smith* 1983 SCCR 100; *Hagen v HM Advocate* 1983 SCCR 245; *Flood v McLeod* 1983 SCCR 400; *Ruddy v Taylor Wilson* 1988 SCCR 193.

9 *Barn v Smith* 1978 JC 17, 1978 SLT (Notes) 3. The proper course in such a situation is either for the allegation to be withdrawn or accepted or for a proof in mitigation to be held.

10 *Russo v Robertson* 1951 SLT 408; *McGivern v HM Advocate* 23 September 1982, HCJ (unreported); *Row v HM Advocate* 11 November 1983, HCJ (unreported).

11 *Sopwith v Cruickshank* 1959 JC 78; *Thom v Smith* 1979 SLT (Notes) 25; *Davidson v HM Advocate* 1981 SCCR 371; *Lambert v Tudhope* 1982 SCCR 144; *Brodie v HM Advocate* 1982 SCCR 243.

However, see also *Simpkins v HM Advocate* 1985 SCCR 30, where the court departed from the comparative principle.
12 *Griffiths v Skeen* 1975 SLT (Notes) 26; *Owens v Heron* 1975 SLT (Notes) 65; *Kindlen v Smith* 1981 SCCR 19; *Wiseman v Hillary* 1981 SCCR 103.
13 *Willms v Smith* 1981 SCCR 257, 1982 SLT 163; *Faboro v HM Advocate* 1982 SCCR 22; *Salehi v Smith* 1982 SCCR 552.

8.56. Manner and time of appeal. A person who has been convicted in the inferior courts may appeal against sentence[1]. Normally this will be by way of a note of appeal[2], but proceedings may be raised by bill of suspension where there has been a fundamental irregularity with regard to the imposition of the sentence[3]. The choice of mode will depend upon whether it is necessary for the High Court of Justiciary to have the views of the sentencing judge before it to determine the appeal or whether on the face of the proceedings there is some obvious error which should be corrected[4]. In the former case a note of appeal is the appropriate mode, but in the latter situation a bill of suspension is likely to achieve the desired result.

An appeal by note of appeal must be lodged with the clerk of the inferior court within one week of sentence being imposed[5]. The note of appeal must properly state the grounds of appeal[6], specifying the reasons why the sentence is considered excessive or inappropriate, and may also crave for bail, a suspension of disqualification, or any other order as necessary[7]. On receipt of the note of appeal the clerk of court must send a copy to the prosecutor and obtain a report from the sentencing judge[8]. The judge's report should 'narrate any facts pertaining to the offence which are relevant to the sentence, describe the substance of any plea in mitigation submitted by or on behalf of the convicted person, and explain the reasoning behind the sentence that was imposed'[9]. Within two weeks of sentence being passed the clerk of court must transmit the note of appeal, the judge's report, a certified copy of the complaint and the minute of proceedings to the Clerk of Justiciary and furnish copies of the report to the parties in the appeal[10]. The sheriff principal may extend the period of two weeks if appropriate[11]. The High Court also has power to extend the period or may hear the appeal without a report, for example if the judge has died[12]. An appellant who is out of time may apply to the High Court through the Clerk of Justiciary for leave to make a late appeal against sentence stating why the appeal was not lodged timeously[13]. If the application is granted the appeal period runs from two days after the High Court interlocutor[14]. At any time prior to the hearing the appellant or his solicitor may abandon the appeal by lodging a minute with the clerk of court or Clerk of Justiciary, depending on the stage the proceedings have reached, and copying the minute to the prosecutor[15]. The Clerk of Justiciary or clerk of court must advise the prosecutor also of the abandonment of the appeal in order that if necessary application can be made to the court for warrant to arrest or imprison an accused who has been released on bail, to serve the remainder of his sentence[16].

1 Criminal Procedure (Scotland) Act 1975 (c 21), s 442(1)(ii) (substituted by the Criminal Justice (Scotland) Act 1980 (c 62), s 34, Sch 3, para 1).
2 Criminal Procedure (Scotland) Act 1975, ss 442B, 453B(1) (respectively added by the Criminal Justice (Scotland) Act 1980, Sch 3, paras 1, 13).
3 Criminal Procedure (Scotland) Act 1975, s 442B proviso (as so added). As to bills of suspension, see paras 8.59 ff below.
4 *Galloway v Smith* 1974 SLT (Notes) 63; *MacNeill v MacGregor* 1975 JC 55, 1975 SLT (Notes) 46; *Handley v Pirie* 1976 JC 65, 1977 SLT 30.
5 Criminal Procedure (Scotland) Act 1975, s 453B(2) (as added: see note 2 above); Act of Adjournal (Consolidation) 1988, SI 1988/110, r 127, Sch 1, Form 76.
6 Criminal Procedure (Scotland) Act 1975, s 453B(1) (as so added).
7 Ibid, s 453B(8) (as so added), applying s 446(1) (see para 8.40 above); High Court of Justiciary Practice Note 29 March 1985, 1985 SLT (News) 120. Where it is sought to challenge a

compensation order imposed with a fine etc, this should be specified in the appeal: *Gray v Allan* 1989 GWD 12–503.

8 Criminal Procedure (Scotland) Act 1975, s 453B(3) (as so added).
9 C G B Nicholson *The Law and Practice of Sentencing in Scotland* (1981) para 9–84.
10 Criminal Procedure (Scotland) Act 1975, s 453B(4) (as added: see note 2 above).
11 Ibid, s 453B(4) proviso (as so added).
12 Ibid, s 453B(5) (as so added).
13 Ibid, s 453B(6) (as so added), applying s 444(3)–(5): see para 8.38 above.
14 Act of Adjournal (Consolidation) 1988, r 130.
15 Criminal Procedure (Scotland) Act 1975, s 453B(7) (as added: see note 2 above). For the style of minute, see Act of Adjournal (Consolidation) 1988, r 127, Sch 1, Form 77.
16 Criminal Procedure (Scotland) Act 1975, s 453B(8) (as so added), applying s 446(5): see para 8.49 above.

8.57. Hearing of note of appeal. The date of the appeal hearing will be fixed by the Clerk of Justiciary in consultation with the Lord Justice-General and Lord Justice-Clerk[1]. An appellant who has been granted bail must appear in person otherwise the High Court will deem the appeal abandoned unless reasons are advanced as to why the appeal should proceed in the appellant's absence[2]. At the hearing the High Court may order the production of any document or article relevant to the proceedings, hear any additional evidence relevant to the alleged miscarriage of justice or order the same to be heard by a High Court judge or other person it may appoint, take account of any circumstances relevant to the case which were not before the judge of first instance, remit to a person to inquire and report into any aspect of the appeal or appoint an expert to sit as an assessor and assist the High Court in its deliberations[3].

1 Criminal Procedure (Scotland) Act 1975 (c 21), s 453C(1) (added by the Criminal Justice (Scotland) Act 1980 (c 62), s 34, Sch 3, para 13); Act of Adjournal (Consolidation) 1988, SI 1988/110, r 137.
2 Criminal Procedure (Scotland) Act 1975, s 453E (as so added).
3 Ibid, s 453B(8) (as so added), applying s 452(4)(a)–(e) (see para 8.51 above); *Hogg v Heatlie* 1962 SLT 39.

8.58. Disposal of appeal against sentence alone. In disposing of the appeal the High Court of Justiciary may either affirm or quash the sentence passed in the inferior court or quash its sentence and pass another sentence in substitution therefor[1]. However, the High Court may not pass a sentence greater than that the inferior court could competently have imposed[2]. Expenses may be awarded by the High Court in respect of the appeal and inferior court proceedings[3].

1 Criminal Procedure (Scotland) Act 1975 (c 21), s 453C(1) (added by the Criminal Justice (Scotland) Act 1980 (c 62), s 34, Sch 3, para 13).
2 Criminal Procedure (Scotland) Act 1975, s 453C(1) proviso (as so added).
3 Ibid, s 453C(2) (as so added).

(E) BILL OF SUSPENSION

8.59. Introduction. Suspension is a form of review in criminal matters with a long history[1]. It is a means of appealing against an allegedly illegal or improper warrant, conviction or judgment issued by the judge of an inferior court[2]. It has been stated that suspension is not open to the prosecutor[3], but the position is more complex, particularly in review of recent decisions of the High Court of Justiciary[4].

1 1 *Encyclopaedia of the Laws of Scotland* (ed Lord Dunedin and J Wark 1926) para 1050; Hume *Commentaries* II, 513; J H A Macdonald *The Criminal Law of Scotland* (5th edn, 1948) p 355; *Jupp v Dunbar* (1863) 4 Irv 355.

2 R W Renton and H H Brown *Criminal Procedure according to the Law of Scotland* (5th edn, 1983) para 16-133. See also the cases referred to there in note 1.

3 *Renton and Brown* para 16-133.

4 *Morton v McLeod* 1981 SCCR 159, 1982 SLT 187; *Durant v Lockhart* 1985 SCCR 72, 1985 SLT 394. See also Forensis 'Appeals by Bill of Advocation' (1986) 31 JLSS 28.

8.60. Competency. Suspension is competent as a mode of review only in summary proceedings[1]. However, it is competent to seek review of a finding of contempt of court which arose in the course of solemn proceedings because this involves the sheriff exercising summary powers[2]. Appeal by way of bill of suspension is competent only where the alleged illegal or improper warrant, conviction or judgment exists or is in force and not where it is merely threatened[3]. Similarly, if a person is illegally detained without a proper court order or warrant there is nothing to suspend and the proper course would be to appeal to the *nobile officium* of the High Court of Justiciary to obtain a remedy[4]. Conversely, even though no further proceedings may have followed upon the obtaining of the allegedly illegal or improper warrant, conviction or judgment, suspension is competent to rectify matters, and the payment of any fine imposed or the serving of a sentence of imprisonment need not be a bar to proceedings[5].

As has been indicated, suspension applies to final judgments and generally is incompetent in respect of earlier stages of a case[6]. However, suspension is a competent method to seek to review the decision of an inferior court to grant a warrant or incidental application, though if it were sought to appeal against the refusal to grant such a warrant or application, advocation would be the proper mode of review[7]. Suspension can also be used to reduce an order granting warrant to remand a convicted person in custody for reports prior to sentence[8]. A third person may also have recourse to a bill of suspension where he has been affected by an order for forfeiture of his possessions[9]. It cannot be employed to seek review of a decision of the judge of an inferior court on the competency of the complaint prior to the conclusion of the trial[10]. Where another means of review is provided by statute, suspension is not necessarily rendered incompetent, but it may be expressly or impliedly excluded by statute[11]. The High Court does have an inherent power to entertain a suspension in cases amounting to a fundamental nullity or to illegality even although review is expressly excluded[12]. It is competent for a convicted person to appeal by bill of suspension where the trial judge is unable to sign the stated case due to death or illness[13]. No such right is given expressly to the prosecutor, and although advocation is competent in certain circumstances[14], it may be that the High Court would entertain a suspension[15].

It can no longer be said that advocation is a remedy only available to the prosecutor and suspension a remedy available to the accused or party affected by the warrant, conviction or judgment. In practice, however, the prosecutor is unlikely to have much need to use suspension, and persons other than the prosecutor are more likely to have recourse to suspension rather than advocation for matters they wish reviewed. Suspension will not be successful if it is in respect of objections to relevancy or competency which were not made timeously in the inferior court[16].

1 The Criminal Procedure (Scotland) Act 1975 (c 21), s 230, precludes appeals by bill of suspension in solemn proceedings. As to review procedures in solemn proceedings, see R W Renton and H H Brown *Criminal Procedure according to the Law of Scotland* (5th edn, 1983) para 16-135, text and note 1.

2 *Butterworth v Herron* 1975 SLT (Notes) 56.

3 *Jupp v Dunbar* (1863) 4 Irv 355; *Lowson v Forfar Police Comrs* (1877) 4 R (J) 35, 3 Coup 433; *Durant v Lockhart* 1985 SCCR 72, 1985 SLT 394.

4 H J Moncrieff *The Law of Review in Criminal Cases* (1877) ch V; *HM Advocate v Lowson* (1909) 6 Adam 118, 1909 2 SLT 329.

5 *Russell v Colquhoun* (1845) 2 Broun 572; *Middlemiss v Lord and Lady Willoughby D'Eresby* (1852) J Shaw 557; *Bell v Black and Morrison* (1865) 5 Irv 57; *Bonthrone v Renton* (1886) 1 White 279.

6 *Morton v McLeod* 1981 SCCR 159, 1982 SLT 187; *Durant v Lockhart* 1985 SCCR 72, 1985 SLT 394.

7 *Bell v Black and Morrison* (1865) 5 Irv 57. Cf *Stallworth v HM Advocate* 1978 SLT 93, and *MacNeill* 1984 JC 1, 1983 SCCR 450, 1984 SLT 157. As to advocation, see paras 8.68 ff below.

8 *Morrison v Clark* 1962 SLT 113; *McKay v Tudhope* 1979 SLT (Notes) 43.

9 *Loch Lomond Sailings Ltd v Hawthorn* 1962 JC 8, 1962 SLT 6; *J W Semple & Sons v MacDonald* 1963 JC 90, 1963 SLT 295.

10 *Morton v McLeod* 1981 SCCR 159, 1982 SLT 187: see para 8.26 above.

11 Criminal Procedure (Scotland) Act 1975, s 455(1), and s 453A (added by the Criminal Justice (Scotland) Act 1980 (c 62), s 34, Sch 3, para 13).

12 *Renton and Brown* para 16-139. See also the cases cited there in note 24.

13 Criminal Procedure (Scotland) Act 1975, s 444(2). See also *Platt v Lockhart* 1988 SCCR 308, 1988 SLT 845 (bill of advocation).

14 Criminal Procedure (Scotland) Act 1975, s 453A (as added: see note 11 above).

15 See *Renton and Brown* paras 16-117, 16-139.

16 Criminal Procedure (Scotland) Act 1975, s 454(1). See also *Skeen v Murphy* 1978 SLT (Notes) 2, and *Pettigrew v Ingram* 1982 SCCR 259, 1982 SLT 435.

8.61. Appropriateness. Suspension is not a suitable mode of appeal where stated case procedure is competent and considered a more appropriate method of enabling the High Court of Justiciary to consider the reasons why the judge in the inferior court took a decision on the basis of evidence before him[1]. However,

> 'when some step in the procedure has gone wrong, or some factor has emerged which satisfies the court that a miscarriage of justice has taken place, resulting in a failure to do justice to an accused'[2],

or

> 'where the relevant circumstances are instantly, or almost instantly, verifiable, and the point sought to be raised is raised promptly, a crisp issue of, say, jurisdiction, competency, oppression, or departure from the canons of natural justice'[3],

suspension is appropriate. Thus suspension is appropriate where defects appear on the face of the proceedings or there has been irregular or oppressive conduct by the judge or prosecutor[4] or, in exceptional circumstances, by the police[5].

In general, the merits of the conviction cannot be raised in a suspension since the High Court does not have before it an authoritative statement of the evidence and the grounds on which the judge proceeded in the inferior court[6]. There have been exceptions to this rule when it was apparent from the bill of suspension and answers that there was insufficient evidence to merit the conviction[7]. However, those exceptions arose when parties agreed on the evidence which had been adduced, and the safer course appears to be to proceed by stated case[8]. Suspension cannot be used as a means of putting before the High Court facts which were not before the inferior court or to obtain probation or other reports[9].

1 *O'Hara v Mill* 1938 JC 4, 1938 SLT 184; *James Y Keanie Ltd v Laird* 1943 JC 73, 1944 SLT 35; *Fairley v Muir* 1951 JC 56, 1951 SLT 237; *Galloway v Smith* 1974 SLT (Notes) 63.

2 *MacGregor v MacNeill* 1975 JC 57 at 60, 1975 SLT (Notes) 54 at 55, per Lord Justice-Clerk Wheatley.

3 *Fairley v Muir* 1951 JC 56 at 60, 1951 SLT 237 at 238, per Lord Justice-General Cooper; *Handley v Pirie* 1976 JC 65, 1977 SLT 30.

4 Hume *Commentaries* II, 514, 515; Alison *Practice* pp 28-32.

5 *McConnachie v Scott* 1988 SCCR 176, 1988 SLT 480.

6 *Rattray v White* (1891) 19 R (J) 23, 3 White 89; *Russell v Paton* (1902) 4 F (J) 77, 3 Adam 639; *Dunn v Mitchell* 1911 SC (J) 46, 6 Adam 365; *James Y Keanie Ltd v Laird* 1943 JC 73, 1944 SLT 35; *Moffat v Skeen* 1963 JC 84; *Rush v Herron* 1969 SLT 211; *Handley v Pirie* 1976 JC 65, 1977 SLT 30.

7 *Lockwood v Walker* 1910 SC (J) 3, 6 Adam 124; *Wright v Mitchell* 1910 SC (J) 94, 6 Adam 287; *M'Shane v Paton* 1922 JC 26, 1922 SLT 251.

8 *O'Hara v Mill* 1938 JC 4, 1938 SLT 184; *Fairley v Muir* 1951 JC 56, 1951 SLT 237.
9 *Farquar v Burrell* 1955 JC 66, 1955 SLT 433. Cf *Hogg v Heatlie* 1962 SLT 39. An appeal by stated case may be brought on the basis of additional evidence: see the Criminal Procedure (Scotland) Act 1975 (c 21), s 442(1)(a), and para 8.37 above.

8.62. Grounds for suspension. Bills of suspension have been sustained on various grounds, of which the following are merely examples: fundamental nullity in the proceedings[1]; want of jurisdiction[2]; want of title to prosecute[3]; oppression on the part of the judge or prosecutor[4]; irregular citation of the accused[5]; objections to the competency of the complaint[6], objections to the relevancy of the complaint where it is alleged the complaint is fundamentally null[7]; admission of incompetent evidence[8] or rejection of competent evidence[9] and refusal of competent questions[10]; objections to the form of the conviction, for example where the charge has been libelled in the alternative and the conviction is a general one[11]; objection that the conviction is ambiguous or unintelligible[12]; objection that the sentence has been altered in the record after being pronounced or that the date of sentence has been altered[13]; objection that the conviction or sentence was not properly authenticated[14]; objection that the conviction was as a result of a plea of guilty tendered in error[15]; objection that the sentence was oppressive or incompetent[16]; objection that the court exceeded or failed to exercise its jurisdiction[17]; and objection that there were irregularities during the trial[18]. Third persons may raise bills of suspension where their property or rights may be affected by decisions reached in a criminal trial[19].

1 Criminal Procedure (Scotland) Act 1975 (c 21), s 444(2), and s 453A(1) (added by the Criminal Justice (Scotland) Act 1980 (c 62), s 34, Sch 3, para 13); *M'Garth v Bathgate* (1869) 1 Coup 260; *Collins v Lang* (1887) 15 R (J) 7, 1 White 482; *Morrison v Peters* 1909 SC (J) 58, 6 Adam 73; *Barr v Ingram* 1977 SLT 173.
2 *McPherson v Boyd* 1907 SC (J) 42, 5 Adam 247.
3 *Simpson v Board of Trade* (1892) 19 R (J) 66, 3 White 167; *Duke of Bedford v Kerr* (1893) 20 R (J) 65, 3 White 493.
4 *M'Kenzie v M'Phee* (1889) 16 R (J) 53, 2 White 188; *Kelly v Mitchell* 1907 SC (J) 52, 5 Adam 268; *Stirling v Herron* 1976 SLT (Notes) 2; *McKay v Tudhope* 1979 SLT (Notes) 43; *Fraser v MacKinnon* 1981 SCCR 91; *Bradford v McLeod* 1985 SCCR 379, 1986 SLT 244; *Harper of Oban (Engineering) Ltd v Henderson* 1988 SCCR 351, 1989 SLT 21. Cf *Mackenzie v Jinks* 1934 JC 48, 1934 SLT 344, and *McPherson v Copeland* 1961 JC 74, 1961 SLT 373, where appeals were taken by stated case.
5 *Stewart v Lang* (1894) 22 R (J) 9, 1 Adam 493; *Dunlop v Goudie* (1895) 22 R (J) 34, 1 Adam 554; *Beattie v M'Kinnon* 1977 JC 64; *Scott v Annan* 1981 SCCR 172, 1982 SLT 90.
6 *Clark and Bendall v Stuart* (1886) 13 R (J) 86, 1 White 191; *Hefferan v Wright* 1911 SC (J) 20, 6 Adam 321; *Morton v McLeod* 1981 SCCR 159, 1982 SLT 187.
7 *Adams v M'Kenna* (1906) 8 F (J) 79, 5 Adam 106; *Smith v Sempill* 1911 SC (J) 30, 6 Adam 348. Cf *James Y Keanie Ltd v Laird* 1943 JC 73, 1944 SLT 35.
8 *Burns v Hart and Young* (1856) 2 Irv 571; *M'Lean v Skinner* 1907 SC (J) 96, 5 Adam 376. Cf *Fairley v Muir* 1951 JC 56, 1951 SLT 237.
9 *Priteca v HM Advocate* (1906) 8 F (J) 66, 5 Adam 79. Cf *Fairley v Muir* 1951 JC 56, 1951 SLT 237, and *Handley v Pirie* 1976 JC 65, 1977 SLT 30.
10 *Falconer v Brown* (1893) 21 R (J) 1, 1 Adam 96.
11 *Reaney v Maddever* (1883) 5 Coup 367; *Aitchison v Neilson* (1897) 24 R (J) 44, 2 Adam 284; *Connell v Mitchell* 1913 SC (J) 13, 7 Adam 23.
12 *Reid v Miller* (1899) 1 F (J) 89, 3 Adam 29; *Macleman v Middleton* (1901) 3 F (J) 70, 3 Adam 353; *Cowans v Sinclair* (1905) 4 Adam 585, 13 SLT 370.
13 *Clarkson v Muir* (1871) 2 Coup 125; *Smith v Sempill* 1911 SC (J) 30, 6 Adam 348; *M'Rory v Findlay* 1911 SC (J) 70, 6 Adam 417.
14 *Simpson v Reid* (1902) 4 F (J) 62, 3 Adam 617.
15 *MacGregor v MacNeill* 1975 JC 57, 1975 SLT (Notes) 54; *Crosbie v MacDougall* Crown Office Appeal Circular A33/89: cf *Healy v HM Advocate* Crown Office Circular A5/90.
16 *Anderson v Begg* 1907 SC (J) 102, 5 Adam 387; *Blair v Hawthorn* 1945 JC 17, 1945 SLT 141; *Lennon v Copland* 1972 SLT (Notes) 68; *McGunnigal v Copeland* 1972 SLT (Notes) 70; *Wilson v Milne* 1974 SLT (Notes) 60; *Galloway v Smith* 1974 SLT (Notes) 63; *Williamson v Farrell* 1975 SLT (Notes) 92; *Devlin v Macfarlane* 1976 SLT (Notes) 5; *Bain v Smith* 1980 SLT (Notes) 69; *Wallace v Tudhope* 1981 SCCR 295, 1982 SLT 218.

17 *Caledonian Rly Co v Fleming* (1969) 7 M 554, 1 Coup 193; *McPherson v Boyd* 1907 SC (J) 42, 5 Adam 247. Cf *Thomson v Smith, Morgan v Smith* 1982 SCCR 57, 1982 SLT 546.

18 *Craig v Steel* (1848) J Shaw 148; *Sime v Linton* (1897) 24 R (J) 70, 2 Adam 288; *Kelly v Mitchell* 1907 SC (J) 52, 5 Adam 268; *Leavack v Macleod* 1913 SC (J) 51, 7 Adam 87; *Aitken v Wood* 1921 JC 84, 1921 2 SLT 124; *Johannesson v Robertson* 1945 JC 146, 1945 SLT 328; *Loughridge v Mickel* 1947 JC 21, 1947 SLT 34; *Barr v Ingram* 1977 SLT 173. Cf *Pettigrew v Ingram* 1982 SCCR 259, 1982 SLT 435.

19 *Loch Lomond Sailings Ltd v Hawthorn* 1962 JC 8, 1962 SLT 6; *J W Semple & Sons v MacDonald* 1963 JC 90, 1963 SLT 295. Cf *Lloyds and Scottish Finance Ltd v HM Advocate* 1974 JC 24, 1974 SLT 3.

8.63. Time for appeal by suspension. As appeal by bill of suspension is a common law procedure there is no fixed time limit for appealing. However, proceedings should be commenced as soon as possible after the warrant, conviction or sentence complained of, and without any undue delay[1]. What amounts to undue delay in a particular case will depend upon the circumstances, but generally any delay of more than two months will require proper explanation if the suspension is not to be barred by the court[2]. Voluntary payment of any fine imposed may be regarded as acquiescence, although if a fine is paid in respect of a minor statutory offence this may be held not to be the case[3].

1 *Low v Rankine* 1917 JC 39 at 41, 42, 1917 1 SLT 292 at 293, 294; *McPherson v Henderson* 1984 SCCR 294 at 298.

2 *M'Lure v Douglas* (1872) 2 Coup 177; *Muirhead v M'Intosh* (1890) 2 White 473; *Watson v Scott* (1898) 25 R (J) 53, 2 Adam 501; *Allan v Lamb* (1900) 3 F (J) 15, 3 Adam 248; *M'Farlan v Fishmongers of London* (1904) 6 F (J) 60, *sub nom M'Farlan v Pringle* 4 Adam 403; *Kelly v Smith* (1904) 7 F (J) 14, 4 Adam 466; *White v Jeans* 1911 SC (J) 88, 6 Adam 489; *Montgomery v Gray* 1915 SC (J) 94, 7 Adam 681; *Carson v Macpherson* 1917 JC 36, 1917 1 SLT 288; *Low v Rankine* 1917 JC 39, 1917 1 SLT 292; *James Y Keanie Ltd v Laird* 1943 JC 73, 1944 SLT 35; *Fairley v Muir* 1951 JC 56, 1951 SLT 237.

3 *M'Lure v Douglas* (1872) 2 Coup 177; *M'Farlan v Fishmongers of London* (1904) 6 F (J) 60, *sub nom M'Farlan v Pringle* 4 Adam 403; *Adams v M'Kenna* (1906) 8 F (J) 79, 5 Adam 106; *Low v Rankine* 1917 JC 39, 1917 1 SLT 292.

8.64. Procedure in suspensions. If the accused is in prison a bill of suspension and liberation must be prepared, otherwise the bill is simply for suspension of the conviction, warrant or the like[1]. The bill should narrate the circumstances, seek warrant to serve on the respondent, ordain the clerk of the inferior court to transmit the proceedings and conclude with the pleas in law upon which the complainer founds his case to have the proceedings set aside. The bill should be signed by the complainer or his solicitor or counsel and lodged with the Clerk of Justiciary. The initial craves in the bill for interim liberation, interim suspension and service may be granted or refused by a single High Court judge[2], but he has discretion if the bill appears to be without substance to remit it to a quorum of judges who may then refuse to pass it. If the bill is incompetent the judge himself may refuse the bill without remitting it to a quorum[3]. If the order for service is granted the bill should be served in the normal way on the respondent, who is usually the prosecutor[4]. Copies of the bill should be printed and delivered as in stated case appeals[5]. Within two weeks after receipt of his copy of the bill the prosecutor may consent to the conviction being set aside[6]. Normally, however, the respondent will lodge answers prior to the hearing.

1 For a style, see R W Renton and H H Brown *Criminal Procedure according to the Law of Scotland* (5th edn, 1983) App C, Form 5, p 608.

2 Act of Adjournal (Consolidation) 1988, SI 1988/110, r 139; Hume *Commentaries* II, 514; *Carnegie v Clark* 1947 JC 74, 1947 SLT 218; *Fairley v Muir* 1951 JC 56, 1951 SLT 237.

3 *Morton v McLeod* 1981 SCCR 159, 1982 SLT 187.

4 See the Criminal Procedure (Scotland) Act 1975 (c 21), s 455(2); *Pirie v Hawthorn* 1962 JC 69, 1962 SLT 291; *Cordiner* 1973 JC 16, 1973 SLT 125; *Durant v Lockhart* 1985 SCCR 72, 1985 SLT 394.

5 Act of Adjournal (Consolidation) 1988, r 136(1): see para 8.50 above.

6 Criminal Procedure (Scotland) Act 1975, s 453(1): see para 8.41 above.

8.65. Hearing. The Clerk of Justiciary fixes a date for the hearing and gives the parties' solicitors at least fourteen days' notice[1]. The complainer must appear at the hearing, otherwise the bill of suspension will be deemed to be abandoned unless special reasons for a hearing in absence can be shown[2]. In hearing the appeal the High Court of Justiciary may order the production of any documents or things relevant to the proceedings, or hear additional evidence, take account of circumstances which were not before the judge in the lower court, remit to a person to inquire and report or appoint an assessor to assist in its deliberations[3].

1 Act of Adjournal (Consolidation) 1988, SI 1988/110, r 137(1), (2).
2 Criminal Procedure (Scotland) Act 1975 (c 21), s 453E (added by the Criminal Justice (Scotland) Act 1980 (c 62), s 34, Sch 3, para 13).
3 Criminal Procedure (Scotland) Act 1975, s 453A(2) (as so added), applying s 452(4)(a)-(e): see paras 8.51, 8.57, above.

8.66. Remits. Normally the facts of the case will not be investigated by the High Court of Justiciary, as suspension is employed to review errors of law. However, the High Court may remit the case to the sheriff principal, sheriff or another fit person to inquire and report on the matter[1]. This may arise where an irregularity is disclosed on the face of the proceedings, or material or relevant averments are either denied or not admitted by the respondent[2]. Normally where there is a conflict between averments and answers the respondent's version will be preferred, although a remit would arise if there was reason to doubt the accuracy of the answers[3]. If gross and flagrant oppression is alleged the High Court may order further inquiries[4]. Much will depend on the tone of the respondent's answers as to whether further inquiries are directed[5].

1 Criminal Procedure (Scotland) Act 1975 (c 21), s 453A(2), applying s 452(4)(d) (s 453A being added by the Criminal Justice (Scotland) Act 1980 (c 62), s 34, Sch 3, para 13); *Barr v Ingram* 1977 SLT 173.
2 *Nardini v Walker* (1903) 5 F (J) 69, 4 Adam 174; *Avery v Hilson* (1906) 8 F (J) 60, 5 Adam 56; *Renwick v M'Dougall* 1913 SC (J) 53, 7 Adam 91; *Ewart v Strathern* 1924 JC 45, 1924 SLT 359.
3 *Neilands v Leslie* 1973 SLT (Notes) 32. Cf *Third Report on Criminal Appeals in Scotland* (The Thomson Report) (Cmnd 7005) (1977) para 9-07.
4 *Wright v Dewar* (1874) 1 R (J) 1, 2 Coup 504; *Russell v Paton* (1902) 4 F (J) 77, 3 Adam 639; *Nardini v Walker* (1903) 5 F (J) 69, 4 Adam 174; *Wright v Thomson* (1904) 7 F (J) 18, 4 Adam 459.
5 *Nardini v Walker* (1903) 5 F (J) 69, 4 Adam 174; *Trotter v Burnet* 1947 JC 151, 1948 SLT 57; *Hynd v Clark* 1954 SLT 85.

8.67. Disposal of bill of suspension. The High Court of Justiciary may pass the bill of suspension and suspend the sentence, warrant, judgment or other order and order repayment of any fine paid. It may refuse the bill and recommit the accused to prison, or it may amend the conviction and sentence or remit to the inferior court to proceed further. The prosecutor may be given authority to raise a fresh prosecution[1]. In quashing sentence the High Court may impose another (but not more severe) sentence in substitution[1].

1 Criminal Procedure (Scotland) Act 1975 (c 21), s 453A(2), applying s 452A(1)(d), (2) (added respectively by the Criminal Justice (Scotland) Act 1980 (c 62), s 34, Sch 3, paras 13, 11).

(F) BILL OF ADVOCATION

8.68. Introduction and background. Advocation first developed not as a mode of appeal but as a means of removing a case to the High Court of Justiciary because of objections to the jurisdiction of the judge in the inferior court or because of the conduct of the judge or the difficulty of the case[1]. Gradually with the development of an independent judiciary in the lower courts and the professionalism of the sheriff there became less need for advocation because of the judge's lack of qualifications and doubts as to his impartiality, and the process developed into a form of review. This procedure was available to both the accused and the prosecutor against alleged errors made by the judge in the lower court prior to the conclusion of the trial and the imposition of sentence[2]. However, because advocations by accused persons would delay the conclusion of outstanding criminal proceedings the High Court generally declined to interfere with proceedings in the lower court other than in exceptional circumstances, preferring to await the outcome of proceedings[3]. At this stage stated case and suspension[4] are competent, and thus in recent times advocation has been used by the prosecutor only. Indeed it was said in 1967 that advocation had become very rare, and for practical purposes was really out of date[5]. Since then there has been steady recourse to the procedure[6], culminating in a reaffirmation that advocation is available to accused persons in appropriate circumstances[7]. The Criminal Procedure (Scotland) Act 1980 also reaffirmed the existence of bill of advocation procedure[8].

1 Hume *Commentaries* II, 510; H J Moncrieff *The Law of Review in Criminal Cases* (1877) p 163.
2 Alison *Practice* p 26; *Moncrieff* p 163; R W Renton and H H Brown *Criminal Procedure according to the Law of Scotland* (5th edn, 1983) para 16-171; *Jameson v Lothian* (1855) 2 Irv 273; *Muir v Hart* 1912 SC (J) 41, 6 Adam 601; *HM Advocate v McKenzie* 1989 SCCR 587; *Crugen v Jessop* 1988 SCCR 182.
3 *Alison* p 26; *Moncrieff* p 163; *Grugen v Jessop* 1988 SCCR 182.
4 See paras 8.27 ff, 8.59 ff, above.
5 *MacLeod v Levitt* 1969 JC 16, 1969 SLT 286.
6 *Skeen v Skerret* 1976 SLT (Notes) 6; *Skeen v McLaren* 1976 SLT (Notes) 14; *Tudhope v Lawrie* 1979 JC 44, 1979 SLT (Notes) 13; *Skeen v Fullarton* 1980 SLT (Notes) 46; *Mackenzie v Maclean* 1980 JC 89, 1981 SLT 2; *MacKinnon v Craig* 1983 SCCR 285, 1983 SLT 475; *MacNeill* 1984 JC 1, 1983 SCCR 450, 1984 SLT 157; *HM Advocate v McDonald* 1984 JC 94, 1984 SCCR 229, 1984 SLT 426; *Jessop v Rae* Crown Office Appeal Circular A7/90. See also *Lees v Weston* 1989 SCCR 177, where, in an appeal by the Crown against the sheriff's decision to refuse a warrant to take the fingerprints of a fully committed accused where the police had failed to take prints earlier, it was held that the public interest outweighed the rights of the accused.
7 *Durant v Lockhart* 1985 SCCR 72, 1985 SLT 394. See also Forensis 'Appeal by Bill of Advocation' (1986) 31 JLSS 28.
8 Criminal Procedure (Scotland) Act 1975 (c 21), s 453A (added by the Criminal Justice (Scotland) Act 1980 (c 62), s 34, Sch 3, para 13).

8.69. Competency and appropriateness. Advocation is an appropriate procedure to seek a review by the High Court of Justiciary of irregularities in the preliminary stages of a case and prior to a final judgment[1]. It can be used to seek review of any proceeding, and advocation may be resorted to despite the absence of a minuted interlocutor[2]. The bill will be refused by the High Court unless special circumstances are made out, and it will depend on the nature of the case as to whether special circumstances are held to be present. Where the accused has presented the bill there would need to be a fundamental nullity present or circumstances 'which outraged all the principles of liberty of the subject'[3].

Where, however, the prosecutor has presented the bill a less rigorous test is applied. As has been explained above, advocation by the accused is likely to delay the proceedings in the lower court whereas advocation by the prosecutor will usually re-raise proceedings which have been terminated in the lower court by the judge[4]. It is incompetent to use advocation to attempt to review the merits of a case or to appeal against a decision repelling objections to relevancy and competency of the proceedings[5]. Where appeal by stated case is not open to the prosecution, advocation is competent[6]. Under solemn procedure bills of advocation require to be in accordance with existing law and practice[7].

Advocation can be used by the prosecutor where a court dismisses an indictment or complaint in part as irrelevant or incompetent or dismisses the case on some other ground[8]. Advocation has been used when the sheriff orders a guilty plea to be recorded which the prosecutor had refused to accept[9], and when an incidental application for warrant to search premises was refused[10]. It has also been used in connection with a decision taken by the court to grant or refuse an adjournment, or with a failure to deal properly with a case, or with a premature finding of not guilty and an incompetent sentence[11]. A decision by the judge not to allow desertion *pro loco et tempore* but to desert a case *simpliciter* could be reviewed by bill of advocation[12]; but advocation against a sheriff's administrative decision to restore a driving licence has been held to be incompetent[13]. Advocation has also been resorted to by the Crown where the sheriff refused to state a case[14].

1 *Smith v Kinnoch* (1848) Arkley 427; *Earl of Kinnoull v Tod* (1859) 3 Irv 501; *MacLeod v Levitt* 1969 JC 16, 1969 SLT 286.
2 Alison *Practice* p 26; *MacKinnon v Craig* 1983 SCCR 285, 1983 SLT 475.
3 *Jameson v Lothian* (1855) 2 Irv 273; *Muir v Hart* 1912 SC (J) 41, 6 Adam 601.
4 See para 8.68 above. See also *Strathern v Sloan* 1937 JC 76, 1937 SLT 503; *M'Fadyean v Stewart* 1951 JC 164, 1951 SLT 382.
5 *Jameson v Lothian* (1855) 2 Irv 273; *Muir v Hart* 1912 SC (J) 41, 6 Adam 601; *Aldred v Strathern* 1929 JC 93, 1929 SLT 312; *McLeod v Levitt* 1969 JC 16, 1969 SLT 286.
6 Criminal Procedure (Scotland) Act 1975 (c 21), s 453A(1) (added by the Criminal Justice (Scotland) Act 1980 (c 62), s 34, Sch 3, para 13).
7 Criminal Procedure (Scotland) Act 1975, s 280A(1) (added by the Criminal Justice (Scotland) Act 1980, s 35).
8 *Craig v Galt* (1881) 4 Coup 541; *Macrae v Cooper* (1882) 9 R (J) 11, 4 Coup 561; *Duncan v Cooper* (1886) 13 R (J) 36, 1 White 43; *Dunbar v Johnston* (1904) 7 F (J) 40, 4 Adam 505; *Nimmo v Lees* 1910 SC (J) 75, 6 Adam 279; *M'Fadyean v Stewart* 1951 JC 164, 1951 SLT 382; *HM Advocate v M'Cann* 1977 JC 1, 1977 SLT (Notes) 19; *Mackenzie v Maclean* 1980 JC 89, 1981 SLT 2; *Skeen v Fullarton* 1980 SLT (Notes) 46; *HM Advocate v Walker* 1981 JC 102, 1981 SCCR 154, 1981 SLT (Notes) 111; *HM Advocate v M'Donald* 1984 JC 94, 1984 SCCR 229, 1984 SLT 426.
9 *Strathern v Sloan* 1937 JC 76, 1937 SLT 503.
10 *MacNeill* 1984 JC 1, 1983 SCCR 450, 1984 SLT 157. See also *Lees v Weston* 1989 SCCR 177.
11 *Skeen v Skerret* 1976 SLT (Notes) 6; *Skeen v McLaren* 1976 SLT (Notes) 14; *Tudhope v Lawrie* 1979 JC 44, 1979 SLT (Notes) 13; *Skeen v Evans* 1979 SLT (Notes) 55; *Skeen v Sullivan* 1980 SLT (Notes) 11; *MacKinnon v Craig* 1983 SCCR 285, 1983 SLT 475; *R S* 27 January 1983 (unreported); see R W Renton and H H Brown *Criminal Procedure according to the Law of Scotland* (5th edn, 1983) para 16-177.
12 *Mackenzie v Maclean* 1980 JC 89, 1981 SLT 2.
13 *McLeod v Levitt* 1969 JC 16, 1969 SLT 286.
14 *MacDougall* 1986 SCCR 128. See also *Singh* 1986 SCCR 215, 1987 SLT 63n.

8.70. Hearing and disposal of bill of advocation. As in stated case and bill of suspension hearings[1], on a bill of advocation the High Court of Justiciary may order production of documents or articles, take account of circumstances not before the judge of the inferior court, remit to a fit person to inquire and report and appoint an assessor to assist in deliberations[2]. At the conclusion of the hearing the bill may be passed in whole or in part or remitted to the lower court to proceed as directed[3]. The High Court may set aside a verdict in the lower court and grant authority for a new prosecution[4].

1 See paras 8.51, 8.65, above.
2 Criminal Procedure (Scotland) Act 1975 (c 21), s 453A(2), applying s 452(4)(a)–(e) (see para 863 above) (s 453A being added by the Criminal Justice (Scotland) Act 1980 (c 62), s 34, Sch 3, para 13).

3 H J Moncrieff *The Law of Review in Criminal Cases* (1877) p 169.
4 Criminal Procedure (Scotland) Act 1975, s 453A(2) (as added: see note 2 above), applying ss 452A(1)(d), 452B (both added by the Criminal Justice (Scotland) Act 1980, Sch 3, para 11).

(d) Miscellaneous Provisions relating to Appeals

8.71. Petition to the *nobile officium*. Over and above the powers of review already mentioned, the High Court of Justiciary (like the Court of Session) exercises a *nobile officium*, an extraordinary and inherent discretion, where no other mode of review appears competent or appropriate, and an aggrieved person may petition the *nobile officium* for redress or to prevent injustice or oppression[1]. This procedure is open to the prosecutor as well as to accused persons[2], and to third persons affected by criminal proceedings[3]. The *nobile officium* will be exercised by the High Court where the circumstances are unforeseen and where there is no other remedy under statute or at common law[4]. In cases involving statutory law the procedure may be utilised even though no appeal procedure is provided unless the statute expressly or impliedly negates a review[5]. A petition to the *nobile officium* has been used after a stated case has been lodged and abandoned[6]. However, this has since been criticised and would not be followed where the procedure seeks to go into the merits of a conviction[7]. The correct procedure in such circumstances would seem to be an appeal by a bill of advocation or suspension[8]. The *nobile officium* cannot be used to rectify a failure to comply with a statutory timetable such as a failure to lodge timeously an appeal against refusal of bail or a stated case[9]. The *nobile officium* can be exercised only by a quorum of the High Court[10].

1 Alison *Practice* p 23; H J Moncrieff *The Law of Review in Criminal Cases* (1877) p 264; *Wylie v HM Advocate* 1966 SLT 149; *Anderson v HM Advocate* 1974 SLT 239; *Ferguson v HM Advocate* 1980 JC 27, 1980 SLT 21; *Mathieson* 1980 SLT (Notes) 74; *Rae* 1981 SCCR 356, 1982 SLT 233; *Kemp* 1982 JC 29, 1982 SCCR 1, 1982 SLT 357. See also C N Stoddart 'The Nobile Officium of the High Court of Justiciary' 1974 SLT (News) 37.
2 *HM Advocate v Greene* 1976 SLT 120; *HM Advocate v Keegan* 1981 SLT (Notes) 35; *Macdougall* 1986 SCCR 128.
3 *Wan Ping Nam v Federal German Republic Minister of Justice* 1972 JC 43, 1972 SLT 220; *Lloyds and Scottish Finance Ltd v HM Advocate* 1974 JC 24, 1974 SLT 3; *Rae* 1981 SCCR 356, 1982 SLT 233.
4 *Moncrieff* p 264; J H A Macdonald *The Criminal Law of Scotland* (5th edn, 1948) p 193; *Vetters v HM Advocate* 1943 JC 138, 1944 SLT 85; *Anderson v HM Advocate* 1974 SLT 239; *Mathieson* 1980 SLT (Notes) 74; *Muirhead* 1983 SLT 208; *Gerrard* 1984 SCCR 1, 1984 SLT 108; *Hughes, Petitioner* 1989 SCCR 490, 1990 SLT 142; cf *McKay, Petitioner* 1989 GWD 31–1412; *Mullane, Petitioner* 1990 SCCR 25.
5 *Hartley* (1968) 32 JCL 191; *Heslin* 1973 SLT (Notes) 56; *Anderson v HM Advocate* 1974 SLT 239; *HM Advocate v Greene* 1976 SLT 120; *Fenton* 1981 SCCR 288, 1982 SLT 164; *Harper* 1981 SCCR 363, 1982 SLT 232; *Berry* 1985 SCCR 106; *MacPherson, Petitioners* 1989 SCCR 518; *Campbell, Petitioner* 1989 SCCR 722.
6 *McCloy* 1971 SLT (Notes) 32. See also *Mathieson* 1980 SLT 74.
7 *Anderson v HM Advocate* 1974 SLT 239.
8 See the Criminal Procedure (Scotland) Act 1975 (c 21), ss 449(2), 453A (the former amended by the Criminal Justice (Scotland) Act 1980 (c 62), s 34, Sch 3, para 8(b), and the latter added by Sch 3, para 13); R W Renton and H H Brown *Criminal Procedure according to the Law of Scotland* (5th edn, 1983) para 16-183, note 5.
9 *Ferguson v HM Advocate* 1980 JC 27, 1980 SLT 21; *Fenton* 1981 SCCR 288, 1982 SLT 164; *Berry* 1985 SCCR 106.
10 *HM Advocate v Lowson* (1909) 6 Adam 118, 1909 2 SLT 329; *Milne v M'Nicol* 1944 JC 151, 1945 SLT 10; *Macdonald* p 193.

8.72. Reference to the European Court of Justice. The Court of Justice of the European Communities has jurisdiction to give preliminary rulings on the interpretation of the Community treaties, the validity and interpretation of acts

of the Community institutions and the interpretation of Community legislation[1]. Where such questions arise a Scottish court may, if it considers a
decision on the matter necessary to enable it to give judgment, request a ruling
from the European Court of Justice, but if the High Court of Justiciary, acting in
its appellate capacity, is the court concerned it must refer the question for a
ruling[2]. In practice it is likely that the question will be referred to the High Court
by way of the normal appeal procedures rather than that lower courts will
directly refer cases to the Court of Justice[3].

A style of reference for a preliminary ruling is prescribed, and a procedure is
laid down for drafting by parties and adjustment[4]. The clerk of court thereafter
transmits the reference and copy proceedings to the Registrar of the Court of
Justice[5]. Once a ruling has been given it will be conveyed to the clerk of court,
who copies it to the parties, and the Scottish court then gives effect to any
directions as to further procedure[6]. Should a court of first instance make a
reference direct to the Court of Justice, any party aggrieved by the decision to
refer may within fourteen days of the order appeal to the High Court of
Justiciary, sitting as a court of appeal, by lodging the appropriate form with the
clerk of the lower court and serving a copy on the other party[7]. Thereafter the
proceedings are transmitted to the High Court, which may sustain or dismiss
the appeal by remitting the case back to the inferior court or give instructions
with a view to the matter being referred to the Court of Justice[8].

1 EEC Treaty, art 177, 1st para; Euratom Treaty, art 150, 1st para. See also the ECSC Treaty, art
   41. And see *Wither v Cowie* (1990) The Scotsman, 22 August, High Ct.
2 EEC Treaty, 2nd and 3rd paras; Euratom Treaty, 2nd and 3rd paras. If a question is raised in the
   High Court in any proceedings on appeal under the Criminal Procedure (Scotland) Act 1975
   (c 21) or on appeal by bill of advocation, or on a petition for the exercise of the court's *nobile
   officium*, the court must proceed to make a reference: Act of Adjournal (Consolidation) 1988,
   SI 1988/110, r 64A (added by SI 1989/48).
3 *Geweise v Mackenzie, Mehlich v Mackenzie* 1984 SCCR 130, 1984 SLT 449 . See Act of Adjournal
   (Consolidation) 1988, rr 63–65, 113–116; R W Renton and H H Brown *Criminal Procedure
   according to the Law of Scotland* (5th edn, 1983) paras 16-184–16-191; and para 8.20 above.
4 Act of Adjournal (Consolidation) 1988, rr 65(2)(a), 116(2)(a), Sch 1, Form 31.
5 Ibid, rr 65(2)(c), 116(2)(c).
6 Ibid, rr 66, 117.
7 Ibid, rr 67(1), (2), 118(1), (2), Sch 1, Form 32; *HM Advocate, Petitioner* 1990 GWD 13–647.
8 Ibid, rr 67(3), (4), 118(3), (4).

8.73. Pardons. Aside from the appeal provisions contained in the Criminal
Procedure (Scotland) Act 1975 (c 21) it is open to a convicted person to petition
the Queen for exercise of the prerogative of mercy[1]. The effect of a pardon is to
free the convicted person from the effects of the conviction, but it does not
quash the conviction[2]. Pardons will be granted only in exceptional circumstances where there is no other remedy open to the convicted person.

1 C H W Gane 'The Effect of a Pardon in Scots Law' 1980 JR 18; C G B Nicholson *The Law and
   Practice of Sentencing in Scotland* (1981) p 117; *HM Advocate v Waddell* 1976 SLT (Notes) 61; C H W
   Gane and C N Stoddart *Criminal Procedure in Scotland: Cases and Materials* (1983) p 596. See also
   paras 1.54, 8.21, above.
2 *HM Advocate v Waddell* 1976 SLT (Notes) 61. For a form of pardon, see *Report of Inquiry into the
   whole circumstances of the Murder of Mrs Rachel Ross at Ayr in July 1969* (the Hunter Report) (HC
   Papers (1981–82) no. 444) para 12.137.

8.74. Compensation. High Court judges and sheriffs are immune from all
actions at law for damages for anything done by them in their judicial capacity[1].
The Lord Advocate and prosecutors engaged in connection with proceedings on
indictment have a similar privilege[2]. Judges in the other inferior courts and
officials cannot be found liable for damages either unless the person suing has

suffered imprisonment in respect of proceedings for which sentence has been quashed, and the judge or official concerned acted maliciously and without probable cause[3]. A convicted person whose conviction has been quashed on appeal may apply to the Secretary of State for an *ex gratia* payment in respect of a period spent in custody as a result of a wrongful conviction, provided it can be shown that the period in custody arose from a serious default on the part of the criminal authorities[4]. Statutory provision is now made for compensation in the case of a miscarriage of justice[5]. Compensation may also be awarded by the Criminal Injuries Compensation Board.

1 R W Renton and H H Brown *Criminal Procedure according to the Law of Scotland* (5th edn, 1983) paras 21-01, 21-02; *Harvey v Dyce* (1876) 4 R 265.
2 Hume *Commentaries* II, 135; Alison *Practice* p 92; *Renton and Brown* para 21-06; *Hester v MacDonald* 1961 SC 370, 1961 SLT 414.
3 Criminal Procedure (Scotland) Act 1975 (c 21), s 456; *Renton and Brown* para 21-07.
4 1986 SLT (News) 43 (House of Commons answer on 23 January 1986). Following the quashing of a conviction in *Preece v HM Advocate* [1981] Crim LR 783, Preece was awarded £77,000 compensation. Following the pardon of Patrick Meehan he was initially offered £7,500: see Scottish Grand Committee debate on the Hunter Report on 7 December 1982, cols 3, 17.
5 See para 8.24 above.

9. CHILDREN

9.01. Prosecution of child offenders. Scotland's juvenile justice system is both radical and unique. There are no juvenile courts; children under the age of sixteen, when prosecuted, are dealt with either in the High Court of Justiciary or the sheriff court, with the district court having no jurisdiction over such children[1]. Prosecutions of children are, however, rare, with the majority of child offenders being dealt with by the reporter to the children's panel whose remit covers not only children as offenders but children as victims of offences and children in need of measures of care[2]. In Scots law a child under the age of eight cannot be guilty of any offence[3]. This section of the title accordingly deals with children over the age of eight. 'Child' is normally defined in criminal proceedings as one who has not attained the age of sixteen[4], but it is possible for a person who is over sixteen and under eighteen to be classified as a child, if he is the subject of a supervision requirement imposed by a children's hearing[5], or if he has been referred to a children's hearing under the provisions[6] relating to the return and removal of children within the United Kingdom[7].

1 Social Work (Scotland) Act 1968 (c 49), s 31(1) (amended by the Health and Social Services and Social Security Adjudications Act 1983 (c 41), s 9, Sch 2, para 7).
2 Social Work (Scotland) Act 1968, s 32(1) (amended by the Children Act 1975 (c 72), s 108(1), Sch 3, para 54; the Solvent Abuse (Scotland) Act 1983 (c 3), s 1; and the Health and Social Services and Social Security Adjudications Act 1983, s 8(1)).
3 Criminal Procedure (Scotland) Act 1975 (c 21), ss 170, 369.
4 Social Work (Scotland) Act 1968, s 30(1)(a).
5 Ibid, s 30(1)(b).
6 Ie ibid, Pt V (ss 69–77).
7 Ibid, s 30(1)(c).

9.02. General guidelines. No child under the age of sixteen may be prosecuted for any offence except on the instructions of the Lord Advocate or at his instance[1]. The Lord Advocate has further directed that no child under thirteen is to be prosecuted without his prior express authority. The Lord Advocate has given general guidelines and instructions to procurators fiscal with regard to categories of offences for which, if committed by a child between the ages of thirteen and sixteen, the procurator fiscal may institute proceedings without further reference to the Lord Advocate. The general guidelines have been accepted as being in accordance with the terms of the controlling legislation and do not require any proof to be led in the appropriate case that authority has been given to prosecute[2].

There are seven categories of offence which the Lord Advocate has indicated may be brought in the ordinary criminal courts. The first relates to the exclusive pleas of the High Court of Justiciary (treason, murder, rape, incest at common law, and deforcement of messengers). The second category relates to the serious offences against the person, namely culpable homicide, attempted murder, assault to the danger of life, sodomy, assault and robbery involving the use of firearms, attempted rape and attempted incest. The third group, and the most common in practice, is where the child is alleged to have committed the offence while acting with an adult. The fourth and fifth groups cover situations in which the children's hearings do not have the appropriate power to deal with the specific circumstances, for example where in the event of a conviction a court would be obliged or permitted to order disqualification from driving or where a court could order forfeiture of an article seized. A children's hearing may not impose disqualification from driving and has no power to order forfeiture of seized items. The sixth category concerns offences alleged to have been committed by children between the ages of sixteen and eighteen in respect of whom a supervision requirement of a children's hearing is already in force. The seventh category relates to offences which are sufficiently serious to warrant the initiation of solemn proceedings notwithstanding the fact that the offence was committed by a child. This general category includes all serious crimes other than those specified in the first two categories and includes such crimes as wilful fireraising, assault to permanent disfigurement and similar crimes. While this category is based upon the view that solemn proceedings are warranted it does not exclude the initiation of summary proceedings in appropriate cases in terms of this category.

In many instances the categories involving acting with an adult, disqualification or forfeiture will be dealt with at summary level. These categories are only general guidelines for procurators fiscal concerning the classes of cases which may be prosecuted, and it does not follow that any offence falling outwith these categories may not be prosecuted, or conversely that every offence within these categories must be prosecuted. With the exception of the first category (the crimes exclusive to the High Court) there will be discussion with the reporter to the children's panel to see whether or not the case could be more appropriately dealt with by him[3]. There is a presumption in law that cases falling within these categories can be prosecuted without the prosecutor requiring to provide evidence to the court that he has the specific authority of the Lord Advocate to proceed with that particular prosecution[4]. It is, however, only a presumption and is open to challenge and rebuttal in appropriate cases. The challenge is made by way of preliminary plea which requires to be stated before any other plea is tendered to the charge on the complaint or indictment, which failing it will not be heard subsequently[5].

1 Social Work (Scotland) Act 1968 (c 49), s 31(1) (amended by the Health and Social Services and Social Security Adjudications Act 1983 (c 41), s 9, Sch 2, para 7); Act of Adjournal (Consolidation) 1988, SI 1988/110, r 142 (summary procedure). The complaint must be at the instance of the procurator fiscal: r 142. For the procedure, see further rr 140–147.
2 *M'Guire v Dean* 1973 JC 20, 1974 SLT 229.
3 For further details of the consultation between the procurator fiscal and the reporter, see *Speedy Justice for Children* (1986), a report published by the Scottish Association for the Study of Delinquency.
4 *M'Guire v Dean* 1973 JC 20, 1974 SLT 229.
5 See paras 680 ff above, and the Criminal Procedure (Scotland) Act 1975 (c 21), s 334(1) (amended by the Criminal Justice (Scotland) Act 1980 (c 62), s 83(2), Sch 7, para 54(a)).

9.03. Notification. One principal difference between prosecutions involving children and those involving adults is the requirement in the case of children to notify two groups of people that the prosecution is to be instituted. First, the chief constable must notify prosecutions of children to the local authority in whose area the court sits, informing it of the day and time when the case is to be heard and the nature of the charge upon which the child is to appear[1]. The local authority on receipt of such notification is required to make investigations and to make available to the court a report containing such information as to the child's home surroundings as appears to it will assist the court in dealing with the case[2]. Failure to notify the authority before the prosecution is instituted is not fatal to that prosecution[3]. Secondly, notification must also be made to the parent or guardian of the child, and if he can be found and resides within a reasonable distance of the court, he may be required to attend the court during all stages of the proceedings unless the court is satisfied that it would be unreasonable to require such an attendance[4]. The particular parent or guardian whose attendance is required is the one having actual possession or control of the child[5]. However, if that person is not the father then the attendance of the father may also be required[6]. Where the child has been removed from the custody or charge of his parents by an order of court before the institution of the proceedings, the parents need not attend[7]. Failure to notify parents before the prosecution is not necessarily fatal to the proceedings[8].

1 Criminal Procedure (Scotland) Act 1975 (c 21), ss 40(1), 308(1). 'Local authority' means the regional or islands council: Social Work (Scotland) Act 1968 (c 49), s 1(2) (amended by the Local Government (Scotland) Act 1973 (c 65), s 214(2), Sch 27, Pt II, para 183), applied by the Criminal Procedure (Scotland) Act 1975, s 462(1).
2 Ibid, ss 40(2), 308(2).
3 *Gershenson v Williamson* 1945 JC 127, 1946 SLT 21.
4 Criminal Procedure (Scotland) Act 1975, ss 39(1), 307(1).
5 Ibid, ss 39(4), 307(4).
6 Ibid, ss 39(4) proviso, 307(4) proviso.
7 Ibid, ss 39(5), 307(5).
8 See *Gershenson v Williamson* 1945 JC 127, 1946 SLT 21.

9.04. Court procedure. In summary proceedings, except where the child is represented by a solicitor or counsel, the court may allow the parent or guardian of the child to assist in conducting the defence[1]. Where the parent or guardian cannot be found, or cannot reasonably be required to attend, any relative or other responsible person may take the place of the parent or guardian in so assisting[2]. Summary proceedings must take place in a separate room or building or at a time apart from normal criminal court business[3] in cases where no adult is being prosecuted at the same time on the same complaint. Precautions are taken to prevent those children attending from mixing with adult offenders[4] or with other children[5]. Every effort is also made to ensure that where a child has been detained at a police station there is no contact at any time with any adult charged with an offence other than an offence with which the child is jointly charged[6]. The procedure in court is very similar to that when dealing with an adult, subject to minor modifications: the substance of the charge should be explained in simple language suitable to the child's age and understanding[7], and where the child, instead of asking questions by way of cross-examination, makes assertions, the court must put to the witnesses such questions as it thinks necessary on behalf of the child and may for this purpose question the child in order to bring out and clear up any point arising out of such assertion[8]. Where the court is satisfied that the child has committed an offence he must be so informed and his parent, guardian or other representative, or the child himself, must be given an opportunity to make a statement[9]. There must also be opportunity for these persons to produce evidence in relation to any report submitted by the local authority for the court to consider[10]. No report of court proceedings made in any newspaper or radio or television broadcast must reveal the child's name, address or school nor contain any other means of identification, including a picture[11].

1 Act of Adjournal (Consolidation) 1988, SI 1988/110, r 143(1).
2 Ibid, r 143(2).
3 Criminal Procedure (Scotland) Act 1975 (c 21), s 366. As to child witnesses etc in solemn proceedings, see ss 165, 166.

4 Ibid, ss 38, 306.
5 Act of Adjournal (Consolidation) 1988, r 147.
6 Criminal Procedure (Scotland) Act 1975, ss 38, 306.
7 Act of Adjournal (Consolidation) 1988, r 144(a).
8 Ibid, r 144(d).
9 Ibid, r 144(f).
10 Ibid, r 144(g).
11 Criminal Procedure (Scotland) Act 1975, ss 169, 374 (substituted by the Criminal Justice (Scotland) Act 1980 (c 62), s 22) (see para 6.18 above). See also the Social Work (Scotland) Act 1968 (c 49), s 58(1)(a), (b).

9.05. Detention or arrest. A child is dealt with in the same way as an adult in all the normal preliminary steps and procedures, but with certain modifications. When a child under sixteen has either been detained or arrested[1] the police constable involved is obliged to intimate without delay to the child's parent or guardian the fact that the child is in custody at a specified place[2], unlike the corresponding position for an adult where the police are entitled to delay intimations of arrest or detention where necessary in the interest of the investigation, or the prevention of crime or the apprehension of offenders[3]. A parent or guardian has a right, unless there is reasonable cause to suspect that he has been involved in the alleged offence, to be permitted access to the child[4].

1 As to detention and arrest, see paras 3.01 ff above.
2 Criminal Justice (Scotland) Act 1980 (c 62), s 3(3), (5).
3 Ibid, s 3(1).
4 Ibid, s 3(3), (4).

9.06. Custody in place of safety. Special rules also apply where it is proposed to detain a child, either with a view to bringing him before the court or, having brought him to court, with a view thereafter to keeping him in custody before trial or sentence. In such circumstances a child must be detained in a place of safety managed by the local authority unless he is over fourteen and certified as being so unruly a character that he cannot be safely committed to its care[1]. 'Place of safety' means any residential or other establishment provided by a local authority, a police station, or any hospital, surgery or other suitable place, the occupier of which is willing, temporarily, to receive a child[2]. Prior to his first appearance the child may be liberated by the police with a view to having him cited to court ultimately, or on an undertaking to appear in court[3], and once in court he can be either ordained to appear at future diets or liberated on bail[4].

1 Criminal Procedure (Scotland) Act 1975 (c 21), ss 24(1), 296(2), 297(1).
2 Social Work (Scotland) Act 1968 (c 49), s 94(1), applied by the Criminal Procedure (Scotland) Act 1975, s 462(1). It should be noted that s 296(2) excludes detention in a police station at the instance of the police.
3 Ibid, s 296(1). See para 3.17 above.
4 As to bail, see paras 3.38 ff above. See also para 9.07 below.

9.07. Unruly certificates. Where a child is arrested and cannot be brought immediately before a sheriff sitting summarily he must be liberated on an undertaking that he will attend any hearing of the charge, given by a parent or guardian, unless a senior officer of police of the rank of inspector or above, or the officer in charge of the police station, having made inquiries into the case, is of the view that it is necessary in the child's interest to remove him from association with any reputed criminal or prostitute, or has reason to believe that the child's liberation would defeat the ends of justice, or unless the charge involved is one of homicide or other grave crime[1]. Where the child is not liberated, the senior officer concerned must cause the child to be in a place of safety, other than a police station, until such time as the child can be brought before a sheriff[2]. He may be detained in the police station only if the senior officer certifies that it is either impracticable to detain the child in a place of safety or that he is of so unruly a character that he cannot safely be so detained or that by reason of his state of health, either mental or bodily, it is inadvisable to detain him in a place of safety, and that certificate has to be produced to the sheriff[3]. Once the child has been brought to court and the court decides that he requires to be kept in custody the court will commit him to a place of safety[4]. However, in both solemn and summary proceedings, if the child is over fourteen and the court certifies that he is of so unruly a character that he cannot safely be committed to a place of safety, the court may commit him to prison pending the further proceedings involved[5]. Thus no child under fourteen may be committed to a prison on remand, and only in limited circumstances may a child over fourteen be so remanded. The place of safety referred to is one chosen by the local authority[5] and not designated either by the police officer or the court. It is the responsibility of the local authority to provide such a place of safety and to look after the child in the interim.

1 Criminal Procedure (Scotland) Act 1975 (c 21), s 296(1)(a)–(c) (amended by the Bail etc (Scotland) Act 1980 (c 4), s 9(a)).
2 Criminal Procedure (Scotland) Act 1975, s 296(2). For the meaning of 'place of safety', see para 9.06 above.
3 Ibid, s 296(2)(a)–(c).
4 Ibid, ss 24(1), 297(1).
5 Ibid, ss 24(1) proviso, 297(1) proviso (amended by the Children Act 1975 (c 72), s 70).

9.08. Reference to children's hearing. A child who pleads guilty to, or is found guilty of, an offence may be referred by the court to a children's hearing[1], unless the charge is one in respect of which the sentence is fixed by law[2], which at present is only murder. If at the time of the court hearing the child is not subject to a supervision requirement imposed by a children's hearing, the court may either remit the case to a children's hearing to be dealt with entirely, thus bringing to an end the proceedings in court, or alternatively may request the hearing to provide advice to the court as to the treatment of the child[3]. If the remit is simply for advice, then the child is brought back to the court for sentence. Where a child is the subject of a supervision requirement at the time of the court appearance, then the sheriff requires to remit the case to the children's hearing at least for advice[4]. The High Court of Justiciary is not subject to the same obligation, although it may so remit the case[5].

1 Criminal Procedure (Scotland) Act 1975 (c 21), ss 173(1), 373.
2 Ibid, s 173(5).
3 Ibid, ss 173(1), (2), 372(1), (2).
4 Ibid, ss 173(3)(b), 372(3) (the former amended by the Criminal Justice (Scotland) Act 1980 (c 62), s 83(2), Sch 7, para 35). For decisions available to the reporter, see R W Renton and H H Brown *Criminal Procedure according to the Law of Scotland* (5th edn, 1983) paras 19-34, 19-35.
5 Criminal Procedure (Scotland) Act 1975, s 173(3)(a) (as so amended).

10. MENTAL DISORDER

(a) Introduction

10.01. Unfitness to plead and the special defence of insanity. Everyone is presumed to be sane until the contrary is proved. Insanity is a question to be decided by the court, not by doctors, though there will in practice always be medical or psychiatric evidence before the court. There are patients who may be being treated for psychiatric disorders who are legally sane and answerable for their actions. Though the court may be guided by medical evidence it is not bound by it, and it is a question of fact for the court to decide whether or not a person is legally insane[1]. Insanity arises in two separate contexts. The first is where the accused is insane and unfit to plead at the time of the legal procedure against him with regard to the alleged crime[2]. The second is where the accused person was insane at the time when the crime was allegedly committed[3]. The two are quite separate, and it may be that the accused was insane at the time of committing the crime but has since recovered his sanity and is now fit to plead, or was sane at the time of committing the crime but has since lost his sanity and is no longer fit to plead. The second case (insanity at the time of committing the crime) is the basis of a special defence and must be pleaded as such[4].

1 See R W Renton and H H Brown *Criminal Procedure according to the Law of Scotland* (5th edn, 1983) paras 20-08, 20-16. It is for the party claiming insanity to establish the fact by corroborated evidence on the balance of probabilities: *Jessop v Robertson* 1989 SCCR 600.
2 See paras 10.02–10.07 below.
3 See para 10.08 below.
4 See paras 4.37, 5.21, above.

(b) Unfitness to plead

10.02. Insanity in bar of trial. The plea that an accused person is unfit to plead is properly called a plea of insanity in bar of trial, albeit that it may be tendered at any time in the legal proceedings and is not restricted simply to the trial diet. The basis of the plea is that because of the insanity of the accused he cannot reasonably instruct his defence as he is incapable of understanding the substance of the charge and the proceedings and of communicating adequately with his legal representatives[1]. This situation may arise at any time in the course of the proceedings, although in practice it is a matter which is usually discovered at the outset of the proceedings.

1 *HM Advocate v Brown* 1907 SC (J) 67 at 77, 5 Adam 312 at 343, per Lord Justice-General Dunedin.

10.03. Decision by prosecutor to take no proceedings. It is not uncommon for the procurator fiscal to be advised either by the police or by the defence solicitor that a person charged with a crime may be unfit to plead. What happens thereafter depends upon the circumstances of the charge and of the accused. If it is a minor charge and the accused, if liberated, is not likely to be a danger to the public, the prosecutor may decide to take no further proceedings or to delay taking proceedings in order to allow the accused to be treated by his own doctor. Should the accused require in-patient hospital treatment it may be possible to arrange for such treatment either on a voluntary basis or on a compulsory basis under the normal civil proceedings[1]. Where the procurator fiscal decides that it is necessary to insist upon prosecution the procedure described below will be adopted.

1 See MENTAL HEALTH, vol 14, paras 1410 ff.

10.04. Procedure where proceedings have commenced. Where the prosecution has commenced in the district court, which has no jurisdiction to deal with a mentally disordered accused, such persons must be remitted to the sheriff court[1]. Alternatively, as the procurator fiscal is the prosecutor in both courts, he could desert the complaint in the district court and raise a new complaint in the sheriff court without going through the remit procedure, which is cumbersome and time wasting. When a mentally disordered accused appears in the High Court or the sheriff court[2], it is necessary to arrange for him to be examined by a psychiatrist as to his fitness to plead before the case can continue further. Depending upon the circumstances the accused may be liberated on bail with a condition that he attend for such examination or he may be remanded in custody pending that examination. The remand may either be in prison or preferably in a psychiatric hospital provided that in the latter instance the court is satisfied there is a bed available in the hospital for his admission and the hospital is suitable for his detention[3]. Furthermore, before the court can make an interim order committing the accused to hospital, the court requires to be provided with the written or oral evidence of a medical practitioner to the effect that the accused is suffering from mental disorder and that a hospital bed is available for him. Most prisons have ready access to the services of a psychiatrist, thus allowing for a prompt psychiatric examination, the early submission of a report to the court and the replacement of the original order committing him to prison by a new order committing him to hospital if that is what the doctor certifies. An order detaining the accused in a hospital is a compulsory order and the accused is not free to leave the hospital should he recover his sanity[4]. The accused must not be remanded for more than the appropriate time limits in solemn or summary procedure without obtaining the appropriate extension of time, although such an extension would normally be granted since illness of the accused is one of the specific reasons for allowing extension of time[5].

1 Criminal Procedure (Scotland) Act 1975 (c 21), s 376(4).
2 See ibid, s 174 (solemn procedure) and s 375 (summary procedure).
3 Ibid, ss 25(1), 330(1).
4 Ibid, ss 25(2), 330(2) (respectively amended by the Mental Health (Scotland) Act 1984 (c 36), s 127(1), Sch 3, paras 24, 31).
5 See paras 4.24, 5.04, above.

10.05. Procedure where mental disorder not discovered until trial diet. The situation can arise where the insanity of the accused person is not discovered until the trial itself or where the question of insanity is not resolved until the matter is brought before a court. The matter can be raised either by the prosecutor or the defence or by the court itself[1]. Normally there will then be a preliminary inquiry into the accused's mental condition in order to decide whether or not he should be called upon to plead and go to trial. Exceptionally, and exceedingly rarely, in solemn cases the judge may call upon the accused to plead, leaving it to the jury at the trial to say whether or not he is capable of pleading, as it is a matter of fact that is open to the jury to decide[2]; but usually the issue is raised as a plea in bar of trial and the procedure is to apply for a preliminary diet[3]. Though the application should be lodged and intimated at least ten days prior to the trial, if the accused is insane, the matter could in practice be raised at any time and even in the course of the trial. In summary proceedings notice of such a plea in bar of trial and of the witnesses to be adduced in support should be given before the calling of the first witness to give evidence[4], but the Crown is not likely to object if no such proper notice is given and the matter becomes apparent during the course of the trial. Whether in solemn or summary proceedings the question of whether or not the accused is insane and unfit to plead is determined by the court on the basis of evidence from two psychiatrists with regard to their independent examination of the accused. If the accused is found insane and unfit to stand trial in solemn proceedings he must be ordered to be detained in the State Hospital at Carstairs or other such hospital as for special reasons the court may specify[5]. The detention is without limitation of time[6]. The effect of the order is that psychiatrists may thereafter determine when the accused is sane enough to be liberated without further recourse to the court. In both solemn and summary proceedings it is competent to have this hearing (to determine whether or not the accused is insane and unfit to stand trial) in his absence, provided no objection is taken by him or on his behalf[7]. In summary proceedings the procedure is the same as in solemn, except that the court order does not involve necessarily the State Hospital at Carstairs, nor is there any requirement for the order to be without limit of time[8].

1 *HM Advocate v Brown* 1907 SC (J) 67, 5 Adam 312.
2 *HM Advocate v Wilson* 1942 JC 75, 1942 SLT 194.
3 See paras 4.40 ff above.
4 Criminal Procedure (Scotland) Act 1975 (c 21), s 375(3).
5 Ibid, s 174(3).
6 Ibid, s 174(4).
7 Ibid, ss 174(5), 375(4).
8 Ibid, s 376(2).

10.06. Restriction orders. Where a hospital order is imposed in either solemn or summary proceedings the court may restrict the discharge of the patient from hospital either indefinitely, that is without limit of time, or for a specified period[1]. The court must consider the whole circumstances of the alleged offence and of the alleged offender including his previous convictions and the risk that he may commit offences as a result of this mental disorder if he were set at large whereby the public would be at risk of serious harm[1]. If such be the case, the court may order him to be detained either without limit of time or during such a period as may be specified in the order[1]. The Secretary of State has power to direct the lifting of these restrictions if he is satisfied that they are no longer needed for the protection of the public from serious harm[2].

1 Criminal Procedure (Scotland) Act 1975 (c 21), ss 178(1), 379(1) (amended by the Mental Health (Amendment) (Scotland) Act 1983 (c 39), s 22(2), Sch 2, paras 33, 36, and the Mental Health (Scotland) Act 1984 (c 36), s 127(1), Sch 3, paras 28, 35): see MENTAL HEALTH, vol 14, para 1455.
2 Mental Health (Scotland) Act 1984, s 68(1): see MENTAL HEALTH, vol 14, para 1458.

10.07. Proceedings on recovery of accused. A person found to be insane in bar of trial has not by definition stood trial and therefore has not tholed his assize[1]. He may therefore be tried with regard to the allegations against him if and when he recovers his sanity[2].

1 See para 4.46 above.
2 *HM Advocate v Bickerstaff* 1926 JC 65, 1926 SLT 121.

(c) Special Defence of Insanity

10.08. Insanity at the time of the offence. The insanity of the accused at the time of the offence is a special defence which, if accepted, results in his acquittal. It is, however, a rather specialised verdict in that he is found to have committed the act charged but acquitted on the grounds of insanity[1]. In solemn matters the result of such a verdict is that the accused must be detained in the State Hospital, or, if there are special reasons to the contrary, in some other specified hospital without limit of time[2], whether or not he has since recovered his sanity. As a consequence a sane person, that is a person sane enough not to be insane and unfit to plead at his trial, may be found not guilty of an offence by virtue of his insanity at the time of the offence and be sent to a mental hospital. The position in summary proceedings is by no means clear except that the verdict is still the same. As to disposal following upon such a verdict, statute permits the court to order detention in hospital in similar fashion as if he had been unfit to plead[3]. However, the terms of the statute are somewhat confusing, and in a sheriff court case it was decided that it was not competent to order hospitalisation of a person who was no longer suffering from mental disorder at the time of the disposal of the case[4]. A hospital order, if imposed, may be made the subject of a restriction order[5].

1 See the Criminal Procedure (Scotland) Act 1975 (c 21), ss 174(2), 376(3).
2 Ibid, s 174(3), (4).
3 Ibid, s 376(3). See, however, C G B Nicholson *The Law and Practice of Sentencing in Scotland* (1981) para 4-10.
4 *Smith v M* 1983 SCCR 67, 1984 SLT (Sh Ct) 28. See, however, R W Renton and H H Brown *Criminal Procedure according to the Law of Scotland* (5th edn, 1983) para 20-17.
5 See para 10.06 above.

(d) Hospital and Guardianship Orders etc on Convicted Persons

10.09. Convicted persons suffering from mental disorder. A person convicted of an offence who was legally sane and fit to plead[1] but who is nevertheless suffering from mental disorder may be dealt with by the court in such a way as to ensure that he receives treatment appropriate for his disorder, rather than being dealt with by another form of sentence. In both solemn and summary proceedings if the court is satisfied on the written or oral evidence of two psychiatrists that the person is suffering from mental disorder of a nature or degree which makes it appropriate for him to receive medical treatment in a hospital or which warrants his reception into guardianship[2], it may, where suitable, dispose of the case by means of a hospital order or of a guardianship order[3]. If the court imposes such an order, it may not impose any sentence of imprisonment, detention or fine or make a probation or community service order upon the accused in respect of the offence, but may make any other order such as disqualification for driving or for forfeiture of goods[4]. The order may not be made unless the two doctors describe the accused as suffering from some form of mental disorder and they must agree as to the form of mental disorder from which he is suffering[5]. It is not necessary that they agree in every detail, in that one may specify more than one form of disorder with which the other does not agree, but provided they are in agreement on at least one common disorder then that will suffice[5]. Before a hospital order can be made, the type of mental disorder must beone whereby treatment in hospital is appropriate; it must be necessary for the health or safety of the accused or for the protection of others that he should receive such treatment and requires compulsory detention to do so[6]. If the appropriate grounds do not apply, then a hospital order cannot be made, even though the person is suffering from some form of mental disorder. The court may restrict the discharge of the patient from hospital by imposing a restriction upon him if, taking into account all the circumstances of the charge, the antecedents of the accused and the risk of further offences if he is set at large, it is of a view that as a result of his mental disorder it is necessary for the protection of the public from serious harm to restrict his discharge from hospital[7]. The order may be either for a specific period or without limit of time[7].

1 See para 10.01 above.
2 See the Mental Health (Scotland) Act 1984 (c 36), ss 17(1), 36(a). For the meaning of 'mental disorder', see MENTAL HEALTH, vol 14, para 1402.
3 Criminal Procedure (Scotland) Act 1975 (c 21), ss 175(1), 376(1) (respectively amended by the Mental Health (Scotland) Act 1984, s 127(1), Sch 3, paras 26, 33).
4 Criminal Procedure (Scotland) Act 1975, ss 175(7), 376(10).
5 Ibid, ss 175(6), 376(9).
6 Mental Health (Scotland) Act 1984, s 17(1).
7 Criminal Procedure (Scotland) Act 1975, ss 178(1), 379(1) (respectively amended by the Mental Health (Scotland) Act 1984, Sch 3, paras 28, 35).

10.10. Guardianship orders. Instead of committing a person to hospital the court may as an alternative place the convicted person under the guardianship of the local authority or such other person approved by the local authority as the court specifies[1]. The rules are similar to those for hospital orders; thus there must be evidence from two psychiatrists who must agree on, or at least have a common agreement on part of, the mental disorder from which the convicted person is suffering[2]; the court must be satisfied that that mental disorder is of a nature or degree which warrants reception into guardianship[3]; the court, taking into consideration the evidence of the mental health officer, must consider it necessary in the interests of the welfare of that person that he should be placed under guardianship; and the local authority or other person must be willing to receive him into guardianship[4]. As in the case of a hospital order, when a guardianship order is imposed the court may not pass any other sentence by way of imprisonment, fine, probation order or community service order in respect of the offence, but may make any other order such as disqualification for driving or for forfeiture[5].

1 Criminal Procedure (Scotland) Act 1975 (c 21), ss 175(1), 376(1). For the meaning of 'local authority', see para 10.03, note 1, above.
2 Ibid, ss 175(6), 376(9).
3 Mental Health (Scotland) Act 1984 (c 36), s 36(a).
4 Criminal Procedure (Scotland) Act 1975, ss 175(5), 376(8).
5 Ibid, ss 175(7), 376(10).

10.11. Interim hospital orders. In 1983 provisions were introduced to enable the court to take more time to consider whether a person is suffering from mental disorder requiring his detention in hospital, or whether or not a restriction order is appropriate. In such cases the court can impose an interim hospital order under the same provisions as for hospital orders[1]. The duration of the order must be for no more than twelve weeks in the first instance, but it may be renewed for periods of up to twenty-eight days thereafter subject to a maximum period of six months[2]. The provisions apply to both summary and solemn procedure, but it is envisaged that the use of these interim orders will be almost completely confined to the solemn courts and particularly for serious crimes. The procedure for renewing or terminating an interim order is for the responsible medical officer to indicate to the prosecutor that he seeks a continuation or termination of the order as appropriate, and thereafter the prosecutor makes an application to the court[3]. A diet is fixed for hearing the application and it is intimated by the clerk of court to the offender or his solicitor[4]. When an interim hospital order ceases to have effect, the court may deal with the offender in any way in which it could have dealt with him if no such order had been made, save that it may not make a new interim hospital order[5]. As in the case of hospital orders, when imposing an interim order the court may not order imprisonment, impose a fine or make a probation or community service order, but may disqualify for driving or forfeit goods as appropriate[6].

1 Criminal Procedure (Scotland) Act 1975 (c 21), ss 174A, 375A (added by the Mental Health (Amendment) (Scotland) Act 1983 (c 39), s 34, and amended by the Mental Health (Scotland) Act 1984 (c 36), s 127(1), Sch 3, paras 25, 32).
2 Criminal Procedure (Scotland) Act 1975, ss 174A(6), 375A(7) (as so added).
3 Act of Adjournal (Consolidation) 1988, SI 1988/110, rr 62(1), 112(1), Sch 1, Form 29.
4 Ibid, rr 62(2), 112(2), Sch 1, Form 30.
5 Criminal Procedure (Scotland) Act 1975, ss 174A(9), 375A(10) (as added: see note 1 above).
6 Ibid, ss 174A(4), 375A(5) (as so added).

10.12. Appeals. Hospital orders, restriction orders, guardianship orders and interim hospital orders (but not renewals of interim hospital orders) are subject to appeal in the same manner as an appeal against sentence[1].

1 Criminal Procedure (Scotland) Act 1975 (c 21), ss 280, 443 (amended by the Criminal Justice (Scotland) Act 1980 (c 62), ss 33, 34, Sch 2, para 32, Sch 3, para 2, and the Mental Health (Amendment) (Scotland) Act 1983 (c 39), s 34).

10.13. Probation and deferred sentences. In practice it is relatively uncommon for courts to have to deal with accused persons who are insane and unfit to plead or whose mental state is so precarious that they require compulsory treatment by way of the various orders discussed in the preceding paragraphs. Much more frequently encountered are persons who would benefit from some form of psychiatric treatment, but to a lesser extent than that envisaged in these formal orders. The desirability of such treatment is one of the factors that can be considered by the court in determining the appropriate sentence to impose on the accused. In appropriate cases the court, having received a report from a psychiatrist, may order the accused to undergo treatment as a condition of probation, which treatment could be on a residential or out-patient basis, or both[1]. Again, the court may defer sentence on the accused on condition that he undergo psychiatric treatment[2].

1 As to probation, see para 7.19 above.
2 As to deferred sentences, see para 7.20 above.

11. FATAL ACCIDENT INQUIRIES

(a) The Fatal Accidents Inquiry (Scotland) Act 1895

11.01. History. In the year 1895 Britain was still at the zenith of her imperial and industrial power. The 1914–18 war was nineteen years away. Such was the background to the passing of the Fatal Accidents Inquiry (Scotland) Act 1895 (c 36), which introduced a completely new concept to the law of Scotland, namely the public investigation by a sheriff and a jury of fatal accidents sustained in the course of industrial employment or occupation.

The Act's only forerunner was the Fatal Accidents Inquiry (Scotland) Bill which was introduced in the House of Commons on 18 May 1893. The Bill passed its first and second readings and was referred to the Standing Committee on Law. Many amendments were submitted for the committee's consideration, including amendments proposed by Mr Keir Hardie MP. However, one amendment, put forward by Sir Charles Pearson, a former and future Lord Advocate and then member of Parliament for Edinburgh and St Andrews Universities, was of fundamental importance and was accepted by the committee. This was to amend the Bill by taking away the right of investigation before a jury, and also by deleting that portion of the Bill which provided that the sheriff should make a finding after the investigation. This emasculation of the Bill not surprisingly provoked considerable protest, in particular from a conference of Scottish trade councils and trade societies which met in Glasgow in August 1893. The conference called upon the government to restore the provisions relating to the employment of a jury and the sheriff's findings, and later that same month a deputation of Scottish trade councils, trade unions and miners visited the Lord Advocate. Mr Keir Hardie was a member of the deputation. The Lord Advocate, the Rt Hon J B Balfour, later Lord Kinross, refused government support for restoration to the Bill of the provisions regarding juries on the ground of the expense which would be incurred, but indicated that the government would be willing to restore the provisions regarding the sheriff's findings. There was some shrieval opposition to the restoration of these provisions and eventually the government took the line of least resistance and on 11 September 1893 the Bill was withdrawn from the House of Commons.

The Fatal Accidents Inquiry (Scotland) Bill of 1895 fared better, largely because scant parliamentary time could be devoted to it. The government of Lord Rosebery had many other problems such as the Budget and the question of Irish Home Rule to contend with. The Bill contained the provisions regarding the use of a jury, and the jury was to return a verdict at the end of the inquiry. The Bill passed all its stages and the royal assent was given on 6 July 1895.

11.02. Scope of the Fatal Accidents Inquiry (Scotland) Act 1895. By modern standards the Fatal Accidents Inquiry (Scotland) Act 1895 was remarkably succinct. It contained only seven sections. The Act extended to all cases of death of any persons, whether employers or employed, engaged in any industrial employment or occupation in Scotland, due or reasonably believed to be due to accident occurring in the course of such employment or occupation[1]. 'Industrial employment or occupation' was defined as employment or occupation for or in the performance of any manual labour, or the superintendence of any such labour, or the working, management, or superintendence, of machinery or other appliances, or animals used in the prosecution of any work[2].

The Act was not to alter or affect the existing law and practice relative to the duties of the procurator fiscal to inquire and report to the Crown Agent in regard to cases of death from accident[3]. Nor was it to alter or affect any powers already vested in the Lord Advocate to cause public inquiries to be held[3]. The verdict returned at an inquiry under the Act would not be competent to be given in evidence, or be founded on in any subsequent judicial proceeding, civil or criminal, arising out of the same accident[3].

1 Fatal Accidents Inquiry (Scotland) Act 1895 (c 36), s 2 (repealed).
2 Ibid, s 7 (repealed).
3 Ibid, s 6 (repealed).

11.03. Petition for inquiry. The procurator fiscal was entrusted with the task of proceeding to collect evidence regarding any death to which the Fatal Accidents Inquiry (Scotland) Act 1895 applied, and thereafter presenting to the sheriff a petition craving him to hold a public inquiry into the death or deaths[1]. If more than one death resulted from the same accident the petition and inquiry were to relate to the whole deaths resulting therefrom[2]. The fiscal also had to furnish to the sheriff clerk, so far as possible, the names and addresses of the wife or husband or nearest known relative and the employer, if any, of each person who had lost his or her life in the accident[3].

1 Fatal Accidents Inquiry (Scotland) Act 1895 (c 36), s 3(1) (repealed).
2 Ibid, s 3(2) (repealed).
3 Ibid, s 3(1) (repealed).

11.04. Holding of the inquiry. Comprehensive provision was made for the procedural arrangements regarding an inquiry under the Fatal Accidents Inquiry (Scotland) Act 1895. After presentation of the fiscal's petition calling for the inquiry the sheriff would make an order directing that a public inquiry be held at a time to be specified in the order 'being a time as soon as reasonably possible, in such court house within his jurisdiction as may be nearest to the place where the accident occurred'[1]. This small provision as to place was of importance in the days before the motor car and when even Britain's railway system, which was the envy of the world, did not reach all parts of Scotland[2].

The sheriff was to grant warrant to cite witnesses and havers to the inquiry[3]. The duty was placed on the sheriff clerk of intimating the time and place of the inquiry to the wife or husband or nearest known relative and to any employer of the person who had lost his or her life in the accident[4]. The widespread employment of women tends to be thought of as a fairly modern development, but at the time of the passing of the Act (and for many years afterwards) large numbers of women were employed in the jute and cotton thread industries. Intimation of the time and place of the inquiry was also to be made by the sheriff clerk to certain government officials and departments[4]. Lastly and most importantly in ensuring that the inquiry was public, the sheriff clerk had to insert an advertisement giving the time and place of the inquiry in a newspaper circulating in the district or, if there was more than one such newspaper, in two newspapers circulating in the district[4].

1 Fatal Accidents Inquiry (Scotland) Act 1895 (c 36), s 4(1) (repealed).
2 It is, perhaps, of interest to note that some eighty years after the passing of the 1895 Act one of the authors of this part of the title received representations that a fatal accident inquiry should be held at a different sheriff court from the one where such inquiries were normally held, the reason for the representations being the proximity of the court to the scene of the accident.
3 Fatal Accidents Inquiry (Scotland) Act 1895, s 4(1) (repealed).
4 Ibid, s 4(2) (repealed).

11.05. The jury. Discreetly tucked away in the Fatal Accidents Inquiry (Scotland) Act 1895 was one of the provisions that had caused so much controversy, namely that 'the inquiry shall be by the sheriff and a jury'[1]. The jury was to consist of seven jurors, made up of five common and two special jurors[2]. Either type of juror had to be between the ages of twenty-one and sixty, and a special juror had either to own heritage anywhere in Scotland of the annual value of £100 or to possess moveable property to the extent of £1,000 or to pay taxes on a house of the annual value of £30[3]. A common juror had to be seised in his own or his wife's right in, or be liferenter of, heritage of the annual value of £5 or have personal property to the extent of £200[4]. The distinction between these types of jurors was later abolished[5], but the number of jurors remained at seven.

The normal procedures for challenges to jurors in civil and criminal cases in Scotland were not to apply, but any person interested in the inquiry could state to the sheriff an objection as to any person balloted to serve on the jury, and if the sheriff considered that sufficient cause had been shown why such person should not so serve the sheriff would not allow that person to serve on the jury[6]. Neither the employers of the deceased nor any person working for the same employers were to be jurors in any such inquiry[7].

The other previously contentious matter concerned the sheriff's findings. The Act departed from this and the jury's verdict was substituted for it. After hearing the evidence, submissions by or on behalf of persons appearing at the inquiry and the summing up by the sheriff, if he considered such summing up necessary or proper, the jury was to return a verdict setting forth, so far as proved, when and where the accident and the death or deaths to which the inquiry related took place and the cause or causes of such death or deaths[8]. The jury of seven was empowered to return a verdict by a majority, provided that at least one hour had elapsed after the jury had been enclosed[9].

1 Fatal Accidents Inquiry (Scotland) Act 1895 (c 36), s 4(4) (repealed).
2 Ibid, s 4(5) (repealed).
3 Jury Trials (Scotland) Act 1815 (c 42), s 25.
4 Jurors (Scotland) Act 1825 (c 22), s 1.
5 Juries Act 1949 (c 27), s 29.
6 Fatal Accidents Inquiry (Scotland) Act 1895, s 4(6) (repealed).
7 Ibid, s 4(6) proviso (repealed).
8 Ibid, s 4(7) (repealed). The terms of the verdict which the jury could return were considerably extended by the Fatal Accidents and Sudden Deaths Inquiry (Scotland) Act 1906 (c 35), s 2: see para 11.09 below.
9 Fatal Accidents Inquiry (Scotland) Act 1895, s 4(8) (repealed).

11.06. Conduct of the inquiry. Detailed arrangements were made in the Fatal Accidents Inquiry (Scotland) Act 1895 for the conduct of the inquiry, which was to be open to the public[1]. Again the procurator fiscal was allowed the leading role in that he was to adduce evidence, including such medical or skilled evidence as he deemed expedient, in regard to the cause or causes of the death or deaths and the circumstances of the accident[1]. The sheriff could competently grant warrant to officers of law to take possession of and hold in safe custody, subject to the inspection of the parties interested, any article or thing which it might be considered necessary to produce at the inquiry[2]. The sheriff could also, with or without the jury, inspect any premises, machinery or other thing which in his opinion might be material for the purposes of the inquiry[3]. He could also grant warrant for such inspection by any person he deemed expedient[3].

The wife or husband, the relatives and the employers of the person who had lost his or her life were all given the right to appear at, take part in, and adduce evidence at the inquiry either by themselves or by instructing counsel or agents or by any other person whom the sheriff might allow to appear on their behalf[4]. This right was also extended to inspectors of mines and inspectors of factories where the accident had happened 'in or about a mine' or in a factory or workshop[5]. The right also extended to any person employed under the same employer and even to any other person or persons whom the sheriff might consider to have a just interest in the inquiry[6].

1 Fatal Accidents Inquiry (Scotland) Act 1895 (c 36), s 5(1) (repealed).
2 Ibid, s 5(2)(a) (repealed).
3 Ibid, s 5(2)(b) (repealed).
4 Ibid, s 5(3) (repealed).
5 Ibid, s 5(3) (repealed). When one considers the number of mines, factories and workshops which were operative in Scotland in 1895, as compared with the present day, one gets some idea of the scope of operation of the 1895 Act.
6 Ibid, s 5(3) (repealed).

11.07. Evidence. The evidence adduced at an inquiry under the Fatal Accidents Inquiry (Scotland) Act 1895 was to be taken on oath[1], thus allowing for prosecutions for perjury if necessary. The witnesses were to be subject to cross-examination and the inquiry was to be conducted as nearly as possible in accordance with the ordinary procedure in a trial by jury before the sheriff court[1]. This appears clearly to relate to a criminal trial by jury since the Act provided for the witnesses being allowed such expenses as were paid to any person attending a criminal trial by jury in the sheriff court[2]. The examination of any person as a witness at the inquiry was not to be a bar to criminal proceedings being taken later against him[3]. Correspondingly, no witness was to be compelled to answer any question tending to show that he was guilty of any crime or offence[3]. The evidence was to be taken down in writing 'either at length or in shorthand'[4].

1 Fatal Accidents Inquiry (Scotland) Act 1895 (c 36), s 5(4) (repealed).
2 Ibid, s 5(6) (repealed).
3 Ibid, s 5(4) proviso (repealed).
4 Ibid, s 5(4) (repealed).

11.08. Verdict. The verdict at the conclusion of an inquiry under the Fatal Accidents Inquiry (Scotland) Act 1895 was to be recorded in the sheriff court books[1]. The procurator fiscal was to obtain from the sheriff clerk a copy of the petition, the recorded evidence of the witnesses, any reports or productions used at the inquiry or copies thereof and a copy of the verdict, and was to transmit these documents and the usual schedule of particulars for the registrar of deaths to the Crown Agent[1]. This matter of reporting to the Crown Agent was later to be of considerable importance in relation to the provisions of the Fatal Accidents and Sudden Deaths Inquiry (Scotland) Act 1906 (c 35)[2]. The sheriff clerk was to transmit to the inspector of mines or inspector of factories copies of the petition and the recorded evidence and any reports (but not apparently the verdict) where the accident had occurred 'in or about a mine' or in a factory or workshop[3].

1 Fatal Accidents Inquiry (Scotland) Act 1895 (c 36), s 5(5) (repealed).

2 See para 11.10 below.
3 Fatal Accidents Inquiry (Scotland) Act 1895, s 5(5) (repealed).

(b) The Fatal Accidents and Sudden Deaths Inquiry (Scotland) Act 1906

11.09. Extension of the jury's task. Two important alterations to the Fatal Accidents Inquiry (Scotland) Act 1895 were made by the Fatal Accidents and Sudden Deaths Inquiry (Scotland) Act 1906.

The first of these was to extend very considerably the task of the jury at an inquiry. No longer was the jury simply to return a verdict setting forth when and where the accident and the death took place and the cause of death[1]. Now its verdict was also to deal with the cause of the accident, the person, if any, to whose fault or negligence the accident was attributable, the precautions, if any, by which the accident might have been avoided, any defects in the system or mode of working which contributed to the accident and 'any other facts disclosed by the evidence which, in the opinion of the jury, are relevant to the inquiry'[2]. This provision imposed a very much higher duty on the jury which might, in later years, in Glasgow or Edinburgh have to deal with five or six inquiries in the course of one day. Perhaps the escape clause for the jury was to be found in the words (used in both the 1895 Act and the 1906 Act) 'shall return a verdict setting forth *so far as such particulars have been proved*'[3]. In many inquiries a formal verdict was returned simply setting forth when and where the accident and death occurred and the cause of death.

1 Fatal Accidents Inquiry (Scotland) Act 1895 (c 36), s 4(7) (repealed): see para 11.05 above.
2 Fatal Accidents and Sudden Deaths Inquiry (Scotland) Act 1906 (c 35), s 2 (repealed).
3 Fatal Accidents Inquiry (Scotland) Act 1895, s 4(7); Fatal Accidents and Sudden Deaths Inquiry (Scotland) Act 1906, s 2 (both repealed) (emphasis added).

11.10. Sudden deaths. The second alteration to the Fatal Accidents Inquiry (Scotland) Act 1895 made by the Fatal Accidents and Sudden Deaths Inquiry (Scotland) Act 1906 concerned sudden and suspicious deaths in Scotland. Neither 'sudden' nor 'suspicious' was defined. The Lord Advocate was given the power, 'whenever it appears to him to be expedient in the public interest', to direct that a public inquiry into such death and the circumstances thereof should be held[1]. The inquiry directed by the Lord Advocate was to take place according to the forms and procedure prescribed by the 1895 Act[1]. The obvious question was how the Lord Advocate was to know about such sudden or suspicious deaths. The 1895 Act had preserved the law and practice relating to the duties of the procurator fiscal to inquire and report to the Crown Agent in regard to cases of death from accident[2]. Once again the procurator fiscal had an important role to play in connection with such inquiries. It was his duty (and still is) to report to the Crown Office a wide range of deaths (which tended to be expanded over the years 1906 to 1976) including deaths in suspicious circumstances, suicides, deaths (usually in hospitals) from what are euphemistically called 'medical mishaps', deaths in road traffic accidents, deaths due to gas poisoning (at one time fairly frequent but due to the discovery of North Sea gas now very rare), deaths in prison or police cells, deaths under anaesthetic in unusual circumstances or if there was a suggestion of negligence, deaths which occurred in circumstances the continuance of which or possible recurrence of which were prejudicial to the health and safety of the public and also when any desire had been expressed that a public inquiry should be held into the circumstances of the death. This last category allowed for the wishes of the relatives of the deceased to be taken into consideration. Some categories of deaths overlapped between the provisions of the two Acts. For example, a man might be killed when driving a motor vehicle. If it was his own car and he was, to use the words of most insurance certificates, using it for 'social, domestic and pleasure purposes', the Lord Advocate might direct an inquiry under the 1906 Act if the place of the accident was an accident black spot or there was some defect in the layout of the road or there was some other factor which affected the public interest or the relatives were very anxious that there should be a public inquiry into the accident. If, on the other hand, the man was driving his employer's van in the course of his employment then an inquiry under the 1895 Act had to be held and the wishes of the relatives were irrelevant.

When the death was reported to the Crown Agent, the Lord Advocate (in practice usually Crown counsel) considered whether or not an inquiry was to be held and directed accordingly.

1 Fatal Accidents and Sudden Deaths Inquiry (Scotland) Act 1906 (c 35), s 3 (repealed).
2 Fatal Accidents Inquiry (Scotland) Act 1895 (c 36), s 6 (repealed): see para 11.02 above.

(c) The Fatal Accidents and Sudden Deaths Inquiry (Scotland) Act 1976

11.11. Introduction. Eighty-one years after the passing of the Fatal Accidents Inquiry (Scotland) Act 1895 (c 36), the Fatal Accidents and Sudden Deaths Inquiry (Scotland) Act 1976 was passed as part of the then Labour government's legislative programme. The Act came into force on 1 March 1977[1]. Both the 1895 Act and the Fatal Accidents and Sudden Deaths Inquiry (Scotland) Act 1906 (c 35) were repealed *in toto* by the 1976 Act[2] which, although containing a number of parallels to the 1895 Act, was not a consolidating Act and introduced a number of changes, one of the most significant of which related to the use of juries: by its silence on this subject the Act effectively abolished juries. The wheel had now turned full circle.

In exercise of his powers under the new Act[3], the Lord Advocate made the Fatal Accidents and Sudden Deaths Inquiry Procedure (Scotland) Rules 1977, which came into force, with the Act, on 1 March 1977[4].

1 Fatal Accidents and Sudden Deaths Inquiry (Scotland) Act 1976 (c 14), s 10(5); Fatal Accidents and Sudden Deaths Inquiry (Scotland) Act 1976 Commencement Order 1977, SI 1977/190. See generally I H B Carmichael *Sudden Deaths and Fatal Accident Inquiries* (1986).
2 Fatal Accidents and Sudden Deaths Inquiry (Scotland) Act 1976, s 8(2), Sch 2.
3 Ibid, s 7.
4 Fatal Accidents and Sudden Deaths Inquiry Procedure (Scotland) Rules 1977, SI 1977/191, r 1.

11.12. Mandatory inquiries. The Fatal Accidents and Sudden Deaths Inquiry (Scotland) Act 1976 provides for the holding of two types of inquiry, mandatory and discretionary. Provision is made for a mandatory inquiry in the case of a death (1) apparently resulting from an accident in Scotland sustained at work[1], or (2) occurring during the time in which the person who died was in legal custody[2].

As did the Fatal Accidents Inquiry (Scotland) Act 1895 (c 36), the 1976 Act extends the provisions in the first of these categories to include not only an employee who died in the course of his employment but also an employer or self-employed person who was engaged in his occupation as such[3].

The inclusion of deaths in legal custody has taken into account an apparently increasing public concern about such deaths. 'Legal custody' is defined as including detention in, or being subject to detention in, a prison, remand centre, detention centre, borstal institution or young offenders institution[4]. It also applies where a person is detained in a police station, police cell or other similar place[5]. To avoid doubt, the Act specifically includes the time during which the person was being taken to any of these places in which he or she was to be detained or from any such place in which immediately before the journey he or she was detained[6].

The mandatory provisions apply to deaths occurring 'in Scotland' after the commencement of the Act on 1 March 1977[7]. However, an important new provision recognised a sphere of employment unknown at the time of the earlier legislation dealing with public inquiries. The growth of off-shore gas and oil industries and the inherent dangers attached to them have led to a specific extension of the inquiry provisions to employment connected with this work. Thus a death or causative accident which occurred in connection with activities connected with the exploration of, or the exploitation of the natural resources of, the shore or bed of territorial and certain other waters[8] or the subsoil beneath them, and, without prejudice to the generality of the foregoing, activities carried on from, by means of or on, or for purposes connected with, certain installations[9], is taken to have occurred in Scotland[10]. To make it quite clear which areas are meant, the Act states that the deaths or accidents in question are to be taken to have occurred in Scotland when they occur in an area or part of an area in respect of which an Order in Council[11] provides that questions arising out of acts or omissions taking place therein are to be determined in accordance with the law in force in Scotland[12]. This provision has resulted in a succession of lengthy and technical fatal accident inquiries in the Aberdeen sheriffdom as the area with which this type of work has been most closely connected.

If an inquiry into any matter or accident causing the death of any person is held under the Gas Act 1965, the Mineral Workings (Offshore Installations) Act 1971, the Health and Safety at Work etc Act 1974 or the Petroleum and Submarine Pipe-lines Act 1975, then, unless the Lord Advocate otherwise directs, no inquiry with regard to that death is to be held under the Fatal Accidents and Sudden Deaths Inquiry (Scotland) Act 1976[13]. Conversely, where an inquiry is to be held under the 1976 Act no inquiry is to be held under the Merchant Shipping Act 1970[14] into a death on or from a ship or the death of a member of the crew of a ship[15].

1 Fatal Accidents and Sudden Deaths Inquiry (Scotland) Act 1976 (c 14), s 1(1)(a)(i).
2 Ibid, s 1(1)(a)(ii).
3 Ibid, s 1(1)(a)(i).
4 Ibid, s 1(4)(a). Borstal training was abolished by the Criminal Justice (Scotland) Act 1980 (c 62), s 45(3).
5 Fatal Accidents and Sudden Deaths Inquiry (Scotland) Act 1976, s 1(4)(b).
6 Ibid, s 1(4)(c).
7 Ibid, s 1(2).
8 Ie tidal waters and parts of the sea in or adjacent to the seaward limits of territorial waters; waters in any area designated under the Continental Shelf Act 1964 (c 29), s 1(7); waters in any area specified by Order in Council under the Oil and Gas (Enterprise) Act 1982 (c 23), s 22(5); and, in relation to installations maintained or established in any such waters, waters in a foreign sector of the continental shelf which are adjacent to such waters: s 23(6)(a)–(d).
9 Ie installations for the exploration or exploitation of mineral resources in or under the shore or bed of such waters, or for the storage of gas there, or for the conveyance of things by pipe there, or for the accommodation of workers there: see ibid, s 23(3)(a)–(d).
10 Fatal Accidents and Sudden Deaths Inquiry (Scotland) Act 1976, s 9(a) (amended by the Oil and Gas (Enterprise) Act 1982, s 37(1), Sch 3, para 34), applying s 23(2).
11 Ie under ibid, s 23(1).
12 Fatal Accidents and Sudden Deaths Inquiry (Scotland) Act 1976, s 9(b) (as so amended).
13 Gas Act 1965 (c 36), s 17(4) (amended by the Fatal Accidents and Sudden Deaths Inquiry (Scotland) Act 1976, s 8(1), Sch 1); Mineral Workings (Offshore Installations) Act 1971 (c 61),

s 6(5) (added by the Fatal Accidents and Sudden Deaths Inquiry (Scotland) Act 1976, Sch 1);
Health and Safety at Work etc Act 1974 (c 37), s 14(7) (as so amended); Petroleum and Submarine
Pipe-lines Act 1975 (c 74), s 27(5) (as so amended).

14 Ie under the Merchant Shipping Act 1970 (c 36), s 61 (amended by the Merchant Shipping Act
1979 (c 39), s 29).

15 Merchant Shipping Act 1970, s 61(4) (amended by the Fatal Accidents and Sudden Deaths
Inquiry (Scotland) Act 1976, Sch 1).

11.13. Waiver of mandatory inquiry. The mandatory provisions may be
waived where the Lord Advocate is satisfied that the circumstances of the death
have been sufficiently established in the course of criminal proceedings against
any person in respect of the death or any accident from which the death
resulted[1]. As any criminal proceedings are normally concluded before the
question of a public inquiry is determined, this proviso could prove beneficial in
obviating any need to have the same evidence adduced twice and in lessening the
risk of adding to the distress of bereaved families. While the Fatal Accidents and
Sudden Deaths Inquiry (Scotland) Act 1976 does not state how the circumstances are to be brought to the attention of the Lord Advocate to consider such a
waiver, the procurator fiscal would appear to be the most appropriate agency,
bearing in mind his duties both as public prosecutor and as the person to whom
investigation of such deaths is entrusted.

1 Fatal Accidents and Sudden Deaths Inquiry (Scotland) Act 1976 (c 14), s 1(2).

11.14. Discretionary inquiries. Apart from the two instances in which an
inquiry is mandatory[1], the decision to hold a public inquiry is at the discretion of
the Lord Advocate. The test which he has to apply (which follows the test laid
down in the Fatal Accidents and Sudden Deaths Inquiry (Scotland) Act 1906[2]) is
whether or not it appears to him to be expedient in the public interest to hold an
inquiry into the circumstances of a death occurring in Scotland on the ground
that it was sudden, suspicious or unexplained, or has occurred in circumstances
such as to give rise to serious public concern[3]. There is thus an unfettered
discretion, and the considerations discussed in connection with the 1906 Act[4]
still apply.

1 See the Fatal Accidents and Sudden Deaths Inquiry (Scotland) Act 1976 (c 14), s 1(1)(a), and
para 11.12 above.

2 See the Fatal Accidents and Sudden Deaths Inquiry (Scotland) Act 1906 (c 35), s 3 (repealed), and
para 10.10 above.

3 Fatal Accidents and Sudden Deaths Inquiry (Scotland) Act 1976, s 1(1)(b), (2).

4 See para 11.10 above.

11.15. Investigation by procurator fiscal and application for inquiry. In
a case in which an inquiry is mandatory, or in any other case where the Lord
Advocate in the exercise of his discretion determines that there should be an
inquiry, the procurator fiscal for the district with which the circumstances of the
death appear to be most closely connected must investigate those circumstances
and apply to the sheriff with whose sheriffdom those circumstances appear to be
most closely connected for the holding of an inquiry under the Fatal Accidents
and Sudden Deaths Inquiry (Scotland) Act 1976 into those circumstances[1]. It is
not clear to whom the circumstances are so to appear, but in practice there is
seldom, if ever, doubt as to which procurator fiscal and which sheriffdom
should be involved.

For the purpose of carrying out his investigation the procurator fiscal may cite
witnesses for precognition by him[2]. If a witness so cited fails without reasonable
excuse and after receiving reasonable notice to attend for precognition at the

time and place mentioned in the citation, or refuses when so cited to give information within his knowledge regarding any matter relevant to the investigation, the procurator fiscal may apply to the sheriff for an order requiring the witness to attend for precognition or to give such information, and if the sheriff considers it expedient to do so he must make such an order[3]. A witness who fails to comply with the sheriff's order commits an offence[4].

Forms of application by the procurator fiscal to the sheriff for an inquiry are prescribed[5]. These forms require the procurator fiscal to narrate briefly the apparent facts of the death and state either that in terms of the Act an inquiry requires to be held or, as the case may be, that it appears to the Lord Advocate to be expedient in the public interest that an inquiry should be held. The forms then ask the sheriff to fix a time and place for holding the inquiry, to grant warrant to cite witnesses and havers to attend, and to grant warrant to officers of law to take possession of and hold in safe custody any necessary productions. Although the instruction to narrate briefly the apparent facts of the death is simple[6], compliance with these instructions can be anything but simple. It is sometimes no easy task to prepare an application which sets out briefly and in neutral terms (that is without apportioning any blame to any person) the circumstances which led up to the death. An example of a relatively simple application for a mandatory inquiry might read:

> 'From information received by the Applicant it appears that AB, now deceased, formerly residing at (*address*) was on 19th December 1988 while engaged in the course of his employment as a labourer with the X Engineering Company Limited at their premises at (*address*) struck by a fork lift truck and sustained injuries from which he died on 21st December 1988 at the Y Infirmary, the cause of death being multiple injuries'.

Even that narration leaves a number of questions to be answered, such as who was driving the fork lift truck, whether the place where the accident happened was subject to the provisions of the Road Traffic Acts and, if so, whether there had been a prosecution? Nonetheless the narration meets the general requirements that it is brief and does not indicate any blame on the part either of the deceased or the driver of the fork lift truck. That is the function of the sheriff and, if he considers it appropriate, he can set that forth in his determination.

Similarly an application for a discretionary inquiry (in this case a medical mishap) might run in the following terms:

> 'From information received by the Applicant it appears that CD, formerly residing at (*address*), now deceased, and who was 69 years of age and a patient in Y Infirmary, on 13th March 1988 fell from a hospital trolley in said hospital and sustained injuries as a result of which he died there on 20th March 1988, the cause of death being broncho pneumonia, immobilisation and fracture of the tibia'.

The application again is brief in its terms and shows nothing about how the deceased came to fall from the trolley, whether because of a lack of nursing supervision or unreasonable behaviour by the deceased (perhaps caused by alcohol), nor does it say anything about why the deceased was a patient in the hospital nor whether or not that condition had any bearing on his death. The mention of the patient's age in this case may be relevant to the post mortem findings which provide the cause of death with a fair degree of certainty.

The occurrence of multiple deaths is again recognised, and an application by the procurator fiscal may relate to more than one death, the subsequent order by the sheriff taking this into account[7]. References in the 1976 Act to a death include references to both or all deaths or to each death, as the case may require[7].

---

1 Fatal Accidents and Sudden Deaths Inquiry (Scotland) Act 1976 (c 14), s 1(1), (3)(a).
2 Ibid, s 2(1).

3 Ibid, s 2(2).
4 Ibid, s 2(3). An offender is liable to be summarily punished forthwith by a fine not exceeding
  level 3 on the standard scale or by imprisonment for any period not exceeding twenty days: s 2(3)
  (amended by the Criminal Justice Act 1982 (c 48), s 56(3), Sch 7, para 11). As to the standard
  scale, see para 2.12, note 1, above.
5 Fatal Accidents and Sudden Deaths Inquiry Procedure (Scotland) Rules 1977, SI 1977/191, r 3,
  Schedule, Forms 1, 2.
6 The Fatal Accidents and Sudden Deaths Inquiry (Scotland) Act 1976, s 1(3)(b), requires the
  application to 'narrate briefly the circumstances of the death so far as known to the procurator
  fiscal'.
7 Ibid, s 1(3)(c), 3(3).

11.16. Notification of inquiry. When the procurator fiscal applies to the
sheriff for the holding of an inquiry, the sheriff is obliged to fix a time and place
for the holding by him of an inquiry under the Fatal Accidents and Sudden
Deaths Inquiry (Scotland) Act 1976[1]. At this stage of the procedure there is a
change in emphasis from the procedure under the earlier legislation in that no
longer is the sheriff clerk obliged to intimate the holding of the inquiry to
interested parties or to give public notice after a diet has been assigned[2]. It is now
the duty of the procurator fiscal to intimate that an inquiry is to be held and the
time and place fixed for it to the surviving spouse or nearest known relative of
the deceased[3]. Such intimation is extended to any employer in appropriate
cases[4] and to such other person or class of persons as are prescribed in rules[5].
These are:
(1) in the case of death from an accident at work, the Health and Safety
    Commission;
(2) in the case of a death in legal custody, any minister, government department
    or other authority in whose legal custody the deceased was at the time of his
    death;
(3) in the case of a death connected with the exploration or exploitation of the
    continental shelf (oil-related deaths), the Secretary of State for Energy; and
(4) in any case where it is competent for a minister or government department
    under any statute other than the 1976 Act to cause a public inquiry to be
    made into the circumstances of the death, to such minister or government
    department[6].
The intimations referred to above must be made by notice in writing in the
prescribed form, given not less than twenty-one days before the date of the
inquiry[7]. Notice given to a spouse, nearest relative or employer informs the
recipient that he or she has the right to call witnesses and lead evidence, and that
he or she may attend in person or be represented by an advocate or solicitor or,
with the leave of the sheriff, by some other person[8].
   It is also the duty of the procurator fiscal to give public notice of the holding of
the inquiry and of the time and place fixed for it[9]. Such notice of the holding of
an inquiry requires to be given in at least two newspapers circulating in the
sheriff court district where the inquiry is to be held, again not less than twenty-
one days before the date of the inquiry[10].

1 Fatal Accidents and Sudden Deaths Inquiry (Scotland) Act 1976 (c 14), s 3(1)(a).
2 Cf para 11.04 above.
3 Fatal Accidents and Sudden Deaths Inquiry (Scotland) Act 1976, s 3(2)(a).
4 Ie under ibid, s 1(1)(a)(i): see para 11.12 above.
5 Ibid, s 3(2)(a).
6 Fatal Accidents and Sudden Deaths Inquiry Procedure (Scotland) Rules 1977, SI 1977/191,
  r 4(2)(a)–(d).
7 Ibid, r 4(1), Schedule, Form 3. As to service, see r 16, and para 11.22 below.
8 Fatal Accidents and Sudden Deaths Inquiry (Scotland) Act 1976, s 4(2); Fatal Accidents and
  Sudden Deaths Inquiry Procedure (Scotland) Rules 1977, r 7(2), Schedule, Form 3.
9 Fatal Accidents and Sudden Deaths Inquiry (Scotland) Act 1976, s 3(2)(b).

10 Fatal Accidents and Sudden Deaths Inquiry Procedure (Scotland) Rules 1977, r 4(3), Schedule, Form 4.

11.17. The holding of the inquiry. The inquiry must be held in public[1] as soon after the making of the necessary order by the sheriff as is reasonably practicable in such courthouse or other premises as appear to him to be appropriate, having regard to the apparent circumstances of the death[2]. This restates the terms of earlier legislation[3], and allows the holding of inquiries in places such as town halls or community halls where they appear to be more appropriate to needs.

However, the inquiry is no longer conducted as nearly as possible in accordance with the ordinary procedure in a trial by jury before the sheriff court[4]. Instead, the rules of evidence, procedure and powers of the sheriff to deal with contempt of court and to enforce the attendance of witnesses are to be as nearly as possible those applicable in an ordinary civil cause brought before the sheriff sitting alone[5]. Nevertheless, it is still the specific duty of the procurator fiscal to adduce evidence with regard to the circumstances of the death in question[6]. This is a natural extension of his duty to investigate the circumstances in the first place and to instigate the inquiry.

A provision which is perhaps of more practical importance than at first appears gives the sheriff the power at any time to adjourn the inquiry to a time and place specified by him at the time of the adjournment[7]. This power is of importance where an essential witness may be working on an oil rig or abroad and not available at the time when the inquiry is first held.

1 Fatal Accidents and Sudden Deaths Inquiry (Scotland) Act 1976 (c 14), s 4(3), which is expressed to be subject to s 4(4), for which see para 11.19 below.
2 Ibid, s 3(1)(a).
3 See the Fatal Accidents Inquiry (Scotland) Act 1895 (c 36), s 4(1) (repealed), and para 11.04 above.
4 See ibid, s 5(4) (repealed), and para 11.07 above.
5 Fatal Accidents and Sudden Deaths Inquiry (Scotland) Act 1976, s 4(7).
6 Ibid, s 4(1).
7 Fatal Accidents and Sudden Deaths Inquiry Procedure (Scotland) Rules 1977, SI 1977/191, r 9.

11.18. Evidence. The sheriff's order grants warrant to cite witnesses and havers to attend at the inquiry at the instance not only of the procurator fiscal but also of any person who may be entitled to appear and be heard[1]. In addition to the procurator fiscal there are other persons who have a right to attend and adduce relevant evidence. This group includes the spouse or nearest known relative of the deceased and, in the case of an accident at work[2], any employer of the deceased, a health and safety inspector and any other person who the sheriff is satisfied has an interest in the inquiry[3]. In the great majority of cases the evidence adduced by the procurator fiscal is sufficient for the purposes of all of the interested parties, and it is seldom that such parties call witnesses in addition to those called by the procurator fiscal. On the other hand there are cases, especially where there is a possibility of criticism being levelled or blame being apportioned, where representatives of interested parties feel that they have to attempt to explore certain avenues more thoroughly, if possible, in their clients' interest. This occasionally lays the system open to the criticism that it is not being used purely for the prime purpose of establishing the circumstances of a death, but also for establishing evidence on which a civil claim might be based or defended, although, as in the Fatal Accidents Inquiry (Scotland) Act 1895[4], there is a provision in the Fatal Accidents and Sudden Deaths Inquiry (Scotland) Act 1976 that the determination of the sheriff is not to be admissible in evidence or founded on in any judicial proceedings of whatever nature arising out of the death or out of the accident from which the death resulted[5].

As in 1895 the legislators have recognised a possible area of conflict. In getting to the truth of the cause of a death, it may be necessary to examine witnesses against whom blame may be levelled. Following the 1895 Act[6], the 1976 Act provides that the examination of a witness or haver is not to be a bar to criminal proceedings being taken against him[7]. Thus the driver of a car involved in a fatal road accident may be called to give evidence at an inquiry under the 1976 Act and may also be prosecuted under the road traffic legislation. To safeguard his interests to some extent, the Act also provides that no witness is to be compellable to answer any question tending to show that he is guilty of any crime or offence[8], a restatement of a well established rule of law in Scotland.

On an application by the procurator fiscal or any other person entitled to appear at the inquiry or at the instance of the sheriff himself the sheriff may grant warrant to officers of law to take possession of any production which the procurator fiscal or any other person so entitled wishes to have produced at the inquiry and to hold it in safe custody pending the inquiry, subject to inspection by any persons interested[9]. On such application the sheriff may inspect or grant warrant for any person to inspect any land, premises or other thing the inspection of which the sheriff considers desirable for the purposes of the inquiry[10].

The procurator fiscal may appear at the inquiry on his own behalf or by an assistant or depute procurator fiscal or by Crown counsel[11]; and any person entitled to appear at the inquiry may appear on his own behalf or be represented by an advocate, solicitor or, with leave of the sheriff, by any other person[12]. Such other person might be an official of a trade union.

There is an important innovation in relation to written, as opposed to oral, evidence. Scots law has for some time been reluctant to admit written evidence of facts, but now a written statement signed by the person making the statement and sworn or affirmed to be true by that person before a notary public, commissioner for oaths or justice of the peace or before a commissioner appointed by the sheriff for that purpose, may be admitted in place of oral evidence provided that certain requirements are met[13]. These are that (1) all persons who appear or are represented at the inquiry agree to the admission of such written evidence, or (2) the sheriff considers that the admission of such written evidence will not result in unfairness in the conduct of the inquiry to any person who appears or is represented at the inquiry[14]. In practical terms this usually relates to the admission of the post mortem report. The cause of death is obviously an important part of the evidence at an inquiry but usually it is not a controversial part of the evidence. Such a statement, on being admitted in evidence, is to be read aloud at the inquiry, and where the sheriff directs that the statement or any part of it is not to be read aloud, he must state his reason for so directing[15]. A certificate that the statement has been so sworn and affirmed annexed to the statement and signed by the person making the statement and the person before whom it is sworn or affirmed is sufficient evidence that it has been so sworn or affirmed[16]. Any document or object referred to as a production and identified in a written statement is to be treated as if it had been produced and been identified in court by the maker of the statement[17].

Evidence at the inquiry must be recorded in the same manner as evidence given in an ordinary civil case in the sheriff court[18]. Where the evidence is taken down in shorthand it will not be necessary to extend the evidence unless the sheriff so directs or a copy of the transcript is duly requested by any person entitled thereto[19]. Such a person may obtain a copy of the transcript on application made to the sheriff clerk within a period of three months after the date of the sheriff's determination[20].

---

1 Fatal Accidents and Sudden Deaths Inquiry (Scotland) Act 1976 (c 14), s 3(1)(b). The citation of witnesses and havers and the execution of citation must be in the prescribed form: Fatal

Accidents and Sudden Deaths Inquiry Procedure (Scotland) Rules 1977, SI 1977/191, r 8, Schedule, Forms 5, 6.

2 Ie under the Fatal Accidents and Sudden Deaths Inquiry (Scotland) Act 1976, s 1(1)(a)(i): see para 11.12 above.

3 Ibid, s 4(2).

4 See the Fatal Accidents Inquiry (Scotland) Act 1895 (c 36), s 6 (repealed), and para 11.02 above.

5 Fatal Accidents and Sudden Deaths Inquiry (Scotland) Act 1976, s 6(3).

6 See the Fatal Accidents Inquiry (Scotland) Act 1895, s 5(4) proviso, and para 11.07 above.

7 Fatal Accidents and Sudden Deaths Inquiry (Scotland) Act 1976, s 5(1).

8 Ibid, s 5(2).

9 Fatal Accidents and Sudden Deaths Inquiry Procedure (Scotland) Rules 1977, r 5.

10 Ibid, r 6.

11 Ibid, r 7(1).

12 Ibid, r 7(2).

13 Ibid, r 10(1).

14 Ibid, r 10(1) proviso (a), (b).

15 Ibid, r 10(3).

16 Ibid, r 10(2).

17 Ibid, r 10(4).

18 Ibid, r 13.

19 Ibid, r 13 proviso.

20 Fatal Accidents and Sudden Deaths Inquiry (Scotland) Act 1976, s 6(5)(b); Fatal Accidents and Sudden Deaths Inquiry Procedure (Scotland) Rules 1977, r 14. As to fees, see r 15(2).

11.19. Protection of young people. The long title to the Fatal Accidents and Sudden Deaths Inquiry (Scotland) Act 1976 states that the purpose of the Act is to make provision for the holding of public inquiries into deaths where, inter alia, the circumstances give rise to serious public concern. The Act provides that such an inquiry is to be open to the public[1], but recognises that there are instances where some protection requires to be afforded to a particular section of the public, namely persons under the age of seventeen. Where such a person is in any way involved, the sheriff may make an order prohibiting the publishing, whether in a newspaper or other publication or by a sound or television broadcast, of a report which reveals the name, address or school or other particulars calculated to lead to the identification of such a person[2]. The prohibition extends to pictures of the person[3], Such an order may be made by the sheriff at his own instance or on an application being made to him by any party to the inquiry[4]. Contravention of such an order is an offence[5]. This provision extends to fatal accident inquiries similar protection to that afforded to young persons in criminal cases by the Criminal Procedure (Scotland) Act 1975[6].

1 Fatal Accidents and Sudden Deaths Inquiry (Scotland) Act 1976 (c 14), s 4(3), which is expressed to be subject to s 4(4).

2 Ibid, s 4(4)(a).

3 Ibid, s 4(4)(b).

4 Ibid, s 4(4).

5 Ibid, s 4(5). An offender is liable on summary conviction to a fine not exceeding level 4 on the standard scale: s 4(5); Criminal Procedure (Scotland) Act 1975 (c 21), s 289G (added by the Criminal Justice Act 1982 (c 48), s 54). As to the standard scale, see para 2.12, note 1, above.

6 See the Criminal Procedure (Scotland) Act 1975, ss 169, 374, and paras 6.18, 6.43, above.

11.20. Assessors. In recognition of the advances in modern technology and the need from time to time to have expert assessment of facts brought out at fatal accident inquiries, the sheriff is empowered to summon any person having special knowledge to act as an assessor at the inquiry[1]. The sheriff's decision to use an assessor may be at his own instance or at the request of the procurator fiscal or of any recognised party to the inquiry[1]. Experience has shown that this provision has seldom been used. A request to the sheriff to summon a person to act as an assessor must be made by written motion lodged with the sheriff clerk not less than seven days before the date of the inquiry[2]. The appointment of an assessor does not affect the admissibility of expert evidence in the inquiry[3].

1 Fatal Accidents and Sudden Deaths Inquiry (Scotland) Act 1976 (c 14), s 4(6).
2 Fatal Accidents and Sudden Deaths Inquiry Procedure (Scotland) Rules 1977, SI 1977/191, r 12(1).
3 Ibid, r 12(2).

11.21. The sheriff's determination. Another significant change from the earlier legislation lies in the sheriff's finding, now known as a determination. There has been a noticeable change in emphasis in the role of the sheriff in investigating the circumstances of deaths. The role of the jury was often a charade. Sudden unanimous findings abounded when the requirement to deliberate for at least one hour at the conclusion of the evidence before a majority verdict could be returned was explained. Without a jury, sheriffs in Scotland now appear to be taking a more active part in the inquiries and by doing so are making them more meaningful.

The presiding sheriff is obliged to make a determination at the conclusion of the evidence and of any submissions made by parties to the inquiry, or as soon as possible after the conclusion and the submissions[1]. Five areas have to be covered in the determination, provided of course that the circumstances have been established to his satisfaction by evidence, which need not necessarily be corroborated[2]. The first two of the five areas are perhaps self-evident, covering where and when the death and any accident resulting in the death took place, and the cause or causes of such death and any accident resulting in it[3]. The bite comes in the remaining areas. The sheriff must in his determination set out any reasonable precautions whereby the death or the causative accident might have been avoided[4]. He must also specify any defects in a system of working which contributed to the death or associated accident[5]. Finally he must list any other facts which are relevant to the circumstances of the death[6].

The sheriff's determination must be in writing and be signed by him[7]. The determination must be read out by him in public except in certain circumstances[8]. Thus he is not required to read out the determination where he requires time to prepare the determination and considers that it is not reasonable to fix an adjourned sitting for the sole purpose of reading out the determination; however, in these circumstances the sheriff clerk must send, free of charge, a copy of the determination to the procurator fiscal and to any person who appeared or was represented at the inquiry, and must allow any person to inspect a copy of the determination at the sheriff clerk's office free of charge during the period of three months following the date when the determination was made[9].

While the determination is not admissible in evidence and may not be founded on in any judicial proceedings arising out of the death or accident in question[10], the findings may be very persuasive in ensuring that precautions are taken or defects are remedied with the result that the public could be protected from some recurring hazard or danger to life.

On the conclusion of the inquiry the sheriff clerk must send to the Lord Advocate a copy of the determination and, on request, must send to any minister or government department or to the Health and Safety Commission a copy of the application for the inquiry, the transcript of the evidence, any report or documentary production used at the inquiry and the determination[11]. The procurator fiscal must send to the Registrar General of Births, Deaths and Marriages for Scotland the name and last known address of the deceased person and the date, place and cause of death[12].

On payment of the prescribed fee any person may obtain from the sheriff clerk a copy of the determination[13].

1 Fatal Accidents and Sudden Deaths Inquiry (Scotland) Act 1976 (c 14), s 6(1).
2 Ibid, s 6(2).
3 Ibid, s 6(1)(a), (b).
4 Ibid, s 6(1)(c).
5 Ibid, s 6(1)(d).
6 Ibid, s 6(1)(e).
7 Fatal Accidents and Sudden Deaths Inquiry Procedure (Scotland) Rules 1977, SI 1977/191, r 11(1).
8 Ibid, r 11(2).
9 Ibid, r 11(3).
10 Fatal Accidents and Sudden Deaths Inquiry (Scotland) Act 1976, s 6(3).
11 Ibid, s 6(4)(a).
12 Ibid, s 6(4)(b).
13 Ibid, s 6(5)(a); Fatal Accidents and Sudden Deaths Inquiry Procedure (Scotland) Rules 1977, r 15(1).

11.22. Service of documents. Provision is made for the service on any person of the notice intimating the holding of the inquiry, the citation of a witness for precognition by the procurator fiscal, the citation of a witness or haver to attend at the inquiry and any interlocutor, warrant or other order of the sheriff or writ following thereon issued in connection with an inquiry[1]. The procurator fiscal or the solicitor for any person entitled to appear at the inquiry, as appropriate, may post the document in a registered or recorded delivery letter addressed to the person on whom the document requires to be served at his residence or place of business or any address specified by him for the purpose of receiving documents[2]. Where the document is issued by the procurator fiscal, a police officer, or in other cases, a sheriff officer, may serve the document personally on the person on whom it requires to be served or leave it in the hands of an inmate or employee at the person's residence or place of business or any address specified by him for the purpose of receiving documents, or put it through the letter box at the person's residence or place of business or any specified address, or affix it to the door of the person's residence or place of business or any specified place[3]. When it proves difficult for any reason to serve any document on any person, the sheriff, on being satisfied that all reasonable steps have been taken to serve the document, may dispense with service of such document or order such other steps as he may think fit[4].

1 Fatal Accidents and Sudden Deaths Inquiry Procedure (Scotland) Rules 1977, SI 1977/191, r 16(1).
2 Ibid, r 16(1)(a).
3 Ibid, r 16(1)(b).
4 Ibid, r 16(1) proviso.

11.23. Sheriff's power to dispense with compliance with rules. In his discretion the sheriff may relieve any person from the consequences of any failure to comply with the provisions of the procedural rules relating to inquiries provided the failure results from mistake or oversight or any cause other than wilful non-observance of the rules[1]. In granting such relief the sheriff may impose such terms and conditions as appear to him to be just[1]. In any such case the sheriff may make such order as appears to him to be just regarding extension of time, lodging or amendment of papers or otherwise so as to enable the inquiry to proceed as if such failure had not happened[1]. Clearly this rule has been introduced to prevent unnecessary adjournment of inquiries because some technicality has not been strictly complied with. Remembering that any inquiry causes considerable strain and distress to the relatives, and possibly to other persons, it is indeed important that inquiries should proceed expeditiously and without delay due to some technical failure to comply with the rules.

1 Fatal Accidents and Sudden Deaths Inquiry Procedure (Scotland) Rules 1977, SI 1977/191, r 17.

(d) Systems in other Countries

11.24. Introduction. While most civilised countries have a medico-legal system for investigating deaths, there is no uniformity in the provisions for inquiries in public. There are even differing views regarding the reasons for and the extent of medico-legal investigations, these views ranging from the sole aim of excluding criminality to the extreme opposite, namely a need to make public the circumstances of all deaths of which the cause was not natural or where the deceased was not currently undergoing medical treatment.

The tendency towards the latter extreme is seen in one of the oldest and arguably the best known of the systems, that involving the coroner in England and Wales.

11.25. Coroners' inquests in England and Wales. The office of coroner is of great antiquity, each officer being responsible for investigating well defined categories of deaths within his district.

Originally, the main duties of the coroner were related to the securing of revenues for the Crown under Norman laws. By one of these early laws, a fine was levied on the lord of a community initially and subsequently upon the community itself where a Norman subject was found dead within that community unless the killer was delivered up to justice within a short period. This principle was later applied to all cases of sudden or unexpected deaths unless there was proof that the deceased was not a Norman. The coroner was involved in such investigations and was responsible for the levying of fines in appropriate cases.

Through the years his duties developed, until in 1887 the Coroners Act 1887 (c 71) laid the foundation for the present system. This Act, as subsequently amended, was consolidated into the Coroners Act 1988, which specifies that where a coroner is informed that the dead body of a person is lying within his district, and there is reasonable cause to suspect that such person:

(1) has died either a violent or an unnatural death, or
(2) has died a sudden death of which the cause is unknown, or
(3) has died in prison, or in such a place or in such circumstances as to require an inquest under any other Act,

the coroner, whether the cause of death arose within his district or not, must, as soon as practicable, hold an inquest into the death either with or without a jury[1]. A jury is obligatory where the death falls within head (3), or occurred while the deceased was in police custody, or resulted from an injury caused by a police officer, or was caused by a notifiable accident, poisoning or disease[2]. A jury comprises not less than seven nor more than eleven persons[3].

In this way, public inquiries known as inquests came to be formalised and now are required in every case in which the death was due to unnatural causes or to violence. The inquest is considered by many coroners as the most important tool at their disposal although the apparent lack of discretion as to which cases merit an inquest could result in a devaluation of this particular investigatory procedure.

The Brodrick Committee in 1971 recommended the abolition of juries in inquests[4], but that recommendation was not implemented although, over the years, there has been a reduction in the categories of cases considered appropriate to be heard by a lay jury.

Another step in the evolution of the coroner system has been away from the investigation of criminality. Until 1977 the coroner had the power to commit for trial any person against whom the evidence at an inquest indicated a prima facie case of criminal homicide, but the power was then abolished[5]. This radical change in the role of the coroner was welcomed by the police as there had always been a danger that the committal procedures could be carried out before police inquiries reached a suitable stage. The change was also welcomed by many coroners, some of whom previously felt that their investigatory powers into deaths were inhibited because of the existence of the power of committal in criminal matters to which the strict rules of evidence and procedure applied. The abolition of this power and the prohibition by the Coroners Rules 1984 of the consideration of such extraneous matters as questions of civil or criminal liability[6] have led to a widening of the investigatory role which now leans more towards statistical medical accuracy and community medicine.

1 Coroners Act 1988 (c 13), s 8(1).
2 Ibid, s 8(3).
3 Ibid, s 8(2).
4 *Report of the Committee on Death Certification and Coroners* (The Brodrick Report) (Cmnd 4810) (1971).
5 Criminal Law Act 1977 (c 45), s 56 (repealed). See now the Coroners Act 1988, s 11(6).
6 Coroners Rules 1984, SI 1984/552, r 36.

11.26. The investigation of death elsewhere. Though many jurisdictions have adopted the solution favoured in England and Wales of appointing coroners or similar officers to investigate sudden deaths, this solution is not favoured by the larger number of jurisdictions in the Civil Law tradition which have adopted an inquisitorial system of criminal law; nor is it favoured in the Scandinavian countries such as Sweden which, like Scotland, has a system of public prosecution.

In these countries, death investigation is entirely in the hands of the police. There are no provisions for public inquiries, the system having settled at the end of the spectrum dealing only with an investigation to show or to exclude criminality. Should there be a case against any individual or individuals, this case is dealt with under the normal criminal law of the country.

This particular type of system has led to a situation in some countries such as Sweden where it is often recognised that the public airing of facts may be necessary. This recognition has resulted, for example, in the prosecution of a driver of a vehicle involved in a fatal road accident even when the investigation reveals no fault at all on his part. The prosecution ensures that the circumstances are made open to the public but this necessity involves accusing someone of an offence in the knowledge that all available evidence points to his exculpation.

The Scottish system with its mandatory and discretionary public inquiries sits neatly between these extremes. Mandatory inquiries ensure publicity in particular areas of public concern but perhaps discretionary inquiries play a greater or more important part in allowing the evolution of a system to take into account current attitudes and public interest in the widest sense.

INDEX

References are to paragraphs

References are to paragraphs

References are to paragraphs

Crown Office
procurator fiscal service, supervision of, 1.40
solicitors to Lord Advocate, 1.39
***Cumulo* penalties**
imposition of, 7.07
Custodial penalties
terms of, 1.63
Custody
appearance in court from, 3.18
appellant in, 8.40
liberation by police, 3.17
person in, rights of, 3.16
place of safety, in, 10.06
time limits—
  eighty-day rule, 4.22
  extension of, 4.24
  generally, 4.20
  hundred-and-ten-day rule, 4.21
  one-year rule, 4.23
Customs and excise
search of premises, 3.15

Death
judge, of, 6.08
penalty, *see* CAPITAL PUNISHMENT
sheriff depute, of, effect on sheriff substitute, 1.15
sudden, 11.10
See also FATAL ACCIDENT INQUIRIES
Defects
shrieval justice, in, 1.12
Defence
case, conduct of trial, 6.48
plea bargaining, 3.34
preparation of—
  Crown productions, examination of, 4.17
  documents, recovery of, 4.18, 5.06
  generally, 4.14, 5.05
  identification parade, 4.15
  intermediate diets, 5.08
  post mortems, 4.16
  preliminary pleas, 5.09
  witnesses—
    examination of, 4.17
    precognoscing, 4.19
    summary procedure, 5.07
requirements of—
  generally, 4.31
  productions—
    examination of, 4.34
    lists of, 4.32
    recovery of, 4.34
  rights of defence, 5.20
  special defences, 5.21

Defence—*contd*
requirements of—*contd*
  witnesses—
    Crown, objections to, 4.35
    lists of, 4.32
  special—
    fair notice, requirement of, 4.38
    insanity—
      generally, 10.01
      time of offence, at, 10.08
    lodging of, 4.36
    meaning, 4.37
    pre-trial procedure, 1.53
    summary procedure, 5.21
    withdrawal of, 4.39
Delay
plea in bar of trial, 4.52
undue, prevention of, rights of accused, 1.52
Deportation
court's discretion to recommend, 7.25
Desertion
pro loco et tempore, 6.06, 6.38
simpliciter, 6.07, 6.39
Detention
child, of, 9.05
competent sentence, 7.14
generally, 3.01
nature of, 3.03
right to detain, 3.04
Diet
accelerated, 3.35
intermediate, 5.08, 5.33
pre-trial, *see* PRE-TRIAL DIET
preliminary, *see* PRELIMINARY DIET
trial—
  solemn procedure, *see under* TRIAL
  summary procedure, *see under* SUMMARY PROCEDURE
Discharge
absolute, 7.22
Disqualification
court's powers relating to, 7.24
District court
constitution, 2.11
creation of, 1.17
criminal jurisdiction, 1.17
generally, 1.04
powers, 2.12
predecessors—
  burgh court, 1.17, 1.18
  justice of peace court, 1.17, 1.19
  police court, 1.17, 1.18
public prosecutor in, 1.38
Dittay
brieve of, 1.48
taking up, 1.48

References are to paragraphs

Documents
service of—
complaint, 5.15
fatal accident inquiry, 11.22
summary and solemn procedure distinguished, 3.52
trial diet, 6.33

Error in law
appeal on grounds of, 8.11
correction of, 8.23
European Court of Justice
appeal against reference to, 8.20, 8.72
Evidence
accused, for, 6.26
additional, 6.27, 8.14, 8.37
competency, 2.04
corroboration, 2.03
fatal accident inquiry, 11.07, 11.18
objections to, 6.45, 8.32
oral testimony, 2.05
precognitions, 1.45
relevancy, 2.04
replication, in, 6.28
solemn trial procedure, 1.56
Examination
first, 4.02
further, 4.04
judicial—
extraneous matters, delection of, 4.09
new-style, 4.03
old form, 4.06
pre-trial procedure, 1.46
record of, 4.07, 6.24
verification of record, 4.08
new-style judicial, 4.03
witnesses, of, for Crown, 6.20
Expenditure
procurator fiscal, of, 1.33
Expenses
appeal, 8.23
criminal proceedings, 7.27
Expert
procurator fiscal, preliminary inquiries by, 3.20

Fair notice
special defence, requirement relating to, 4.38
Fatal accident inquiries
Act of 1895—
history, 11.01
scope, 11.02
Act of 1906, 11.09–11.10
Act of 1976, 11.11–11.23
application for, 11.15

Fatal accident inquiries—*contd*
assessors, 11.20
conduct of, 11.06
coroners' inquests, England and Wales, 11.25
discretionary, 11.14
documents, service of, 11.22
evidence, 11.07, 11.18
holding of, 11.04, 11.17
investigation of death elsewhere, 11.26
jury, 11.05, 11.09
mandatory—
generally, 11.12
waiver of, 11.13
notification of, 11.16
petition for, 11.03
procurator fiscal, investigation by, 11.15
sheriff—
determination, 11.21
rules, power to dispense with compliance with, 11.23
sudden death, 11.10
systems in other countries, 11.24–11.26
verdict, 11.08
young people, protection of, 11.19
Fines
amount of, 7.15
conditional offer, 7.26
fiscal, 7.26
imposition of, 7.15
payment of, 7.15
procurator fiscal, powers of, 3.29
Fingerprinting
arrest, following, 3.11, 3.13
Fireraising
criminal jurisdiction, 1.16
Fiscal
meaning, 1.30
See also PROCURATOR FISCAL
Fixed penalty
prosecutor's discretion to offer, 3.28
Forestry court
minor criminal jurisdiction, 1.04
Forfeiture
court's power to order, 7.23
Franchise court
abolition, 1.04, 1.20, 1.25
bailiery court, 1.23
barony court, 1.22
generally, 1.20
jurisdiction, 1.20
regality court, 1.21
replegiation, 1.24
stewartry court, 1.23

References are to paragraphs

References are to paragraphs

References are to paragraphs

References are to paragraphs

References are to paragraphs

References are to paragraphs

References are to paragraphs

References are to paragraphs

References are to paragraphs

References are to paragraphs

References are to paragraphs

STOP
DREAMING
START
LIVING

This book was an inspiration for me. I found working through the exercises so fascinating that I completed the whole thing in one day. The most amazing thing about the experience was that I discovered what I really wanted in my life and this enabled me to make a start putting things in place. Since completing *Stop Dreaming Start Living* I have embarked on a college course, changed my attitude to my work and am about to get married!

Katharine Harris, business manager

Stop Dreaming Start Living really is an exciting book. Not only did the exercises bring clarity, they also created feelings of great energy and optimism. This programme revealed the various fears that sabotaged my work, and allowed me to accept that my recent fiction awards were deserved, not just flukes. The clear methods of discovery led me to plan a strategy to give my own work the same dedication I have applied to other people's.

[This book is] a real treasure, and should help many people clarify just what their issues really are, and how they can change direction in life. (It is *so* important not to be told, but to *discover*.)

I really am no longer 'just dreaming'. The living has begun.

Kristina Amadeus, writer, former New York theatrical agent

[Elizabeth's workshop] was very productive. It allowed us to look inside ourselves and dream a little, and everyone needs to dream. It gave me hope. People don't realise how valuable it is to be able to see clearly what you need. And the value increases over time. I urge anyone who can to try it for themselves. If you can't meet Elizabeth in person, then read her book.

Marie Coleman, grandmother

I used to dream about making things, and now I have a go and get on with it. The Stop Dreaming Start Living programme really helped me make better use of my time, and now life is never boring.

Adele Coleman, mother and craftswoman

I had a role as a mother. I had a role as a wife. But I felt I had lost the 'ME' in my life. It is easy to make changes when you know what you want from your life. Dr Mapstone's Stop Dreaming Start Living workshop showed me exactly what it was I needed. I needed pleasure! Once I had discovered this fact, the rest was easy – from time for long soaks in the bath to arranging childcare for me to have restful weekends away, and all of this without the 'guilt factor'. As Dr Mapstone says, 'when you've made decisions, you *can* do what you've decided!'

Patricia Hoare, counsellor and mother

The exercises are very practical and useable, and really did help me find a different way of thinking. Since then I have changed my life quite considerably.

Ann Truscott, professional mediator

STOP
DREAMING
START
LIVING

DISCOVER YOUR HIDDEN POWERS –
AND TRANSFORM YOUR LIFE

ELIZABETH MAPSTONE

Vermilion

1 3 5 7 9 10 8 6 4 2

Grateful acknowledgement is made for permission to reprint copyrighted material from *A Return to Love: Reflections on the Principles of a Course in Miracles* © 1992 by Marianne Williamson, published by HarperCollins Publisher Ltd. Reprinted by permission of the publisher.

First published in the United Kingdom in 2004 by Vermilion,
an imprint of Ebury Press
Random House UK Ltd.
Random House
20 Vauxhall Bridge Road
London SW1V 2SA

Random House Australia (Pty) Limited
20 Alfred Street, Milsons Point, Sydney,
New South Wales 2061, Australia

Random House New Zealand Limited
18 Poland Road, Glenfield,
Auckland 10, New Zealand

Random House (Pty) Limited
Endulini, 5A Jubilee Road, Parktown 2193, South Africa
Random House UK Limited Reg. No. 954009
www.randomhouse.co.uk
Papers used by Vermilion are natural, recyclable products made from wood grown in sustainable forests.

A CIP catalogue record is available for this book from the British Library.
ISBN: 0091894611

Printed and bound in Great Britain by
Mackays of Chatham plc, Chatham, Kent

To John, as always, and to Michael, Lise and Akita who are making their own dreams come true

Acknowledgements

I am immensely grateful to all those who so generously gave me permission to quote them. As promised, those quoted in the body of the book remain anonymous, but they know who they are.

I also acknowledge my debt to those numerous others – colleagues, clients and teachers – who, over the years, have taught me so much.

Particular thanks are due to Jane Turnbull, a very special agent, to Julia Kellaway for her patience, and to Amanda Hemmings, who returned to editing at just the right time.

Contents

CHAPTER 1

What this Book is About

Our deepest fear is not that we are inadequate.

Our deepest fear is that we are powerful beyond measure.

It is our light, not our darkness, that most frightens us.

We ask ourselves, who am I to be brilliant, gorgeous, talented and fabulous?

Actually, who are you *not* to be?

You are a child of God.

Your playing small doesn't serve the world.

There is nothing enlightened about shrinking so other people won't feel insecure around you.

We are born to make manifest the glory of God that is within us.

It is not just in some of us; it's in everyone.

And as we let our own light shine, we unconsciously give other people permission to do the same.

As we are liberated from our own fear, our presence automatically liberates others.

Nelson Mandela, 1994 inaugural speech

from *A Return to Love: Reflections on the Principles of a Course in Miracles,*

Marianne Williamson

We all reach places in our lives when we are not quite sure what to do. Sometimes it is as though we have reached a crossroads, and we have to choose whether to turn right or left, or carry straight on. We know we must make a decision, but cannot help feeling worried that it could be the wrong one.

At other times, we may find ourselves trapped, imprisoned by other people's expectations, and unable to see a way out. Or we may simply feel bogged down on our life's journey, as though we are in a bad dream where the sleek car we are driving has turned into a primitive cart, with the wheels sinking deeper and deeper into the mud, while the horse struggles unsuccessfully to drag us out of the mire.

You may, of course, have reached a pleasant place in your voyage through life. Why would you want to move on? And yet inside your soul, you know that this is not quite enough. You don't want to spend your entire life on holiday, not ever doing quite what you would like to do, waiting…for something, you are not quite sure what.

Decision time. You are anxious, excited perhaps but apprehensive. How are you to decide? This book is for those moments we all have to face when we know that the time has come to choose.

This book is about how you can learn to see clearly what you want, what you need, and how you can find the courage to choose what is right for you.

Perhaps you are thinking, 'I'd love to take control of my life, but that's only for exceptionally lucky people. The rest of us have to put up with what fate doles out.' It is true, life very often does look like a lottery. But don't despair, don't give up now, for you too can discover the secrets of success, and they don't depend on luck. They depend on you.

Every one of us has choices. All through our lives, from our teens right into old age, we are faced with moments of decision. Whatever we opt for at those moments – whether we decide to act positively or stick with what we know – these choices influence our wellbeing and happiness, and the happiness of those we love.

You too can learn to make the right choice at the right time, discover a way out of self-doubt into self-belief. You too can escape the prison of other people's expectations, break down the bars of your own limitations on your life, become fulfilled as the person you really are. You can stop dreaming, and start living a life that suits *you*.

Knowing How to Choose

Opportunities for change appear suddenly throughout our lives. It is up to us to have the courage to recognise them and take the plunge. We are not stuck for ever with choices we made before we knew what we really wanted. Believe it or not, it is realistic to consider transforming your life maybe every 10 years.

But so often we don't know *how* to choose, so we 'fall into' things, 'stick with the devil we know', until one day we wake up and realise our youth has gone – then our middle age has gone – and we're not quite sure what we did with our lives.

Think about it …

At 15 or 16, you are asked to decide what you want to do in the future. Are you leaving school or staying on into the sixth form? Which subjects are you going to study? Are you going to university? What are your plans for a career?

For people who haven't got a special talent that everyone recognises – and that means most of us – this is the beginning of a life-long battle with the thought: *'Dear God, I've got to decide what I want to do for the rest of my life! How can I do that when I don't even know what I want to do next week?'*

How indeed? Why *should* a choice made at 15 – or even 21 – dictate the rest of your life? It shouldn't. More importantly, it doesn't have to.

Maybe you left school as soon as you could because you hated being a pupil and wanted to start earning money. Perhaps you now regret the education you never got. Well, it's not too late, if that's what you want. Lots of people go back to school as adults – that's what evening classes and the Open University are all about.

Then there are the struggles to find a job, choose somewhere to live, pay the bills and 'enjoy life' the way magazines, newspapers and television adverts suggest everyone else does. Perhaps you fall in love and wonder if it is 'the real thing'. Some of you decide to get married and have children.

For many people, the decision to get married is the one big moment when they really do choose freely, and know they have done so. Marrying this special person is what they want more than anything else. It doesn't really matter what anyone says, because they know that this is the right thing to do for themselves.

But then life goes on, gets in the way, and that delicious sense of having the freedom to choose drowns in our everyday struggles to survive.

This book is about rediscovering that freedom of choice.

Perhaps, though, you have never experienced that freedom. It's true that some people just 'find themselves' getting married, falling into it because it's easier than choosing not to. Perhaps you have never dared to choose for yourself, have simply gone along with what other people want you to do, because you have never felt strong enough – or worthy enough – to take your own desires and wishes seriously.

Now is your chance to take a close look at what you would really like to do with your life. This is your opportunity to listen to your inner being, get in touch with your secret self, and taste the flavour of your true thoughts. Discover that glorious sense of freedom when you make a choice, even if you have never experienced it before. And learn how to choose what is right for *you* when the opportunities for change arise.

How I Developed this Programme

I know it can be done, because I have tried this programme – many times!

For many years I too had a dream. As a girl, I had wanted to become a doctor, but my father didn't believe in higher education for girls (this was in the fifties), so I left home at the earliest opportunity, went to Canada and became a journalist. There I discovered psychology.

This was the beginning of a life-long love affair. I read

voraciously, studied modules at various universities, attended seminars and eventually undertook a training analysis to become a Jungian psycho-analyst (by this time I had moved to Belgium). But all the time, I had a secret longing to do a proper full-time science degree at university – not in medicine now but in psychology – because I wanted to know the true scientific basis for all the different theories about the human mind. It was not until I was 44, and my youngest child had gone off to art college, that I was finally able to turn this dream into reality by enrolling as a mature student at Oxford University, to read Experimental Psychology.

Those long years of study stood me in good stead, however. Instead of being trapped in one school of thought, I began to see how all the different approaches to psychology fit together, and so was able to evolve a much deeper understanding of the human mind. And that is how I came to develop this simple but revolutionary programme to help individuals help themselves.

Most self-help methods rely on exhortation, getting the individual to 'commit' to themselves, or even (in my view, mistakenly) to the writer. Initially, these methods may appear to work quite well, because hope inspires a rush of adrenalin and the writer's words boost the reader's self-esteem. They believe they can do it. Alas, adrenalin and hope are not enough. They are like taking aspirin or sleeping pills – they make you feel better but do nothing about the root cause.

My method may look undemanding, but these simple exercises allow the individual to tap hidden depths, in the same way as in a psychotherapist's consulting room. I have adapted many of the techniques of the psychotherapist, so that each individual may discover how to confront directly those hidden demons that prevent life being lived to the full. At the same time it is safe – certainly better than putting yourself in the hands of a not-so-well-trained counsellor, because you work at your own pace. If you are not ready to deal with some painful trauma in your past, you can note it is there but let it alone until you feel brave enough to confront your own truth. (You will see that it is a good idea to let the daylight in on those dark fears, because they are more powerful in the dark – sometimes just bringing them out into the light of day will make them shrivel away.) This programme is at the same time broadly based, and includes techniques borrowed and adapted from new 'voice therapy', cognitive therapy, Beck 'mood therapy' and Rogerian 'client-centred therapy', as well as using many insights from experimental psychology.

That is how I came to develop this Life Planning Programme. Each time I came to a crossroads – or felt frustrated and trapped, as though I was going nowhere – each time I felt I just didn't know which way to go, which choice would be best and whether I should abandon all my dreams as unworkable – each time I worked through this programme, changing it as I learned more about psychology. And I found the answers.

The answers to my problems were always inside me.

And the answers to your own dilemmas and conflicts are inside yourself. The difficulty is always how to find those answers.

Putting Yourself in the Picture

Some people may feel that the exercises in this book encourage people to be selfish. It *is* true that we cannot always choose to do what is best for us if it would be harmful for others. However, the exercises I will describe do in fact require you to take account of all those affected by your decisions.

The real problem most people have is not that they are too selfish. It is that they are not selfish enough.

Selfish people don't need a book like this because they take it for granted that what *they* want is what is right. And if they change their minds, they don't worry about that either. Let other people pick up the pieces while they move on, doing their own thing. This book is not for them. They couldn't be bothered to read it anyway.

There is an exception to this. If you were born into a wealthy family, you may have had to make fewer difficult choices because so much has been possible for you. You want a car – you buy one. You change your mind and want a different car – not a problem. You want a boat, to travel, to go to college, to drop out – nothing matters, because money can be thrown at almost any problem. This *does* make a person deeply selfish and, very often, supremely unhappy. Running round seeking thrills in order to feel alive is yet another way of not confronting who *you* are, and what – deep inside your soul – you really require of yourself.

We all need time to commune with ourselves, put ourselves centre stage, under the spotlight. We must learn to recognise who we are, and what we truly need to become a whole person.

*It is your life, dear reader. So every time you make a choice –
and you make choices every day – ensure your own needs and
desires are put in the balance too.*

This book asks you to find the courage to concentrate on
you. If it makes you feel selfish, then you will look at that
feeling too. And if you must think about other people, ask
yourself how you want them to behave towards you, so
that you can be happy.

Synchronicity

It is an extraordinary psychological fact that when we are
honest with ourselves about ourselves, and when we are
clear about our needs and our wants, things move together
to make it possible for us to choose what is right for us. This
is known as *synchronicity.*

Synchronicity requires us to be truthful, sincere and
candid in our inner thoughts, and to find a balance within
ourselves between what we know to be good and what we
know to be our failings. We discover we can be at one with
ourselves and with the world. This is what Eastern
mystics call 'being in Tao', and what the poet T. S. Eliot
described as 'the still point of the turning world'.* I think
of it as being completely in tune, like a stringed instrument ready to make music: a glorious moment of being
absolutely at one with the universe. It may last only for a
short while, but for that brief interlude we are in balance.
And in that moment the events in our lives seem to work
together in harmony.

*'Burnt Norton', *Four Quartets*, line 62

For the less mystic and more ambitious, Shakespeare put it cogently:

> 'There is a tide in the affairs of men,
> Which taken at the flood, leads on to fortune.'*

Enthusiastic surfers will recognise that superb feeling when you catch a swelling wave at just the right moment, and the power of the sea carries you forward.

Achieving balance requires us to be honest with ourselves, and the straightforward techniques I describe in the rest of the book can help everyone be just that. These simple exercises will help you focus, clarify your fears and open doors to possibilities. They offer the opportunity to discover what you really want now, at this stage in your life. Only you have the answers.

*Julius Caesar, Act 4, Scene 3, lines 216–17

This book could be seen as a *travellers' guide* to your voyage through life. It will help you work out where you have got to so far, and whether you like the direction you are moving in or would prefer to go somewhere else. It provides crucial information you are unlikely to find anywhere else about how to deal with major difficulties and dangers along the way. You will be given a route map through the 'valley of the shadows' and learn how to deal with your personal demons so that they no longer prevent you from fulfilling your dreams. You will discover your personal powers and how to give yourself permission to use them to the full. You will develop your own skills of map-making, and create your own route to fulfilment. Use the simple techniques in this book and you really will find the way to stop simply dreaming and start to live.

CHAPTER 2

How to Use this Book

Each chapter presents one or more simple paper-and-pencil exercises. You may like to complete them before going on to the discussion that follows in each section.

Although the exercises are perfectly straightforward, no one ever completes them in quite the same way. In each section, I have therefore given some examples of answers from people who have done Life Planning Programmes with me (their names have been changed to maintain their privacy – see the section *Introducing the People*, page 26). Many people find it useful to compare what they have done with what others have come up with. This often stimulates new ideas and creates new possibilities in their minds. It can also be helpful to discuss each exercise with someone else, so you might like to go through these exercises with a friend.

You may prefer, though, to read through the book first and see what it's all about before you commit yourself to the exercises. That's fine. Or if you feel like jumping in and having a go, that's fine too. Whatever suits you.

A Warning!

These exercises may look simple, but they are amazingly powerful. There are two important things to bear in mind:

1. **You should go through each exercise** *in the order given* **and you should** *write down your answers.*

Some people have tried to avoid the bother of writing down their answers, thinking that it is the same if they just do the exercises in their head. It is not. Believe me, I have tried it myself – and heaven knows, I'm more familiar with these exercises than with the inside of my fridge! If you just *think* about your answers, you will never need to confront what you really believe about yourself and your life. You will never surprise yourself, never move on.

So, to benefit from these easy exercises, do take the trouble to write down what comes to mind. Keep your answers for future reference – you may well want to guard them in a safe place, away from prying eyes. The best approach is to get a new folder to store the papers in, and a pile of fresh A4 paper – or a pad, if you prefer – and then you can answer each question on a fresh sheet. Label and date each one. Then you will always be able to look back at where you were and what you were thinking when you last did these exercises.

2. **Once you start, and certainly once you get to Chapter 4, you really should try to get through to the end of the book.** *If you stop in the middle, you will find you are more depressed and unsure of where you are going than ever...not a good idea.*

As you will see, it is essential to examine what prevents you fulfilling your dreams. But if you stop there, you may feel 'What the hell am I doing wasting my time on this rubbish?' *because that is what your inner demons want you to think.* Then you will not have benefited at all from the painful experience of meeting the devils inside your head.

Most self-help books seem to assume that by exhorting you to success, you will feel good and get there. I know from years of experience, however, that the inspiring words *may* lift your spirits and appear to galvanise you into action, but the effect doesn't last long. If you really want success, you need to know what your inner demons are telling you in the quiet of the night. You need to find out how they prevent you achieving your own ambitions. Then you must learn some pretty effective techniques for getting rid of them for good. In Chapter 10 you will see what happens to someone who allows his inner demons to wreck his opportunity to confront them, and so fails to get rid of their insidious, destructive poison.

So do carry on, right to the end. If you are brave enough to confront your secret demons and see them for what they are, you will find that it is worth all the discomfort, pain and even agony. You will discover how to stop your private fears and misconceptions getting in the way of your dreams.

If you have no interruptions, it may be possible to go through all the exercises in one day. However, that doesn't give you much time to absorb the discussions in each chapter or to, well, just ponder. Better still would be a long weekend devoted entirely to thinking about *you*.

When I last did these exercises, I took off for a break of five days, entirely alone, in my favourite place – the Scilly Isles. I took paper and pens, and a reminder of the exercises in their proper order, and spent each day walking and thinking and completing the exercises in an orgy of concentration on *me*. The changes I was contemplating were so important and far-reaching, I needed to be sure I had given my inner psyche a proper opportunity to express its needs.

I still do these exercises from time to time, as things change over the years. Even though I know these simple techniques inside out and have used them to help many clients, I can still be surprised at what they reveal to me. You will also find that they stand you in good stead throughout your life.

Introducing the People

Here I introduce a few of the people who have tried this Life Planning Programme, and whose answers to one or more of the questions appear somewhere in the book. All are genuine participants, but their names and situations have been changed. As you will see, some of them chose to do the programme because they were feeling low, depressed and couldn't see any way out of the miserable place they were in. You may find just reading about them makes your life look a whole lot better by contrast.

Some of these people have done the programme recently, so we can only know about the hopes they left with. Others are older now, and so by the end of the book we will discover that many of them did manage to transform their lives. Here they are, in order of age:

Mark was just 13 and hated school. He was in trouble with his parents and his teachers because he was refusing to study. He couldn't sleep and apparently didn't enjoy anything except playing computer games late at night.

Annie was 14 and also hated school. She believed she was overweight and ugly, and was generally unhappy. Her parents were in the throes of an acrimonious divorce.

Jenny was 18 and studying French and German at university. She was good at languages, but 'hated the course'. She didn't want to be at university at all, but was continuing her education to please her mother.

Wendy was 27, a lone parent of two children, a boy and a girl. She felt she 'could never make decisions', and that everyone 'looked down' on her because of her situation. But when a friend offered to take the children for the day so that she could attend a Life Planning Day, she said, 'I knew I mustn't let this opportunity go by.'

Celia was 29 and also a lone parent of a two-year-old boy, though she had expected to marry his father 'who does help out'. She had travelled widely, but now lived in a dreary council flat in a drug-ridden part of her city. She was looking for a way to escape.

Diana was 33, the mother of two children, aged 10 and 12. She dreamed of being a painter but was feeling anxious and guilty because she had quit work, and was therefore totally dependent on her husband.

Irene was also 33, the mother of two children, aged 8 and 5, divorced and recently remarried. She felt it was 'time to take a bit of control', but was afraid of making the wrong choices.

Floyd was 34, an executive with a big international company, and proud of his success in climbing out of his working-class background. He had just been offered a major promotion which involved moving to the United States. He wanted to marry his girlfriend, but hadn't yet asked her.

Frances was also 34, and worked in an art gallery. She just wanted to 'find out what I want to do that I don't know about'.

Teresa was 35 and a secondary school teacher. She said she was curious, open to new ideas. We discovered she was at an important crossroads in her life.

Rose was just 40 ('a frighteningly pivotal age'), widowed and the sole support of three children. She felt her life could be less stressful, but couldn't see how.

Stella, another 40-year-old, was a former bank clerk, married for the second time and now the mother of one young child. She said she always relied on other people to make her happy, and had decided it was time to find out how to do this for herself.

Lynne was 45, another high-powered executive with a major company, and mother of two children. She said she knew what she wanted to do, but couldn't reconcile what she wanted with what she believed she *should* be doing.

Dorothy was 47, and said she led 'an extremely complicated life, with people leaning on me'. She felt suffocated, and wanted something for herself. She had written a book, 'the one thing I am proud of', and wanted time to write more.

Martin would not reveal his age, but was probably in his late 50s. We learned that growing old and possibly helpless was a major problem for him. He said he craved knowledge and wanted to discover how to 'usefully spend the next 30 to 40 years'.

Barbara was 59, a 'wife, mother and grandmother'. She worked as a solicitor and saw her Life Planning Day as 'pure selfishness'. But she felt ground down, even though she was sure there was no good reason for this.

Elizabeth was 63, married, a mother of three and grand-mother of five, a chartered psychologist and frustrated writer.*

Tyler was 75 and proud of his age because he had 'begun my third career'. He said he wanted to make the most of his remaining years, and felt pressured by needing to do too many things and having less energy to do them.

You will notice that the majority here are women. Although these examples were arbitrarily chosen from the small, select group who were actually asked to give permission for me to quote them, these numbers do reflect reality. It is true that most participants in Life Planning Programmes *have* been women, though there is no reason why men should not enjoy and benefit from the course.

Age is intriguing too, and again there is a gender differ-ence. Although we can all find that we reach a crossroads at

---

*As I write this, I am 64, moderately successful as a psychologist in private practice, but secretly frustrated because I want to write books. So last summer, I made myself do all these exercises. It was what I discovered as I went through the exercises that made me reduce the individual counselling and psychotherapy sessions I give, refuse all new clients and concentrate on writing. This is the first book to result from that decision, so I hope you will enjoy it.

almost any age, here we see men longing to make life-transforming decisions at the extremes – one man in his teens and two men refusing to accept they are so old they must be consigned to the scrapheap. The single exception in this group is a young adult man facing two major life-changing decisions at once: moving to another country and getting married. My interpretation of this is that until recent years, men have had to decide on a career and then stick to it. More recently, I have had several men in their late 30s and 40s longing to make a change, and wondering if they dare. None of them was willing to be quoted – which is another gender difference.

Except Patrick. He is 42, a successful building contractor and father of four children. Patrick was very anxious to prevent *anyone* knowing that he had come to see me. He was feeling so desperate about how his life was going, he summoned up all his courage to ask for help. He did the Life Planning Programme in individual sessions, and wouldn't let me quote from what he discovered along the way. But three years later, once he had not only learned what he needed but had also done something about it, he told me that he didn't care who knew now. The Life Planning Programme had saved his life. So you will meet Patrick in the final chapter, and find out what happened to him. Men seem, on the whole, to be much more wary than women about acknowledging a need to look at their own psyche.

Women's lives tend to be more fluid, probably because they so often try to combine family and career. Almost anywhere between the ages of 30 and 50 we find women asking themselves important questions about whether they are going to have 'lived life' the way they want. The 40s are particularly crucial for women who have chosen to devote their early years to their children and family: as the children grow up and leave home, many a woman finds that the time has come to think about herself.

We have examples of people from all age groups. There are no ages, in fact, at which you need think 'I'm stuck, I can't change things', if you are not happy with what you have got.

Whatever your particular reason for deciding to look at this book the techniques outlined in the chapters that follow can be useful to you at any stage in your life.

CHAPTER 3

Meeting Yourself

We are born originals and die as copies.

Søren Kierkegaard

We all are individuals, with our special talents and personal powers. Yet everything in our lives from our earliest days in our mothers' arms persuades us that we must learn to be like everyone else. And this can be difficult because we are not all alike. We are different from one another. We are born originals.

Society needs us all to conform to a certain extent so that we can live together in harmony. The process of changing the squalling individualistic infant into a civilised adult is known as socialisation, and is essential for a peaceful and safe society. We all know how dangerous and unpleasant it can be when selfish people refuse to live by the rules, and simply take what they want without regard for others. But being civilised and being a clone are not the same thing. The trick is to learn how to live peacefully in society and remain – or allow yourself to become – your own special self.

So where has this socialisation left *you*? The exercises in this chapter will help you explore how you experience who you are. How you see yourself, how you think about and judge yourself, how it feels to be you and whether it tastes and smells good – these factors all determine how you live your life. You will be asked to look at your own ideas about yourself, to weigh up your good and bad traits, to listen to what the voices in your mind say about you, and to discover how you feel inside your own skin.

Please note, this chapter is not like one of those personality questionnaires you find in many newspapers and women's magazines. You know the kind of thing – answer (a), (b) or (c) and, after 10 questions, the expert can tell you all about yourself. That sort of thing is great fun, but not very realistic nor much help. What can help, though, is to concentrate your attention entirely on yourself so that you can discover what you see and what you really think and feel about being you.

Many of us are good at intuiting how other people feel and what they need, but we tend to be out of touch with our own feelings. This doesn't mean that we don't react. Some of us may shout, scream or weep, express fury, frustration and misery. But we still may not know how to *use* our feelings, our emotions, our anger and distress to help us make wise decisions in our lives. This chapter is just the first step in your journey to find the real you.

Don't skip over this chapter. It is important. In the rest of the book you will be trying to sort out what you really want to do and what is getting in the way of you fulfilling your dreams. But do you like yourself? Do you think you are the sort of person who *should* lead a happy and fulfilled life? We shall see.

exercise 1
who are you?

List 10 or more things that you are. Write down as many as you can.

Now examine your list.

Wendy said the first thing that came to mind was 'stupid', but then she crossed it out because she knew she wasn't really stupid – *that was how she thought other people saw her*. This is a valuable insight. Many of us find ourselves paralysed by other people's criticism, imprisoned by their expectations, unable to see any way out of the trap of believing that what other people think should come first.

Stella couldn't come up with 10 things to begin with. She listed 'kind, healthy, neat' and came to a halt: she was focusing on attributes other people might see. Lynne found the same thing – but her list was all to do with relationships and functions: she wrote 'mother, wife, daughter, business executive'.

Most people start by thinking of how other people perceive them – whether it be what they do, how they behave, or in terms of their most important relationships. And the things they come up with first are often significant in their own relationship with the world.

But it is worth going beyond those very first thoughts and considering other possibilities. There are many different ways in which you might see yourself. For example, have you considered:

• Roles?
• Abilities?

- Qualities?
- Relationships?
- Experience?
- Physical characteristics?
- How you direct your attention and energies?
- How you evaluate your experience?

Are there any items you now want to add to your list? It helps to think about all the different aspects of your life in case you have left out something so central it didn't even occur to you to give it a mention.

It is not a good idea to alter your list to fit someone else's perceptions, so don't make changes just because you think you *should*. Remember, this is entirely a question of how you see you, how you experience being you, what it feels like being inside your skin. So do make sure you include items that mean important aspects of you to *you*.

exercise 2
creating a self-portrait
From the list you made in Exercise 1, select the 10 most important descriptions of who you are.
Put them in order of importance.

This exercise should provide a good picture of what you consider most central to being *you*. As you do this, you may find you want to change your original list. Go ahead. The more you probe, the more likely you are to discover the really important things you feel are essential to being you. You are painting a word portrait of your own self.

When you are happy that you have included all the most important aspects of being the person you are, it is time to examine your self-portrait from a different angle.

Do You Like You?

Do you like yourself? Are the qualities you have listed good – or bad? Look at this list made by Annie:

Annie, 14
Overweight
Will-powerless
A pupil
Plain-looking
Lazy
Unkind to people I don't like
A liar
Loud-mouthed

Poor Annie doesn't seem to like anything about herself. Unfortunately, many teenage girls do struggle with this kind of devastating self-image. Psychologists in the United States and in Britain have found that self-esteem can be at a reasonably high level in girls of about 9 or 10, but as they enter adolescence, their self-esteem seems to plummet. This is a serious social problem, and a painful psychological burden for huge numbers of girls. So if you happen to be a teenager, and have produced a similarly self-critical self-portrait, you can at least tell yourself you are just like everyone else.

However, if your list *is* mainly a litany of self-criticism and bad qualities, do stop for a moment and ask yourself if this depressing portrait can really be all there is. Don't you have *any* good qualities?

Of course you do. Courage for a start, or you wouldn't be doing this exercise. And a valuable sense that you can make changes in your life. So keep aware as you go through the rest of the exercises that you have a nasty, carping critic sitting on your shoulder, dripping poison in your ear. Look out for ways to dislodge that carping critic later in the book so that you can finally enjoy being who you really are.

Why Are These Aspects Important?

Many people find their list combines social roles (e.g. nurse, teacher), relationships (e.g. husband, mother, lover) and descriptions of how other people see them (e.g. kind, critical). Ask yourself why these different aspects are important to you. It may be that most – or all – represent what makes your life worthwhile.

On the other hand, it could be that you are anxious to fit into a social mould that you secretly feel you may not suit. Jenny, for instance, had spent much of her life living abroad and hated any sense of not belonging, not fitting in. 'I like to get along with people,' she said. So nearly every item on her list (*'female, student, British, single, sister'*) described her as just like all her friends.

Asked to think about what she had *left out* – all those more personal qualities that make her the individual she really is – Jenny became anxious, and confessed, 'I want people to like me'. She didn't think 'being different' was a good idea. But then she added to her list *'bored all the time'* and *'frustrated'*. Her need to feel accepted by her group was clearly not making her happy.

It may be, like Dorothy, that the combined list of feelings and roles creates a coherent description of the life situation you would like to change.

Dorothy, 47
Overburdened
Daughter
Sensitive
Wife
Writer
Caring
Worried
Employee
Artistic
Healer

If you read this list downwards, you can see that she is describing herself as burdened with an elderly mother and a husband who suggests she is 'over-sensitive', and as a caring but worried employee. But buried in the middle of the list is Dorothy's ambition to be a writer, and her belief in her gifts (*'artistic, healer'*) has not been lost.

Discover the Hidden Messages

Examine your own list to discover its hidden messages, the secret knowledge that comes only from looking at things from a slightly different angle. *Where* certain items occur in your list may be significant. Diana's list is a good example.

Diana, 33
Mother
Friend
Painter
Lover of art
Female
Alive
Lover of music
Wife

Diana's first two items emphasise her relationship with others. Her list then reveals her dreams of being a painter, her sense of being aware of art and music, of being herself, of being alive. And last is her relationship with her husband. This list illustrates what Diana herself only really understood later when she painted a picture, using her preferred images instead of words: it showed her at her easel, painting, with music playing, and all around was a fence guarded by her children and husband. Just as she revealed herself in her list hemmed in by her roles as mother and wife, so she in fact felt trapped and imprisoned. All this can be discovered from just a list!

It is worth examining your own list to see if you too have shown your dreams as hemmed in by other important aspects of yourself.

Are Your Fears Clearly There?

Those worries and fears that interfere with your desire to stop dreaming and start living may be perfectly clear to you, and need no symbolic placement in your list. Martin knows perfectly well what his problems are. His pen portrait describes how he sees himself: a man with talent and experience, unable to discover how he can start living again.

Martin
Scientist
Educator
Philosopher
Wasted ability
Wasted potential
Actor
Forcibly retired at 50
Frustrated
Stressed

Martin is angry at being forced out of a job he enjoyed, and the failure of certain business ventures he subsequently embarked on. He is frustrated and stressed by his inability to make things happen the way he wants them to through lack of money. There is little worse than to approach old age realising that your abilities and potential are being, or have been, wasted.

If you are angry, stressed or frustrated, try to stand back and see how these feelings are interfering with your ability to think creatively. Just be aware. The exercises in the rest of the book will help by revealing unexpected ways to deal with these destructive feelings.

If you are happy being you, appreciate your good qualities and feel you do deserve to stop dreaming and start living, hold on to that positive feeling.

exercise 3
seeking transformation

**Which aspects of yourself would you like to change?
Make a list.**

Unassertiveness

All of us have something we want to change. It may be a major aspect of your way of doing things. For example, Dorothy wrote, *'My unassertiveness – I never say "no".'* This is an important insight for someone in her situation. Lots of people, and especially women who are expected to care for others, have difficulty saying 'no'. Just remember: each person has freedom of action. You are free to say 'no' to a request, but equally the other person is free to ask. So your aim is to refuse to do whatever it is you don't want to do without rejecting the other person, or being annoyed at being asked. It takes practice to get the balance right, so it is a good idea to start now.

Wendy wrote: *'Be kinder to myself'* and *'Look after my own needs'*. It is essential to be kind to yourself if you are to start living. And of course you must look after your own needs – everyone must do that.

You are at least as important as everyone else in your life.

Losing Your Temper

'Stop losing my temper' is a frequent item on people's lists, especially those of women, and particularly mothers of young children. Part of the problem is that society has a foolish social attitude to anger. It is still widely believed that women are less liable to feel anger than men, so it is more

acceptable for men to lose their temper than for women. This is absurd and factually wrong. Anyone and everyone can feel anger, at any age. Indeed, you are *allowed* to feel angry if the situation seems to call for it.

The real issue is what you do with that anger when you feel it rising inside you. You are entitled to feel what you feel. But you are not entitled – no one is, male or female – to inflict suffering and misery on others because of what you feel. So learning how to control *expression* of anger is a valuable resolution. Allow and acknowledge your own angry feelings, but learn to tell others that you feel angry when they behave in certain ways without losing self-control. (For more on anger, see Chapter 8 of my book *War of Words: Women and Men Arguing*.)

Taking Control

A related problem is wanting to control others. This looms large for many people, and is particularly difficult for mothers. How are they to know what constitutes setting necessary boundaries for their children, and what is being a control freak? It may help to know that this goes with the job – mothers never get it right.

Lynne said, 'I don't *want* to control my family. It's just that there's this vacuum, and someone has to fill it.' And a bit later, 'I'm so afraid whatever I do will damage my children.' Others agreed.

Letting go as children grow older, allowing them to make all those mistakes you have learned from, permitting them to invent the wheel all over again takes enormous self-control. So if trying to manage others is a factor for you, try turning it round and applying the control to yourself – stop yourself from saying anything that smacks of you trying to run their lives.

The opposite difficulty confronts some parents. Many realise and accept that teenagers must be allowed to take increasing control of their lives as they near legal adulthood, but do not know how to insist on reasonable behaviour. The fundamental issue is: does their growing freedom of choice interfere with the rights and freedoms of others? Adolescents should be allowed choices, but not to rule the family. Every parent should insist that they have rights too, and no child of whatever age should be permitted to violate these while they live 'at home. This is yet another aspect of our need to stand up for ourselves and refuse to be treated shabbily by those nearest to us.

Wanting to be Better

Being 'better' at whatever we do is a normal desire. Many women wrote that they wanted to be *'a better mother'*. If you have written something like that – or *'be kinder'*, *'think more of others'* and so on – just keep in mind that this admirable ambition could also be the voice that prevents you fulfilling your dreams. We don't know yet. But you may find that what you think you want to change is exactly what you are frightened to change because *other people* might not like your dreams. You may really be an excellent mother, an effective contributor at work, a kind, generous and thoughtful person, but it may be that these good qualities are stifling your own fulfilment. A dreadful thought, but perhaps you have to learn to be more selfish, not less.

Worry and Fear

Lynne wrote, *'Worry – everything I want is blocked by worry about the consequences for the children.'* Very often we are prevented from turning our dreams into reality by concern for others – and we will look at this question in more depth later in the book. But if this sort of fear has surfaced explicitly in your own list, you already know in some part of your mind that this is *you*. You know it is your own way of construing the situation, and that somehow, if only you knew how, you can discover a new way of seeing things. This is a valuable first step because, yes, you *can* learn to construct your own reality differently.

Other fears may be more disguised. Jenny, for instance, wrote a long list of things she wanted to change about herself. All were different aspects of her *real fear* which was of what other people would think if she did what she wanted to do.

Fear of what others might think could be leading you into real danger. Floyd, who had been offered a major promotion overseas, was worried about *'being a slouch'*. We learned that Floyd worked for 10 to 12 hours a day, and took work home at weekends, and yet he still worried about being lazy! Floyd believed that he *should* be able to work like that because that was the culture in his big international organisation. So he felt guilty when he wanted to rest, enjoy a day sailing, maybe cook a meal for friends. No wonder his self-confidence was ebbing away – by accepting the unreasonable demands of his employers, he had actually set himself up for failure.

This may sound extreme, but in my view workaholism has become as serious a mental illness in young to middle-aged businessmen as anorexia in young women – and just as deadly, though the process is slower. If you work that many hours every day, and simply don't know how to stop, then your life is seriously unbalanced, your health is being undermined and you need psychological help.

Guilt

Guilt was a major obstacle for many participants. Stella said she had been angry with her husband that morning because he had raised last-minute difficulties, but she was sure it was because she had felt guilty about leaving her three-year-old with his father. 'Part of me feels it is wrong.'

Martin said he thought this was a gender issue: as a scientist, he didn't have feelings of guilt, he was looking for practical solutions. It is true that women are more likely to experience guilt when thinking about themselves. Guilt arises when you have children and other family members depending on you, and you feel you must put their needs and wishes first. Men with families suffer the same kind of guilty feelings when they want to change course. Those without dependents do not tend to experience guilt as a major hindrance.

No one likes a feeling of guilt, but it is there because you have not resolved certain dilemmas. Keep aware of it, and exercises later in the book should help you find a way through.

exercise 4
recognise your good qualities
Which aspects of yourself are you happy with?
Try to list at least five aspects.

Considering what you like about yourself is not as easy as it might first appear. Most people are quickly able to think of what they want to change, but hesitate when considering what pleases them about themselves.

When you realise, though, that you *do* have attractive qualities, that there *are* aspects of your life that give you happiness, that you *have* achieved some things of which you can be proud, then your spirits rise. You feel lighter, colours are more vibrant, a song may even come into your mind, perfumes fill the air and life tastes sweet. Pleasure is enormously valuable for your mental and physical wellbeing, and being able to take pleasure in being yourself is a significant achievement.

Annie, who had produced a self-portrait full of self-disgust, discovered to her delight that, yes, she *did* have some good qualities after all. This is her list:

Annie, 14
Strong
Patient
Friendly
Understanding
An equal

She said the items on her original list were all true, but now she could see that the things that pleased her about herself were more important than she had thought. She *liked* the feeling that she was strong and patient and friendly, and really just as good as other people. We all rejoiced when she decided her first self-portrait should be changed.

Wendy too discovered that there were many things about herself that pleased her, and not least among them was her decision to do this programme. This is her list:

Wendy, 27
Striving to change
Do new things
Honest
Not frightened of people (as I used to be)
Good mother

Many who had expressed anxiety about being 'a better mother' also found that having children was one of the good things in their lives, and the older ones added *'being a grandmother'*. Lynne wrote: *'sometimes I'm a good mother.'*

Some people's lists were short, but everyone was able to discover something about themselves with which they were happy. Teresa wrote: *'sensitivity, passion, awareness'* and Frances's list was similar: *'awareness, empathy, love of nature'*, while even Martin, frustrated and angry though he was, wrote: *'decreasing stress, having moved to Somerset, beginning to do something useful.'*

exercise 5
consider a desert island...

**Take your 'self-portrait' – your list of the 10 most
important things about you that you created in
Exercise 2.**

**If you were living on a desert island, which of these
aspects would you change?**

This exercise is to help you determine the extent to which
you are dependent on other people for your sense of self. So
look back over your answers to the questions in this chapter
and ask yourself, 'If I were all alone on a desert island, how
would I like to be?' Is this how other people want you to be?
Does it matter?

All of us have to live with others to some extent so we
cannot leave out of account what other people seem to
want. But before you think about other people, you need to
be clear in your mind about what *you* think about yourself.

You are the only person you have to live with all your life. We
tend to forget this.

Perhaps you have already changed your self-portrait
because of what you discovered in Exercise 4, as Annie
did. But now, imagining yourself on a desert island, you
are really face-to-face with the person you would really
like to be.

Some people find this exercise very difficult, because it
can be frightening to imagine life without other people,
especially those you love. Diana had no difficulty, however,
for she realised that a desert island would give her the
freedom to paint – her roles as mother, friend and wife

could be set aside for the sake of this exercise, and she was left with the core of herself – a creative lover of art and music.

Rose said it would be restful to be alone, and realised that her situation as a widowed mother of two was full of stress. Her original self-portrait was:

Rose, 40
Mother
Bereaved
Good worker
Worried
Good sense of humour
Good cook
Organised
Good with people
Lonely
Tired

Nearly everything in her list, she said, was because of others, and a period on a desert island would make her 'relaxed. I'd have enough sleep, and nothing to worry about except how my children were getting on. I'd miss them, of course, and I'd still miss my husband. But it wouldn't be so much of a burden'.

If the thought of escaping people produces images of pleasure and relaxation, this is a clear sign that you are not taking your own needs sufficiently into account. Just keep this in mind for now. You have been alerted, and later in the book you will discover ways of putting this right.

Irene, on the other hand, said that she would find it very hard to live without people; 'I need an audience. I like to make people laugh.' As we will see, this was an important insight for Irene who does indeed thrive best when on a stage. But knowing this also allowed her to see that she tried to conciliate people because, like Jenny, she wanted them to like her.

'Deary me,' she said. 'I've a backbone made of blancmange!'

Most people find there is something they would change about themselves if left all alone. Sometimes they are not sure whether other people would be happy about such a change. But bear in mind what you discover here. It will be important later.

exercise 6
a brief first glance at your dreams
What has been your dream since childhood?
Have you pursued or deferred this dream?
Who or what has held you back?
Who or what has helped you the most?

You may not feel you need to write down your answers but it helps to put it all on paper. Especially important are the last two questions. Make yourself look at who or what has been holding you back, however important, central and impossible to change these aspects of your life may appear. Write down in detail how you see the barriers to achievement. Hear the injunctions, feel the weight of the chains, taste the bitterness of hindrance, smell the sour air of an unfulfilled dream. Your words will take the obstacles out of your mind and objectify your thoughts and feelings on the paper in front of you. Eventually, when you have completed more exercises and are ready, you will be able to examine your prison coolly and objectively, and discover a way out.

Consider that last question carefully. Who or what has helped you in the past? What are the circumstances in which you begin to feel strong, resilient, able to overcome all obstacles? When have you believed – just occasionally, in some tiny secret place inside you – that making those dreams a reality might be possible after all?

Be honest with yourself. No one else need know. Your dreams are an important part of what makes you *you*.

This time, I will use myself at two different stages to show you how this exercise works.

Elizabeth (age 40)
As Rose said, 'Forty is a frighteningly pivotal age', and like many people, I started to panic that I would never turn my dreams into reality. These are my answers at that time:

Childhood dream? Ever since I went into hospital at the age of six, I dreamed of being a doctor.

Pursue or defer? Unable to pursue this, ever. When I discovered psychology, I changed to dreaming of becoming a psychotherapist. I managed to pursue this – slowly – by part-time study while living in Montreal, Canada, and then by undertaking a training analysis in Brussels, Belgium.

What held you back? Firstly, my father's unyielding refusal to allow me to go to university. (Younger readers should remember I am talking about a *pre*-feminist era.) Secondly, the need to earn a living and look after three children. Finally, returning to England where I have run out of money.

Who or what helped the most? Woody (a professor at McGill University) who believed in me, and persuaded me to keep trying. He also influenced my need to find the scientific underpinning to psychoanalytic theories, which is now making me feel uneasy about the path I am following.

I realised that I could make things happen if I was absolutely certain I was going in the right direction. But I had lost faith in the 'rightness' of Jungian theory, even though I had found the personal analysis valuable and illuminating. What I really dreamed of doing now was attending a university full-time and studying the most up-to-date scientific research. And when I had completed the rest of the exercises, I eventually found a way to do just that.

Elizabeth (age 63)
Dream? I was six when I wrote my first 'book' and sent it to my father, who was in Germany (during World War II). Hidden beneath the dream of helping people has always been the dream of Being a Writer.

Pursued or deferred? I have always written; I became a journalist in Montreal and kept my children by writing, translating and teaching. I was founding editor of *The Psychologist*, combining my Oxford degree and journalistic experience.

Held back? Definitely lack of self-confidence. I need to be asked, almost never offer to write articles, books, etc. Have written three novels, 12 short stories, three plays, all gathering dust on my shelves. Why? Perhaps it's fear. I may not be good enough.

Helped? My first editor on *The Montreal Star* gave me confidence (at the time). John (my present husband) encourages me, and Lise (my daughter) is a good critic. They make me feel I *can* write. I feel strong when what I have written seems to work.

I was astonished at how long this ambition had been simmering away beneath the surface, and how ready it was to break through given half a chance. I also realised that, whether through fiction or non-fiction, I wanted to write about everything I had learned over more than 40 years of studying psychology. My two dreams were coming together.

CHAPTER 4

Confronting Your Inner Demons

You've heard of walking through the valley of the shadow of death*, and struggling through this chapter will feel a bit like that. This is where things get rough. Dark clouds gather and you may hear wailing and the gnashing of teeth.

This chapter focuses on all the things that bother you, those pressures and demands that get in the way of your happiness, those fears that paralyse your thoughts and prevent you from achieving your dreams. You are not likely then to feel good. Life is unlikely to be looking sunlit at the end. You will probably not be hearing heavenly choirs, delicious odours of roses and honeysuckle are unlikely to assail your nose, and the taste in your mouth is unlikely to be sweet.

Nevertheless, toiling through this chapter is an essential step towards taking control of your life. It really is necessary to take a good hard look at how you see the difficulties in your way. You do need to listen to the voices that clamour in your mind so that you can find a way to shut them up.

Because this chapter is long and difficult to work through – for anyone, however generally happy and well-

---

* Psalm 23, verse 4, King James Authorised Version (also Revised Standard Version, 1952)

balanced they are – it is a good idea to choose a time when you are feeling strong and able to face up to unpleasant truths. Know that you *will* be able to get through this dark valley of shadows unharmed. But it does take strength and lots of courage to make your way through the darkness of your own fears, to listen to your own cruel demons and feel them claw at your heart. You know they are there. Now you need to find the courage to face them, look at them and hear them, so that you can discover how to make them go away.

So, once you have gathered all your strength, be brave. Have a go. Try to work through this chapter without stopping, so that you can really get the benefit of the exercises. Then move on to the more positive and enjoyable chapters that follow.

This is a particularly long chapter because I have given a lot of examples from other people. Obviously, your own discoveries are more important to you, but you may find that some of these examples resonate in your mind and give you further insight into your own difficulties.

exercise 7
vexations, plagues and harassments

List the things in your life that bother you most.

You will probably find that you have between three and six main items. If you find your list is a lot longer, see if you can put one or two items together to make a single category. For example, you might have listed *'mortgage, bills, money'* – the sort of thing anyone who is really worried about finances is inclined to do – so they could be grouped together as *'finances'* or *'money'*. Try to produce a manageable list of no more than six items.

Many of the items may well be the same as those you listed in Exercise 3 – *aspects of yourself you would like to change*. Many will not. It doesn't matter – just focus on the question 'What are the things in my life that bother me most?'

One Big Worry

You may find that everything adds up to one major worry that is dominating your life at this moment.

For many people, the central worry is upsetting others who are important to them. Jenny, for instance, hated being at university but didn't want to distress her mother by leaving. Diana worried about neglecting her children and her friends by devoting her energies to painting. Lynne was convinced that fulfilling her own ambitions would deprive her family. This sort of concern is shared by many people, especially women, as we will see in more detail a bit later. Worrying about other people can be very distressing, particularly once you have become an adult and taken on the responsibilities of a spouse, children or caring for an elderly and/or sick relative. Now you *know* that other people really do depend on you for money, time, physical and psychological care, and so on. How can you let them down?

Other major anxieties can be relationships and a sense that one has been rejected as 'not good enough' by important people. Frances and Stella describe different aspects of this, as we will see.

Double Trouble

A real double bind can arise when you have two major worries, and can do nothing about either without the other rearing its ugly head. Mark, for instance, was about to sit the Common Entrance Examination because his parents wanted him to go to public school, and he was scared of letting them down. He was convinced he was not clever enough to pass, so there wasn't any point in working, and he was refusing to study. That way he could always tell himself that he *could* have passed if only he'd been able to get down to learning – an attempt to protect his self-esteem that was having dire consequences. He was in trouble at school and at home, which is how we met in the first place.

Mark was in an agonising double bind: if he pleased his parents and teachers and buckled down to study, he'd have no escape when he failed his exams, as he was sure he would. Yet he was so terrified of actual failure, he couldn't sleep at night.

Mark's particular situation may be unusual, but the dread of failure is shared by many people, young and old. We need to recognise that children usually have a good reason when they defy parents or teachers – a good reason in terms of their own understanding and fears, that is. Mark did not *want* constant turmoil and conflict, but deep inside it felt safer than doing what other people asked.

Fear of failure may plague us throughout our lives. It can be especially painful at the end of a lifetime of struggle, when you feel, as Martin did, that your skills are no longer wanted by anyone. His list included '*insecurity, no money, society doesn't want me, loss of face and purpose*'. Lack of money becomes a major issue for older people who don't have occupational pensions, and both Elizabeth and Barbara were worried about this. But while everyone can understand the practical problems of financial insecurity, Martin expressed the more unbearable distress of feeling rejected by society as a whole just *because* he was ageing. All his experience of living appeared to have no value.

Does Your Age Make a Difference?

Age plays a large part in what distresses us at every stage in our lives. Teenagers are bothered both by hormones and fears of what might lie ahead. Young adults worry about relationships, mature adults are concerned about responsibilities and sometimes the realisation that they might never achieve something they can look back on with pride. Older people worry about the prospect of becoming incapacitated, dependent on others and unable to make choices through lack of money.

Tyler, the oldest person who has done this Life Planning Programme, listed *'failing physical powers, weakening memory, loss of concentration, tendency to rages'*. He said he was inclined to fly off the handle at trivial things, such as dropping a cup or banging into a table. Larger issues were much easier to deal with. Getting angry about trivia is a definite sign of stress or anxiety. Anyone who is worried about problems that seem to have no solution may find their irritability increases. Tyler's rages may well have a lot to do with his sense of increasing nearness to death and his desire to do more with his life. This is what the poet Dylan Thomas meant when he wrote:

Do not go gentle into that good night,
Old age should burn and rave at close of day;
*Rage, rage against the dying of the light.**

All the fears the people express here are realistic. This book is not an attempt to deny that relationships, unfulfilled ambitions, money, age and encroaching death can be serious concerns, nor does it try to pretend you do not have to find ways to deal with them. No – the purpose of this book is not to deny reality or create a fantasy world. It is to examine what each individual might realistically choose to do about their difficulties in the clear knowledge of who they are, and what skills and possibilities are available to someone brave enough to move on.

First, though, you need to discover what these fears and anxieties are saying to you.

exercise 8
the circle of demon voices

This is a very important exercise.

1. **Take a sheet of paper and draw a large circle.**
2. **Divide the circle up like a pie, giving each of your major worries an appropriate share of the circle.**
3. **Label each section.**
4. **Label the page 'My Circle of Demon Voices'.**
5. **Write alongside each section of the pie what that worry is saying to you.**

*Dylan Thomas, 'Do Not Go Gentle into that Good Night', 1952

Let your conscious mind defocus, sink down, go limp and receptive. Listen to those nasty critical voices and write down what you hear. Don't stop to argue or question – you need to be able to hear exactly what your inner critics are saying in the depths of your mind. Try not to feel silly about this unusual exercise. Just let those critical voices take over – and write down their unpleasant thoughts.

If you do this properly, you will almost certainly be feeling *awful*. Sometimes in a group session, one or two participants find themselves in floods of tears. This is distressing, but stick with it – it means you are doing it right. You wouldn't be in difficulties and looking for help in finding a way out if you didn't have some pretty negative ideas about yourself or your situation.

When you look at what you have written and find you have really heard what those inner voices say about you, you will probably see that they all add up to one general theme. In some way, you have failed or you are just not good enough, or you are a fraud or no one wants you.

Console yourself with the thought that you are not alone. This happens to *everyone*. Everyone has an inner critic – or two, or more – that undermines their self-confidence and makes them feel they might as well give up trying. *But don't stop now. This is as bad as it gets. If you have done this exercise properly, you will find it can only get better from now on.*

Let's look at some of the circles other people have created.

DOROTHY
'Don't be selfish'

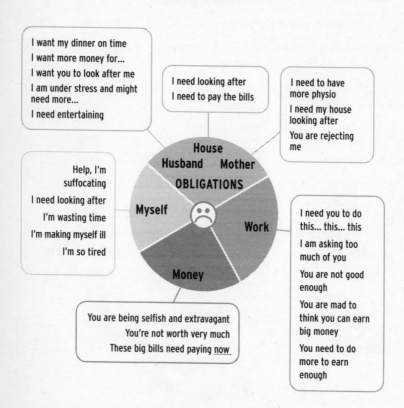

I want my dinner on time
I want more money for...
I want you to look after me
I am under stress and might need more...
I need entertaining

I need looking after
I need to pay the bills

I need to have more physio
I need my house looking after
You are rejecting me

House
Husband   Mother
OBLIGATIONS
Myself
Work
Money

Help, I'm suffocating
I need looking after
I'm wasting time
I'm making myself ill
I'm so tired

I need you to do this... this... this
I am asking too much of you
You are not good enough
You are mad to think you can earn big money
You need to do more to earn enough

You are being selfish and extravagant
You're not worth very much
These big bills need paying <u>now</u>

Dorothy's voices are all making demands: *'I want...'* and *'I need...'* This is how she experiences her husband, her mother, her house, her work. Deep inside her, their hassles never stop. Deeper still is the tiny voice of her own self crying out for help and attention. She does indeed feel suffocated by all the demands being made on her time and energies. Loudest of all is the voice that says, *'Don't think of yourself. That's being selfish.'* She didn't need to write it down.

'I hear it shouting at me all the time,' she said.

Money, of course, might be a way of getting more time for

herself – she might be able to pay someone to do some of her chores. But again her voices tell her she is not good enough to earn more money, and if she does spend any money to help herself, she is being selfish again. No wonder she is tired.

LYNNE
'You're not good enough'

You will be poor in old age
You will be a burden

Not good enough to make a living at growing things

You must dress the part...
Don't spend the money

Not enough money to make others happy

You don't fit in
You don't belong

If you spend money on greenhouses, you are depriving husband and son of what they want

MONEY

WORK

You're not good enough to be on the Main Board

Your children need the best education.
If you don't send them to private school, their lives will be <u>ruined</u>

FAMILY

Job wants your entire time
No time to do what you want

You're too old to find a new job
You're not good enough to find a job

Must have a nice house
Husband won't be happy in a 'commonplace' house

Lynne didn't draw any lines in her circle to divide it up into a pie. As you can see, all her worries merge into one another. She is indeed going round and round in circles inside her head.

In terms of career and money, Lynne is probably the most successful woman to take this course, yet even she feels she is '*not good enough*' to succeed. She earns a big salary, but this means she has to travel much of the time, so she feels constantly under pressure with no time for herself or her family. Nevertheless, she is convinced that her family *needs* her income, and if she doesn't devote herself to this demanding job, they won't have everything they require. Most important of all, she believes she *must* make enough money to send her children to private schools or they will not get the best education possible and their lives will be ruined.

Lynne knows what she wants to do. She is a skilled horticulturist and wants to spend more time growing exotica. However, she feels she could never make an adequate living doing this, and that she is just being selfish (again) whenever she spends money on this hobby. She would like to find a job that doesn't demand so much travel, but despite her success, feels '*too old*' and '*not good enough*'.

Hearing your inner critics saying you are 'not good enough' is the horrible fate of enormous numbers of people. If you have discovered this in your own inner demons, just remember *it is not The Truth* – it represents the fears that even the most successful among us have to contend with.

Fear of Failure

Floyd, is young, ambitious and about to take up a big promotion with salary to match.

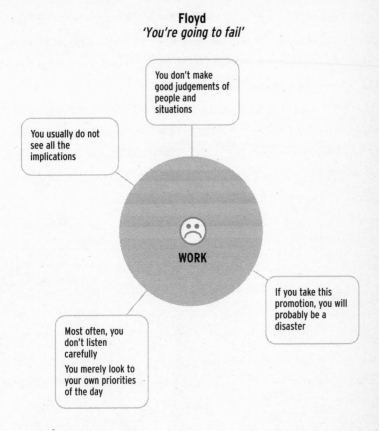

Floyd
'You're going to fail'

You don't make good judgements of people and situations

You usually do not see all the implications

WORK

If you take this promotion, you will probably be a disaster

Most often, you don't listen carefully

You merely look to your own priorities of the day

Floyd is scared. All he can hear in his head at the moment are voices telling him his bosses have got it wrong, that his judgement is weak and he'll never make the grade in the United States. He has no divisions in his circle because everything is in one great turmoil – it's not a pie, it's a stew.

While Floyd listens to those voices without knowing how to answer back, he will be unable to make any sensible decisions. But at least he knows quite clearly what it is he is afraid of. Just like the adolescent Mark we met at the beginning of this chapter, Floyd is afraid of failure.

Problems of Love

Fear of failure does not apply only to work, though. It can apply to relationships too, and Frances discovers that this is part of her difficulty.

FRANCES
'You're not enough'

The first and major thing Frances finds is that the man in her life is rejecting her *in her mind*. It is important to remember that all these voices are simply your own voices in your own mind. They are *not* the actual voices of the people you hear – they are your *interpretation* of what these people are saying to you. You need further information before you can know whether what you are hearing is really what is intended. So Frances hears him saying to her in her mind, *'You are my enemy'* and *'You are my scapegoat'*. Not surprisingly, she feels rejected by the one person she wants to feel close to.

At the same time, however, Frances finds another voice saying *'You don't let yourself belong'* and *'You stop spontaneity'*. And she realises that in truth she does not like to let go. She fears being vulnerable if she is not in control. A little later, Frances said: 'I really am always afraid that if I get what I want, I'll get hurt. I have to be able to withdraw.'

Is this you too? Loving someone never comes with guarantees, so you might get hurt. But at the same time, mutual love cannot exist without vulnerability – on both sides. That is why love can be both wonderful and terrifying at the same time.

However, Frances might be accurate in her interpretation of her lover's attitude. He may well be treating her as his enemy and scapegoat. This Circle of Demon Voices signals that something is seriously wrong in this relationship, and points to the areas where she needs to look more carefully.

When you are in an unhappy relationship, you do contribute your share. But as Robin Norwood pointed out so clearly in her book *Women Who Love Too Much*, this may be because you have chosen exactly the right person with whom to reproduce those miserable experiences you have learned to expect. The Circle of Demon Voices can alert you to the need to explore your own contribution to your distress.

Unwanted Childhood Legacies

Relationships are frequently a major source of worry. Stella's circle is a splendid example of the kinds of fears and suspicions that interfere with many people's happiness, especially for women.

Stella is beautifully presented, her hair carefully styled, her nails manicured, her deliberately casual clothes neatly fitted. She looks painstaking, meticulous, fastidious. And she is. She does not dare face the world without the armour of careful make-up, neat clothes, shining shoes. Deep inside

STELLA
'You're nothing but a fraud'

Younger people have more fun
Men don't like old women

Men will make you happy

All marriages don't work
You have to have a miracle to have a good one

Money makes you happy
Money gives you power

AGE

All men are selfish

MONEY   RELATIONSHIPS

Moneyed people are better than poor people

If you don't have a relationship you are not perfect

I can't have money because I have to be hard to get it!

TIME

Routine is everything
Time must not be wasted

Don't interrupt

If you don't have a clean house you are a slut
You have to give your kids 100% of the time
You have to feed people to nurture them

Women are subordinate to men
Women have legs to walk from the kitchen to the bedroom

Most people don't get what they want and they die unhappy

Women take men's jobs
Women who do what they want are hard and selfish

she believes she is not good enough for anyone really to like her, as her Circle of Demons shows, so she must protect herself by looking as though she is an acceptable person. But then, of course, she is a fraud, and if anyone were to get to know her, they would discover the truth and she would be lost again.

'I realise now,' she said, 'why people get the wrong impression of me. I never show them the real me, I wouldn't dare. But I do so hate the woman they see…' And she was in tears.

Why does Stella have this devastatingly poor self-image? We can see that she must have been brought up in a family that despised women. She told us it was her father who said that *'Women have legs to walk from the bedroom to the kitchen'*, an old-fashioned and seriously demeaning attitude to grow up with. Indeed, it appears she learned all the ideas that adorn her circle from her parents. Her parents' voices torment her, even into her 40s, because she has never before realised that she can separate herself from them, write these thoughts down, and see if they really are ideas she welcomes inside her head.

As a girl, she dreamed of escaping the prison of sub-servience that was all her parents offered. She was sure the way out was money, but money was for men. Money was for people who were better than her. Women who got money were hard and unfeminine. A whole series of double binds was created in Stella's mind as she listened to her parents. A strong-minded young woman, she left home, decided her parents' attitudes were totally unsuited to the modern world and, without realising it, buried their beliefs in the depths of her unconscious so that they could continue to torment her for the rest of her life.

This is one reason why the exercises in this chapter are so valuable. If you too have buried unwanted legacies from your childhood in your psyche, you may well find that some of them resurface in your own circle.

How to deal with them? Well, the first step is to recognise they are there. Look at them as though they do not belong to you. They simply exist as powerful ideas in your head. *They do not have the power of truth.*

The second step is to get rid of them. We will look at different techniques for discarding unwanted rubbish, and various other ways of coping with demon voices in Chapter 9. Meanwhile, just note that this stuff is there. You may find that just becoming aware that these ideas are left-over detritus from your childhood will rob them of their power, and they will begin to wither and fall away.

Braving Your Shadow

Let us look at what Barbara calls 'a biggy'. She accuses herself of hypocrisy, which is a pretty big failing in most people's eyes. However, the importance of this section for you is not so much this particular fault, but the general issue of whether you have discovered a major flaw in your personality and what to do about it.

Barbara does not tell us why she feels hypocritical, though if we look at the detail of her circle, we can see her Demon Voices call her *'lazy, intolerant and morally weak'*, and that these disparaging comments are linked to her relationships with her two daughters and her friends. Perhaps she

BARBARA
'You're guilty'

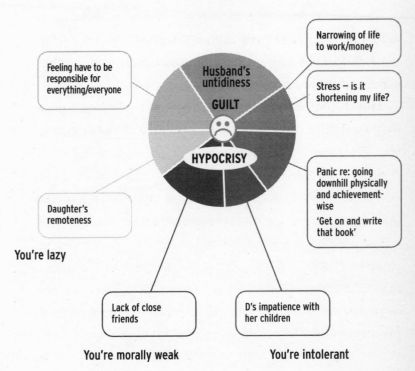

The Hypocrisy is a 'biggy' — why minimise it? Confront it.

feels she never tells them her true thoughts, and so these relationships are fundamentally sterile.

Many people also find that they are required to behave insincerely, even deceitfully, at work. This can undermine their feeling of integrity. If you find yourself in this situation, it may be time to consider a change of occupation. To feel forced into pretence and hypocrisy is to negate your own value as a human being. You need to ensure you can live according to your own standards of morality, not succumb to other people's when they are lower than yours.

But Barbara is a mature woman, and it could equally be that she is trying to confront and deal with the dark side of her nature. All of us have a dark side, what Carl Jung called 'the Shadow'. The Shadow contains all those aspects of ourselves we don't really want to acknowledge, all those traits we hate in other people and couldn't possibly accept are ours. Dealing with the Shadow is difficult and takes a long time, partly because we really don't want to see it, and partly because the Shadow has greater power to operate when we are unaware it is there, and so actually resists our efforts to confront it.

Let me give you an example of the Shadow at work. Libraries everywhere suffer from book thieves, and nowhere more so than at universities. Which group of students would you guess to be the worst offenders? The librarian at my university told me those who steal the highest number of books are students of divinity. I was astonished, until I understood about the Shadow.

The problem is that every good quality has its other – bad – side. Divinity students spend a great deal of time thinking, writing and praying about leading a good, moral life. For them, acknowledging any aspects of their own personality that are not good and moral may undermine their belief in their calling. So these not-so-good aspects get pushed back into the subconscious, ignored, and then flourish in darkness. When a student of divinity steals a book from a university library, he is hardly aware of it. Somehow it becomes acceptable, because he really knows that he is not the sort of person who would steal books. The human psyche has a wonderful way of deceiving itself.

Barbara is determined not to deceive herself any more. She wants to confront the nasty and unacceptable parts of her psyche. Her sense of being hypocritical is, of course, a major part of her feeling guilty. Nothing she does is right, and at her age, she 'should know better', yet still she fails all those who are important to her – and herself.

If you have reached this stage in life, you may have found that some major, deadly sin has appeared in your Circle of Demon Voices. This will certainly bring you moments of self-doubt and even self-loathing. But remember that you are not alone. We all have that dark side, so don't despair. The way can be difficult when you truly discover your Shadow, but you *can* learn to live with it. And this discovery may help you finally fulfil your most important dreams.

The Problem of Trivia

Like so many people we meet in this book, Barbara has a secret ambition. Yet again, like so many, she doesn't have time to indulge her own desires. She feels trapped on a treadmill, needing to earn a living, yet finds that the relationships she believes should bring her pleasure simply increase the guilt. And looming over all this unhappiness is her husband's untidiness.

Why should a husband's untidiness take up so large a portion of Barbara's circle? We all know how another person's habits can drive you mad, especially when you live with them. If one of you is tidy-minded and the other is not, you have a recipe for constant niggling irritation, and it can get so bad that it overwhelms everything. Especially if you are a woman who feels that keeping the house clean and tidy is *your* job. Especially if you are tired and stressed. This is definitely molehill into mountain stuff, but to the sufferer it feels truly momentous.

Most of us must have been in a situation at some time when a small thing transforms you from an apparently normal, sensible human being into a hopeless, snivelling wreck. You are trying to cope with a whole series of major worries, and someone coming along with one more thing for you to deal with, however trivial, can be like the last straw on the camel's back – insignificant in itself but potentially destructive in effect. An untidy husband, a recalcitrant child, a car that won't start – any such thing can tip you over the top.

So be careful. If you find yourself in a permanently stressful situation, do take precautions. Bursting into tears or losing your temper may make you feel bad, but a car accident might be infinitely worse. And car accidents are exactly what occur when people are over-stressed, as Barbara is.

Unfulfilled Ambitions

You will see from the next – and final – example that busily getting on with a job, however successfully, when you have an unfulfilled secret ambition can lead to serious stress and undermine your confidence.

ELIZABETH
'Really you're a failure'

This circle is mine, drawn in the summer of 2000, after a period in which, objectively, I had experienced quite a number of successes. I had been approached by the University of Exeter to give lectures and workshops; I had been asked to act as Expert Witness in a number of distressing childcare and custody cases; my book on the psychology of argument had gone into paperback and I had received letters and cards from former clients, bringing me up-to-date on their now happier lives, and thanking me for my help. But I didn't feel like a success inside. I was working long hours and neglecting my friends and family.

My body constantly ached, and somehow I never seemed to make enough money. I felt as though everything I did and tried to do was doomed.

I remember the sinking of my heart when I realised that the summary of what my inner critics were saying was: *'You are a failure.'* This devastating sense of inadequacy was undermining everything.

It was true that I still had a mouldering scrap of childhood rubbish to dispose of. My father had written in my autograph book when I was 14, 'Nothing is so demeaning as failure. Except success.' This intensely discouraging maxim resulted from his own discovery that getting what he thought he wanted made him even more unhappy. I had known his story, but had not realised until I did this exercise that his depressing words still reverberated in my unconscious. Better to think of myself as a failure than risk the disaster of success.

But most of my demons' undermining criticisms came out of an escalating awareness that I was spending all my time *not* doing what I wanted to do, and that the fateful sister with the scissors might soon cut the thread of my life. What I really wanted to do, and have always wanted to do, was write books. One consequence of the growing success of my practice as a consultant psychologist was that I had no time to write at all.

Perhaps this is happening to you? Very often we can embark on a promising career, but find after some years that a part of ourselves remains unfulfilled. This was what was happening to me. I love psychology. I think it is the best subject anyone can ever study, and I really enjoy giving lectures and workshops so that others can discover it too. I enjoy helping people with therapy. I find being an Expert Witness very worthwhile, and know that it is a valuable service. But somehow I still felt I was not taking account of what I myself wanted, deep down. That, of course, is what this Life Planning Programme is all about.

Move on Quickly

Now you have given your inner critics a chance to air their views, the time has come to set them aside for a while. Nasty, carping voices that they are, they must not be allowed to remain the only thing filling your mind. We will deal with them later. So put this Circle of Demon Voices away inside your folder, and go on quickly to the next chapter. Think about the next exercise before you take a break.

CHAPTER 5

The Pleasure Principle

The exercise in this chapter will be much more fun to do than the last one, and should be tackled as soon as you have finished dealing with your Circle of Demon Voices. It is a serious error to spend too long listening to those carping critics, and you need to do this next exercise as an antidote to the poison they are pouring into your mind.

So, quickly, turn your mind to some of the good things in your life.

exercise 9
all about pleasure

What gives you pleasure?

What are you doing when you feel alive?

Write down everything you can think of.

Teresa said, 'Oh that was easy.' She read us a long list of things that gave her pleasure and made her feel alive: '*running in the rain, playing sports, having friends round, playing the flute, having a candlelit bath...*' The mood around the table lifted, and the people in her group started smiling. Laughter chased away the blues of the previous exercise. Pleasure in life can be contagious, and Teresa is fortunate in being able to enjoy so many things.

But she is not alone. While her pleasures might be summed up as *'sensuous freedom'* (her words), other people feel alive in different ways. Allow these other lists of pleasures to inspire your own. See if you can find one word or phrase that summarises what makes *you* feel alive. Victoria (you have not met her before) described her own pleasures as *'standing bare-breasted in the wind'*, a wonderfully vivid image, though perhaps too chilly for everyone's taste.

For **Lynne**, pleasure in being alive was summed up as *'participating – doing it'*, and she loved:
Plants and soil
Laughing with my son
Dancing in the kitchen
Making the children dance with me
Giving presentations
Making things happen
Complicated problem-solving

Wendy said she felt alive when combining *sensual pleasure with communication*. Her list included:
Dancing
Signing for the deaf
Languages – the way words are so different
Singing
Kissing and cuddling boyfriend
My children
Theatre
Making things
Music
The feel of nice clothes

For *Frances*, pleasure was *'freedom'*, and though her list
included *'being with friends'*, her pleasures were mainly
solitary:

Nature

Being alone

Meditation

Being still – non-doing

Music

Extreme weather conditions

There are so many ways of enjoying being who you are.
Most people can produce lengthy lists of things that give
them pleasure and make them glad to be alive.

Recently I came across an article in *She* magazine
entitled 'Comfort and Joy', in which they asked people –
famous and not-so-famous – to describe their own ways of
finding joy at Christmas time. Again, the variety of sources
of pleasure was enormous:

- **When it starts getting cold outside, curling up on the
  sofa with my huge cashmere shawl.**
- **Closing the front door after I get in from work,
  standing still and just listening to the silence.**
- **I love spending hours wrapping my presents beautifully – the outside often looks better than the actual
  gift.**
- **First thing every morning, I pad quietly into my little
  boys' bedroom and take a peek at them. Just the sight
  of them makes me ecstatic with happiness.**
- **Being with my family after I've been away. That and a
  glass of champagne.**

- Going for a walk on a winter evening when it's getting dark, and the snow sparkles under the streetlights – you'd need a heart of stone not to be moved.

To quote the *She* editor, 'Joy isn't complicated. Comfort doesn't cost. It's a smell, a taste, a feeling…simple things.'

Having Difficulties?

If you find you really can't think of things that make you feel good, and nothing in these lists made by other people brings the slightest frisson of enjoyment to you, then you may be seriously depressed.

Try thinking about each of the five senses in turn – one of them at least should be a source of pleasure to you.

- What do you see that gives you pleasure? What feasts your eyes?
- What sounds bring you happiness?
- When do you get a glow out of things that touch your body? (And yes, having sex does count!)
- What tastes delight you?
- What smells, scents, perfumes please you?

But pleasure doesn't need to be sensual. Our thoughts can stimulate our brains to promote physical wellbeing too. (Unfortunately, the opposite is also true, and negative thoughts can lead to negative effects, but that is what focusing on pleasure is designed to avoid.) Most people find they include in their lists those uniquely human qualities of intelligence and laughter. So also ask yourself:

- What makes you feel alive and glad to be exercising your brain?
- What are the things that really make you laugh?

If after all this you still feel you enjoy nothing, really nothing, then please go to your doctor and tell her or him you are miserable and need help.

Everyone who has taken this Life Planning Programme with me has been able to make a list of things that give them pleasure. Even Martin, whose first reaction was, 'I can't do that'. Martin's frustration and anger at not being able to do many of the things he enjoyed in the past were uppermost in his mind. But persuaded to have a go, he came up with the following:

Martin
Achieving something worthwhile
Helping people
Being independent
Being self-sufficient
DIY and modelling
Writing
Thinking

You may have noticed that many of the pleasures people have listed can be enjoyed alone. This is important and valuable, for if your happiness and enjoyment of life depend entirely on other people, you are always vulnerable and can never be content to be alone. This does not deny the importance of other people. We are, after all, social beings, and loneliness and isolation can be painful. Indeed, solitary confinement is one of the worst forms of psychological torture.

But life is lived within our own bodies. All our senses – sight, hearing, touch, taste, smell – contribute to our capacity to experience joy, delight and happiness. The ability to find pleasure in being *you*, and feel happiness inside your own skin is crucial to your wellbeing.

Pleasure as the Key to Mental Health

I have discovered that the key to mental health is to ensure that your mind and body have at least 30 minutes in every day during which they can relax from the demands of everyday life. The best way to do this is through sensations of pleasure. Our body chemistry requires this. Just as we need sleep to sort out the experiences of the day and reorganise our memory banks, so too we need to restore the chemical balances in our bodies by allowing the senses to relay messages of wellbeing to our brain.

While we're busy dealing with our lives, our brain keeps us alert and ready for action by calling for that well-known stress hormone, adrenalin. But when it's time to stop, if we don't send the right messages to our brains, that 'fight or flight' hormone will continue to circulate in our blood, preventing us from relaxing properly, even interfering with our sleep. If we continue to live with high levels of adrenalin, our health will suffer. The best way to avoid adrenalin overload is through pleasure.

Pleasure alerts our brain to reduce adrenalin and increase the output of serotonin, a natural chemical that

The Pleasure Principle

Daily Prescription: 30 minutes of pleasure

reinforces a general feeling of calm and happiness. Serotonin is Nature's Prozac – an ecologically sound self-medication under our own control and without any nasty side effects.

Pleasure is important. Everyone needs pleasure. You should make sure that you do something that gives you pleasure for at least 30 minutes every day. It doesn't matter what it is, so long as it brings you a sense of wellbeing inside your skin. This is why you need to know what kind of activities – or non-activities, 'non-doing' in Frances's words – give you a sense of being alive.

Now I do know that some of you may feel it is wrong to indulge yourself, that you don't deserve to enjoy life. But if you wait until you think you deserve happiness, then you may never feel ready to have any. Remember those carping critical voices that are going on at us all the time deep inside our heads. They can make sure that you never believe it is time to think about yourself.

Be aware of how you prevent yourself from achieving a state of serene calmness. Take note of all the times you find some reason why – just today – you can't manage to indulge in some form of sensual pleasure. All of us do this. But it is a mistake. Thirty minutes out of 24 hours is a tiny proportion, and we can all find that much time to devote to our own selves if we really try.

Remember your list of sources of pleasure. Look at it regularly and select at least one item from it every day. You will feel wonderful after a while, and not the least bit guilty. Because it is what you *need*. And everyone in your life will benefit.

CHAPTER 6

Picturing Your Life

Here you are asked to draw on a different part of your brain. Instead of listening to voices in your mind, this exercise invites you to use your visual imagination. What sort of images are conjured up when you look at your life? How could you summarise your life in visual terms? You will discover that the simplest drawing, even a diagram, can reveal aspects of your own life that you need to know if you are to stop dreaming and start living.

exercise 10
drawing pictures
Draw a picture of your life.

This chapter is full of diagrams and pictures so it may be very tempting to look at how others have depicted their life. But before going any further, just think about how *you* would draw a picture of your own life.

The ability to draw – or, more usually, a conviction that one just *can't* draw – is unimportant. What you are trying to do is discover how you see your life up to now. Remember I mentioned Diana's picture in Chapter 3? She painted a vivid image of how she saw herself at that time: a painter, fenced in by all the people in her life – her children, her husband, her friends.

Some people draw cartoon strips, depicting important episodes over a lifetime. Others just produce diagrams.

Have a go yourself. If you need inspiration, well, have a look at the following examples.

Life as a Time Line

The simplest approach is a time line. This is how both Irene and Tyler drew their life pictures.

IRENE

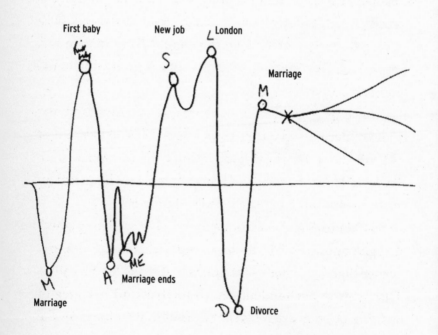

Irene sees her life as a series of peaks and deep depressions. Every time she reaches a happy place, life comes along and clobbers her, leaving her tumbling down to a new low.

In this picture she sees herself as starting out at a mid-point, then falling steeply when she makes a mistaken marriage. Each of the peaks and troughs is labelled: the first high point is her first baby, which she said made her very happy. Then her marriage ends, and she goes up again, finding a job and moving to London, both of which make her happy and glad to be alive. But then comes a rapid and steep decline to her divorce, which apparently was the worst time in her life. 'No one who has ever been through a divorce would recommend it to anyone else,' she says. But she remarries, and more happily, so her second marriage is another high point. Now she is at a crossroads, marked X, trying to decide which way she should go to remain at a high level. She is hopeful, but not confident of making the right choice.

Those peaks and troughs represent a highly dramatic view of her personal tribulations as well as an element of self-mockery. As she completed her drawing, she said, 'Woooh! I knew my life was a soap opera, but this is ridiculous. Look, I've actually reached Crossroads.'

Her amusement was contagious and everyone laughed. Laughter appears to be an important part of Irene's life, and comes high up in her list of things that make her feel alive. Discovering her tendency to dramatise and her love of making people laugh becomes important to Irene by the end of this Life Planning Programme, as we will see.

Tyler's approach is very similar, but his peaks and troughs are not quite as dramatic. He too labels the high points: the first is a boyhood triumph, the second when he won a

TYLER

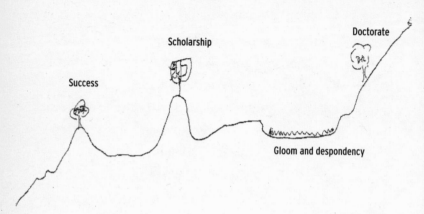

scholarship to Oxford University (what looks like a tankard of beer is apparently his college crest!) Evidently he spent much of his adult life in a Slough of Despond, but then climbed out, went back to university and got a doctorate, and apparently has not stopped climbing. A very positive picture, rising to the edge of the page, shows Tyler is optimistic about life at this stage.

He made a discovery too: 'I had never quite realised before how achievement-oriented I have always been.'

Life as a Graph

Floyd gives us a more elaborate form of timeline, one undoubtedly influenced by his experience in business where graphs of different lines are common.

You can see that he has labelled each of the lines. He sees his earnings rising rapidly in parallel with experience, and his energy remains mainly constant or better. His satisfaction with his life, however, is not keeping pace, while his self-confidence is dropping.

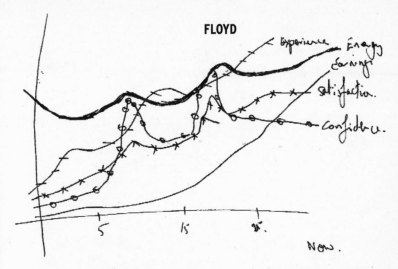

FLOYD

Floyd knew he felt like this – to a certain extent. But until he actually drew the graph for himself, and tried to express how he really saw his life, he was not fully aware of how his happiness and self-confidence were ebbing away. He saw quite clearly then what had led him to undertake the Life Planning Programme.

Finding Your Inner Landscape

Rose combines the notion of time line and a depiction of herself. She drew her life as a continuous series of mountains to climb.

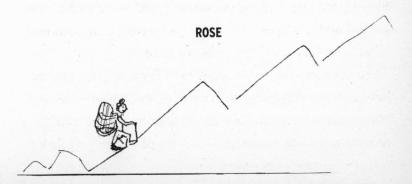

ROSE

Here she is, steadily climbing alone, an enormous pack on her back, the mountains stretching ahead, ever higher. She looks cheerful enough, and determined, but the going does look tough.

Rose said she knew she felt as though she 'could never rest on her laurels', but hadn't quite realised before how far the mountains stretched ahead in her mind. She decided she needed to find a way to change the landscape of her imagination.

Life as a Strip Cartoon

Many people combine the time line with pictures, and create a cartoon strip with small scenes from all the important events in their lives. Jenny has produced a lovely example, and even if we can't follow all the different events (because she has not told us everything), we can see that she has illustrated her life from birth to her 18th birthday. That, it appears, was a crucial moment for Jenny because she believed she was then an adult, and might choose for herself.

She starts with herself as a baby in the pram. Then we see various aeroplanes that took her around the world, and the different kinds of places she lived in. She shows her happy family splitting up. Then we find her first love, and his tears as she goes off to university. We see her looking miserable surrounded by pens, paper and books. We see her in a happy family again, and Christmas, leading to that all-important birthday when she believes she can decide what she really wants to do.

JENNY

Time Standing Still

Dorothy left out the time line altogether and produced an overall image of how she feels her life is now. She used coloured pencils, and each of the colours appears to be significant (though sadly not reproducible here).

The first thing we can see is that Dorothy has given herself no face, no eyes to see, no mouth to tell, no ears to hear, and no legs to walk away. She is centre-stage, but all she feels is pain and oppression. This is a very sad image.

This is Dorothy's own explanation of the picture:

'The central figure is me with a black cloud over me of worry and responsibility and pain inside (both physical and emotional). Orange figures (on left) are my husband

DOROTHY

and my mother, both asking a lot from me, and giving something in return. The brown squiggles are the burden of money, work, bills etc. Turquoise is my 'spiritual' colour, so the blue and yellow (above centre and right) stand for the work I am doing with meditation, reading, reiki etc, which brings me a lot of joy, peace and hope. This helps me continue to feel love (hearts) for the 'responsibility' side of my life and gives me hope it will all work out. The big heart is how important I think love should be, and on the right are books for my inspiration, and lots of friends and people I meet like you who are extending love, help and support. A lot of empty space – which I think means that a lot is missing. I'm still working on bringing the pieces together to make my ideal life.'

Note that Dorothy did not fully *know* all this when she started drawing her picture of her life. She discovered some important insights as she was working on it, and more afterwards as she showed it to me and gave her interpretation.

This is the value of creating an image of your life as you see it. Aspects emerge that you know about at one level, but are not entirely aware of until you actually see what you have drawn.

Taking Snapshots

A similar attempt to create a single picture as a sort of snapshot of her life led Stella to produce not one but three pictures of her life: her childhood, her young adult life and now.

STELLA

1. Childhood   *2. Young Adult*

Her first picture is in pencil, 'which is probably significant', she said. She says she did not have a happy childhood, but she looks pretty strong, standing four-square with a toy drum. The second picture is in pencil too, but with touches of colour added – the letter for WORK coloured lightly in yellow because she enjoyed it, a series of little red hearts surrounding the aeroplane, which represents a lost love, and a big red heart on her sleeve.

3. Now

The image of her life now is in coloured pencil, which is difficult to reproduce, but presents a much happier picture. She and her husband stand hand-in-hand, with their young son, and a big heart symbolising love above them like the sun. She has drawn their home on the bottom left, a tree in spring-time on the right, and a stream teeming with fish – both major symbols of burgeoning life – and the butterfly that appeared in both the earlier pictures is now in colour. She worked on, drawing a path to their future which went over the page, and there she drew a large butterfly in beautiful colours, and a great arrow up to the stars and moon.

Earlier, Stella said she was feeling angry, lonely and miserable. But deep inside, her image of her present life is very positive. Unlike Dorothy, who puts on a brave face but whose picture shows she is oppressed by depression and misery, Stella feels she now has a deeply satisfying life, which she can choose to make better by taking action for herself.

Finding the Meaning

You can see that there are many ways in which people choose to picture their lives. None of them is the 'right' way. Each one has a purpose for the person whose choice it is. Your own image should come out of your psyche, and therefore be right for *you*.

If you allow your unconscious some free rein, and draw without too much interference from your rational mind (which would like to prevent your imagination running away with you), you will produce an image that should bring you insight into your present situation.

I have done this exercise at various stages of my life, and each time I used a different technique. The first was a simple time line of peaks and troughs, very much like Irene's; then a feeble attempt at a cartoon strip; and finally, I produced an overall picture of how I see my life now. Here it is.

ELIZABETH

I realised, once I saw what I had done, that my life is very much the way I thought I wanted it. And it is static. There I am, at my desk, with books and computer, with my husband at my side. My past is represented by my children and grandchildren who are happily getting on with their own lives, not depending on me, and I see I have included a clumsy depiction of my daughter Akita's exceptional sugar sculpture which I admire. In the corner is my very steep garden, which is my preferred approach to regular exercise. And there is the cat. When I looked at my picture of my life as it is right now, I thought, 'I am a very fortunate woman'.

But that static image also showed me just why I was feeling frustrated. It included all my important past, and pleasant present, but showed no promise for the future.

Perhaps you have reached a similar stage to me, or recognise yourself more easily in Diana's situation, fenced in by other people's demands and expectations. Or maybe you relate more to Floyd, fearing failure in the future, or Irene, at a road junction without a map. Whatever your picture of your life, the important thing is to be aware of *how you see you*. It doesn't matter what anyone else says about your situation. It is how *you* see your life that counts.

Where are the Demons?

Once you have completed your picture, dig out that nasty Circle of Demon Voices again. Are the demons in your picture? Or have you created an image which leaves them out?

This is a significant moment, in which you discover whether and to what extent you have pictured your inner demons. Whatever the answer, it can be important to you in the next chapters.

Floyd's picture is an exact representation of how he *feels* about his life right now, and his worries and fears do appear in graphic form. This is a good example of how a very rational man can analyse his inner feelings. Using a graphic technique with which he is very familiar, he makes his feelings concrete, so that he can see and discover them fully. His demon voices are part of his everyday life, and created in his current situation – so the feelings they engender (lack of self-confidence, growing unhappiness) are depicted here. This means they need to be countered by active measures, and the exercises and techniques in the following chapters will help do just that.

Dorothy too finds her demons are part of her picture, and therefore part of what is true for her today. However, on her left (a significant place for inner change) and above her (also significant) are symbols of what gives her hope. So she has been able to picture an appreciably large proportion of her life very positively, and this can give her the strength to fight her demons more effectively.

Pictures like Irene's are more difficult to interpret in this way. I understand the crossroads as a sign that she is aware of demons lurking, but is not quite sure whether they represent rubbish or whether they are central aspects of her life today. In my own picture, too, the demons are lurking in the background, preventing action. So I can wallow in the pleasure of having a loving husband and children and grandchildren, enjoy my reputation as a psychologist and take pleasure in my garden, but I know that I need to move on, out of this lovely but static situation and do something positive about publishing my books. Those lurking demons need to be countered and rendered harmless by the various exercises and techniques in the following chapters.

Those whose pictures are essentially happy, though, may find that many – perhaps most – of their demons represent rubbish that can simply be discarded.

Stella presents an excellent example of someone whose demons could be exorcised to allow her to enjoy the happy life she pictures. In Chapter 9, we will discover what Stella – and you – can do to rid herself – yourself – of parents' or teachers' tormenting voices.

CHAPTER 7

Discovering Your Personal Powers

Now the time has come to examine all the skills, abilities and aptitudes that you personally have at your disposal. These are manifestations of your personal powers. When you are fully aware of what you are good at and what you do well, you will see more clearly how to direct your powers towards goals that will allow you to stop dreaming and start living.

exercise 11
identifying your strengths

What do you do well?
What are you good at?
Make a list of as many things as possible, under both headings.

You may feel both the above headings are the same, but ponder the question in both ways because it might inspire you to think of other aspects of your abilities. Some of the items on your list may already have appeared on your list of *'things you are'* in Exercise 1, Chapter 3. If you included skills and abilities in your verbal self-portrait, that's splendid, but please list these and other talents here too, on a new sheet of paper.

This exercise is designed to help you explore those powers that lie hidden in your psyche so that you can understand and appreciate what you do really well, what you are good at, where your natural talents lie. We all have weaknesses – they are like the dark side of the moon, the flip side of the coin – so we need to know how to protect our weaknesses by using our strengths. Give your mind an opportunity to be creative with your knowledge, skills and talents so that you can draw on all your special powers when you come to make changes in your life.

When you are completely satisfied that you have thought of everything you can do, like to do, are skilled at doing – even things you would like to learn to do because you know you would be good at them – then the time has come to consider what these skills tell you about yourself in relation to the world.

Are You a Square Peg or a Round One?

Let's look at two people who are just like the proverbial square pegs trying to fit into round holes: Mark and Jenny. It's not surprising that both these young people are in trouble because their parents are apparently urging them to do something for which they have the wrong skills. Their stories might illuminate your own difficulties. We all have strengths in particular directions, and it is a psychological fact that individuals tend to use their intelligence in different ways.

Mark said that he is *'good with people, good at making friends. I like making people laugh. People think I'm good at that'*. If you have the ability to make friends, entertain them, make them laugh, you should realise this is an enormous asset that not many people have. Mark's tension eased as he realised that this is a real talent. He would often rescue clumsy newcomers who lacked the gift he has in such strong measure. Teachers, alas, are inclined to distrust the popular boy who appears to prefer clowning to knuckling down to study, but Mark needs to know what his strengths are as well as what others perceive to be his weaknesses. Jenny, too, appears to have developed 'people skills' to a high degree, and her strongest motivation is *'to get along with others'*.

So because Mark and Jenny are skilled in understanding people, it is quite probable they find the more formal logic of science and mathematics and academic study much more difficult to grasp. Understanding people and understanding science use essentially opposite kinds of logic.

Thinking and Feeling Types

This is one aspect of Carl Jung's theory of psychological differences, which I will explain as simply and briefly as I can. Jung argued there are two opposing ways of evaluating the world we live in, and both have their own internal logic: one is what he called *Thinking*, and deals in rational logic and cause and effect; the other is what he called *Feeling*, and deals in the logic of values. Mark and Jenny are Feeling persons, and so they are very likely to find much of their work at school or university difficult, wherever it calls on their weaker skills of rational Thinking.

> **Thinking Type**
> Likes formal logic, cause and effect
> Rational, tries to work out logical outcomes
> Objective, detached
> Looks for information before making decisions
> Enjoys problem-solving
> Assumes everyone should be able to follow line of
>   reasoning
> Likes discussion and argument
> May be good at maths, science, engineering
> May be baffled by emotions

Mark has the additional difficulty of not fitting in to the stereotypical view of male and female: males are *supposed* to be good at rational thinking, and not good at the logic of feelings. As I have pointed out in my book, *War of Words: Women and Men Arguing*, being cast in a stereotyped gender role when you just know that you don't fit that picture at all can make you want to scream with frustration. Poor Mark was driven to near despair as he struggled to fulfil his parents' and his teachers' demands that he be good at what was for him a baffling way of thinking. No wonder he was convinced he was not intelligent enough to pass exams. He *is* intelligent – above average in fact – but his preferred evaluating approach will make him better at subjects such as literature, history and perhaps even psychology, rather than formally logical subjects like maths and science.

Feeling Type

Uses value judgements in choices

Good at the logic of human feeling

Empathetic

Listens rather than asking questions

Needs to know how other people see a situation

Tends to assume others will reciprocate

Rarely insists on own way

Dislikes conflict, seeks harmony

May feel bamboozled by rational argument

May be afraid of science and maths

Jenny too is well above average intelligence, and her people skills help with languages. However, this does not mean that she can be happy struggling with the kind of academic, disciplined approach needed at university which calls on a kind of logic she doesn't fully understand. Knowing this, she should be able to move on from castigating herself because she dislikes academic study – as it's her weak side, why would she enjoy it? – to find something that combines her skills with people and other abilities.

It is very useful to know which is your preferred way of evaluating and making decisions. If you are a Thinking person, you probably try to weigh up the pros and cons, ask a lot of questions, try to work out logical outcomes, and can be very critical of those who fail to understand the rightness of your way of going about things. If you are a Feeling person, on the other hand, you are much more likely to trust your own responses to a situation, and to use value judgements in your choices. Where a decision involves other people, you need to know they are all happy with what is decided, and you are liable to go along with others rather than insist on your own preference.

Many of you will recognise yourself in one of these descriptions. However, many of you will not, because you know you use *both* ways of reaching decisions. Your response may well depend on your age. As far as we can tell, we are all born with a tendency to prefer one particular way of evaluating the world, but can develop the opposite ability to a certain extent as we mature. Mark and Jenny are young people and we would not expect them to be able to use their weaker Thinking ability adequately. This is a pity because that is precisely the ability that schools and universities so often require. This developmental lag undoubtedly contributes to the unhappiness of many young people.

Sensation and Intuition Types

As well as opposing ways of evaluating and deciding, Jung found there are two opposing ways of perceiving the world in the first place. Obviously, we must take in information about the world via our five senses, but just as we know that some people are touchy-feely, others watch and others listen, so we seem to have different ways of focusing on the outer world.

You have all heard of 'not seeing the wood for the trees'. Well, some people tend to see each individual tree in detail; other people tend to see the whole wood, and never get down to noticing the separate elements and features that

Sensation Type
'Tree' people who are aware of detail
Efficient detailed perception by all senses
Focus on what is 'real', tangible, actual
Organised, tidy, dislikes muddle
Likes to know facts, hates to go beyond what is
  known
Practical, likes to make things work
Learns through practical experience
Likes traditional ways of doing things

fascinate the others. The *tree* people, those who see the details, are using what Jung calls the *Sensation* faculty: their senses efficiently inform them of every attribute, as though using a zoom lens on a camera. Obviously, if you are focusing in close, you are hardly likely to see the big, overall picture. The *wood* people, on the other hand, very rarely see the minutiae because their camera is in wide focus, and specific details are blurry. They are using what Jung calls the *Intuition* faculty.

If you don't already know which of these faculties you tend to favour – and many people will be reading this with a sense of recognition – one method of finding out is to think of what you do well *and* what you do badly.

Stella, for instance, wrote *'neat and tidy, organised'* among her skills. For these to be strong abilities, she is almost certainly a Sensation person. Intuition people find they tend to create untidiness, even chaos around them,

> **Intuitive Type**
> 'Wood' people who are aware of the overall
>   picture
> Often not immediately aware of sensory input
> Likes to find connections, wider meanings
> Loves brainstorming
> Often 'senses the mood' of a meeting or group
> May 'know' things without being able to say why
> Tends to be untidy, may appear to work in chaos
> Likes new ideas, change for its own sake

and that *things* are a constant nuisance. But Stella told us she is good at keeping things in order and hates muddle: Intuition people tend to thrive where disorder is tolerated.

So, what is your preferred way of gathering information about the world? Sensation people rely on concrete facts, dislike speculating beyond what is known, focus on detail and are good at learning by 'doing'. Many scientists, engineers, car mechanics, gardeners, builders and craftspeople are Sensation people. Charles Darwin spent 20 years collecting enough evidence for him to feel sure enough to publish his theory of evolution. His Intuition was his weakest side, as well as the source of his creativity, so although he eventually produced one of the world's most revolutionary ideas, his strong Sensation side would not permit him to go public until the facts he had gathered were overwhelming. Even then, he was precipitated into going public before he wanted to by a young upstart scientist, Alfred Russell Wallace, who had relied on his intuitive grasp of the patterns he observed in nature, and actually published two papers on 'the survival of the fittest' and 'evolution by natural selection' based on a small fraction of Darwin's painstaking accumulation of evidence.

Each way of perceiving the world has its strengths and weaknesses. Intuition people tend to 'know' things and are not always able to explain why, which can infuriate strong Sensation types. Intuitives are more likely to 'go beyond the information given', see connections and patterns; as indeed, did young Wallace who threatened to pip Darwin to the post. Intuitives are good at 'sensing the mood' of a meeting, and pick up information about people without being able to explain how. Many psychotherapists and counsellors are Intuitives, as are successful entrepreneurs like Richard Branson.

This does not mean Intuition is the same as fey. In fact, you should be very cautious if you feel you have 'other-worldly' intuitions. While it is true that strong Intuitives seem to have a sort of sixth sense that allows them to intuit knowledge about people and events in a way difficult to explain, not all psychic experiences relate to a true reality. Sometimes, belief in psychic phenomena can be a sign of some deep-seated neurosis which is wielding too much power in the psyche, demanding you pay attention to the voices within. If this sounds a bit like you, I recommend you find a psychotherapist to discover exactly who or what from your past is interfering with your present.

Creativity

Many of those who choose to do the Life Planning Programme nurture strong, unfulfilled yearnings to be creative – as writers, painters, musicians…or as warm, loving, life-enhancing human beings. As you investigate your personal powers, it will help to discover where your own creativity comes from.

Jung believed that creativity arises out of one's weakest area – the opposite pole of one's strength. To help you understand how this works with the aspects of personality we have discussed so far – the different ways of perceiving the world and evaluating it – I have presented this idea in a diagram.

Because Thinking and Feeling are opposites, as are Intuition and Sensation, we can present these aspects of personality in the form of a cross. Each person starts out using one of these areas to learn about the world, and which one of the four probably depends on your genes. Strangely, even though we clearly need to be able to both perceive and evaluate things around us, it appears that any one of the poles can be your strongest faculty. In other words, your greatest strength may lie in perceiving the world (Sensation or Intuition) or in evaluating it (Thinking or Feeling).

Very early on, however, we develop a second strength. If you started out with one way of perceiving, then you develop one of the ways of evaluating. Or if you started with evaluating, then you quickly develop one of the ways of perceiving. Again, the choices are probably down to our genes.

A diagrammatic view of two dimensions of personality: perception and evaluation (after C. G. Jung)

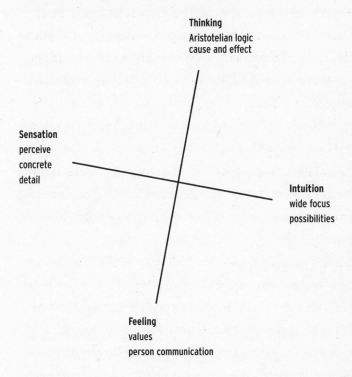

Thinking
Aristotelian logic
cause and effect

Sensation
perceive
concrete
detail

Intuition
wide focus
possibilities

Feeling
values
person communication

You will see in the diagram that the cross is tilted to indicate that development of these different faculties is somewhat unbalanced. One is always stronger than any of the others, we then develop a second and eventually, as we mature, we can to a certain extent develop a third. Always, though, one of these faculties remains somewhat out of reach of our conscious volition and, however far we mature and develop our abilities, is the source of our weaknesses – and our creativity.

This simple diagram for finding your way around the psychology of personality might be compared to the cardinal points of a compass, though in the geography of the psyche there is always one pole to which you can never travel. It is as though each of us begins at the equator of our inner world, and sets out towards one of the poles. On the way, areas to one side are explored and, some time later, areas to the other are explored too. By the time we become mature, we have reached, say, the North Pole (which, as we know, is tilted on our spinning world and represents our strongest faculty). From this high point, we can notionally command everything down to the equator – that is, we have control over our strongest faculty (let's say, Intuition), over our secondary faculty (let's say, Thinking) and now most of our third faculty (in this example, it has to be Feeling). But everything below the equator is out of sight.

Below the equator lies our weakest faculty – in the above example, Sensation – with some of the third faculty which can never be fully developed – here, Feeling. These weaknesses reside in our subconscious, out of reach.

SOURCES OF CREATIVITY

Strongest Faculty	Secondary Faculty	Third Faculty	Weakness/ Creativity
Sensation	Thinking	Feeling	Intuition
Sensation	Feeling	Thinking	Intuition
Thinking	Sensation	Intuition	Feeling
Thinking	Intuition	Sensation	Feeling
Intuition	Thinking	Feeling	Sensation
Intuition	Feeling	Thinking	Sensation
Feeling	Sensation	Intuition	Thinking
Feeling	Intuition	Sensation	Thinking

The way to find out where you are in this table is to think of both your strengths and your weaknesses. We have seen that both Jenny and Mark have highly developed Feeling faculties. They showed every sign of suffering misery because of being expected to use the opposite pole – logical Thinking – which was essentially out of reach in their subconscious. Other aspects of their exercises confirmed that they would be able to develop both Sensation and Intuition to some degree (first one and then the other, which is how our brains seem to work), so these two people were strongest on the Feeling end of the evaluation dimension.

Floyd believed he must be a Thinking type because he had focused all his energies on logical Thinking for his success in business. His inventory of strengths, however, made clear that his Sensation faculty was his greatest strength, the one he didn't even need to think about, *and* that he had begun to develop a third faculty, Feeling. How did he discover this? He realised that he had been working on improving his people skills, and that they had recently become much easier to use. When he focused on what he found most difficult, though, it was Intuition. He felt he never quite knew what was going on in meetings, could never figure out the unspoken nuances that others, good Intuitives, always seemed to pick up. This was his weak area and the source of a large part of his fear of failure in his new job.

So it's good to know what your weak area is, but not to spend time worrying about skills you are never going to be able to develop fully. Better by far to know what your weakness is, and protect it by emphasising those areas you are really good at.

By contrast, Tyler's weakest area has always been Sensation, which makes him a strong Intuitive type. He says that he prefers to live in the world of books, and has long believed that Count Axel, the hero of a 19th-century prose poem, had got it right when he said: 'Live? our servants will do that for us.'[*] The minutiae of everyday life – coping with cooking and shopping, washing and ironing, making fires or maintaining a boiler, clearing up dirt and muddle – all these are burdensome for many Intuitives, especially introverted Intuitives like Tyler. However, he has turned his weakest side into a source of creativity by developing, in his old age, a new ability to write popular books which make accessible to others all the erudition he has acquired over 70 years of reading.

Extroversion and Introversion

You will have noticed that I added a further dimension when describing Tyler – introversion. One reason people are so different is that there are many ways of relating to the world, and a third dimension concerns how you direct your energy – are you extroverted or introverted?

Most people understand *extroversion* as being gregarious, a party person. But there is more to it than that. You are likely to be an extroverted person if your energy is usually directed from you outwards, to other people. You like

[*]Quoted in *Axel's Castle*, a book of literary criticism by Edmund Wilson, 1931 (Fontana, 1969, p.209). It is quite typical of Tyler that he would cite such an erudite source in our Life Planning session – *and* that he would insist on giving me the correct reference when I said I wanted to quote him.

Extroverted

Energy directed outwards

Initiates social interaction

Enjoys sharing thoughts and feelings with others

Sociable, gregarious

Wants to participate, be where the action is

Enthusiastic

Prefers to communicate face-to-face

interacting with others and communicate by talking and listening. You find that you initiate exchanges, discover your own thoughts while expressing your views to others, want to be where the action is and participate in what is going on. This is precisely what Lynne said about herself: she feels alive when 'participating – doing it'.

Introversion, on the other hand, does not mean you dislike people. It means, rather, that your energy comes from outside to inside. You have an inward focus, preferring to work alone, and feel it is wrong to share your interests and feelings with everyone. You like to communicate in writing, and prefer quiet, peaceful places. Parties may make you uncomfortable, and you much prefer in-depth, one-to-one relationships. Frances said that she is 'a loner', likes to stand back and observe rather than participate. For her, feeling alive is summed up as 'freedom' – freedom to be separate, not too close.

Throughout our lives, we may develop both ways of directing energy, but for each of us there tends to be one pre-

Introverted
Energy directed inwards
Prefers to work alone
Feels it is wrong to burden others with feelings
Enjoys in-depth one-to-one relationships
Prefers quiet, solitude
Independent, task-oriented
Prefers to communicate in writing

ferred way, a 'home base' to which we retire when weary, and from which it may be less of an effort to cope with problems. It is useful to understand your preferred way of dealing with what life throws at you: where you can, *it is always best to work with your strengths and protect your weaknesses.*

Planning and Emergent Types

Finally, there is a fourth dimension to be considered: how you organise your life. This is an extension of Jung's original theory of types, and has been developed by two American psychologists, Isabel Myers and Katharine C. Briggs, in their famous Myers–Briggs Type Indicator. Inconveniently, they call this dimension Judging and Perceiving. Because these terms may easily be muddled with those other dimensions we have already examined (how you evaluate the world and how you perceive it), I prefer to label this dimension *Planning* and *Emergent*.

Those who prefer *Planning* are happiest with a well-structured day. They like to plan ahead, know exactly where they are going, and what they need to have done to have completed a task. They like routines and hate to feel rushed and in a muddle.

Rose wrote that she was good at 'organising time', which made those in her group who were not good at time-planning gasp in admiration. Rose realised as others talked that she has highly developed powers of organising, planning and structuring work, and that this dimension of her powers was a major reason her employers valued her. These skills are probably essential for the supervisor of 70 workers in a factory, but because they were almost second nature to her – she *preferred* to plan, organise and structure her work – she had never before realised that other people might find it easier to work in what she considered a muddle.

'I can feel a huge burden falling off my shoulders,' she said, laughing suddenly. 'They actually value me for what I'm good at. What a wonderful thought.'

Planning Type

Likes to plan ahead

Prefers routines

Hates to feel rushed or in a muddle

Good at organising time

Good at structuring work

The opposite pole of Planning is what I call *Emergent*. People who prefer this way of organising their lives dislike monotony and try to vary how they deal with routine matters so as not to die of boredom. They try not to plan ahead too much and enjoy the adrenalin rush of having to complete work at the last minute. They get pleasure from surprises, like to feel they can keep their options open, feel comfortable if they can 'go with the flow'.

Martin, who tells us he has '50 projects on the go', finds meticulous planning a headache, but is highly skilled at juggling multiple tasks. He knows how to handle surprises, cope with change, discard unnecessary elements of a task, and use his inner timing mechanism to choose when to move into high gear to meet a deadline. The opposite pole – Planning – is a weak area for Martin, and may be a handicap for someone who is in business for himself. But knowing what you are good at allows you to work from your strengths, so that you can find a way to protect your weaknesses.

Emergent Type

Dislikes fixed plans, prefers to keep options open

Enjoys surprises

Hates monotony, tends to disrupt routines

Likes to do things at the last minute, use
  adrenalin rush

Enjoys spontaneity

Relies on an inner sense of timing

Finding Your Personality Type

This analysis of personality leads to 16 different personality types, all of which have their own particular set of strengths and weaknesses. It is useful to have a clear idea of where your true strengths lie. Even if you have worked hard at developing those areas that are more difficult for you, you will always find you return to your natural 'home'. *Your strengths are what give you your personal power.*

Working out how all these different dimensions interact can be difficult at first, so I will give a very brief description of the personal powers of the 16 types. None of these will describe you exactly, of course, but I hope you will recognise yourself somewhere in these brief sketches.* And because change is inevitable if you are to stop dreaming and start living, I will also include the four major motivations for different personality types to make changes in their lives.

Extroverted Sensation

Motivation for change: 'It's not working. But if it ain't broke, don't mend it. Let's not change more than is practically necessary.'

Extroverted Sensation Thinking Planning These people are 'task oriented', like to roll up their sleeves and get things done. Logic and reason are their guides. They focus on the realities of the external world and like to plan,

---

* These are adapted from the work of C.G. Jung, Isabel Myers and Katharine Briggs.

anticipating what is needed and what might go wrong. Stella is a good example of this type. She is careful, meticulous and likes a structure to her day. If she needs to make changes as a result of this Life Planning Programme, she will make them promptly, but will only change what isn't working properly. What she likes about her life, she will leave well alone.

Extroverted Sensation Thinking Emergent These people want to be where the action is. Like Lynne, they want 'to participate'. They too like to get on with a job. They are pragmatic and realistic, quick to understand a situation, and resourceful and ingenious when things go wrong. Perhaps they tend to be a bit sharp with those who are not as quick-witted, and can unintentionally hurt feelings with their blunt comments. But this is the person you will want with you in an emergency – practical, down-to-earth, able to turn disaster into victory.

Extroverted Sensation Feeling Emergent These people also want to be in on the action, but more because that is where other people are. They are friendly and outgoing, their natural energies flowing out to others with exuberance. At work, they are at their best if their liveliness and need for fun can be harnessed. Irene, as we shall see, is a good example of this. Frustration at not using their powers can make these people try to create situations that call on their natural talent for humour, and make others feel they are 'stirring it'. If you do this, you are probably a round peg trying to fit in a square hole, and may need to move on.

Extroverted Sensation Feeling Planning These people value harmony, 'getting along with people' as Jenny put it. They always keep promises and carry out commitments, and expect others to do the same. They are warm, friendly, concerned for others' wellbeing, and like to work in a structured situation where everyone knows where they are. Rose is a good example: she likes structure and organisation (as does her employer), but she makes choices determined by human values and is concerned that her co-workers are comfortable in the tasks assigned to them (so they like her too).

Introverted Sensation

Motivation for change: 'If change will produce better results, then it is the sensible and responsible thing to do. But every step should be evaluated, and no more changed than is necessary.'

Introverted Sensation Thinking Planning These people are careful, methodical, painstaking and hardworking. In the right job, they are valued employees who work well within a recognisable hierarchy, always complete their assignments and are especially good at detail, keeping track of information, ensuring goods and services get to the right place at the right time. Because they tend to be guarded and wary, they prefer things to stay the same. This is probably the reason why I cannot give an example from those who did the Life Planning Programme. This description is of one of my early clients, whom I will call Carol.

Carol was unhappy. She had tried for years to be the perfect wife and mother, but her marriage had failed. Now she needed a job. After I got to know her, I suggested she'd been trying to be what other people thought she *ought* to be, and had been ignoring her own special gifts. Her powers of logic, attention to detail and appreciation of organisation and structure might make her, for example, a good book-keeper. She was dubious. This idea didn't fit the picture of herself she'd always had. But synchronicity was at work. An old friend asked for her help in his office, and whether she would be willing to learn book-keeping. She said she would give it a go. A year later, she telephoned to say her life was transformed. She loved the job (which was now permanent and full-time). It called on all her own personal powers, and because she was doing what she was good at, she had found the strength to make the rest of her life work too. Magic! Being true to your true self really can work wonders.

Introverted Sensation Thinking Emergent These people are creative problem-solvers who thrive in situations where their quick grasp of essentials is needed. They are practical, rational beings, who hate to be tied down by routine, tight structures or schedules. They often get frustrated with other people who don't think in their way, but they are always willing to listen to new information and enjoy discussing creative solutions. Floyd is a good example of this type.

Introverted Sensation Feeling Emergent These people are quiet, gentle and compassionate, more inclined to think of others' needs than of their own. Dorothy is a good example.

They are modest, self-effacing, dislike argument and conflict, and have a talent for creating beauty and harmony around them. They do have enormous difficulty in giving their own needs sufficient priority, and others may often take unfair advantage.

Introverted Sensation Feeling Planning Very much like the previous group, these people are inclined to make sacrifices for the benefit of others, especially their family. They are happiest in a role where there is a clear hierarchy and they understand the rules, especially if they feel they are upholding tradition. They like to provide practical help to people and are often to be found in voluntary and charity organisations.

Extroverted Intuition

Motivation for change: 'This is an interesting new idea. Let's have a go, right away. Never mind if it doesn't work, we'll try something else.' Here are people who are excited and stimulated by something new.

Extroverted Intuition Thinking Planning These people like to take charge. Where there is confusion and muddle, they will move in, create order and structure, and zoom to the top. Not surprisingly, I have not seen many people of this type in my Life Planning sessions as they are supremely confident that they can sort things out themselves. They are great entrepreneurs, strong at strategic planning. If this is your type, you may legitimately anticipate material success.

Extroverted Intuition Thinking Emergent These people may also be entrepreneurs, pushing against boundaries that inhibit others, inspired by a faith in their ability to overcome all obstacles. They are supremely independent and value creativity, innovation and imagination. They hate routine, hierarchies and bureaucracy – anything that stifles new ideas. They love complexity and are good at inventing strategies to guide their vision to fruition. Martin is a good example. People in this group may also fail spectacularly because they get bored by the routine maintenance necessary to keep going. If this is you, watch out for the negative hidden side, the opposite of faith in your ability, which is despair. Recognise your weakness and protect it by calling on that amazing creative, innovative strength.

Extroverted Intuition Feeling Emergent These are also people keenly aware of possibilities. Their strong Feeling values lead them to enthuse others, stimulating and energising co-workers with a vision of a better future. They are often charismatic leaders, bringing joy and zest to the workplace. They are at their best when the situation is fluid and in flux. Teresa has the enthusiasm and energy of this personality type.

Extroverted Intuition Feeling Planning These people are easy-going, tolerant and appreciative of others' efforts. They are at their best where they can apply their warmth and understanding to people's needs and develop plans to help them achieve their goals. They like organisation and structure, and are skilful facilitators in the workplace. Despite the self-doubts created by her desire to get to grips with her hidden negative Shadow, Barbara appears to be a good example of this group.

Introverted Intuition

Motivation for change: 'This fits my vision of the future. I need to think about my values, my principles, so that everything moves towards a future that is right.'

Introverted Intuition Thinking Planning These people are strongly individualistic, perhaps more than any other type, though this may not always be clear to those around them. They like to keep their thoughts to themselves, but work quietly and persistently at developing their ideas. They are rapid thinkers and have insights they may not reveal. Many academics are in this group, and Tyler is an example.

Introverted Intuition Thinking Emergent These people are individualistic thinkers too, and they spend much time seeking universal truths and logical purity. They think quickly and clearly, and appreciate elegance and clarity in communication. What 'everyone knows' is of little consequence to them, for they are seeking ultimate truths. They are good at building conceptual models or developing complex ideas. Their creativity may make them innovative writers, artists or musicians. Diana may belong in this group.

Introverted Intuition Feeling Emergent These people may seek a lifestyle in keeping with their deepest values, and rarely give up what is important to them. They are gentle and usually have a delightful sense of humour which draws people to them, though they may be difficult to get to know. They are creative, thriving on new ideas and possibilities. Wendy may belong here.

Introverted Intuition Feeling Planning These people seek to understand human nature through discovering themselves, and require solitude to reflect on their deepest ideals. Frances appears to belong to this group. They have deep compassion and work quietly to achieve harmony with others. They do not like to draw attention to themselves, and are at their best when they can concentrate on new ideas which may inspire them to creativity.

exercise 12
neglected talents
What abilities do you have that you neglect or use too little?
List as many as you can.

Now you have a clearer idea of where your strengths lie, it's time to examine those abilities you don't use, or use too little. Many of us waste talents we are endowed with.

This exercise can be rather difficult as you may have dreams you feel you haven't the ability to fulfil, or you may have already listed your talents in the previous exercise under 'what I do well'. So take a good look at your list of talents and abilities. *Are* you using them? I, for example, was not using my skills as a writer to the full when I last did this exercise – which was the reason for doing the Life Planning Programme in the first place.

I remember a nightmare I had many years ago, which I will relate to you as a horrible warning. I dreamed that I went to a high cupboard where I had hidden something precious, saving it for the future. But whatever was hoarded there had dried up and shrivelled. As I opened the cupboard door, it tumbled out in a heap and smashed on the floor. In my dream, I knew I had wasted my talents by not using them, and now they were gone.

This is much like the biblical parable of the talents, of course, and is only a dream. Nevertheless, it shook me at the time, and I hope it will alert you to the possibility that unused talents may wither and not be available to you for ever. The moral is – as doctors say of our muscles – *use it or lose it*.

How these Exercises Fit Together

Martin refused to write anything down at this stage, but when we talked, he acknowledged that at least part of his reason for doing the programme was that he felt frustrated and unfulfilled because his talents were under-used. This section provides a different perspective on what you established about yourself earlier. Don't get impatient – there *is* a purpose in going over the same ground from a different direction. Let's look at a couple of examples of what you can discover by combining exercises.

Irene decided that she must be extroverted because she needed fun and laughter, and how can you have laughter without people? Then, when she thought of talents she could use more, again *'sense of humour'* headed the list. She also thought that she was good at understanding people, and this too was repeated in Exercise 12.

Like so many of us, Irene found she was not using her personal powers to the full, even though they gave her the greatest pleasure. Her sense of humour, her tendency to dramatise and entertain, and her quick grasp of other people's feelings all came easily and naturally, so she had never before *valued* her gifts. Now, when she put together the answers to different exercises, she began to see more clearly that they were central to being her. Laughter comes high up in her list of what makes her feel alive. Her picture of her life, with its dramatic peaks and troughs, was a self-mocking, highly theatrical view of her personal tribulations, which she created both to express her own feelings and to entertain those in her group. The brief excursion into personality types made her realise that, yes, she does tend to create dramas in her home life, and that perhaps the time had come for her to turn her need for laughter and excitement into something more practical.

She began to wonder if she could use her sense of humour to make others laugh in a constructive way that would give her a real sense of achievement. Humorists and stand-up comics have to have some pretty well-developed psychological skills, and Irene saw herself as good at empathising with people. She resolved to use her gifts, for they were what made her unique.

Rose also wanted to develop her ability to create fun. Her talents are different from Irene's, though. Rather than a need for drama and excitement, she has a deep desire to create happiness for those around her. This demonstrates that words have different meanings for different people, and you can only discover your own true needs and abilities by looking at yourself.

'I am really happy with my job and don't really want to change that,' Rose said. 'It's the burden of my own worries – my children, my house – that's what I want to get to grips with.'

Remember Rose's picture of herself, carrying an enormous pack alone, climbing mountain after mountain? Carrying on gallantly after her husband died and bringing up three children alone is an admirable achievement – but cannot have been much fun. Her answers to this exercise and the previous one suggest that fun is something she is both good at and needs to have more of. And yes, *'having fun'* is on her list of what makes her feel alive too.

You may now begin to see how these different exercises start to fit together. Take another look at your own lists of what makes you feel alive (Exercise 9, Chapter 5), what you do well (Exercise 11) and perhaps build up your list of skills you could use more/talents you could develop (Exercise 12). When you really feel satisfied you are fully aware of your personal powers and potential, it will be time to move on to the next exercise – in which those skills and untapped talents may become fruitful.

CHAPTER 8

A Window on the Future

At last the time has come to look at your dreams. You may feel it's taking a long time to get there, but the fact is most of us have an awful lot of debris to clear out of the way before we can stop dreaming and start living. Now it is time to open the window and enjoy a view of the future.

exercise 13
the future of your dreams
Make detailed notes for a day in your ideal future – say three to five years from now. If you prefer a visual image, create a picture instead.

If you could have the life you dream of, what would you be doing three, four or five years from now? Be honest with yourself. You are asked to think of a typical day, not a special holiday.

This chapter may turn out to be a crucial stage for you. Whatever image you create of your future life may determine how that life actually turns out! So think carefully, and try to ensure that the details really please you. Don't get hung up on how you get there. Focus instead on what you see around you, the scents that perfume the air, the sounds that fill your ears, what you touch, where you are and how you feel being you in your dream future.

Create a Positive Vision

Martin said, 'I can't do this exercise. I'm not in charge of my life.'

We tried to persuade him to imagine what it might be like if he *were* in charge. It is important for people like Martin, who feel hamstrung by unfair circumstances, to have a positive vision of the future. Visualising this ideal day in the future is not just a game. It is a crucial step in the progress towards giving up dreaming and starting to live.

Dreaming means you are *not* in charge of your life. You are essentially supine, asleep. In order to stop dreaming and start living, you need to take charge. Deliberately. Actively.

This book is designed to help you discover:

(a) what is keeping you lying down, dreaming but not doing;

(b) where you really want to go when you get up off that comfortable couch;

(c) how you can tap into your personal powers to find the energy to take control of your life.

You can do it. It only takes courage, honesty and willpower. That's all!

The Power of a Positive Image

I warn you now that describing your ideal day in the future can have a powerful effect. The first time I did this exercise – nearly 30 years ago – determined how I saw my life for a long time. It is the reason I have been living for 28 years in an isolated house in the wilds of North Cornwall. That vision of a peaceful place where I could be creative has had so much power in my psyche that I will need an equally powerful vision to make me move.

Your own vision of the future could help determine your life too. Writing down every detail can make it seem real, until it becomes real. So think about it with care. But do think about it. Without a vision of the future, you are unlikely to turn your dreams into reality.

Does Your Dream Depend on You?

If you have difficulty getting to grips with this exercise, it may be because you still have longings, worries and conflicts that have not been exorcised by the previous exercises.

Celia found she couldn't even start.

'What I really want,' she said, 'is to be able to fly around the world to exotic places, lie in the sunshine on golden sands, bathe in blue seas and meet interesting people. I want to be part of the jet set.'

Isn't this just a romantic fantasy? Celia lives in a council flat, on social security, with a young child. Until she discovered the new government programmes designed to help women in her position develop new skills and build confidence, it was difficult for her even to get out of the house. No wonder, then, that she dreams of escape. But she *has* travelled the world, stayed in exotic places and met unusual and interesting people, so she knows what she is missing. Why *shouldn't* she be able to get there again?

The real question is, could she make this dream of hers come true herself?

'Aha,' I can hear you saying, 'you told us not to get hung up on how we get there. Now you've contradicted yourself, by asking Celia to think of practical solutions.' Well, yes and no. The issue here really is, *does Celia's dream depend on herself or does it depend on someone else?*

She could see only two practical options: one, she must marry someone with enough money to allow her to join the jet set; or two, she must make enough money herself. Sadly, she decided neither was on. So she lowered her sights and said she would consider training as a hair-dresser, which she thought she would really enjoy. However, she was truly unhappy at losing her dream, which depended not on her but on the man she had hoped to marry. The father of her child was a wealthy man, and the jet planes and sunlit beaches symbolised the glorious life with him she had imagined and knew was never going to materialise.

Take a close look at your own dream day. If achieving it depends entirely on someone else, it may be just a glorious fantasy. But if your dream day depends on *you*, you may hope to find a way to make it come true. Success in many ventures may depend on other people as well – you can't make a living if no one wants your goods or services – but *the prime mover has to be you*.

Are You Just Pretending?

Reality and dreams may clash in other ways too. As the hero of Ernest Bramah's delicious tale *The Wallet of Kai Lung* points out, 'It is a mark of insincerity of purpose to spend one's time in looking for the sacred Emperor in the low-class tea shops.'

Annie, for example, confessed that she had always dreamed of being a ballerina. When sent to formal ballet classes as a young child, she was ecstatic. She still keeps her first pink ballet tights, shoes and tutu hidden in a box under her bed.

'Noel Streatfield's *Ballet Shoes* was my favourite book for years,' she said. 'I was so jealous when my sister was taken to see *The Nutcracker*, I thought it should have been me. But my Mum took me to *Swan Lake*, and to *Romeo and Juliet*, and lots of others. It was wonderful.'

But Annie is 14, a schoolgirl at an ordinary comprehensive and not in a special ballet school. Is her dream another fantasy? 'Nobody thought I was any good really,' she said sadly. 'I enjoyed the classes and practised a lot, but I suppose I wasn't good enough.'

This is an example of the kind of dream that depends – alas – on exceptional innate ability and early training. To be a ballerina demands a special talent that very few people have. You will know what I mean if you have ever had a similar experience to this one of mine. As a teenager I was good at swimming. At 14 or 15, I was possibly the best in the school. Then a new girl arrived, a member of the junior Olympic team, who came to our school so that she could be nearer the training pool. Yes, I was good – but she was outstanding. She left us all awestruck, watching open-mouthed as she sped through the water as fast and smoothly as a hunting shark.

Many dreams depend on whether you have the talent and the skill in the first place: being a professional footballer or tennis player, for instance, or a concert pianist, or opera singer. Most skills that rely on physical prowess require innate ability and need to be developed early. If your dream future depends on a skill or talent of this kind, you need to be cold-blooded and ruthless with yourself. What evidence do you have that you could make this into your life's work? Are you fantasising, or could you really develop your innate abilities? Or are your abilities in your chosen area not enough for you to become a professional, but can nevertheless bring you great pleasure in an amateur way? Have you been indulging in dreams and fantasies that you actually *know* you can never turn into reality?

If, however, your dream future depends on skills you have already, and that *can* be sharpened and improved as you grow older then you are probably not fantasising at all. You may dream of writing, for instance, or a career in horticulture. Running your own business or becoming a counsellor could be your dream, or training as a pharmacist, an astronomer, a hairdresser or any of hundreds of other occupations. Don't give up just because developing these skills is difficult and requires hard work.

Don't Put Up with Second-best

Even though it can be difficult to get started, most people enjoy this exercise – visualising the future of their dreams. Once you have got all the detail down on paper, you will find your energy levels seem to rise. This is what you want to make of your life, and somehow you will succeed.

If your energy levels remain low, however, you may find you are trying to deceive yourself. Listen to Teresa as she started to tell us about her day in the future.

Teresa

'I wake refreshed in a nice bedroom, then I get stuck into my day. I teach in the morning but leave my work at work. I am running my own timetable. I enjoy being with my family but use my home as a base from which to do other things. Like it was at university…'

But then she screwed up the sheet of paper, put her head in her hands and confessed that this wasn't really what she wanted at all. This scenario was her attempt to make the best of second-best. A year ago, she had a major opportunity to do what she has always dreamed of – study medicine – but she had to turn it down.

'It's still sitting there. It's my destiny,' she said.

She was prepared to risk everything and borrow the necessary money, but she needed her husband's backup – and he couldn't give it. This is a major crisis in anyone's life and marriage. If one partner has a clear-cut ambition that feels like 'destiny', then *not* being supported when the opportunity arises to fulfil that ambition can lead to disaster. Teresa gave up her place to please her husband, but then found the sacrifice was not acknowledged or appreciated. To give up your dearest ambition, something immense is required as compensation. Very few relationships can carry that burden – and, in the end, Teresa's marriage failed.

It is worth realising that the loss of a personal dream of this importance will feel like an amputation for the rest of your life. Somehow, Teresa must find a way of financing her studies because she will never be able to live happily with the loss of both marriage and long-standing dream.

Create Your Vision First!

Practical issues – like money, time, other people's needs – are, of course, important, but they should be dealt with later, after you have a vision of what an ordinary day in an ideal future *could* be like. Only when you have this vision can you find the energy to overcome real, factual, down-to-earth obstacles. One other example will illustrate this point.

Lynne
'I start the day by opening the greenhouses and checking on my plants. They are all thriving and my new cuttings are looking good. The orchid house is a wonderful sight, and I breakfast on their glorious colours and textures. I am running a successful business, with lots of decision-making and problem-solving. I have helpers whom I am training in horticulture. My family is happy and I don't worry about them.'

Lynne has a glorious, detailed, complete vision of her future. All she needs now is the courage and determination to make it happen. Lynne says she knows it is possible. She could do it, but is worried about the financial aspect. Of course! But that practical aspect of *how* to make your dreams reality is for a later chapter.

Money is obviously a problem for anyone who dreams of starting up a new project as a way of earning a living, just as it is for Teresa who wants to undertake long-term training. Someone pointed out that Lynne is an expert in financial affairs and surely could manage to sort out her own money problems. Lynne laughed. The fiscal tribulations of a major international organisation are apparently fun for the expert, while taking on one's personal business worries is a headache. This is much like the traditional tale of the cobbler's children who have no shoes: we all find it much simpler to apply our skills to other people's affairs than to our own.

I am a psychologist, not a financial expert, and have no intention of offering any advice on financial matters. Once you know what you really want to do – which is what this book is about – it is then up to you to find out *how* to deal with practicalities. But the really difficult part is the psychology – when you give yourself permission to turn dreams into reality, anything is possible.

Some people, like Frances and Dorothy, dream of a life in which they can fulfil their own creativity without necessarily having to earn a full-time living from it. Their dream days may not depend entirely on the dreamer, for we all must have enough money to live on, and families may continue to be problems. But when you know what you really want to do, you can make changes in the right direction. Dorothy, for example, can start making time for herself so that she can write for part of the day. Did we not see how stifled her poor starved self feels?

It is an interesting psychological fact that when you start to make space for yourself in your everyday life, and do not immediately stop your own activities the minute some member of your family demands your attention, those demanding others begin to learn that they have to take account of your needs too. You may believe they *should* think of you without being asked – but they probably won't. Your job is to think of yourself *yourself* – and make sure you too have time to do your own thing. Turning dreams into reality takes many different kinds of effort.

So take a cool look at your dream and see if you are willing to do what is necessary to make it come true. If you are, that powerful vision of the future will carry you through all the trials and tribulations that beset the visionary, and you will succeed in the end.

CHAPTER 9

Inside the Pressure Cooker

Now that you have an inspiring vision of the future, you will be able to find the energy to go through one last difficult chapter. The time has come for a proper spring-cleaning of your psyche, tossing out the rubbish, examining all the impedimenta, washing, sweeping and scouring into the darkest corners until all is in readiness for you to create your happy future.

Console yourself when the going gets rough: this is the last bad patch. You've got this far and survived, so just how ghastly could it possibly be?

You need to take another look at the pressures in your life and the demands they are making on you. Here you will finally dispose of unwanted rubbish from the past, clear, clean and polish your inner space so that *you* can make all the choices from now on. This is where you discover how to put your own needs into the balance, allow your desires a say and give them due weight. Here you learn how to tell that Circle of Demon Voices just what it can do with all that insidious carping. If you have the courage to make this final effort, you will discover your own way out of the valley of shadows into the sunlight of hope.

Get through this last ordeal and you will be well set to stop dreaming and start living.

exercise 14
the obstacles in your life

1. **Make a list of the pressures and difficulties that interfere with your life. Write down what comes to mind now, without referring to anything you wrote earlier.**

2. **Then compare this with the list of 'Things that bother you' that you wrote for Exercise 7 (Chapter 4). Are they the same?**

Pressures that Change their Shape

Many of your pressures and difficulties will be all too familiar, but sometimes the lists may show striking differences. Take a look at your list of *things that bother you*. Do any of these *not* appear on your new list? Perhaps they are not important pressures. Can you set them aside as not so significant after all? What do they say to you? What is your reply?

Celia said: 'It genuinely bothers me that I'm an unmarried mother. I thought that was the most important pressure in my life. But not having a partner doesn't come through as a pressure. Funny that.'

When Celia joined the group for her Life Planning Day, her thoughts about her difficult situation were focused on other people – the lover who had let her down and the social stigma of being a mother but unmarried. But by the time she reached this exercise, she had begun to think in ways that would help her take control of her life. Just thinking about your problems and difficulties in unusual ways can help to break down the bars of your prison and show you a way out.

Celia's earlier list of 'things that bother me'
Being alone
Being an unmarried mother
Money
The terrible place we live in
Keeping Sam happy

Celia's new list of pressures
Money
Getting a job
Moving to a decent place
Decent childcare for Sam

You can see that most of the same difficulties are there but Celia has discovered a different way of thinking about them. All her pressures now appear in a form that requires her to do something.

'It's making a life for me and Sam that's important,' Celia said. 'I'd *like* a partner, I'd like a proper husband, but I'm not going to let that be a pressure any more.' Was she sure? 'It's what I want, but there's not a lot I can do about it. I can see that now. So I'm letting go.'

Celia had made a giant leap forward. Most people want love and companionship in their lives, and being let down by a lover who seemed to promise everything you ever wanted is seriously painful and damaging to your self-esteem. But while you cannot undo what other people do, and you cannot *make* another person love you, you most certainly can choose how you deal with rejection or betrayal. Celia chose to pick herself up, take stock of what she had going for her, and make her own way, proudly, on her own. She was taking control. Hurray!

Cleansing the Augean Stables

You may have noticed that the poison of the demon voices has been seeping away, draining into channels created by your active participation in these exercises. Guilt and shame accumulate in our psyches, hidden in the shadows, amassing piles of filth and stench until the lower reaches of our subconscious resemble those Augean stables that required a Hercules to clear them out. But just as Hercules diverted a river to wash out the stables, so you can divert the cleansing power of your thinking mind to clear out the mess. Yes, it's a Herculean task – but you can do it!

Simply taking part in these exercises is often enough to start the process of moving years of mucky accretions.

Stella, for example, said that she felt things had changed for her since the earlier exercise. 'My need to have the perfect house, to have money – it's become personalised. Now I've owned the problem, I can see I have a need to produce money myself. I feel empowered.'

If you have not found a great deal of change, however, despair not. As we will see shortly, there *are* ways of taking direct action to deal with those demon voices that have so much power inside your head.

exercise 15
getting inside the pressure cooker

1. **Draw a large circle on a new sheet of paper. In the middle, draw a small circle with ME inside. Label the sheet 'Inside the Pressure Cooker'.**
2. **As you have done in previous exercises, take your latest list of pressures and difficulties, and divide up the circle into appropriate portions.**
3. **Again, get those pressures to talk to you and tell you want they want.**
4. **This time, answer back. What do you say to these pressures? Do you accept what they say, reject it or require compromise? Write down your answers.**
5. **When you have completed this task, retrieve the earlier Circle of Demon Voices and compare the two.**

Again, you are likely to be feeling pretty bad about things when you have finished. Those demon voices are still dripping venom, and life looks pretty bleak. This time, however, you may have been able to push beyond the guilt and fears, and discover what it is you really feel is being demanded of you.

What's the Point of this Exercise?

Martin said he couldn't do this exercise. 'Too many voices, too many ideas and people inside me, contradicting me. I can't do this.'

If you feel like this too, please believe me – and all the other people who have done this course – it is worth making a real effort to get to grips with those nagging voices in your head. You may find you are like Jenny. When she sat down with a pen in her hand, she found she wrote almost an essay for each of her pressuring problem areas, as we will see.

The more voices and contradictions there are, *the more necessary it is for your mental health to get it all down on paper.* That way it is no longer stewing and churning in your head. It is then all outside yourself, so that you can look at the thoughts that have been undermining your wellbeing and self-esteem, and decide whether you are prepared to give 'head room' to any of these ideas.

You may find it difficult. You may feel a bit silly. You may have a nagging fear that actually listening to voices in your head means you are going mad. But be reassured – the kind of 'voices in the head' that mean you are deluded are quite different. If you believe that real external entities – God, the Devil, an angel for example – are talking to you, giving you instructions, then perhaps you *are* suffering delusions, and should consult a psychiatrist. But if the voices are those nagging, carping demons we have all had to live with – personal thoughts that torment and criticise – then these are not evidence of madness. They are evidence that you are perfectly normal – but need suffer no longer if you have the courage to write down what they say.

First, listen. With a pen in your hand and paper (lots, in case your voices are unstoppable, like Jenny's), sit quietly and let your mind sink down. Write exactly what comes into your head. Don't stop to edit or argue. Don't allow any thoughts of being silly or deluded get in the way – write such judgements down if they appear. They are part of what your inner critics want you to think. Keep writing until the thoughts dry up.

Then take a deep breath and read what they say. And answer back. You don't have to accept the unacceptable any more. Write down what you really think about these pressures, demand compromise if you wish, or reject totally. Then use the techniques discussed in this chapter to deal with the notions you really don't want to keep as part of your life. Remember – the choice is yours.

It is time for you to fight back, think for yourself, answer your critics and reject unwanted pressures.

Let's now consider what can be done.

First, let's deal with two kinds of poison that might be clogging up your thoughts, neither of which have any business being in your mind. You may already have succeeded in clearing some of it away, but here are some effective techniques for cleansing those Augean stables.

Getting Rid of Childhood Rubbish (1)

The first technique is very simple. It is to challenge those ideas you recognise as not belonging to you but to faceless 'others': to the media, to politicians, to society.

Celia and Wendy's difficulties with society's picture of 'the unmarried mother' stem essentially from gender-role stereotyping. Gender stereotypes permeate everyone's thinking without our being fully aware of it. (See my previous book, *War of Words: Women and Men Arguing,* for an extensive discussion of its ramifications.) We will see shortly that many women have to exorcise some aspect of this destructive thinking from their lives before they can move on.

Part of the debris we all inevitably need to push aside has been dumped on us by other people: parents, teachers, books, magazines, television, society in general. So we all grow up in Western society 'knowing' (among lots of other things) that:

(a) women are caring and nurturing;

(b) men are cool, logical and naturally aggressive;

(c) being loved means you are a good person;

(d) children need parents who are married, love each other and stay together;

(e) failing to provide your child with this is proof you are immoral;

(f) this is a Just World so if misfortune hits, you must have deserved it.

None of these beliefs is true.

But even if, intellectually, you are prepared to accept that these ideas are wrong, untrue and damaging, deep down inside you, you will discover that you learned to believe these things from a very early age.

Facts:

(a) Some women are good at caring and nurturing, and so are some men. Some women are awful at it, and would really rather do something else.

(b) Some men are cool and logical, and so are some women. Lots of men are irascible, hot-tempered and fly off the handle (ditto women). Most people can learn to think and argue rationally, but it takes education (which used to belong to the males in our society, but not any more). There is some truth in the notion that males are naturally more aggressive than females, as testosterone is nature's chemical stimulant. However, this genetic difference is most noticeable in adolescence, and is rapidly overridden by cultural learning. By their 20s, men and women are acting and reacting in ways they have *learnt*, not as they have been programmed.

(c) Being loved means you are fortunate. Lots of very unlovable people are loved by others, while many warm, delightful, generous beings are not.

(d) Children need consistent love, affection and support. In our society of nuclear families, it may be best if the parents are married, love each other and stay together, but it is not essential. Many children grow up with a single parent (having lost the other for many reasons) and develop into happy, well-balanced, productive adults.

(e) Failing to conform to what a vociferous minority claims is 'the proper way to behave' is not proof of immorality. Immorality is dishonesty, cruelty, using others for your own ends.

(f) This is not a Just World. It would be nice if it were, but it is not. If you find yourself thinking, 'Why me?' when disaster strikes, then you probably function with a Just World belief. The answer to that question is, 'Why not?'

All these beliefs – gender stereotypes, moral imperatives, being sure we'll be rewarded if only we are good and so on – need to be recognised as second-hand, outdated rubbish, dumped in the bin and put outside for garbage collection.

Both Celia and Wendy had to acknowledge that some people 'look down on' them, and criticise them for being 'immoral, good-for-nothing spongers'. But they also learned that they could reject these demeaning ideas and not allow them any place in their own minds.

Getting Rid of Childhood Rubbish (2)

In the chapter on demon voices, we saw a lot of evidence that our minds are cluttered with rubbish from our formative years, and that there is another kind of ancient, rotting garbage that might be jamming our thoughts. This we discovered in its clearest form in Stella's Circle of Demon Voices: destructive or demeaning ideas wished on you by your parents, whose carping criticisms live on in your mind without you being fully aware of it. Destroying these voices may require a major effort.

It often takes time to realise that you have been acting under the influence of old ideas you thought you had rejected many years ago. But now you have them down on paper – outside yourself – objectified, something you can see, and so can others if you dare let them, you can treat them as not part of you. You can decide which elements, if any, are worth hanging on to, and which you are going to eliminate from your psyche for good.

You could tear up your Circle of Demon Voices, but that would mean losing your record of how things were at the moment you completed it. Another way is to write those elements you wish to get rid of in large print on a separate piece of paper and ceremonially destroy them. Burning them – a 'bonfire of the vanities' – is a good method. We act symbolically in lots of ways, and this symbolic act of destruction should remain in your psyche.

A different technique used successfully by several of my clients is to consider these ideas as mental garbage, which must be disposed of mentally. Visualise yourself tipping all this psychic rubbish into a big basket. When everything you want to obliterate is in the basket, visualise yourself and the basket on top of a cliff, overlooking the sea. A huge coloured balloon, filled with hot air is attached to the basket. You release the guy ropes and, slowly and steadily, the balloon rises into the air, carrying your basket of psychic rubbish out to sea. You watch it float away into the distance, and you know it will come down in the ocean, hundreds of miles from land, where it will sink and do no one any harm. You are rid of it for ever.

Exposing Your Real Problems

Putting the demon voices together with this pressure cooker circle leads to both pain and catharsis. When you put your own two circles together and compare and contrast what you have written down, you will achieve insights into your own psyche you probably don't want to share with others.

As before, we will look at a few examples of how other people dealt with this task to help you appreciate how this powerful exercise can work. Let's start with Diana.

Diana's list of difficulties and pressures has not changed, but the demands have. Her earlier circle dripped with the poison '*You do nothing right*', smearing everything

DIANA
'Pay attention to ME'

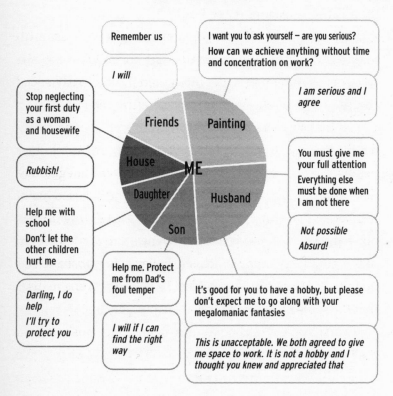

she valued with blame and guilt. Now, though, she can 'hear' what those pressures are demanding of her, and decide whether or not she is happy to comply.

As you can see, she accepts the pressures from her painting, her children and her friends because she finds them reasonable and consonant with what she wants. She is serious about her art, and knows she must concentrate to achieve. No longer are her friends' surrogate voices in her mind loading her with guilt; they are simply asking her to remember them. Her children are no longer stabbing her with the conviction she is a bad mother; they are now simply asking her to be aware of their difficulties and try to help.

Like so many women, Diana finds her house still making unreasonable demands – in her mind – and she recognises immediately the unwanted junk of early social conditioning. As she so rightly comments: *'Rubbish!'*

Her major problem area is now exposed. She experiences her husband as expecting her full attention, and as rejecting her own dreams of being a successful painter as 'megalomaniac fantasies'. Earlier, her demon voices had accused her of neglect, selfishness, even betrayal. Now she has dug deeper, however, she has discovered that beneath the mucky scum of the guilt being laid on her, she believes her husband has no faith in her vocation or talent. To her horror, she realises that the selfishness and betrayal are possibly his.

Diana's problem is not one of money. Her husband did offer to support her, agreeing to the proposal that she give up her job and concentrate on painting. But such an arrangement between partners carries with it more than a simple contract by one to support the other. It also assumes good faith, moral support and joint responsibility. Verbally, he agreed to support her ambitions in every way, but once she became a full-time painter, his attitude changed and he saw her as a full-time housewife with a pleasant hobby.

There was some discussion around the table when she revealed this, and one woman suggested that she 'should be grateful to him' for being willing to support her. Diana was incensed, and this was at least in part because her earlier Circle of Demon Voices had said much the same thing.

'I *was* grateful to him because I thought he loved me and appreciated my talent. I'm not bloody grateful for being treated like a silly little woman with childish fantasies.'

Was this really her husband's attitude? Well, only Diana and he can know that. But there was no doubt that his behaviour towards her had led her to infer this attitude, so they would have some very serious talking to do when she returned home.

How to Lighten the Load

Rose has a very different problem. Her husband died five years earlier, leaving her with three children, a house and a mountain of debts. She has had an uphill struggle to survive. Remember her picture? She was alone with an enormous pack on her back, climbing mountain after mountain. So we can expect her to experience pressures.

We can understand why she pictures herself carrying an enormous burden. She finds demanding voices inside her head that insist everything – her job, her children, her house, even her loneliness – is her problem, her task. Oh dear – her shoulders must be breaking under the strain.

Very sensibly, Rose allows herself to answer back.

Her house is looked after perfectly adequately. She pays someone to keep it clean, and rejects the insidious notion that torments so many working women that they are somehow 'wrong' if their home does not resemble a touched-up photo in a glossy magazine. Shove that idea out, dump it in the bin. It's a relic of the 1950s and the years following the Second World War when society wanted women to stay home and leave the jobs to the men.

ROSE
'It's all up to you'

You have a beautiful house and should look after it properly

Don't expect Ivy (cleaner) to be able to clean as well as you can

---

I give you quite enough attention

Ivy is fine

I will not be made to feel guilty

I am a working woman

So there!

You have to prove yourself

You're lucky to have this job and you know it

They expect a lot of you, you mustn't let them down

You are neglecting us

We don't like it if you are tired when you come home from work

You can't ask us to help you, we are just children

I want you to come and watch me at Sports Day

I want you to help me with my homework

I want you to listen to me, and cuddle me more

I want you to look after me as you did before

House

Work

ME

Children   *Loneliness*

No

I don't have to prove myself any more

I am liked and respected. I am told that at every assessment

Time you were over his death

You know he loved you, that should be enough

You don't need a man

You sound like dreadful spoiled brats! Of course you should help out at home

I will give you lots of hugs and I really will try to listen

We have to love each other

It's not enough

I miss him

But I do have some wonderful memories. They make me happy

Her work, too, need not be a source of pressure. Rose realises this when she examines those rumbling, nagging fears that undermine so many of us in the secret recesses of our minds. Most of us have wondered at some time: am I good enough? Will I let them down? Do they really think I can do the job? Rose has been in her current position for more than four years and *knows* – when she allows herself to relax – that she is liked and respected for what she does. She should be aware of this because she is told so by her boss at frequent intervals. Whenever you find yourself being undermined by nagging fears that you are inadequate, allow yourself to remember all your successes, those times you know you did well, those moments – however rare – when someone said, 'Well done!'

Her children are inevitably a pressure and a problem as all children are to some degree. But I like Rose's answer to her own: *'You sound like dreadful spoiled brats! Of course you should help out at home.'* Of course!

I am firmly of the opinion that children should be part of the family, not a separate unit that gets all its whims catered to. In a family with working parents, any child old enough should be encouraged to play a part in the family economy, an approach which engenders a sense of responsibility, cooperation and positive feelings of achievement. Even a child of three can help with setting a table, preparing food, clearing away afterwards, putting toys and clothes away, preparing for a quick start in the morning. As children get older, they can be given responsibilities. In the excellent television series *The 1940s House*, which re-enacted family life during the Second World War in England, the 10-year-old boy was given the task of ensuring the family did not use more than its tiny ration of fuel each day. He took the job very seriously indeed, keeping records and proudly announcing when on one occasion they had achieved the impossible by using less than the daily ration.

In more modern households, you might find it useful to have a regular, perhaps weekly, round-the-kitchen-table session in which all the children have a say, and during which all the jobs for the week are assigned. Listen to what they say – just as you listen to the cruel voices in your head. In the same way, decide whether what your children say is reasonable, or merely a bit of rubbish gleaned from their mates or television. Just as democracies declaim, 'No taxation without representation', so children might cry, 'No responsibility without discussion', and everyone should have a right to say what they think.

Love is a Restorative

Rose does acknowledge that her children need her loving attention. It may be that you discover in your own circle that – in your mind – your children are calling out for your love. This is another difficulty for many working parents. Many people, especially mothers, get so utterly fatigued and worn threadbare, they feel they have nothing left to give their children when they finally get home.

But love is a restorative. Happy children will raise your spirits, allow you to relax in their warming care, renew your energies. Listen to them, and ask them to listen to you. Tell them how tired you feel and why (without laying any guilt or blame on them). If you have a son or daughter old enough to make a cup of tea, it is probable he or she will already have thought of this loving gesture. If so, enjoy it. If not, gently suggest that a cup of tea would restore you to the mother they expect, and see if you can persuade one of them to make it for you. Such a gesture is so much more than it seems – an act of love by the giver, and by the receiver who accepts its value as intended (drink it up, with enjoyment, even if the giver made a disgusting brew!) Children love to care for their parents, if only they are given some idea how to do so.

Loneliness is a 'biggy', as Barbara put it. The death of a loved one is never easy to cope with, and I'm not sure it is reasonable to expect to 'get over it' completely. Some losses are experienced as a mutilation, like the loss of a limb, and life can never be quite the same afterwards.

But Rose is right. Though she misses her husband, she is now able to remember the good times they had together, and feel happy in her memories. This is good. Good in itself, and a good antidote to the nagging voices that fill her with guilt because she still longs for him in her lonely midnight hours. She longs for him because they had wonderful times together, and she still has her memories of those.

Now that the dripping poison of guilt and a sense of inadequacy seem to have dissipated, Rose discovers that the pressures in her life are realistic – but don't have to be experienced as quite such an enormous burden. Her face brightened, and her voice sounded lighter, more musical: 'All these pressures on me are actually hiding some pretty good things,' she said. 'I think the children and I are going to have some good times now.'

Being True to Yourself

Not all pressure cooker circles produce such satisfactory results, however. Jenny, for example, discovers that underneath her guilt and fear of letting other people down is a deeply depressing conviction that life is futile.

JENNY
'Grow up and accept what life really is'

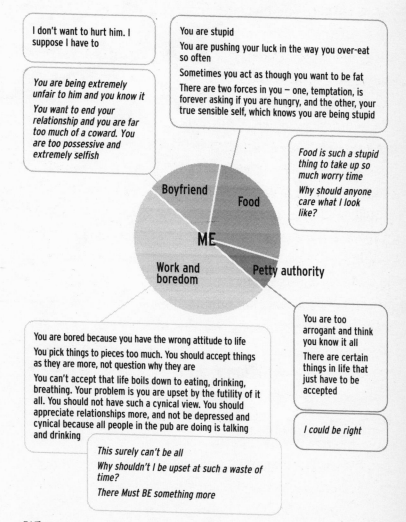

I don't want to hurt him. I suppose I have to

You are being extremely unfair to him and you know it
You want to end your relationship and you are far too much of a coward. You are too possessive and extremely selfish

You are stupid

You are pushing your luck in the way you over-eat so often

Sometimes you act as though you want to be fat

There are two forces in you — one, temptation, is forever asking if you are hungry, and the other, your true sensible self, which knows you are being stupid

Food is such a stupid thing to take up so much worry time

Why should anyone care what I look like?

Boyfriend

Food

ME

Work and boredom

Petty authority

You are bored because you have the wrong attitude to life

You pick things to pieces too much. You should accept things as they are more, not question why they are

You can't accept that life boils down to eating, drinking, breathing. Your problem is you are upset by the futility of it all. You should not have such a cynical view. You should appreciate relationships more, and not be depressed and cynical because all people in the pub are doing is talking and drinking

This surely can't be all
Why shouldn't I be upset at such a waste of time?
There Must BE something more

You are too arrogant and think you know it all

There are certain things in life that just have to be accepted

I could be right

When Jenny started to write down what each of the pressures was saying to her, she didn't stop. Each one was nagging, nagging, nagging, until she had produced almost an essay for each one. The circle shows just a short extract from each, to give the flavour. We can see that Jenny is deeply unhappy, feeling that if she were mature and would 'grow up', she would be able to accept what everyone else appears to accept. But she can't. So the voices go on and on and on.

In the demon voices exercise, Jenny found she was overwhelmed with guilt and shame, worried about letting her mother down, terrified of failure and not being loved. Here, though, we get down to the real source of the problem: she is denying the validity of her own experience.

'*Work and boredom*' take up half the circle. We know that Jenny is doing a university course she dislikes, but her dislike of studying is revealed as something a great deal more. She is trying to work out what life is all about, and she doesn't like what she finds. Everyone else, however, apparently knows better.

Her voices batter her with *should*s: she *should* be able to accept what everyone else seems to accept. She *shouldn't* think for herself and pick things to pieces. She *should* resign herself to what seems futile. She *should* appreciate relationships that leave her feeling alienated.

'Should' is a word that spatters guilt and shame in the way a gritting lorry spreads icy roads with sand and grit. And 'should' always demands the question 'why?'.

Why should Jenny accept what seems to her deeply unacceptable? Answer: because everyone else does.

Is that a good reason? Answer: no!

Jenny reminds me of the character played by Julie Walters in the film *Educating Rita*. Poor Rita was bored – by life with her husband, by long evenings in the pub, by everyone's assumption that her life would consist of working, drinking and producing babies. She wanted something *more*. So does Jenny. Rita's solution was to enrol in classes at university, which doesn't seem quite to be Jenny's eau de vie! But there is no reason to suppose that Jenny would fail to find something to suit her, if only she is willing to acknowledge that her own feelings and beliefs are more valid for *her* than are anyone else's.

Jenny also has a boyfriend who wants to marry her. She knows this would be a disaster, yet finds it impossible to end the relationship, which is now tedious and dull. Three-quarters of her circle represents boredom and frustration – is it any wonder she finds herself obsessed by food when she gets very little pleasure from anything else?

The nagging voices were so strident and insistent, and Jenny had so much to write down to their dictation, that at first she was unable to answer back. Persuaded to try, she did at last acknowledge that her own feelings *might* have validity. She *could* be right. If most hours in her life felt like a waste of time, why shouldn't she be upset? Yes, there *must* be something more. She just had to give herself permission to look. As for her boyfriend, she realised that she had been trying to protect him from the inevitable, but that this was unfair – to both of them.

Jenny's pressure cooker circle reveals the true nature of her difficulties – that *she is denying her own truth.* This important insight will allow her to make sensible choices about what to do next. She crossed out the words '*and accept what life really is*' on her paper, and wrote with a flourish: '*Make something of your life!*' In a later chapter, we will see that she did.

Acknowledging Unpalatable Facts

Tyler's pressure cooker circle is another that reveals an important truth, but for him the struggle is rather different. He discovers that to be true to himself he must acknowledge an aspect of life he would rather deny. What is a fundamental lesson for one person may be quite a different story for another.

TYLER
'Get on with it'

You make these commitments, so get on with it
Stop procrastinating
People are relying on you

I don't want people to rely on me

You must perform. People expect it of you
You must be a good host

Stop being lazy

Am I lazy?

You should exercise more. Get on with it

I know

Stop leaving everything to B (wife)

I don't

Gardening would be good for you

Maybe, so long as it's gentle

Don't take on so much work if you can't cope

I feel so weary sometimes

Social contacts

Deadlines

ME

Jobs in house

Fatigue

Tyler's pressures are all making demands on him to 'get on with' things, and spattering him with guilty *shoulds*. Now the important fact here is that Tyler is 75 years old, and therefore inevitably has less energy than he had as a young man. Like most people in this situation, he resents this fact of ageing. He has been pressuring himself to ignore fatigue, meet deadlines, do more in the house, be the excellent host he always was. But he is tired, and the more he listens to those pressure cooker voices, the more weary he becomes, and the guiltier he feels.

You can see that he finds it very difficult to answer these pressures back in any positive way. The central truth is that he needs to find a way to reject most of the pressures, put them out of his life and acknowledge that he cannot do as much now as he could when young. This is very hard for many people, and Tyler continues to resist: 'But I have a real tendency to be lazy,' he protested. This from a man who proudly announced he began his third career, as a writer, at 70! This is reminiscent of Floyd (see Chapter 4) who works 10 or 12 hours a day and accuses himself of being 'a slouch'.

Where do these accusations of laziness come from? They may be left over from childhood, or they may be – as we saw with Floyd – internalised pressure from a workaholic culture. Western society is permeated with ideas that can lead to workaholism, among them what is known as the 'Protestant Ethic'. This, according to the *New Oxford Dictionary* (1998), is 'the view that a person's duty and responsibility is to achieve success through hard work and thrift'. Nothing is fundamentally wrong with that, until it takes over and becomes a core head of steam that threatens to blow your pressure cooker up. If this is one of your problems, take a good look at where your own pressure to work comes from. Desire to achieve is good if that is your own chosen ambition. But if it originates from some outside influence, junk it.

Tyler resisted any suggestion that he reduce the pressure by undertaking less. Persuaded to dig deeper and explain why he felt he couldn't stop pushing himself, he realised that as a child and youth, he had been expected to succeed. He felt he had never really lived up to the promise everyone had seen in him, so he had to make up for wasting his talents all those years. This is an *internalised pressure* that originates in other people's expectations, and therefore should be considered as rubbish to be discarded.

He said urgently: 'But I haven't got much time! There's so much I want to do!' Ah, this is true. He does hear the sound of 'Time's winged chariot hurrying near'.* But he did not put *this* concern in his circle. Why not?

Tyler's answer was that he doesn't experience his desire to write books as a pressure. It represents the major part of what makes his life so pleasant. If we look back to his picture of his life, we do see that the success of his third career has brought him a great deal of happiness. 'I have so many more books I want to write before I die,' he said.

It would be absurd for anyone to suggest that knowledge of encroaching death does not pile on the pressure, particularly if you have ambitions you want to fulfil before the end. But Tyler needs to see that the desire to write more

*Andrew Marvell (1620–1678), 'To His Coy Mistress'

books – a positive aspiration – is separate from the pressures he experiences from the other aspects of his life. His increasing age, his decreasing energy and his literary ambitions all need to be given due importance in his thinking so that he can dismiss the 'shoulds' and the 'musts' and the general sense that his remaining energies 'should really' be dedicated to other people. Yes, I do advocate an important element of selfishness, especially in old age. It is not sensible or admirable to deny your own needs.

As you will see in the next chapter, if you fail to deal with those demon voices, and your pressure cooker continues to increase the load on your psyche, you will be unable to move on. Complete the task in this chapter, allow the difficult elements in your psyche free rein so that you really *know* what you are up against, and then deal with them as suggested. Then, and only then, will you feel free enough to stop dreaming about a happy life and really start living.

CHAPTER 10

Putting Yourself Centre-stage

Now we have examined the demons poisoning your life, analysed the pressures and difficulties that prevent you from fulfilling your dreams, and taken steps to rid your psyche of some of the worst excesses of your inner tormentors, it is time to move out of the shadows and into the sunlight. The time has come for you to take positive action towards transforming your life.

'At last!' you may be thinking. Yes, it has taken a long time to get here, but now you are well armed, you know your inner enemies and have found ways to neutralise them or dismiss them from your mind. The next step is to turn it all around and make everything work *for* you, so that you can turn dreams into reality.

exercise 16
putting it all together

1. Turn back to Exercise 9 (Chapter 5), where you examined what gives you pleasure, what makes you feel alive. If you haven't already done so, choose a word or phrase that sums up what makes you feel alive.

2. On a new sheet of paper, draw a large circle and put a smiley face in the middle. Draw another circle around this, and write in the word or phrase that makes you feel alive. There you are, in the middle of the circle, feeling good.

3. Divide the circle into segments that represent the most important factors in your life. Label them clearly. Then write down what they would say to you to ensure you remain in the smiley circle, feeling alive and happy. This will almost certainly be different from what they have been saying – in your head – up to now.

4. Consider what you could say – or do – to get this response.

If you have difficulty with this exercise, it may be that you have not completed the Herculean task of cleaning out the dark corners of your inner psyche. You may need to go back to the pressure cooker to find out what is still cooking up a head of steam down there. That exercise was designed to scour out the debris of the past and get rid of deeply buried fears that get in the way of your happiness.

Terrorists in your underworld may have successfully

evaded your explorations, and now be indulging in guer-rilla warfare. If you find you just can't think of anything those important factors could say to keep you centred and smiling, then your demons have hijacked your thought processes. Let's look at Martin, as an example.

In the previous chapter, we saw that Martin opted out of the pressure cooker exercise, and that he had still not dealt with those 'too many voices, too many ideas and people inside me, contradicting me'. So his most powerful demons were still interfering with his ability to plan sensibly for his future. Persuaded to attempt this exercise, he drew a splendid graphic image of how he sees his situation.

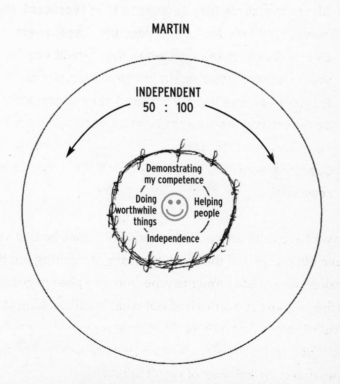

Go 'round, not over: lateral thinking

He knows what makes him feel happy and alive. There he is, in the centre of the circle, demonstrating his competence, doing worthwhile things, helping people, being independent. Typically, Martin has also resisted summing up his sense of being alive in one word or phrase. He wants to hold on to *all* the elements, just as he wants to hold on to all the different projects that might help him be and remain independent. Does Martin really want to have the stress of 50 to 100 projects on the go at once? Or might there be one thing that would make him genuinely happy?

Unfortunately, Martin's refusal to dig deeper in the previous exercise has stopped him from dealing with the Mafia in his underworld that prevent him from starting to live as he desires: the Brotherhood of Big Money. Surrounding him, and far too close for comfort, is a barbed-wire fence represented by pound signs, showing him kidnapped, imprisoned and held to ransom by the need for money he hasn't got.

His group tried to persuade him to talk to the barbed-wire, to try imaginatively to think what that fence might say to make him happy.

'Nothing,' he said.

'Imagine it rusting away,' one suggested.

'I can't do that,' he protested. 'I can't make it rain.'

'You could in your head,' said someone else, and another said, 'Come on, use your imagination. Think positively, that's what this exercise is about.'

He agreed to have a go, and wrote himself a big note: '*Go 'round not over: lateral thinking*'. Alas, that won't work either, for you can't go round something that is round you. The only way for Martin to destroy that barbed-wire fence is to take it to bits, recognise it as a mental construction out of his own mind and dismantle it by examining all its component parts. Those pound signs are all menacing strong-arm hoodlums in Martin's head. He has refused to deal with the major demon – Money – in any of the ways suggested in the previous chapter, so it remains in charge, dominating his mind, overwhelming all his thoughts, and preventing him from thinking in new ways.

If you find yourself in Martin's position – unable to think because you are paralysed by a lack of finances – you really do need to listen to what your fears are telling you. For your difficulty is not just money, it is the emotional baggage the whole idea of money brings with it inside your mind.

Finances *are* a problem, of course they are. But they pose a practical problem that must be solved in some concrete way, once you have given yourself permission to do so. Before you take steps to sort out *how* to deal with finances, you must deal with your own psychology. You need to exorcise your demons, fight terrorism in your psyche, rid your mind of its own Mafia.

You also need to know what you really want to do; what you would do if finances were not a problem. Barbara knows what she would do.

The Psychology of Self-belief

Money appears to be a major difficulty for Barbara too. She is worn out, stressed and tired because she longs to stop working full-time so that she can devote some of herself to

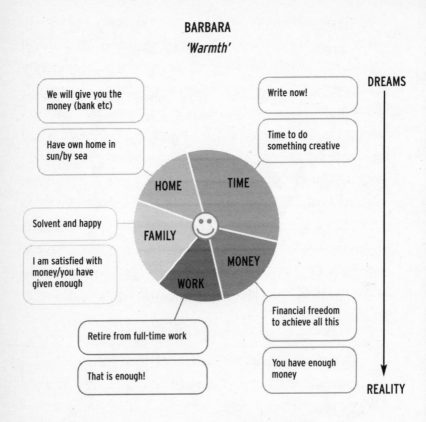

BARBARA
'Warmth'

DREAMS

We will give you the money (bank etc)

Write now!

Have own home in sun/by sea

Time to do something creative

HOME

TIME

FAMILY

Solvent and happy

I am satisfied with money/you have given enough

MONEY

WORK

Retire from full-time work

Financial freedom to achieve all this

That is enough!

You have enough money

REALITY

being creative. She knows what she wants to hear. She longs to be told her family does not need her to give them money any more, that there is enough money to live on, that she has done enough.

However, finding a way to get these important parts of her life to say to her what she wants them to say seems too difficult. We see that *'Dreams'* and *'Reality'* are linked by an arrow, but she has not yet discovered what she can say to her family – and herself – to get the reply: 'You have enough, you have done enough.'

What *might* she say? This is always a difficult exercise. Part of the reason is that we would really like people –

husbands, children, parents, friends, colleagues, bosses – to offer us what we want without being asked. In an ideal world, our loved ones would be sympathetic, considerate and generous, our bosses would be appreciative and rewarding, our colleagues admiring, our friends empathetic and supporting. When we don't get these ideal responses, we all tend to feel it is our fault and there must be something wrong with us. Unfortunately, people very rarely give you what you want and need without being asked. Indeed, they often fail to give you what you want and need even when you *do* ask. The fact is that, unless you are extraordinarily lucky, you have to persuade the people in your life to let you have what you want and need. That is where psychology comes in.

> **The most important lesson of this entire Life Planning Programme is:** *when you know what you want and need, then you must take steps to ensure you get it.*

Human psychology is very strange. These days there is a widespread belief among top athletes and sports people that who wins and who loses is essentially a question of psychology. This is because they know, from long experience, that they can be as fit and prepared as the best, but if they don't have a total conviction that they will win, if they cannot visualise ultimately winning through all the brilliant performances of their opponents, then they will defeat themselves.

A perfect example of this occurred in the Wimbledon women's singles final in 1997, when Jana Novotna appeared to be heading for victory against Martina Hingis. Novotna had won the first set easily, 6:2, and looked as though she was unbeatable until halfway through the second, when her opponent fought back with determination. For the first time in the match, Novotna lost her service game. This was a blow from which she never recovered. Her sense of invincibility crumbled before Hingis's valiant onslaught, and for some reason – some psychological reason – her play deteriorated from that moment. To everyone's amazement, Martina Hingis came from behind and won the championship.

This is what happens to us when the people in our lives do not live up to our expectations of how a husband, wife, daughter, son, parent, friend *should* behave. We lose confidence in ourselves. But just as a tennis player or javelin thrower has to deal with the reality of other people's behaviour, and fight back even harder when the opponent is tough, so we need to deal with the people in our own lives in the knowledge of what we require of them. They cannot know if we are not clear. But if we are honest with ourselves, we have a greater chance of getting what we want and need.

Barbara wants her family to say, *'I am satisfied, you have given enough'*. In order for this to happen, she has to *believe* it. Assuming she does believe this, she must then *behave* as though she does. That means, for example, that she can choose an appropriate moment to tell her family: 'I have decided to retire (or work part-time) in (say) two months'. Any discussion of consequences must also include firm statements from her to the effect that she has helped her family as far as she can, and now it is time to consider her own future retirement. Requests for money should be denied firmly, without anger or emotion. 'I'm sorry if you still feel insolvent, but I am afraid I cannot help any more.'

The Choice is Yours

If Barbara believes in her dream, she will know that she can no longer fritter her resources on others – and that includes the resource of time as well.

Sounds selfish, you think? Good. That's what Barbara, and others like her, need. Remember, right at the beginning, I pointed out that selfish people are unlikely to feel a need for a book like this. It is those of us who spend our lives thinking of other people first who need to be encouraged to be selfish for a change. There is a happy balance, and most people find they fall on one side or the other.

Tyler objected that this approach is over-simplistic. 'We all need to do things we don't want to.' No, we don't – or at least not nearly as much as most of us think. My point is that each of us needs to *choose freely* what we do, and not do anything just because we believe we *should*.

So Barbara can choose whether or not to support her family further. If she believes in her heart she has given them enough and her needs are greater, so be it. And Tyler can choose freely whether he will submit to all the pressures in his life or acknowledge his need to conserve his energy. 'That's asking me to break the habits of a lifetime,' he said. Yes! Hard work, but the results will be worth it. Tyler's precious resources – in his case, energy – are far better spent defending himself than being frittered away on other people.

It is yet another fact of human psychology that those on whom we squander our precious time and energies are usually quite unaware of the sacrifices we make, and only start to take us seriously when we put ourselves centre-stage.

Dealing with Demanding Others

Dorothy's circle is a good example of what might happen when a self-sacrificer decides to think of her own needs too.

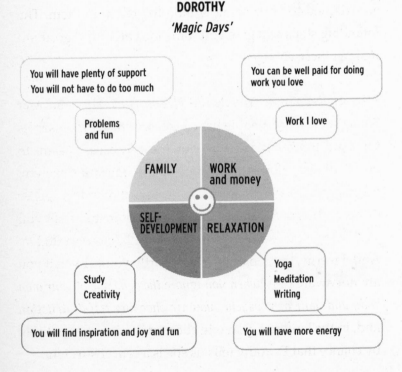

DOROTHY

'Magic Days'

You will have plenty of support
You will not have to do too much

You can be well paid for doing work you love

Problems and fun

Work I love

FAMILY

WORK and money

SELF-DEVELOPMENT

RELAXATION

Yoga
Meditation
Writing

Study
Creativity

You will find inspiration and joy and fun

You will have more energy

You may remember that Dorothy has been oppressed for a long time by the burden of self-sacrifice. She has an invalid mother, a demanding husband, an ill-paid and stressful job and a sense that any desire to think of her own needs is to be selfish. If she considers doing what would make her happy, however, she realises that her family would support her more and make fewer demands. She would be earning money while doing something she enjoys, and half her circle would be devoted to what gives her a sense of achievement and wellbeing.

What might Dorothy say to her family to get the kind of response she longs for? Again, it is never easy to get family members to change, especially when everyone has become accustomed to your being willing to give in to them. The following steps will give you some idea of how to go about making these changes.

Step 1: Recognise You Have Needs that Must be Met

Sometimes, when people have been sacrificing themselves for years and can see no way out, the only escape seems to be in illness. Stress undermines the immune system, leaving you more vulnerable to serious illness like cancer or heart disease. There often comes a moment when you almost feel you could *choose* to become ill if you wanted to. And it is true, the choice is at least partly yours. Even if you are not aware of it, *when you ignore the demands of your own body and your own psyche, you are choosing self-destruction* and, in the long run, you will succeed. It cannot be entirely by chance that Dorothy tells us she is a cancer survivor.

Step 2: Be Quite Clear about What Your Needs Are

Now Dorothy can see in this happy circle precisely what she needs to keep her happy and in balance – and that includes help and support from her family.

It is a good idea to examine closely what you mean by 'help and support' from others, because if you are vague, they will be vaguer – and you won't get it. Don't forget, if the help were forthcoming spontaneously, you wouldn't need to ask in the first place.

Step 3: Ask This is an important and challenging step. You can say, 'I realise I need your help and support', but that simply raises difficulties for other people without their knowing quite what to do. Better to be more specific. Present a problem that can be put on the table and jointly examined.

You could say, for example, 'I realise that having a full-time job, caring for an invalid and doing all the things in the house are just too much for one person. It really would help if you would take on doing X or Y'.

Try to phrase the difficulty in as objective a way as possible but without denying what is reality for *you*, and then make specific requests for help. The objective is to persuade those involved to look at what is a problem for you, and help you find a solution.

Of course, the callous answer may be, 'So what do you want me to do about it?' That is often the first reaction of people who realise that the comfortable life they have been used to is about to be disrupted. They are negative, discouraging change at all costs.

You must refuse to be discouraged, and insist that change has to be made. The only way you can do this in the face of the emotional turmoil you will be offered is to be sure in your own mind that you are right. You *must* defend yourself. Dorothy needs to rescue her poor, starving, suffocating self and allow her to live, breathe and thrive.

Step 4: Make Changes and Stick to Them If you have said, for example, 'It would really help if you did the shopping', then assume that the other person will do the shopping. Provide a complete and detailed list and try to get agreement on when the task is to be done. Discuss alternatives if necessary: 'Would you find it easier to go on Friday evening or Saturday morning?' Be calm, reasonable and assertive. You must have help. Assume it will be forthcoming.

It is true that family members are sometimes unkind and refuse to cooperate. Usually, though, they are just testing your resolve. When they see you really mean what you have said and are sticking to it, they generally acknowledge the justice of the new arrangement and get on with it. If this works for you, reward your cooperative family members with warmth, smiles, hugs and anything else that suits!

If you have really mean, selfish family members, then they have to be discouraged from their nasty ways. *Reward good behaviour, do not reward bad.* For example, you could withdraw treats or stop ironing shirts. As an extreme example, make it clear that you will not continue to provide meals for those who absolutely refuse to help out. They will have to fend for themselves. You will know what might get them thinking.

Picture your uncooperative family members as recalcitrant dogs that need training. Anger doesn't work, nor does aggression. Just positive rewards when the right thing is done, and penalties when behaviour is bad. It works in the end, every time.

Of course, you will feel remorseful and apologetic. You have no experience of standing up for yourself, and will feel guilty when your selfish family points out how unkind you are being. They may go further and suggest you are mentally ill, going round the twist, having a nervous breakdown. Reject it all. See all this emotional turbulence for what it is – your family's blind struggle to get back to the comforts of having you squander all your energies on *them*.

You can see that making crucial changes in how you relate to members of your family may lead to some uncomfortable times at first. Spoilt children, badly behaved dogs and selfish adults will always fight back when what they are used to is taken away. But why should their bad behaviour continue to be rewarded? You need to be firm and strong. Just keep in mind your hard-won knowledge that you need change, soothing your nerves with your image of you in the middle of the circle, glad to be alive. Remain calm and focused. They will learn. And eventually, you will *all* be happier.

Beware the Pride of Humility

One other aspect of self-sacrificing behaviour needs to be addressed: it is that those who give up their own lives to serve others may actually be feeding on a strong sense of moral superiority. Some people feel a real gratification in knowing that they are needed, and that others depend on them for their wellbeing and happiness. They may feel pride in the knowledge that no one else is as thoughtful, nurturing and caring as they are, and believe that their sacrifices make them better people. You may have to dig very deep to discover this one, because this demon – Pride – masquerades as an angel.

This demon is extremely powerful and often defeats the self-sacrificer who aspires to freedom. The Christian Church has long been aware of the dangers and difficulties for those whose besetting sin is the pride of humility and self-sacrifice. If you do discover this demon in yourself, please avoid wallowing in guilt and swathing yourself in sackcloth and ashes. It is just one more demon to be exorcised.

Be kind, generous, thoughtful, loving to others, yes – but put your needs in the balance too. They must be given due weight. And consider that it may not even be kind or generous or loving to prevent your loved ones from learning the important lesson that they too must take responsibility for their actions.

Finding a Balance

Lynne appears to have succeeded in exorcising her major demons. When she started this Life Planning Programme, all her worries were going round and round in a circle inside her head (see Chapter 4) and she just couldn't think straight. Now, however, she knows what would make her feel happy and alive. When she puts herself centre-stage, she finds the major elements in her life can be in balance.

You will see she hasn't thrown in her job, which provides both a good income and a lot of satisfaction. She has put it in perspective and given it its right amount of

LYNNE

'Participating. Doing it'

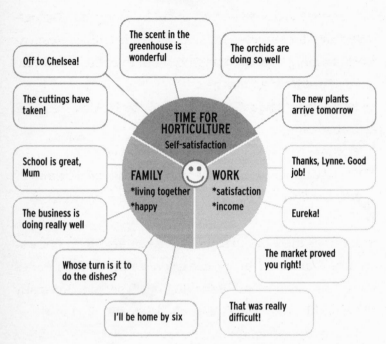

Off to Chelsea!

The scent in the greenhouse is wonderful

The orchids are doing so well

The cuttings have taken!

The new plants arrive tomorrow

TIME FOR HORTICULTURE
Self-satisfaction

Thanks, Lynne. Good job!

School is great, Mum

FAMILY
*living together
*happy

WORK
*satisfaction
*income

Eureka!

The business is doing really well

The market proved you right!

Whose turn is it to do the dishes?

I'll be home by six

That was really difficult!

space. At the same time, she assigns a third of her circle to her dream of horticulture, and plans to ensure her job does not swallow up every moment of the day so that she can undertake some big projects in the greenhouses. She envisions her family contentedly getting on with their lives, and being there all together in the evening. This would mark an enormous change, as Lynne has been having to work away from home for a large proportion of the time up to now.

What does she need to say to get the positive responses that adorn her circle? She smiled and said, 'I just have to make it happen'. It is true that most of the responses would arise essentially out of her own sense of achievement, her

own will to succeed and her own psychological prepared-
ness, which would affect everyone around her.

'I know exactly what you mean by being psychologically ready for success,' she said. 'I do this with my team at
work, helping and encouraging them to believe in themselves. I just forgot about me!'

Remember the quotation, borrowed by Nelson Mandela,
at the beginning of this book?

Our deepest fear is not that we are inadequate.
Our deepest fear is that we are powerful beyond measure.
It is our light, not our darkness, that most frightens us.

Sometimes the fears that prevent us achieving happiness
are not a dread of being considered selfish. Sometimes
those fears are a dread of making other people, especially
those we love, feel inadequate and insecure.

Like many extremely successful women, Lynne makes a
great deal more money than does her husband. This had put
her in a double bind. On the one hand, she didn't want him
to feel inadequate, and encouraged *him* to fulfil his dream of
starting his own business, with her financial help. On the
other, she felt the enormous burden of supporting the
family. She believed she had to justify the demands of her
high-powered job by providing everyone with expensive
goodies, a beautiful house, cars, holidays abroad, a horse for
her daughter, a computer for her son. This obviously meant
she had to work harder and harder, for longer and longer
hours. No wonder she felt she was 'not good enough' (see
Chapter 4). Who could ever be, especially if you keep
moving the goal posts?

But now Lynne has a vision of the future that allows her to lead a more balanced life. Yes, she will continue to work, because she loves her job, but for shorter hours, and not spending all week, every week travelling away from home. If her bosses don't like the change of attitude, then she will change jobs. Her sense of her own abilities is no longer being undermined by those demon voices insinuating that she is 'not good enough'. She knows she is very good at the work she does. She is not afraid of undermining her husband because she appreciates his good qualities, and they are different from hers. Remember the words quoted by Nelson Mandela:

Your playing small doesn't serve the world.

There is nothing enlightened about shrinking so other people
won't feel insecure around you...

And as we let our own light shine, we unconsciously give
other people permission to do the same.

Letting Your Own Light Shine

Stella's own chart was so original and creative, it has been reproduced exactly, so that you can see how one person went about this exercise, thinking about and writing down her solutions to her own particular issues. Stella has decided to let her own light shine. She has realised that she can take action to make the changes she wants. She does not have to be the passive 'good little woman' that her inner demons had required. Her happy circle is surrounded by warm and loving comments that will make her feel good.

What does she need to do to get these warm, positive responses? We can see she has already given herself permis-

STELLA
'Sensual'

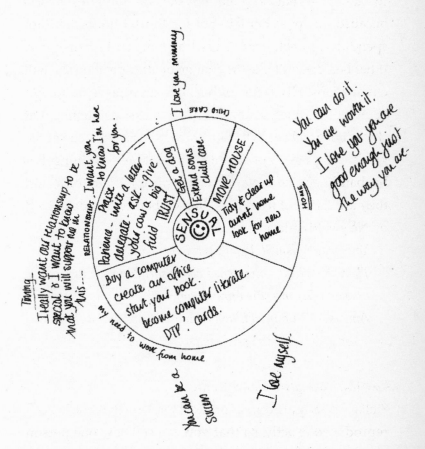

sion to ensure her own happiness. Her actions are given inside the circle, surrounding her happy, smiling, sensual self.

The largest section of the circle is devoted to her need to earn money for herself, to become free of the sense that only men are allowed to do this. As we saw earlier, Stella felt empowered by her discovery that she could take responsibility for her desire for a perfect house, for her need to have wealth. She has decided that it is up to her to do something about them and produce an income for herself. So she plans to *'buy a computer, create an office, start her book, become computer literate'*, maybe even discover how to publish herself.

Another large section of her circle is labelled *'Move House'*. Where she lives is clearly of importance to her, as it is for many people. Having discovered that a dream house is part of her vision of a happy future, she is determined to take action. She resolves to *'tidy and clear up current home, look for a new one'*. She wants to believe she is *'good enough'* just as she is, and *'worth it'* so she *can* achieve her own dream of her ideal home.

These two items are inevitably related to her ambivalence over childcare. Earlier, Stella revealed problems with her own – and possibly her husband's – belief that a 'good mother' must be with her child 24 hours a day. Now that Stella has taken charge of changing her life and is determined to earn money and move house, she will need some regular childcare to release time for these projects. She does not anticipate any problems from her son, however, as she hears him say, *'I love you, Mummy'*.

This leaves a major section of the circle labelled *'Relationships'*, which here almost certainly means principally her husband. Stella discovered that the demon voices in her head told her that active steps to achieve a loving relationship were up to the man, and if he didn't show her love, it was because she didn't deserve it. But now Stella realises – not just intellectually, because we all *know* this, but at a deep level – that a relationship between two people takes two. She must contribute, not be a passive recipient.

So she has clearly been thinking about her husband's own needs, of ways in which she can make him happy and get the response from him she desires. She will lavish praise on him, not wait for him to make the first move. She will write him a love letter, ask for what she wants, trust him.

The Psychology of Love

'*Give your cow a big field*' Stella wrote, and explained: 'He needs space. I realise that now. I have to trust his love, not cling to him as though he might run away. He won't. I know he loves me. It's up to me to help him show it.'

Now, of course, we don't know anything about Stella's husband. But if we assume she is right, and she knows that he does love her and wants to have a mutually loving relationship if given the freedom to choose, then Stella has definitely got the right idea.

The psychology of love says you can never force anyone to love you. You can coerce or manipulate someone into *pretending* affection – through fear, perhaps, or because you offer something important that the other wants. This could be company for someone afraid of loneliness, a refuge for the frightened, a home for the homeless, a source of income for the weary, social status, wealth, sex, free housekeeping, free childcare. There are lots of reasons why people pretend to love each other and stay together in loveless relationships. But as you are reading this book, you probably want better than that. Stella's image of 'giving your cow a big field' is a splendid picture of how you find out if your love is worthy of your protection.

What is your reaction when someone says, 'I need you'? I know that mine is very negative indeed. I have never said that to my husband, nor he to me, and I would be ashamed to do so. I might occasionally say, 'I do need you to understand how I see X.' But needing another person in an emotional way is a big NO.

Now I am not talking about real needs. Babies and small children, for instance, *need* loving care, as do victims of disaster or serious illness, and those who are growing very old. No, I am talking about the notion of psychological need that so many people associate with love. 'I need you' from one adult to another is supposed to be proof of deep, undying, romantic love. However, love between adults can only be truly deep and happy if it really *is* between adults, and not with one of them playing the role of inadequate infant.

Stella has shown us a perfect example of a woman who began the Life Planning Programme with a real sense of her own inadequacy, and therefore an inability to love her husband as an equal. It followed, then, that she needed him more than he could need her, and in her Circle of Demons she discovered why. She had internalised all those destructive and antiquated notions about what makes the 'perfect woman' – which, let's face it, none of us could ever be, so there's failure for a start. Having begun with what turned out to be rather extreme versions of what most of us learn about the differences between women and men, she inevitably feared no man could love her if she ever revealed to him what she is really like in her inner heart. So, having found a man whom she truly loved and could marry, how could she dare let him know about her secret inner needs? If she asked for anything, she would be demonstrating her unfitness for his love. And because she could never let him know what she wanted, he inevitably failed to say the right thing, or make the right gesture at exactly the right time. Poor Stella felt desperate, half wanting to cling to this man and half expecting him to walk out and leave her because she didn't deserve to be loved. What dreadful double binds we get ourselves into.

You can see that Stella has come a long way. Learning new habits is always difficult, and that is perhaps why she requires herself to show patience. She is absolutely right, of course. When you change your behaviour, it comes as a shock to those nearest and dearest, and they usually wait anxiously for you to revert to your previous ways. So both, or all of you, need time – and space – to absorb the changes and see what difference they make to your everyday lives. Stella plans to allow her husband the freedom to love her, in his way. It is amazing how much easier it is to love someone who doesn't demand it as a right.

Remaining in Balance

Putting yourself centre stage is not as easy as it might appear. Many of us have been bombarded for so long with the message that it is selfish and immoral to put ourselves first that we no longer have that innocent egocentricity that we all began with as children. Not that I am advocating a return to egocentricity – and we all know people whose selfishness is so great they appear never to have grown up.

No – I am advocating simply the valuable realisation that we are *all* important, each one of us, and that we must sometimes put our own needs under the spotlight, centre-stage, so that they are taken into account.

Once you discover that you are just as important as everyone else, you experience a great sense of liberation. Stella, for example, does not need to cling on to her husband out of fear because she has realised they can stand apart and love each other as equals. Dorothy, too, has found that she requires her family to consider her, help her and support her, just as much as they apparently expect her to do things for them. When she puts herself centre-stage, she sees that half her circle can be given over to *her* needs, the activities that make *her* happy, while she can devote the other half to caring for her family and earning the money they all want. And Lynne has discovered that she can fulfil her own desires and be happy while keeping her family and her well-paid job in proportion.

Put your own needs on to the scales and discover how to be not too selfish, but just selfish enough. The key is balance.

CHAPTER 11

Turning Dreams into Reality

If you have had the courage to complete all the exercises fully, you will have achieved a great deal by the time you reach this chapter. You will have discovered how to confront your demons, learned ways to release the steam in your pressure cooker and have a clear idea of what you need to feel happy and alive.

Now – how are you going to take the final steps so that you can stop dreaming and start living?

exercise 17
looking to the future

Think again, in some detail, about your ideal day in the future – say three or four years from now. Write down what you will be doing, what you will be feeling and what important others in your life are doing too.

Your task now is to imagine just how your life would look and feel if you were doing what you – the deep-down real you – really want to do. What do you see when you wake up in the morning? Where are you and where do you spend your day? How do you feel inside your skin as you carry out your daily occupations? What do you hear? What do you smell? What do you taste? What do you touch? Try to

live through an entire day in your imagination and discover the real truth about your dreams of the future.

Don't restrict yourself to what you feel is 'realistic'. Now
you know so much about yourself, what would you be
doing if you could make your dreams real?

This is where you genuinely examine your dreams and
consider what you could be doing with your life if only you
had the courage to make it happen. The only 'realistic limitation' is that making your dreams come true must depend
principally on *you*.

Teresa said, 'I just don't know how I could raise the
money.' It is, of course, absolutely true that lack of finances
is a limitation that seems to interfere with many people's
dreams. However, once you are clear about what it is you
truly need to do to be fulfilled, sorting out *how* – and that
includes finances – is the next step. We deal with this in
Exercise 18 (see page 198).

Simple Transformations

Some people find that the changes they need to make in
their lives are not as enormous or as terrifying as they had
previously thought. Rose, for example, realises that her life
is essentially the way she wants it to be once she can accept
that her beloved husband is no longer with her, except in
memory. It is her attitudes towards the different elements
in her life that need transformation. She dreams of continuing her life's journey through a very different landscape
now, leaving the mountain ranges behind and moving into
wide, verdant valleys, with trees, flowers and rushing
waters. Her children are with her, laughing, enjoying the

journey, and her enormous burden has been discarded.

For Rose, the most important change has been to transform the landscape in her mind. Relieved of the heavy burden of guilt, remorse and constant worry, she feels she can allow herself to stop dreaming of the past and what might have been, and give herself – and her children – permission to enjoy what is good in their present.

Irene, too, does not want to make radical changes in her everyday life, but realises that she needs to create opportunities for herself to have fun and entertain other people. Her dream day in the future reveals an ambition to perform before an audience that she has only hinted at before. She isn't sure what she will do with this ambition, but promises herself she will no longer pretend it isn't there.

Floyd and Tyler are also among those who discover that the principal changes they need to make are in their own minds. Both of them, in their very different lives, belabour themselves with sticks, like cruel coachmen flogging horses that have already given their best. Both are doing work they really enjoy, both are apparently successful, and both create their own stress, tension and misery through fear of being thought lazy. Floyd's worries go even further, for he is afraid of failure. But when they examine their dream day in the future, they are both able to realise that their ambitions are perfectly realistic. What each man needs in order to achieve his dream is to have confidence in himself. Each man, too, finds he has included a lot of pleasure in his ideal day: Floyd has found time to go sailing for two hours, and Tyler anticipates good royalties, walks on the moor to see the sunset and reading poetry to his wife.

Radical Changes

Other people have more radical changes to make. We have already seen that Dorothy will have a major task ahead of her if she is to stop simply dreaming and start living.

When your ideal future entails important changes that involve other people, your resolve can be sorely tested. I found that it was one thing to decide that I would no longer take on individual clients, and quite another actually to turn people away when they phoned. Often I would be tempted to make an exception 'just this once', and had to keep reminding myself of my long-term goal – that ideal day in the future when people would be reading my books and enjoying them.

This is why it can be so valuable to have a clear and detailed picture of how you envisage spending a day three to five years from now. Whenever you vacillate in your resolve, bring your ideal day into your mind. It will inspire you.

Ending a Relationship

Sometimes that ideal day in the future reveals to you that you are in a relationship you want to end. Patrick (whom you have not met before) realises that his dreams do not include his wife. Like so many couples, they remain together because of the children, and he has been trying to deny he has been wanting to leave her for years. He runs a successful business, which he enjoys, lives near his parents whom he sees frequently, and has a good social life in a village where he has lived most of his life. His ideal day shows that he wants to change very little, and that his life would be happy if only he were not tied to a woman he now rather dislikes. Patrick said firmly that leaving is not an option, and so he has to find a way to reconcile this decision with his discovery – and it *is* a discovery because he has not wanted to face it – that his marriage is the source of his physical and mental misery.

He had come to me in the first instance because he had begun to suffer from claustrophobia to an increasingly debilitating degree. It was getting so bad, he couldn't go in a lift, on a bus or train, or indeed anywhere where he might be hemmed in – by walls or by people. When we had eliminated childhood trauma and other possible causes of his difficulty, we were left with but one – his marriage. His refusal to acknowledge that he felt trapped in an unhappy marriage left him psychologically enclosed in a dark place, with no way out. As I have mentioned on several occasions, we all tend to live symbolically, and Patrick's experience is an extreme example of how the psyche takes revenge when you will not pay attention to its needs. We will see how Patrick dealt with his problem in the next chapter.

Taking Responsibility for Love

By contrast, Stella began the Life Planning Programme feeling angry, resentful and lonely, obviously worried that her marriage might be a source of her difficulties. But as we have seen, the exercises revealed that her life with her husband was essentially happy and that she planned to do her part in keeping it that way. Her ideal day showed all the important elements of her life in balance, and she saw herself as having taken the necessary steps to make her dreams reality.

Be honest with yourself. There is no point in going through all the agonies of confronting demons and the difficulties of reducing tension in your pressure cooker if, at the end, you refuse to face the crucial and fundamental needs of your psyche. If this entails radical change, is it not better to *know*? Then at least you can make a choice. If radical change is not needed, and what is required is a change of mental attitude and focus, then you need to know that too. Sometimes changing one's habitual ways of thinking is the hardest task of all.

exercise 18
detailed action plans
Make lists under the following headings:
Wishes I need to turn into plans
What I need to start doing now
What I need to stop doing now

More on Money
Teresa's desire to study medicine is clearly a wish that needs to be turned into a *plan of action*. Part of her plan naturally involves investigating all the possibilities of raising money for her training. A bit of lateral thinking is in order here. Perhaps there are bursaries available for needy students, or perhaps a relevant professional organisation or commercial business might sponsor her. Perhaps there are government grants she doesn't know about. People who are determined are able to raise finances for extraordinary projects – sailing round the world single-handed, for example, walking the Great Wall of China or exploring the Amazon jungle – so failure to raise enough money may often be a failure of nerve and imagination.

I remember Annabel, a young woman I met many years ago, who was determined to send her three children to private schools, even though her husband was struggling to start a new joinery business and she was an ill-paid musician. *Three* children? I'd have thought it impossible to send *one* to private school in those circumstances. But no, not Annabel. She was adamant. Her children had to have the best education possible, and she was convinced that a private school was the way.

So she researched the subject thoroughly, discovered what scholarships, bursaries and supported places were available and where, and set out to arrange one for each of her children. Successfully. I remember listening open-mouthed to her account of how she had gone about her campaign. If truth be known, I was a little shocked. Wasn't she being, well, grasping and greedy? I didn't *say* so, of course, but she must have sensed my disapproval.

'Why not?' she demanded. 'Why shouldn't my children have the best education? Those grants and bursaries are there – so why shouldn't my children have the benefit?'

I realised she was absolutely right. She wasn't stealing. She didn't take anything to which she and her children were not entitled. But what she did do – and what might be an inspiration for us all – was expend a lot of effort and time in doing the research into what, in her view, she needed. The real point is, she found out what we could all discover if only we had the nerve and the gumption to look.

Turning Wishes into Plans

People's wishes vary enormously, as do the plans they need to make. Jenny, for example, wanted to leave university, to break up with her boyfriend and 'do something exciting'. Perhaps the first two items demanded more courage and determination than they required planning. Jenny smiled.

'I do have to work out the best way because I have to make sure no-one changes my mind. I shall probably tell my mother over the phone, when it's too late. I know she'll be upset, but I've got to do it. I shall tell my tutor as soon as I get back. That's it!'

Her group was a bit concerned on her behalf. 'Where will you go? What will you do? You haven't any qualifications for a job.' She laughed. 'No problem. I've got it all planned.' As we shall see in the next chapter, she had.

Celia wasn't quite sure what she would be doing in three years' time, but 'I will certainly be independent'. It had become clear to her that her first thought of hairdressing wasn't really her thing. Her plan now was to investigate government training schemes for young mothers, which had started at 'just the right time' for her. 'I'm also going to make sure we move somewhere better for Sam. And I am going to investigate nursery schools for him. I think he needs other children.'

Floyd's plans included making sure he had a lot more time to relax, and especially to go sailing. 'I think sometimes we just keep on working, even when the brain has got so tired it's just idling. I'm fed up with it. It doesn't help me climb the ladder. It's really just being on a treadmill.'

He was right, of course. This was some years ago, before the widespread understanding that everyone needs exercise and relaxation in order to be able to work productively. This was a good strategy for workaholic Floyd. He also expected to ask his girlfriend to marry him. He smiled as he said this, obviously believing that her answer would be yes. 'The graph of my self-confidence is taking an upward turn.'

Rose intended to involve the children more in how they ran their lives. 'I like the idea of a family conference to make plans and share jobs. I think they'll enjoy being more part of my life, and I certainly would feel less alone. They miss their dad too, and I think I sometimes forget that.'

Lynne had already decided what she had to do to make her ideal future a reality. 'I don't think there will be any difficulty at work really,' she said. 'I realise that I was trying to convince them I should be made up to the main board, but it isn't going to happen. And now I don't even want that. I want to be with my family. We need my income, but it's not going to dominate my entire life.'

Stella's strategies are already written out in her happy circle, as we saw at the end of the last chapter. Dorothy intends to make more time for herself, and for her writing. She also plans to take steps towards being able to do the sort of work that would make her happy. Elizabeth decides to refuse all new individual clients and start writing a book. Tyler proposes to cut down on social activities and to concentrate on writing another book. There are rather a lot of writers involved in this Life Planning Programme!

Deciding What to Start – and What to Stop

Many of the action plans you make will show you what you need to start doing without delay. Each of those participants quoted had made resolutions that involved them immediately doing something concrete and positive. Writing things down and making sure you can see how to progress your plan step by step will help enormously. This is especially helpful in the first stages, particularly if you are proposing to transform your life radically. If your changes affect other people, they will inevitably react. During the emotional turbulence you will need to be clear at all times that you are going in the right direction.

Dorothy, for example, will have a difficult time if she is to take action to make her dreams reality. She will need to start by making her own wishes clear to her husband, in particular, and to her mother. As I have shown in the previous chapter, it is never easy to persuade those who are used to you running round after them that you no longer plan to do this and that, on the contrary, you expect them to think of you. She also needs to stop doing everything, and to start expecting some help. She needs to begin experimenting with that hazardous word 'no'.

Saying 'no', however charmingly, is a major hurdle for many of the people we have met. It may be a difficulty for you too. Remember that you are a person who has rights as well, and it is up to you to assert them – not aggressively, but firmly. If you prefer to lie down and be a doormat, well, the choice is yours, but is it good for those other people to think they can walk all over you? Beware of martyrdom. And if you never say 'no', what is your 'yes' really worth?

Keep your plans and dreams in mind and don't let other people's unreasonable demands divert you. Go on. If you've got this far, you can do it!

Dealing with Fear, Frustration and Failure

Learning to live the life that suits *you* demands courage and determination. Synchronicity may occur at crucial moments. At others, however, life will turn around and clobber you, just to keep you on your toes and test your resolve. Your loved ones may come up with some ingenious ways to frustrate you, the world economic climate may turn cyclonic, natural disaster may strike... There are numerous ways in which your courage may be stretched to its limit. We are extraordinarily fortunate to be living in the Western world, and rarely do we have to think simply of survival. But even here life can be weighed down with difficulties, and anyone who promises you an easy way forward is lying.

Fear is the greatest danger confronting you when you try to transform your life. Fear is natural, and useful when it persuades you to be cautious and look before you leap. However, fear can also paralyse and keep you stuck in the old, comfortable rut. So face that fear, feel it – and go out and do your stuff anyway.

Fear can be exhilarating if you let it. All those hormones rushing through your blood can inspire you to notable achievement. Every time you do make a step forward, you will feel a huge rush of excitement. Overcoming fear, using the feeling to spur you on, can bring you immense enjoyment. It can help you discover that your potential is considerably greater than you ever imagined.

When failure threatens, take time to consider your options, to remember your abilities and qualities, to tap into your inner strengths. Then get up and grapple with those demons, Fear and Failure. Be prepared to do whatever it takes to hold on to your dreams. Grit your teeth and believe in yourself. You will win through.

exercise 19
learn how to relax and meditate

Meditation and relaxation are important skills for anyone who wants to stop dreaming and start living. Both are skills you can use every day.

Relaxation

The ability to relax all your muscles at will is enormously helpful when dealing with difficult situations because body and mind always work together. I recommend you take up any opportunity of learning how to do this with an instructor. However, the technique is quite simple – it just takes lots of practice. Do start now as it takes several weeks or months to derive the full benefit. It really is worth it.

The best way to relax completely is to lie down on a carpet or thick blanket, with just a book about one inch thick under the back of your head. Sounds uncomfortable, I know, but this is the most helpful position for you to relax *all* your muscles. Make sure you are warm enough and wearing comfortable loose clothing and no shoes. Wiggle your body on the floor until you start to feel reasonably comfortable, then lie still. Then follow these steps:

1. Tighten the muscles in your right foot and toes. Let go, and feel the tension leaving your toes and foot. Do the same with your left foot.

2. Tighten the muscles in your right calf, then let go. Do the same with your left calf. The aim is to feel the difference between clenched muscles and relaxed ones. Then tighten the muscles in your right thigh, let go, and do the same on the left. Your legs should now be feeling relatively relaxed. If they are not, do the whole thing again.

3. Now concentrate on your belly, your buttocks and abdomen. Tightening the muscles there will be easier, but letting go is not always as effective. Do this tightening and relaxing gently several times until you can really feel a difference.

4. Tighten and relax your fingers and hands, then your arms.

5. Find the muscles in your back, shoulders and abdomen, which can be rather tricky. Try to feel the difference between tight muscles and relaxed ones in each of these areas.

6. Finally, concentrate on your neck and face. Screw up your face and let the muscles go. Let your tongue fall to the base of your mouth – if it is touching the roof, it is not relaxed.

7. When you feel you have covered your whole body, and it is reasonably relaxed all over, you should repeat the exercise to find an even deeper level of relaxation. Feel yourself sinking into the floor. If one or two muscles are complaining, just tense and relax them, and carry on discovering how it feels to let go completely.

Once you discover how to relax totally, you will find this position on a hard (but carpeted or blanketed) floor remarkably comfortable. You should lie there for at least five minutes. The moment to move is when you feel you never want to move again!

Several weeks of regular practice will allow you to relax all your muscles at will, all together. Don't waste time trying to do this at first – you will just get frustrated and never learn this remarkable skill. It's so easy to do once you have learned it, and so difficult to achieve in the first place. It is highly recommended by anyone who has succeeded – and is useful even in the dentist's chair.

Meditation

Meditation is basically a form of relaxation for the mind. Just as relaxation allows you to remove tension from your body deliberately, so meditation allows you to choose to set aside worries in your mind. Meditation is essentially a form of self-hypnosis, which allows you to be in control at all times while letting go of everyday concerns.

There are many ways to get to this calm and pleasant state. I will describe one simple method, which you can adapt to your own needs:

1. Sit comfortably, where your back can be held upright. Those who do yoga will often meditate sitting cross-legged on the floor, but if you are not an adept at this, it is better to sit in a chair with your back supported. You don't want to be distracted by bodily discomfort of any kind. For the same reason, you should make sure you are warm, in loose clothing, preferably without shoes, and that you will not be interrupted.

2. Close your eyes and watch your thoughts. They skitter back and forth, jostling for attention. Try to stand back, so to speak, and simply observe. Your aim will eventually be to still these busy thoughts and allow your mind some peace – a daunting task for most of us whose minds are full of insistent voices. Beware of being caught up in a series of coherent thoughts.

   You will soon tire of watching, or will have found you cannot stop thinking about problems you must solve. This is the difficulty that must be overcome. The best way appears to be to *have one single thought or idea to take the place of all that busyness.*

3. Each of us has a preferred sense – yours might be sight, hearing, smell, taste or touch. Whichever is yours, that is the form the single thought or idea should take.

You have probably heard of yogic meditators humming the word 'OM' over and over. If your preferred sense is sound, then repeating a word or phrase in your head will help you relax your mind. Buddhist monks repeat the mantra 'OM MANI PADME HUM'. This may be translated as 'the jewel in the heart of the lotus', with the sound 'OM' representing the great roar of the universe and the eternal silence of pure being. True Buddhist meditation would take a person from the sound of the words deep into the profound meaning of the mantra, a sophistication that takes many years of assiduous practice. You should choose a word or simpler phrase that suits you.

You may find that creating a visual image stills your mind better. Think of a peaceful place – a tranquil beach in moonlight, perhaps, a quiet woodland glade or a green field high on a hill – somewhere that pleases you. The choice is yours. Take yourself there in your imagination. Notice all the details of the place – the colours, the shapes – and remain there in your mind. Choose a place you can revisit happily every time you meditate.

Those for whom smell is important may find that burning incense helps them clear the mind of thoughts. Concentrate on the elements of the perfume, savouring the scents. If your mind keeps talking, choose a suitable word or phrase to repeat in your mind as you focus on the incense.

If your preferred sense is touch, try to concentrate on your heart. Feel it beating, sense the blood coursing through your veins and arteries. Notice how it speeds up as you focus on it, then slows down, steadily and rhythmically pumping the blood around your body. Or you may like to focus on your breathing, becoming aware of how the air enters your nostrils and runs down into your lungs. Feel them expanding, pushing the diaphragm down, raising your chest and abdomen, then how they deflate, slowly, steadily, until your body automatically breathes in once more. Try to remain detached but aware. Don't *do* the breathing; just let it happen. Be there as the air enters your body and leaves it again.

You may have to experiment to find which approach suits you best. But once you have discovered which sense can bring you peace in your mind most easily, then use it – every day. You may wish to change the image, elaborate on it perhaps, but not too much. Make it easy for yourself. The more frequently you concentrate your mind on a simple image – or sound, or smell, or touch – the easier you will find it to relax your mind, and move deeper into a peaceful place where you are *you*.

Meditation is for every day, but most especially for those days when you feel you have no time to meditate. Remember – *when you know you just can't take time out, that is the most important time to meditate*. Twenty minutes is all it takes. With 30 minutes of pleasure and 20 minutes of meditation each day, you will find you have the strength of 10. Don't let the clock deprive you of what you need most.

What Next?

We have reached the end of the exercises. Now it is up to you to use the discoveries you have made along the way, turn them to account, make even the painful revelations work for you. Keep central in your mind an image of yourself smiling and happy and feeling alive. Everything you choose to do from now on must be informed by that image, and what you know you need to keep yourself within the circle of pleasure.

These exercises are to be *used.* Remind yourself from time to time of your abilities, talents and skills. From your list of pleasures, choose activities that make you feel alive, and make sure you experience pleasure every day. Meditate. Listen to the voices in your head, and consider frequently whether they are talking sense or simply undermining your plans with insidious criticism you can discard as rubbish. Keep focused on *you*, what makes you glad to be alive. Don't let others – real others or imagined voices – prevent you from making your dreams come true.

Take action to make those dreams reality. It may take a while to transform your life – if your dream were to walk across America, you would still have to take one step at a time. So have faith in yourself. Start living. You can do it.

As you will see in the final chapter, others have succeeded in taking control of their lives and in being true to themselves. They have discovered they have strengths, abilities and skills, and they feel good about themselves.

If they can do it, so can you.

CHAPTER 12

Where Are They Now?

We have followed a number of people through this Life Planning Programme, sharing many of their difficulties and dreams. Perhaps you wonder how successful they have been. Have they stopped dreaming and started to live?

I can't tell you what has happened to everyone. Some I have lost touch with, others have only recently taken part in the programme. But here is an update on some of those you have met.

Mark

When we met him, Mark was terrified of the looming ordeal of the Common Entrance Examination. He passed – well enough to get into the school he was aiming for.

'Makes me wonder how well I might have done if I had worked,' he said to me afterwards. Then he laughed ruefully, realising that he had always claimed that 'I am working, really' though we had both known these had been placatory words designed to get parents and teachers off his back.

He telephoned two years later to tell me his news and to say thank you. He was happy at school, had lots of friends, and 'even the teachers like me, most of them'. He found that realising he had strengths and abilities transformed his attitude. Now he has few problems studying and plans to go on to university.

'I've decided I want to study Psychology,' he said, 'or Marine Biology, one of the two.' What a wonderful compliment!

Annie

Annie was a very unhappy teenager when we met her, but she discovered that she was not to blame for everything that went wrong in her life. Nor was she 'born unlucky' – her constant refrain, and a favourite ploy of people who don't want to take responsibility for their lives. She also discovered that she has talents – she can be creative and is an excellent cook. Her exam results were fairly average, with the shining exception of a grade A for Art, and two of her paintings were on show in a local exhibition. This raised her morale. She decided to study hairdressing at a local college. Several years on, she is a successful senior stylist in a big salon, is married and has a son.

'My love life was a bit chaotic in my teens,' she told me, 'and I still have trouble with my weight. But my husband seems to like me cuddly, so I've given up worrying about it.'

Did she feel the Life Planning Programme had helped?

'It made me realise how much of a victim I felt. I hated that. It had to change. And I did learn to use my strong points. There *are* things I'm good at, and I try to use them where I can. It's really nice to be able to like myself.'

Quite right.

Jenny

Jenny did go away from the Life Planning Programme and transform her life. As soon as she returned to university, she saw her tutor and said she was going to leave. 'The worst of it was,' she told me afterwards, 'I had come top in all the end-of-term exams, and he didn't want me to go. But I didn't let it make a difference.'

She then arranged to go and stay with a friend living near London while she looked for a job, and only then did she telephone her mother. 'She *was* a bit upset, but when she saw it was too late, she just wished me luck.' And within a week Jenny had found a job, for which she had absolutely no qualifications except intelligence and determination. 'I told them I'd learn whatever skills they needed in my own time.'

Jenny appears in my book, *War of Words: Women and Men Arguing*, as Jenifer in the chapter entitled 'Women who feel they are winning'. This interview was about eight years later, and she provides a wonderful example of a woman in her 20s who feels she can achieve anything if she tries hard enough. From being a girl concerned to fit in and be like everyone else, Jenny has become a self-confident young woman, determined to stay in control of her life.

What did she take away from the Life Planning Programme? 'Really it was about trusting myself,' she said. 'I know I'm intelligent, but I didn't want to go to university like my parents and my brother. I like real problems. I love working in an office, I love being busy, and I get on really well with everyone at work. They like me as I am. I like me as I am!' She laughed. 'Sounds awful, doesn't it? But I know you understand.'

Indeed I do, and I am delighted. There can be no greater achievement than to be able to say, truly, 'I like myself'.

Celia

We saw Celia defeat a major demon that was trapping her in dreams of 'what might have been', and preventing her from getting on with life. She realised that she need not cower under the blow of being let down by her lover. She could take control herself. Six months later, she phoned to say her life had been transformed.

'We moved. That was the first thing I had to sort out, and I feel so much happier. It's only a flat instead of a house, but we even have a small garden where Sam can play safely. He now goes regularly to nursery school, and loves it. I think he's better now he can play with other children – not so clingy. He hardly has any temper tantrums now.'

What about herself? 'I've discovered computers.' She laughed: 'I never would've thought it. I went on one of those government schemes for learning IT, and I just love it. *And* I've got a part-time job. It's so good to get out of the house and talk to other people. You don't know what a difference it's made.'

I can certainly guess. And her love life? She didn't say, and I didn't ask. But a few months later I heard on the rumour machine that she was going out with another man. Celia is moving on.

Diana

We left Diana with a major problem to confront: her husband's attitude to her ambitions as a painter. She said it took her a while to sort out the right way to approach him – and to find the courage – but that she precipitated a show-down when she decided to take her painting seriously herself.

'I realised when I looked back over the exercises that I always let other people's needs come first,' she said. 'I wrote myself a note and posted it on the fridge:

If you don't take your work seriously, who will?

Of course, it was illustrated, with me at my easel, and a clock showing me working from nine to five. I knew I just had to make myself think of it as a full-time job, even if I was ready to stop most days when the children came home. I needed them – and me – to realise that painting is my *work*.'

A good move, I thought. But inevitably this meant that jobs in the house could not be done in the day – shopping, washing, ironing, cooking, cleaning – those chores we all have to cope with somehow, whatever our working lives. But a husband who is supporting his wife financially apparently does not expect to contribute anything to these chores. (In fact, we know that lots of husbands contribute very little, even when their wives are employed full-time, but that's another issue.) Indeed, Diana's husband felt justified in complaining that his shirts were not ironed and the vacuuming not done.

'The real crisis came when I said I couldn't go to a stupid coffee morning his boss's wife was holding. I said I would be working. He said I was letting him down. I said it would make absolutely no difference to how his boss saw him and his work, that I didn't want to go and act in some command performance, that I would be bored out of my mind. And anyway, I was busy. He said it was important to him. I said he'd never have asked me to do something so trivial when I was teaching. He said, "That was different. I wouldn't expect you to take time off from work for a coffee morning." This made it so crystal clear, I felt he had punched me in the face.'

The outcome of Diana's story is perhaps not as satisfactory as we could have hoped. She and her husband tried to sort out their differences, but he thought she was fantasising about her talent, and she was not able to accept his disparagement of what was to her a serious ambition. Eventually they parted, and she had to go back to teaching to support herself and keep a home for the children. He did, of course, contribute, but no more than required by law.

Diana still paints and has a regular schedule: during term time, she gets up at 5am and paints for two hours before everyone gets ready for school. In the holidays, she works from 6am to 2pm most days, and has the afternoon and early evening for her family. She exhibits regularly and sells. She has not yet been discovered by a major gallery or art critic, but is seriously considering risking that final move of quitting her job and painting full-time now the children are about to leave home.

'I don't regret any of it,' she said. 'I am so glad I was able to see the truth, and it was that awful pressure cooker exercise that really made me see. Much better to face the truth than live a lie.'

Doing the Life Planning Programme takes courage – and it can take courage to confront what you discover. 'But I would never have had the success I have now,' Diana said. 'I would have carried on being frustrated and angry, and everyone would have been miserable. It was worth it. Really it was.'

Irene

Irene had seen herself at a crossroads. When I heard from her several years later, she did seem to have chosen the right way forward for her. She discovered she had a talent for drama and humour, and that she needed to have – and to create – more fun. The Life Planning Programme left her with a real appreciation of her needs, but a great deal of apprehension too, because she and her new husband were moving to a small village. How was she to develop her desires there?

Synchronicity was at work. Without realising it, they had chosen a community with a thriving amateur dramatic society, one that welcomed new talent with enthusiasm. Irene's comic skills became much in demand. She told me that a local playwright who regularly creates plays for the society wrote a part specially for her. She felt she had come home.

Was she still swerving up and down on her mental rollercoaster? She laughed. 'Only when a new production is coming up and I'm shaking with fright. Me noives is terrible. My lovely husband gives me flowers and hot drinks and stays out of my way.'

And the Life Planning Programme? 'Brilliant!' she said. 'I'd never have dared do this acting lark, I'd have been too scared. We *all* thank you – my husband, my kids. We all like me so much better now.'

Floyd

As we know, Floyd was due to leave for the United States, to take up a major promotion that secretly terrified him, so I heard very little from him. He did write a note to say that he realised he needed to find a balance between work and relaxation, and that he felt his self-assurance rising. He would remember the exercises whenever he lost confidence, and was grateful. And his girlfriend had said yes, and they were to be married.

Dorothy

It is only a short time since Dorothy took part in the Life Planning Programme but she has already started making changes. She telephoned me to ask about courses in psychology and counselling. She believes she would be much happier doing such work, and it would use many of the caring and empathic skills she knows she has.

As for her pressure cooker, well, she's working on making things better. 'I'm less depressed than I was,' she said. 'It's a major change from where I was a few months ago.'

Dorothy has a very difficult task ahead of her but she sounds determined. We have seen how gruelling it can be to persuade demanding members of a family to give *you* due consideration, and transformation in attitude is rarely achieved overnight.

A few weeks after her call, she wrote: 'I have begun a Basic Counselling Skills course, which is proving very interesting, so I'm concentrating on enjoying that before deciding what to do next.' Very sensible. Important life changes must be taken seriously.

Stella

Stella also attended the Life Planning Programme a short time ago, but she told me over the phone that she has already put her plans into action. All of them. She now has a computer and is writing a book, the sort of guide for parents she wishes she had been able to find when she first had her son. She sounded happy and in control.

'My life is transformed,' she said. 'When I realised I could junk all the rubbish from my childhood, I felt liberated. Empowered. Everyone should do your exercises. I know I can do it. I really can. And I don't even have to clean the house before I start work in the morning. You have no idea what a liberating thing that is for me. I feel wonderful.'

Patrick

Patrick bought a dog for companionship and to give himself a reason for going on long walks. I taught him relaxation and meditation, and every morning he would spend half an hour with his dog in a secret place in the woods, meditating, calming his psyche and listening to its needs. We met by chance about three years later, and he told me he had 'taken the plunge' and left home. He still lives in the same village and sees his children nearly every day. He is happy and so are they.

'Doing that work with you was the best thing I ever did,' he said. 'I tell everyone now that learning to relax and meditate saved my life. I didn't want them to know I'd seen a psychologist, but now – well, I don't care who knows. Everyone can see how much better I am these days.'

Patrick went through all the Life Planning exercises in individual sessions, and was terribly anxious not to allow anyone else to know he was seeing me. For nearly three years he was unable to acknowledge that he could have got to such a low ebb that he actually saw a *psychologist* – a GP is acceptable, but a psychologist, dear me no. And then, as he dared be honest – first with himself, then with his wife and family – he realised that there was nothing wrong with admitting you had got into a tight spot in your life, and even that it was *sensible and intelligent* to be able to admit you could do with a bit of help. So he eventually found the courage to make the changes he needed and allow himself to stop dreaming and start to live.

So now it's your turn. Are you another success story, or are you still wondering if it's worth plucking up the courage to have a go? All these people show that if you start thinking about your problems and difficulties in new ways, you can take control. You can vanquish your hidden demons, confront your fears and escape from that pressure cooker. It takes time and effort, of course, but you too can learn to stop dreaming and start to live.

Elizabeth Mapstone's revolutionary method adapts the techniques of the psychotherapist, and allows each individual to confront directly and safely all the hidden demons that prevent life being lived to the full.
The programme includes techniques borrowed and adapted from new 'voice therapy', cognitive therapy, Beck 'mood therapy', and Rogerian 'client-centred therapy', as well as using many insights from experimental psychology.

Dr Mapstone may be contacted by email via her website: www.elizabethmapstone.com

Also available from Vermilion

The Art of Leading Yourself
Tap the power of your emotional intelligence
Randi B. Noyes

This thought-provoking book, full of case studies and exercises, puts the theories of emotional intelligence into effective practice, explaining how everyone can use their emotions and gut feelings to improve and guide their logical thinking and their actions.

Confidence in Just Seven Days
Practical strategies to transform your life
Ros Taylor, Dr Sandra Scott and Roy Leighton

Lacking in confidence? Here's how to get it in just seven days!

Some people are just plain shy, but even the seemingly most confident and successful people find certain areas of their life difficult to negotiate. In *Confidence in Just Seven Days*, three experts offer their most effective techniques for conquering shyness – in just seven days.

The Secrets of Happiness
100 Ways to True Fulfilment
Ben Renshaw

Full of witty and practical tips, and written in a positive, uplifting style, this delightful book brings succinct advice on finding fulfilment and peace of mind from Britain's answer to John Gray.

Who Moved My Cheese?
An amazing way to deal with change in your work and in your life
Dr Spencer Johnson

Over 10 million copies sold!

What began as a 94-page self-help book has grown into a major international bestseller. Written for all ages, this story takes less than an hour to read, but its insights last for a lifetime. The book is the work of MD turned management guru Dr Spencer Johnson, whose *One Minute Manager* sold more than 7 million copies.

The message is simple – 'change isn't everything, it's the only thing. Embrace change; don't fight it.'

❏ **The Art of Leading Yourself**	0091889731	£8.99
❏ **Confidence in Just Seven Days**	0091856655	£7.99
❏ **The Secrets of Happiness**	0091887542	£4.99

Who Moved my Cheese?

❏ (paperback)	0091816971	£5.99
❏ (hardback)	0091883768	£10.99

FREE POSTAGE AND PACKING

Overseas customers allow £2.00 per paperback

BY PHONE: 01624 677237

BY POST: Random House Books
C/o Bookpost, PO Box 29, Douglas
Isle of Man, IM99 1BQ

BY FAX: 01624 670923

BY EMAIL: bookshop@enterprise.net

Cheques (payable to Bookpost) and credit cards accepted

Prices and availability subject to change without notice.
Allow 28 days for delivery.
When placing your order, please mention if you do not wish to
receive any additional information.

www.randomhouse.co.uk